To this day, my family is in disagreement as to precisely when the nightmare began. For me, it was the morning Daddy and Luther discovered Marvin, beaten, shot, and dying, in the Klan's stomping grounds off Round Lake Road. My brother Ren disagrees. He points to the small cluster of scars that begin just outside his left eye and trail horizontally across his temple to the top of his ear. Ren claims it started when the men in white robes took the unprecedented step of shooting at two white children. Others say it was when Mr. Thurgood Marshall of the NAACP and Mr. Hoover's FBI came to town.

Mother and Daddy shake their heads. In their minds, the real beginning was much earlier. . . .

LAY THAT TRUMPET IN OUR HANDS

"In this deceptively simple tale of a girl's maturity during evil times, McCarthy shows us something more: a community banding together under fire, and a family willing to shoulder a terrible responsibility. *Lay That Trumpet in Our Hands* is, in microcosm, what the civil rights movement meant—and means—to all the men, women, and children involved."
—Laurie R. King, author of *Folly*

"Evocative . . . The sincerity of her tale and its simple telling would make the book as interesting to young adult readers as it will be to those who remember or want to learn about the tangled moral questions of the '50s." —*Publishers Weekly*

"Poignant and beautifully written."
—*The Lebanon (MO) Daily Record*

LAY THAT TRUMPET IN OUR HANDS

Susan Carol McCarthy

Bantam Books

New York   Toronto   London   Sydney   Auckland

LAY THAT TRUMPET IN OUR HANDS
A Bantam Book

PUBLISHING HISTORY
Bantam hardcover edition published February 2002
Bantam trade paperback edition / April 2003

Published by Bantam Dell
A Division of Random House, Inc.
New York, New York

For Dad, Mother and Gam.
And for all the others whose
time in the fire was Florida
in the early '50s.

Prologue

Most of the Southern Belle states chose their widest, wildest rivers and seduced them into hardworking husbandry. In Big Delta marriages that still prosper, Mississippi claimed her namesake, Alabama her Mobile, and Georgia her Savannah. But Florida—skinny, flat-chested baby sister to the Belles—had slimmer prospects. Rejecting old Suwannee, Florida chose the Orange Blossom Trail, not a river at all but a slick 600-mile highway that knew how to dance.

The Orange Blossom Trail, also called Route 441, snake-charmed poor Florida, from her redheaded Georgia border through the skinny, sink-holed waist of the state to the wild abandon of her southern tip. While romancing her with dreamy visions of life in paradise, the Trail openly auctioned Florida's best beaches to the highest Yankee bidders. Later on, in a scandalous orgy of profit-taking, her lesser parts were tendered, cheaply, placing liberal Northerners, Orthodox Jews and devout Catholics cheek-by-jowl amongst the grandchildren of Confederate aristocrats, raging Crackers, and dirt-poor blacks who sought work wherever they could. "It's the social equivalent of a Molotov cocktail," my father liked to say.

In the spring of 1951, that cocktail combusted, blowing the roof off our state for nine nightmarish months. What happened is historical fact, and, now that the State Attorney has unsealed the Grand Jury documents, public record:

Florida's Klansmen, who for twenty years had confined their activities to assault and battery of adulterers and the occasional cross-burning, turned murderous. In March of 1951 they grabbed, stabbed and shot nineteen-year-old Negro citrus picker Marvin Cully. Then, in a high-speed chase down the Trail to the Orlando airport, they attempted to abduct N.A.A.C.P. Attorney Thurgood Marshall (future Supreme Court Justice Marshall). Later, with little attention and no intervention from law enforcement, Klansmen blew the hell out of the Carver Village Housing Project for Negroes with two 100-pound bundles of dynamite, set off blasts at the Coral Gables Jewish Center, the Hebrew School, and several Catholic churches. The horror seemed endless until finally the brutal double murder, by dynamite, on Christmas night got the attention of President Harry Truman, vacationing in Key West.

To this day, my family is in disagreement as to precisely when the nightmare began. For me, it was the morning Daddy and Luther discovered Marvin, beaten, shot and dying in the Klan's stomping grounds off Round Lake Road. My brother Ren disagrees. He points to the small cluster of scars that begin just a hair outside his left eye and trail horizontally across his temple to the top of his ear. Ren claims it started when the men in white robes took the unprecedented step of shooting at two white children. Mother and Daddy shake their heads. In their minds, the real beginning was much earlier when, as brash young newlyweds on a Florida honeymoon, they let a fast-talking agent entice them into twenty-seven acres of "prime grove land in the charming town of Mayflower."

It was afterwards that our family, the only Northerners left by then, and our circle of secret friends contrived the showdown between Mr. Hoover's F.B.I. and the central Florida K.K.K. *When* it all began and *why* remains debatable. So much lies buried with Marvin and the others and with their white-robed killers. In the end, all we have, all we can take refuge in, is *how*, for each of us, one thing led to quite another.

Chapter 1

Luther's on the back porch knocking on the door. Inside my cocoon of bedcovers, first thoughts, like moths, flutter. Temperature's dropped and the men have come to work the smudge pots. I see them in my mind, dark, bundled bodies shuffling, soft calls anticipating the all-night battle against a freeze, gloved hands passing shiny thermoses filled with fresh, hot coffee, maybe something stronger. No, no, the dusky wings whisper: winter's gone, the trees long into bloom, new fruit already the size of sweet peas. I wake with a start. *What is Luther doing here, now?*

There it is again, his distinctive *tappety-tap-TAP*. Across the hall, Mother and Daddy's voices arc in surprise, recognition, then concern. Daddy's feet hit the floor. I hear him yank on pants, belt buckle jangling, jerk open their door, and stride to the back. In my room Buddy's tags jingle at the window, nose pressed against the screen, tail gently slapping wood. I slip down beside him as, suddenly, the porch light slants across the tangerine tree outside my window. A breeze carries the scent of blossoms and the sound of voices into my room.

"Good Lord, Luther, what is it?" Daddy asks.

"It's Marvin, Mist'Warren. He ain't come home. Armetta's about worried herself to *death*. The boy went out 'round eight, telling his mamma he'd be back 'fore midnight. Ah been looking for him since one. Run into Jimmy Lee just now, swears he saw Klanners cruising the Trail where Marvin's s'posed to be."

"The Klan? Where on the Trail?"

"Joe's Jook, up to Wellwood. Marvin's sweet on one of them girls up there."

"Marvin had any run-ins with the Klan?"

"Nawser, but the girl say he left 'round 'leven."

"What do you think?"

"Ah'm hoping we could check on Mistuh Myer's Valencia grove this morning, drive slow-like past Round Lake, take a look."

"Come on in. I need to get my shoes on and some coffee."

Opening my door, I see Mother, a blur of dark curls and blue robe, flash through the hall and into the dining room. Buddy and I trail her into the kitchen.

Luther's at the table, chair nearest the door, staring down into the frayed innards of his field cap. Daddy's at the stove fumbling with the coffeepot. Mother moves to help him. Touching her elbow in thanks, he turns to retrieve his work boots from the porch.

"Sorry to bother you, MizLizbeth," Luther says to Mother's back. "Hey, Roo," he says to me, abbreviating his usual greeting. Everything about him, normally cola-colored, is gray-cast: his eyes glow darkly in ashy nests of wrinkles; a frost of unshaved stubble smudges his chin; his clothes, usually pressed and proper, hang loose and rumpled. Buddy pads over to him, tail wig-wagging, and rests his muzzle on Luther's knee.

"Luther and I need to take a drive, honey," Daddy says low-voiced to Mother. "Marvin's missing and it's cruise night on the Trail."

"But, Marvin's *not* . . ." Her eyes zigzag between the two men.

"Thought we'd check on Myer's Valencias, swing by Round Lake," Daddy says calmly, talking code in front of me.

"Can I go?" I ask.

"ReesaRoo, we don't know what's out there." Daddy lifts a booted foot onto the side bench, tying leather laces. "Besides, aren't you supposed to be watching for the DeSoto? She's due in today and your mother says her room's not ready." *Thrust and parry, Daddy's a master at it.*

"Your mamma comin' in today?" Luther asks, his smile showing a glint of the 24-karat canine Marvin calls his "golden dog."

"Yep, we get her for Easter this year," Daddy replies, tying the other boot.

"She *some*thin', Miz Doto is. And Ah *love* that car!"

"Fits her perfectly, doesn't it?" Daddy says, shrugging into his jacket.

My grandmother's DeLuxe, drive-without-shifting, custom DeSoto coupe is the source of our family's nickname for her. Once, when I was two or three, I answered my parents' request to "watch for the DeSoto" with an eager "Here comes Doto!" and the name stuck.

"Coffee's ready, sugar's on the table." Mother lays spoons and two steaming mugs in front of them. "Get you anything else?"

Luther's eyes thank Mother for her kindness, then dart to Daddy's.

"I think we'd best get going, honey," Daddy answers, not sitting, swigging coffee deeply.

Luther stands, visibly relieved, and ducks out the door, tossing "See y'all later" over his shoulder.

Daddy throws his good arm around Mother and pulls her to the barrel of his chest. "Warren, take Buddy with you," I hear her urge in a whisper.

"Don't worry, Lizbeth," he replies with a kiss. "Bye, Roo, don't forget the hospital corners on Doto's bed. Here, boy!" As the shepherd jingles after him, I see Mother check the time on the kitchen clock.

"*Where* on Round Lake?" I want to know.

"Reesa," she sighs, clearly unsure how much she wants to tell, "there's been talk about a lemon grove, one of Mr. Casselton's, but . . ."

Mr. Casselton. In our county, where local boosters declare citrus is king, Emmett Casselton, owner of the sprawling Casbah Groves, considers himself the area's crown prince. In our house, where the only thing worse than an "arrogant son of a bitch" is an "ignorant damn Cracker," Emmett Casselton is both.

"You mean the Klan's taken Marvin to the Casbah?" My voice, my whole throat quivers on the phrase favored by local biddies, black and white, to reel in wayward children . . . "You better be good," they warn, "or the Klan'll take you to the Casbah!" I never understood it, never connected it to Emmett Casselton's vast acreage—until now.

"I don't know, Reesa. I doubt it. I *do* know, however," Mother says, retreating behind her Poker Face, "in the time it'll take me to fix breakfast, you can finish your grandmother's bed. Go on now. I'll call you when it's ready." Gentle hands turn me toward the door.

The window at the top of the stairwell glows oddly orange; daybreak's flaming the treetops of the back grove. *Marvin, where are you?*

Both my younger brothers lay sound asleep in Mitchell's room. I switch on the light in Ren's room opposite, its windows facing west and the driveway. *Daddy and Luther should just about be there by now.*

Ren's mattress is bare, except for the tidy stack of Doto's pink sheets. During the nine months she's elsewhere, our grandmother's sheets, two sets of them, sit folded in the upstairs linen closet. The sheets are from downtown Chicago's Carter-Ferris-Mott store. "I can't sleep on *any*thing else," I heard Doto tell Mrs. Ruth Ferris at last year's Florida Party at the big Ferris house south of town. From there, she launched into "My aunt Ethel was a Carter, of the Cape Cod Carters; I'm sure we're related to your father-in-law's partner." *If he's in that lemon grove, Buddy will find him.*

Southerners set great store by their ancestry, but it's a rare Rebel who can go toe-to-toe with my Yankee grandmother and win. Doto dotes on her lineage the way other old ladies delight in dahlias or Staffordshire teacups. Given half a chance, she blatantly brags she named Daddy, her firstborn, for "Richard Warren of the *Mayflower*"; her daughter Eleanor for "the wife of William the Conqueror" and Uncle Harry for "the Revolutionary War hero General Light-Horse Harry Lee, of the New York Lees, not those people in Virginia."

Shouldn't they be back by now?

Stuffing and fluffing Doto's pillows, I hear, *finally*, the roar of the truck engine, Buddy's barking and the urgent blast of Daddy's horn. I run to the open window and yell, "Daddy, what's wrong?"

He jumps out onto the driveway and shouts, "Roo, get your mother. We need blankets, towels—quick!"

Hurtling down the steps two, three at a time, I nearly crash into her, arms full of linens from the downstairs closet. Together, we race out of the house to the truck.

Luther's on his knees in the back. Daddy grabs towels and blankets, yells "Stand back now!" and springs to the sideboard, bending low. A raggedy moan rises from the shadows of the truck bed. Mother steps forward to peer over the side and, with a sharp gasp, spreads her arms like wings and folds them backwards, trapping me behind her. I wiggle away and dash to the tailgate. Jumping up on the back bumper, I see with a shock the blood-covered body in the back.

Marvin Cully, who I've known all my life, who taught me to pick tangelos without ripping the fruit cap, who showed me the secret of steering a go-cart, who started the game of rhyming my name, lies drenched in blood in the bed of my father's truck. His head and eyes are covered with something, a familiar fabric, one of Ren's striped T-shirts, turned into a terrible blood-soaked turban. Bright red, dark brown, dried black blood is everywhere: congealing in cuts on his jaw and neck, seeping through rips in his shirt and pantlegs, oozing out of scrapes on the tops of his bare feet. "Marvin! You all *right*?" I cry as the sickening sweet smell heaves my stomach into my throat. His lips, bleeding in a bright red trickle onto his chin, don't move, can't answer.

"G'wan now, Roo!" Luther yells in a garbled plea, replacing a stained picking sack with a soft towel under Marvin's head.

"Lizbeth!" Daddy barks, settling blankets over Marvin's chest.

Mother's hands, like claws, yank me down, turn me around, clutch me to her chest. "No, Roo, no!" she cries, walking stiffly backward toward the house. Her heart, like mine, drums in my ear.

"Lizbeth, call Doc Johnny! Tell him we have a bad case of Klan fever, *really* bad! We'll be at his back door in ten minutes. Okay?"

"Okay," Mother says, steering us onto the walk. "Go!"

"Damn them," Daddy swears. "Damn those damn Klanners to hell!"

The truck engine growls and jerks into reverse down the driveway. As the front porch door slams behind us, two figures float in the bright sunlight now filling the stairwell. "Mother?" the boys call, sleepily scratching themselves.

"Ren, take Mitchell into the kitchen," she commands, waving them off to the back. She reaches for the phone to dial Doc Johnny and as she does so, lets me go. At my side, a dark, damp nose sniffs its concern; I feel myself sinking, sobbing into the furry softness of Buddy's neck.

Chapter 2

Our house is old, "turn of the century," my parents say. "New England saltbox in a Miss Scarlett petticoat," Doto always calls it, meaning the wide screened porches that flounce around the ground floor with the kitchen, like a bustle, in the back. When my parents bought it from old Mr. Swann, the house had two big bedrooms upstairs but, after Mitchell was born, they converted the broad side porch into a downstairs bedroom for themselves, with a smaller one in the back for me.

After Mr. Swann sold it to them, he just walked out, leaving his linens, china, dining room table, his piano in the living room—everything but his clothes—behind. Said he wouldn't need them where he was going. As it turned out, Daddy says, that piano was a lifesaver. When Daddy caught the polio, the summer I was born, playing the piano helped him regain the use of his right hand and most of his right arm. It also kept him from going nuts, he says. Still does.

Daddy glances at me when I enter the living room, but keeps on playing, nodding his okay to join him on the bench. He's dressed for the funeral in white shirt and dark tie; his suit coat hangs off the mantel, like a strange, coal-colored Christmas stocking.

Strangeness has descended on our house like a winter fog bank, blurring the lines between the last few days: *Marvin's dead, gone forever,* the words singsong in my head trying to convince my heart they're true; Doto here, finding everything in an uproar; Doc Johnny unable, or unwilling, to state the cause of death; Constable Watts shrugging it off as a jook-joint fight, stopping just short of calling Daddy a liar about Round Lake Road. "Besides," the string-bean Cracker laughed, tall and rangy in his constable uniform, "everybody knows the Opalakee Klan don't kill niggers like they *use* to." Daddy came home fuming. "In the old days," he told us, meaning before the polio, "lawman or not, I'd have pretzeled that pecker-wood." Before I was born, they say, my father had a torrential temper, huge as a hurricane, fast and physical. But the polio, he says, taught him patience. The man I know is more circumspect, with a temper that veers toward geological. When Daddy's upset, he turns to stone, granite-faced, flinty-eyed. Now, he sits rock-like at the piano, a one-man Mount Rushmore, fingering his thoughts.

The song "I am a poor wayfaring stranger" is one of the saddest in the Mayflower Baptist hymnal. We'll sing it on Palm Sunday, the week before we sing the happiest song, "Up from the grave He arose, with a mighty triumph o'er His foes."

"Daddy," I ask him, "is it true, what Doto says about Richard Warren being called the Stranger?"

"Yes, honey. On the *Mayflower,* the Pilgrims were the Saints and they called the people like Richard Warren, whose company was paying for the voyage, the Strangers."

"When we studied them last fall, Mrs. Beacham said she never heard of such a thing."

"True story, Roo," Daddy says, fingertips teasing out the chorus.

"Doto says she's afraid she jinxed you by naming you after him."

"Maybe so, Roo. Sometimes I know exactly how he felt."

"Will the funeral last long?"

"Several hours, I guess. There's the service and the burial, then the gathering at Luther and Armetta's. Afterwards, there's a meeting with Reverend Stone and some elders."

"What about?"

"Options, Rooster."

"You mean about finding out who killed Marvin?"

"The Klan killed Marvin, Roo. The question is why. And what's to be done about it."

"But you've always said the Klan was nothing to be afraid of, just a bunch of good ol' boys playing boogey-man."

Daddy lifts his hands off the keyboard and drops them in a ball in his lap. His back, ramrod straight when he plays, curls forward, shoulders falling. The right one, his "polio shoulder," dips lower than the left. His chin juts forward in a craggy outcrop.

"Like Doto says, we are strangers in a strange land. The Klan's been around here for years—stupid stuff mostly, burning crosses, pestering couples parking in the dark, picking on Negroes they thought were getting uppity, whatever that means. But this week, they crossed the line."

"But May Carol's Daddy's in the Klan. May Carol says it's nothing but a card club, an excuse to play poker. And, Armetta works for them in their house!"

"Lord, Roo, it's a complicated mess," he says, straightening up again, chest expanding, blue eyes blazing. "I wish we'd known more about it before we bought all this property and—"

"Warren?"

Mother's voice, the scent of her shiny, shampooed hair and the unzipped back of her black dress hush him. Daddy stands to help her. She turns with a murmured thanks, lifting a handful of dark curls off her neck. Normally playful and softly pretty, Mother's face looks stiff and drawn today, like she's steeling herself to get through these hours.

"Roo, make sure you finish up the breakfast dishes before Doto does," she says. Then, leaning forward, with a glance upstairs and a flash of dimple, she whispers, "If she starts putting things away, it could easily turn into a 'let's clean out the cupboards' project."

"Okay," I say, grateful for the reminder.

Doto is the queen of clean. Since arriving on Thursday, she's been "spot cleaning," a corner here, a closet there, all in the name of "helping your mother out." Mother's handled this with distracted grace, thankful for the help. Daddy's accused Doto of marking her territory, like a dog does its yard.

"We should be going, don't you think?" Mother says, checking her wristwatch.

"Yep," he says as he grabs his coat and strides to the stairwell. "We're leaving, Doto. Bye, Ren, Mitchell," he calls in the direction of the boys' upstairs whining. "I'm sure those kids have the cleanest ears in town by now," he tells us. A wide, roguish grin gleams suddenly, whitely against his tanned face.

"You look like a pirate," Doto told him the other day, stepping regally out of her new DeSoto.

"At your service, m'lady," Daddy had laughed, extending his hand, bending in a low Errol Flynn-like bow.

They make a handsome couple, I think, as my parents cross the front porch and turn to call, "Bye, Reesa. Be good."

Ears scrubbed, breakfast dishes stowed, porches swept, my brothers and I gather at the kitchen table with our grandmother, who's investigating her wallet for "cash on hand."

"Now, about lunch," Doto says. "I'm thinking clam chowder might hit the spot. What do you all think?" We all know that the only place for miles around that serves such a thing is the Lakeview Inn in Mount Laura, which means huge hot fudge sundaes for everyone.

"Sure! You bet!" we say, delivering the response she's after.

"Let's take a little drive then, shall we?"

We pile into the big DeSoto, the boys sinking into the white leather back seat, inhaling greedily the smell of new car.

Doto fits her DeSoto like candy in a wrapper. This one, a special order, is Mediterranean blue, which looks like turquoise to me, white interior, and chrome everywhere. Doto's glasses are cat-eyed in a shape almost identical to the DeSoto's taillights; her hair, permed and combed in twin side waves, reminds me of the car's back fins. Between us, in the front, is her brown leather map box, containing the Triple A's most up-to-date routing from her home outside Chicago to Mayflower, Florida; Mayflower to Bozeman, Montana (Uncle Harry's home); Bozeman to Baltimore (where Aunt Eleanor lives) and back again to La Grange, Illinois.

The DeSoto's engine purrs like a happy cat as Doto backs

carefully out of our driveway and noses north to the crossroad off Old Dixie Highway, then onto the Orange Blossom Trail. Unlike the larger towns of Opalakee south of us and Mount Laura to the north, Mayflower is little more than a place where the Trail picks up a couple side streets, Old Dixie on the east side and Citrus on the west. Dead center, where most places have a courthouse or a city hall, stands the Mayflower Citrus processing plant, Emmett Casselton's giant co-op, turning most of the local fruit into trainloads of frozen Jiffy Girl juice concentrate.

Across the street, "like a wart on old Emmett's nose," Daddy says, is our family's small, fancy-fruit packinghouse. "Independent Grower—Packer—Shipper" it says on tall billboards facing the traffic both ways. Passing by in the DeSoto, we see the signs Mother and Daddy put out on their way to Marvin's funeral. "Closed for the Day" they say, blocking both entrances to the gravel parking lot. Beside the packinghouse is our Trail-side grove, which runs to Mr. Fred Turnbull's Standard Oil station, then his grove, then the office of "Buy a Patch of Paradise!!! J.J. Jenkins, Real Estate & Insurance." At the north end of town is Tomasinis', the small store run by our friends Sal and Sophia Tomasini, the only other Northerners in Mayflower, and the source of meat, milk, bread and other staples for the residents of The Quarters. Voight's, at the south end, is where most white people shop.

Just beyond Tomasinis' is the entrance to The Quarters, the steeple of St. John's African Methodist Episcopal Church and the funeral assembly of old, smudge-colored cars and trucks. Our parents' Chevy Styleline wagon is the only white-owned vehicle there.

Doto shakes her head as we pass by. "That poor young man. Such an abominable waste!"

We all fall silent, thinking our own thoughts of Marvin, his long easy stride, his wide-as-the-world grin, his love of a rhyme and a joke. He and his father have picked fruit for us forever, and since that awful morning two days ago, I've used my best memories of him to try to push away that picture of his body in Daddy's truck. Marvin was the one who turned my real name, Marie Louise, and my nickname, Reesa, into "Reesa-Roo-How-Do-You-Do," "Rooter-Tooter-Where's-Yo'-Scooter" and, my favorite, "Rootin'-Tootin'-How's-Yo'-Shotgun-Shootin'." Marvin was always good about letting me in on things that everybody else seemed to know already, like the fact that Luther wasn't his real daddy. Marvin's real daddy died or ran off when he was little, but "that's all right," he told me, because "Luther's *twice* the man mah real daddy was." It was Marvin and Luther who gave us our German shepherd Buddy, because "nobody oughta live in the middle of an orange grove without a good dog." When we first got Buddy, he sometimes vanished back to Luther and Armetta's house in The Quarters. Marvin would tie a rope around Buddy's neck and walk him home to us. "Hey-Root-Hog-Lost-A-Dog?" he'd call from our back porch.

Only Marvin could tell me when it was officially spring. "It ain't oh-fishal 'til the granddaddy bird calls it's time to '*Whip-Poor-Will!*' and the big bull 'gator bellows back, '*You leave ol' Will alone fo' Ah come over there, give yuh what fo'!*'"

"Who's Will and what did he do?" I'd ask each year, mock suspicious.

"I don't know, but *whatever* it was, his wife was in on it, too," he'd say, looking at me sideways.

"Now, how do you know that?"

" 'Cause, Roo, the other birds cry '*Whip-Will's-Widow!*' "

"Marvin, I never heard the birds say that!"

"Oh, *lots* of folks hear, but only a *few* listen," he'd reply, dropping his chin, narrowing his eyes at me.

The sky is bright, bird's-egg blue, cloudless; the sun March-warm, not yet summery hot. The DeSoto glides past the pure geometry of the groves. So my grandmother won't see or say anything about my tears, I turn away, tapping out the rhythm of the green rows flying past the window, haunted by the awful singsonging inside my head: *Marvin's dead, gone forever.*

North into Lake County, we reach the historic New England-style mansion that's the Lakeview Inn. The Inn sits between two stands of navel trees still in full bloom, on a slight ridge above pretty Lake Laura. As we pull into the driveway, the smell of orange blossoms and fried food fills the car. The azaleas, blazing pink against the wide white porch, look like they'd smell good, too, but I know they have no scent at all.

"Your grandfather and I used to winter across the lake from here," Doto tells four-year-old Mitchell, reaching out to rub his buzz-haired head. "The first time I brought your father here, he was a babe in arms."

Mitchell squints up at her, knitting his pale brows at the idea of a baby Daddy in Doto's arms. We call him our human fireplug because he's about that high and wide, and bursting with me-too energy. Spitting image of your uncle Harry, Doto says. Eight-year-old Ren, on the other hand, is lean and lanky, with Mother's curls and easygoing disposition except, Doto says, for the streak of the daredevil that's pure Daddy.

The Inn's hostess, who's older than Doto and remembers her, greets us loudly, exclaiming over how big we've grown, and settles us in a booth with a view.

Outside, the lawn runs down to the lake. People stroll on white crushed-shell pathways admiring more pink azaleas, late red camellias, lavender clusters on the lolly-popped chinaberry trees and the sweet, sun-colored jessamine trained over a trellis. Beyond the lake, orderly rows of blossoming trees march up and over the rolling hills. This is the Florida the snowbirds fall for.

The menus, the size of newspapers, dwarf us. We know what we want so we slap them shut right away and order as soon as our waitress appears. Doto sips her iced tea and Ren and I carefully suck our Coke straws. Mitchell's another story. Since our baby brother is not yet accustomed to Doto's strong opinions on table manners, the appropriate use of a straw and napkin, she quietly lectures him. Just after the waitress delivers our food——clam chowder for Doto, fried clams and French fries for us——a loud burst of male laughter from the booth next door startles us.

"The hell of it is, they grabbed the wrong nigger!" roars one of the men.

Doto's soup spoon freezes midair; her eyes slit at the man's language.

"They cruised the juke joint and saw him, young buck leanin' up against this white Caddy with New York plates. Uppity-ass burr-head smart-talked Jimmy Sims at his garage. They got the bastard, shut him up right quick and headed for a little stompin' party at Round Lake."

The man telling the story stops for a noisy swig of his drink.

"Reed Garnet, y'all know him? Got there little late and that half-dead nigger looks up at him and whimpers, 'Mr. Reed, Mr. Reed, it's *me*, Marvin!' "

Again the table laughs, this time at the storyteller's high-voice impersonation of the Negro dialect. Doto glares at us around the table, hazel eyes beading the unmistakable message *don't make a sound.*

"Well, Reed, he was hoppin' mad, called those boys a bunch of morons, told them this boy's mamma works in his house and now what were they gonna do? J. D. Bowman, y'all know that crazy Opalakee boy, just got back from Korea? Well, J.D. he just laughed, pulled out his pistol and shot that nigger boy in the head. 'Problem solved,' he told ol' Reed."

At this, the table's other occupants guffaw, slapping the tabletop in high humor. The speaker snickers, "I saw ol' Reed at the Wellwood Cafe, said I hoped he wudn't too broke up about it. It's good t' kill a nigger every once in a while, keeps the rest of 'em in line."

More murmurs and loud laughter follow.

"Way *I* look at it . . . one less nigger makes the world a cleaner place. Mary Sue, honey, it's my turn to buy these ol' boys their pie and coffee."

We sit in our booth, silent, lips tight, chests rising and falling in long, slow breaths. Tears collect inside my eyelids; I fight them off by pinching the back of my hand so hard the pain takes my mind off crying. The waitress brings the check to the men next door, hidden by the flowered curtain between our booth and theirs. The speaker pays; coins rattle as she makes change from her apron.

Three men slide and rise out of their booth, backs to us, hitching up their pants. The one closest to us, the storyteller, has on matching green-gray shirt and pants. As he ambles out of the dining room, he lifts his hat—the wide flat brim of a Lake County Sheriff's Deputy—onto his head. The men disappear out of the dining room, their boots clomping across the hardwood floor like dry thunder rolling off the horizon.

Doto sucks air deeply, bends forward, cat eyes glinting behind her glasses. She hisses: "Not a word until we're in the car."

"Awful quiet crew today," the redheaded waitress tells us with a smile. A curly wire pin on her uniform spells out "Mary Sue." Pink apron pockets bulge with order tickets and change. "Y'all save room for dessert?"

Ren and I cut our eyes at Mitchell, who's salivating for his hot fudge sundae.

"Just the check, please," Doto says with a frozen smile.

Chapter 3

Our family huddles around the kitchen table as Doto re-tells the story we heard in the restaurant. Her lips curl in distaste at the words she must use to tell it exactly. Beside her, Daddy's jaw mirrors hers in its hardening. Mother's eyes, red-rimmed from the funeral, stay on his; the single dimple in her left cheek missing in a mask of sadness. Beside me, Ren twists a buried fist in the pocket of his baseball glove. Doto is livid.

"To hear that idiot talk about Marvin like the boy was an animal, a dog to be put out of its misery, I swear I could have killed him with my bare hands."

The image of my 110-pound grandmother throttling that 200-pound Deputy flickers through my mind. The eyes behind her cat glasses are shooting sparks.

"I want you to call that Opalakee Constable and get him over here. This has got to be an important clue in his case."

"The Constable has no case, Doto," Daddy tells her in a flat voice that puzzles me.

"Well, this ought to give him one," she retorts.

"The Constable is a card-carrying Klan member. His standard line with anything involving a colored is 'We'll look into it' and he never does."

"But, Daddy," I say, "Marvin's *dead!*"

"Can't you call the Sheriff, or one of the County Commissioners?" Doto demands.

"The Sheriff, the Commissioner, the Opalakee Chief of Police, they're all Klan members. Even goddamn Governor Fuller Warren is one of them!"

"Governor *Warren*," Doto snorts. "That's one Warren that is no *possible* relation of ours!"

Shoving herself up and out of her chair, she paces the yellow linoleum. "The Klan *owns* this state like Capone owned Chicago," she rails, turning like a teacher, finger raised to make her point. "He owned the city, the county, the state, but . . ." Her eyes lock onto Daddy's. "You remember how they got rid of *him*."

Daddy studies his mother and I can see the wheels begin to turn. He leans forward, elbows on the table, chin on top of his folded hands, staring at the squiggly pattern in the blue Formica.

"The F.B.I.," he says. "I don't know how Mr. Hoover feels about the Klan, but I know he's no fan of cold-blooded killing. We could try to contact him . . . but how?" The veins in his temple jump. "We couldn't possibly call him," he says. "We'd never get through. Besides . . ."

"Maybelle . . ." Mother says it quietly.

"Would likely listen in and blab all over town," Daddy nods, completing her thought.

Our family has the unfortunate fate of sharing a party line with our two-doors-up neighbor Miss Maybelle Mason, who's also the town postmistress and perpetual old biddy. Miss Maybelle listens in on other people's phone calls as a form of entertainment. At the post office, where everybody has a box, she takes it personal if anyone dares receive a letter without a proper return address. It's rumored she opens such letters to verify their claim to space in her postal slots.

"That old bird lets out writing a letter as well. If the F.B.I. wrote us back, we'd never hear the end of it. But . . . Buuut . . ." Daddy says. "We *could* send a registered letter from downtown Orlando and use your address in LaGrange for the return."

"Of course." Doto lights up in support of the plan. "Blanche would forward it here inside my weekly packet."

"It could *work*," I say, seeing it all inside my head.

"It will work!" Doto declares.

"Blanche," Mother adds softly, "is our trump card."

"That's the plan then," Daddy says. He leaves the kitchen and goes into the small office off the living room. We hear the snap of paper rolling into his typewriter and the clack of the keys punching out the story of Marvin's murder for Mr. J. Edgar Hoover of the Federal Bureau of Investigation.

Doto walks to the refrigerator, patting her hair waves. "Lizbeth," she says, opening the Frigidaire, "I believe I owe these children some ice cream. Got any fudge sauce?"

Chapter 4

I did not go to school the Thursday Marvin died, or the day after that. The funeral was on Saturday; and Sunday went by me in a blur.

"Please," I begged my parents this morning, "don't make me go! I don't want to, not today, not *ever* again."

The idea of returning to a place where most people's lives have flowed right along uninterrupted by blood-wet bodies and bald-faced lying and bad people doing awful things; the thought of playing Red-Rover-Red-Rover-Can-Reesa-Come-Over as if Marvin's alive and laughing as he should be, and his poor old parents aren't sitting broken-hearted in their house—"I can't," I cried, "I just *can't!*"

Doto, ever the diplomat, replied, "I don't blame you. I couldn't ride in that smelly old school bus either. How about we drive down in the DeSoto? Maybe you'll feel differently when we get there."

My grandmother is the reason I'm here this morning, trying to pretend like I belong. I sit in the same desk, surrounded by the same children who were here before. Up front, Mrs. Beacham carries on in her same old brown suit and ugly lace-up shoes. But no one, none of it, feels the same.

Sunlight floods through the wall of windows, brightly white. I sit, deliberately opening my eyes to the whiteness, then closing them to ghostly black; seeing day full of life, then, behind flickering eyelids, trying to imagine death.

The idea that life is as fragile and full of holes as a lace curtain terrifies me. The other kids in this room have no idea. Well, maybe one of them does.

I see her two rows over, three seats ahead of me, but we've avoided each other's eyes all morning. May Carol Garnet knows about Marvin. She has to because Armetta works in her house. Beyond housekeeping, Armetta mothers May Carol in ways Miz Lucy Garnet never could. I can tell from here, by her unstarched dress, her plain, unplaited ponytail, that Armetta, May Carol's other mother, has not yet returned to work at the Garnet house.

May Carol and I know each other. We've spent time at each other's houses, made cookies with Armetta, laughed with Luther, endured Marvin's big-brother-like teasing our whole lives. But we are not friends.

Maybe it's her "Southern-ness" that gets in the way. The tendency to sort everything and everyone according to appearances. But maybe, just maybe, it's my sense of "other-ness," an in-the-blood inability to be a joiner. Like Doto says, our family runs long on being in, but not of, the places we call home.

Outside, a row of orange trees lines the school playground. Six days ago today, I saw Marvin for the last time, standing by the trees that edge our backyard.

"Looky here, Rootin'-Tootin'," he'd called to me, "here go

Mistuh Bee payin' his respects to Miss Angel Blossom. You know the story, don't yuh? 'Bout how Mistuh Bee got his stripes, and his wings, too?"

"Tell it to me, Marvin," I remember asking.

"Well, it goes like this," he said, sitting on an orange crate. "After God got done creatin' the world and everythin' in it, He was mighty proud of the way things turned out. 'Course, His angels was mighty curious 'bout what God done. So, God told 'em, 'Y'all g'wan down there, angels, take a look-see.' Now, angels, like humans, come in all different measures and band together with others they size. So, the band of littlest, tiniest, tee-ninchy angels flew down together and landed in a orange grove 'bout like this one, made it smell like heaven on earth. When those angels looked down on God's new-made ground, *what* did they see? The first big ol' fire ant, red as the devil, beatin' up the first big ol' black bee with a cat-o'-nine-tails, saying '*Ah's* your Massa now, bee, get to work!' Well, that whippin' is what gave Mistuh Bee the stripes on his back. And what made the leader of the tee-ninchy angels fly down and cry, 'You ol' devil ant, get back underground where you belong 'fore Ah tell the Massa of the Universe what you done!' Now, that fire ant high-tailed it into his hole right *quick*! Then, the angel no bigger than a blossom turned to poor Mistuh Bee and noticed God had forgotten to give him wings. 'Here, Mistuh Bee,' that angel say, 'you take mah wings, Ah'll grow some more. You take these wings and you fly 'way up high in them trees, make your home where they *ain't* never no evil ants.' That's how Mistuh Bee got his stripes, and his wings, in a single day. And that's why, ever since, when the groves grow blossoms that smell like heaven, Mistuh Bee flies back, pays his respects to the Angel Blossoms that set him free."

"Marie Louise!" Mrs. Beacham's voice in my ear, her big brown shoes on the floor beside my feet, make me jump.

"Shall I ask the school nurse to schedule a hearing check?" Her face is like a walrus, fleshy folds wobbling off her chin.

"Pardon me?"

"Here's your worksheet: Transportation Systems of the Ancient Egyptians. There are others that we covered in your absence. Meet me at my desk, please. May Carol Garnet, you may as well come, too."

While the rest of the class works at their desks, we stand together in front of Mrs. Beacham. I notice with a shock May Carol's fingernails. Usually shiny and shell pink, the polish is chipped, nails bitten to the quick. Her hair, normally braided, slips limply out of her ponytail. She's a small thing, pink and pretty (unlike me who's a medium everything— medium brown hair, middle-of-the-road size, looks I know are "fair to middlin' "). I'm surprised to hear May Carol's missed as much school as I have; and to see that her eyes, like mine, are sunken and dark-circled.

I'd like to ask what she's upset about—Marvin's death or Armetta's absence?—and tell her things I'm *sure* she doesn't know—about her daddy being there that night and all. But of course that's not possible. She's the daughter of a Klansman and I'm to keep my mouth closed.

Chapter 5

It's an ironclad tradition. On Palm
Sunday, the congregation of Mayflower Baptist, the only white church
in town, has dinner-on-the-grounds.

Under the ruthless direction of Miss
Maybelle Mason, the old snapping turtle
who runs the post office, Ren and the boys
from the Royal Ambassadors bivouac the
long tables under the big live oaks beside
the sanctuary. While Miss Maybelle fumes
over straight lines and wide-enough walk-
ways, Miz Naideen West, the preacher's
pinch-faced wife, fusses over the white
sheets she calls tablecloths (which are the
exact same ones she calls drapes during the
Children's Christmas Pageant). On top of
the sheets, she spreads long palm fronds
for decoration. After church, the women
will cover them with their specialties.

Everyone knows who cooks what best,
and for weeks now, when the church ladies

pass each other at the post office or in Mr. Voight's grocery store, they fawn and nod with exaggerated politeness. "You *are* makin' your fried chicken, your baked beans, your carrot Jell-O salad, aren't you?" they chirp like birds to one another.

When they see Mother, these women have one thing on their minds. "Lizbeth, you are bringin' that *scrumptious* fruit cocktail cake of yours!" It's always the first dessert to disappear.

Unlike most people around here, we weren't born Southern Baptist. Doto and her family are self-described Lukewarm Methodists and Mother's from a long line of Congregationalists, which is practically Episcopalian. When my parents arrived in Mayflower, they were newlyweds, barely past twenty, and kept to themselves. The following year, though, it was obvious that Mother was expecting me and, even more so, that Daddy got the polio. After Doto and Doc Johnny (and Luther, of course), Miss Maybelle Mason, eyes like a hawk, was first on the scene. Of course, she organized the church ladies in nothing flat and the casseroles arrived, like clockwork, for months. As Mother recovered, and Daddy improved, they were honorbound to repay the brigade for their diligence. The price was membership in Mayflower Baptist Church.

Of course, the major prerequisite is baptism. But it's an often-told, true story that Daddy caught the polio in the very lake where the baptisms take place, and refused to enter it again or allow Mother to, either. Citing some sort of "Biblical precedence," the minister agreed, and my parents' waterless entry into the congregation gave new meaning to the term "dry Baptists."

It was afterwards that Miss Maybelle, who always has her ears open, heard Daddy playing the piano and revealed his talent to the community. Long story short, Daddy got roped into leading the Mayflower Baptist choir, a job which he vows is infinitely preferable to being a Deacon.

Although we attend every Sunday, my parents take "the long view" on a number of church tenets, the most notable being the ban on alcohol. Daddy, a quick Bible study, never minds pointing out that the Apostle Paul encouraged Timothy to "drink a little wine for thy stomach." "Surely," Daddy says, "*Paul* enjoyed a glass of the grape and *so* can I."

On Mother's part, she just bakes her fruit cocktail cake exactly as her mother does, flooding the coconut and pecan mix on top of the cake batter with a generous cup of rum, then covering all with brown sugar and dots of butter.

None of this means my family's not *spiritual*. (Though what happened to Marvin has put me at odds with God these days.) To their credit, our parents have spent considerable time discussing the difference between Faith—the abiding belief in a Divine Creator that's as plain a part of a hundred-year-old oak tree, or a fiery red sunset, as the nose on your face—and Religion—which is the rigamarole that makes *some* folks figure they've got a leg up on everybody else.

Usually, my favorite part of Palm Sunday is the young people's Bible Drill, the hotly contested game of who-can-find-it-fastest, played in the lag time between the end of church and the blessing that begins dinner-on-the-grounds. Usually I love the competition, and to tell you the truth, usually I do quite well.

But this year, because of Marvin and all, I didn't feel like competing. In fact, I'd made up my mind *not* to participate until Doto told me about the prize—four tickets to the glass-bottom boat ride at Silver Springs—and suggested, if I won, I might give them as a thinking-of-you gift to Luther and Armetta.

It was Marvin, after *all*, who turned me into a first-class Bible Driller, by sharing his secret.

"Think of the Bible as a rainbow, Roo," he told me. "See the books in colors. The beginning ones are red: Genesis and all the begets and begats and the Moses books through Judges, *scarlet* red. After that comes the name and story books starting with Ruth and going through the poem books to the juicy Songs of King Solomon. They navel orange. After that, you got the four major prophets, Isaiah, Jeremiah, Ezekiel and Daniel, plus a whole batch of minor prophets, twelve actually, Hosea through Malachi. They daylily yellow, and *that's* the end of the Old Testament.

"Up next, they's the Jesus stories with the four Gospels and the Acts, they your green section with the words 'spoken by our Lord and Savior' in red letters—green and red like Christmas, y'see. Then, they's the Apostle Paul's letters to *all* the different churches all over the ancient *world* starting with the Romans through the Hebrews. They blue, Mediterranean Sea blue. At the hind end of things, you got the other letters from James, Peter, John and Jude; they's violet. No need to give the Revelations a color, *everybody* knows where they is." Marvin was a patient and inventive teacher.

Today, in his honor, when our Sunday school teacher Miz Agnes Langford calls "Time for Bible Drill!" I join the others elbowing their way into formation in front of the food tables. I prefer, and take, the end.

"Attention!" Miz Agnes commands and we straighten up like good Christian soldiers, Bibles at our thighs, pinned in the curve of our right palms.

"Draw swords!" comes next, which means Bible front and center, face-down on left palm, right hand on top, thumb at the ready.

After that, Miz Agnes calls book, chapter and verse: "Ezekiel 34:12."

Yellow, I think, *middle of the book*, and take a breath.

She calls it again: "Ezekiel 34:12," then gives the command: "Charge!"

I breathe out, thumb the Bible open to the middle, check book name and chapter, top right corner, check verse numbers bottom left, and step forward.

"Reesa?" she says.

"Ezekiel 34:12," I say, then read, *"As a shepherd seeketh out his flock in the day that he is among his sheep that are scattered; so will I seek out My sheep, and will deliver them out of all places where they have been scattered in the cloudy and dark day."*

Miz Agnes *always* picks out comfort verses.

"That's right, Reesa, and what a comfort. Attention!"

I step back into the line and we start again. The person who finds the most verses first wins.

One Sunday, only once, she let me call the verse. To amuse the others, I picked a recent discovery from the orange section, Song of Solomon 7:2: "Thy navel is like a round goblet that wanteth not liquor: thy belly is like a heap of wheat set about with lilies."

Miz Agnes was not comforted and spoke to my parents afterwards. Later, Daddy laughed and asked if I was trying so hard to shock Miz Langford, why didn't I go with the one about *I am a wall and my breasts are like towers?*

"Be bold," Daddy told me, "or what's the point?"

Today's Palm Sunday Bible Drill comes down to a tie breaker—me versus Billy Roy Sparks, who's two years older and can say the books of the Bible backwards. I'm not worried. Truth is, I usually beat him.

The others stand back, while Billy Roy and I square off for the final selection. The adults are hungry, their interest roused by whiffs of rapidly arriving country ham, fried chicken and cinnamon sweet potato "sue-flay." Miz Naideen and several other ladies stand sentry, using long palm fronds to wave the flock of greedy flies and wandering fingers away from the food platters.

Miz Agnes shushes the crowd, holding up two plump hands, palms forward, for quiet. She turns to face us, raises a dramatic, sausage-shaped finger and calls "Attention!"

Billy Roy and I straighten in front of the crowd.

"Draw swords!" she cries.

Ready.

"John 12:12 and 13," comes the call.

Green section, red letters.

"John 12:12 and 13. Charge!"

I thumb and scan and step out in a flash, but Billy Roy is there, one plaid-shirted, Vitalis-shellacked hair ahead of me.

"Billy Roy?"

"John 12:12 and 13," he says, and reads, "*On the next day, much people that were come to the feast, when they heard that Jesus was coming to Jerusalem, took branches of palm trees, and went forth to meet him, and cried, 'Hosanna: Blessed is the King of Israel that cometh in the name of the Lord!'*"

As everyone applauds, I'm not mad at Billy Roy. I'm really not. But I could kick myself for not seeing *that* one coming, it being *Palm Sunday* and all.

"You have to think ahead," Daddy says. I should've known.

D inners eaten, dishes gathered, the ladies of the church having duly noted which pots and pans were picked clean and which weren't, whose had gone first and whose hadn't, Mother and Doto wave me over.

"Reesa, please go round up the boys and see if Daddy's ready to go," Mother says, her fruit cocktail cake with rum long gone. Not even crumbs are left.

The boys are bent over a hot game of Acorns, jacks played with sticks and nuts scavenged from the feet of the big oaks. I holler at them to finish up and find Mother.

Daddy's with the men gathered in the deep shade beside the sanctuary. As I walk up, one, a tall, paunchy citrus man named Ralph MacElvoy, is saying:

"Luther and Marvin've picked my tangerines for years. Those boys're damn fine pickers, 'scuse me, Reverend. Fast, too. How's ol' Luther takin' it?" he asks, nodding in Daddy's direction.

"Hard as any *man* would who lost his only son," Daddy says, his careful choice of words glinting in Ralph MacElvoy's direction. My father can't abide the Southern custom of calling a grown man a *boy*.

Mr. MacElvoy gives Daddy an odd, sharp look. His eyes narrow slightly, then slide hastily away from my father's steely gaze. Daddy's not a large man, but he has the presence of somebody much bigger.

"I think this business up in Lake County's made the Opalakee Klanners a little trigger happy," Aldo Brass, one of the church deacons, says in his slow, thick Alabama drawl.

I learned all about this Lake County *business* when I got my pre-Easter perm at Miz Lillian's Beauty Parlor. Not that Miz Lillian told me directly, but it was all the other ladies talked about. The story started a year or so ago, when a white couple was driving home after dark and their car broke down on a back country road. Another car with four young Negroes stopped to help and offered them a ride to the gas station. The man didn't want to leave the car, so the woman went for help.

"Though what white woman in her right mind would get in a car with four Negroes, I want to know!" Miss Iris, Miz Lillian's assistant, said, eyes wide in the large mirror that runs the length of the shop.

"And what *husband* would let her!" Miz Lillian wondered, raising a perfectly penciled eyebrow.

The woman didn't come back, but the next morning, her husband found her talking to the man at the gas station. The woman and the man told her husband she'd been kidnapped. The day after that, she said those Negroes had *bothered* her.

Southern ladies use the word "bother" to mean anything from an inappropriate glance to rape, which is, apparently, *a fate worse than death*. The more serious the infraction, the further they drop their chins and their voice tones. From the steep descents surrounding me, the woman obviously claimed *the worst*.

All the white men in Groveland got riled up about that and Sheriff Willis McCall deputized the whole bunch into a posse. The posse searched the county for the men who the papers called "the Groveland Four." One man was shot "trying to escape," but three others were caught and stood trial together.

An all-white jury declared them guilty, sentencing two to The Chair and the other one, who was only fifteen, to Life in prison. When the N-double A-C-P got wind of it, their New York attorney, Mr. Thurgood Marshall, said the trial was unfair and filed an appeal. The Florida Supreme Court said the trial was fine, but Mr. Thurgood Marshall took the story all the way to the *U.S.* Supreme Court. The U.S. Supreme Court said it wasn't fair *at all*, on account of the jury being all white men and the local newspaper getting everybody all riled up about it. Miz Lillian read us the part in *Time* magazine where Justice Robert Jackson said, "This is one of the best examples of one of the worst menaces to American justice I've ever seen." So, now there's to be a new trial for the two men on Death Row.

"And don't you bet Sheriff Willis McCall is fit to be tied about that!" Miz Lillian's long, red-tipped fingers expertly flip the elastic cords off the pink and green curlers on my head.

"Isn't he some muckety-muck with the Klan in Lake County?" Miss Iris asked, wrist-deep in Miz Sooky Turnbull's henna rinse.

"Nuthin' I heard about him'd surprise me a bit," Miz Lillian replied.

"I know some folks don't think much of the Klan," Miz Sooky, our across-the-street neighbor, called from the sink, "but as a *woman*, I have to say I sleep better knowin' the Klan's around to keep the Nigras from goin' *wild*."

In the mirror, my face flushed furious at Miz Sooky's ignorance. Miz Sooky's not a bad person. She really isn't. She's always doing nice neighborly things like bringing over fresh-baked banana bread or sharing home-grown tomatoes. But, like a lot of people around here, she's got a gigantic, gaping *hole* in her head when it comes to Negroes. Fact is, never *once* in my life have I seen Miz Sooky that she hasn't worked in some reference to what she calls their "dark danger to Southern womanhood."

Miz Lillian, who's as smart as a whip, pursed her red lips at me in the mirror and together we shook our heads. Miss Iris made a face at Miz Sooky's lumpy old sack-dressed body, reclined headless at the sink, her square-cut hands like turnips, spotted and gnarled from gardening without her gloves on. *As if any man, besides old Mr. Fred, would want to bother your frumpy old bones,* I thought.

"Sooky?" Miz Lillian said, changing the subject firmly, "You bringin' your sweet corn salad to dinner-on-the-grounds this Sunday?"

D eacon Brass leans against the big oak tree like a scrawny stork, jacked up one-legged, perched on his heel. After a long, slow drag on his Pall Mall, he lifts his chin, blows smoke and drawls, to no one in particular, "Re-trial or not, those two boys are gonna *fry.*"

And what about that murdering J. D. Bowman? Will he fry, too? Or, I want to scream at him, at all of them, *does Justice wear a hood on top of a mask?*

Daddy, seeing my face, intercedes. Smooth as molasses, he asks, "Your mother ready, Roo?"

I nod, mute, feeling the familiar catch in my throat, the pinch in my chest that comes from not being able to speak my mind.

"Gentlemen," Daddy says, throwing an arm around me that's half warning, half comfort, and nods our goodbye to the men in the shade.

Chapter 6

At four-thirty, Ren and I race to the brick-front post office at the end of our street. *This is it,* we've decided, one week to the day since Doto's friend Blanche forwarded the notice that Mr. J. Edgar Hoover had received Daddy's letter. This is the day we'll receive his reply.

Together, we duck through the heavy, half-glass door, hoping to avoid our postmistress' evil eye. Hands on the counter, Miss Maybelle Mason unpleats her neck, squinting into the afternoon sun, an old turtle sniffing for trouble.

"Marie Louise!" she snaps, stopping us in our tracks. "You two want to explain why you're not in school today?"

"Easter vacation, ma'am, all week," I say, wondering why she'd hit us with such an obvious question. The front porch of the post office is also our school bus stop.

Each school day, Miss Maybelle watches us and the Samson boys like a hawk, making sure we don't sit down on either of the two benches out front which she informs us are "U.S. Government property!" I'm sure she keeps track of school vacations closer than we do.

"How old are you now?" she demands, giving me the once-over.

"Twelve, going on thirteen in July," I say, resenting her greenish-yellow gaze.

"Good. My niece from Virginia is comin' to town next month and she's bringin' her daughter who's about your age. I'm callin' your mother to have you two play together while my niece and I visit."

Miss Maybelle stops, not having asked me if I'm interested or anything, but clearly expecting a reply. As if, in addition to the P.O., she's the boss of the *world.*

"I'll tell Mother you'll be calling her, ma'am," I say lamely, hating how she makes my blood boil.

"Don't forget! Now, what kind of trouble you two gettin' into with no school all week?"

"No trouble, Miss Maybelle, just playing at the packing-house or down at Dry Sink." Ren's scratching the back of his left leg with his right foot.

"Dry Sink! There's no place around here called Dry Sink. What are you talkin' about?" she demands. Nothing sets her off like an inaccurate address.

"You know it, ma'am," I say. "That big, dry sinkhole in the back grove behind our house."

Miss Maybelle's age-spot-speckled face creases briefly into her snapping-turtle smile. "*That* what you call it? When I was a girl, it was Little Lake Annie, the local swimming hole."

"Dry Sink? A swimming hole?" we ask, truly amazed.

"Certainly was. We had a rope off the big old oak tree on the side, used to spend hours swinging off it into the lake," she cackles.

Ren and I look at each other, dumbstruck.

"You kids today have no idea what *real* fun is!" Miss Maybelle huffs. "Go on, now. Marie Louise, tell your mother she'll be hearing from me."

Ren and I beat a path around the corner to P.O. Box 122, second section, third row from the top. Moving fast, to escape Miss Maybelle and recover the conviction that "This is the Day!" Ren misdials the combination the first time and has to do it again. Finally, the little glassed door springs open. There it is—the large manila envelope from La Grange, Illinois, and a handful of small ones. I grab them all and, after cat-walking carefully past the front counter, we fly the half-mile back to the house.

Doto's where we left her, enthroned on the screened front porch with the large leather journals she calls her "bookwork." In the blue one, she records her "monthly updates" from the trustee who administers her father's estate. In the red book, she tracks her "income and outgo."

We burst through the screen door and our grandmother looks up, cat eyes twinkling. We thrust the envelope into her hands, grabbing our sides and gasping from the run.

Slowly, she takes her silver letter opener and slits open the top. Mother, having heard the door slam, appears expectant on the porch, reading glasses in hand. As Doto removes the stack of smaller envelopes from their enclosure, we eye each one for an official-looking clue. Quickly, she spreads them fan-wise like a bridge hand, scanning the return addresses in the upper left corners. Her face falls in the message *it's not here.*

"Look again," we insist, as she deals the stack, one by one, face up on her ledger book.

Not there. Even though last week's packet gave notice that our registered letter had been duly delivered to F.B.I. headquarters, even though he's had a whole seven days to respond, Mr. J. Edgar Hoover has not yet found time to reply.

"Damn," Ren says glumly. As the three females surrounding him look at him sharply, he levels his eyes, obviously feeling justified.

"Double-wide Hoover dam," Doto tosses the compliment to what she calls his *mettle*.

"Triple-toed beaver dam," he tosses back.

"Daddy's in the car barn." Mother sighs, veiling her disappointment. Ren and I run to deliver the news.

E aster Sunday, Miss Maybelle nabs me in the vestibule. "Marie Louise, I hope you haven't forgotten our social plans?" she says, squeezing a face-crease in my direction. "My grandniece Maryvale will be here the second Saturday in May and I'm sure she can't wait to play dolls with Miss Reesa McMahon!"

"Dolls!" I grouse to Mother once we're seated in the church pew. "You think Maryvale is some little bitty old biddy like Miz Maybelle?"

"I doubt it, Roo. I'm sure the Good Lord broke the mold after He made Maybelle," Mother murmurs. "Now, sit up straight, here comes Daddy and the choir."

Chapter 7

Easter night, Mother and I are peeling eggs when all of a sudden Buddy, asleep by the door, shoots to his feet and winds up his tail. At Luther's *tappety-tap-TAP*, Mother calls, "Come in!"

"Evenin', MizLizbeth. Howdy-Doo-Roo," Luther calls back. His over-bright smile's a poor mask for the dark grief lines crisscrossing his face. "Y'all have a nice Easter?"

"Okay, how about you?" Mother asks gently.

"Good as could be, all things considered," Luther says, dropping his eyes quickly to pat Buddy. My throat tightens at his sideways reference to Marvin, and following his lead, I swallow *hard*. After a moment, Luther looks up again. "How'd the program go?"

Under Daddy's direction, the choir performed an Easter cantata.

"Came off well," Mother says and leaves it at that.

The Easter service had been agony for me. I'd gone unprepared for the effects of the familiar story—the bright young man, so kind and gentle, so gifted at storytelling, the murderous mob, the uncaring officials, the terrible sorrow of his family and friends. Of course, Jesus' story turned out considerably better than Marvin's. The rousing finale, *Up from the grave He arose with a mighty triumph o'er His foes,* left me sobbing. Miz Sooky Turnbull, sitting in the pew behind us, reached up and patted me encouragingly, heartened, I'm sure, by the hope that I'd somehow blundered my way into salvation. It wasn't that at all, of course. Jesus rose, *a victor o'er the dark domain.* Marvin's dead, *gone forever.*

"How about yours?" Mother asks him.

Few white people realize that besides being the best citrus pruner in the county, Luther's choir director at St. John's A.M.E. And nobody, outside our family and his choir members, knows that the choirs of both churches often perform similar programs, courtesy of sheet music passed between the two directors.

"It was fine," Luther says, his eyes appreciating Mother's kindness.

I watch the two of them, marveling at the way they tiptoe around each other's pain, like the way your tongue probes yet protects a toothache.

"Armetta do her solo?" Mother inquires.

"Ah wish you could've heard her." Luther's smile is real this time. "Not even Paul Robeson hisself coulda sung 'bout the balm of Gilead any better. The whole church-house was lifted up, lifted right up."

"Wish we could've been there. Please tell Armetta I'm thinking of her," Mother says, laying a soft hand briefly on his forearm. "Reesa, show Luther in to Daddy, please."

Luther trails me into the living room where Daddy sits at the piano working on his new piece.

"Evenin', Mist'Warren. What we got here?" Luther takes his reading glasses out of his shirt pocket and puts them on his nose. "Rhap-so-*dee* in Blue," he reads. "How's it go?"

"You know this, don't you?" Daddy asks. "I used to. Forgot all about it 'til Doto showed up with the sheet music."

"Can Ah hear it?" Luther asks with the briefest flash of his old self. Daddy sees what's coming. Settling in on the sofa, so do I.

"Play it for me, Mist'Warren," he chides Daddy gently.

Musically, Daddy and Luther are different as night and day. While Daddy works hard mastering his pieces, Luther has the ability to hear a song once and play it back, perfectly at first, then even better, embroidered with whatever he hears inside his head. In the comfortable, comforting game they've played for years, the rules are simple: Daddy plays first for Luther, then Luther returns the favor.

When Daddy lays his hands on the keyboard, everything about him elongates. His head rises above an upright back. His legs extend flatly to the floor, right foot on the pedal, left toes gently tapping. His fingers stretch out on the keys, wrists flat.

"Rhapsody in Blue" is my new favorite song. When Daddy plays it, I imagine I'm in a place far away from here, where people are nothing but nice to each other. I see it clearly inside my head:

A beautiful ballroom, the handsome, tuxedoed gentleman and the charming Miss Rhapsody—a vision in sky-blue chiffon, swirling about her, around them as they dip and float across the polished marble floor. The sound of sophisticated music, the perfume of jasmine and orange blossoms fill the air, and her hair, with sweetness.

"That's a *fine* song. You played it right elegant!" Luther tells Daddy at its end.

"Thank you, sir." Daddy nods, ceremoniously yielding the piano bench to his old friend.

Luther sits. His long, loose-jointed body curls over the keyboard, palms pressed together briefly as if in prayer. Lightly, he lays one finger, then another, on the keys, tickling out the La-Da-Dee-Da of the opening. Then, fanning his fingers like a faith healer, he plays. Once the basic line is laid, he begins his embroidery, threading twice as many notes as Daddy did. Elbows, arms and his entire right leg pumping, angular yet effortless, like an ibis taking flight. Mother appears in the doorway. Doto, Ren and Mitchell crowd the upper stairwell.

Luther's version of the song is local—less Rhapsody, more Blue. His lady lays sobbing-hearted on her bed, waiting for the one who has not come. Memories of their last perfect dance together fall like leaves onto the crumpled heap that was her party dress, now abandoned on the floor. At one point, she gets up, suddenly alert, certain he's come. But, *no*, she realizes. *No*body's there. Sinking back into bed, sadder than before, she knows he's *not* coming, not tonight, not *ever* again.

Oh, Marvin . . . Remember when I said I wasn't looking forward to teenage dances because I didn't know how; and you said, "Don't worry, li'l Rooster. Ah'll teach yuh t' Car'lina Shag with the best of 'em!" Who's going to teach me now?

When Luther finishes, my entire family applauds him wildly. He looks up, dazed and distracted by a sorrow so thick it's seeped out his fingertips. He nods, thanking us all. "No, Luther, thank *you*," Doto calls from the top of the stairs. "That was wonderful."

"You's most kind, Miz Doto," he says softly.

Doto says goodnight and herds the boys back into their bedroom. Mother returns to the kitchen and I remain, temporarily forgotten, on the sofa.

In a voice worn and tired, Luther says quietly to Daddy, "Mist'Warren, Ah come for your help."

After their first year in Mayflower, my parents say, they asked Luther to stop addressing them with the customary *Mistuh* and *Miz* attached to their names. "We're friends," they told him, "our first names will *do*." But Luther wouldn't have it.

"Ah 'preciates what you saying, and Ah'm proud to call you friends 'cause you's quality folk; but you's in the South and got to get use to they ways. If Ah was to call you jus' Warren and Lizbeth, the white folks 'round here bound to think *you's* crazy, and they'd laugh at you and leave you alone. Worse'n that, they'd take a notion that *Ah's* getting uppity and that don't bring nothing but trouble, Ah *mean*!"

Eventually my parents surrendered to Luther's logic, yet, in his way, Luther rebelled against it, pruning the customary *Mistuh* down to *Mist'* for Daddy, grafting *Miz* and *Lizbeth* into a single word.

What is it, Luther?" Daddy asks, sitting in the chair nearest the piano bench, leaning forward.

"Armetta's plum grief-struck over losing our Marvin. Since it was the Klan that kilt him, and Mistuh Reed Garnet's a member, Armetta swears she can't never set foot in they house again. Miz Lucy Garnet's been up to our house with they little girl crying, *please* come back, saying Mistuh

Reed had nothin' to do with it, it was the Lake County devils that kilt our boy. Armetta won't take a listen—though she loves that li'l May Carol like her own, such a sweet child. But, Mist'Warren, Armetta's use to working, she *needs* to work, take her mind off funeralizing. Ah'm wondering if you might have something for her to do. Not in the house. We know MizLizbeth likes to tend her own. But, maybe at the packinghouse, cleaning up, clearing out. Just enough to get by 'til she finds herself a new fam'ly to work for."

Daddy sits silently, thinking.

Yes! I think. *You must say yes!*

"We don't usually hire help this time of year, except for Robert, who sweeps up a couple times a week. But . . . it has been several seasons since the showroom had a thorough cleaning. We could keep Armetta busy for a week or so, maybe two. That help?"

Luther's and my shoulders sag in relief. "Bless you, Mist'Warren. Thank you. Can she start tomorrow?"

"Eight o'clock, before it gets too hot."

Luther looks down at the keyboard, then back at Daddy. "They's something else . . ."

Daddy's nod tells him to continue.

"Ah had a visit from Mistuh Harry T. Moore. You know who he is?"

"Leads the N-double A-C-P over in Brevard County, doesn't he?" Daddy says. "Helped the Negro teachers get a bigger paycheck?"

N.A.A.C.P.? Marvin used to joke that those letters meant Negroes Annoyed by the Abuse of Colored People.

"That's him, 'cept he's the State leader now. Mr. Moore heard 'bout Marvin and come to see me and Armetta, asking what the authorities been doing 'bout it. Ah told him Constable Watts says he's 'looking into it,' which is 'bout like a diamondback wonderin' where that rattlin' noise come from."

"Exactly."

"So Mistuh Harry T. Moore say he talk to Mistuh Thurgood Marshall 'bout what happened. You know him? Head lawyer for the national N-double A-C-P in New York City?"

"Know *of* him."

"Mistuh Moore say since we was together when we found Marvin, Mistuh Marshall be wanting to talk to you, Mist' Warren. Mistuh Moore say Ah need to ask if you'd be willing to talk to them."

"Of course, Luther. I'd welcome the opportunity to speak with either of those gentlemen."

"Mistuh Moore say Mistuh Marshall been a good friend of the coloreds in Florida. He say Mistuh Marshall has big friends in Washington, D.C., might be able to get the local authorities to pay more attention to this."

"Tell Mr. Moore I'll be happy to help, any way I can."

"The hang of it is," Luther says, his voice all of a sudden choked, and his eyes glimmer, "Jerry Tee heard some of those ol' Crackers talkin' at the gas station. They say the Klan wasn't even after Marvin. They just confused him with somebody else in a white Cadillac with New York plates."

Luther's head drops, his shoulders fold in on it as he begins to sob. Daddy's eyes are watery as he puts his arm around Luther's bent-over back. I feel hot tears rising, their wetness racing down my cheeks.

"I heard that, too," Daddy tells Luther softly.

Luther tugs a large plaid handkerchief out of his pants pocket and wipes his eyes and his nose.

"Mist' Warren, the Klan done kilt-dead our boy for nothin'."

Daddy takes a shuddery breath. "I know, Luther, and I can't even begin to tell you how bad I feel about it."

"Thank you," Luther says, blowing his nose and wiping his eyes again. "Ah couldn't tell Armetta 'bout that, and Ah warned Jerry Tee he better be muffle-jawed in her direction; her heart's done broke enough already. Ah 'pologize for spoiling your evening. It's just been a rope . . ."

God! How did You let this happen?

"No apologies, Luther. Armetta's isn't the only heart that's hurting around here," Daddy says sadly, catching my eye across the room.

"Folks in The Quarters are scared outta they wits; most of 'em grabbin' they chil'ren off the street at the least li'l noise or the motor-by of a white man's truck. The chil'ren are having night terrors, too. Hardly a night goes by that Ah don't hear a couple of 'em, up and down the way, waking up screaming in they beds."

"Luther, these people must be stopped. There *has* to be a way."

"Ah wish they was, Mist' Warren. Ah sincerely wish they was."

But who? my heart cries. *How?*

Chapter 8

I'm running through the dark grove to keep up with the others. Just ahead of me, a woman hoists a boy roughly to her hip. I watch him bury wide, frightened eyes into her bony shoulder. Just behind me, the voice of one man urges on another, in words I don't understand. On both sides, trees like fountains tunnel the row; their leaves too long and too thin to be citrus, with round red fruit I think may be pomegranates.

The way is steeply uphill. I'd like to stop and catch my breath, but I'm afraid of getting trampled by the heavy feet hammering the hard ground behind me. Chest heaving, back wet with sweat, *finally* I reach the tree break.

A crowd surrounds the hill's rocky crest. Without stopping, I squirm my way into them, past rough elbows and dark, cutting eyes, desperate to reach the center. I know this scene by heart. I've flipped past it a million times, green section, middle of the book, above small block letters that spell GOLGOTHA. *Except*—and the shock of this hits me like a fist—on the towering, rough-hewn cross, red neon lights flash JESUS SAVES. At the base of the cross, a circle of angry men are kicking and hitting the man on the ground; horrible movements made spastic by the pulsing red lights. "*Some*body! *Help* him!" I scream, outraged at the strangers craning their necks to see. "Marvin!" I cry, pushing, kicking, clawing through the crowd, "Marvin, it's *me*, Reesa!"

"Reesa, wake up! You're all right, honey, wake up!"

In the small constellation of our family, Daddy may be the sun, but Mother is our moon. Hers is the face that lights the night's shadows.

"You were dreaming. What happened?" Mother asks, the sound of her voice and scent of her hair proof that the nightmare is over.

"I was trying . . ." I sob into the softness of her shoulder. "Trying so hard to save Marvin. But they wouldn't . . . I couldn't get to him."

"Nobody could, honey. I'm sorry."

"Jesus couldn't save him. And neither could I," I tell her darkly.

"It was a dream, Reesa. Nothing but a bad dream," she says, smoothing my hair. "Poor thing, you're all right now. Lay down. I'll stay here for a while and rub your back. Go to sleep now, honey. Good night, sweet girl." Under Mother's soothing lunar light, I drift back into shallow sleep.

The mid-morning light paints the white walls of my bedroom silvery. Outside, a breeze threads the needles of the pine tree by the car barn. A lone bird calls loudly from the top of it.

That bird sure wants somebody's attention, I think. *Whip-Poor-Will*, he cries again and my eyes fly open. Somewhere, off in the direction of Lake Opalakee, another sound seems to answer him, low, rolling like thunder but more alive, the bellowing of the lake's notoriously big bull 'gator.

It's officially spring, I remember. *Oh, Marvin, I heard it! I listened and I heard. Can you hear it, too, wherever you are?*

The house is uncommonly still. This late, Mother and Daddy are long gone to the packinghouse. The boys are off, too, on a field trip with Doto to the plane show at Orlando's airport.

In the kitchen I see Mother's left a place mat, napkin and bowl in front of the Shredded Wheat. I eat my breakfast in the sunny kitchen, listening again for the whippoorwill, wondering who taught Marvin all the things that he taught me. *Maybe I'll ask Armetta*, I think as I head out the door. She'll be at the packinghouse today. *Maybe not*, I reason, remembering Luther's visit. Apparently, unless they bring it up directly, care for a grieving person is best done sideways.

Outside, under a bright bowl of spring blue, the world seems soaked with color. Green grass laps like a river around Mother's island of rosebushes. Pink, coral and scarlet blooms cast a net of fragrance over bright orange butterflies that dip and bob as if tied by an invisible tether.

Across the street, a pair of redbirds hop along the pitched roofline of the Turnbulls' old house, the crested male singing bravely to his mate. That house is rented to the Carmichaels: Miz Evelyn Carmichael sings alto in Daddy's choir and, a lot of folks say, is a dead ringer for Ava Gardner. But her husband, poor pale-faced Mr. Frank Carmichael, they say, doesn't look a thing like Frank Sinatra. Their teenaged son Robert works for us part-time at the packinghouse. He calls my parents Mr. and Miz Mac, and me Macarooni. Robert wears white, rolled-sleeve T-shirts, like Marlon Brando on the movie posters for *Streetcar Named Desire*. He has a motorcycle which he's forever riding or working on in the Carmichaels' garage.

Next door, in front of the Turnbulls' new house, modern concrete block with shiny terrazzo, a pair of scrub jays complain bitterly to Miz Sooky Turnbull and I don't blame them. Miz Sooky stands with her back to me surveying the all-white Easter garden that's been the talk of the town for weeks. White azalea bushes, in full flower, flank the sides of a giant magnolia tree serving up milky blooms the size of soup bowls. In front, a stand of pearly Easter lilies trumpet behind the row of white-starred bushes Miz Sooky calls cape jasmine. Mother calls them gardenias.

On Easter Sunday, Mother and I were standing in a circle of ladies outside the church when Miz Esther Hall raved, "Sooky, your Easter garden is to die for! Whatever made you think of an all-white display?"

"You'll probably laugh," Miz Sooky trilled, "but I was at the station, taking Fred his lunch, when a carload of Nigras pulled in for gas. It was hot, so they piled out of the car thirsty, but, of course, none of them had enough money for Coke-Cola so they headed for the water fountain. Fred pointed out the sign, and of course, you never know if they can read, so he told them 'Whites Only, No Coloreds!' Well, that's when it came to me . . . a white-only garden without a *stitch* of color!"

As the rest of them tittered on about how lovely the whole thing looked and smelled, Mother and I left in search of Daddy. Truth is, I was mad at Miss Sooky, at all of them, for shoveling out their comments like a bunch of garbage on Marvin's grave.

In her new henna rinse and green gardening smock, Miz Sooky looks like an overgrown stamen in the heart of a fat white swamp flower, its scent impossibly concocted. To me, the whole white garden thing's unnatural and that's what the squawking blue jays are trying to tell her.

Fortunately, she doesn't see me. I stick to my side of the street until I'm past her—I do not want to talk to her, I do not trust what I might say—then sprint into the Turnbull orange grove. There's a dirt road running across it that we call "Fred's shortcut" because it connects the Turnbull house on Old Dixie Highway to the Turnbull station next to our business on the Trail. I've used it forever to walk between home and the packinghouse.

Like most of the groves around here, the Turnbulls' navel trees are trailing late bloom from treetop to grove floor, like a bride's veil. Gratefully, I slip away from Miz Sooky into the close, sweetly scented passageway.

"Ah heard our preacher waxing on poetical 'bout 'the lilies of the field,'" Marvin said once. "Personally, Ah hain't never seen no field full of lilies but Ah shore do love a grove in Blossom Time. Ol' King Solomon hisself wudn't 'rayed such as these!"

The leaves on the trees are full and richly green, lighter and finer than they'll be later, in the high heat of summer. Soon, I think, sniffing blossoms, the last of the bright white petals will fall, taking their heavenly scent with them. The little green vases inside will swell in Green Time, from pea-sized globes to full-size fruit, golden and juicy at Orange Time. That won't happen until November. And it wouldn't happen at all, I remember, if Mistuh Bee and Miss Angel Blossom didn't do their part.

At the end of Fred's shortcut, the scent of orange blossoms gives way to the reek of high octane and hot asphalt at Turnbull's Standard Oil. Just inside the work bay, next to the Coke cooler, I see the cold-water fountain and notice, for the first time in my life, the sign Miz Sooky talked about. It hangs, fat black letters on white cardboard, a good head higher than me, at adult eye level.

Is it new? I wonder. The curling edges of the cardboard, a diagonal smear of old grease give me my answer. Without stopping, as I always have before, I wave politely to old Mr. Fred, who nods above his newspaper, feet up on his desk, in front of the electric fan. Seeing that sign, realizing it's been there forever, I feel suddenly embarrassed. Like I've been an ignorant player in an awful game. *Shame on you*, I tell myself, resolving never to drink from that fountain again. And I feel it, the bee sting of shame on me.

At the highway, I quicken my pace. In the fall and winter, when our navel trees are heavy with fruit, the big billboards invite the snowbirds to "Pick An Orange Free!" and "Send Some Florida Sunshine To The Folks Back Home!" Earlier this month, Daddy and Robert changed the panels to pull in the warm weather folks with "Ice-cold Orange Juice, Fresh-squeezed," "All-You-Can-Drink For A Dime! (Limit 3)." Nobody in their right mind has any business drinking more than three glasses of orange juice. If the bulk of it doesn't make you sick, the acid will.

Across from me, the tall gray tanks and buildings of Mayflower Citrus climb like turrets of some medieval castle, quiet this time of year, after winter's roar of fruit juice processing. At its highest peak, like an eagle's nest, is the room with windows all around and a clear view of every operation: the private office of Mr. Emmett Casselton. You can't see him from here, but everyone knows he's there—pulling all the strings in town. Emmett Casselton is head of Mayflower Citrus, king of Casbah Groves, and, no doubt, chief of the Klan that murdered Marvin.

My thoughts, like arrows, fly at Casselton's wide-open windows: *A truckload of shame on you, too.*

Chapter 9

There you are!" Mother dimples as I enter our showroom. She sits on her stool behind the register, paperwork piled neatly in front of her. "Find your breakfast?"

"Yes, ma'am. Thank you."

"Armetta brought you something to-day," she tells me in a voice that says *mind your manners*.

I follow her gaze to the back of the showroom where Armetta Cully, Luther's wife, my friend Marvin's grieving mother, stands at the top of our stepladder. White cloth and spray bottle in hand, she's tackling the high glass shelves of the marmalade section, dressed in the white uniform and thick-soled shoes she used to wear at May Carol's house in Opalakee. It's the first time I've seen her, since Marvin and all, and I approach her, fearful of saying the wrong thing.

"Hey, Armetta," I call softly, shyness suddenly clogging my throat.

"ReesaRoo," she croons, setting aside her cloth and climbing quickly down. "Gotta getta a look at *you*!"

I can't help but smile, reminded that "Ol' Gonna-Gotta-Getta" was one of Marvin's pet names for her.

"Girl! You weren't no bigger than a minute when you was born . . . you a pretty half-hour now!" Armetta exclaims, a grin brightening her face, tiny gold tendrils curling around her teeth.

Maybe it's her smiling eyes, so like Marvin's but not exactly, her teasing tone, or the gentleness with which she places her palm under my chin and lifts it to look at me; all of a sudden, an ocean of sorrow slams over me, stealing my breath away. Worse yet, the four terrible words that have bashed against my brain, beat like wild birds caged inside my chest, fly out my mouth. "Oh, Armetta," I cry, before I can stop myself, "Marvin's *dead, gone* forever!"

All at once, I fall and am pulled sobbing into the wide, warm circle of her arms. Armetta's twice the size of Mother. In the soft talcum-scented saddle between her breasts, I feel, rather than hear, the beat of her great heart.

Behind us, crunching gravel, car doors open and slam, signaling the arrival of a carload of customers.

Armetta walks me quickly into the cool quiet of my parents' office, hidden in the crook of the L-shaped showroom.

"Oh, child," she says, stroking my hair, softly weeping. "Mah boy, he loved you like a sister."

"He was my best friend," I sob. "He was the best friend in the whole world and, and . . ." I try to stop crying but I can't. "*Everything* seems all upside down without him."

Armetta holds me, anchors me, as my head spins with the

awful truth that the world I knew, bright and warm and fun, has spun and quaked and fallen *away* to reveal something infinitely less simple, more dangerous and complicated than I ever imagined.

She holds me close, then, after a time, she pushes me just far enough away to see my face. Sternly, she says, "Reesa, lemme tell you somethin'. When Ah was 'bout your age, Ah lost someone, too. My old grandmamma told me somethin' Ah've never forgot. God is the potter, she said, and we clay in his hands, soft and weak which don't do at all. It's our time in the fire, don't y'see, that gives us strength and shows His purpose. Without that, we couldn't hold water. Y'understand?"

I bite my lip, unsure. God and I aren't exactly on speaking terms these days.

"God has His plans, honey, for all of us—you, Marvin, me, your mamma and daddy, everybody. And, He gotta prepare us. Time in the fire don't burn us, y'see, it helps us be ready for whatever's ahead."

"But Marvin's gone for*ever*," I wail in protest.

"His work was done, Reesa. His time come."

"But why couldn't he just die natural? Why'd it have to be so *aw*ful?" I want to know as the terrible memory of him groaning, bleeding in the truck bed flashes through my mind.

"Oh, child, there's no explainin' the meanness in this world." Armetta shakes her head, wipes wetness off her cheek, then cradles my hands in her palms. "But there's goodness here, too. You can't never lose sight of that, hold on to it. It's the goodness that gets us through."

"Do you . . . really *believe* we'll see Marvin again . . . up there, I mean?"

"Ah do, child, Ah *do*," she says gently. Her eyes seem lit from within, her great face shines with faith. "In the meantime . . ." she says, dropping her chin like Marvin used to, "Ah brought you some snicker doodles, and, since those boys done traipsed off to O'landah, Ah 'spect you get the whole plate to your own self."

"Snicker doodles?"

"Your mamma put 'em over there," she says and points to the desk in front of the showroom window, "next to your puzzle."

"Thank you, Armetta," I say, hugging her, "for . . . well, everything."

"Have some cookies, girl. Ah gotta get myself back to work," she says, but holds me real tight a moment longer before she goes.

I sink into Mother's desk chair. The crunchy sweetness of a snicker doodle can't cover the taste of bitter grief in my mouth. Staring through the shelves of the shell-lamp section, I hear Mother making change for a customer.

Beyond her, in the driveway, a second car wheels in and parks beside the people just leaving. I recognize, with surprise, the big blue Pontiac that is May Carol's mother's car.

Miz Lucy Garnet, blonde hair, pink shirtwaist and big black sunglasses, steps out of her car alone. As she greets my mother, I wonder where May Carol could be.

"Hey, Lizbeth. How you doin' today?" Miz Lucy calls, tucking her glasses with a snap into a small white purse.

"Trying to stay cool," Mother says. "How about you? Looks like it's heating up pretty good out there."

"Yeah, probably, I had the air conditioner on." Miz Lucy sounds distracted as she scans the showroom, spotting Armetta at work on the honeys and marmalades. "Listen, Lizbeth, would it be okay with you if I have a li'l conversation with Armetta? Won't take a minute."

Mother, apparently not wanting to speak for her, turns toward the stepladder and calls, "Armetta?"

Through the office window, I can tell Armetta's noticed Miz Lucy but elected to keep on cleaning.

Miz Lucy strides, high heels clacking across the concrete floor, around the rack of postcards, past the three big show-cases of small souvenirs, to the great wall of glass jars in the back. "Armetta, could we talk a minute?" Miz Lucy calls up the ladder.

"Ah got lots to do here, Miz Lucy."

"Armetta, *please?*"

Armetta carefully, quite deliberately sets aside her spray bottle. She lumbers down and off the ladder, keeping the white cloth in her hand. Miz Lucy cups her elbow and point-ing to the shell-lamp section, just in front of me, says, "How 'bout over there?"

The two women move to a spot in front of the open win-dow. May Carol's mother is a fragile, pretty woman, a South-ern Belle who married well. Next to her, Armetta stands at least a head taller, her arms thick and powerful next to Miz Lucy's frail white ones.

"Armetta," Miz Lucy says urgently, in a voice so low that both Armetta and I incline our heads to hear. "I'm about to go out of my *mind*. May Carol can't sleep, won't eat, won't hardly do a thing 'cause of missin' you. Durin' the day, that girl's like a haunt, wanderin' from room to room. Every night, she just cries and cries. What can I *say*, what can I *do* to get you to come back to us?"

"Miz Lucy, you know this has nothin' to do with you and that chil'."

"Yes, Armetta, and you have to know that Reed had nothin' to do with Marvin's death."

"No, ma'am, Ah can't know that. Ah'm not saying Mistuh Reed pulled the trigger, or nothin' like that. But Ah know it was the Klan that kilt mah Marvin and that Mistuh Reed's a member."

"But, Armetta, there's three different Klan dens around here. Reed's is just a card club, bunch of overgrown boys playin' poker."

Armetta looks off into the sunshiny distance outside and breathes deeply. The broad planes of her face are still when she turns back to Miz Lucy.

"Miz Lucy, Ah can't. Ah just can't feature comin' back to your house, cleanin', cookin', puttin' clothes in the closet, seein' that white robe hangin' in there."

"Armetta, I could make him keep his robe at his mother's house. I could bring him to you and he'd *swear* on the family Bible that he had nothin' to do with this. Reed said he would if it'd help you feel comfortable comin' back to us."

"Ah'm sorry, Miz Lucy—"

But Miz Lucy cuts her off, whispering like a cry, "Armetta! Don't you see I'm *beggin'* you *here*!"

Armetta takes another long, slow breath. "Miz Lucy, Ah'm just as sorry as Ah can be. Ah'm sorry for you and Ah'm sorry for li'l Miss May Carol and Ah'm sorry that mah Marvin lies rottin' in his grave at age nineteen with cuts on his body and a bullet hole in his head. Ah could never, *ever*, again work in the house of a Klan member."

Miz Lucy Garnet, whose blue eyes are full of wobbly tears, takes a step backward. She fumbles with her white purse, finds and pulls out her big black sunglasses. Putting them on, there inside the showroom, she says, light-voiced, "So, you goin' to be workin' permanent for Warren and Lizbeth now?"

"This is jus' temporary, cleanin' mostly, gettin' things ready for the summer season," Armetta answers.

"Then what?"

"Ah hope to find me another family to work for."

"In Opalakee?"

"Yes, or here or Wellwood, it don't matter. Ah'll find somethin', some place."

"I'm sure you will, Armetta. And I'm sorry we couldn't straighten this out."

"Marvin's killin' is somethin' that won't stand straightenin', Miz Lucy."

"Goodbye, Armetta." Miz Lucy says it quietly. She turns to go, but stops midway and turns back. Removing her glasses, she's obviously remembered something.

"May Carol asked me to say 'hey' for her," she says, biting her pink lip.

"You tell that chil' she's a angel, tell her Ah said she'll always be a precious li'l angel to me."

"I, uh . . ." Miz Lucy looks up at the ceiling, bosom rising, as if she's collecting herself from the very air. "I, uh . . . don't suppose I could get a copy of your snicker doodle recipe for her? May Carol, uh . . . she asked me to ask."

"You know it's outta my head, all my recipes are; but . . ." Armetta's face softens. "Ah'll try. If Ah can figure out the measures, Ah'll write 'em down and send 'em to you."

"Thank you, Armetta. We'll watch for it."

Miz Lucy Garnet turns on her white patent-leather heel and strides quickly out of the showroom. Passing Mother, she waves vaguely in her direction. "Lizbeth," she nods and keeps on walking out into the sun shining on the Pontiac, high heels crunching the gravel driveway.

Armetta shakes her head and treads slowly back to the

marmalade wall, climbs steps, picks up her spray bottle and resumes her work.

"Time in the fire," she'd told me. *Seems to me some people get more than their share.*

"You all right?" Mother calls to her.

"Ah'll be fine, MizLizbeth. 'Ventually Ah'll be jus' fine."

Chapter 10

Somewhere, someone must have put grieving to music. There must be a song that, when you hear it, helps your heart heal its aching hole. I don't know that person, and I don't know that song. But, I do know, mine has lyrics—*Marvin's dead, gone forever*—and that my brother Ren's is a simple series of beats—*Bhhh-dmmm (pause) pfff;* sometimes harder, *BHH-DMM,* sometimes softer, *Buhhhh-dummmm,* with a varying pause, and a final *pfff.*

Ren's grief song is the sound of a solitary person throwing a baseball that hits the ground, bounces against the car barn wall, arcs through the air and into a lonely glove. The rhythm, sometimes fast, sometimes slow, changes with the distance between the ball and the wall, which alters the arc and the glove pocket's answer.

I can see my brother outside my bedroom window, a lean little figure facing a big, blank wall, on the bright opening day of Major League play. For baseball fans across the country, this is a personal holiday. But for Ren and Marvin, it was a holy day in the sacred celebration of Heaven on Earth.

Marvin gave me nicknames, Bible Drill secrets, Mistuh Bee stories. But his gift to Ren was baseball.

Two years ago, on my brother's sixth birthday, Marvin gave Ren his first glove and the great love of his life. He had Daddy's permission, of course, because Daddy can't play—the polio withered the muscles required for an overhand throw. So it was Marvin who taught Ren to catch a ball, fire a pitch, hit a curve, follow a game on the radio and love the Brooklyn Dodgers.

Marvin wasn't alone, of course. Old Sal Tomasini, the Italian grocer who grew up in Brooklyn, was in on it, too. The same year Ren got his glove, the Dodgers won the 1949 National League pennant, Marvin's hero Jackie Robinson was picked Most Valuable Player, and Sal and Marvin christened Ren their lucky charm.

Above Sal's small store, which caters to the folks from The Quarters, is the cheerful, cluttered apartment where he and Sophia live. Rising above that is the twenty-five-foot radio antenna that connects Sal and the fans who gather behind his store on game days to the Brooklyn Dodger Radio Network.

No doubt, they're all there now, sitting on the benches under the scrub pines, watching the game in their minds with the help of the Dodger's honey-toned storyteller, The Rhubarb, Red Barber.

Old Sal was here earlier, offering Ren a ride. But Ren refused.

"We can'ta open widout you!" Sal had said in his thick Milano-by-way-of-Brooklyn accent. "You are our lucky charm! Besides," he'd pleaded, "It's Preacher Roe pitching; you don't wanna miss *him*."

Ren said nothing, and everything, with a shake of his head. Chin on his chest, face unreadable under the bill of his blue cap, he'd mumbled, "Sorry," and turned away, walking resolutely down the drive to face the car barn wall.

Sal's eyes, behind his thick glasses, grew pained; their sadness magnified by the high-power lenses. His white mustache drooped over lips pursed in disappointment.

"Sorry, Sal," I'd told him, by way of comfort.

He'd thanked me with a wave of his small hand, adjusted his own ancient Brooklyn cap and driven away.

Bhhh-dmmm (pause) pfff. The lonesome sound of Ren's solitary play is a world away from the complex chatter of catch with Marvin.

For the past two summers, the driveway where Ren stands now, facing the wrong way, was his and Marvin's playing field. In front of an imagined crowd (Ebbets, of course), the two of them, fifteen feet apart, re-enacted baseball's greatest plays, playing multiple positions as their personal heroes. Marvin was most often Jackie, the great Jack Roosevelt Robinson, white baseball's first black player. Ren was sometimes Preacher Roe, the Dodgers' league-leading pitcher, sometimes himself as a grown-up pitcher, Ren "Rocket Man" McMahon. ("When Rocket Man's on the mound, nobody orbits the bases!" he'd crow.)

"But can The Rocket do it again?" Marvin would taunt, his throw finding Ren's glove with a firm *Thwap!* Ren would squint, hard, and hurl the ball back—*Thwap!*—and the imaginary game would begin, with Marvin, imitating Red Barber, calling the play-by-play:

"Rocket Man's held the flock scoreless, folks, through

eight innin's. Bottom of the ninth, one away, with Reese on first. Snider steps in to face McMahon.

"Rocket Man checks Reese, an' delivers. Duke swings—*Thwap!*—It's a blue darter over the shortstop's outstretched glove. The left fielder picks it up an' rifles it to second—*Thwap!*—No, suh! *Too* late!

"Listen to those fans as Jackie Robinson approaches home plate. Jackie leads the league in runs scored, an' bases stolen. PeeWee's on second, Snider's at first. Here's The Rocket's windup, an' the pitch—*Thwap!*—It's a bullet back to the box. Rocket Man snags it, turns and fires it to second, doublin' off a surprised PeeWee Reese!—*Thwap!*—Oh-ho, doctor! Rocket Man McMahon has single-handedly *won* the game!"

"Waa-hooo!" Ren would holler, tossing his glove high in the air, tipping his cap to the imaginary crowd.

What's he thinking now? I wonder as the sound of Ren's vigil echoes in my room. *BHH-DMM (pause) pfff.* He's not much of a talker, even on good days. Mother says he gets that from her side of the family. Oh, he can go on forever about baseball and his precious Brooklyn Dodgers. But when it comes to something personal, like "You missing Marvin, too?," forget it.

I asked Marvin once, "What's the big deal about baseball, anyway?"

He and Ren were taking a break, sitting in the shade beside the house.

"Well, Ah'll tell you, Roo," Marvin replied, rubbing his chin. "Ah heard Red Barber say 'baseball's like life.' His life, maybe. Not mine. Ah'd say baseball's a bit of Heaven on Earth and Ah can prove it, too. Wanna see?"

"Sure," I said, sitting down beside him.

Marvin drew a diamond in the dirt. "Looky here. If this is

heaven, y'got to have the Father, Son, and Holy Ghost, right? Well, the pitcher's like God, standin' highest on the mound, playin' catch with The Son behind home plate. Backin' God up is the Holy Ghost, the shortstop who's all over the place. With me so far?" Of course I was. "Okay! Now, behind these three, there's two bands of angels, three each: Cherubim on the bases, Seraphim in the field. Heaven on Earth!" He laughed. "But, Roo, wouldn't be Heaven without a pearly gate and that's right here," he said, stabbing home plate. "And behind the gate is St. Peter hisself, dressed in a suit. Also called the umpire," he said, as if I didn't know.

"Now, jus' like Heaven, a batter comes knockin' at the pearly gate, askin' God and St. Peter, 'Can Ah come in?' 'We'll give you three tries,' the two of them say. God loves threes, don't y' see—three around the mound, three bases, three outfield, three outs. So the batter tries his hardest, and his teammates try, too. But here's the best part, Roo: Once you get in, you jus' as good as anybody else. In Heaven, they don't count the color of your skin, or the cut of your clothes, or whether your shoes are shined or not. In Heaven, a black man can out-hit, out-run, out-field a white man and live to tell about it. A black man, black as Jackie Robinson, can be picked Most Valuable Player, over hundreds of white men. That ain't like life, Roo. That's Heaven on Earth!" Marvin had grinned, and sat back satisfied he'd proved his point. Looking at me sideways, he'd flashed me his V-for-Victory sign which, for Marvin, meant *I know what I'm talkin' 'bout here*, or simply, *gotcha!*

Wait 'til next year!" Marvin promised Ren last October, after the Dodgers lost their pennant to the "Whiz Kids" from Philadelphia.

Baseball's next year begins today: Jackie Robinson's a Cherubim on second base, Preacher Roe's passing judgment on the mound, the fans are assembled in Ebbets Field and under the pines behind Tomasinis' store. But Ren's outside facing a big, blank wall. And Marvin?

Marvin's dead, Buhhhh-dummmm, gone forever, pfff.

Chapter 11

The month of April falls with the
last of the orange blossoms into
May. Armetta's gone to work for
Mr. and Miz Charles Clark in
Wellwood. Miz Clark is the former Patsy
Lee Berry, youngest daughter of the Well-
wood Berrys, who are fine folks with no
apparent Klan connections. Mr. Clark is
from New Orleans and as nice as can be.
The Clarks' first child, Parlee Berry Clark,
has just arrived and her parents need
Armetta's steadying hand.

Ren and I continue our daily dashes to
the post office but, to tell you the truth,
I'm starting to think Mr. J. Edgar Hoover
couldn't care less about a cold-blooded
murder in the middle of an orange grove.

On a night in early May, Mother, Doto,
Ren and I sit around the kitchen table attempting Pinochle. Under Mother's patient tutelage, we've worked our way up

from Go Fish and Old Maid through Crazy Eights, Rummy, Hearts, and Canasta, to Pinochle, her prerequisite for instruction in Bridge.

Daddy, with a sleepy Mitchell slung over his good shoulder, ribs Mother, "You know, you're probably this town's only serious card-playing Baptist."

"Don't forget Lillian!" she mock-protests.

"Twice a year does not a card shark make," Daddy calls on his way upstairs. "Besides, you taught her everything she knows."

Mother grins, cuts and deals.

All of a sudden, Buddy, our live alarm system, scrambles up and runs to the back door. Nose to the crack, his tail ticktocks welcome while, at the same time, a small warning growl rolls around his mouth.

Luther's knock follows and, opening the door, I see the source of his mixed reception. Behind him, just outside the circle of porchlight, stand two white shirtfronts split by dark ties, men dressed for business.

"Evenin', Roo. Y'all finished supper?" Luther asks quietly.

"Yessir, we have."

"Ah brought a couple people to see your daddy."

"Please come in," I say, pulling the screen door wide.

Mother and Doto look up and hastily collapse their card hands.

"Evening, MizLizbeth. Ah'd like you to meet Mistuh Thurgood Marshall and Mistuh Harry T. Moore."

"Gentlemen, welcome," Mother says, rising from her chair and extending her hand. "Please meet my mother-in-law, Mrs. Dorothy McMahon."

"How do you do?" Doto stands, offering her hand in that queenly way she uses whenever she meets anybody.

"And this," Mother continues, "is Marie Louise."

Although they seem to be about the same age, the two strangers are quite different. Mr. Marshall's a great golden bear of a man. His hand swallows mine in a firm, hearty shake. Mr. Moore hangs back, slim, dark, dignified. He meets me with his eyes before offering his grip.

"Also known as Roo, I hear," Mr. Moore says. His smile is warm and kindly. N-double A-C-P, I remember, from Daddy and Luther's talk.

"Pleased to meet you," I say.

"And our son, Warren, Jr., who we call Ren," Mother says. Ren does Daddy proud, shaking hands firmly, level-eyed.

"It's a pleasure meeting all of you," Mr. Marshall says, openly surveying the kitchen. Unlike Luther and Mr. Moore, his hair is straight and brown. He sports a handsome, close-clipped mustache and a taffy-colored tweed jacket, an unusual fabric for Florida, but of course he's the lawyer from New York.

"You're a long way from home, Mr. Marshall," Doto says.

"I've had business at the Lake County courthouse all week," Mr. Marshall explains in a voice that seems to rumble around the room. "Spent today with Harry registering voters. Heading home tonight."

"Looky here!" Luther says, grinning gold. He pulls a small white card out of his shirt pocket. "Says *here* Ah'm a duly registered Democrat in the County of Orange, State of Florida. Come next spring, Ah get to vote in the primary elections. After that, Ah'll help pick the President of the United States."

"Haven't you voted before, Luther?" Ren asks.

"Nope," Luther says.

Mr. Moore explains smoothly, "Orange County's been a little slow in giving us the vote, but thanks to Mr. Marshall here, we're back in the registration business."

"Good Lord, that amendment passed, what? Twenty years ago?" Doto asks Mr. Marshall.

"Thirty, actually!" Mr. Marshall's laugh is hollow. "But," he tells Doto, "I doubt you need me to tell you the pace down here is a bit behind the rest of the country."

Doto shakes her head in weary agreement.

"How's the voter registration coming?" Mother asks Mr. Moore.

"Pretty good, so far." A shy grin widens his narrow, thoughtful face.

"Harry's being modest," Mr. Marshall booms. "Before he got involved, less than four, four and a half percent of the Negroes in this state were registered. Now, we're up to nearly thirty percent, which is *twice* the rate of any other Southern state!"

"Good for you!" Mother says. "I'm sure it hasn't been easy."

Mr. Moore nods, offers a honey-toned thank-you, then adds gently, "Ma'am, I need to get Mr. Marshall to the airport in about two hours. Luther said your husband might have a word with us?"

"Of course. He's upstairs putting our youngest—"

Before she can finish, Ren and I are up and in motion. "We'll get him right away," we say and race out the door.

"Would you like some iced tea, coffee?" Mother asks as we tear through the dining room and up the living room stairs.

"Daddy!" we tell him on the landing. "Luther's here . . . Mr. Harry T. Moore, Mr. Thurgood Marshall . . . to see you."

"Here? *Now?*" he asks.

"Isn't this great?" I ask, heart pounding. *At last, somebody's going to do something about Marvin's murder!*

"Yes," Daddy says. Suddenly, he's all business. "You two stay up here while the adults talk," he tells us curtly and heads down the stairs.

Ren and I gape at his back, at each other, in surprise. It's not like him to exclude us from living room conversation. *Aren't we witnesses to the conversation at the Lakeview Inn?* I sulk. Together, my brother and I sink into the dark of the upstairs landing, lean against Doto's bedroom door, and listen to the introductions downstairs.

"Mr. McMahon," Mr. Marshall begins.

"Please, call me Warren," Daddy says warmly. He sounds glad they're finally here.

"Warren, we're compiling a file on what happened to Marvin Cully. I'd like to hear your story and that of your mother."

"Hold on. Let me get my notes."

I hear Daddy's steps into his office, the slide of a file drawer opening and closing, and his quick return to the living room.

"What I have here are four documents: The first is the notes I made on Thursday, March eleventh, the day Luther and I found Marvin on Round Lake Road. Except for poor Marvin, the scene looked pretty much like there'd been a party . . . beer cans, cigarette butts, a couple of broken branches on the orange trees, lots of wheel tracks nearby."

I hear the sound of rustling papers as the sheets change hands.

"How'd you know to go to this place?" Mr. Moore asks.

"Everybody knows where the Opalakee Klan takes people," Luther says.

"If we hadn't found him there, we'd have checked the

Ocoee Klan's stomping grounds off Winter Garden Road," Daddy adds.

"Harry, can you research these properties, find out who owns them?" Mr. Marshall asks.

"Oh, I can tell you that," our father says. "Emmett Casselton's a big citrus man around here and long-time Klan member."

Talk about how the Klan's been taking people to the Casbah for years! I urge Daddy in my head, but he's not listening.

"Good. What else do you have?" Mr. Marshall asks. Though we can't see him, his presence rolls up the stairwell. This is a man who, one way or another, makes things happen, gets things done.

"These are Doc Johnny's notes on Marvin's condition when we brought him in. I've called the coroner a couple times for his report. I'm not even sure there *is* a report."

As he reads the notes, Mr. Marshall makes little clicking sounds with his tongue against the roof of his mouth. I'd asked to see the notes—after Daddy finally finagled them out of Doc Johnny's nurse—but Mother said no. "She's seen too much already," she told Daddy. *As if reading about it would be any worse than the real thing,* I'd told Ren.

"Here's a transcript of the conversation my mother and the children heard at the Lakeview Inn on Saturday, March thirteenth. My mother and I sat down afterwards. She dictated, I typed. As you can see, I'm not the world's best typist."

Again, there's the sound of paper shuffling and a silence.

"Did you get a look at this Deputy, ma'am?" Mr. Marshall asks.

"Unfortunately, only from the back," Doto answers. "He was a burly man, about your size, with big brown freckles all over the back of his neck and hands. Big-boned, too. I'd guess Irish descent."

"And the waitress. Can you remember her name?"

"No," Doto says, "I'm sorry."

"Mary Sue!" I cry out, and six pairs of eyes seek me mid-stairwell. Leaning over the banister, I explain, "She had a curly pin on her uniform that said 'Mary Sue' plain as day. And that's what the Deputy called her when he asked for the check."

"You're very observant, young lady." Mr. Marshall nods, making a note. "Anything else?"

"The other two men wore grove boots, like Daddy's. One was tall and real skinny, stooped like Ichabod Crane; the other was older, with dark hair like Mother and a big bald spot on the back."

"That's right, Reesa," Doto says. "I'd forgotten."

"Any other details?" Mr. Marshall asks.

Ren's voice at my elbow startles me. "The deputy's gun had a fancy handle."

Mr. Marshall's eyes shift alertly up to Ren. "What do you mean, *fancy*?"

"It was white, like the inside of a shell," Ren tells him.

"Like a pearl?"

"Yes, like that, and marked, carved maybe?" Ren says.

"Donnelly," Mr. Marshall says grimly. "Deputy Earl the Pearl Donnelly. It figures."

"Ren, Roo, you've been a big help. Thanks." Daddy's look sends us back into the dark recess of the landing.

"Warren, do you know these people Donnelly mentioned?" Mr. Marshall asks Daddy.

"I know Reed Garnet; but I'm sure Armetta can tell you more than I can."

"Yes, we've spoken with her."

"J. D. Bowman's another story. I know his father. The old man's a loudmouthed bigot, worked for Emmett Casselton for years. Has a grove of his own, but since most of the local pickers won't work for him, Bowman hires migrant labor instead. I don't really know J.D., but he has the reputation of being a wild hare, a real chip off the old block. I don't doubt for a minute that what my mother heard is exactly what happened. This last is a copy of a registered letter I sent J. Edgar Hoover mid-March."

"Heard anything back?"

"Not a word."

"Doesn't surprise me. The Director's had his hands full, and he's not exactly color blind," Mr. Marshall says, and I think his voice sounds careful. "Plus, this situation's a little tricky. Here in Florida, murder is a state crime. If local lawmen choose not to act, the feds have to be creative because they lack the authority to get involved. If you would, Warren, I'd like a copy of all this."

"I typed everything with carbons, in triplicate. Take whatever you'd like."

"Warren, how would you compare the Orange County Klan to the group I'm dealing with in Lake County?" Mr. Marshall asks.

"Well, the first difference is the sheriff," Daddy says without hesitation. "Willis McCall is a racist son of a bitch—'scuse me, ladies—and his deputies are pond scum."

"I have to agree with your assessment." Mr. Marshall's tone is weary.

"Not that our sheriff's much better," Daddy continues, "but he's a lot less arrogant. The second thing is there are three different Klans here in Orange County. I don't know much about the one in Orlando except they seem to have the good sense to leave the folks in Eatonville alone. There's another Klan in Ocoee-Winter Garden and that crowd's a lot like the Crackers in Lake County. You know about the signs, don't you?"

"What signs?" Mr. Marshall asks.

"You mean the ones in Ocoee?" Luther says.

"What signs, Luther?" Mr. Marshall asks.

"Driving in and outta town, they's signs on both sides sayin' '*Nigger—If you can read this: Don't let the sun set on your head in Ocoee.*' "

"Harry, make a note," Mr. Marshall says with a rumbly sigh.

"The Opalakee Klan's a little different," Daddy says. "The names I know read like the town's social register. Most of the oldest families are involved. Their grandfathers brought The Klan with them from Georgia and the Carolinas. The fathers are pretty sedate, but the sons . . . Well, before the war, they mostly pulled college-boy pranks on young couples parked in cars and old coloreds whose fear amused them. Obviously, they're men now . . . veterans, with experience in killing."

Despite the fact that six adults sit in it, our living room is silent.

Ren and I exchange looks. What's happening down there? Finally, Mr. Marshall clears his throat. "Warren, Luther said you'd be a big help and you certainly have been. I can't make any promises. The problem is the state's jurisdiction and the lack of hard evidence. If the coroner removed the bullet, if the bullet happened to match J. D. Bowman's gun . . . Well, we'll see what we can do."

"Marvin was a good friend, not just to me and Lizbeth, but to our children. We'll do whatever we can to help."

People are standing, shaking hands.

We hear Mr. Moore quietly singling out Mother. "Thank

you for the coffee, ma'am, and for opening your home to our little meeting." Daddy, meanwhile, is insisting that Luther and Mr. Marshall, turning toward the kitchen, leave by way of the front door. Doto opens it for them and bids Mr. Marshall a warm "Good night and safe journey."

As our parents and Doto head back to the kitchen, Daddy tosses up the stairwell, "You two go to bed!"

"Now, we're *getting* somewhere," I tell my brother, punching his shoulder in celebration. I feel light-headed with tonight's progress.

But Ren is less confident, his face pinched in disappointment. "Not exactly Dick Tracy and Sam Catchem, are they?" he pouts, wanting more from Mr. Marshall than "We'll see what we can do."

"No, they're *not*," I tell him, "but since nobody else seems to give a good damn 'bout Marvin, they're all we've got!"

Chapter 12

A t quarter 'til one on the steamy hot Saturday before Mother's Day, I amble over to Miss Maybelle's to meet her grandniece Maryvale. Miss Maybelle's on her lunch hour from the post office and I've been told to be prompt. Expecting the worst, I'm relieved to see that the girl swinging her bare legs on Miss Maybelle's front porch is dressed like me in shorts, T-shirt and sandals. And there's not a doll in sight.

"Hey, there," I call as I open the wood-and-wire front gate.

"Hay's for horses; try grass, it's cheaper!" the girl calls back. Her face is full of freckles and her brown eyes crinkle beneath red-brown bangs when she grins. "You Reesa?" she asks.

"That's me. You Maryvale?"

"Puh-lease call me Vaylie. I've been Maryvaled to death this week!"

I figure the pretty woman opening the screen door is Vaylie's mother. Miss Maybelle's in full steam behind her, jangling keys to the post office in hand.

"You two met already? Good." Miss Maybelle takes charge as usual, brisk in her postmistress' uniform. "Marie Louise, this is Maryvale's mother, Miz Laverne Carrollton."

Miss Maybelle acts surprised that I know enough to step forward, shake hands, and say "Pleased to meet you, having a nice trip?"

Miz Laverne's more redheaded than her daughter and her teeth are bright white against the reddest red lipstick I've ever seen. Her skin is pearl-colored with tiny lavender veins showing through. Although she wears makeup like a movie star, I see dark purple circles under her eyes. There's a small bruise like a violet-colored butterfly on the ivory inside her wrist.

Miss Maybelle checks her watch and spouts orders. "Laverne's keeping me company at the post office while I sort the afternoon mail. Marie Louise, you must return Maryvale at precisely five o'clock. I went over this with your mother in case you forget."

"Yes, ma'am," I say nicely, hating her.

As we trail them down the walk, I marvel at Miz Laverne's ability to walk so smoothly in spiky heels next to Miss Maybelle's MacArthur-like march. At the street, they turn right toward the post office and Vaylie and I peel left, toward home.

"That woman's a witch," Vaylie says. "She always like that?"

"Pretty much." I grin. "Our school bus picks us up every day in front of the post office. No matter what the weather, boiling hot, freezing cold or pouring rain, she never lets us wait inside. 'I'm runnin' a branch of the United States Post Office, *not* a nursery school! This building is for official *business* only. You hooligans stay off those benches, too. They're official government property!' You'd think the fate of the entire nation rests on those benches staying empty."

Vaylie's laughing at my version of Miss Maybelle's ornery old attitude. "She wanted us to stay over a few days, but our Atlanta cousins warned us that an afternoon was 'bout all we could stand."

"Where you headed next?"

"Over to Winter Park to stay with a school friend of Mamma's. We're *on tour*, Mamma says, but mostly we're takin' a break from Daddy."

"Is your father sick?" I ask.

"Sort of. I mean, he's all right most of the time. But sometimes he gets to feelin' melancholy and then he drinks and turns mean as a snake. Usually only lasts a couple weeks, but when Mamma sees his melancholy comin', she tells Whit and Claudette to take over and we go on tour."

"Who are they?"

"Whit and Claudette? They're our colored maid and butler, been takin' care of Daddy since he was a boy. Claudette says melancholy runs in Daddy's family, but Whit says it was *The War* that did him in. Whatever the reason, Mamma and I leave town 'til they get Daddy back on track. Where you takin' me?" Vaylie asks as I turn down the grove road.

"Dry Sink. It's this old, dry sinkhole where my brother Ren and the Samson boys are waiting to have a rattler race."

"What's that?" Vaylie asks, breaking into a run beside me.

"Ren and Roy and Dwayne have been out in the palmetto scrub all week with their fork sticks looking for rattlesnakes.

Caught some and trapped 'em in burlap bags. First, we all climb up the tree, then we lower the bags and let 'em free. The rattlers race for cover into the brush outside the sinkhole. You won't believe how fast they go!"

In the clearing, where, on one side of the hole, our grove stops and, on the other side, the Samson palmetto scrub begins, Vaylie declares she's never seen a sinkhole before. "Where'd it come from?" she pants.

We wave to the boys, who are already up in the giant oak, and run around Dry Sink to join them.

"Daddy says this whole state's just a thin layer of limestone floating on a million underground rivers. Every once in a while, either a river rises or the ground sinks, then you wind up with a big hole like this one," I explain.

"Swell!" Vaylie hoists herself easily onto the lower branches of the tree, yelling "Hey" to the boys above us.

"This is Vaylie," I tell them. "Don't drop those snakes 'til we get up there!"

Ren, Roy and Dwayne are champing at the bit to get started. "What took you so long?" Ren grumps.

"Got here as soon as we could!" I blaze back at him. "Get this show on the road!"

Vaylie and I scramble above them, cushioning our seats with the Spanish moss that hangs like lace around us. Vaylie wrinkles her nose. "This stuff stinks."

"That's not the moss; it's *rattler* taint!" I say, watching her eyes balloon open.

Each of the boys holds a squirming burlap bag with two ropes attached. Side by side, the three of them lock their legs on the tree limb and "skin the cat." Now upside down, like a trio of acrobatic puppeteers, they use the ropes to lower the bags into position, behind the starting line drawn in the dirt.

"Now, Roo, *now*!" Ren hollers.

"On your mark," I yell. "Get set! *Go!*" The boys yank on one of their ropes to release the slip knot on the other. Instantly the snakes are free, their terrible beauty churning the pale gray dust. From our tree, we watch and hoot and yell as the fat brown diamondbacks coil and uncurl, tail bells rattling, split tongues flicking, angry, hooded eyes surveying each other and the barren sinkhole for cover.

"Won't they kill each other first?" Vaylie gasps, mesmerized by the drama below.

"No, watch! They want to run for cover, but the big one—see him?—the race won't start 'til *he* says so."

The biggest one, diamond head high above the others, twirls himself into position, twisting a giant coil across the necks of the other two, then, darting and dancing, presses their heads down into the dirt.

Dominance established, Ren's snake, the smallest, is first to quit the dance. It stretches out flat—at least four feet— and wriggles its way toward Dry Sink's side and the stand of palmetto. The other two join him and the race begins. Screaming, we cheer them and howl as Roy's snake, the big one, pulls ahead and vanishes into the scrub, with Ren's and Dwayne's just behind.

All of a sudden, the boys punch each other in victory and defeat, a big clap of thunder yanks our attention to the sky. While we were looking elsewhere, a dark mound of clouds has boiled itself into a surly black storm bank. Out of nowhere, lightning flashes on top of us, sparking a mad scramble out of the tree. A high branch in a giant live oak is no place to be in a Florida thunderstorm. Gasping at the splat of raindrops the size of soup spoons, flinching at the roar of the thunder, the boys veer left through the scrub toward

Samsons'. Vaylie and I run right, through the grove toward home.

In the kitchen, Doto looks up from her letter-writing. "When I heard the thunder, I knew you'd be home soon. You must be Maryvale," she says, regally extending her hand.

"*Vaylie*, please, ma'am. Vaylie Carrollton."

"I've driven through the town of Carrollton in Virginia. Any relation?"

"Yes, ma'am, my daddy's family's lived there forever, raisin' horses and growin' tobacco."

"You may call me Doto."

"Dodo? Like the Dodo bird?" Vaylie is puzzled but polite.

I laugh. "No, Doto, like DeSoto, the kind of car she drives."

"Pleased to meet ya," Vaylie says, stretching her freckles in a smile.

"Likewise, I'm sure," Doto nods. "If you girls want a snack, there are Oreos in the jar and milk in the Frigidaire," she says, turning her attention back to her letter.

"Mind if we sit out the storm in the attic?" I ask.

"Be my guest," Doto waves.

The roof of our house is heavy-gauge tin, and the third-floor attic, accessible only through Doto's room, is the best possible place to enjoy a good storm. The slant of the rain, the wind, the thunder and lightning create what I call the tin-tin symphony. Vaylie and I spread out a quilt on the wood plank floor and, like the Sorcerer's Apprentice in *Fantasia*, conduct the elements with our cookies dipped in milk. After a while, when the storm dies down to a slow drone, Vaylie's attention turns to the attic.

"This all y'all's stuff?" she asks, picking her way around an old trunk.

"Nope, most of it was Mr. Swann's. He used to own this house. Mother keeps threatening she's going to throw it all out."

"Who's this?" Vaylie's holding up a picture of a serious-looking lady in a big black hat.

"No idea."

"Kinda ugly, isn't she?" she says, setting down the dusty gold frame.

"Sort of, but like Mother says, 'pretty's only skin-deep.' "

"Yeh, and my mamma says, 'Sometimes pretty's all you got.' " Vaylie says, smearing her hands on her shorts.

"I think your mother's *very* pretty," I say.

"Well, *of course* she is. She was Miss Richmond at age eighteen, went on to become Miss Virginia, 1937. She was the prettiest girl in our state, that's why Daddy married her." Vaylie's picking through an old button box.

"My father married Mother because she was a Bridge Champion," I tell her proudly.

"What's that?" Vaylie frowns, holding a pair of silver buttons up to her ears.

"Well, it's someone who's really good at the card game called Bridge. He met her at a country club tournament. It was a member-guest event, and she was the guest of another member. Daddy says Mother beat the socks off everybody there, in spite of the fact that her partner was a dummy. He says that after she demolished his hand, he had to ask for hers."

"Your daddy proposed to your mother because she *beat* him at cards?" Vaylie asks, not believing me.

"That's what he says, and because right before she wins, she flashes him her Judy Garland grin."

"Your mother looks like Judy Garland?" Vaylie's impressed.

"Well, yes, *we* think so."

"Whoa, what's this?" Vaylie asks, standing tiptoe to pull a fat hatbox off the top of an old armoire.

"Hat, maybe?" I wonder, moving closer to see.

The box top's pattern is barely visible under its thick coat of dust. Vaylie lifts it and the eyes of a handsome young man in military uniform smile back at us. "Neat," Vaylie says, lifting the photo to reveal a flag folded in a triangle, and a stack of yellow papers.

"Let's turn on the light," I say, stepping around an abandoned rocker to reach the switch.

The top newspaper clipping is somebody's death announcement.

Lieutenant Richard Randall Swann, U.S. Army, Slain in Second Battle at River Marne, the black headline reads. We check the date. September 28, 1918.

"This stuff's ancient," Vaylie says, sorting quickly through the rest of the stack.

"He must have been old Mr. Swann's son. Looks a lot like Tyrone Power, don't you think?"

Vaylie doesn't answer. Instead, she gasps. "My Gawd, Reesa, look here!"

The party scene cut from the yellowed newspaper is of a cluster of ladies behind a lace-draped table topped with a big silver punch bowl, a party cake and a tall vase of flowers. Below it, the line of print says *Miss Maybelle Mason to Wed Local Hero*. Dead center, a pretty young woman smiles broadly for the camera. The date is September 15, 1918. Vaylie reads me the story:

Mrs. Blanche Ogden Swann entertained at her home on Old Dixie Highway Saturday night in honor of Miss Maybelle Mason, who will wed the highly decorated

Lieutenant Richard Randall Swann on Sunday, October 15th. The affair was a variety shower and the bride received many beautiful and useful gifts. After a delicious supper was served, the ladies entertained themselves with games. A mock wedding was the source of much merriment. Guests included: Mrs. Caroline Mason, Misses Bertine Turner . . .

". . . and a whole bunch of other names." Vaylie hands me the article.

"Oh, Vaylie," I say, comparing dates, "he died ten days after the party, two weeks before the wedding!"

"How *aw*ful for Great-Aunt Maybelle!" Vaylie exclaims, looking back at the smiling bride-to-be. "Poor thing, how'd she ever get over it?"

"Maybe she didn't, Vaylie. Some things, well, *some* things you never get over."

"I know," she says darkly. "Like people being mean to each other who ought not to."

"And getting killed," I add, "for no reason at all."

"Girls!" Doto calls from the bottom of the stairs. "It's four forty-five. Doesn't Vaylie have to be at Maybelle's by five o'clock?"

"Oh, Lord," Vaylie says, holding up the hatbox, "think we should take this stuff to her?"

"I don't know. It might . . . well . . . mightn't it bring up a batch of memories best left alone?"

"You're probably right." Vaylie sighs, replacing the lid very carefully, returning the box to the top of the armoire. "It explains a lot, though, don't it?"

Outside, the road has switched from the dry, baked asphalt of a few hours ago to a shiny wet ribbon reflecting us. Rain-washed leaves glitter in the sun. Walking back, we talk quietly about our secret discovery under the dust in the attic. Vaylie promises to quiz her grandfather, Miss Maybelle's brother, for more information; both of us swear to be pen pals for *life*.

In the driveway, Vaylie's mother leans against her big blue Cadillac. Purse and keys in hand, it's clear she's ready to go. Miss Maybelle checks her watch as we enter the gate.

"Not bad, Reesa. Your mother have to remind you?" she queries, her metal-rimmed glasses glaring in the sun.

"Doto did, actually." Vaylie grins widely. "But we had the *best* time together! Thank you for *thinking* of it, Aunt Maybelle!" she says and, with a great rush of feeling, flings her arms around our wrinkled old postmistress.

Miss Maybelle freezes inside Vaylie's embrace, then pats her, stiff-handed, on the back, wanting to be let go.

"You're welcome, Maryvale," she says formally, smoothing the front of her post office uniform, almost as if wiping off Vaylie's warmth.

"I'll write you the very first second I can," my new friend vows as she hugs me goodbye.

With the best of intentions—to somehow comfort an ancient heartache—Vaylie's left Miss Maybelle plainly unsettled, a step off her usual statue-like control. As the two of us stand awkwardly by the road, watching the blue Cadillac disappear, I want to tell Miss Maybelle, *Vaylie didn't mean to make you uncomfortable, she's never lost anyone so she doesn't understand.*

Grief, I think, signs you up in a separate, invisible club, members selected at death's awful randomness. "Gone forever" is our password, lingering sorrow our secret handshake. If you haven't lost someone important to you, you can't begin to know the rules. Truth is, you don't even know the club exists.

As my own grieving heart recognizes another, my life-

long view of Miss Maybelle as the angry old snappir
shifts. Opening the gate for her, calling a soft yet proper
"good evening, ma'am," I resolve to treat her more kindly
from now on.

A ll of a sudden, Doto's three big suitcases appear from
under her bed, lined up, mouths open, across her window seat. I'm sorry to see her go, but she's promised Uncle
Harry she'll leave this week, crossing the country to Montana
before the Memorial Day traffic hamstrings the highways.

"I'll be back for Christmas, though," she promises Ren
and me, "and, of course, I'll call right away if we hear anything from Mr. Hoover."

A few days later, Vaylie's letter arrives, addressed in a
fat loopy script that could only be hers. It's post-
marked Carrollton, Virginia and bears, in the top left corner,
where the return address belongs, the heart-shaped greeting:
Hello, Great-Aunt Maybelle!!!

Miss Maybelle, who's placed the envelope under her
counter rather than in our box, points out the infraction
sternly. "The U.S. Postal System frowns on *any* implication
that one of its workers is taking familial advantage," she lectures me.

"I'll write Vaylie right away and explain," I promise.

"That won't be necessary, as I've already informed her
mother!" Miss Maybelle snaps back.

"I'm sorry, Miss Maybelle," I say, attempting the appropriate remorse on Vaylie's behalf. Miss Maybelle eyes me
sharply, grading my sincerity. Apparently, I pass.

"*You* didn't do anything," she says with that wave that means *get on about your business.*

"Thank you, ma'am," I grin, then call, stopping her in mid-turn, "and, Miss Maybelle?" She scowls, impatient. "Thank you for introducing me to my new pen pal. I've never had one before."

"You're welcome, Reesa," she says, creasing her face briefly, not so business-like, in my direction.

Inside the offending envelope, Vaylie writes:

Dear Reesa,

Whit and Claudette tracked us down in Winter Park, said c'mon home, so here we are! Boy, was Daddy glad to see us! He surprised Mamma with a new dinner ring, a big emerald the size of a snake eye! The real thing, not the marble—I've seen a rattler race and know the difference. Mamma was as happy as could be until I opened my present—a new Jack Kramer tennis racket.

"The child's already got more freckles than a field hand, why would you give her something that keeps her out in the sun, instead of away from it?"

"'Cause it's what she wanted," Daddy said, and after that, they had a big ugly fight that I refused to listen to and left the room.

I did talk to Mamma about coming back to Florida next time Daddy has a "spell," but she said if it happens this summer, we're heading north out of the heat and if it's not 'til fall, she'll have to take me someplace educational since I'd be missing school. Boston maybe, or Washington, D.C.

Oh, Reesa, didn't we have the BEST time together? I just

hate that we live so far apart. Please write me just the SECOND you get this.

Love, VAYLIE

P.S. Do you think I have too many freckles?

P.P.S. What kinds of things do your parents fight about?

Chapter 13

To tell you the truth, before Marvin's murder, and the visit to our home by Mr. Harry T. Moore and Mr. Thurgood Marshall, I didn't read the newspaper much, had no idea *who* they were. But now that we're familiar, I notice their names often. The paper doesn't think much of Mr. Moore's efforts in Negro voter registration. It thinks even less of Mr. Marshall ("Mr. Civil Rights," they always call him) for forcing the retrial of Walter Lee Irvin and Samuel Shepherd, the two young Negroes accused of raping a Groveland white woman last year.

Since we met them, both Mr. Moore and Mr. Marshall have stopped by our packing-house almost regular. When you compare the paper's descriptions of them as the "strident insurgent" and "pugnacious parliamentarian" to the well-mannered gentlemen we've come to know, you have to wonder if the reporters ever actually talked to them.

Sometimes they drop in together, sometimes separate, to exchange papers with Daddy, enjoy a cool drink and use our bathroom in the back.

"You've *no* idea how rare access to a clean rest room is to a man of my color in this part of the country," Mr. Marshall says.

Mr. Harry T. Moore, the former schoolteacher, never fails to ask Ren and me about our homework. One day, he helped Ren master long division. Another time, when I was writing a report on Ancient Rome, he proved quite knowledgeable about the Caesars, Julius and Augustus.

"Although," he told me, "I much prefer the Greeks to the Romans."

"Why's that?" I asked, curious.

Mr. Harry's eyes lit up like twin headlamps. "Rome was a republic where only the rich had rights. But Greece! Greece gave us democracy—one man, one vote—the fairest form of government on earth! Greece gave us Plato, Socrates and Aristotle. Do you know Aristotle, Reesa?"

I'd never seen Mr. Harry so spirited. "Not really," I answered.

"Aristotle was brilliant!" he declared. "Aristotle said democracy rises out of one very important notion—that those who are equal in *any* respect are equal in *all* respects. 'Democracy,' Aristotle said, 'is best attained when all persons alike share in the government to the utmost.'" Mr. Harry stopped and raised his eyebrows in that teacher way that means *Are you getting this?*

"And that's why registering Negro voters is so important?"

"You betcha, girl!" he beamed, and told Daddy I'd earned "an A for the day!"

Fortunately for Ren and me, this school year's wound down to its inevitable end, the Friday before Memorial Day weekend.

"It's wrong to live in a state that's half water and not *enjoy* it!" Mother exclaims, cajoling her wary, unwilling family out the door. Nobody wanted to come on this Memorial Day Picnic, but here we are.

To Mother, a "picnic by the shore" on Memorial Day is an ironclad tradition, cast in her Midwestern childhood. To Daddy, Memorial Day, or any military holiday for that matter, is a painful reminder that his private war with polio left him unfit for the important battles against Hitler, Mussolini, and Hirohito. Daddy prefers a private observance, away from the marching bands, strutting veterans and cheering crowds lining Main Street Opalakee today.

The quiet cypress-rimmed cove off the St. John's River seems no different from the last time we came, last year. But none of us are quite the same. Mitchell, for instance, can swim. He and Buddy plunge in eagerly after Ren, whose passion for baseball has been re-channeled into a daily scrutiny of the Brooklyns' box scores. Last summer, Ren and Marvin hit no less than a hundred fly balls a day.

Mother and Daddy, having set up camp, sit in the shade of our beach umbrella. Daddy scans one of the three newspapers he's taken to reading regularly, clipping stories with his small fruit knife. These days, he's constantly compiling files for Mr. Harry, answering lists of questions from Mr. Marshall. I don't know what the questions are, but I do know that every answer must be three times verified by separate, unwavering sources. What will become of the answers puzzles me, too; but their careful completion has become my father's second occupation.

Beside him, Mother, festive in her blue polka-dot sundress, plays solitaire, shuffling and sorting, shifting and stacking. Now that Doto's left us for Montana, and the awful events of the spring have given way to summer, she's hoping, Mother says, for "some sort of normal."

A ways from my parents, I stretch out on my beach towel watching the water. The surface of the cove shines like metal, with dark emerald sparkles between the knees of the cypress trees. These days, I find myself watching *everything*, with the clear hope of not being caught unaware. Ever since Marvin's murder, I've come to despise surprises:

There in the cypress shadows, for example, a small, smooth log turns. Is it really wood? Or the slow, oily coil of a deadly water moccasin?

Beyond the splashing boys, two dark bumps surface among the sheltered water hyacinths. Another log? Or the dangerous, double-lidded eyes of an alligator?

Except for the turbulence trailing the boys, the water is a mirror, reflecting a bright blue sky, cottony clouds and the green lacework bowing the heads of the kneeling cypress. On its surface, the cove's as peaceful as a prayer. *But nothing is truly as it seems*, I know. Not me, not Mayflower, not the whole entire world. And especially not old Miss Maybelle two doors down the road.

I pull out Vaylie's letter and read, again, the sorry sequel to the already sad tale:

Dear Reesa,
  I just got back from a big family dinner at my
Granddaddy's. It was fun, cousins galore, but nothing like a

*rattler race which, by the way, nobody believes I really saw!
After dessert, I got the chance to ask Granddaddy the real scoop
on Great-Aunt Maybelle.*

*Oh, Reesa, it's even sadder than we imagined. The battle her
fiancé was killed in was the very last one of the war. Even
though he was supposed to come home before it, he <u>volunteered</u> to
stay! Granddaddy says the news hit Great-Aunt Maybelle so
hard she wouldn't leave her room for months, not even for
Christmas dinner. When she finally did come out, she told the
family she didn't want to talk about her fiancé or what
happened—ever again! And as far as Granddaddy knows, she
never has.*

*Granddaddy told me the young man was Mr. and Mrs.
Swann's only son and that his mother was so upset that she
died the next spring of a shattered heart. Isn't this just the
<u>saddest</u> thing you ever heard?*

*I asked him if that's the reason why Great-Aunt Maybelle
is so mean to everybody and all he'd say is "Everybody's got
their reasons, Vaylie, whether you know 'em or not."*

Are you excited that summer's here? Write SOON!!!

Love, VAYLIE

*P.S. If what Granddaddy says is true, that we all have our
reasons, I've been trying to figure what mine are. Do you know
yours?*

I've brought pen and paper with me to reply:

Dear Vaylie,

*If your grandfather's right, if everyone has their reasons,
then somebody stole my share.*

*These days, the reasons behind just about everything baffle
me. Like what really happened to Miss Maybelle and why?*

Or, how can a bunch of men murder my friend Marvin and the whole of Mayflower act as if it never happened?

Marvin's mother Armetta says, "Time in the fire prepares us for what's ahead." But that doesn't make sense to me. Did God kill Miss Maybelle's fiancé so she could spend her life sorting envelopes? Protecting U.S. property from my brother and me? Did Marvin die so those of us who loved him could suffer while his killers walk around scot-free?

What do you think, Vaylie? Do bad things happen because God wills it so? Or is evil something else, with a mind of its own? Like the serpent in the Garden of Eden, or an alligator at the edge of a swimming hole?

Down here, people think of alligators as "a necessary evil." "Take the good with bad," they say. Do you think maybe good and bad are stuck together, like two sides of a dime?

I'm sorry for going on about this. But every question I come up with just seems to lead to another one. Most days, I feel like a dog chasing its tail.

If you come up with any answers, or reasons either, please let me know. And write again <u>soon</u>!

Love, Reesa

Chapter 14

Summer's heat settles on us like a mother hen. We locals know enough to stay in the shade, but the summer tourists, skin white as eggshells heading south, are blistered stiff going north and reeking of Coppertone applied too late.

Today, Mother and I are tending customers in the showroom while Daddy and Luther prune the last of the spring-bearing Valencia trees in the grove out back. The big fruit-processing equipment on the raised platform behind the showroom walls is quiet: the washer with its giant water tank and big bristle brushes; the waxer with its rubber rollers, preservative spray, drying fan and hood; and the long conveyor belts that transport the washed-and-waxed fruit to the sizing bins are all at rest between summer's relaxed, twice-a-week runs.

Mid-morning, the big black pickup truck wheels into the parking lot, oversize tires splaying gravel, large chrome bumper and Confederate flag plate glaring in the sun.

Local, I think at my post behind the juice counter; *nobody I know*, seeing the packed metal gun rack behind the seat.

The driver gets out, skinny, on the short side, with an upright stride that's soldier-like. *War veteran,* I guess. Although he's a stranger to me, the two same-size boys with different clothes and identical faces with him are familiar. *The Bowman twins*, I remember, *first graders*, and the only identical twins in the history of Opalakee Elementary. I've helped them find picture books in the school library.

The three of them move quickly into the shade of the front awning, get their bearings, then strut over to me.

"We'd like some of that ice-cold orange juice you're advertisin'," the man says, pulling a forearm across his forehead to wipe back the sweat. He has the flushed red coloring and the slow-rolling accent of people from south Georgia. "Three for a dime, right?"

"No, sir," I say with a smile. "It's all you can drink for a dime, limit three per customer. We say that to keep the tourists from drinking too much and getting sick to their stomachs."

"You tellin' me you want *thirty cents* instead of a dime?" His eyelashes are thick and orangey around pale eyes that have turned suspicious.

"Yes, sir." I smile again. "A dime apiece. After your first glass, you can have two more each, if you want." The boys are staring at me, trying to sort why I'm familiar. The man sees it, too.

"Y'all know this girl?" he asks them.

The boys nod and say, "Yes, from school." "The library, right?" They have the habit of finishing each other's sentences.

"*You* go to their school?" the man asks me, leaning forward to get a closer look.

"Yes, sir. I've helped your boys find their library books."

"That's funny," he says without smiling. A fat drop of sweat pops out at his hairline. It swerves down the flat of his temple, the hollow of his cheek, and hangs off his jaw. "I didn't think we had any *Jew* girls at our school."

"Pardon me?" His tone turns my arm trembly. Without my telling them to, my hands grip the edge of the counter.

"Well, anybody that advertises three glasses for a dime then tries to charge thirty cents *must* be a *Jew*." His glint across the counter is ugly. The drop of sweat falls off his chin and splats on the counter between us.

"*No*, sir, we're Baptists." My heart's pummeling my chest with a fear I don't understand. What if I *was* Jewish? What would be wrong with that?

His eyes sweep the showroom, taking in Mother and the customers in the shell-lamp section.

"Well, looky here, little Baptist Jew girl," he drawls in a voice that pricks the back of my neck. "I think we've changed our minds about that juice. I think we'll just head on down to Voight's for some Coke-Cola. C'mon, you two. *Git* in the truck." His words cut the space between the twins like a knife. The boys quit and run, fast, toward the truck.

The man glares at me across the counter some more, then slowly, like a dare, parts his fat pink lips into an unpleasant smile. He turns, unhurried, on his boot heel, and swaggers away, under and out from the awning. When the sun hits his back, I gasp. Mother, returning to the counter carrying a conch lamp for checkout, turns. "Reesa? What's wrong?"

As the man's boots crunch across the gravel toward the truck, the letters "J.D.," tooled on the back of his black leather belt, get smaller, harder and harder to read.

"Reesa, what is it?" Mother asks, coming close to look me in the eye.

"That man, that's J. D. Bowman, the one who shot Marvin."

"Good Lord, Reesa, are you all right? Did he *say* something? Did he *do* anything to you?"

"He called me a Jew."

That night, the nightmare, the horror where I'm trapped in the crowd and can't save Marvin; that dream changes. Now, one of the men in the center of the circle stops and turns to scan the spectators. In this new nightmare, J. D. Bowman singles me out, points and yells, "Grab her, too. She's a Jew!"

The next day, at the border between two Miami neighborhoods, all hell breaks loose.

Daddy's family, genetically inclined toward quick thinking and fast acting, are the first to call. I answer the phone and Uncle Harry, in a voice that sounds like Daddy's, mistakes me for Mother.

"Lizbeth, what the *hell's* going on down there?" he wants to know.

That night, we hear from Doto and Aunt Eleanor.

"Warren, you've had fourteen years to whip that state into shape. What the hell's wrong with it?" my father's only sister demands.

"The hell" they refer to, the one *every*one's talking about, is the bombing of the Carver Village Housing Project for Negroes in Miami. The story's all over the news. Bombs gutted two buildings in the recently refurbished section of what used to be all-white Knights Manor. "The largest blast ever detonated in the state of Florida," the papers say, "possibly the entire Eastern Seaboard." The boom of it pitched people living five blocks away out of their beds, and rattled the balcony windows of the fancy hotels down at the beachfront.

One picture in the paper shows the garage owner across the street from the project pointing at the mangled cars, which leaped eight feet in the air, crashing their roofs against his ceiling.

Despite the fact that a number of people suffered cuts and bruises from flying glass, block and wood, everybody swears it's a miracle nobody's dead. The lucky thing is, the two eight-unit buildings were empty; their new occupants hoped to move in next month.

"My guess is that the local whites weren't inclined to form a welcoming committee," Daddy tells us grimly. "This thing's got the Klan written all over it."

When the investigators uncover the remains of two 100-pound bundles of dynamite, they find a third bundle of eighty sticks which failed to explode. One war veteran, looking things over, tells reporters it reminds him of "the blockbuster bombs we used to rout the Krauts out of Bastogne and Coblenz."

On the radio, the Miami police chief says he's certain the Ku Klux Klan "had no involvement *whatsoever*"; in fact, he has "reason to believe that *Reds* are responsible." One Negro has been arrested.

"Idiots!" Doto rages on the phone (so loud the whole family can hear her) and declares she's calling her Congressman *first thing* in the morning.

After Doto rings off, we hear from our mother's only brother, Gordy, and our other grandmother, Nana. Like Mother, they're the sensitive side of the family:

"We're just a nervous *wreck* over this, Lizbeth. Aren't *you*? Why not pack up the kids and come back to Chicago for a few weeks? We'll have a nice visit while the police settle things *down* down there."

Mother and Daddy hand the phone back and forth, each reassuring the other's family, "*Every*thing's fine, we're all *fine*."

As bad as the bombing appears to be, there is, in fact, the slightest flicker of a silver lining in this storm cloud. In today's paper, the remarks of Mr. Harry T. Moore and Mr. Thurgood Marshall are startling:

"I call on Mr. J. Edgar Hoover and the Federal Bureau of Investigation to come to Miami, help us sort this thing out," Mr. Moore, Executive Secretary of the State N.A.A.C.P., is quoted as saying.

"And when they get here, I have a list of other things to look into," Mr. Thurgood Marshall, attorney for the National N.A.A.C.P. said, "including the mistreatment of my clients, Walter Lee Irvin and Samuel Shepherd, in Lake County's Raiford Prison, and the murder of Marvin Cully, a fruit picker, outside Opalakee, in central Florida."

It is the first official acknowledgment of anything to do with Marvin, who was killed three whole months ago. And, to me, it means, it surely *must* mean *something* will happen now.

Chapter 15

In the middle of July, at the peak of our summer season, here's what *should* have happened:

At six o'clock, Daddy, having placed the big "Closed For The Day" signs out front, should've joined the rest of us at the already bustling party in the back.

Our friends Sal and Sophia Tomasini, having closed their own store an hour earlier, should've been holding court over the stove's steaming, boiling, baking pots, bubbling Italian, brimming laughter. Armetta should've been basking in our communal admiration for her heavenly cloud cake—three light-as-air layers floating in creamy coconut—the very one Marvin calls her "Ain't-None-Betta Cake." Luther and Marvin should've been corralling the boys to take their turns cranking the homemade strawberry ice cream. My parents should've looked and felt young again when, after our dinner, we laughed until we cried at the stories of that other summer thirteen years ago:

They remember the swim in the lake followed by polio's headaches, high fever and paralysis. But it's Armetta who tells the one about Doto best. "Miz Doto was a wildcat. You shoulda seen ol' Doc Johnny go bug-eyed when she tol' him, 'What kinda doctor *are* you? I want those splints off Warren's arm and leg this *minute*! Moist heat and massage is what he needs, you old *fool*!' She was right, too!"

Old Sal should've told the one about the big day itself: the men tending Daddy's muscle spasms in one room; the women helping Mother with her contractions in the next while, downstairs, Doto railed at the doctor on the phone, "They're coming *too close*! We'll never make it to Orange Hospital in Orlando, *get* in your damn car and get over here *now*!" It was serene Sophia who held Mother while Armetta "caught" me on my birth day. Doto was downstairs at the door, hauling in poor Doc Johnny, who luckily arrived in time for cleanup. "It's a wonder he's even speaking to us," Mother should've said.

After dinner and the stories, Marvin should've turned on the radio and coaxed us all out to dance, something lively and fun like Teresa Brewer and the Dixieland All-Stars "Choo'n Gum." This very minute, we should've been howling at Marvin trying to teach a shuffling Sal the latest fancy dance step.

Truth is, all of this *should've* happened and *would've* happened—as it always had on this particular day—if only Marvin hadn't been murdered, and the Klan stayed out of everybody's business in Miami.

Instead of loud music, the radio plays low, everyone half

listening for the latest news update. Instead of funny stories, my parents, Sal and Sophia, and Luther and Armetta sit softly discussing the latest fearful developments. Last month's massive bombing of Carver Village was only the beginning. On the Fourth of July, dynamite bundles were hurled at the steps of the Miami Jewish Center and, just today, a blast blew up the doors of St. Stephen's Catholic Church.

"First da Negroes, den da Jews, now Catholics." Sal's eyes behind thick glasses sink into the shadows of his bushy gray brows. Next to him, Sophia, his wife, bows her silver-streaked head.

"It's the Klan's holy trinity of hate. Nobody else is so obviously ecumenical," Daddy says.

I wonder if it occurs to him how nearly our little group resembles that triangle. Luther and Armetta are Negroes; the Tomasinis, Catholic transplants from New York; and we've been called Jews by the very man who murdered Marvin!

Except for Daddy who's angry, we're an anxious, apprehensive group. As Ren and Mitchell quit us to search outside for fireflies, it's Luther who lays out the night's most troublesome question.

"How long 'fore the Opalakee Klan stirs things up 'round here again?" he asks quietly.

"Hard to say, isn't it?" Daddy says. "Since nobody's doing anything to stop the Miami crowd, this business could easily get out of hand. It's not surprising their police are looking the other way—they're probably half Klanners themselves. We know Thurgood and Harry are doing all they can. But you'd *think* the big hotel owners would be screaming their heads off. It won't be long, it *can't* be long before the wealthy tourists start making other plans. Once the cancellations start rolling in, the Miami bigwigs will be howling for the governor, *somebody*, to do *some*thing. Nothing like an endangered pocketbook to help a businessman find his conscience."

"In the meantime . . . ?" Mother's eyes are dark with worry.

"In the meantime, what are *we* supposed to do?" Daddy wonders, his stare challenging the table, his jaw hardened in frustration. "What choice do we have but to sit tight and keep our heads down?" he asks in a tone that tells me that's the *last* thing he wants to do.

I was Mitchell's age when the Japanese bombed Pearl Harbor. I have no memory of President Roosevelt saying the day will live in infamy, but I know he said it. I was Ren's age when we dropped the A-bomb on Hiroshima. These were Acts of War. Everybody knew it. What with Europe, Japan and Korea, my country's been at war with somebody, somewhere, practically my entire life. But it was today, July 14, 1951, that the Klan bombed St. Stephen's Catholic Church and declared war on the people of this state. It was a lousy gift in the worst year I've ever known. It ruined my thirteenth birthday, which, by all rights, *should've* been a happy day.

The one and only bit of good news this month comes from Ren: the Brooklyn Dodgers, who captured first place in their league in April, and held on to it throughout May and June, win ten games in a row in July. At midseason's All-Star break, they're still way ahead of everybody else—which, Ren says, "is a sure sign they'll win the pennant and make it into the Series!" Ren, old Sal, and the fans from The Quarters go crazy when a record seven Brooklyn Dodgers make it onto the National League's All-Star team, including Negroes Jackie Robinson, Roy Campanella and Don Newcombe. These days, what Marvin called "baseball's Heaven on Earth" offers the only hopeful respite from our real lives in central Florida.

Chapter 16

The high, humid heat of August presses on us with an unkind hand. This is, officially, the hottest Florida summer on record. Everything, from traffic on the Trail to Buddy's tail-wagging, has slowed to a crawl.

In Miami, denied protection by local police ("We will not make night watchmen out of our officers," the chief says), Jewish war veterans patrol their communities to protect their families from further bombings. In the Negro neighborhood surrounding Carver Village, leaders request but are denied the same privilege.

The F.B.I., citing "no apparent violation of any federally guaranteed civil rights," remains elsewhere. The bombings continue.

This week's explosion is at the Coral Gables Jewish Center, seven miles southwest of Miami. As usual, the police report no suspects. No official actions are taken.

Inside the showroom, the air hangs as limp and damp as a washrag. Daddy brings out the three big pedestal fans, normally in the back, and places them in opposite corners to create a cooling air flow. The fans are noisy. Ren and Mitchell, playing darts in the office, yell to us, "Hey, sounds like there was a wedding in Wellwood!"

The familiar sounds of a squealing lead car followed by a flock of honking well-wishers pull Mother, Daddy and me outside and onto the walkway, peering north.

What we *expect* to see is a pair of newlyweds, their car decorated with ribbons, cans, signs and all, followed by loudly celebrating family and friends.

What appears *instead* stuns us.

In the lead, a sleek black Chrysler New Yorker, speeding wildly, weaves in and out of the slow-moving traffic. No decorations, no signs, four Negro occupants, two in front, two in back, *obviously* in flight. The Hertz logo on the car's front plate tells me it's a rental, probably from the airport. The lockjawed concentration of the driver and the flat-out frantic movements of the others inside makes it clear—*this* is no party game. The four people flying past us in the Chrysler are terrified. When you see what's behind them, you can't blame them.

The first of the three chase vehicles roaring down the Trail is a big black Ford pickup, oversize bumpers polished to blinding brightness. Two men inside wear the ghostly white of the Ku Klux Klan. Out one window, the rider brandishes a double-barreled shotgun. Out the other, the driver waves a high-powered rifle, using his inside forearm to press against the truck horn. Both men are hooded, but there's no mistaking those bumpers and Confederate flag plate. Passing in front of us, pursuing the Chrysler, is J. D. Bowman, the man of my nightmares.

Behind him, about a hundred yards, a red Dodge truck tears toward us. Three riders lean forward in the front. Two more stand in the back, clutching the cab and waving weapons. The sleeves of their robes flap in the wind, the crests of their hoods blow back, flat against their heads. One lets out an eerie, high-pitched cry, the unnerving howl of the Rebel Yell.

In the last truck, a shiny blue Chevy, the white robes of three men glow against its dark interior. These figures brandish no weapons, honk no horns, make no battle cries. These men sit calmly, the driver coolly maneuvering in and around the traffic, the riders patient like observers or judges or law enforcement officials. A large Confederate flag draped and taped to the driver's side covers the logo we all know is there: the golden script of Emmett Casselton's Casbah Groves.

As this terrible parade flies past us, Mother and Daddy look at each other in disbelief. The fearful faces of those in the front car, the hateful menace of their white-robed pursuers leaves me numb. I *know* the Klan is a group of white men capable of doing horrible things; what they did to Marvin is etched in my mind till I die. But to tell you the truth, I'd somehow imagined that adults dressed in sheets might look like a grown-up Halloween party. The sight of them in full pursuit, in broad daylight, sickens me.

Mother pulls me close. Daddy, behind us, grips us both. Mercifully, the boys have remained inside, choosing dart play over the supposed "wedding party." My parents and I stand stiffly together, listening to the horns race out of town. Then two carloads of customers pull into our driveway. We follow them, dazed, into the showroom.

"You see that Big Chase?"

"What was it all about?"

"Was that the Ku Klux Klan?"

"Where were the cops?"

"Who was in the Chrysler?" the tourists want to know, peppering us with the very questions we have for each other. For the next few hours, we collect details like puzzle pieces.

"That car flew past us, doing at least ninety outside Wellwood, nearly scared my wife and kids to death!"

"I don't know where it started. We stopped to get gas in Tangerine and that Chrysler nearly crashed into us when we were pulling out of the station. We stopped, tried to pull out again, and here come the trucks. My wife made me wait fifteen minutes, just to be sure it was safe to get back on the road."

"That black pickup ran the car ahead of us off the road outside Lockhart!"

On Sunday, at church, the congregation is buzzing.

"Did you see—?"

"Where were you when those trucks went through?"

"I recognized that big black truck, didn't you? Blue one, too."

"Any idee who was in the car?"

"Had to be folks from up north. Rented from the airport. Wonder what they did?"

After Sunday's midday dinner, we drive to Opalakee for ice cream. Mother and Daddy buy an Orlando paper and search it for clues. We listen to the car radio. We ask a few Opalakee people (not many out in this heat) what they know.

"Oh, it went right past *here*, smack-dab through the middle of town! Chief of Police was parked over there, front of the bank building. Leaned against his car and watched it with the rest of us. Didn't do a thing."

Of course not, but who were they? Are they okay?

It's not until Luther stops by, after that night's supper, that the pieces tumble into place. He comes in carrying a bulging brown paper sack.

"Evenin', y'all!" he beams. "Mah cousin Sylbie was visitin' from Valdosta this weekend, brought us a case of sweet Georgia peaches. They won't last the week in this heat, thought y'all might take some off our hands."

"Luther, there's nothing in the world better than a ripe Georgia peach," Mother says, brightening. "Thank you! You kids want one?"

Ren, Mitchell and I sit at the table smacking through our peaches, catching the sweet juice running down our chins with pink paper napkins, when Daddy asks Luther, "You hear anything about the Big Chase?"

"Well, actually, Ah did." Luther leans back in his chair, his gold dog tooth glinting in a grin.

Daddy leans forward, hanging on his every word.

"Y'see, Mistuh Thurgood Marshall was s'posed to be in Tavares yesterday, filin' for the hearin' on the big *re*-trial. The Opalakee Klan got wind of it, thought they might kidnap Mistuh Marshall, or at least give 'im a scare on his way to the *a*'port. They was waitin' for him to cross the county line. Chased his car all the way down the Trail to O'landah. Lost 'im in the a'port traffic."

"Luther, how in the *world* do you know this?"

"Mist'Warren, half mah choir works in the homes of the Klanners 'round here, *have* since most of these young bucks were chil'ren. Those folks so use to havin' they colored women in the kitchen or workin' 'round the house, they forgit to watch what they say."

"You mean to tell me, you heard all this from your *sopranos*?" Daddy's flabbergasted.

"Well, *some* of 'em are altos," Luther says, "but, yes, Ah did."

"Why, Luther, you're head of a spy ring," Daddy says, impressed.

"Ah s'pose Ah am," Luther nods.

"You know . . ." The corner of Daddy's mouth twitches. "You could call it the Choir Intelligence Agency, your own private *C.I.A.*"

"Oh, that's good, that's real good!" Luther's booming laugh bounces off the kitchen walls. Then he turns serious. "Ah'll tell you somethin' else . . ."

"What?" I ask.

"What those Klanners don't know is that Mistuh Thurgood Marshall wudn't even in that car."

"What do you mean?" Mother asks.

"Mistuh Marshall had to cancel and send his assistants. The people in that car were his staff, plus a couple Yankee reporters hitchin' a ride to the O'landah airport!"

"You're kiddin' me!" "Really?" "Can you believe it!" we exclaim as the implications of this news race around the table.

"But wait a minute . . ." Daddy's tone cuts off our delight. "Luther, if the Klan lost the car in the airport traffic, how do *you* know who was in that car?"

"You a quick one, Mist'Warren." Luther narrows his eyes at Daddy, dropping his voice. "Ah got *that* information from Mistuh Harry T. Moore, who sends y'all his regards, by the way. Mistuh Moore says those redneck Klanners have no idee how much they helped the cause of the Florida Negro yesterday."

In the wake of Luther's revelations, I'm relieved that the people in the black car got safely away. *Maybe* the involvement of two Northern reporters will call attention to a bad situation that's clearly grown worse. "Evil is contagious," Doto told me once. Like some Biblical plague, the Klan's particular kind of evil has taken over Miami and headed north, back up the Trail, parading past our very doorstep.

That night, as my parents enter their bedroom across the hall from mine, I hear Mother echo my worry.

"I thought Marvin's murder was a mistake, the show-off act of a madman," she tells Daddy, "but *this* was *organized*, Warren! If the Klan's grown brazen enough to attempt a kidnapping in broad daylight, what's next?"

I can't hear, I can only imagine my father's stone-faced reply.

What will the local Klan do next? I wonder, curled tight in my sheets. There aren't any Negro housing projects or Jewish synagogues around Mayflower. They wouldn't dare dynamite The Quarters or Opalakee's Colored Town, would they? But if they tried, who'd stop them? Not the local law, of course. We learned that last March. Then who? And I find myself praying for the first time in months. *Oh, God, if You're up there, could You arrange a little help down here?*

Chapter 17

The answer is no. God doesn't care what's happening in Florida. And, apparently, Mr. J. Edgar Hoover doesn't either. (Of course, in little Mitchell's mind, God and Mr. Hoover have become one and the same.)

Without Anyone's intervention, the Miami Klan continues to terrorize that city's non-white and non-Protestant neighborhoods. You can read all about it in the newspaper; though, since the big blast last June, the stories are buried in a back section . . . as if it's perfectly *normal* to have dynamite blow up another Catholic church, or a Jewish synagogue, or Negro housing project.

Everyone says it's a miracle nobody's been killed. *Yet.*

Last Saturday, the Orlando Klan jumped in, blowing up a perfectly good ice-cream stand called the Creamette. We drove over the next day and I could not believe my eyes. What was once a nice little drive-up business is now a heap of rubble, as if a nasty-tempered giant monster stepped on just *that* place and flattened it to nothing.

Daddy talked to the owner and his wife, who were picking through the piles, shaking their heads. "Somebody called us," they told him, "a man's voice telling us we better stop serving white people and Negroes from the same window. We only had the one window to hand out the ice-cream cones. *What* were we supposed to do?"

The Orlando paper says the blast hurled concrete blocks two hundred fifty feet in the air. The lady across the street said she spent the entire day picking up rocks, pieces of metal, paper napkins and the little white wrappers they put ice-cream cones in, scattered all over her yard.

Everybody's talking about it: the people at church, the customers at Voight's, the last of the summer tourists heading home for Labor Day and, of *course*, the ladies at Miz Lillian's Beauty Parlor.

Miz Maggie Brass, wife of Deacon Aldo, is on the same Labor Day–Christmas–Easter perm schedule I am. (Nobody gets a summer perm. The weather's so hot and heavy that everybody's hair frizzes, perm or not, so why bother?)

"It's hurricane season," Miz Maggie says. "Got everybody on edge, doin' crazy things with dynamite."

"No, no, it's the Nigras gettin' *uppity*, movin' into their fancy housing projects," says Miz Opal Taylor, in for her weekly shampoo-and-set. "The Klan's just keepin' 'em in their place. I'm inclined to agree with Mr. Eugene Cox, that

Georgia Congressman, y'all know him? He says it's the *hand of Stalin* behind these Nigra uprisings."

"*Up*risings?" Miz Lillian laughs, coaxing Miz Opal's top curls into place with a red rat-tail comb. "Far as I can see, the Negroes haven't done a thing! It's the Klan that's *doin'* it all."

"And why'd they bomb the Jewish synagogues and the Catholic church? None of 'em have a *single* Negro member," Miss Iris, Miz Lillian's assistant, wants to know.

"Be*cause*, Iris," Miss Opal, sounding aggravated, says, "those left-wing liberals are *agitators*, givin' the Nigras *ideas* about livin' next to whites. Next thing y'know, they'll wanta be eatin' in our *restaurants*, usin' our toilets," Miz Opal says.

"Maybe even comin' to our beauty parlors." Miz Lillian winks at me in the mirror, aggravating Miss Opal right back.

"Lillian! You're not about to let a Nigra woman in here!" Miz Maggie barks, her voice rising out of the rinsing sink.

"I don't know, Maggie. I never had the chance to work with that kind of hair. Might be interestin'," Miz Lillian says, stifling herself.

At supper, I relate Miz Opal's "hand of Stalin" comments to my family.

"That's ridiculous," Mother says, Miz Opal being one of the church ladies she regularly avoids.

"Devil's trick, my dear," Daddy says, shaking his head.

"What do you mean?" Ren asks, making a face at the spoonful of succotash Mother's placed on his plate.

"If you're the bad guy, people are *against* you, right?" Daddy asks, pointing a fork full of limas in Ren's direction.

"Right," Ren nods.

"Best way to get people rooting *for* you is to accuse your enemy of being something worse than you are."

Ren frowns. "You mean if people think that Negroes are turning Communist . . . that's supposed to make it okay for the Klan to blow up their houses?"

"Exactly," Daddy tells him.

"Mother's right. That's the stupidest thing I've ever heard," Ren mutters, turning his attention to his meat loaf.

"But will it work?" I want to know.

"I certainly hope not," Mother says.

"Depends." Daddy leans forward, both elbows on the table. All of sudden, he's very serious. "Sometimes, this kind of thing starts out small, like a new plant, a vine like kudzu, for instance. If nobody pays attention to it, it grows and grows, and before you know it, it's taken over a whole hillside, choked the life out of every other plant around it."

"Warren," Mother says, in a way that means *quit scaring the children.*

"Forewarned is forearmed," Daddy shoots back at her. "These are devilish times we're living in, Lizbeth. There's no hiding that from anybody, especially these children."

At Daddy's stinging tone, Mother retreats behind her Poker Face, gets up and clears the table. It's their last exchange of the evening.

To tell you the truth, I'm worried about my mother. Ever since we went to visit the Creamette, or rather the place where the Creamette used to be, ever since we toed our way through the rubble of what's left of that other family's business, she's not been herself. Fact is, none of us are.

Chapter 18

The number eighty-six school bus lumbers to a squeaking stop in front of the post office. The bill of Taddy Carver's green John Deere cap turns profile, nodding toward the steps. Taddy's big hand cuffs and thrusts the handle. The doors split open and the boys—Ren plus Roy and Dwayne Samson—tumble out ahead of me, barking and romping like bloodhounds released from their cages, eager for the woods.

Over the din of their cries for weekend adventure, Taddy's cap dips a silent "See you Monday" to me. The doors swish closed and the bus, clutch complaining mightily, heaves itself back onto the road. The Samson boys cut left toward their house, but I amble right, behind the bolting bird dog that is my brother. *It's a relief to be back in school,* I decide, feeling the first-week jitters crowd out this summer's insanity.

As the front porch door slams behind us, the phone is ringing in that jingle-jangle way that means it's a party-line call. Ren, knowing it could only be Miss Maybelle at the Post Office or Miz Sooky across the street, tears into the bathroom.

"Reesa! Where's your daddy? I *need* him, *quick*." The voice is Miss Maybelle's and it's urgent.

"He's not here, ma'am, probably at the packinghouse."

"You've *got* to find him. I need his help *now!* Understand?"

"Y-Yes, ma'am." Something is very wrong. There's no doubt about that.

"He must come right away!"

"Yes, ma'am," I say, sensing no time for questions. "I'll find him."

Mother answers on the first ring.

"Where's Daddy . . . something's wrong at the post office . . . Miss Maybelle needs him," I tell her in a rush.

"He's gone over to Winter Garden to pick up a tractor part. Reesa, what is it?"

"She didn't say. Just that he needed to come quick!"

"Weren't you just there, Reesa? Did you see anything wrong?"

"Nothing out of the ordinary." What could it be?

"Robert's due any minute," Mother tells me. "I'll send him along as soon as he gets here."

As I hang up the phone, Ren demands an explanation. Getting it, he turns without a word and heads out the door.

"Where are you going?" I yell, running after him, then, realizing his intent, race to catch him.

The front of the post office is as dead as usual this time of day, at least two hours before the mail is sorted and available for pickup. There are no cars or trucks, front or back, no sign of anything or anyone outside. Carefully cracking the door, we peer inside, then back at each other. One whiff of that musky-sweet scent and we *know*, without asking, what's wrong.

"Damn, need my fork stick!" Ren whispers, tiptoeing in with a hunter's grace. The lobby's empty, but over the counter, in the shaft of sunlight slashing across the backroom floor, I see the diamondback rattler, coiled and spitting at a frozen Miss Maybelle. The rattler whorls in the dusty light, dead center between Miss Maybelle, who's trapped at the front counter, and the room's only exit at the back.

"Where's your daddy?" Miss Maybelle asks us desperately, nothing moving but her mouth.

"He can't come, but Robert's on his way," I assure her, watching Ren size up the situation. Over his shoulder, something in the corner catches my eye.

"Can you use the push broom?" I ask and point.

"Yes!" he says. "Help me up, then hand it to me."

"What are you two doing? Don't come in here!" Miss Maybelle cries out of the side of her mouth, eyes glued to the snake.

I hoist Ren up on the counter and he squirms quickly across it and to the right, out of the snake's line of sight. Quietly he says, "Don't worry, Miss Maybelle, I've caught a *million* snakes. You stand real still now. *I'll* get him."

With great care, I pass him the long-handled push broom, then reach across to put my hand over Miss Maybelle's ice-cold claw clinging to the counter's edge. As Ren mountain-climbs across the wall of mailboxes and steps lightly, gingerly onto the worktable, the snake senses something and bobs his hood. Miss Maybelle's bony fingers find mine and crush them so tightly I cry out, a sharp yelp of pain.

Ren raises a finger to his lips, then inches down to his knees. He twirls the broom into position, brushes up, rail-side down. Holding it like a pool cue, eyeing his mark, he rams it down onto the back base of the snake's skull, pinning it, tail wildly flopping, to the floor.

He looks up, grinning ear to ear. "Can you toss me an empty mail sack, Miss Maybelle?" he asks her.

"Is it safe to move?" she wants to know, still clutching my hand.

"Perfectly," he tells her.

Miss Maybelle lets go, grabs a soft canvas sack from under the counter and with a nervous jerk heaves it Ren's way. Catching it with one hand, maintaining pressure on the flat, trapped head with the other, Ren slides off the table and scoops up the writhing body, tail first into the sack. With a practiced flick, he lifts the broom and yanks the drawstring, securing the rattler inside.

"Safe and sound, Miss Maybelle," he says, holding the sack, like a prize, up in the air.

Relief wilts her. "Oh, my dear boy, thank you, thank you," she says.

"No problem," Ren tells her. "How'd he get in, in the first place?"

"Must have snuck in during the afternoon delivery. I turned around and it was just *there*." She shudders. "Will you take it out and kill it?"

"*Kill* him? He was just looking for a safe place to sleep. Naw, I'll let him go, out in the scrub where he belongs."

Out front, we hear the sudden rumble and heave of Robert's motorcycle. The big front door bangs open. "Miss Maybelle, Miz Mac says there's trouble. What's wrong?" Robert growls, ready for action.

"Not a thing," she answers, her eyes lighting on Ren. "Not anymore."

Ren, still holding the squirming sack, recounts his heroics for Robert. The sun streams through the window, bathing Miss Maybelle in light. As she thanks us again, I find myself blinking at her powerful resemblance to the pretty bride-to-be in the photo in our attic.

V aylie's postcard arrives the following week, her choice an unfortunate one for our postmistress. The picture on front shows a coiled diamondback rattler, tail and triangular head erect, pointy fangs like drapery hooks ready to strike. Red letters on the front say GREETINGS *from the Natural History Museum, Washington, D.C.*

On the back, she writes:

Guess who's on tour again? Is Junior High great? I hate missing the first few weeks, takes forever to catch up. Did you know a rattlesnake is part of the Pit Viper family? I told Mamma that since she always calls Daddy's mamma "the old viper" that must make me part rattler. Maybe I'm related to the bunch we saw in ol' Dry Sink. If you see one, tell 'em "hi" from Cousin Viper! Will write more when I can.

Love, VAYLIE

You've got something there, Vaylie, I think. There's a bit of the rattler in all of us. But as far as I've seen, human snakes are a whole lot meaner than the reptile kind.

Chapter 19

Octtober third is a summer day with an autumn date. Ren and I spent the morning helping Sal and Sophia get ready for this afternoon's crowd. In the scrawny shade under the scrub pines behind Tomasinis' store, over a hundred people are assembling to cheer their beloved Jackie Robinson, and the Brooklyn Dodgers, to pennant glory over the nasty New York Giants.

After a season that, according to Ren, was pretty much a one-horse race, with the Dodgers in the lead April through September, the Giants came out of nowhere to force a pennant play-off, the three-game cockfight that, one way or the other, ends today.

Already, we've raked the dirt free of pinecones and rearranged the rough-sawn benches into semicircles facing the back of the store. Against the wall, Sal's perched his small black-and-white TV set on a plywood shelf, suspended by ropes out of the window of their upstairs apartment. We've stood on the ground below while Sal fiddled with the twenty-five-foot antenna, yelling our opinions on the screen's reception from the faraway Atlanta station. We've stocked the Coke-Cola cooler and arranged the charcoal in the side-split fifty-gallon barrels where Sal will barbecue, and we will serve, his secret-recipe, all-beef frankfurters, "like da Stahl-Meyers at Ebbets Field, only betta."

Luther and Armetta are among the first to arrive just after noon, with Reverend Stone from St. John's A.M.E. I see Jerry Tee, Jimmy Lee and Natty and others who work on our picking crew are here, and old ladies and young mothers and children who, lacking real Dodger baseball caps, wear blue cotton kerchiefs tied to their heads. They race around like a band of miniature pirates.

The hot dog work before the game is fast and furious. The talk around me is all baseball. *Marvin would have loved this*, I think with an ache around my heart, as old Sal, the only person present who's actually been to Ebbets Field, holds court: One boy asks, "Mistuh Sal, Big Nate says they usta be the Trolley Dodgers? What's a trolley, anyway?" Some young men challenge Sal to "tell Willie 'bout Babe Ruth's fastball in the 'sixteen Series 'gainst the Red Sox." A man in an old brown Grays cap wants to argue: "Babe Ruth? Smokey Joe Williams could outplay Ruth any day of th' week!"

At five minutes before game time, in a move that's an important part of this behind-the-store ritual, Reverend Stone rises for the opening prayer. Reverend Stone is a wiry man with a big, booming voice. He holds a blanched palm high above the crowd and we all, even the youngest children, respectfully bow our heads.

"Lawd, **Lawd**, *we thank You for Your son* **Jesus**,*"*
the Reverend says, and a chorus of scattered voices say, "Amen."
"And, on this day especially, we thank You
for our **people**'s *son,* **Jackie**.*"*
At this, the "Amens" become noticeably more enthusiastic.
"Now, Lawd, we know **better** *than to ask*
Your involvement in **petty** *sports.*
But in Your Son's **glorious** *Sermon on the Mount, He told us*
'Enter ye in at the **straight** *gate.*
Straight *is the gate, and* **narrow** *is the way,*
and **few** *there be that find it.'*
We ask, Lawd, Your blessing on young Don Newcombe,
our starting pitcher.
We ask that **his** *gate be straight and narrow,*
and that there be **few** *today that find it."*
Amens and muffled laughter ripple through the crowd.
"Lawd, we thank You for the four apostles who
*spread Your good word—***Matthew, Mark, Luke and John**.
And we praise You for the good wood of four
*others—***Jackie, Campy, Duke and Gil**.
May their bats ring loudly the gospel of hope, faith, fairness
and the equality of **all** *men at the plate!"*
"AMEN!"
"We know it's best, Lawd, not to hope too high."
Reverend Stone pauses to eyeball the zealots in the crowd.
"And we **promise** *You, Lawd, that,* **whatever** *today's outcome,*
we **will**—*now and forever—praise Your* **holy** *name!"*

"AMEN and PLAY BALL!" the crowd yells enthusiastically.

Jerry Tee clambers up the stepladder to turn up the
TV's volume, loud, and the game begins. It's a shock to hear
a voice other than the honey-toned Red Barber's, but Ren

explains to me, since they're playing at the Giants' Polo Grounds, their man Russ Hodges is announcing the game.

Because I don't follow baseball as fanatically as the people around me, I find myself watching them for clues as to what's going on. Throughout the early innings, the fans are nervous, wringing their hands, shaking their heads over every pitch, hit and play. By the end of the seventh inning, the teams are tied at only one run apiece. People cast worried eyes at the TV screen and each other.

In "the top" of the eighth inning, when Maglie—the Giants' pitcher who nobody likes—makes a mistake, a bad throw, and a Dodger named PeeWee runs home, 2–1, the fans cheer loudly. Then Maglie walks Jackie Robinson, and the crowd erupts. "Steal second, Jackie!" they holler. "Steal 'em all!" Miz Coralie Brown—the tiny old lady with a face as round and crinkled as a walnut, sitting next to Armetta—crows. But before Jackie can steal anything, batter Billy Cox hits a two-run homer and stretches the lead to 4–1. The fans are *thrilled* by that, and by the fact that in "the bottom" of the inning, the Giants don't score a thing.

Now, in the ninth inning, the Dodger batters don't score either. But the fans are hopeful as the teams change places. "Three more outs and we get our Series!" Ren yells in my ear, then, turning back to the screen hunched over and intent, wipes wet palms on his pants. Reverend Stone dabs his upper lip with a huge white handkerchief. Old Sal nervously taps his false teeth. And Miz Coralie holds up crooked arthritic fingers, double-crossed for luck.

The crowd is hushed and unhappy when first one, then another Giant batter gets on base. A third batter hits the first one home, bumping the score to 4–2, with two men still on base. Suddenly, there's a great roar of disapproval as the

Dodger manager walks out to remove Don Newcombe from the pitcher's mound. "Leave 'im in!" Jimmy Lee and many others holler. "Let 'im be!" Miz Coralie wails.

The announcer Hodges identifies Newcombe's replacement, a young pitcher named Ralph Branca.

Beside me, Ren is stunned. "Branca? *Nooooo!*" he howls as, beside him, old Sal mutters, "Is no good, Dressen, no good."

The crowd is still grumbling as the Giants' next batter, Bobby Thomson, comes to the plate. "Shhhhhhh, hush, now," the old people hiss, some watching the screen, some merely listening, seeing the game inside their heads. Branca's first pitch is a good one. "Strike one off the knees," Hodges says. Ren and Sal eye each other in guarded relief. At the second pitch, the voice from the Polo grounds says, "Here's a long fly . . . it's gonna be . . . I believe . . ." And, then, a pause and the unbelievable, heart-stopping news, "The Giants win the pennant! The Giants win the pennant! The Giants win the pennant!"

Ren jumps up, slams his fist against the wall. "No," he cries, "*no, NO!*" Old Sal buries his head in his hands, hiding his tears but not the moan in his throat.

Several people, including Miz Coralie, openly weep. Armetta turns to her with shiny wet cheeks. Luther and Reverend Stone stand to comfort them; Luther with a soft squeeze on his wife's shoulder, the Reverend with a sorrowful "The Lawd giveth, and He taketh away."

As the dejected young men, the disappointed parents and their silent children, the pairs of old people rise and turn to tread sadly home, I want to protest.

It would have been divinely *right* for these Dodgers, seven All-Stars among them, to have won this pennant. But apparently, Marvin has no damn pull in heaven. It would have been morally *just,* for Jackie Robinson especially, to have played the Series, and shown the world that Negroes are the equal of anybody. But, instead of the Dodgers' brilliant Don New-combe standing victorious, today black-hearted Sal Maglie—who viciously bean-balled Robinson all season—is the pennant-winning pitcher.

To my mind, because of Marvin, God owed us this win, owed the Dodgers their stay in Heaven on Earth. But, for reasons beyond me, God came down on the wrong side of right. And made baseball, as Red Barber says, "just like life."

The late-afternoon sun pierces the pines with sharp orange swords of light. The departing fans trail long, lonesome shadows. Dusk comes fast and is wintry red.

Chapter 20

On Monday afternoon, November fifth, Mr. Thurgood Marshall wheels his rental car into the packinghouse lot. Leaving his suit coat in the car, he strides into our showroom, tie loosened, starched white shirtsleeves rolled back against the heat.

"Did you hear about the cold snap in New York?" he asks, patting his forehead with a folded white handkerchief. "There were icicles hanging off our front stoop when I left," he tells us with a throaty chuckle.

"Welcome to paradise," Daddy says, turning the small electric fan on the counter in his direction. "Time for another tango with Sheriff McCall?"

"Ackerman, the defense counsel, has filed for a change of venue; Judge Futch is going to rule on it day after tomorrow," the big man tells us. News of the Supreme Court-ordered retrial—of the two young

Negroes accused of raping a white woman up in Groveland—
has been all over the papers for months.

While I pour Mr. Marshall some fresh-squeezed juice, I
listen to him tell Daddy they're hoping to get Prosecutor Jess
Hunter removed for calling the N.A.A.C.P. "a subversive and
Communist organization." He wants to transfer the proceed-
ings to Marion County, where Lake County's notorious Sheriff
McCall "has fewer friends."

"Better there than Miami," Daddy says, and the two men
shake their heads over the most recent string of bombings—
three more since Labor Day.

"What the hell's taking the F.B.I. so long?" Daddy rails.

Mr. Marshall's face falls. "Your guess is as good as mine.
We've called everyone we can think of, *twice*. And that in-
cludes the President and the former First Lady!"

"And, unfortunately, old give-em-hell Harry's up to his
eyeballs in Communists?" Daddy asks, raising an eyebrow.

"We're standing in a line that's gets longer every day,"
Mr. Marshall tells him sadly, finishing his juice. "If you have
the time," he adds, "you're welcome to attend Wednesday's
hearing in Tavares."

"Really?" I say, avoiding Daddy's eye. "Me, too?" I ask,
hoping to confirm my seat from Mr. Civil Rights himself.

Far too smart to be caught between a teenager and her
parents, Mr. Marshall shakes his head. "That's for your parents to decide, Reesa."

After he's gone, my begging begins. The trick is to press
hard enough to get a yes, but not so hard I get a no. "Please,
Daddy, please. After all I've read, all the things the paper's
said, you have to let me go! It's history!"

My father, no slouch at smartness either, gives me the sly
eye. "We'll discuss it with your mother, later."

I t should have been, it *would* have been, something to see Mr. Marshall at work, defending Walter Lee Irvin and Samuel Shepherd, two of the four young Negroes who stopped their car to help a white couple and were later accused of raping the woman. But, on November sixth, on their way to the courthouse, both Walter Irvin and Samuel Shepherd were shot. Shepherd was killed. What happened that night, on a lonely road in Lake County, depends on who you choose to believe.

In the local paper, Sheriff Willis McCall tells his side of things:

In the late afternoon of November sixth, the sheriff and his deputy James Yates drove up to Raiford State Prison in Union County to pick up defendants Irvin and Shepherd. The lawmen's court-ordered task was to deliver the two Negroes back to Lake County's court in Tavares. When they left the prison, the defendants were handcuffed together in the front seat next to the sheriff. Deputy Yates sat in the back.

"Fearing interference from a lynch mob," Sheriff McCall explained, he drove Deputy Yates to Weirsdale to pick up a second car. "By that time, it was dark, so I sent Yates ahead to watch for roadblocks. On the way," McCall said, "a tire went flat and needed fixing. When I opened the car door to get the prisoners out, Shepherd grabbed my flashlight, smashed me on the head with it, and yelled to Irvin to get my gun." Sheriff McCall pulled his revolver and shot each prisoner three times. Then he radioed for Deputy Yates to come back and to call a doctor. When the doctor got there, Samuel Shepherd was dead. Walter Lee Irvin looked dead, but was not.

Instead, Irvin's in the hospital with tubes draining blood

from his chest cavity, and a bullet lodged forever in his kidney. Miraculously, he's able to talk. In an interview, headlined "Who Lied?," twenty-three-year-old Irvin tells his story:

"The sheriff and the deputy began talkin' on the radio a little bit. The sheriff told him to 'go ahead and check' and so the deputy sheriff went on a short ways in front of us and he says, 'Okay' . . . The sheriff shimmied his steering wheel and said, 'Something is wrong with my left front tire.' "

Irvin said McCall reached under the seat for his flashlight, got out and kicked the front wheel. "Then he opened our door and said, 'You sons of bitches get out and get this tire fixed.' . . . So Sammy—he was by the door—he takes his foot and put it out of the car and was gettin' out, I can't say just how quick it was, but he shot him. It was quick enough, and he turned, the sheriff did, and he had a pistol and he shot Sammy right quick. Then he shot me. He reached and grabbed me, and snatched me, and Sammy, too. He snatched both of us and then threw us on the ground.

"Then I didn't say anything. I didn't say nothin'. So later he snatched us, he shot me again in the shoulder, and still I didn't say anything at all, all that time. And I knew I was not dead.

"In about ten minutes, the deputy sheriff was there. And the deputy he shined the light in my face and he said to the sheriff, 'That son of a bitch is not dead.' And then he said, 'Let's kill him.' The deputy sheriff pointed his pistol on me and pulled the trigger, snapped the trigger, and the gun did not shoot. The deputy took it around to the car lights and looked in it and shined the light in it. He turned it on me again and pulled it and that time the gun fired. It went through me here," indicating his throat, "and then I began to bleed out of my mouth and nose. I didn't say nothin' and didn't let them know I was not dead. And some people came . . ."

There isn't a doubt in my mind that Walter Lee Irvin is telling the truth. And that Sheriff McCall is, like Daddy says, "a lying sack of cesspool slop."

But, like Daddy also says, "These are devilish times."

At the end of the week, an all-white Lake County Coroner's Jury hears nine hours of testimony and decides, after just thirty-five minutes of deliberation, that Samuel Shepherd's death was "justifiable homicide," and that Sheriff McCall fired "in self-defense and the line of duty."

Even the most conservative people we know can hardly believe it. But no one is more disgusted than Harry T. Moore.

"This thing stinks to high heaven," he tells Daddy, asking us to join him in a statewide letter-writing campaign demanding that the Governor suspend Sheriff Willis McCall.

"A total whitewash!" Daddy agrees, reading a copy of Mr. Harry's own letter to Governor Warren.

"Florida is on trial before the rest of the world! Only prompt and courageous action, by removing Sheriff McCall, can save the good name of our fair state," the normally reserved schoolteacher warns our Governor.

"This is great, but, Harry," Daddy locks eyes with the soft-spoken leader of the state N.A.A.C.P., "I hope you're watching your back."

Good Lord, I think, stunned, *who would even think of harming Mr. Harry?*

"There have been threats," Mr. Harry says, jutting his chin, "but I've got a .32 caliber in my car, and, if it comes to that," he declares, "I'll take a few of them with me."

Chapter 21

December snuck up on me. I should've seen it coming but I was busy with other things.

From the middle of November to the end of December, the packinghouse is a crazy place. We have long lists of standing mail orders to pack and ship, big wooden baskets of Florida Sunshine, fresh-wrapped fruit, to get to somebody's Aunt Mabel, or Cousin Larry, or, my special favorites, the children's wards of quite a few hospitals.

Aside from school, we do everything but sleep in the big back work area behind the showroom, helping our parents "make pay while the snow falls."

The radio is constantly on, providing a rhythm to our work, and there must have been a time when the Christmas carols began, but I didn't notice it. I did notice, however, the point at which my mother, planner of picnics, singer of songs, initiator of card games, disappeared, permanently it seems, behind her Poker Face.

The radio announcement on the morning of December fourth was brief: In Miami, at three A.M., an explosion blew up yet another Carver Village apartment building. Thirty minutes later, another building in that very same housing project exploded and fell in the night. Half an hour after that, a blast at the Miami Hebrew School and Congregation shattered forty-four stained-glass windows, a memorial to family members lost in Hitler's Holocaust. Exactly thirty minutes later, a fourth blast destroyed a Jewish community center, sending nearby residents screaming into the street.

"What a nightmare!" I say, mad as can be.

"When will it end?" Mother says, but she's not asking me.

And I watch it happen: As if somebody pulled a plug, her brightness fades, her dimple disappears. Only her Poker Face—the careful, studied expression, the hazel eyes that see everything and say nothing—remains. She shifts her attention back to the task, wrapping and packing fruit in the basket between us, working as hard, harder, than anybody. But she has drawn the curtains and retreated to some private, inside place.

Even a week later—when U.S. Attorney General Howard McGrath decides, *finally*, to act, ordering Florida's F.B.I. agents to "investigate to see whether they can investigate" violations of anyone's federally guaranteed civil rights—my real mother does not return.

Even when we hear that Mr. Harry T. Moore—the F.B.I.'s most vocal critic, the Negroes' most powerful advocate, the compiler of civil rights case files that local law enforcement conveniently overlooked—has been invited to Miami to brief the federal agents. Even then, she doesn't respond. Not really.

Even as the rest of us sit around the break table, expressing our hopes that, maybe now, the bombings will stop. Maybe now, the tidal wave of evil will ebb. Maybe now, Marvin's murderers will be brought to justice. And the winter tourists, who should be choking the Trail with traffic by now, will change their minds and decide it's safe to come to Florida after all. Even now, she holds herself apart, playing Solitaire at the table's other end.

I wonder, I worry, I even think about asking her directly, "What's going on behind that Poker Face of yours?" But it wouldn't do me a bit of good. My mother, the expert card player, never tips her hand. "You think *I've* got a Poker Face," she told me once, "you should have seen my *father's*!"

My mother adored her father, the soft-spoken accountant whose thick spectacles and thinning hair made him look older than he was. He taught her everything there is to know about card playing—from how to count the cards to how to calculate, in her head, statistical probabilities. The summer she turned sixteen, a bad strep throat kept her daddy home from work. She helped him pass the hours, that stretched into days, with their own special versions of Pinochle, Gin Rummy and double-handed Bridge. While she sat by his bedside playing by the rules, and he did everything the doctor ordered, that strep throat turned into scarlet fever, a child's disease, that somehow became rheumatic and masked the pneumonia that, in the middle of the night, stole him away from her forever.

I know, from my own father, it was a terrible shock and a devastating loss for her. And, I can't help but wonder if it's playing on her mind now, the way it is on mine. Is she worried, too, that something awful is sneaking up on us the way that pneumonia did? I'd like to ask her about it. But I have the distinct feeling she'd tell me to "breast your cards," which is cardplayer talk for "mind your own business."

Chapter 22

In the store windows and on Christmas cards, Santa Claus shows up as a
round little man with a white beard
and a red suit. At our house, Santa is
a feisty old lady with silver-toned cat-eye
glasses and mink-colored hair.

"You're a sorry sight for sore eyes,"
Doto tells us and she's probably right. The
events of the past seven months, since
she left us last May, have made us "all hol-
low-eyed" and "too thin," she declares.
Mother's "just skin and bones" and "obviously, these children need more ice cream."

Doto's like a tonic. In the span of a
single week, she's bullied us out of the
backroom to cut down a Christmas tree (a
Florida pine from the woods off Wellwood
Road); she's unearthed the decorations,
opened her pack (from the trunk of the
DeSoto) and infused our lives with much-
needed holiday spirit.

Heaped under our tree are gifts from her and from our cousins in Montana and Maryland. There are gifts from our mother's side, our cousins and grandmother outside Chicago. And there are the small gifts which we children have for our parents and each other, thanks to Doto carrying us off for an afternoon's shopping at Woolworth's and the Opalakee Five-and-Dime.

On Christmas morning, we plow through our presents like half-starved entrants in a pie-eating contest. Afterwards, our opened piles are full to bursting with possibilities: board games, science sets, puzzles, new underwear and outfits for all, plus a bright red Radio Flyer wagon for Mitchell, a Schwinn bike for Ren, and a pink portable record player for me. For the first time in recent memory, it feels like some kind of normal has returned.

The last gift to be opened is a very large box tagged *To the whole family. Love, Doto.* My brothers and I have been eyeing it ever since she arrived, trying to guess what it could possibly be. Daddy drags it from behind the tree to Mother, who invites us to help her unwrap it. With each of us posted on a different side, we tear back the colored paper, racing to see who will solve the mystery first. It's Mother who realizes it's a television, a beautiful dark-wood cabinet with an oval screen the size of a turkey platter, the much-talked-about black-and-white eye on the rest of the world. Doto has topped herself! We surround her, hugging her, calling our thank-yous.

"Hurray! Now we can see *Howdy Doody*!" the boys cry.

"And *I Love Lucy*!" I say.

"What's *I Love Lucy*?" Doto wants to know.

"It's new. Miz Lillian says it's her favorite," I explain. "Miz Lillian never goes *any*where on Monday nights anymore because she doesn't want to miss Lucy."

"We'll just have to check it out then, won't we?" Doto grins.

As Daddy looks over the manual for hooking up the television, Ren, Mitchell and I organize our gifts into individual piles under the tree. Doto and Mother clear away the box of wadded-up wrapping paper and curled ribbons, then head into the kitchen to check on the turkey, already in the oven.

At noon, Sal and Sophia arrive carrying a round box of panettone, Italian Christmas cake, for the adults and a red tin of Amaretto cookies for us. I know that later, after dinner, Sal will show us how to twist the paper cookie wrappers and light them so they take off and fly like tiny angels.

During dinner, the adults entertain us with their favorite Christmas stories. Doto tells about the morning she received her very own pony, complete with wagon. Doto was one of two children, but after her only sister, Hettie, died of scarlet fever, her parents spoiled her *terribly*, she says. Shy Sophia, egged on by the rest of us, tells about the time when, as a child in Rome, she attended midnight mass at St. Mark's Cathedral. But old Sal's story is my favorite. It's about a big fire on Christmas Eve that destroyed his apartment building off Brooklyn's Flatbush Avenue, how all the people and families from his building were adopted by other big families on the street, who shared their dinner, clothing and gifts with those who'd lost everything. At the end of the story, both Sal's and Sophia's eyes are watery.

"That's really what Christmas is all about, isn't it?" Daddy says, smiling around the table.

"Yes, is about good neighbors," Sal agrees, "and about moving on, what Sophia and me, we must do."

The crack in Sal's voice, the look on his face, prompts

Daddy, who's all of a sudden solemn, to ask, "What do you mean?"

"Sorry." Sal drops his eyes and shakes his head. "I didna mean to speak of this in fronta the children."

"Please, Sophia, are you moving?" Mother's tone is urgent, concerned. Doto is frowning.

Sophia closes her eyes, unable to speak. She puts a shaking hand on Sal's arm, a mute request for him to explain.

"The phone calls," Sal tells us, nearly in a whisper. "They started lasta month. First, justa name-calling, a man with a Southern accent saying, 'Fish-eaters!,' 'Pope-lovers!'—baby stuff nexta what I heard in Brooklyn as a kid. Then, the calls, they got worse. Insults, threats about us and the coloreds, saying leave, 'or else!' Lasta night, a stick wrapped in paper thrown through our big window. We hearda the crash, ran downstairs, and found—the stick was dynamite. On the paper, the words: 'Next time, this will be lit.' "

Across from me, Ren goes bug-eyed. Beside me, Doto gasps.

Mother's eyes fill with tears. "Oh, Sal, Sophia, how horrible!"

"Have you talked to anyone else about this?" Daddy asks Sal.

"I called the Constable's office lasta week, also the week before. Constable Watts came, but when I talked, he kept interrupting. 'Speak English! I can't understand you!' he says. Then he shrugs. 'A little phone call never hurt nobody,' he says. I think now, if I showed him the dynamite, he'd shrug again and say, 'It don't hurt if it ain't lit.' "

"What will you do?" Doto, angry, wants to know.

"If I was a younger man . . ." Sal's voice trails off. His eyes find Sophia's, then return to Doto. "Sophia and me, we boarded up the window and putta sign on the front door, 'Closed, Out of Business.' We called her sister in Tampa. We go there, for now, this afternoon. Afterwards, who knows?"

Sophia is sobbing into her napkin. Mother moves to put arms around her and leads her away from the table, into the kitchen. In the silence, Doto stands. "Children, it's time we took a look at Reesa's new puzzle. Everybody out on the front porch, *now!*"

We drop our napkins beside our plates and follow her quickly out of the dining room, leaving Daddy and Sal alone. Looking back, I see my father, stony-faced and rock-hard, turning slowly in his chair to face his old, suddenly frail-looking friend.

This place has gone to hell in a handbasket, I fume inside my head to Whoever's listening, which, as near as I can tell, is nobody.

The morning after Christmas, the rumble of Daddy's truck engine wakes me. I hear women's voices in the kitchen, Mother's, Doto's, and, surprisingly, a third one with an accent. Sophia, I remember. She and Sal spent the night in Mitchell's room, the boys camping out on the couch in the living room. The Plan.

Instantly, it comes back to me. My parents persuading them not to leave for Tampa yesterday afternoon; Daddy and Sal's trip to The Quarters to meet with Luther, Armetta, Reverend Stone and the elders from St. John's A.M.E. Last night, after Doto led Sal and Sophia upstairs, my parents explained The Plan. It goes like this:

Sal and Sophia wanted to leave town immediately, abandoning everything, walking away from the contents of their beloved store, and the sunny, furniture-filled apartment above it. Daddy convinced them to wait one day, to attempt to salvage as much of their lives as possible.

Their Christmas night meeting in The Quarters proved fruitful. Luther and Reverend Stone agreed to rally the residents to purchase as much of the store's perishable goods as possible in a special sale this very morning under the big oaks behind the church. Daddy and Sal left early to load the truck with the store's stock of dairy, meat and produce. The elders of the church will oversee the sale. Luther and the Reverend offered to stock the church's choir room with the store's canned goods, sell them to the locals as needed, then turn over the proceeds to Daddy for forwarding to Sal and Sophia in Tampa. On top of that, Armetta volunteered to take on collecting from their credit customers in The Quarters.

The Tomasinis seemed overwhelmed by the willingness of their customers to help them. "We know all about the Klan, Mistuh Sal," the elders said. "You and Miz Sophia have been nuthin' but good to us ever since y'all came here." By way of thanking them, old Sal presented Reverend Stone with his hastily disconnected twenty-five-foot antenna which, the Reverend told him, would make a fine addition to St. John's steeple.

I head into the kitchen where Sophia sits at the table, fingering her black rosary beads. With her big eyes, made larger by dark, worried circles, and her long hair hanging loose instead of in her usual bun, she looks like a little lost soul instead of our Sophia.

"Everything will be fine," Doto tells her, patting her shoulder. "Warren said they'll be home by noon."

"Mother, Doto, look at this!" "Come here, quick!" The

boys' cries pull us out of the kitchen and into the living room, where they point wildly to the television.

On the screen, a man is talking: "*. . . from Mims in Brevard County. Agents from the Federal Bureau of Investigation arrived this morning and cordoned off the scene of last night's explosion. Local lawmen suspect dynamite destroyed the home of the state's N.A.A.C.P. leader and his wife. According to relatives, Harry Tyson Moore died on the way to Sanford Hospital. Doctors report his wife suffered severe internal injuries. Her condition is critical.*"

"Santa Maria, Madre di Dio!" Sophia cries, beads to her chest. Tears slick her face.

"*Relatives say the blast occurred after the Moores returned home from a family party celebrating Christmas and their twenty-sixth wedding anniversary. The Brevard County Sheriff's Office states that although the F.B.I. has no jurisdiction in this case, murder being a state crime, the local authorities will give Mr. Hoover's G-men their full cooperation. At this time, there are no known suspects.*"

"This is a nightmare," Doto rages.

"That poor man and his wife," Mother murmurs, to none of us in particular.

Mr. Harry. Dead? My mind flashes with pictures of him, vibrant and alive: His first visit to our house with Luther and Mr. Marshall; his patient help with my homework ("Democracy is the fairest form of government on earth," he'd said); the jut of his chin when he told Daddy about the death threats and the .32 caliber under his car seat.

I remember telling Daddy once it didn't fit, the soft-spoken schoolteacher with the loaded gun under his seat. But Daddy said Mr. Harry was *made of steel.* "Any man who travels up and down this state registering Negro voters right under the noses of all these Klanners is *solid steel*, through and through," Daddy told me.

As we stare at the screen for more information, it's obvious the reporter cares more about the arrival of Mr. Hoover's G-men than what happened to Mr. Harry. Doto fiddles with the knobs and the V-shaped wires she calls rabbit ears in search of another station. Frustrated, she and Mother move into the kitchen for a radio update.

Ren and I run out front to retrieve the morning paper which, because everyone was worried about Sophia and all, lies forgotten in the driveway. Outside, we rip off the rubber band, scan through the sections for something, any kind of mention of the Moores. Nothing. Ren runs to take the paper in to Mother, but all of a sudden, *I can't move.* Just then, at that very moment, all of it, every single, stinking, heart-hurting detail of Marvin in the bed of Daddy's truck comes bolting back on me.

Collapsing on the lawn, I see it *all*, all over again—the cuts, the wounds, the striped blood-soaked turban hiding his eyes. I hear his raggedy breath, bubbling on bleeding lips, knowing now what I couldn't know then, that it was one of the last breaths he'd ever take on this earth. And I smell, in a memory more sharp, more painful than all the others, the smell of his life's blood oozing out of him onto the filthy truck bed.

For what? I want to know. *For WHAT!* I rage at the Rock of Ages who, as far as I can determine, has turned His back on this whole stupid mess called the State of Florida. *When will this nightmare end? And why, WHY is ALL this happening?*

Sophia stands on the front steps, frantically fingering her beads, watching the driveway for signs of the truck. We hear it, she from the steps, me from the lawn, roar onto the property. I watch her fly down the walk to the far side of the drive, and, as Sal climbs from the truck, fling herself into his arms.

The minute I see Daddy's face, I can tell he's heard the news. Wrenching his door open, he strides right past me, asking, in a voice like granite, "Your mother in the house, Roo?" But he does not look or, taking the steps two at a time, listen for my reply.

Chapter 23

The most frightening part of a hurricane is its eye.

Like the giant blade of a buzz saw broken loose, a hurricane spins wildly; its outer edges blow and bite and dump barrels of water and dangerous, wind-whipped bits of wood and trash. After that, closer in, comes the *real* rain and the horrible sound of the wind cracking hundred-year-old oak trees in two. If you're lucky, locals say, the hurricane only glances in your direction and whirls off, moving on to the next community, the next state or, better yet, back onto the ocean where it came from.

If you're *not* lucky, if you have the unfortunate luck of living *directly* in its path, the center of the storm, *the eye*, engulfs you in terrifying silence. You wait, and watch, and wonder *when* it will pass, when the crack of old trees, and the rain, and the winds, and the barrels of water will return, all over again. It always does.

In the ten terrible days after Christmas, after the murder of our friend Harry Moore, after Sal and Sophia left Mayflower for good, the Klan's silence is deafening. Not a word, not a *sound* from the men in white who, everybody knows, spent the last nine months whipping the state into frantic frenzy.

For ten days, during which the F.B.I. sorts and sifts through the Moores' ripped-up floorboards, the shattered ceiling planks, the tinsel of Christmas glittering in the yard, and finds too few clues as to *who* did *what*, we wait. Ten days after her husband died, the day after his funeral (where Reverend J. W. Bruno pronounced "You can kill the prophet but you cannot kill his message"), Mrs. Harriette Moore dies, too.

Mrs. Moore's death is the first sign that this hurricane's overquiet eye has passed. A flurry of increasingly loud events follows:

Mr. James Ferris, the wealthy Chicago retailer whose family owns the winter estate just south of town, calls Daddy to ask if "there's still martial law in Miami."

"No," Daddy tells him, "never was."

"Ruthie's been after me to visit the Bahamas," Mr. Ferris tells Daddy. "We thought we'd try there this year, put off Florida 'til next year, when things are more settled." His is the first of many calls from longtime big-spending customers who "just aren't comfortable" coming to Florida this year.

After that, we have an odd, unsettling encounter with Mr. Barrett of Barrett Hardware in Orlando:

Daddy has dynamite. He and most citrus growers around

Mayflower use it to blow the stumps of old dead orange trees in preparation for planting new seedlings. The powerful variety, called ditching dynamite, is also used to rout the stubborn tentacle roots of a stand of palmetto. Above ground, there's nothing friendly about a palmetto. Underground, its roots are as mean as an army of octopi, thick as a man's arms and impossible to dig up.

On a Saturday afternoon in mid-January, Daddy and I drive down to Orlando to the big Barrett Hardware Store. Daddy, an avid subscriber to *Popular Mechanics*, read about a new kind of electric fuse which makes igniting ditching dynamite "a heck of a lot safer.

"Usually, you just dig a hole as close to the root center as possible, put in the sticks, light the fuse strings and let her go," Daddy explains to me. "A fuse string burns at three seconds a foot, so you have time to run away before it blows. Sometimes it fizzles, or you think it has. If you walk in too soon to check it, you risk getting yourself blown up or blasted by flying palmetto. These new electric fuses are expensive but a lot more reliable than the strings."

"Is that what you think the Klan used on Mr. Harry?" I ask him.

Daddy takes a deep, raggedy breath. "Maybe. Especially since the boom sticks were hidden under the house."

"Daddy," I say, feeling my tongue grow thick, "I can't believe they did that to him."

Daddy is quiet a minute. Then he says, "He knew there were risks, honey."

"But his wife . . ." The words get stuck in my throat.

"There's no accounting for that level of cowardice," Daddy says, wheeling abruptly into the parking lot, his eyes clouding with contempt.

I trail him through the front door of Barrett Hardware, through the big aisles, to the back counter where Mr. Barrett handles special requests. Mr. Barrett is very tall and thin with a helmet of white hair, "a real Southern gentleman," my father says.

He listens patiently to Daddy's request, nodding in recognition and understanding, but in the end he shakes his head. "I know what you want, young man, but I can't help you."

"Is it something you could order for me?" Daddy asks.

"As of this week, as the result of a visit by high law-enforcement officials, I am out of the powder and explosives business. And you should be, too."

"What do you mean?" Daddy asks.

"Just what I said. My basement which has, in the past, been stocked with powder and explosives to meet the needs of my agricultural customers is now empty. My purchase records have been appropriated."

From the sweep of Mr. Barrett's hand, I gather "appropriated" means taken away.

"Who was it? The F.B.I., the County Sheriff, who?" Daddy asks, immediately curious.

"I'm not at liberty to say, young man," Mr. Barrett says. "Only that these items are now in the possession of *high* law-enforcement *officials*." Mr. Barrett lifts up his open palms in that way that means *I've said all I care to*. "Like I said, *I'm* out of the dynamite business and *you*, sir, should be, too."

Daddy's always said that the reason they called Stonewall Jackson "Stonewall" was because it's near impossible to get a Southerner to do or say anything he doesn't want to.

Daddy and I walk out, unanswered and empty-handed.

A week later, when the plain black Ford pulls into our parking lot, Ren and I watch it through the office window. Both doors open at the same time and two white men in white shirts, dark ties and pants step out of the car and shrug themselves into their suit jackets.

"Definitely not tourists," Ren says.

"Salesmen, maybe?" I wonder.

"Naw, salesmen are usually alone. Mormons?"

"No Bibles or books," I point out.

We watch the men cross the gravel, enter the showroom and approach Mother at the counter.

"Mornin', ma'am," the older one says. He's got a wide red face atop a body shaped like a barrel. His shoes are very shiny.

"Good morning," she replies. "May I help you?"

"We're lookin' for a Mistuh Warren McMahon. This his place?"

"It's ours. Warren's my husband and he's in the back. May I tell him your business, please?"

The older man puffs out his chest and hikes up his belt, like it ought to be obvious his business is important. He reaches into his coat pocket and flips out a black leather wallet. "Agent Thomas Elwood of the Federal Bureau of Investigation. This here's Agent Odom."

"Ma'am," the younger man says, dipping a pointy chin at Mother.

"Reesa, Ren, please get your father off the platform," she calls in our direction as the agents' eyes skim the showroom for our hidden location.

Without a word, Ren and I fly out of the office, across the showroom to the side door, up the steps, around the big waxer to the washer machine, where Daddy's upending boxes of grove fruit into the cleaning tank.

"Daddy, the *F.B.I.'s* here! Two of them. In the showroom with Mother!" we pant.

"What?" he says, looking at us like we're crazy, like we've just told him the Martians have landed in Mayflower.

"Mother wants you *now*. They've got badges and everything!"

We follow him off the platform and into the showroom.

"Gentlemen, Warren McMahon," Daddy says, extending his hand with a smile. "My children tell me you have F.B.I. badges. I have to tell you, they won't sleep tonight if they don't get a good look at one."

Young Agent Odom grins at us, pulls out his wallet, flips it open and lets us see. *Agent James S. Odom,* the card says beside the shiny silver shield that spells out *Federal Bureau of Investigation*.

"You a G-man?" Ren asks him.

"Yessir, I am!" Agent Odom seems hardly old enough to be anything.

"Ever met Mr. J. Edgar Hoover?" I want to know.

"Not personally, but we teletype a report to 'im every night."

"Okay, you two, thank the gentlemen, then make yourselves scarce," Daddy says, waving us off, away from the counter.

Kneeling on chairs inside the office, Ren and I quickly fold ourselves over Mother's desk, straining to hear the adult conversation.

"I didn't catch how you happened to know my name?" Daddy asks the two agents.

I catch my breath, sure the G-men will say that it was Mr. Hoover himself who sent them, because of Daddy's long-ago letter about Marvin's murder.

"We understan' y'all have some dynamite." Agent Ellwood's clearly the boss. "We had an interest in knowin' what y' plan to do with it?"

"Same thing every other citrus grower in the county does with it—blow stumps, try to win the war against palmettos."

All of a sudden, Daddy's got his guard up and I think I know why. For years, Ren and I have played a game called "Accents," where we listen to the way customers talk and guess where they're from. Some accents are harder to peg than others, but Agent Ellwood's is pure Florida panhandle, the heart of Cracker country.

"Would y'all have any other uses for it?" Agent Ellwood drawls.

"You mean, like blowing people up, or destroying private property? Gentlemen, my wife and I aren't Klan members. In fact, you can probably tell from our accents, we're not even Southerners," Daddy says, throwing his arm protectively around Mother.

"But y'all are familiar with Klan activities 'round here?"

"Well, they killed a young friend of ours last March. I wrote your boss a letter about it but never heard anything back. At Christmas, the Klan ran the only other Northerners in town out of here because they were Catholic and made the mistake of being too nice to the local Negroes."

They killed Marvin in Emmett Casselton's lemon grove! They scared old Sal and Sophia into leaving here forever!

"What was it y' say the Klan did 'round Christmas?" Agent Ellwood asks sharply, his fat blue pen poised over his small black notebook.

Just like that, they've brushed past Marvin's murder as if it doesn't count!

"Christmas *Eve*," Daddy says, "which is twenty-four hours before the event I imagine you're interested in. On Christmas *Eve*, they threw an unlit stick of dynamite through our friends' store window, warning the owners that if they didn't leave town, the next one would be lit."

"What'd the owners do?" Ellwood asks, putting his pen down.

"They left," Mother says quietly.

It's clear their only interest is the Moores' murder. To hell with anybody else.

"Mistuh McMahon, you friends with local Klansmen?"

"I know a lot of the local men, do business with them from time to time, and, in general, try to get along with everybody." Daddy's tone is even more guarded than before. "We have property here, a business, and—as you can see—children who attend the local school. We get along. But we're not what I'd call *friends*."

"Looky here, Mistuh and Miz McMahon, we're on a sort of fishin' trip, officially to determine if all citizens are re-ceivin' equal protection under the law. Unofficially, we got some suspicions 'bout the Opalakee Klan. Y'all be willin' to speak with our supervisor?"

"Regarding?" Daddy asks, politely.

"Oh, jus' the general lay of the land 'round here, how things work in Orange County and Opalakee?" Ellwood says.

"I'd be willing to speak *generally* about just about any-thing, Agent Ellwood. What's your supervisor's name?"

"Jameson, sir, James Jameson's his name. Can he call y'all at this number?" Ellwood says, pocketing one of our business cards from the little plastic holder on the counter.

"I'd prefer to speak with the gentleman in person," Daddy tells him. "I like to see who it is I'm talking to."

"I'm not exactly sure when he'll get up this way. He's operatin' outta Orlando, though, and he jus' might want to stop by."

Daddy shrugs. "We'll be here."

Agent Ellwood hikes his pants again, an important man off to more official business. "Thank y' for your time, Mistuh McMahon. Ma'am. Y'all have a real nice place here."

"Thank you." Mother nods stiffly.

Agent Ellwood and Agent Odom, who hasn't said a word since showing us his badge, turn and walk out into the sun. At the Ford, they shrug off their jackets and lay them on the back seat like they were babies. As the frowning Agent Ellwood starts the engine, Agent Odom shoots a shy smile and a small wave in our direction.

Florida Crackers bearing the badges of Mr. Hoover's F.B.I. . . . it's clear the other side of this hurricane has begun to blow.

Chapter 24

The word is out. You'd have to be a hermit not to 've heard that Florida has "race troubles."

I sit in the showroom office, flipping through the clippings sent from our far-flung relatives. It doesn't matter which one you look at—*Time, Reader's Digest, Saturday Evening Post*, newspapers from Maryland to Montana—they all say the same thing. Under the swaying palm trees, inside the orderly orange groves, Florida leads the nation in cases of race prejudice and violence. Also, despite six weeks of intense investigation, the F.B.I. has not a single suspect in the Christmas night murders of Harry and Harriette Moore.

I study the pictures of Mr. Harry and his wife. She was a schoolteacher, too, he'd said. We never met her, but she has a pretty face and the same kindly look in her eyes that he always had.

In the showroom, I hear my mother sidestep questions from the troubled tourists.

"You expect this sort of thing in Mississippi or Georgia," a lady with an up-east accent is saying. "But Florida?"

"Hard to believe," my mother lies.

In my hand, a Chicago clipping tells the truth: "Even in the 1920s, Florida, not Alabama or Mississippi, led the South in lynchings in proportion to population." I wonder who did the math.

The husband and wife driving the big Pontiac Chieftain with New Jersey plates exclaim, "It was front-page news in the *Times*. We almost didn't come!"

"We're glad you did," Mother, wearing her guise of Cheerful Saleslady, assures them.

We are, after all, a family of shopkeepers; like Daddy says, "merchants on the South's most lucrative trade route." In exchange after exchange, my mother models "proper showroom behavior." The rules are simple, and older than I am: These people are on vacation, they've left their real lives behind and have no interest in ours. Never complain, never explain, just politely present the Florida of their fantasies. It makes me sick.

Isn't it wrong, I used to ask Marvin, to pretend niceness you don't feel? Especially to people who are rude, or, sometimes, downright mean?

"Cock-a-doodle, li'l Rooster!" Marvin mocked, narrowing his eyes at me as if I was a fool. "Try being colored," he'd grinned. The truth—that my complaints were ridiculous, his, impossible—popped up between us like some jeering jack-in-the-box. We both laughed, shamefaced, and hastily, awkwardly, moved on to other things.

Oh, Marvin, things are much worse now than they were then.

Some days, I'm glad you're not here to see it. Most days, though, I'd give anything to have you here to talk to.

At Mr. Marshall's invitation, Armetta joins a group of over two hundred N.A.A.C.P. representatives from fifteen states at an emergency meeting in Jacksonville.

"They're hoping," Daddy tells me, "to turn their outrage over the Moores' murders into something meaningful."

Together, the group creates and unanimously adopts the Jacksonville Declaration, a single sheet of demands for "seven basic rights of full citizenship."

Proudly, Armetta thrusts mimeographed copies of the document into our hands. The Declaration calls for:

"One—the right to security of person against the organized violence of lawless mobsters or irresponsible law-enforcement officers;

"Two—the right to vote as free men in a free land;

"Three—the right to employment opportunities in accordance with individual merits;

"Four—the right of children to attend any educational institutions supported by public funds;

"Five—the right to serve unsegregated in the armed forces of the country;

"Six—the right to travel unrestricted by Jim Crow regulations;

"And seven—the right to go unmolested among fellow Americans as free men in a free society."

Daddy calls it a *manifesto*. He ribs Armetta that "all good Communists have to have one." I sit, dumbfounded by my own stupidity.

Nothing, not *one* thing, on their list seems the least bit

unreasonable to me, but the fact that the list exists must mean, can *only* mean that these things are not currently available because, and only because, of a person's *skin* color? Does the entire country—the land of the free, the home of the brave—*know* this? Is ignorance like Miz Sooky's, arrogance like Emmett Casselton's, outright lunacy like Sheriff Willis McCall's so widespread that people like us, *we* are in the minority?

To tell you the truth, it had never occurred me. The signs were all around and I never saw them. I knew we lived in a place, a state, gone crazy, where good people had been killed for no good reason. I knew our nation's leaders had been preoccupied with other things. But the reality, the day-to-day dangers and restrictions that define a colored person's life anywhere in this country, had never struck me before. The shock and shame of it leave me staring, flabbergasted, at Armetta's proud document.

"Try being colored," Marvin had told me. And I couldn't. Even in my wildest imaginings, I wouldn't have come up with the picture painted by Armetta's seven points. And that sickens me, truly.

For her part, Armetta is *transformed*. The weary, weeping soul who attended both of the Moores' funerals in Mims has become someone else. She's fired and filled up. Seeing the change, feeling my own sense of fear and frustration, I can't help but ask her, "Armetta, how *can* you be so hopeful?"

She looks at me steady, without smiling. "Hope's like food, Roo, like air . . . there's no real livin' without it. This world's not perfect, not even close. But everythin' we want, everythin' we're hoping for," she says, "is ahead of us. You can't move forward lookin' back."

S he's right," Doto tells me later when I show her the Jacksonville Declaration. "We *can't* change the world overnight, Reesa. But we begin by changing the way we *choose* to live in it."

T hat same week, I'm relieved to hear, at last, from Vaylie.

Dear Reesa, she writes.

Thanks so much for the silver friendship bracelet. I love it! It was my favorite part of a very crummy Christmas.

Mamma and Daddy got into a big fight on Christmas morning. Over me, of course. Well, actually, it was over their presents to me. Mamma gave me a whole new wardrobe specially ordered from New York—I was hoping for a pink shirt with matching poodle skirt or maybe something with polka dots. Anyways, everything I got is either bright red, blue or green. My looks are "coltish," Mamma says, and with my freckles, I'm so polka-dotted already, she says, I can only wear solid bright colors like "racing silks." I hate every single thing she got me, Reesa, and I wouldn't be caught dead in any of it!

Daddy's gift was a small box with a little porcelain pony inside. It was his way of telling me that he'd given me a horse! My very own Tennessee Walker! I was so excited but Mamma about blew a gasket. "I told you absolutely NO on this horse thing, Gerald!" she yelled. "I can't believe you did this to me!" and started crying up a storm. Daddy just looked at her, kind of squinty eyed, and hissed, "If you're gonna make the girl dress like a goddamn jockey, the least you could do is give her a goddamn horse to sit on!" I'll spare you the details except that, after they quit yelling at each other, Daddy dove into his Bloody Marys and Mamma took a couple of her nerve pills and they both passed out before we'd even had our breakfast. I had to call my daddy's mamma and tell her they were "too indisposed" for us to make it to Christmas Dinner. Fortunately for me, Claudette came by with a pan of her Christmas gingerbread. She knows it's my favorite. When I told her what happened she called Whit and he came all the way from Colored Town with a plate of their Christmas dinner just for me. Claudette and Whit both sat down with me in the kitchen while I ate and it was __so__ good! Ham, sweet potato pone, collards with fatback and a huge slice of pecan pie after. This might sound crazy but I think I'd be a whole lot better off if Whit and Claudette were my parents instead of the ones I got stuck with. (And, wouldn't my daddy's mamma have a big fat cow if she heard that one!)

Have you made your New Year's resolutions yet? I have two but you're the only soul I'm telling them to. The first is to catch up with my school work. After missing the whole month of September, plus two weeks in November "on tour," my grades are just awful. My daddy's mamma got a look at my report card and suggested I might be better off at a school for __slow__ kids! I wanted to tell her I know I'd make honor roll if I could stay in town for more than a couple months at a time, but she won't listen to anything that has to do with Daddy's "spells."

My other resolution—well, __wish__ is more like it—is that Mamma and Daddy will just stop fighting and get a divorce. Reesa, I hope I don't get struck by lightning for saying this, but I think we'd all be a lot happier without each other. 'Course, Mamma would have to change her ways without all Daddy's money, but we'd get by. And Whit and Claudette would take care of Daddy just like they always have. The thing is, right now, Daddy and Mamma and me are just like those three rattlers in your clearing, coiling and rattling and hissing at each other, then racing away as fast as we can to get out of the big old hole we're stuck in.

It's a New Year, Reesa. I wish I could believe it'll be a HAPPY *one. Write* SOON*!!!*

Love, VAYLIE

Grabbing paper, pen and a jacket, I head out of the house.

Dear Vaylie,

Do you remember the big old oak tree next to Dry Sink? I'm sitting in it now on the same big branch we sat on last spring. My friend Marvin told me everybody ought to have a tree and this one's been mine ever since I can remember; especially after Marvin told me about its heart. You didn't get to see it when you were here but it's carved in the trunk about ten feet higher up, a small heart with the letters "R.S. + M.M." in the center. All my life, I've thought that heart was some kind of magical message just for me. Marvin told me he found it when he was a boy, but I've always been sure that M.M. was for me (Marie McMahon) and that R.S. was a sign, the initials of the man I'd marry someday. But, just now, thinking about our day here and in the attic, it hit me that M.M. wasn't me at all, that the letters stood for Miss Maybelle Mason and her dead fiancé, Richard Swann!!!

Oh, Vaylie, aren't a whole lot of things not at all what they seem? Like your grandmother thinking you're slow when you're as smart as can be. And like Whit and Claudette acting more like proper parents than your real mamma and daddy. It's happening here, too, in the way a whole lot of white people think their skin tone makes them better than colored people—

when the truth is some of the finest people in the world aren't the least bit white!

My daddy calls the whole rotten mess "growing pains." "No pain, no gain," he says. Personally, I see the pain, but where's the gain in your mamma and daddy being so mean to each other, or in Miss Maybelle's heartbreak, or innocent people like my friend Marvin shot, and others—a colored couple named Harry and Harriette Moore—killed in their beds? I don't get it.

Mother sees things different. She tells me God's like the dealer in a giant card game. Because of luck, some people wind up with better cards than others, but the important thing is to do the best you can with the hand you're dealt. That's what you're doing, Vaylie—the best you can!

One thing for sure (I know because I've tried it both ways) is we can't give up hope. Marvin's mother says hope keeps us going, Vaylie. My mother says it keeps us in the game. 'Til luck, like the tide, turns. It always does, she says.

Give yourself a Happy New Year's hug from me, Vaylie. And know I'm sending you all the love and hope and luck I can spare!

xxxooo, Reesa

Chapter 25

To celebrate George Washington's birthday (and show off her new swimming pool), May Carol Garnet's invited our entire seventh-grade class to a Pool Party at her house.

"I don't want to go," I tell Mother. "Just yesterday, I heard our teacher scolding the boys for playing *eeny-meeny-miny-mo, catch the nigger by his toe, light the sticks and watch him blow.* If they try that in front of me, I'll have to hurt somebody," I warn Daddy.

But my parents are insisting I attend the party. "It's the entire class, so your absence could appear an affront, Reesa. Besides, Lucy Garnet will keep the boys in line. You'll be fine," they say. "Just go on and get along."

When Doto drops me off at May Carol's in Opalakee, she reminds me that Daddy and Luther will pick me up at three, on their way home from checking out a grove for sale, south of town.

May Carol's house is a split-level, with wall-to-wall carpets and sliding glass doors. The pool's what they call
kidney-shaped with curved steps at one end and a big slide
and diving board at the other. (Mr. Reed Garnet's in real estate and does *real* well.)

Since it's practically against the law to live in Florida and
not know how to swim, most of us are good swimmers and
divers, too. I join Joan Ellen Marks, who's sitting on the side,
feet dangling in the shallow end, watching the boys show off.
Their goal, of course, is to leap off the diving board, wrap
themselves into a "cannonball" and create a big enough
splash to get the girls at our end wet. I don't know the blond-
headed boy climbing up the ladder.

I poke Joan Ellen. "Who's that?"

"He's May Carol's cousin Randy, Randall Jefferson Holt
the third, a real Georgia jackass."

I love Joan Ellen. She's the only girl I know who swears
out loud and gets away with it. She gets it from her mother,
who's foul-mouthed but so funny about it and so well connected around town that nobody seems to care.

"Kind of favors her, don't he?" says Lottie Ann Louis,
meaning that Randy's pointy features and pale skin tone's a
lot like his cousin's.

Randy proves to be the king of cannonballs, splashing
every single one of us.

"Told you, didn't I?" Joan Ellen says as we peel off our
cover-ups and spread them on the grass to dry in the sun.

Miz Lucy Garnet appears on the patio with a large platter
of fried chicken. Behind her, a short, yellow-skinned woman
uses pot holders to carry a pan of baked beans, long strips of
bacon still sizzling on top.

"Anybody hungry?" Miz Lucy calls. "We got a bunch of
Selma's fried chicken here and, boy, is it good!"

Selma is the Garnets' new maid, hired last spring to replace Armetta. Selma lives in Opalakee Colored Town, west of the train tracks that divide the white area and downtown businesses from the Negro community.

All the boys rush forward to the table where Miz Lucy's placed the platter of chicken beside the heaping bowls of potato salad and cornbread and the stack of paper plates and napkins.

"Gentlemen, step back now. It's ladies *first* at our house, as I'm *sure* it is at yours," Miz Lucy chides the boys with a smile.

"Ain't no ladies at *my* house," Cousin Randy yells.

"No gentlemen, neither," Joan Ellen tells him, grinning at me.

The boys shuffle to the end of the line which we girls have politely formed.

Filling my plate, I decide that fried chicken and bacon-topped baked beans are only two of the many differences between my family and that of my Opalakee classmates. My mother bakes, never fries, our chicken. Our beans are "Boston-style," cooked in a round brown pot and served with round dark brown raisin bread instead of the buttery yellow cornbread Miz Lucy serves.

After lunch, May Carol and Miz Lucy organize a game of Pin the Tail on the Donkey.

Still enjoying her jackass joke, Joan Ellen looks from the game Donkey to Randy and asks "Which one?"

The boys win that game.

Next, we play Simon Says in the pool and, fortunately, we girls win that one. The tie-breaker game is a relay involving diving and swimming the length of the pool to hand off the baton to your team members at the opposite end. We put Lottie Ann, our best swimmer, last. Even though she narrowly beats out red-faced Randy, Miz Lucy calls it a tie.

Since it's ten 'til three and Daddy's due soon, I get out of the pool, visit the bathroom, grab my sun-dried cover-up from the lawn, and hunt for May Carol and Miz Lucy to thank them for inviting me. They're not in the pool area or the kitchen, where I see Selma and thank her for the delicious fried chicken.

"Thank you, honey," she says. "You're that McMahon girl, aren't you, from Mayflower? Your family helped out Armetta after she left here?"

"I think my parents would say that Armetta helped *us*; but, yes, I'm Reesa McMahon. Pleased to meet you," I say.

"Pleased to meet *you*, Reesa! You see much of Armetta and her husband Luther?"

"Well, actually, Luther and my father are picking me up any minute, which is why I was looking for May Carol, to say goodbye."

"I b'lieve you'll find Miss May Carol and her mamma in the back bedroom. And, Reesa . . ."

"Yes, ma'am?"

"Would you ask Luther to have Armetta give me a call?"

"I'll tell him as soon as I see him. Thanks again for the chicken. Bye!"

Racing down the hall, I hear Miz Lucy lecturing May Carol loudly, something about "conduct unbecoming a lady" and then the sound of a stinging slap. I rap loudly on the door and, without opening it, make my goodbye quick. "May Carol, it's Reesa! I'm going now; thanks for inviting me!"

"You're welcome, honey," Miz Lucy calls back, in a voice like sugar.

I turn and walk quickly down the hall, thankful for yet another difference between my mother and May Carol's.

Passing through the living room on my way out the door, I hear that Cousin Randy's organized the boys into a pool game like one I've played with my Chicago cousins. It involves one shut-eyed person calling out the word "Marco" while the others, trying to keep from getting caught, call back "Polo!" The big difference, however, is that shut-eyed Randy is calling out "Nigga!" and the others are calling back "Massa?"

Jackass is right, I decide, remembering Joan Ellen's words, and feeling my blood boil. Through the dining room, I see Selma in the kitchen—*no doubt she's hearing him, too*—and all of a sudden, as a loud "Nigga!" bursts through the house, this is *more* than I can *stand*!

A large green watermelon on the kitchen counter gives me an idea. I tear through the dining room, rush into the kitchen, scaring Selma, and say, "Knife! Grab the biggest knife you can find and follow me!"

Lunging out onto the patio, I yell, "Randall Jackass Holt the third, think *fast*!" and hurl the big melon straight at his stupid chest. It lands, just inches in front of him, with a huge splash that shocks him silly. On reflex, he scoops it up and now stands cradling it like a baby, glaring up at me from mid-pool.

For the briefest moment, I glare back, then smile real sweetly and say, with my best fake simper, "Miz Lucy says it's time for the seed-spitting contest out back. She's put Selma in charge of cutting and wants you to carry it out for her, please." "Bye, now," I call to the girls on the lawn and to Selma who, giant knife in hand, grins back at me, eyes very bright.

On the drive home, I tell Daddy and Luther all about it.

"Lawdy, you a bold little Rooster," Luther tells me. "Wonder where you got *that* from?"

"She's her grandmother's granddaughter, I'm afraid." Daddy shakes his head.

Luther chuckles. "Wait'll Ah tell Armetta. Better yet, think Ah'll let Selma tell her."

"Boy, can *she* cook," I tell him. "Selma's was the best fried chicken I've ever had."

"Uh-oh, you turning Southern Belle on us?" Daddy teases.

"No, sir, not if that's what Miz Lucy's trying to make May Carol."

"You *know*," Luther says, raising his eyebrows, "Armetta could tell some *tales* 'bout Miz Lucy . . . that woman is *high strung!*"

"I sure wouldn't want to cross her," my father agrees.

"Oh, she'd pull your hair out, for *sure*," Luther tells him.

Daddy's chuckling as he turns to back the truck up to the packinghouse platform, but all of a sudden, his look changes. "What do we have here?" I hear him ask under his breath.

A man, a stranger, is standing on our platform. He's medium-built, with the untanned look of someone who spends his days indoors. He's dressed for business in a white shirt, dark pants, and a tie that's been loosened in the afternoon heat. In his hands is a notebook and he's watching our truck.

Chapter 26

Mother, spotting us from the showroom, appears tense-faced on the platform. As we pile out, she says, "Warren, this is James Jameson from the F.B.I."

"Warren McMahon," my father tells him, extending his hand. "This is my daughter, Marie, and our friend, Luther Cully."

"Jim Jameson, sir, in the flesh, as requested."

"Excuse me," Mother says, "I've got customers in the showroom."

Mr. Jameson smiles at Mother and says, "Thank you, ma'am."

"Reesa?" Mother says, meaning I'm to come with her.

"I'll be right there," I tell her, stalling for time.

"Mr. Jameson, my assistant, here," Daddy says, nodding to me, "doesn't let me talk to law enforcement without seeing some identification."

"I heard about that. Miss McMahon, my badge," he tells me, not smiling, and flips open the black wallet from his back pocket. "And here's my card," he adds.

I examine his badge and the small white rectangle. "Says here he's official, Daddy."

"Where's he from?" Daddy asks, catching my eye.

Daddy heard it, too. Mr. Jameson's accent—the shape of his vowels especially—is a revelation, and a relief.

"Well," I say, "his address is Orlando, but he sounds like Ohio to *me.*"

"Cleveland," Mr. Jameson nods.

"Can we talk to him, then?" Daddy asks me.

"Fine by me," I tell him. *Ohio*, I think, *is a definite step up from those other two agents who were here before.* We have many long-time customers from Ohio. Mother loves them because "they order early and their checks are always good. Ohioans," she always says, "are as *good* as *gold.*"

"Well, thank *you*, ma'am," Mr. Jameson tells me, very serious. "Okay to sit here?" he asks Daddy, pointing to the bench by the washer's big water tank. "Can Mr. Cully join us, too?"

Daddy and Luther nod, grab chairs and sit, facing the agent on the bench.

"Your deputy staying?" Mr. Jameson asks, meaning me.

Daddy studies me a moment. Then he says, "Reesa, your mother's expecting you in the showroom."

I leave them real reluctantly and walk slowly around the waxer's large metal hood that runs sideways to the washer, six feet high and eight feet long. On the far side, I can hear their voices through the hood's air vent. If I peer through the vent,

I can just see Daddy's and Luther's profiles through the other air vent on the opposite side.

"Mr. McMahon, Mr. Cully, I'm here to tell you that you have friends in high places," Mr. Jameson of Ohio says, rustling his papers.

"Really? Who would that be?" Daddy asks.

"Well, let's start with my boss, Mr. Hoover. And while we're at it, let's add a Mr. Thurgood Marshall of New York City."

"Okay . . ."

"And, Mr. Cully, you're the father of Marvin Cully, shot and killed last March?"

"Yes, sir." Luther sounds nervous. He glances at Daddy.

"Don't worry, Mr. Cully, you're not in any trouble. In fact, truth be told, *I'm* the one in trouble," Mr. Jameson tells him.

"What do you mean?" Daddy asks. Luther stays silent.

"Well, as you know, two people were assassinated, by dynamite, over six weeks ago. So far, my elite corps of crackerjack agents have produced precious little evidence, and not a lot of suspects. Mr. Hoover is, shall we say, not happy; particularly since Mr. Truman of the White House, Mr. Marshall of the N.A.A.C.P., assorted influential people from the Civil Rights Congress, the Anti-Defamation League of B'nai B'rith, and the Florida Board of Tourism are all breathing down his neck."

"Is that so?" my father says mildly.

"Believe me, it is very much *so,*" Mr. Jameson says.

"What's this have to do with us?" Daddy asks him.

"We're operating in a bit of a vacuum here. Although your state's assorted departments of law enforcement promised 'full and complete cooperation,' they've done nearly nothing to help us get to the bottom of anything. In spite of that, we have some extremely compelling reasons to believe that the Opalakee Klan has direct knowledge about the murders of Mr. and Mrs. Moore. The problem is, we have no inside sources. According to Mr. Marshall, you have a very clear handle on things around here, Mr. McMahon. I don't suppose you'd consider joining the Klan for us?"

"Me? A Klanner? Mr. Jameson, I'm a Yankee, for starters, and a man who speaks his mind pretty clearly. Even if they'd *have* me, which they wouldn't, I couldn't do it. It would take me—what d'you think, Luther—three, maybe four, minutes to blow my cover?"

"I figured you might say that. But here's the *real* reason I've come . . . Mr. Marshall says that between you and Mr. Cully, you have a circle of friends who, let's see, how'd he say it, 'would put the F.B.I and the C.I.A. to shame.' "

In my narrow view, I see Luther stiffen. At his side, Daddy shoots him a quick look, then turns back to face Mr. Jameson, who says, "What I'd like to ask you is this . . . I have a list of names we believe to be members of the Opalakee Klan, cross-referenced from several other sources. What I'd like you to do, and you don't have to say yes or no this minute . . . what I'd like you to do is look over this list and have your circle of friends look over it, too, and simply cross off anyone who's not a known Klan member. Of course, if you see any glaring omissions, and you'd like to add a name or two, that would be fine. But at this point I'm merely looking to delete anybody who's not a Klan member. Is that something you might be willing to do to help us catch young Cully's and the Moores' killers?"

"*If* we agree to look at your list, Mr. Jameson, what happens to it when we're done with it?" Daddy's tone is careful, not saying yes or no.

"Well, I've thought about that. I've placed two pieces of paper in this envelope." I hear the rustle of more papers. "The first sheet is the list we've been discussing. The second is a short summary of an event that occurred last August fourth. A high-speed chase between a black Chrysler and three pickup trucks. Did you see it?"

"Didn't everybody?" Daddy replies.

"The second sheet merely describes the incident. You may write in any comments you deem appropriate. As you can see," Jameson says, handing the envelope to Daddy, "it's already stamped and addressed to Mr. James J. Smith—that's me—at P.O. Box 12 in Orlando. All you have to do is look things over, make your comments, then seal it and mail it as soon as you can."

Daddy turns again to face Luther. Slowly, without moving, Daddy raises an eyebrow and, it appears, Luther drops his chin in a nod.

"We'll take a look," Daddy says, standing up. Luther and Mr. Jameson stand, too.

"And mail it?" Mr. Jameson asks.

"I'll deliver it myself into the hands of our lovely postmistress," I hear Daddy promise as I duck hastily out the side door and into the showroom.

A fter Mr. Jameson leaves, Daddy and Luther want to tell Mother what happened. But she stops them.

"Why," she wants to know, "didn't you send Reesa down here with me?"

"I did," he says.

"Well, she wasn't here," Mother tells him. All three adults turn their eyes on me.

Uh-oh, I think. I was hoping she hadn't noticed.

"But . . ." Daddy's stare is turning to a glare.

"But little Miss Big Ears stood on the other side of the waxer spying on you and the F.B.I.," Mother says in that tone that will brook no excuses.

"Well, why not?" I say, blistered by her calling me Little Miss anything! "It's about time Mr. James Jameson showed up. And what could he possibly say that would be any worse than what I've seen or heard already? I saw what the Klan did to Marvin, same as you. I heard that deputy in Mount Laura tell how it happened. I heard him say how, if Mr. Reed Garnet hadn't shown up late, Marvin might still be alive. And *I'm* the one who had to go make nice at the Garnets' house this very afternoon! It's not fair for you to treat me like a baby. I'm *not* one—not anymore!"

I realize, when I finish, that I've embarrassed Luther, who's now studying his shoes, and I feel bad about that. Daddy's looking at me with admiring eyes, but Mother's face stays a blank.

"She makes a good point," Daddy says softly, but in that way that leaves everything up to Mother.

"Oh, Reesa, when I was your age"—she shakes her head sadly—"it was the middle of the Depression. I worried every single day that my father would lose his job and we'd wind up in the soup lines. My mother told me not to worry, that worrying was her job, that children should have fun, and I should be carefree. But I worried anyway. So I guess it wouldn't help for me to tell you the same thing. I'm just sorry we didn't do a better job protecting you from all this. And for the record," she says, "you're not full grown, just more than halfway."

"Yes, ma'am," I say with as much earnestness as I can muster, considering Daddy's winking at me behind her back.

At his suggestion, the four of us go into the office off the empty showroom. It's late in the afternoon and doubtful that we'll have any more customers today. As we gather 'round his desk, Daddy opens Mr. Jameson's envelope, pulls out two sheets of paper, and sets them side by side on his blotter.

Luther responds to the first one with a low whistle.

Daddy was right, I think, *when he told Mr. Marshall that a list of Opalakee Klan members would read like the local social register.* Most of the two dozen or so names are all too familiar.

Across the desk, Mother's eyes meet Daddy's. For the first time in a long time, the curtain of her composure parts. In her face, I see fear and the flare of resistance, like a little flame leaping up.

"You agreed to do this?" she asks him carefully.

Daddy's jaw juts. "We both did," he tells her, nodding in Luther's direction.

Her eyes drift back to the paper on the desk. She stands very still, then looks back up at Daddy. His face is firm, his eyes steady. With the slightest shake of her head, she registers her worry and retreats from a fight. The curtain drops, closing us out again. Closing herself in?

Don't worry, I itch to tell her, but it's clear she will. *Besides, we can't back out now. This is important! Mr. Marshall himself sent Mr. Jameson our way. Mr. Marshall and the F.B.I. wouldn't put Daddy, Luther and the maids in any danger, would they?*

The list is arranged alphabetically. As Daddy and Luther pore over it, the most obvious omission is at the top. With a ballpoint pen, Daddy adds: *Bowman, J.D.*

"How the hell did they miss *him*?" he wonders aloud.

Exactly what I was thinking.

Beside the name of *Casselton, Emmett* are the initials *E.C.*

"For Exalted Cyklops. The big cheese," Daddy explains to me.

The second change is further down. There are three entries with the same last name, a prominent father and his two sons. Daddy crosses off the younger son's name. He lives down the road from us and is a deacon in our church, always has a roll of Life Savers in his pocket in case somebody gets a coughing attack. His father and older brother live further south and attend Opalakee First Baptist.

"I've had many conversations with him," Daddy tells Luther. "He's a good Christian and absolutely against the Klan's tactics. Even told me once that the rest of the family kid him about it, calling him 'medium rare.' "

"What's that mean?" I've never heard the term applied to a person before.

"That's their way of saying he's soft and a little pink, meaning Communist."

"He's a *Communist*?" I ask quickly, balking at the idea.

"Of course not," Mother says. "It's just their way of insulting him because he's chosen not to join the Klan."

The second sheet is a lot more interesting. At the top, the title says "Attempted Abduction, 8/4/51." A paragraph about the Big Chase follows. Below that are four numbered sections.

The first section is about the Chrysler New Yorker and the four people who were in it—two N.A.A.C.P. attorneys and two Northern reporters.

The other numbered sections contain descriptions of each of the three pickups. All three sections say "occupants," followed by blank lines. There is a question mark at the beginning of each line. All three truck sections have an area marked "vehicle owner." Two of the three have the owner's name filled in correctly. (We aren't the *only* ones who know an Emmett Casselton Casbah Groves truck when we see one, even with the name covered up.) In the section for the big black Ford pickup, the "vehicle owner" line is blank with another question mark. Daddy fills in the name: *J. D. Bowman.*

"That's it for us, Luther," he says, carefully replacing the two pages into the envelope and handing it over. "The rest is up to the ladies of your C.I.A."

Luther takes the envelope and nods. "Looks like there'll be a special choir practice after church tomorrow."

Chapter 27

Bloom time, which used to be my favorite time of year, is back. For most people, it's the perfumed time of new beginnings. For me, it's the anniversary of Marvin's death. I am in gloom time. And, most certainly, *not* the girl I was last time the tangerine tree outside my window wore its band of Angel Blossoms. I can never be that girl again, so safe, so sure of everything and everyone. I long to feel that comfortable inside my skin, but I will never be *her* again.

It's been one whole week since Daddy and Luther mailed Mr. Jameson's envelope to his Orlando P.O. Box. I felt sure we'd have heard something by now. But as the days drag by, as the date Marvin died comes and goes with no hint of resolution, the nightmare I thought I'd outgrown returns.

I wake screaming. The run through the grove, the crowd on the hill, the flashing red lights are all the same. But this time, after I kick and claw my way to the front, after J. D. Bowman sees me and yells "Grab her, too!" because "She's a Jew!," the men in the circle yank me between them. Their faces, now familiar from the F.B.I. list, surround me, contorted in anger, eyes hard, teeth bared, as a hideously laughing J. D. Bowman raises a rattlesnake whip high above my head . . .

This night, Mother and Daddy are out for the evening. It's Doto who hears me and holds me tight. Turning on the light, she sits down beside me and we talk quietly for some time, going over every awful detail of the dream.

"All right, then," she says, "I have an idea. Will you wait here while I get you something?"

Within moments, she returns with the spare set of her special pink bedding. Together, we strip my mattress of its usual white cotton and remake it with my grandmother's sheets, ordered just for her from Chicago's Carter-Ferris-Mott. Slipping between them, I relish the silky pink softness, the scent of Ivory Snow, and I thank her with all my heart.

"I'm sure I'll sleep perfectly fine now."

She nods, cat-eye glasses winking in the light; then, lifting my chin between her fingers, she asks, "How come I never heard about this bad dream before?"

"Kept it to myself," I say.

"Because?" she wants to know.

"Because Daddy's got enough to worry about without taking me on, too."

"And you figure you can fend for yourself?"

"Yes!" I shoot back, then, meeting her gaze, tack on a respectful "ma'am."

"Oh, Reesa," Doto says, "you, your father and me . . . we are cut from the same quarry, rock-hard and marble-headed."

"Not at all like Mother," I say.

Doto doesn't like my tone and leans in so she can eye me more directly. "Your mother's a different kind of strong than we are, young lady."

"What do you mean?"

"I mean," she says, "we McMahons are the stuff that mountains are made of. But your mother . . . well, your mother's more like a river, which is stronger still. Do you understand?"

I don't and tell her so.

"No, of course you don't. You live in a state without a decent-sized mountain or river in sight. I'll tell you what: Next spring, I'll take you west with me to your uncle Harry's. We'll go to the Grand Canyon, and when you stand on the rim and see that sight carved out of solid rock by water and ice, you'll know exactly what I mean. We'll follow the Colorado River north. You'll see how fresh water makes the difference between a livable valley and an impossible desert. Maybe then you'll understand the kind of strength your mother has."

"Yes, ma'am," I say, needing to think about it.

"You're lucky to have the parents you have, Reesa. Don't you forget that," she says, squeezing my hand in goodnight. "Do you want this light on or out?"

"Out," I say. "I'll be all right."

"Of course you will," my grandmother chuckles. "Sleep tight."

Two days later, Mr. Jim Jameson of Ohio parks his brown Dodge on the side driveway, away from the prying eyes across the Trail, and spends an hour or so talking to Daddy in the back. At one point, Daddy leads him into the showroom to point up and out the side door, at the spot that can only be Emmett Casselton's eagle's nest, the windowed office high above the tanks of Mayflower Citrus on the other side of the road. When they're finished, the two of them amble up to Mother and me at the front counter.

Mr. Jameson makes cheerful small talk, about the weather, the upcoming primary elections. Mother tells him she's on the fence between Stevenson and Kefauver, if, of course, Stevenson ever gets off the fence to run.

Daddy's a Kefauver man all the way. He relished the newspaper accounts of Kefauver's Senate Crime Investigating Committee hearings in Miami. Just last year, Kefauver's committee had a field day with Dade County Sheriff "Smiling Jimmy" Sullivan, who couldn't quite explain how, during five years in office, his personal assets jumped $65,000 while his sheriff's salary was never more than $12,000 a year!

"Believe me," Mr. Jameson laughs, "I've a stack of files six feet high on that one."

Kefauver's committee also uncovered that William H. Johnston, one of the Governor's cronies and a major state contractor, was a close associate of the Capone gang.

"You know," Daddy says, "Governor Warren was furious over that. He's vowed he'll never let Kefauver set foot in this state again."

"Won't that be interesting come primary time in May?" Mr. Jameson grins. "Though I should be *long* gone by then."

"Are you really that close?"

"Oh, there's some very interesting irons in the fire," Mr. Jameson replies. "Things are heating up. People are getting nervous. I anticipate a fair amount of action in the next couple weeks."

Chapter 28

That Friday, Ren goes home after school with his friend, Petey Smith, who lives out in the country, a few miles east of Mayflower.

Daddy and I are set to pick him up before supper, around five.

Since the County Dump is just a mile or so past Petey's house, Daddy asks Robert to load up the truck with a bunch of stumps that've been cluttering our grove road for weeks. Daddy and I head out around four. At the Dump, the old Negro caretaker named Horatio Sykes ambles over and helps us unload. The dump *stinks*. Everywhere's that sweet sickening stink of things rotting, dying or in full, dark earth decay. Daddy tells me to breathe through my mouth, but I still feel the sting of it in my throat.

Afterwards, we double back to pick up Ren. Petey's house is deep in a grapefruit grove that belongs to Emmett Casselton. The blue and gold Casbah Groves signs glint at us from mile markers beside the road.

"Looks like old Emmett forgot to spray for leaf curl," Daddy says, noting the brown-tipped leaves as our truck weaves and bumps down the narrow dirt road toward Petey's house.

As we enter the clearing, Ren bolts out the screen door and into the yard. He's waving his arms frantically for us to stop. He's got a bandage around his head and Petey and his father hot on his heels.

"*Now* what?" my father says, heaving himself out of the truck.

"Daddy, Daddy, the Klan, a man . . . *shot* at us, shot *me*, just playing, '*gators*! He—"

I've never, in my life, seen Ren so flustered.

"Hold on, now, what's this all about?" Daddy's looking over Ren's head to lock eyes with Petey's father.

"Warren, you would not b'lieve it!" Mr. Smith, who everyone calls Smitty, says. "These two boys been playin' fine 'round here all afternoon. 'Bout a hour ago, they asked if they could run over to that ol' sinkhole lake in the grove, you know the one with Mr. Casselton's fishing camp on the landing in the middle? Well, they jus' wanted to see if they could spot a 'gator or two. Climbed up the water tower to get a better look. Ren, tell your daddy what happened next."

"We got up there, Daddy, and saw a whole bunch of men in white robes." Ren's face beneath the bandage is beet red, shiny with sweat. His voice has risen to a pitch like a girl's.

"It was the Klan!" big-eyed Petey puts in.

"They were marching, three across," Ren says, "down the big ramp and into the camp. They looked stupid in their pointy hats and all . . ."

"Like a bunch of fat ol' ghosts," Petey adds.

"Well, Petey and me . . ." Ren pauses to catch his breath. "We had us a couple pieces of irrigation pipe. We were just poking fun, making noises through the pipes. You know, like *Woooooo!*, like ghosts. Well, one of them started waving at us to stop."

"Big white sleeves flappin' like a crane." Petey demonstrates.

"We should've stopped, Daddy, I *know* that, but he just looked so funny waving his arms at us . . . we started laughing."

"And we just couldn't stop!" Petey says earnestly.

"Another man came out and started *shooting* at us! I mean pointed both barrels right at us and *shot*! When something bounced off the water tower and hit me in the head, I thought I was going to *die* up there!" Ren's hand flies to his heart, his chest heaves beneath his dirty T-shirt.

Petey's father Smitty shakes his head. "I heard it from the house and went runnin'. I was so *damn* mad, Warren, I ran straight through the saw grass to get there." He shows the slashes on his hands and arms from the razor-sharp grass. "Would've gone right in the middle of those guys if a big guard hadn't stopped me with a sawed-off shotgun. 'What the *hell* do you think you're doin'?' I yell at him. 'Since when does the Klan take to shootin' at a couple of kids?' I was mad, I tell you! The guard . . . he says he's sorry, says 'There's big stuff goin' on and the Grand Dragon from Jacksonville's in town. The boys are a little edgy,' he says, 'but they had no business shootin' at children. Those kids were lucky,' he tells me, 'the guy who shot at 'em was loaded with bird shot, coulda been a whole lot worse with *buck*shot.' "

Daddy is silent. Then, gently lifting the edge of Ren's

bandage to inspect his head, he says, "Let me see, son." Bloody red scrapes begin a hair outside my brother's left eye. They run across his temple to just above the top of his ear.

"Smitty says if it'd been a little to the right, I might've lost an eye. I thought I was dead for *sure*," Ren says gravely.

Daddy pulls him close, but says nothing.

"You're telling me that fishing camp is the Klan's *head-quarters*?" he asks Smitty.

"Can you b'lieve it? Lived here a year and a half and never seen a thing. Usually meet at night, I guess. Today was some-thin' special, 'cause of the Grand Dragon and all."

"Old Emmett's going to be hearing from me on this." Daddy's voice tells me he is more than *mad*. He is *furious*.

When we get him home, Ren explains everything all over again to Mother and Doto. Mother's eyes flit be-tween Ren and Daddy. After Ren's done telling his story, Mother wraps him in her arms and herds him off to the bath-room to clean and Mercurochrome his head. Mitchell, fasci-nated by Ren's wounds, tags along after them. We can hear him pestering everyone with questions, punctuated by Mother's "Hush now, Mitchell," and Ren's loud "Ooow, that hurts!"

In the kitchen, Doto is fuming in Daddy's face. "Jesus H. Christ, Warren!" *Doto never swears; Daddy's clearly as shocked by it as I am.* "First these maniacs get away with *murdering* Mar-vin; then they run off Sal and Sophia. No doubt they had *something* to do with blowing up the poor Moores. And now, *now*, they're taking potshots at our own flesh and blood? This is outrageous! Beyond barbaric! Are you going to *do something* about this? Because if *you're* not, *I AM!!!*" Behind her cat-eye glasses, Doto's ready to explode.

Mother appears in the kitchen doorway. "Now what?" she asks wearily.

Daddy's become a boulder. Everything about him, his neck, his voice, is solid rock.

"Now, I tell Emmett Casselton what I think of men dressed in sheets shooting at children," he says, stone-faced. "I also tell Mr. Jim Jameson that there's going to be a little fireworks at the Opalakee Klan headquarters."

"Warren, can we talk about this?" Mother pleads.

"We'll talk *later*, Lizbeth," he grits between his teeth. "Right now, I have a couple calls to make." My father, the human mountain, strides toward his office off the living room. I hear him firmly, deliberately close the door behind him.

"What's he going to *do*?" I ask Mother. My heart is pounding so hard I'm afraid she'll hear it.

"Lizbeth," Doto says, "the Klan has pushed Warren one step too far today. He's *got* to push back."

"But *how*?" I want to know, wishing I could stop the trembling in Mother's hands, wanting the flutter in my stomach to fly away.

"I guess we have to wait and see," Mother says, turning her face away from me. Doto motions for me to leave them alone.

In the living room, I find Ren where Mother left him, watching cartoons on the couch with Mitchell.

Mitchell jumps up when he sees me and, clutching his tummy, asks, "We going to eat soon, Reesa?"

Poor thing. In all the commotion over Ren, we've forgotten supper. "Run into the kitchen," I tell him, "Doto will feed you."

Ren remains slumped on the couch, his eyes glued to the

TV screen. The bright orange streak of Mercurochrome on his head reminds me I should probably feel sorry for him. But what I really feel is *mad*.

"What in the Sam Hill were you thinking, Ren?" I hiss at him, deliberately standing between him and his show.

"Don't want to talk about it."

"Of course you don't! Because it's probably the dumbest damn thing you've ever done in your life! Standing on a water tower, yelling at the Klan. You heard what they did to Marvin, you know they killed the Moores. What did you think they'd do to you?"

"Nothing," he mumbles. He's refusing to look at me.

"Nothing? You mean you *thought* nothing, or they'd *do* nothing?"

"I thought we were safe." He's pouting.

"And where in tarnation did you get that idea?"

"I thought we were safe," he says, meeting my eyes for the first time. "Because we're *white*!" He hurls the words at my chest.

There it is. The ugly truth that had been circling 'round my stomach, creeping up my spine, sneaking around the edges of my mind. The bald fact that skin color—the paper-thin veil that made Marvin an easy target and gave Ren his air of invincibility—no longer matters. With the Klan's attack on two white boys, the rules have abruptly changed; their evil is no longer limited to Negroes, Jews and Catholics. The Klan's crossed its own hate line. Now, *any* of us, even *children*, can be targeted. It's a dreadful thought. And I hold my brother completely responsible.

"This is all your fault!" I lash. "You've got Doto about to have a *heart attack*, Daddy on the phone saying *God-knows-what* to Mr. Casselton, and Mother worried out of her head! I hope you had your fun, Ren, because you've most certainly ruined *everything* for the *rest* of us!"

It was a mean and hateful thing to say. I aimed for his heart, and I could see by his face, I hit dead center. I'm glad and sorry at the same time. And, for the first time in my life, I am quite afraid.

Chapter 29

Nobody's talking this morning. When Ren got up and Mother saw his head, its cluster of cuts round and ripe like a bunch of table grapes, his eye socket swollen like a small plum, she packed him in the car without a word and headed, we assume, to Doc Johnny's. Doto's carted Mitchell off to who-knows-where. And I'm left to help Daddy open up the showroom. *Divide and conquer—it's a sure sign the adults are upset with each other.*

Daddy and I make the short drive to the packinghouse without talking. As we enter from the back, I'm the first one to see it—the brown Dodge parked outside.

"Somebody wants their orange juice awful early," I say.

"Oh, I think he wants more than orange juice," Daddy says as he unlocks and slides open the big front doors. "Agent Jameson, I presume?"

"Mr. McMahon," Mr. Jameson says, reaching out his open window to shake Daddy's hand. "Do I need to present my badge again?" he asks me as he enters the showroom.

"No, sir," I say. It's obvious he's trying to keep things friendly.

"Mr. McMahon . . . may I call you Warren?"

Daddy nods, but says nothing. He's a stone wall.

"I got your message very late last night, drove over from the coast first thing this morning. What's all this about fire-works?"

"I thought you should know that the Opalakee Klan is about to get a taste of its own medicine," Daddy says flat-out.

"What do you mean . . . medicine?" Mr. Jameson asks.

"The very same substance they administered to the Moores."

"Dynamite? You're going to dynamite the fishing camp?"

"Yes, I am," Daddy says, locking his jaw.

"Hold on, Warren, our agents have appropriated pretty much all the dynamite in the county." Mr. Jameson's smile's gone a little wobbly.

"Nobody's appropriated mine!" Daddy tells him.

A noise in the back room startles the three of us. Mr. Jameson wheels around, as Daddy and I realize it's only Robert, come as usual to sweep the floors and rake the gravel.

"Our employee, Robert Carmichael," Daddy tells Mr. Jameson, nodding toward the back.

"Warren . . ." Mr. Jameson's voice has totally dropped his friendly-fellow routine. "I have no business telling you this, but I'm going to . . . The U.S. Attorney General has agreed to convene a Grand Jury in Miami the first week of April. We'll be presenting everything we have on the Opalakee Klan, its involvement in the deaths of the Moores, as well as the Gordon Klavern's bombings in Miami."

What about Marvin? I want to scream, my hands fisting so hard my fingers hurt.

"If you take *any* aggressive action now," Mr. Jameson tells Daddy, "you could destroy our hopes of ever bringing these Crackers to justice. The subpoenas are already typed, and we're set to deliver them on Monday."

"They shot at my son, nearly took his eye out," my father says, flint-faced.

"They're fools, Warren. You want to know why the Grand Dragon's in town? To try to calm them down. We've been all over these guys like stink on"—he glances in my direction—"*feces*. Some of them are worried about having their precious family names dragged into court, so they've quit, surrendered their robes and their dynamite and quit. The Opalakee Klan is going *down*. You can't ruin this for us."

"Nobody shoots at my children without retaliation."

"You want to *retaliate*, Warren? I've got just the job for you."

"What?" Daddy asks, eyeing Mr. Jameson.

"Since last time we talked, we've found an insider, an older gentleman who says there's a hidden compartment inside the fishing camp building which could put nails in a whole lot of coffins. Membership records, treasurer's books, things like that. That's *legal* dynamite, Warren, a whole lot more powerful than the stuff you want to plant."

"So why don't you just go in and get it?"

"No judge in this county would give us a warrant. What we're talking about here . . ." Mr. Jameson looks down at his shoe, then up. "Well, to be honest, what we're talking about is illegal break-in and entry."

"I'll do it."

Mr. Jameson doesn't seem to understand.

"I was going in to plant some dynamite," Daddy says

quietly. "If you're telling me I can't do that, I have to do something."

"Well, uh, we sort of see this as a two-man job. One to go in and find the stuff and one to stand watch."

"I'll go with you." Robert emerges from the back. He's carrying the push broom diagonally, like a rifle, in front of him.

"This is a *man's* job, son," Mr. Jameson tells him.

"'Scuse me, *sir*," Robert says, blue eyes blazing. After all, he *is* seventeen. "The reason we moved here was to get away from the Klan in South Carolina. They practically *killed* my father because somebody confused him with some man dating a Klanner's ex-wife. They beat him with a cat-o'-nine-tails and left him for dead right on our doorstep. I *hate* the Klan. If Mr. Mac needs me, I'm *in*."

Mr. Jameson stares at Robert for a long second, we all do, then turns back to Daddy and lifts both hands, palms forward, in a way that I know means *your call*.

"How much time do we have?" Daddy asks him.

"Why?" Mr. Jameson asks.

"Well, I'd planned to go the next moonless night, which, according to the calendar, is eight days from now."

"You've got *that*, but not much more. We need to have all the evidence in hand as soon as possible."

"Do I call you when I have it?" Daddy wants to know.

"No. No calls. Let me get you something from the car."

Mr. Jameson strides to the Dodge and pulls out a stiff flat canvas bag, about the size of a TV tray. When he hands it to Daddy, I see the mailing label is addressed to the P.O. box in Orlando.

"I don't know how much postage you'll need, but there's a twenty inside to cover it. Send it first class, okay?"

"Right, as if I'm going to break into Klan headquarters and send whatever I find by parcel post?" Daddy shoots back.

"I am, uh, authorized to pay you two hundred fifty dollars for your trouble," Mr. Jameson says.

"I don't want your money," Daddy tells him right away. "The only thing I do want is your word that you'll strike any mention of my name, or Luther's, or young Robert's here, from your files."

Mr. Jameson nods. "Warren . . . if you get caught, I never heard of you. If you live, make sure your attorney packs the jury with tenderhearted parents of boys your son's age."

"I'm way ahead of you." Daddy's extending his hand. "Will we see you again?"

"Only in the funny papers," Mr. Jameson says, returning his grip. Then, "You're doing us a tremendous service, you know."

"Let's hope so," Daddy answers.

"Pleasure to see *you* again, young lady," Mr. Jameson tells me. "Stay out of trouble, young man." He cocks and points his fingers like a gun at Robert, then walks out into the sun.

The months of hand-holding and head-ducking are over. The weeks of waiting for *some*one to do *some*thing are done. My father has finally found his way into the fight.

He turns, signaling to Robert to follow him up the stairs and onto the platform. I'm left in the still-dark showroom to turn on the lights, unlock the cash register, and deal with the tornado of feelings—pride, relief, terror—whirling around me.

Outside, off one of the big specimen trees planted by the drive to impress the tourists, an overripe grapefruit falls to the sand. The sound's like a heavy fist hitting flesh.

Chapter 30

Daddy's decision to help the F.B.I. sparks off a slew of other choices: He, Mother and Doto choose not to demand a police investigation of Ren's shooting ("The Constable was probably standing there in his sheets when it happened, anyway," Doto sneers); not to discuss the details of the shooting outside our family ("I've told Petey the same thing," Smitty says, "after I spoke my piece with Mr. Casselton." "Who is, after all, his landlord," Daddy reminds Mother); not to disclose his F.B.I. plans to Ren and Mitchell ("They're too young," Mother says, "and they know way too much already"); and, finally, to ask Armetta and the maids for help.

The decision to keep the source of Ren's injury a family secret hits the boys hardest. Ren was hoping for some center-of-town showdown between Daddy and the Klan, like in *High Noon* with Gary

Cooper, Ren's favorite actor. And Mitchell remains mesmer-ized by the mechanics of the "bad guy's bird shot" bouncing off the metal water tower to hit Ren in the head.

"I saw the very same thing on *Hopalong Cassidy!*" he in-sists, till I want to throttle him.

The day after Daddy agreed to help Mr. Jameson is a Sun-day.

I've got Mitchell by the hand on our way into Sunday school when eagle-eyed Miss Maybelle intercepts us with "Where's my hero this morning?" (That's what she calls Ren ever since he rescued her from the rattler.)

"He got shot!" Mitchell blurts out.

"No, no, *caught,* Mitchell, Ren got *caught* by a branch climbing up the big live oak out back. Scraped his head from here to here," I show her, all the while squeezing Mitchell's hand, *hard.*

"Swoll up like a balloon," Mitchell says, finally getting into it.

"Purple as a plum," I say as Miss Maybelle continues to give me the eye.

"Goin' to miss school tomorrow?" she wants to know.

"Maybe a day or two," I tell her. "But Doc Johnny says he'll be good as new by next weekend."

Later that afternoon, it's Mother who has to run interfer-ence with a concerned Miss Maybelle. "He's sound asleep," Mother tells her at our front door, accepting a plate piled high with "feel-better brownies."

Now, about the maids: It was a lifetime ago that Daddy joked to Luther about his personal spy ring, the circle of choir members who work as maids in the homes of area Klansmen. Before Marvin's murder, the circle was mostly social. Afterwards, it turned political, seeking and sending information to Armetta, who in turn fed it to Mr. Harry Moore.

Along the way, Armetta and Mr. Harry and his wife, Harriette, became friends. It was Armetta who invited the Moores into The Quarters and helped them register eligible adults to vote.

Fueled by the Moores' murder, it's Armetta who convinced the ladies of the choir to fill in the blanks on the F.B.I.'s list of Klan members. It's Armetta who expanded the circle to include several other maids from the Colored Town in Opalakee. "It's Armetta," Daddy assures Doto, "who'll find out if Monday, March twenty-fourth is a Klan meeting night or not."

Luther argues strongly that he should be the one to go with Daddy. "Robert's jus' a boy. Ah know those groves like the back of mah hand."

"No, Luther," Daddy argues back. "If you and I got caught, a Negro and a Yankee in Klan headquarters, neither of us would live to tell about it. With Robert, I can play the upset father and probably talk my way out of any trouble."

"Ah'm driving y'all then," Luther insists. "Ah know jus' where to let y' off and the safest place to pick y'all up."

"And what if they run into you, alone in the middle of a white area in the dead of night? You'd never see daylight. This is a two-man job and you can't be one of them. All I need is for you and Armetta to confirm that the twenty-fourth is clear."

Whatever objections my mother has to Daddy's plan—I can tell she's not the least bit happy about it—have been raised outside my hearing. Daddy's resolved, a man on a mission. And Mother is real quiet, more Poker Faced than ever.

It's two days before Buddy's tail wagging and the familiar

tappety-tap-TAP on the back door tell us Luther has Daddy's answer.

The boys have left the table already and are plopped in front of the television laughing at Allen Funt's *Candid Camera* show. I'm at the fridge, refilling our tea glasses, so I let Luther in.

"Evenin', Rootin'-Tootin'!"

"Hey, Luther, pour you some tea?"

"That'd be fine, real fine, thank you. Evenin', MizLizbeth, Miz Doto. How y'all tonight?"

"You're in high spirits," Daddy says and invites him to "have a seat" in Ren's empty chair.

"You bet Ah *am*! There are Grand Jury subpoenas showin' up all over the place, at some of the finest homes and oldest names in Opalakee. The ladies say they ain't never heard the blues sung so bad; the folks with the white robes hangin' in their closets are whinin' to beat the band. People callin' each other back and forth, wantin' to know what they s'posed to say, where they g'wan to stay, how long they g'wan to be gone, and how the hang did the Governor let this happen. Well, of course, they not sayin' 'hang,' but Ah won't repeat what they really sayin' in front of the ladies."

Daddy nods. "Jim Jameson said the subpoenas'd be there."

"That he did and that they are," Luther agrees. "And as long as we're talkin' 'bout what's happenin' where, looky here what *Ah* got."

Luther unbuttons his shirt pocket and pulls out a small, folded piece of paper. Carefully, he opens it to full letter size, laying it on the table in front of Daddy, smoothing out the creases with the flat of his hand. I peer over Daddy's shoulder to see.

It's a flyer announcing a "Kounty-wide Klonverse," inviting "all members of the Orange Kounty Klaverns of the Invisible Empire" to gather on the north shore of Lake Eola in Orlando, Friday night, March twenty-first—three nights from now!

"Where in the world did you get this?"

Luther looks at Daddy sideways. "You know, Mist'Warren, any laundress worth her salt checks the pockets of the dirty clothes before puttin' things in the washer. Ah got four more just like it if you want extras."

"So, instead of the twenty-fourth, we'll go in on the twenty-first. Luther, tell Armetta this is a Godsend!"

"You got *that* right, Mist'Warren." Luther's smile is wide and golden. "Could be the first time the good Lawd sent word by way of a laundry chute!"

T he seventy-two hours between Luther's arrival with the flyer and Daddy and Robert's March twenty-first "invasion" of the fishing camp pass me in a blur. The days at school roller-coaster in and out of crazy. Although our teacher, Mrs. Loreen Finney, promised last September, "I won't put up with any foolishness," she's still having trouble controlling the boys in our class. Most seem bent on seeing who can get sent to the principal's office first, ahead of the others. The nights make my stomach churn, as Daddy, Luther and Robert sit on the front porch suggesting, rejecting and arguing over details of The Plan.

At *last*, late Thursday, March twentieth, everything finally seems set. The ladies of the C.I.A. have confirmed that most all the Opalakee Klan members are committed to attending "the Rally in Orlando" the next night. The flyer outlines the meeting time "from eight o'clock until midnight," so The Plan is this:

At nine P.M., Luther will stop by the Dump to see his old friend Horatio Sykes, Negro caretaker there. Together, they'll unlock the Dump's little-used back gate. At nine-thirty Daddy and Robert will enter the back gate, park Daddy's truck behind the shed, and climb through the barbed-wire fence into the grove closest to the camp.

As Daddy and Robert approach the fishing camp from the south side, Luther and his friend, driving Horatio's truck, will cruise into the driveway on the north side of the camp and make sure there are no vehicles parked on the property. (Horatio often picks up trash at the camp and is certain they'll be safe.) If everything looks good, at ten o'clock, Luther will flash a single "go" sign with a flashlight across the lake toward the ridge where Daddy and Robert will be waiting.

Daddy and Robert will wade across the small lake which, Horatio swears, is no more than four feet deep in the center. The wide rim of razor-sharp saw grass on each side prohibits any kind of hike-in entry. They'll enter the camp's main building from its blind side.

Once there, Robert will stand guard by the front door while Daddy looks for the hidden compartment. The Plan allows for twenty minutes of search time; they must be out of the camp no later than ten-thirty, wade back across the lake, get through the grove, return to the truck and be home by eleven, at the latest.

On the face of it, everything makes sense to me except one part. For thirteen years, I've begged my father to swim with us in any number of lakes around here. Not *once*, not *ever*, has he done it.

"Swimming pools and oceans are fine, Roo," he's always

said, "but ever since the polio I just can't bring myself to get wet in a Florida lake."

"So why are you willing to wade through this one?" I want to know.

"This is different, Roo," he tells me, calm as calm can be. "*This* is war."

Chapter 31

Early Friday night, Doto herds the boys out of the house for dinner and a movie, a new Gene Autry, The Singing Cowboy, Western. As planned, I stay home to keep Mother company.

At 8:14, Daddy and Robert sit at the table, dressed in old dark-colored clothes and shoes, ready to go. Mother's silent. I'm tightrope anxious and trying hard not to show it.

Mother and I jump at the sound of Luther's knock. Letting him in, I'm surprised to see him dressed in a white shirt, dark tie and suit, as if for church. Behind him, Armetta in a navy blue dress carries a fat canvas bag by its cloth handles.

"Brother Luther, welcome," Daddy hails him. "You, too, Armetta?"

"Luther and I thought y'all could use a

little company while the men are out gallivantin'."." Armetta's eyes are on Mother. "Were we wrong?"

"Not at all. Thank you," Mother tells her and I can see she's grateful. "I appreciate you thinking of us."

"Thinkin' of myself, too. Waitin's hard work, unless you have comp'ny to distract you." Her comment conjures up something Luther told Daddy the night Marvin was missing. "Armetta's about worried herself to *death*," he'd said. I want to hug her for being here.

"Luther, how come you're dressed like that?" I have to ask.

"Well, y'see, Roo," he says, enjoying himself, "mah friend Horatio at the Dump has a sort of bad reputation, mainly 'cause he likes to cook up a li'l moonshine now and then. A lot of people might find it hard to b'lieve a churchgoin' man like mahself would visit a man like Horatio, unless, of course, it was to witness to him about his terrible evil ways. Horatio and Ah decided it'd be best, for *his* reputation and for *mine*, if Ah played the part of Brother Luther tonight. Got mah Bible in the car and everythin'. If we get caught at the lake or if anybody asks any questions, Ah might have to claim that Brother Horatio has *seen the light* and wants t' be baptized there and then!"

Somewhere during Luther's explanation, I realize everybody at the table's grinning but Mother and me. Armetta reaches over and pats my hand. "It's okay, honey, the Lord's got a sense of humor jus' like anybody else. Even King Solomon did a li'l play-actin' . . . for a good cause."

Luther looks down at his watch. "Y'all got 8:25?" he asks. As Daddy and Robert check their wrists, I eye the time on the kitchen clock above the stove.

"Ah b'lieve," Luther says, "we could do with a word of prayer b'fore we go."

"I think so, too, Luther," Daddy agrees. "Please."

"All right, then." Luther spreads his palms out to me on his right and Daddy on his left. Wordlessly, we join hands around the table and bow our heads. Luther's hand on my left is strong and calloused, his grip firm. Armetta's hand, on my right, is velvety, smooth and comforting.

"Lawd," Luther says, low and respectful,
"You been watchin' over us for a **long** *time,*
from our first breath to this one.
You know our **hearts***, Lawd.*
And, You know we have **no hope**
of accomplishin' our task tonight
without Your help.
We **feel***, Lawd, like old Joshua, when You took him*
to the great walls of Jericho and told him
to let Your trumpets **blow.**
Blow those trumpets, You said,
and the great walls of Jericho will come tumblin' **down.**
Old Joshua b'lieved You, Lawd, and so do we.
We ask You tonight:
Lay that trumpet in our hands.
We all know our part, Lawd, and we gonna do the best we can,
But it's Mist' Warren and young Robert here
who need Your help the **most.**
Guide they steps, Lawd.
Protect they path.
Show them the way to the secret hidin' place and, **Lawd,**
Lay that trumpet in they hands.
Give it to 'em, Lawd, then bring 'em **home***, safe and sound.*
We **thank** *You for the help*
and for the hope that fills our hearts tonight.

*We **bless** You for the privilege of doin' this in Your name.*
*And we **praise** You, Lawd, tonight and forever.*
Amen and thank God."

I hear my parents and Armetta echo Luther's "Amen," and both Luther and Armetta squeeze my hands before letting go.

"Well," Luther says, standing, "Ah best be goin'. Watch for the light on the lake at ten. Lord willin' and the Klan don't rise, Ah'll see y'all back here at 'leven o'clock."

Beside me, I hear Armetta suck in a soft breath as Luther leaves. Daddy and Robert, with thirty minutes to kill, decide to walk out and see him off, check the gear on the truck one last time.

Just before nine, they come back inside. Their goodbyes seem ordinary—Robert's, a shy wave around the table, Daddy's, a quick kiss for Mother and a confident "be right back" for Armetta and me—as if they were headed to the hardware store instead of into the very heart of the Klan's secret headquarters. As if life, as we know it, doesn't hang in the balance of what happens out there tonight. My chest feels clenched like a fist, like I'm sucking breath through a straw.

As the screen door slams shut behind them, Armetta lifts her canvas bag up onto the table.

"Reesa, Ah got somethin' you might be interested in. Know what this is?" She's holding a plastic container with a large brown glob inside.

"No'm," I tell her, straining to hear Daddy's pickup drive away.

"Well, with a little baking, *this* is a batch of my world-famous snicker doodles. You think you could find us a cookie sheet, maybe set the oven to three hundred an' fifty degrees?"

As I search for and set out the cookie sheets, I feel suddenly chilled. In all the debates over tonight's plan, nobody's dared mention the real danger Daddy's walking into. *What if the fishing camp isn't empty? What if somebody sees Daddy's truck driving into the Dump? What if they recognize Luther's car, too, and put two and two together? Everybody knows Daddy and Luther are friends.*

My hands, fiddling with the cover on the cookie dough, feel thick and stupid, like I've forgotten how to move. Armetta reaches over and covers them, warming me like a fire.

"MizLizbeth, I brought my sewing box along. I know with all these chil'ren, you *must* have some clothes that need mendin', socks that need darnin'. If you'd like to help Reesa with the snicker doodles, I'll be happy to sit right here and do a little mendin' for you."

Mother looks at Armetta's face, searching, I think, for the words she'd like to say. Her hazel eyes are wet-rimmed with feelings.

"It's all right, MizLizbeth. I'm an old hand at passin' time. Could you bring me that mendin' please?" Armetta says softly, opening her sewing box.

Just after ten, the cookies are done. Mother pours cold milk all around. As we sit down to sample our still-warm efforts, Armetta tells me she was my age when her Mississippi grandmother taught her the recipe.

"Have you always lived in Mayflower?" I ask her.

"Oh, no, chil', I was born and raised in Ocoee."

"Ocoee! There aren't any Negroes in Ocoee."

"Not *now*, but there used to be a whole community, like The Quarters here in Mayflower, only bigger."

"What happened to it, Armetta?" Mother asks.

"Election Day 1920 happened, and a man named Mose Norman, our neighbor, drove downtown to vote," she says, leaning forward, her eyes and voice calling us into careful attention. "The local Klan was mostly Dixiecrat and they were worried that day because *most* Negroes were votin' Republican.

"The Klan showed up at the polls and started pushin' and shovin' our people away. Well, Mose Norman got hit and that made him mad. Mose drove over to O'landah to complain to a lawyer man, Mr. Cheney.

"Mr. Cheney told him to drive back and write down the names of *anyone* interferin' with the vote, and anyone else who got turned away. Long story short, it turned into a mob scene and that night, the Klan showed up and set fire to our houses."

"I remember hearing about this," Mother says. "Didn't the locals call it the Ocoee Riot?"

"Oh, they called it a lot of things, not much of it true." Armetta eyes her mending.

"Late that night," she continues, "there was a big gun battle at the home of July Perry, who lived in the middle of his own orange grove. At the time, he was the most influential Negro in town. Now, July Perry hadn't done a *thing* but the Klan came after him jus' the same, said he was hidin' Mose Norman in the house. 'Course, by that time, old Mose was *long* gone.

"When July Perry asked to see a search warrant, the Klan opened fire. July Perry tried to scare 'em off by showin' 'em his high-powered rifle, but it didn't help. When two white men attacked his daughter, he shot 'em. Sheriff tried to haul him into jail, but the mob lynched July Perry, on the big oak tree outside his house."

"Armetta!" Mother exclaims. I hear the tremble in her voice and know she's thinking of Daddy.

"The rest of us jus' scattered, scared outta our wits by burnin' crosses and flamin' houses. For a couple hours, my family—Mamma, Daddy and the six of us kids—hid out in a orange grove, listenin' to the sound of gunfire and people yellin' and cryin' in the streets. Then my daddy decided it was safe to move and we started walking. It was *pitch-dark* that night. Most of us had been asleep in our beds when the trouble came, so we were barefoot. We walked all night, through the palmetto flats outside Ocoee, through the piney woods around Lake Opalakee, then *finally*, just before sunrise, we made it to Mayflower, where our cousins took us in."

"How old were you?" I ask.

"A year less than you, honey." Armetta's eyes glow like embers. She seems at once both here and back there walking barefoot through the pitch-dark wood. "You remember Selma, works at the Garnet house now?" she asks me.

"Yes," I say, nodding her on.

"*Her* people were in Ocoee, and they went to Opalakee. Others went to Kissimmee or to Eatonville outside O'landah, wherever they had fam'ly or friends. All in all, 'bout fifty people died that night, includin' my best friend, Jolily Johnson." She stops, then says, "But *no*body never did anythin' about it. The F.B.I. came into town later, took statements from all the *white* men involved, didn't even *bother* talkin' to a single Negro."

"But what about your things, your property?" Mother asks.

"*No*body ever went back. At first, we were scared to. Later on, we just didn't want to." Armetta picks up her needle, pulling thoughtfully at the thread. "We keep in touch, though," she says, her face softening as if she'd remembered something pleasant. "Matter of fact, a bunch of us get together fairly reg'lar, not to dwell on what we *lost*, mind you. But to remember they's *some* things can't nobody take away, no matter *what*."

My eyes stray up to check the clock. Mother sits staring at the plate of fresh-baked cookies, untouched between us.

Chapter 32

At 10:33, we hear the purr of the DeSoto coming down the driveway. Mother and I hurry out to help Doto with the boys, who are both asleep in the deep leather seats. I carry Mitchell, Mother half carries, half walks Ren up the stairs to their beds.

The kitchen clock shows nine 'til eleven when we hear Luther's truck, followed by his careful tap at the back door. Mother gets up quickly, stiffly, to open it.

"Should be right behind me, MizLizbeth," Luther tells her quietly. He's loosened his tie, left his jacket in the car. Walking in, he pauses beside Armetta to place a hand on her shoulder. She covers it with one of her own.

"Be here any minute now," he says and the five of us—Mother, Doto, Luther, Armetta and me—sit silent, listening for the truck. I watch the second hand hop around the clock, nudging the minutes from 10:57 to 11:03 to a full ten after.

Luther checks his watch and shakes his head. "I *saw* 'em," he says, "walkin' outta the lake and into the grove. Shouldn't've taken but another *five* to reach the truck."

Mother stands and leaves the room. I hear her walking back and forth on the porch. Luther and Armetta follow her. As I get up to join them, Doto stops me, tells me to "sit down and stay put." *What's wrong? Where are they?* I want to scream.

Doto remains confident. "Calm down. Your daddy's smarter than any ten of those men put together. He'll be here."

Like a wave, fear rises up to choke me. *What if you're wrong?* I wonder. As if she's read my mind, Doto glares at me to keep the faith.

At 11:30, worry, like a magnet, pulls Doto and me out of the kitchen and onto the porch. Nobody's talking. Out in the yard, the crickets rub their wings and my nerves together, a pair of bullfrogs croak our concern, and a lone night bird cries for its mate.

I stand beside Doto, willing Daddy home. *It's a ten-minute drive; you should be here NOW!* My heart bangs inside my chest. For another lifetime, we stand and wait, watching the dark, not wanting to acknowledge the possibilities that swirl like demons around us.

And then, we hear it . . . the roar of the truck entering the driveway, its headlights arcing into view. Mother flies down the steps. Daddy brakes, leaps out and grabs her tightly. I wait my turn to hug him.

"Tire!" he says. "Goddamn *flat*. Picked up a nail on the way in . . . flat as a pancake when we got back."

"They're *fine*," Doto announces, queen to her court.

"Right as rain," Luther says, shaking off dark thoughts.

"And just about as wet," Daddy says, tossing Robert a towel and swinging his waterproof ditty bag onto the table. "Sorry for scaring you all. Everything was fine until that tire. Never changed a flat so fast in my life."

"We made it through the grove in *no* time, saw Luther's light and headed down the beach," Robert tells us.

"Didn't see a soul," Luther tells him. "Ev'ry one of them Klanners musta been at that big rally downtown."

"The lake wasn't any more than three and half feet deep," Daddy says. "We waded right across it, holding the bag and the shotgun over our heads. Only thing was, in the middle, Robert looks at me and, quiet as can be, asks, 'Did Ren ever say whether or not there's *'gators* in this lake?' "

As Mother gasps, Daddy smirks, "Let's just say it's a good thing my pants were already wet. We picked up the pace after that. Made it to the fishing camp fine, but as we walked up onto the beach, Robert nearly stepped on a *water moccasin*."

A shiver snakes up my spine. Unlike a rattler, a deadly water moccasin will strike without warning, just as soon kill you as look at you.

"Scared me half to death," Robert says. "Didn't dare shoot it, though. Mr. Mac's next to me whispering, 'Stand *still*, stand *real still*.' Now how am I s'posed to stand still when I'm shakin' like a leaf?"

"Snake was as scared as we were," Daddy says. "After a while—"

"He means *forever*," Robert interrupts.

"—it slithered off. After that, we expected just about anything. Crept up to the door of the building and started searching for a padlock. Robert tries the handle and the door *opens*—we walked right in!"

"Tell 'em about *that*," Robert says, nodding Daddy on.

"Damnedest thing I've ever seen. On the outside, that building's just plain pine clapboard, badly in need of paint. Inside, we switched on our flashlights and it's varnished tongue-and-groove cypress, paneled like a high church or a courtroom. There's a small anteroom, like a vestibule, in front and a big paneled door; beyond that, a fairly large meeting hall."

"You wouldn't *believe* it," Robert tells us.

"Black, red and gold everywhere," Daddy says. "Like a House of Horrors, with a big square painted on the floor. In the middle of that, some kind of altar."

"Gave me the *creeps*." Robert mock-shivers.

Daddy nods. "On three sides of the square there are chairs, some kind of ceremonial seats. And on the far side, opposite from where we came in, there's a throne on a raised dais, big as a church pulpit but painted blood-red and black."

"With a *huge* Florida longhorn cow's skull above it." Robert holds his hands wide apart to show us the size of the skull and horns. "I told Mr. Mac, 'Wouldn't surprise me to see the Devil himself sittin' up there.' "

"Made my skin crawl," Daddy agrees. "I went one way, Robert went the other, tapping the paneling with our ballpeen hammers, looking for a hollow spot. Took us about ten minutes, but just behind a small table on a side wall, we found it—hollow panel, about waist high, with a sliding door concealed in the woodwork. We got that open, and inside, there was a shelf and a good-sized tin tackle box. We opened that and found three books and a zippered bank pouch. The top book was a Bible."

"Presented to Mr. Reed Garnet, on the occasion of his confirmation into Opalakee Presbyterian Church," Robert tells us.

"Age twelve, by his loving mother." Daddy grins.

"Oh, Lord," Mother moans, "wouldn't Hannah Garnet just die if she knew where that Bible ended up?"

"Maybe, maybe not." Armetta purses her lips.

"We left it there, along with the pouch, which had a little bit of cash in it, and took the other two books with us," Daddy says.

"What were they?" I ask, hardly able to breathe.

"Not much." Daddy shrugs. "Just the Membership and Attendance Records. And the Treasurer's Log."

"Ohhh, if that don't beat *all!*" Luther is grinning, slapping his thigh.

"*Then* what happened?" Doto demands.

"We put the hammers and the books in our bag, slid that tin box back inside the secret panel, closed the door, waded back across the lake, crossing our fingers that if there *were* any gators they *weren't* hungry, ran through the grove, changed the flat and hightailed it home!"

"Were you scared?"

Daddy turns to face me. "Terrified," he tells me softly.

"Can we see what y' got?" Luther asks.

"You bet!" Daddy empties his bag in front of us.

Maybe because I was expecting big leather-bound volumes, like Doto's ledger books, the black-and-white cardboard composition books, like Ren and I use in school, surprise me.

Daddy opens the Membership Book first. There, in someone's tidy handwriting, is the list of names far longer than the F.B.I.'s list I saw last month. This one has columns with years of dates across the top and checkmarks showing who attended which monthly meeting. Apparently, the last meeting was just five nights ago, with all but a few members present and accounted for. After that, there's a section listing Klan Offi-cers. Emmett Casselton's at the very top, as Exalted Cyklops, above a list of strange-sounding titles like Klaliff, Kludd, Klokard, and others with the letters KL.

The second book, the Treasurer's Log, has neat, numbered entries for dues paid and fines collected. Armetta is the first to notice that in the back of the Treasurer's Log, there are a few odd enclosures. All of a sudden, she freezes, eyes wide, nostrils flaring, hand flying to her throat.

"What is it, Armetta?" Mother asks her.

Slowly, carefully, without removing it from its place, Armetta points out the newspaper clipping. "I have a copy of this at home. It's the story about the Moores registering vot-ers in The Quarters. My name's in it, too." Turning the page like it will tear if she touches it, she uncovers another sheet taped into the book. A rough pencil drawing. "Good God Almighty! You realize what *this* is?"

Daddy leans forward, studying the bunch of squares and rectangles with letters inside. I see "P," "K," "LR," and, in one, a "BR" with a circle around it.

"Luther! Don't you recognize it?"

"Recognize what?" Luther says, his eyes darting from the drawing to Armetta's face and back again.

"It's the Moores' house!" Armetta says, pointing. "See here, 'P' is for porch, 'K' for kitchen. This 'LR' right here is the livin' room. You and I sat right there last October visitin'. This 'BR' over here, the one with the circle, is the bedroom where the dynamite went off."

"Are you *sure* about this?" Daddy asks, his blue eyes bor-ing into her brown ones.

"Dead sure," she says, returning his gaze steadily.

Daddy sits back in his chair. I find myself staring at the open window over the sink, wishing it was closed.

After a few long seconds, Daddy leans back in. "Anything else?"

"These last two sheets aren't taped . . . let's look." Armetta unfolds the two sheets and places them in the middle of the table. The first one is a duplicate of the flyer inviting Klansmen to tonight's Kounty-wide Klonverse in Orlando. The second one is titled *Why the Klan liKes IKe!* It calls on "Good Democrats and Real Southerners" to support Eisenhower for President. The flyer cites Ike's record as "an enforcer of racial segregation in the U.S. armed forces," his "opposition to civil rights legislation," and his "support of immigration laws which bar Colored Races from entering the country."

"Jim Jameson was right, this stuff *is* dynamite," Daddy says. "Lizbeth, where's the pouch?"

As Mother retrieves the mailing pouch Mr. Jameson gave Daddy, Armetta folds and replaces the flyers in the book. Daddy brings Armetta a plain sheet of paper and asks her to write a note to Jim Jameson stating that the drawing in the Treasurer's Log appears to be the floor plan of the Moores' home which she visited last fall. After she writes the note and signs it, Mother and Daddy sign it, too, as witnesses. Daddy puts the note on top of the two composition books, slips them inside the mailing pouch. He seals it and hands it, along with Mr. Jameson's twenty-dollar bill, to Luther, who's agreed to mail it from the Wellwood post office first thing tomorrow morning.

"Once you put that pouch in the mail, we've done our part. Now, we just have to hope that the Good Lord and the Grand Jury do theirs," Daddy tells him.

"Amen to that," Luther echoes.

"I still wish we could've blown that place up tonight," Robert says on his way out the door.

"Back to hell where it came from?" Daddy asks. "Me, too."

Robert grins and waves goodnight.

"We'll see y'all later," Luther and Armetta call quietly as they disappear into the night.

In the kitchen light, my parents' faces seem drained of the excitement that filled the room just minutes ago. I'm dead-tired myself, not wanting to think.

"And now we wait," Doto says, so softly I almost don't hear her. I've never seen her look so old.

"Now," Daddy says, helping her up, herding me out of the room, "we try to get some sleep."

The Saturday morning after Daddy and Robert went into the Klan fishing camp, Ren (who knew nothing about their efforts) did the second most foolhardy thing of his life.

Privately, he and I had decided that the man who shot at him was most probably J. D. Bowman, the same trigger-happy Klansman who murdered Marvin. "But, of course, we'll never know for sure," I told him, trying to let that particular sleeping dog lie.

Well, Ren, applying the kind of cockeyed logic that only a boy is capable of, got up and took himself off to Carney's Coffee Shop, the flat-topped fried-food restaurant across from Voight's Grocery Store. Everybody knows Carney's is where Mr. Emmett Casselton, King of the Klan, regularly holds court with two or three other men in the big corner booth facing the street.

Ren walked in, sat himself at the counter, ordered a hot apple fritter and a glass of milk, and settled in to eavesdrop on Emmett Casselton's conversation!

"I was hoping they'd talk about the shooting and who did it and all," he brags to me later, cocky as can be.

"Are you *crazy*?" I yell, dumbstruck by his brashness. "The Klan almost blows your head off and, first chance you get, you're off to Carney's pestering Emmett Casselton?"

"I wasn't pestering him, I was just listening. But all he talked about was money, price of fruit, price of juice, price of land. Hardly worth the trip."

"And that's *all* that happened?"

"Well, yeah, until they got up to pay and Mr. Casselton noticed my Dodger cap. I had it pulled way down so he couldn't see my head." Ren's scrapes have healed into beet-red welts.

"*And?*" I'm ready to strangle him.

"And he asks me, 'You a Brooklyn fan, boy?' "

"And you said . . ."

"Well, nothing at first. He's kinda scary-looking. Got these pale alligator eyes with no lashes, big old nose with gray hairs sticking out the holes, and skin like leather with sun spots all over him."

"So, you didn't answer him?"

"Yes, I did, too. I said 'yes, sir.' And, he said, 'The Brooklyns are bums. Goddamn nigger lovers never won a Series, never will.' "

"Oh, *God*! And you said . . ."

Ren grins. "I gave him Marvin's V-sign and said, 'Maybe this year, sir.' "

I *groan*.

"And he didn't say nothing, just looked at me like I was an idiot."

"You *are* an idiot!" I rail, shaking him. "If you don't swear this *minute*, Ren McMahon, on the Holy Bible, that you will *never* go near Carney's again, I'm going to tell Daddy *and* Doto, and you know they'll make *mincemeat* out of you!"

"Leave me alone. Lemme go!"

Because our family seems so different from other people's in Mayflower, Daddy's always joked that we are strangers in a strange land. Somehow, Ren twisted that into believing he was anonymous or, worse yet, invisible. I have no idea whether Emmett Casselton recognized him as "the McMahon boy" or not. But I'm worried that Ren's visit to the coffee shop draws attention to our family at a time when, Daddy says, "we need to be laying low."

Chapter 33

M onday, April first, Fool's Day, the Federal Grand Jury convenes its investigations into Ku Klux Klan activities in the state of Florida.

By Tuesday morning, the news from Miami crackles through the school hallways like an electric current. Fourteen Klansmen have been subpoenaed statewide, twelve of them from Orange County, nine of them from Opalakee.

Before the first bell rings, Joan Ellen Marks broadcasts the morning report to a group of us lined up outside our classroom.

"Miz Lucy came over last night, mad as hell and wailin' like a banshee," Joan Ellen says. "I guess Mr. Reed thought there'd be a bunch more people from a bunch more Klans. But there aren't but a few who aren't from Opalakee. Miz Lucy's 'bout gone 'round the bend ravin' that Mr. Reed's gonna wind up in *jail*! If *that* happens, Miz

Lucy swears, she'll never be able to hold her head up in this town again; she and May Carol'll wind up in the *poorhouse*, or else livin' with Mr. Reed's mother, which Miz Lucy says would be a *fate worse than death*. It took Mamma most of the night to calm her down."

"What about May Carol?" I ask, remembering her mother's stinging slap at the Garnets' pool party.

"She spent the night with me but went home to Miz Lucy this mornin'. Don't think she'll be in school today."

In class, everybody wants to talk about the same thing, peppering our teacher with questions about Grand Juries and U.S. Prosecutors. Mrs. Finney, smelling an opportunity for some real-life Social Studies, puts aside Americanism versus Communism and begins a comparison of States' versus Federal Rights.

"At the heart of this week's events in Miami is the question of *jurisdiction*," Mrs. Finney says, writing the word on the board. "Who can tell me what that means?"

My classmates, several of them related to the Klansmen now in Miami, appear well versed in the differences between state crimes (robbery, assault and battery, murder) and federal ones (the infringement of someone's Constitutional rights).

"The jurisdiction of a Federal Grand Jury applies only to areas governed by *federal* law," Mrs. Finney tells us. "Unless the Federal Prosecutor can prove that a federal crime has been committed, the people subpoenaed to Miami will have a nice vacation and come home in a few weeks, okay? May we move on to mathematics now?"

The news passed on from the maids to Armetta to us is pretty much the same. The nine members of the Opalakee Klan as well as the five others from the Orlando, Ocoee and Miami Klans were expecting many more Klansmen to be subpoenaed. Safety, so to speak, in numbers. They remain confident, however, and have been advised by no less than the state's Grand Dragon himself that no federal jurisdiction applies.

Apparently, the Klansmen are free to discuss their testimony outside the courtroom and, according to the maids, call their nervous wives at home almost every day. "Loose lips sink ships," the saying goes. They certainly destroyed Miz Lucy Garnet.

We hear the story from Armetta, who got it from Selma, who was *there*. "It's pure pitiful," Armetta tells us, "hurt my heart to hear it." Mine, too.

After ten days of cooling his heels in a Miami motel room, Mr. Reed Garnet finally got his turn to testify.

Miz Lucy was a nervous wreck waiting to hear from him, smoked a pack of cigarettes nonstop before Selma even had time to clear the breakfast dishes.

After taking the oath and his seat, Mr. Reed answered the first question put to him by the Federal Prosecutor ("Are you a member of an organization known as the Ku Klux Klan?") with a confident "No."

Then the prosecutor, open file folder in hand, asked his second question. "Are you not presently a member in good standing of the Opalakee Klavern of the Ku Klux Klan?"

Again Mr. Reed said "No."

After that, the prosecutor turned to shuffle through the stack of file folders on his table. That's when Mr. Reed saw it, the briefest flash of a familiar black-and-white pattern. At first, he told Miz Lucy, it reminded him of a schoolboy's composition book. But as the prosecutor turned to ask his third question ("Are you not a former Exalted Cyklops of the Opalakee Klavern of the Ku Klux Klan?"), it reminded him of something else.

An hour later, during the morning recess, Mr. Reed called home, fuming to beat the band. Miz Lucy took the call in the kitchen, a scant five feet from where Selma stood cleaning out the oven.

"Lucy, listen to me carefully," he said in a tone Selma said was way beyond upset. Mr. Reed was *riled*. "Call Emmett. Tell him to check the fishing camp. I think they've got our record books! How the hell could they have our record books?"

"What record books?" Miz Lucy asked him.

"Membership, attendance, the goddamn list of officers. We keep them at the camp, but I swear I saw them here in the prosecutor's files!"

"Oh, Reed, what does this mean?" Miz Lucy wailed, sinking like an empty sack into the kitchen chair.

His answer was loud enough for Selma, scrubbing the oven, to hear every word. "It means I just fucking *perjured* myself in front of the goddamn Grand Jury! Hang up the phone and call Emmett *now*!"

Miz Lucy did as she was told. Her call to Emmett Casselton included a strident retelling of every word Mr. Reed had said, followed by fifteen minutes of frantic pacing and chain-smoking, waiting for the return call.

Emmett Casselton's confirmation ("They're gone") sent Miz Lucy into orbit. Two more calls—one to her brother, an attorney in Macon, and a second to Miz LouAnn Marks, her best friend next door—pushed her spread-eagled, sobbing hysterically, onto the sofa.

"If I'd been there, I'd have known what to do," Armetta tells us sadly. "Poor Selma'd never seen her that way, hadn't the slightest idee how to handle things."

Miz LouAnn arrived shortly, grabbed a bottle of bourbon and hauled her friend back into the bedroom. An hour later, Miz LouAnn emerged, told Selma, "Miz Lucy's resting. Under no circumstances, is she to be disturbed."

Mid-afternoon, Miz Lucy stumbled into the kitchen in search of some ice. She found Selma serving May Carol an after-school snack and told May Carol that when she's finished she's to run next door and play with Joan Ellen. Then she asked Selma to leave early, she needed peace and quiet "to rest," she said. Both Selma and May Carol did as they were told.

That evening, Miz LouAnn brought her friend supper on a tray. When her knock on the door went unanswered, she let herself in and found, to her horror, that Miz Lucy, aided by the bourbon and her barbiturates, had rested herself into peace and quiet of the most permanent kind.

The news of Miz Lucy's suicide casts a pall over Opalakee, and puts thoughts in my head that I'd rather not think about.

Armetta's worried sick about May Carol. "That chil's gonna need all our prayers to survive life as a Garnet without her mother," she says, shaking her head.

I remember last March, how fragile and upset May Carol looked when Armetta, her other mother, left. Now she's lost her real mother, too. What's to become of her if Mr. Reed goes to jail? Why is it, in this whole mess, ever since Marvin, innocent people are the only ones suffering?

M r. Reed Garnet, granted temporary leave by the Grand Jury, returns home to bury his wife. My parents, knowing the small Opalakee Presbyterian Church will be packed with wary Klansmen and their heartsick wives, send flowers but elect not to attend.

After the funeral and the paying of respects at the Garnet home, Joan Ellen and May Carol sit quietly on the patio just off the living room while Miz LouAnn suggests to Mr. Reed that May Carol move in next door.

In the girls' locker room, Joan Ellen shares what happened next:

"So Mamma says to May Carol's Daddy, 'Reed, that child's been through so damn much. Why don't you let her stay with us for a while, at least 'til this business in Miami's cleared up?'

" 'Might be longer than you think,' Mr. Reed says with a smirk. '*Besides*, she's goin' to Mother's,' he says, meaning May Carol's grandmother, Miz Hannah Garnet. Y'all know what Miz Lucy used to call Miz Hannah, don't ya? *H-R-H*, which Miz Hannah always thought stood for *Her Royal Highness*, you know, like the Queen? But Miz Lucy told Mamma it really meant *Hannah Right outta Hell!* They did *not* get along!

"Anyway, my mamma says, 'Reed, you can't let that old hellcat have that child!'

" 'It's a done deal, LouAnn,' he says. 'And Mother's already arranged May Carol's transfer to Mount Laura Academy.'

" 'Dammit, Reed, *no*!' Mamma tells him. 'You know every time Miz Hannah brought up that prissy-ass boarding school, it made Lucy crazy. You know how *set* she was on keepin' May Carol home!'

" 'Well, Lou,' Mr. Reed says, just as *mean* as could be, 'if she was *that* set, she should've stuck around instead of climbin' into the booze and her little pill bottles!'

"*Well*," Joan Ellen reports to us, rolling big eyes around our circle, "when he said *that*, I thought my mamma was gonna strangle him. And poor May Carol, sitting right next to me, heard every word!

" 'Reed Garnet,' my mamma says, 'you *knew* Lucy was havin' a hard time of it. If you'd spent *one damn minute* thinkin' about *her* instead of yourself . . .'

" 'Ain't a problem anymore, is it, Lou?' Mr. Reed says.

" 'You are every bit the *animal* she always said you were!' my mamma told him.

" 'Well, then,' he says, in a real *ugly* voice, 'you'll excuse me, but I have a plane to catch. The Miami *zoo*keeper's waiting for me to crawl back into my *cage*.' And with that, he opened the door and told Mamma to '*Go home!*'

"Last time we saw May Carol, he had her all packed up and on her way to Miz Hannah's house. Damn jackass didn't even give us a chance to say goodbye."

Chapter 34

In the gray days after Miz Lucy's suicide, there are no further updates out of Miami. Reporters camped outside the Federal Courthouse pester the Federal Prosecutor for news. "Patience," he chides them. "This process will not be rushed." The papers are guessing another two to three weeks before "justice is served."

The big question I have is "Who's saying how much, about what?" Backed into the corner of perjury versus self-preservation, how long before these human snakes bare their fangs at each other? *It has to happen, doesn't it? They can shed their skin, but not their nature, right?*

Mother believes the longer the proceedings run, the better. "It takes time," she tells me, "to draw everyone's cards out on the table."

Hope has begun to glimmer at our house like the flame of a small candle. I see it first in Mother. Or, rather, when the woman who looks like my mother but hasn't acted like her real self for months invites me to play a game of Gin Rummy. The first hand is awkward, but, after the third, she catches my eye when I say "gin," and grins. My mother's lopsided, dimpled grin.

I don't dare acknowledge it, for fear of somehow scaring her away again. But as I gather and sweep the cards in her direction, with a quiet "your deal," I feel the pieces of myself fall back into place, and my heart welcomes her home.

While the small towns surrounding Orlando wait for the results of the Grand Jury face-off in South Miami, another confrontation draws our attention north to Tallahassee. Presidential candidate Estes Kefauver is on his way, back onto Governor Fuller Warren's forbidden ground.

Everyone's anticipating the fray, including the ladies at Miz Lillian's Beauty Parlor:

"They say Governor Warren's goin' to meet him at the border with the state troopers," claims Miz Ethel May Burch, cut and curling. "Goin' t' tell Kefauver to turn around and take his coonskin cap and his redheaded wife back to Tennessee."

"I hear he's flyin' into Miami," Miz Lillian says. "Goin' t' cavalcade right up the Trail, all the way to Jacksonville."

"What color red is his wife's hair?" Miss Iris asks.

" 'Bout the same as mine," Miz Lillian tells her.

"Outta the same *bottle*?" Miz Ethel May asks wickedly.

"Now, now, Ethel May, only my hairdresser knows for sure," Miz Lillian shoots back, patting her copper-red French twist.

"I personally think it's *foolish* of Governor Warren to make such a big *deal* outta this," Miz Agnes Langford, my old Sunday school teacher, says. "Any of y'all see Senator Kefauver on television during the hearings in New York? That man tore that thug Costello to pieces. If Governor Warren thinks Kefauver'll be a pushover, he's likely to be surprised."

"You for Kefauver, Aggie?" Miss Iris asks.

"Well, I'm just not sure I'd be comfortable with a Cracker like Russell in the White House, or if the rest of the country would be, either. Personally, I think Kefauver's got a better chance of beatin' that warmonger Eisenhower in the fall."

Everyone at Miz Lillian's knows Miz Agnes has a son in Korea and is anxious to get him home.

The following week, both Democratic candidates, Senator Kefauver of Tennessee and Senator Russell of Georgia, come calling on the voters of Florida. Not long after Kefauver's arrival, Governor Warren openly challenges him to a twenty-one-question debate.

"I'd be happy to talk to the Governor," Kefauver replies, "but a debate's sort of a *candidate* thing. Last time I looked, I didn't see the Governor's name on the ballot. Is it there? Did I miss it?" Kefauver asks the press.

Both Senators tour the state, shaking hands, making speeches up and down the Orange Blossom Trail. I'm at the packinghouse when Senator Russell's parade passes through Mayflower. A dozen state trooper cars, lights flashing, sirens blaring, announce their arrival and departure at both ends of town. In the middle, the Georgia Senator and the Governor wave like kings from the air-conditioned comfort of their shiny gold Mercury.

Kefauver's pass-through was much smaller, Daddy tells us, riding in an open convertible with him and his pretty wife smiling and waving at the people beside the Trail. Mother confirms that Nancy Kefauver's hair is very much the same color as Miz Lillian's. Whether or not Miz Kefauver's a natural redhead, she couldn't say.

O n May fifth, the day before the Presidential primary, Luther stops by with questions about the voting process. This will be his very first time at the polls. He wants to make sure he knows *exactly* what to do.

Daddy says he's not surprised that Luther and most of the folks in The Quarters are backing Kefauver.

"Ah like the way he talks about cleanin' up the gov'-ment," Luther says. "Wish he'd start right here with Gov'nor Warren. That man has deviled poor Mistuh Kefauver up and down this state with his 'Twenty-one Questions,' like it was Mistuh Kefauver caught buyin' concrete from Al Capone! Ah hope he gets his chance to clean house in Washin'ton. God knows Ah'd be willin' to lend him a hand with a broom!"

The next night, I stay up late with the adults to watch the results roll in on the television. As expected, the larger cities and the eight counties around them go for Kefauver. The country counties, especially those in the panhandle, tip heavily toward Russell.

In the end, Russell wins, nearly 360,000 votes to Kefauver's 285,000. Despite the fact that their man lost, Daddy and Luther are jubilant. "Governor Warren promised Kefauver a humiliating defeat," Daddy explains. "But thanks to th' *Negro* vote, he didn't get it!" Luther boasts. "We kep' things fair an' square." *Like a democracy should be*, I decide. *Wouldn't Mr. Harry've been proud to see that?*

As both candidates head north with less success than either had hoped for, attention turns south, back to Miami.

T he headline on the front page of *The Miami Herald* says it all:

TRAIL OF VIOLENCE LAID TO KLANSMEN

Daddy reads the lead story aloud:

A federal grand jury Wednesday submitted "a catalog of terror that seems incredible" in a report of Ku Klux Klan activities that ran the gamut from murder and arson to beatings and bombings.

Two White girls were severely beaten for bathing in the nude; a Negro man was shot in the back; the home of a Negro woman in Miami was burned; a Negro man and his wife were killed when their home was bombed;

"Mr. Harry and his wife!" I cry.
"Yes," Daddy nods. "Let me finish . . ."

a White man was beaten for neglecting his family; a Negro worker was thrashed for union activities.

"Nothing about Marvin?" I'm fuming. Daddy gives me the eye and continues.

These are only some of the acts attributed to the KKK by the jury in its roundup of terrorism dating from 1943.

Only those acts to which one or more Klansmen admitted participation were attributed to the KKK by the jury as it recited a long list of unbridled acts of violence in Greater Miami and central Florida . . .

The jury said the list it submitted to Federal Judge John W. Holland in its partial report is far from complete. "Details grow monotonous through sheer repetition," it explained.

The story Daddy reads says that, after a brief recess, the Grand Jury will hear more witnesses and *"consider criminal aspects over which there may be federal jurisdiction."* Their statement indicated that the jury expects to return indictments when it reconvenes.

After seventeen paragraphs outlining the gruesome list of confirmed Klan activities, the Grand Jury has this to say about the KKK:

> It is founded on the worst instincts of mankind. At its best, it is intolerant and bigoted. At its worst, it is sadistic and brutal. Between these two poles it has its existence.
>
> Out of the wells of prejudice, it draws its inspiration. It is a foul pollution in the body politic. It is a cancerous growth that will not be cured until the hand of every decent man is raised against it and the whole power of the law is marshaled to stamp it out.

At the tail end of the story, buried at the bottom of page 10, are the three sentences that quickly become the talk of Mayflower:

> The jury revealed for the first time that two years before the Moore murders, a floor plan of the Moore house was exhibited at a meeting of a Central Florida klavern. The report stated, too, that newspaper clippings of Moore's activities were read at klavern meetings and that mention of him was made on other occasions and in other places. The jury said the Central Florida klaverns were "known to have a malevolent interest in Moore."

Chapter 35

Doto stands on the back porch, inhaling the warm May air.

"What a beautiful day!" she calls into the kitchen. "Why not have Sunday dinner out here?"

"Why not?" Mother calls back. "Reesa, will you set the picnic table, please?"

Doto and I wipe down the backyard table and chairs. She helps me spread the cloth and place the plates, glasses, napkins and flatware. While Mother calls Daddy and the boys to dinner, Doto and I carry the platters and bowls outside to the shaded backyard: pork chops fragrant with rosemary, mashed potatoes and brown gravy, fresh green beans and applesauce.

"It's dinner-on-the-grounds just for us!" Mitchell crows, his blond buzzed head aglow in the sunlight.

We gobble up our food, gab about the Sunday service. Ren reports that the Dodgers' best pitcher, big Don Newcombe, has been drafted into the army and is on his way to Korea. Doto praises Mitchell for his much-improved table manners. As we sit sipping the last of our tea, we hear, then see, Luther's old Dodge at the head of the driveway.

He and Armetta get out of the car, still in their church clothes.

"Well, ain't y'all a picture?" he calls, smiling. "Enjoyin' this pretty Sunday?"

"Sure are," Daddy calls back. "Ren, pull those lawn chairs over here for Luther and Armetta. You two eaten?"

"Jus' finished." Luther patts his belt buckle.

"Had a potluck with the choir," Armetta says, sitting down in the shade. "Lord, was it good!"

"The choir?" Daddy asks, looking curious. "Any gossip from the good ladies of the C.I.A.?"

"Actually, that's why we've come." Luther accepts the glass of tea that Mother's poured for him. "Somethin' pretty important," he says, leaning forward. "Y'all know the Gran' Jury's out on recess, which means the Klanners have come home for a few days. There's been a bunch of little parties and barbecues for 'em which, of course, the ladies have prepared."

Armetta looks around and tugs her chair closer to the table. "Mist' Warren, the question everyone's been chewin' on is 'Who stole the record books with the clippin's and the floor plan and gave 'em to the F.B.I.?' They've been 'round and 'round, tryin' to figure it out. Middle of last week, one of the men remembered somethin'. Somethin' about the men shootin' at some chil'ren and the fathers bein' fit to be tied about it. The talk's been all over Mistuh Emmett about who that was and could they be the one?"

Daddy leans forward, elbows on the table, resting his chin on his upright, folded hands. His jaw's gone concrete.

"The Klan's been chewin' on it all weekend, talkin'

amongst theyselves. They've ruled out the other boy's father; Mistuh Emmett says Mistuh Smitty'd never have the *nerve*. They've decided, well, what they're *sayin'* is, since you're a Yankee, and mad and smart enough to pull it off, they thinkin' it was *you*. . . ."

"What's that mean?" The sun glints off Doto's cat-eye glasses.

"Well, not much, we thought," Luther says. "With as much trouble as they in already, we figured they wouldn't dare try anythin' else . . ."

"But?" Daddy, his face still expressionless, eyes Armetta.

Inside, I feel a trapdoor open and my stomach fall through it.

"But," she says, "last night, Polly—she works for Miz Hannah Garnet, Mistuh Reed's mamma—Polly heard Mistuh Reed talkin' to Mistuh Emmett about 'callin' out the Klavaliers.' "

"What are the Klavaliers?" Mother's hand reaches over to curl under Daddy's arm.

"That's a Klan term for the men who jump you with axe handles and ball bats," Luther says quietly. Daddy draws a breath.

"Mistuh Emmett said *no*, it was time to *lay low*, but Mistuh Reed said he'd already called 'a couple of the O'landah boys, just a little walk and talk.' "

"Which *means*," Luther says, "a little rough stuff but no killing."

"Are you saying the Klan's coming after Warren?" Doto blazes.

"I'm sayin' there's *talk*," Luther tells her.

"What can we do?" Mother's face is drained of color.

"You can pack up and leave *right now*," Doto replies

firmly. "Take a vacation, a *long* one. You said you had a pretty good winter, you can afford it. If you can't, *I'll* pay!"

"It's not that, Doto," Daddy says calmly. He squeezes Mother's hand. "If we turn tail and run, the Klan'll make sure we have nothing to come back for. We can't afford to lose *everything*."

I hold my breath.

After a moment, Mother straightens, squaring her shoulders. "Luther, Armetta, you know these men better than we do. What do you suggest?"

Luther leans in, hands on his thighs. "Well, Ah'll *tell* you: Ah know you have a scatter gun," he says to Daddy. "Load it and take it with you wherever you go. Take the dog, too," he says, pointing at Buddy. "These things tend to happen at night, so don't go out unless you absolutely have to. If you do go out, go as a fam'ly, never alone. The Klanners think of theyselves as Southern gentlemen. They don't usually attack a white man in front of his wife or chil'ren."

"This is *abominable*!" Doto fumes, fire in her eyes. "I'm hiring some security guards. If we can't find them local, I'll get some Pinkertons down here from Chicago, armed to the *teeth*!"

"No, Doto, no," Daddy tells her quietly. "It's probably just talk. And, if it isn't, we'll deal with it ourselves."

"Mist'Warren, MizLizbeth, Ah'm sorry to spoil your Sunday dinner like this," Luther says gently, "but Ah told Armetta you'd want to know right away."

"You were absolutely right," Daddy tells them both. "Thank you, and *please* thank the ladies for their help."

So begins my family's final nightmare.

Chapter 36

Since the first of the year, my friend Vaylie's postcards reveal that her father's "spells" have gotten more frequent. She's been "on tour" more often than not—to Savannah, Plymouth Rock and Cape Cod, Charleston, South Carolina, and last month, Quebec, Canada. I'm delighted when, at last, an envelope containing a real letter arrives:

> *Dear Reesa,*
>
> *I'm sorry it's been so long since I wrote you. As you can tell from my postcards, Mamma and I have been away, a __lot__! The bad news is, no matter how hard I've tried to keep up, I've already flunked seventh grade and will have to repeat it. The __good__ news is Daddy's gone to live in a sanatorium and we get to stay home.*
>
> *How this came about is a very long*

story. I'll give you the short version: With Mamma and me out of town so much, Daddy's mamma had to deal with him a whole lot more than usual. After he wrecked her car, stumbled into church drunk, and got mad enough one day to shoot my horse, his mamma decided he might have a problem after all. She got the best doctors in Richmond and Washington, D.C., to examine him. All of them said the same thing: Daddy's a "manic depressive," which means when he has a bad spell, he's completely out of control. (Somehow, my daddy's mamma believed the doctors over what Mamma and me have been trying to tell her for years.)

The sanatorium is just as nice as can be. You'd never know it was a nut house for rich people. Mamma and I visit him every Saturday, and Whit and Claudette go three times a week. With his medicine and the "treatments" (I think they shoot electricity into his head, but nobody will tell me for sure), Daddy seems to be pretty happy. Once a week, on Sundays, if the doctors say he's been good, his mamma takes him out to her horse farm. He loves to watch the horses run, seems to have forgotten what he did to mine.

Mamma seems much happier, too. She's stopped taking her nerve pills and is starting to look and act like her old self again.

As for me, I have to thank you for that letter you wrote me, sitting in your tree. I carry it with me wherever we go, and read it whenever I feel really bad. Thanks to you, I never gave up hope. Because you believed in me, I figured I was honor-bound to believe in myself. My new tutor, Mrs. Bradford, says that if I work extra hard, there's a slight chance I might catch up with my old classmates. I KNOW I can do it, Reesa. My luck, like the tide, has turned!

Love, VAYLIE

Dear Vaylie,

I was so glad to get your letter and to hear you're home for good! I'm sorry about your daddy, though, and about what he did to your horse. It must have been awful for you.

Do you like your surprise? It's a rattler skin, of course. One of your "cousins" shed it in the scrub behind the old sinkhole. It means he's grown a brand new skin, with one more rattle on his tail to boot. When I found it, it reminded me of you, of all you've been through, and how you've made it through without losing your way.

Oh, Vaylie, I wish I could say the same for me.

Things are as bad as they can be here, and getting worse. And, I can't begin to see a way to wiggle our way out.

What's happened is this: My father got involved with the Federal Bureau of Investigation, helping them find out who killed the colored couple, Mr. and Mrs. Harry Moore. It was the Klan, of course. Everybody knew it. But not a single white person was willing to do anything about it—except Daddy. What he did was a good thing, the absolute right thing to do. But now the Klan's found out about it. And we hear they're sending some men after him to get even.

Vaylie, there's not another person in the world I can tell this to: I'm as scared as I can be. My parents try to act as if everything's okay, but I know it's not. I can see in their eyes that they're scared, too. Worse yet, so's my grandmother, Doto, and she's never been afraid of anything in her life!

The worst thing, Vaylie, is the upside-downness, the inside-outness of things. Like the crazy people rule the world and they're after us because we're *not* nuts. For the first time, I understand why your mother took you on tour so much. I wish somebody would take us out of here until everything's over.

But that's not my parents' way. "We'll get through this,"

they say, and I wish I could believe them. But the truth is, I'm not sure who, or what, to believe right now.

I don't know if you're a praying person, Vaylie. We've never really talked about it. But if you are, please, please, please, put an extra word in for my family, and for me.

Your tried and true friend, Reesa

Chapter 37

There's just no describing the infinite difference between everyday life lived unawares and the agony of keeping watch for strange men who want to hunt and hurt your father.

It's the little things that loom largest: the lock on the back door that hasn't worked for years and *who knows* where the key is anyway; the after-dark carton of milk that normally Daddy would run and get, turned into an awkward family outing; the two-minute drive between church and home, after Wednesday night's choir practice, now too risky to be taken alone; the swishing sound outside, maybe not the wind rustling the palmettos.

Nights especially last an eternity. Somehow, my family gets through them, avoiding the obvious with small, coded conversations and polite I-don't-mind alterations in long-established routines:

Doto, the queen of hot fudge sundaes, gives up her favorite dessert rather than have Daddy risk an after-supper run to Mr. Voight's freezer section. And she seems to have a huge amount of paperwork which keeps her at her post on the front porch whenever we're home.

Mother, who hasn't sung in the choir for years, rejoins the sopranos in the second row. She rides to and from practice with Daddy, and Buddy stands sentry, tied to the choir loft door.

Buddy, who's spent most of his life sleeping in my room, moves, at my suggestion, to the rug at the foot of my parents' bed.

Ren and I keep an eye out for anything, everything the least bit out of the ordinary. And Mitchell wears his cowboy six-shooters everywhere, "in case," he tells us, "the bad guys come."

Just before Memorial Day, the Grand Jury, having reconvened its proceedings in Miami, hands down its indictments.

Seven men from our area are ordered to surrender on June nineteenth for arraignment before the Federal District Court. Starved for resolution, I gobble up the details of the *Miami Herald* story:

> They were charged with lying under oath when they denied to the grand jury that they were members of the Ku Klux Klan, or that they took part in a series of violent acts in Central Florida from 1949 to 1952.

J. D. Bowman leads the list of those indicted! The charges against them range from denying membership in the Klan to denying involvement in a number of incidents, including the attempted abduction of two N.A.A.C.P. lawyers and two Negro reporters, the beating of a local Negro for union activities, the flogging of another and the burning of a shack occupied by a man accused of molesting small girls.

When Daddy reads the article, he tells me, "It's important to note that they're *not* being charged for actually *committing* the crimes, but for *lying* about them to the Grand Jury, Reesa. There's your lesson in the difference between state and federal jurisdiction."

Justice, by a thin thread called perjury, has been served. Even though the indictments carry no direct mention of Marvin or the Moores, it seems that, at least, *right* has won out. After weeks of self-enforced confinement, the need to celebrate pushes my family out of the house.

We pile into Mother's station wagon, Buddy in the back, and drive to Orlando and the new Ronnie's Restaurant for hamburgers and ice-cream sodas all around. The evening floats, light, optimistic, party-like, until Doto suggests that "now that this is over, I can think about heading home." The boys and I howl in protest.

On our way home, my brothers fall asleep against Doto in the back seat; Mother and I remain alert, out of habit, in the front. We enjoy the night, the familiar sights, as Daddy wheels north up the Trail, onto Old Dixie and into our driveway.

Halfway in, however, Mother hisses, "Warren, *stop the car!*"

Chapter 38

Hands fly out in front of me as Daddy hits the brakes and Mother cries, "*There*, behind the palmetto."

From the floor of the back seat, the boys elbow their way up sleepily, asking, "Whuh? Whuh's that?"

"Shhhh!" Daddy flicks the headlights to bright. There, in the narrow space below the big palmetto beside our walkway, are two pairs of dark pantlegs with heavy boots.

Daddy slides his shotgun from under the seat, says softly, "Doto, on the count of three, open your door and lean to the right. Buddy's coming through."

"One, two, *three*!" As his door and Doto's fly open, front and back, Daddy yells, "*Get 'em*, Buddy, *get* 'em!"

Buddy bounds over the back seat, out Doto's door and tears up the driveway, barking like a banshee. Two men appear in the shadows, running, axe handles in hand. Daddy springs to the front of the car, carrying his shotgun, and rests an arm on the hood to steady his aim. I hear the small click as he releases the safety. Panic yanks me to the dash.

"Buddy," I cry. "Don't shoot Buddy!"

Suddenly, one of the men, shorter, gray-haired, stumbles on a tree root and falls. Grabbing his ankle, he turns and freezes in our headlights, a grizzly face pinched in pain.

Buddy closes in, snarling. I gasp as the other man slams Buddy's head with his axe handle and yanks his partner to his feet. Buddy collapses, yelping, on the drive.

Without a word, with both men clearly in his sights, Daddy slowly shifts his aim up, above their heads, and fires both barrels into the night.

We watch them run, three-legged, away from us and around the car barn in the back. Buddy staggers to his feet, still whimpering in pain, and runs after them.

In a blur, Daddy hurls himself back into his seat, dropping the shotgun onto the floorboard, and jabs the car into gear, engine racing, up to the house.

"Quick, quick, quick!" he hollers, yanking arms, elbows, and Mitchell's whole body up the walk, across the porch and into the living room, away from outside doors and windows.

Ren and Mitchell sit stunned on the sofa. I perch, numb, on the arm of Daddy's chair. The adults race around the house checking locks and latches, crimping curtains, tucking blinds to seal out the night.

"Warren," Doto blazes on the porch, "you had a clean shot! *Why* didn't you take it?"

"I had two thoughts . . ." Daddy tells her flatly. "If I took the shot, I'd've killed them. If I'd killed them, the Klan would kill me, probably before I made it to Orlando to report the crime. Where would that leave Lizbeth and the kids?"

"Oh, Warren, what *now*?" Mother whispers. I've never seen her so pale.

Outside, somewhere in the back grove, an engine roars to life and recedes. Buddy's hoarse bark turns into the howl that usually means whoever was here has left.

I shoot to my feet without thinking and run to the back door.

Daddy joins me and whistles for him from the porch. We hear his woof acknowledging the whistle. Then Buddy, tags jangling, tail wagging raggedly, limps out of the darkness.

"Good boy!" I say and drop down to pet and hug him. At my touch, Buddy yelps in pain.

Daddy moves in to inspect the bump on Buddy's head, the gash on his shoulder and his apparently tender rib cage. "He's bruised pretty bad," Daddy tells me, "but nothing appears to be broken."

What kind of monster beats a dog with an axe handle? I want to rage, but the truth hits me, Buddy was not their intended target. And an even more awful idea follows: *This is what they did to Marvin.*

"C'mon, honey," Daddy says softly as he leads Buddy and me back into the living room. "Those men are gone and there's nothing more to do about it tonight. How about you kids watch a little television before you go to bed?" He turns it on and switches channels to an old movie, James Cagney tap dancing in *Yankee Doodle Dandy*. "We'll be in the kitchen for a while," he says, as Mother and Doto trail him out of the room.

I fall back within a whirling chair, straining to hear them in the kitchen. They decide to leave the bright overhead light off "just in case." Their chairs scrape as they take their seats at the table. The talk is low-voiced, urgent. I know the topic is what do we do now. And, I can tell by their tones, they are *not* in agreement.

After half an hour or so, the boys have nodded off. My parents return to carry them upstairs, bidding Doto a strained goodnight. Without a word, my grandmother mounts the steps, heavily, to her room.

Mother comes down first to see me off to mine. Her face is still pale, her eyes overbright. Her fingers under my chin, as she tells me "Buddy will sleep with you tonight," are ice cold. When Daddy lets him in a few minutes later, calling softly "Goodnight, Rooster," Buddy curls with a heavy sigh in his old spot, beside my bed.

In their bedroom, I hear Mother and Daddy undress without a word. Then, for what seems like hours, I hear my parents argue in the night.

Daddy thinks Doto's right, Mother should take us home with her to Chicago. Nana's there, too, he says, she'll have plenty of help. Mother insists no, *that's* not her home, *this* is, and she won't leave him here alone. Back and forth, the argument goes: Daddy insisting, pleading, blazing, begging; Mother refusing, no matter *what* we will not go without him, she will not leave him or allow him, or Doto, or *anyone*, to split up our family. It would be like a death sentence. "These children need their father," she tells him and I hear in her voice, as he must, the pain of her own too-early loss.

My grandmother's pink sheets provide no refuge to me this night, as the very fabric of our lives stretches toward its breaking point. Everything I've ever known or valued seems to hang in the balance of my parents' argument.

Worry, like a vise, tightens my chest. *Please, God,* I think, unable even to whisper a prayer, *I've not been good at this faith thing, I don't even know the words. Please, please help us, help them, know what to do.*

Daddy's tried everything, every argument or approach he can think of; but the stronger-than-stone woman that is now my mother *is* not, *will* not be moved. Silence like a cavern sits between them until, at last, he gives into her. "All right," he tells her, "we'll get through this together."

"We survived the polio," she tells him, "we'll survive this. Somehow, you'll figure our way out."

I hear tears in their voices and, burying my head in the pillow, cry my own.

Next morning, at Mother's insistence, in the face of Doto's poorly masked exasperation, any discussion of what happens next is "tabled until further notice."

"Daddy needs time to think," Mother tells us.

It takes him a week.

Chapter 39

Ren and I watch him from under our eyelashes, ears open wide for a clue, a sign, some kind of indication as to what he's thinking.

He shows us the piece of dark cloth he pulled from Buddy's mouth, and we tag along after him as he checks the dirt beside the old car barn. We see the tracks where Buddy caught up to the men the second time. There's blood in the dirt where someone was bitten. One of the men dragged one foot behind the other. Daddy points out the tire tracks where they parked, and more where they drove off through the grove onto Wellwood Road.

Later, we see Daddy enter the car barn. Ren races outside, pretending to look for Buddy, and passes the door, peering slyly in.

"He's unlocked the chest where he keeps the dynamite and he's counting the sticks," Ren reports to me, winded, having run all the way around the house, through the front rooms, then back to my bedroom.

We hear him whistling for Buddy and from my room's window watch him stride, carrying the shotgun, into the grove behind the house. We follow him, as quiet as we can, and find him standing at the outer edge of Dry Sink, staring into the hole's old, dried-up center as if there was something there to see. We try to sneak back before he sees us, but Buddy sniffs us out, tail wagging and barking. Daddy scowls when he sees us and tells us to "go home."

We ride with him in his truck, aware that he slows unnecessarily as we pass Carney's Coffee Shop, where Emmett Casselton and a few other Klansmen meet for breakfast.

In the morning, while we get ready for school, Daddy sits at the piano playing slow, quiet songs I've never heard before. He's playing them from memory, without sheet music.

At supper, he seems himself. But afterwards, instead of joining us in the living room, he sits in the dark on the porch, sometimes front, sometimes back, cradling the shotgun with one arm, scratching Buddy's ears with the other, staring off into the night.

Luther drops by twice, but not to see us. He and Daddy sit together on the pitch-dark porch, talking. We're not allowed to interrupt.

The waiting, the not-knowing grates on Ren. He argues about stupid, long-settled things: who sits where on the sofa, who clears the table, who bathes the dog. He picks on me and gets nowhere, then turns on Mitchell and makes him cry, which brings the wrath of Doto down instantly on both of them.

On her part, Mother's mostly quiet. I watch for the signs of her slipping away from us, but she's surprisingly peaceful and still present. Her belief that Daddy will "find our way out" shields us from Doto's darker doubts. My grandmother's not talking. But her face, when she thinks we're not looking, says volumes.

My habit over these days has been to escape to the shelter of the old tree beside the sinkhole, or, after supper, the privacy of my room. I have the oddest memory from the other night, after the men left and my parents argued and decided to stay together. I heard something inside my head. A sort of whisper—not by my parents, not by me. But clearly: *Be still and know*, the whisper said. These four words, half of a half-forgotten Bible verse, hum inside my head—not singsong, more like a circle—*Be still and know*, the circle says. And somehow, it helps.

Today, I've climbed the old tree higher than I've been in years, past my favorite limb shaped like a hammock, past the heart carved in the trunk, up into the newer, younger branches where the tree spreads out below me as if upended. The sky has flattened from a bright blue bowl into a pale gray plate. Charcoal thunderclouds crowd its rim. Rain falls in a smoky river from the sky onto the palmetto flats east of here. South toward Opalakee, patches of blue show through breaks in the cloud cover. And there in the west, sunlight pours through a great wide crack; slanting columns of light turning the grove tops glittering emerald.

This patchwork sky suddenly reminds me of my family: Doto's stormy doubts, Ren's rainy anxiety, and Mother's shining faith in Daddy's bright promise. All of us appear so different. Yet we're stitched together in a crazy quilt, draped across the blueness that shields us from the black beyond.

It's the blueness that gets me. Vast enough to create and sustain this bowl brimming with life, rimmed with death;

bright with sunlight, dark with rain. It's the blueness I feel, coursing like a river through this tree and me, from wherever I came from, to wherever Marvin went. Not a driving force. But a pull, like a magnet, that knows the way from here to that place where all things end, and begin again.

Is this, I wonder, sitting perfectly still, *is this what the whisper in the dark wanted me to know?*

O n Saturday morning, Daddy stops me on my way out the back door to the big oak. "Find Ren," he says, "and meet me in the truck."

Chapter 40

I sit on the truck seat beside Ren, wondering what's next, watching my parents. Daddy walks Mother to the station wagon, opens the door for her, closes it after she slides in. He leans in and kisses her, not in the usual way, but longer. She starts her engine, backs out and drives away. Daddy walks toward us carrying his shotgun.

"This is it, boys and girls," Daddy says as he climbs into the truck, and lays the gun across our laps. "Reesa, Ren, I know this has been hard, not knowing what's going on, but your mother and I decided it was best. After today, hopefully, it'll all be over. We'll get our lives back on track."

"What are you going to do?" Ren asks him, quietly, man-to-man.

"What *we* are going to do is have a chat with the Exalted Cyklops. We all have a part in this. Let me tell you yours."

W hen Daddy, Ren and I drive by the coffee shop, we see them clearly, in the corner where they always sit. As our truck passes, one of them stands up with the check in his hand and walks to the cash register, pulling out his wallet.

"Good," Daddy murmurs, wheeling the truck left to circle the block.

When we pull up again, I see Mother's station wagon parked at Voight's across the street. She's sitting behind the steering wheel, but none of us wave. On the opposite corner, Luther stands talking to Miz Lillian, looking at the half-dozen citrus trees in front of her beauty parlor as if they're discussing a pruning job.

Daddy's timed it perfectly. Two of the men have left the coffee shop and are driving away. Emmett Casselton, moving slower, stands beside his truck. The gold lettering of Casbash Groves on the door glitters in the sun.

Daddy pulls in crosswise behind him. As Mr. Casselton looks up, Daddy says evenly, "Good morning, Emmett. Might I have a word?"

Emmett Casselton's eyes rake over Daddy, then Ren, then me last. His weathered face is expressionless but his pale, lashless eyes show a hint of surprise. He plants his feet, folds his arms across his chest, then he nods.

Daddy opens the door and gets out. Emmett Casselton's alligator eyes take in the shotgun pointing out, across Ren's lap and mine. He doesn't blink. *He's not a monster, he's a man, same as me*, Daddy had told us.

"Had a visit from your friends the other night," Daddy tells Mr. Casselton. "Unfortunately, their stay was cut a little short."

Emmett Casselton doesn't move, except for the tiniest squint.

"The way I see it, Emmett," Daddy says, "your men started this thing when they fired on my son. Take a look at his head and you'll see he was about two hairs shy of losing an eye."

As the older man shifts his pale stare to Ren, my brother stares back. His summer-buzzed head shows the trail of red welts from his eye to his ear.

"You can't tell me you wouldn't have done the same as I did, or worse, if someone took a shot at your flesh and blood."

Daddy waits to let his argument sink in. I watch the old man for some sign of agreement. Without changing his expression, Emmett Casselton drops his chin, a definite nod for Daddy to *go on*.

"At that point, I would've called us even, but clearly you didn't agree. You sent those Klavaliers after me. Which unfortunately, Emmett, makes it *my* turn."

Daddy takes a step closer and drops his tone. "I know a few things, Emmett. For instance, I know for a fact that the F.B.I. took all your dynamite. But they didn't take mine. I've got *plenty*, more than enough to blow one, maybe two buildings sky-high. There's your fishing camp, of course. And there's the building you own in downtown Opalakee. And I know you have a warehouse over on Votah Road. What I *thought*, Emmett, is since you went and made it my turn . . . you might help me decide."

Emmett Casselton's eyes drill into Daddy, who doesn't flinch a bit. "You threatenin' me, McMahon?"

"Oh, no, not at all. But you're the Exalted Cyklops, aren't you? The big decision-maker, right? Who better to help decide where we go from here?" Daddy asks.

"Where would you like us to go?"

"Well, that depends on you . . . Emmett. Other people seek your counsel, so do I."

"You askin' me to pick?"

"I'm asking your opinion, looking for advice. You could say here or there. Or, you could suggest something else entirely."

"Entirely what?"

"Well, you could surprise me by suggesting we declare this thing over, right here, right now. We could make an agreement that it's ended. Of course, I'd want your word on it, as a gentleman. You give me yours, I'll give you mine. Then we'd both be done with this."

Old Emmett Casselton stares at Daddy for forever. I realize I'm holding my breath, and when I let it out in a loud hiss, Ren glares at me. Daddy stands steady, ready for anything.

"What guarantee do I have that you'll keep yours?" Emmett Casselton asks.

"I figured you might have a problem with the word of a Yankee. I could arrange to deliver you a guarantee in . . . well, let's say fifteen minutes? If you'd wait right here, I could do that."

"What kind of guarantee?"

"You have to trust me on that, Emmett. Do we have a deal or not?" Daddy asks.

Emmett Casselton's eyes troll over the parking lot. They flicker to Ren and me and the shotgun. They slide back to Daddy standing firmly, legs wide apart. I try to breathe slow and stay calm, like Daddy told me. But inside I'm churning like Mother's Maytag.

A lifetime later, Emmett Casselton slowly, deliberately,

extends a bony hand with enormous black freckles. My head spins as the two men clasp and shake each other's hand.

Without another word, Daddy turns to the truck. He gets in beside Ren, closes the door and starts the engine. As he leans with his right hand to shift into first, he lifts his left wrist out the window, indicating his watch. "Fifteen minutes," he nods to the man standing by his truck.

We exit the parking lot, glancing at Mother in her car across the street, then turn off the Trail toward the Old Dixie Highway and home. Passing Luther and Miz Lillian, Daddy lifts just the first two fingers of his right hand up off the steering wheel, in Marvin's "V-for-Victory" sign. At the house, we head down the driveway, past the car barn, onto the dirt road that leads to the lower grove. Luther's old Dodge appears behind us.

Together we walk into the clearing that surrounds the old sinkhole. Doto and Mitchell stand in the deep, dry center, beside Mitchell's red Christmas wagon.

"So far, so good," Daddy says as he and Luther unload the dynamite onto the dirt. "Wait a minute, Doto, we're missing some. Where are they?"

"We left them in the car barn," Mitchell says proudly.

"Just in case," Doto adds, with a defiant look.

"In case of what?" Daddy asks, carefully stacking the sticks.

"In case your Southern gentleman turns out to be a scalawag," she shoots back.

"Doto," Daddy eyes her, "I had no idea you could be so suspicious." He and Luther twist the fuse strings into two separate cords. "How's our time, Roo?"

"Four minutes," I say, checking the watch he'd handed me in the truck.

"Okay, grab the wagon and head for the hills," Daddy

tells us, pulling a lighter out of his pocket. "Way over there, sit down behind the truck."

"Is that far enough?" Doto asks. "Are you sure the children will be safe?"

"They'll be fine, Miz Doto," Luther tells her. His lighter is out too.

"Sit down, on the ground," Daddy calls as we run across the clearing. He waits until we disappear behind the truck.

"All set over there?" Daddy yells.

"Okay," Doto hollers back.

We duck and watch between the wheels as Daddy and Luther light the extended fuse cords, then run our way. They squat down beside us; Daddy quickly, quietly counting seconds. I hold up the watch and one finger, for one minute remaining. It's been fourteen minutes since we left the coffee shop. Daddy keeps counting: seven-one thousand, six. We cover our ears and join him, mouthing five . . . four . . . three . . . two . . .

The blast of the dynamite rocks Daddy's truck like the floor of a fun house. The noise is loud beyond anything I've ever heard. Dirt clods fly above us, raining dust and dirt and small stones onto the truck, the trees. Later, we learn they heard it in Wellwood three miles north, and five miles south in downtown Opalakee. It rattled the shopping carts in Mr. Voight's grocery store and rang the church bell at St. John's A.M.E. But now we wait and watch for Mother.

We hear her wagon and at last I see her, stumbling through the dust.

"What'd he do?" Luther asks her anxiously.

"He *waited*," she answers. "Stood there, staring at his boots, and once in a while checked his watch. It was fifteen minutes *exactly* when we heard it. People came running out of everywhere, Voight's, Carney's, Lillian's, yelling 'What was that?' "

"And Emmett?" Daddy asks her.

"Stood there for a second or two," Mother says, "then threw back his head and laughed."

"He laughed?" Luther says, smiling.

"Yes, he did." Mother's grinning back at him.

"Laughing's good?" Doto asks, still shaken by the blast.

"Believe it or not, Doto, it's *great*," Daddy says, tracing a smile onto Mitchell's dirty face.

"Warren?" Mother's eyeing the thick fog of dust on the other side of the truck. "Is there anything left of our grove?"

"I think it's safe to take a look," he replies.

We stand up and peer over the truck bed into the mist where the clearing should be. That's when I hear it. Over the sound of dust softly sifting down through the trees, there's a sudden upward rush of . . .

"Warren?" Mother says, uncertainly.

But Daddy doesn't answer. He grabs her hand, pulling her around the truck and through the trees that rim the old sinkhole. The rest of us plunge after them into the dust-clouded clearing.

We hear it first. Then, pressing closer, we see it. In the center of a sinkhole that's been dead dry for thirty years, where minutes before Daddy and Luther stacked and lit our sticks of dynamite, a fountain of fresh water gushes up and onto the earth.

Water glitters and sparkles and splashes onto us. I reach out my hands to catch it, icy cold against my palms. I form a cup to drink it, surprised by the sharp taste of rocks and leaves and the roots of old trees. I stand in wonder as the underground river somewhere deep beneath my feet, released, rushes up to greet the treetops. High above my head, all the colors, Genesis through Jude, arc across the blue, blue sky.

Revelations

The seven local Klansmen who were indicted by the Grand Jury found a friend in
Federal Judge George W. Whitehurst. In
December 1953, the judge granted their
motion to quash the indictments because,
he said, "the Federal Grand Jury has no
jurisdiction to investigate the acts about
which the suspects allegedly lied." The
Klansmen walked free.

But long before the men returned quietly to Opalakee, it was clear, in the days,
weeks, and months that followed the blast
in our back grove, that Emmett Casselton
was a man of his word. The Opalakee Klan
not only left my family alone, it left the
rest of the community, black and white,
alone as well.

Some people said the Klan disbanded
because of Emmett Casselton's say-so. "The
old man got tired of it," they claimed, and after all, he was the Exalted Cyklops *and* the
area's largest and most powerful employer.

I liked the version Armetta came up with better, that it was the *wives* and *mothers* of the Klansmen who decided they'd had enough of the Invisible Empire. "No more late-night meetings at the fishing camp," "no more political rallies downtown," "no more white robes in and out of the dry cleaners," the women told their men, eager to shore up what little social equity remained in the fine old names that had been "dragged through the mud." Somebody heard one ex-Klansmen joke "the Gran' Jury was nothin' compared to my wife."

Years later, I heard a third version. I was in law school then and had driven home for Miss Maybelle Mason's funeral service. Old Miz Sooky Turnbull, the ancient gardener, her face powdery and pocked like a huge potato, told me, "Y'know, Marie Louise, after that big boom behind your house, Maybelle marched right over to Casbah Groves warehouse, told Ol' Emmett she'd got *wind* of his shenanigans. Told him if the Klan harmed so much as another *hair* on your brother's head, or anyone else's for that matter, she'd report certain rather *large* discrepancies in Casbah Groves' Railway Express waybills to the I.R.S.! Y'know, Maybelle moonlighted as bookkeeper for the R.E.A. station for *years*. She told Emmett if he didn't think she'd do it, he had another *think* comin'. For some reason, Maybelle thought *the world* of your brother and you," Miz Sooky said.

"Imagine that," I said, sorting my memories of Miss Maybelle and Miz Sooky like suits in a Bridge hand, hearts from spades, diamonds from clubs.

Not long after Daddy and Emmett Casselton's gentlemen's agreement, the fishing camp in the middle of the lake became just that.

The children of The Quarters returned to the communal

fun of "hide-and-whoop," "chick-mah-chick," and other favorite out-in-the-street games. After nearly sixteen months of
having to hover near their houses since Marvin's death, they
relished their restored freedoms.

My brothers and I and the Samson boys dove in, literally,
to new games of our own made possible by the disappearance
of Dry Sink beneath the surface of the resurrected Little Lake
Annie. Once again, as Miss Maybelle had claimed happened
so long ago, kids leaped from the big limbs of the giant live
oak and swung from ropes into the clear, ice-cold, spring-fed
swimming hole.

One day, I invited Miss Maybelle to come see for herself
the little lake. And she did, too, walking stiffly through the
grove after work, in her sensible shoes and crisp gray-blue
postmistress uniform. She stood outside the range of our wild
splashes, arms folded over her chest, shaking her head from
time to time.

When I swam over to her and got out of the water to ask
what she thought, I noticed two things:

The first was that sometime over that summer, either I'd
grown or she'd shrunk, but now we stood eye-to-eye and I
wondered at the reasons I'd spent so many years *aggravated* by
this little old lady.

The second thing I saw was that, instead of looking at the
lake and the boys' high jinks, her attention had drifted to the
giant live oak. I followed her gaze up the huge trunk, then I
turned to her and said, "It's still up there, Miss Maybelle."
She looked at me sharply, but I didn't cower under her gaze as
I might have.

"What's still there, Reesa?" she asked.

"The heart carved into the trunk. It's still there, about
two-thirds of the way up."

Miss Maybelle's eyes slipped away from mine and lingered on the old tree. Her face gave up a shy smile. "Imagine that," she said.

I n the years that followed 1952, before I left Florida for good, a number of curious things happened on a nearly regular basis:

People came to our house. The hesitant tap, never a knock, after supper or before breakfast, announced their need. And, for quite some time, their location, front or back, told us their color. I know Daddy never directed anyone to our front or back door. They sorted themselves, according to their custom.

He wasn't a minister, a lawyer or a psychologist, yet somehow my father became chief counselor to Mayflower's downtrodden. Sometimes it was a letter in need of reading or writing, or a legal form, or a government notice. A man from church in shock over the receipt of "divorce papers," a young woman from The Quarters heading north to Detroit, or a couple having difficulty collecting on a relative's insurance.

The people at both doors trusted my father to help them sort things out, decide what to do. No money was ever offered or expected, nor would it have been accepted. He simply gave them a few minutes of careful listening, some logical, intuitive counsel and an occasional investigative phone call to the proper authority.

And they thanked him in ways they felt appropriate. To those same porches, front or back, they delivered a crate of just-picked white corn, a fresh-baked peach pie, a half-dozen jars of homemade rhubarb jam, and, once, a lactating nanny goat for the child (my little brother Mitchell) who developed an allergy to cow's milk. We were no longer strangers in the strange land we called home.

Another curious thing involved the ladies of Luther's "C.I.A.," our guardian angels who, for their own various reasons, we never came to know. There were many, many black women who worked in the homes of white people in Opalakee, Mayflower and Wellwood. I'd see them all over in their white, pink or pale gray uniforms walking down a road, sitting on a park bench, or waiting patiently for the bus.

Privately, I'd wonder, "Was *she* one of them?" "How about *her*?"

"I wish I knew," Daddy would say, "I'd like to thank each and every one for their help."

One day, Daddy and I were out riding in his pickup truck, the name of our family business brightly emblazoned on both sides. An older maid in a white uniform and thick-soled shoes sat alone on the green wood bench that was her bus stop, both hands resting on top of the big black purse in her lap.

Daddy and I saw *her*, and obviously, she saw *us*. The question ("Could *she* be one of them?") so prominent in our minds must have shown up on our faces. She looked at us squarely, crinkled her eyes, and ever so slowly raised two fingers of her right hand off her purse top, into the "V-for-Victory" that was Marvin's special sign.

Daddy smiled the wide ear-to-ear grin he was known for and nodded his acknowledgment. She did the same, in a secret, silent ritual that was to be repeated by so many other hardworking black women, again and again, for many years.

I will never forget that first exchange of signs and smiles. It was, for me, an homage to the exceptional dignity and grace of my heart's first and unforgettable best friend. Although Marvin Cully died horribly years ago, he will live for-ever, for me, in the hope-beyond-hope of his parents and oth-ers turned luminous by "time in the fire," in the free flight of a honeybee and the whippoorwill's insistent first call to spring.

It was Marvin, I remember whenever I smell orange blos-soms, who showed me my stripes and gave me his wings.

Epilogue

Revised March 27, 2007

The March 1951 murder of central Florida citrus picker Melvin Womack (whose death inspired the fictional life of Marvin Cully) was never officially investigated. His killers have never been named.

The assassination of Harry T. and Harriette V. Moore in Florida, four years before the Montgomery bus boycott, twelve years before Medgar Evers' murder in Mississippi and seventeen years before the killing of Martin Luther King in Memphis, made them America's first Civil Rights leaders to fall in the contemporary fight for equality. For well over five decades, their senseless killing—explored by a Federal Grand Jury in 1952, by Geraldo Rivera in 1991 and again by the Florida Department of Law Enforcement in 1992—remained an unsolved mystery.

Upon its completion, the 3,000-page record of the Grand Jury's deliberations in Miami, along with twenty boxes of F.B.I. support files, were shipped to the State Attorney's Office and, by court order, sealed for forty years. When re-opened in 1991, they revealed that Agent "Jim Jameson" was also a man of his word.

Although the files clearly reference the Ku Klux Klan materials which my father, teen-aged "Robert" and clever old "Luther" liberated from the fishing camp, and which eagle-eyed "Armetta" helped identify, there is no mention of their names or of the secret circle of maids who, in a mutual, miraculous leap of faith, brought the walls of the "Opalakee" Klan tumbling down. Our celebrations of these things were small and quiet.

There were, however, loud Hallelujahs all around when, in October 1952, 1953 and 1955, Jackie Robinson and the Brooklyn Dodgers made it to the World Series. And, in 1955, finally brought home a victory, for all of us.

More recently, four years after the original publication of this book, there came another cause for celebration.

In early 2004, Florida's then Attorney General Charlie Crist (now Governor Crist) decided to re-open an investigation into the Christmas Day 1951 murders of Civil Rights pioneer Harry T. Moore and his wife Harriette. Twenty months later, on August 16, 2006, Crist announced:

"The investigation, led by the Attorney General's Office of Civil Rights in conjunction with the Florida Department of Law Enforcement (FDLE), points to extensive circumstantial evidence that the Moores were victims of a conspiracy by exceedingly violent members of a Central Florida Klavern of the Ku Klux Klan. Following extensive review of available information, more than 100 additional interviews, the most detailed excavation of the crime scene ever undertaken and extensive analysis, investigators concluded that at least four individuals are thought to be directly involved."

In the presence of Evangeline Moore, the Moores' only surviving daughter, Crist named the names of Earl J. Brooklyn, Tillman H. Belvin, Joseph N. Cox, and Edward L. Spivey. All four, deceased. All four, members of the Apopka (which I call "Opalakee") Klavern of the Florida Ku Klux Klan.

Others, closer to the case than I, have questioned Crist's motive and political timing—he was, after all, running for governor—and called his investigation "deeply flawed." Although many murky questions remain unanswered, I choose to focus on the shy, relieved smile of my dear friend Evangeline. She was twenty-one when she lost both her parents to the Klan's homegrown terror. She was seventy-one when I first contacted her to bless my efforts to tell the story of both our fathers. Now, at seventy-six, with her parents finally receiving the public acknowledgment and respect they were always due, Evangeline Moore is at peace. As to the murderers, Evangline says, "God has taken care of them, and they are resting in hell." Amen.

Author's Note

Every family has its stories. This one was my father's to tell. Anyone who knew my father and mother, or my paternal grandmother, will recognize the inspiration for Warren, Lizbeth and Doto. And anyone who lived through the period, or takes the time to research it, will note my efforts to render historical events and figures as real as I could.

However, this *is* a work of fiction. For two very important reasons, many of the principal and secondary characters—especially Reed Garnet, his wife and daughter, J. D. Bowman and his twin sons—are pure fiction with no resemblance or relation to anyone who ever lived. In the first place, I wasn't even born when bombs lit up the skies above Miami. In the second, the real Klansmen who roamed the back roads and groves of our area, including those who were indicted by the federal grand jury, have their own families and stories. Which are, of course, theirs to tell.

Acknowledgments

When I was in my mid-twenties, visiting relatives outside Chicago, my paternal grandmother overheard me tell someone, "I grew up in central Florida." Not long afterward, she pulled me aside. "Wild plants and animals—and some unfortunate children—simply grow up, Susan. *You* were *raised!* A whole lot of people invested a whole lot of time and effort in your upbringing. Don't deny them the credit they deserve for the way you turned out."

I turned out to be a writer. And credit for that is long overdue to a handful of teachers who, early on, insisted I take my writing and myself seriously. Thank you to Gladys Wilson, Aronelle Lofton, Sara Harvey, Janet Connelly and Myrtle Hubbard. Belated thanks also to the fistful of professionals who, later on, challenged me to write hard and fast (and paid me for the privilege of doing so): W. R. "Mac" McGuffin, publisher of my hometown newspaper; Wilson Flohr in Orlando, Alan Goldsmith in Atlanta, John VanderZee in San Francisco and Tom Sharrit in San Diego.

Of course, I might never have moved from point A (writing Advertising) to point B (attempting a Book) without the inspiration of Diane Dunaway and the San Diego Writers' Conference. And, I might not have finished the manuscript properly without the help of Elizabeth George and my fellow writers in her Masters' Class at the Maui Writers' Retreat.

From beginning to end, the reference departments of the local libraries in Carlsbad and Oceanside were a huge and constant help to me. The archivists at *The Miami Herald* and *The Orlando Sentinel* could not have been more patient or accommodating. Mr. Frank Meech, retired F.B.I. and one of the lead agents on the Moore murder case, was a generous and enjoyable source.

My book club read the early draft with insight and enthusiasm. And, afterward, became the best cheerleaders any writer could hope for. Bless you, Kathleen Bernard, Mary Blaskovich, Jan Brownell, Lindsey Cohn, Francie Droll, Rosemary Eshelman, Valerie Gilbert, Peggy Martinez, Kitty Meek, Debbie Moyer, Audrey Piper, Tricia Rowe, Monika Stout and Cris Weatherby. Also, Blye Phillips, my favorite contrarian who demanded, "Tension! I need more tension!"

Eternal gratitude to Lane Zachary for becoming my agent and my friend. Lane reads with an editor's eye and an artist's heart. She also, according to Bantam's Kate Miciak, "writes one of the best cover letters in the business." Kate is my editor. Everyone says Kate is brilliant and, in my experience, everyone's right. She's also fun, funny, and a writer's dream to work with. Kate connected me to the big, boisterous Bantam family who, sight unseen, embraced me as one of their own. Heartfelt thanks to attorney Matthew Martin, managing editor Anna Forgione, copyeditor Pat Crais, art director Jim Plumeri, and book designer Laurie Jewell, for your time and efforts on my behalf.

Thanks, above all . . . to my sister-friend Joanne who lent me her passion for baseball and the most patient ear possible. To my husband Paul and our sons, Travis and Connor, who made time and space in our lives "so Mom can write" and let no good news go uncelebrated. To my mother who provided liberal amounts of horticultural detail and maternal encouragement. And to my father. This project began as a present for Dad's seventy-fifth birthday. In the six months of almost daily long distance phone calls, discoveries, and heart-to-heart discussions before he died, it became, clearly, his gift to me. Thanks, Dad. You, more than anyone, get the credit for the way things turned out.

Susan Carol McCarthy
January 2001

About the Author

SUSAN CAROL McCARTHY was born and raised in central Florida. She lives in California and is also the author of *True Fires*.

Old Glory

Old Glory

A VOYAGE

DOWN

THE MISSISSIPPI

JONATHAN RABAN

VINTAGE DEPARTURES
Vintage Books
A Division of Random House, Inc.
New York

For Linda Taylor

FIRST VINTAGE DEPARTURES EDITION, JUNE 1998

Copyright © 1981 by Jonathan Raban

Grateful acknowledgment is hereby made to quote previously published material as follows:

Lines from the poem "The Dry Salvages" from *Four Quartets* by T.S. Eliot, copyright 1943 by Esme Valerie Eliot. Reprinted by permission of Harcourt Brace Jovanovich, Inc., for the U.S. and Faber and Faber Ltd., London, for Canada.
Song lyrics from "People" by Bob Merrill and Jule Styne, copyright © 1963, 1964 by Bob Merrill and Jule Styne. Chappell-Styne, Inc., and Wonderful Music Corp., owners of publication and allied rights throughout the world. Chappell & Co., Inc., sole and exclusive agent. International copyright secured, all rights reserved, used by permission.
Song lyrics from "Love Me Tender" by Elvis Presley and Vera Matson copyright © 1956 by Elvis Presley Music. All rights administered by Unichappell Music, Inc. (Rightsong Music, Publisher). International copyright secured, all rights reserved, used by permission. Song lyrics from "Second-Hand Rose" by Grant Clarke and James F. Hanley. Copyright © renewed by Fisher Music Corp.
Untitled poem by Gavin Ewart (*New Statesman*, 1979), used by permission of the author.

Library of Congress Cataloging-in-Publication Data
Raban, Jonathan.
Old Glory : a voyage down the Mississippi / Jonathan Raban.
p.   cm. — (Vintage departures)
Originally published: New York : Simon and Schuster, c1981.
ISBN 978-0-375-70100-9
1. Mississippi River—Description and travel. 2. Mississippi River Valley—Description and travel. 3. Raban, Jonathan—Journeys—Mississippi River. 4. Boats and boating—Mississippi River.
I. Title.
F355.R3   1998
917.704'33—dc21   98-11006
CIP

Author photograph © Jean Lenihan

Random House Web address: www.randomhouse.com

Printed in the United States of America

Contents

7

I do not know much about gods; but I think that the river
Is a strong brown god—sullen, untamed and intractable,
Patient to some degree, at first recognised as a frontier;
Useful, untrustworthy, as a conveyor of commerce;
Then only a problem confronting the builder of bridges.
The problem once solved, the brown god is almost forgotten
By the dwellers in cities—ever, however, implacable,
Keeping his seasons and rages, destroyer, reminder
Of what men choose to forget.

T. S. Eliot, *The Dry Salvages*

One man may paint a picture from a careful drawing made on the spot, and another may paint the same scene from memory, from a brief but strong impression; and the last may succeed better in giving the character, the physiognomy of the place, though all the details may be inexact.

J. F. Millet, on landscape
painting from memory

True and sincere travelling is no pastime but it is as serious as the grave, or any part of the human journey, and it requires a long probation to be broken into it.

H. D. Thoreau, *A Week on the Concord and Merrimack Rivers*

1

The River

*I**t is as* big and depthless as the sky itself. You can see the curve of
the earth on its surface as it stretches away for miles to the far
shore. Sunset has turned the water to the color of unripe peaches.
There's no wind. Sandbars and wooded islands stand on their exact
reflections. The only signs of movement on the water are the lightly
scratched lines which run in parallel across it like the scores of a diamond on a windowpane. In the middle distance, the river smokes with
toppling pillars of mist which soften the light so that one can almost
reach out and take in handfuls of that thickened air.

A fish jumps. The river shatters for a moment, then glazes over. The
forest which rims it is a long, looping smudge of charcoal. You could
make it by running your thumb along the top edge of the water, smearing in the black pines and bog oaks, breaking briefly to leave a pale
little town of painted clapboard houses tumbling from the side of a
hill. Somewhere in the picture there is the scissored silhouette of a
fisherman from the town, afloat between the islands in his wooden
pirogue, a perfectly solitary figure casting into what is left of the sun.

It is called the Mississippi, but it is more an imaginary river than a
real one. I had first read *Huckleberry Finn* when I was seven. The
picture on its cover, crudely drawn and colored, supplied me with the
raw material for an exquisite and recurrent daydream. It showed a boy
alone, his face prematurely wizened with experience. (The artist hadn't
risked his hand with the difficulties of bringing off a lifelike Nigger
Jim.) The sheet of water on which he drifted was immense, an enameled pool of lapis lazuli. Smoke from a half-hidden steamboat hung over

an island of Gothic conifers. Cut loose from the world, chewing on his corncob pipe, the boy was blissfully lost in this stillwater paradise.

For days I lay stretched out on the floor of my attic room, trying to bring the river to life from its code of print. It was tough going. Often I found Huck's American dialect as impenetrable as Latin, but even in the most difficult bits I was kept at it by the persistent wink and glimmer of the river. I was living inside the book. Because I was more timid and less sociable than Huck, his and my adventures on the Mississippi tended to diverge. He would sneak off in disguise to forage in a riverside town, or raid a wrecked steamboat; I would stay back on the raft. I laid trotlines for catfish. I floated alone on that unreal blue, watching for "towheads" and "sawyers" as the forest unrolled, a mile or more across the water.

I found the Mississippi in the family atlas. It was a great ink-stained Victorian book, almost as big as I was. "North Africa" and "Italy" had come loose from its binding, from my mother's attempts to keep up with my father's campaigns in the Eighth Army. North America, though, was virgin territory: no one in the family had ever thought the place worth a moment of their curiosity. I looked at the Mississippi, wriggling down the middle of the page, and liked the funny names of the places that it passed through. Just the sounds of Minneapolis . . . Dubuque . . . Hannibal . . . St. Louis . . . Cairo . . . Memphis . . . Natchez . . . Baton Rouge . . . struck a legendary and heroic note to my ear. Our part of England was culpably short of Roman generals, Indians and Egyptian ruins, and these splendid names added even more luster to the marvelous river in my head.

The only real river I knew was hardly more than a brook. It spilled through a tumbledown mill at the bottom of our road, opened into a little trouty pool, then ran on through water meadows over graveled shallows into Fakenham, where it slowed and deepened, gathering strength for the long drift across muddy flatlands to Norwich and the North Sea. All through my Huckleberry Finn summer, I came down to the mill to fish for roach and dace, and if I concentrated really hard, I could see the Mississippi there. First I had to think it twice as wide, then multiply by two, then two again . . . The rooftops of Fakenham went under. I sank roads, farms, church spires, the old German prisoner-of-war camp, Mr. Banham's flour mill. I flooded Norfolk, silvering the landscape like a mirror, leaving just an island here, a dead tree there, to break this lonely, enchanted monotony of water. It was a heady, intensely private vision. I hugged the idea of the huge river to myself. I exulted in the freedom and solitude of being afloat on it in my imagination.

Year by year I added new scraps of detail to the picture. I came across some photographs of the Mississippi in a dog-eared copy of the *National Geographic* in a doctor's waiting room. Like inefficient pornography, they were unsatisfying because they were too meanly explicit. "Towboat *Herman Briggs* at Greenville" and "Madrid Bend, Missouri" gave the river a set of measurements that I didn't at all care for. I didn't want to know that it was a mile and a quarter wide, or that its ruffled water wasn't blue at all but dirty tan. The lovely, immeasurable river in my head was traduced by these artless images, and when the doctor called me in to listen to the noises in my asthmatic chest I felt saved by the bell.

Then I saw a painting by George Caleb Bingham. It showed the Missouri, not the Mississippi, but I recognized it immediately as my river. Its water had a crystalline solidity and smoothness, as if it had been carved from rosy quartz. The river and the sky were one, with cliffs and forest hanging in suspension between them. In the foreground, a ruffianly trapper and his son drifted in a dugout canoe, their pet fox chained to its prow. The water captured their reflections as faithfully as a film. Alone, self-contained, they moved with the river, an integral part of the powerful current of things, *afloat* on it in exactly the way I had been daydreaming for myself. The French fur trader and his half-caste child joined Huck Finn—the three persons of the trinity which presided over my river.

Crouched under the willow below the mill, I lobbed my baited hook into the pool and watched the water spread. The Mississippi was my best invention; a dream that was always there, like a big friendly room with an open door into which I could wander at will. Once inside it, I was at home. I let the river grow around me until the world consisted of nothing except me and that great comforting gulf of water where catfish rootled and wild fruit hung from the trees on the towhead islands. The river was completely still as the distant shore went inching by. I felt my skin burn in the sun. I smelled sawn timber and blackberries and persimmons. I didn't dare move a muscle for fear of waking from the dream.

Now, thirty years later, the river was just a hundred miles ahead.

The road was empty—not a truck or a car in miles. If it hadn't been for the bodies of the dead racoons, I might have taken my rented mustard Ford for the only thing on the move in the whole of Wisconsin. The coons had the dissolute repose of sleeping tramps, their splayed limbs hidden under rumpled coverlets of greasy fur. Poor coons. Supremely talented, in a schoolboy way, at night exercises, at noisy raids on garbage cans, at climbing trees, they had no gift at all for crossing roads. Bright lights mesmerized them, and they died careless hobos' deaths on the wooded edges of tiny unincorporated towns.

Hunting for company, I twiddled my way through the burble on the radio.

"Good afternoon to all you Labor Day weekenders out there in northern Wisconsin . . ." The announcer sounded like a naval captain in a 1950s movie, a honey-bass throbbing with authority and inner calm. "This is WWID, Ladysmith. Your Good News station."

The road sliced through a broken, hilly landscape of forest, corn and cattle. It had been like this for hours: the white-painted farms set back behind good fences, each one with its grain silo topped by an aluminum cone like a witch's hat, the long sweep of freshly harvested valleys reduced to hog's bristle, the slaughtered coons. No one about. In Goodrich and Antigo, Ruby, Bloomer and Cornell, there'd been the same Sunday somnolence in the standing heat.

At Goodrich I'd stopped for gas, and had had to wake the station's owner, who was asleep under the funnies section, framed between his ice chest and his Coke machine. "Shit," he'd said; then "Where you going?"—as if my presence on the highway were a violation of some Sunday blue law.

From the hillbilly fiddles, electric harmoniums and tabernacle choirs on the radio, a woman's voice broke through with manic brightness and clarity.

> *A song of peace, a song of joy,*
> *A song for every little girl and boy,*
> *A song that says, "God loves you!"*

She dropped to a bedtime whisper. "God loves you," she crooned, while the strings and triangles went *hushabye, hushabye* in the background. "He really loves you." Stroking and snuggling her way into the hearts of the Labor Day weekenders, she said, "This isn't just a song for children, darling. Adults need love just as much, too." I squirmed in my car seat while she went on murmuring *He loves you, He really loves you, He loves you,* and faded out, leaving the airwaves full of breathed kisses.

"Carol Lawrence," the announcer said. "Born-again Christian lady. 'Tell All the World About Love.' The love of God. That's what we're here to share on WWID, twenty-four hours a day, except for Monday mornings. Telling the Good News. And we tell everybody because faith comes by hearing it. We have to get it out. It's twenty-two before six."

Swaddled and babied by the Good News station, I drove on west. I was full of that receptive good humor which marks the beginnings of journeys—a time when everything is coated with the bloom of newness, and one's eyes and ears skitter like minnows, seizing excitedly on every humdrum scrap. A sleeping dog! They have sleeping dogs in Wisconsin! A pile of cut wood! They cut wood here! Look, cows! Look, a water tower! Look, a gas station! Everything shapes up to the same astonishing size. The Falcons had beaten the Saints, the Bears had beaten the Packers, a hurricane called David was making its way up the Florida coast. Key Biscayne had been evacuated. In Dominica, four hundred people sheltering in a church had been swept to death when a river changed its course. And a group called the Lonstroms were singing:

> Well, I've found something that money can't buy,
> I've found a gold mine beyond the blue sky,
> I've found the land where I'll live when I die,
> I've found the Lord—a rich man am I.

The cows were casting longer shadows now, and when the trees met over the road they formed a dark church nave. In the farmhouses, lights were coming on one by one, and their white barns were turning black against the sun. Connorsville. Forest. Somerset. New Richmond. Then the steep climb down into the valley of the St. Croix River.

"Christian witness . . ." said the announcer. "Here's Len Mink." Len Mink was a sobbing tenor backed by a choir of lady angels.

> I have returned to the God of my childhood,
> To the same simple things as the child I once knew;
> Like the Prodigal Son, I long for my loved ones,
> For the comforts of home and the God I outgrew.

He returned and returned and returned. He went back to the God of his father. He went back to the God of his mother. After half a dozen stanzas he was returning to "the Yahweh of Judah," his voice breaking down in the effort to recapture that lost Eden of the spirit. Finally he was shouting, "I have returned! I have returned! I have returned!" in an exultant, if implausible, carol from the womb.

Well, I was returning too. I had never quite given up dreaming of the river and still found comfort in the idea of that lovely, glassy sweep of open water. The rivers I fished, on weekend escapes from the city, were always shadowed by another, bigger river, broad and long enough to

15

lose oneself on. Once, I'd actually seen the Mississippi, but it was from the window of a jet thirty thousand feet up, and the river looked as remote and theoretical as the twisty black thread in the family atlas. One sip of a Pan American highball, and it was gone.

Its afterimage lodged obstinately at the back of my head. In London, I had gone stale and dry. I felt that I'd run out of whatever peculiar reserves of moral capital are needed for city life. I couldn't write. For days on end I woke at five, confused and panicky, as the tranquilizers that I'd taken lost their grip. I listened to the jabbering sparrows in the yard and to the restless surf of overnight traffic on the road beyond. I lay clenched, struggling to get to sleep, and found myself thinking of the river, the great good place of my childhood. It was still just visitable. The dream was heavily overgrown now, and there were prohibitive signs and stretches of barbed wire to pass before one could get back to the old spot where the water spread away for miles, then dissolved into sky. Here, already half asleep, I let myself drift out into the current and watched the rising sun loom like a gigantic grapefruit through the mist.

Going down the river turned into an obsessive ritual. I had to relearn the child's trick of switching instantly into an imagined world. Soon I could work the magic with a few bare talismanic symbols—a curling eddy, a reedbed, an island, and a canister of photographer's smoke. It wasn't long before these daily dawn voyages began to suggest a real journey and a book.

The book and the journey would be all of a piece. The plot would be written by the current of the river itself. It would carry me into long deep pools of solitude, and into brushes with society on the shore. Where the river meandered, so would the book, and when the current speeded up into a narrow chute, the book would follow it. Everything would be left to chance. There'd be no advance reservations, no letters of introduction. I would try to be as much like a piece of human driftwood as I could manage. Cast off, let the Mississippi take hold, and trust to whatever adventures or longueurs the river might throw my way. It was a journey that would be random and haphazard; but it would also have the insistent purpose of the river current as it drove southward and seaward to the Gulf of Mexico.

It's hard to make travel arrangements to visit a dream. The voyage I was planning was on a river which existed only in my head. The real Mississippi was an abstraction. I studied it with impatience, feeling that the facts were just so many bits of grit in my vision of a halcyon river. I learned, without enthusiasm, about the construction of the lock-and-dam system. Figures began to swim in my head where the dream ought to be. In 1890, thirty million tons of freight had been carried down-river; in 1979, after a long and catastrophic decline in river trade, business was up again to forty million tons. The Civil War and the coming of the railroads had almost smashed the river as a commercial highway, but the oil crisis of the 1970s had brought the Mississippi back to life. A river barge, I read, "can move 400 tons of grain a mile on a gallon of fuel, compared with only 200 tons for a locomotive"; and a lot of people were now wanting to move a lot of tons of grain, because the United States had raised its quota of grain exports to Russia. So the port of New Orleans was busy with ships carting Midwestern wheat and corn and soybeans off to Murmansk and Archangel. To someone somewhere, I suppose, this kind of information has the ring of indus-trial poetry; it didn't to me. It was reassuring to find that the river was important again, a central artery linking north and south in a drifting procession of towboats and barge fleets, but I found the details of its renascence grindingly dull. They threatened to contaminate that great, wide-open stretch of level water which was far more actual for me than these tawdry scraps of intelligence from the real world.

I went for long walks by the Thames, following the ebb tide as it ran out through Kew, Chiswick, Barnes, Putney, watching the way it piled against the bridges and came to the boil over deep muddy holes in the river bottom. It was the simple movement of the water that I liked, and its capacity to make the city which surrounded it look pre-carious and makeshift. The pastel cottages on the bank, with their bookshelves, net curtains, standing lamps and potted plants, stood on the lip of a real and dangerous wilderness. A freak tide, a careless shift in the current, and they could be swept away. The river, as it sluiced past their doorsteps, carried plenty of evidence of its deadliness. There were dead dogs in it, and stoved-in boats, and the occasional bloated human corpse. Once I found the body of a drowned woman. She was spread-eagled on the shore; her coat, of sodden leopard skin, had ridden up over her torso and covered her head. There were runs in her tights. Her boots were very new. At the coroner's inquest on her death, I heard that she'd left a note. It was rambling, disjointed, full of resentment and depression, but it didn't actually say that she in-tended to kill herself. It seemed rather that she had come to the river without knowing what she was going to do. Perhaps she believed that the mess and tangle of her life would somehow resolve itself if she could put it in perspective beside the bleak placidity of all that drifting water. It was probable, said the coroner, that she'd thrown herself into the river without premeditation; not really meaning to commit suicide, merely trying to assuage her misery and confusion in the comforting void of the Thames. He announced his verdict: death by misadventure.

I felt I understood what had drawn the woman to the river. I wanted to lose myself too. I had no intention of landing up in some small Mid-western city morgue, but I ached to run away from the world for a while, to put myself in the grip of a powerful current which would make my choices for me, to be literally adrift. The woman had gone to the river for solace, and had ended up drowning in it; I was going for much the same motive, but meant to stay afloat.

I hardly gave a thought to the mechanics of the voyage. It was, after all, a dream journey, and like a dream it was supposed to unfold spontaneously without effort on my part. Obviously I would need a craft of some kind, but I knew almost nothing at all about boats. A raft would turn the trip into a piece of quaint playacting; canoes cap-sized. I vaguely assumed that somewhere at the top end of the river I'd come across a leaky tub with a pair of oars, and cast off in that.

To make the voyage come true, I began to talk about it. At a party in London I met a man who had seen the Mississippi at St. Louis and had gone on a half-day tourist cruise up the river.

"It was amazingly depressing," he said. "Totally featureless. An awful lot of mud. You couldn't see anything over the top of the banks except dead trees. The only bearable thing about the entire afternoon was the ship's bar. It was full of people getting dead drunk so that they didn't have to look at the sheer bloody boredom of the Mississippi."

"That was just around St. Louis, though."

"Oh, it's all like that, I gather. That's what it's famous for, being very long and very boring. The only reason people ever go on the Missis-sippi at all is because after you've spent a couple of hours looking at that horrendous bloody river, even a dump like St. Louis starts to look moderately interesting. I think God made the Mississippi as a sort of warning, to prove that things really can be worse than you think."

He had an air of mighty self-satisfaction, having delivered me at a stroke from the lunatic fantasy with which I'd been possessed. Actually, I'd been rather excited by his description of the river. It had given it something of the melodramatic awfulness of a landscape by John Martin, a touch of *Sadek in Search of the Waters of Oblivion* with its dwarfish hominid scrambling into a world of treeless crags and dead seas.

"I suppose you thought you were going to do it in a *rowing* boat," the man said, snuffling with amusement at the notion. I didn't like the way he had consigned my trip to the past subjunctive tense.

"No, no. I'll have a . . . an outboard motor." I had had one experi-ence with an outboard motor. I had driven myself from one end of a small Scottish loch to the other, where it had coughed and died. It had taken me three hours to row back through a rainstorm.

"You'd get swamped. Or be run down by one of those tow-things. When we were in St. Louis, people were always getting drowned in the river. Went out fishing, never came back, bodies recovered weeks later, or never recovered at all. So bloody common that it hardly ever made the local news."

Some days afterward, I ran into the man again.

"You're not still thinking of going down that river, are you?"

"I've written off about getting a motor."

"It'd cost you a hell of a lot less if you just swallowed a packet of razor blades. According to the Euthanasia Society, putting a plastic bag over your head is pretty much the best way to go." He introduced me to the woman he was with. "He's going to go down the Mississippi in a *dinghy*," he said.

"What a lovely thing to do," she said. "Just like Tom Sawyer—or was that Huckleberry Finn?"

The man smiled with exaggerated patience. It was the smile of a lonely realist stranded in the society of cloud-cuckoos.

That smile. I'd got used to it over the last few weeks. It said I was a jackanapes. Now, studying my route in the pale glow of the car map light, a scramble of lower-case names—*otisville, houlton, lakeland, hudson*—I imagined the smile broadening. In Minneapolis a boat was waiting for me. I was going to ride the river for as long and as far as I could go, and see whether it was possible to stitch together the imaginary place where I had spent too much of my time daydreaming and that other, real, muddy American waterway.

I was being interviewed by the radio pastor of WWID, Ladysmith.

"Have you said yes to Jesus yet?"

No.

"It's by His grace you're saved through faith. Exercise your faith and say, 'Lord, I'm receiving You as my Lord and Saviour.' "

My headlights picked out the twin marmalade eyes of a racoon in the road. I swerved just in time.

"Henry Slotter tells the news at nine, straight up, and then *Sunday Hymnsing* to follow, on this second of September, Labor Day Weekend. Now hear this. The Oklahoma Baptist Festival Choir. 'It Is Well with My Soul.' That says just about all that needs to be said, folks. It Is Well with My Soul . . ." The opening chords on the electric organ quivered with pious tremolo; then came the voices, the sopranos sounding as if they were crying for joy, the baritones and basses adding a counterpoint of moderation and common sense, as if getting on the right side of the Lord were just good business practice. I turned up the volume and joined the Interstate, singing my way into Minnesota along with the Oklahoma Baptist Festival Choir. After all, I was in no position to jeer at other people's dreams of personal salvation. I had my own hopes of becoming a born-again something, even if it wasn't a Christian. *It is well with my soul, pom, pom . . . well with my soul.*

I was jolted back into an America I recognized without affection. The bald glare of the sodium lights over the highway had flattened the landscape and robbed it of shadow and color. The exurban fringe of the twin cities of Minneapolis and St. Paul was the usual mess of neon doodles. Curlicues of mustard. Trails of ketchup. The motels, taco houses, Radio Shacks and Pizza Huts stretched away in a bilious blaze of American mock-Alpine. I remembered poring over the Victorian atlas, playing with the exotic syllables of Minneapolis as if they spelled Samarkand. Even now I wasn't quite prepared for the thoroughgoing charmlessness of this five-mile strip of junk food, porno movies and the kind of motels where you expect to find blood running down your shower curtain. There was a brief, merciful break of darkness. Then the illuminated crap began again.

It was only after I had gone on another mile or so that I realized I'd crossed the Mississippi. I had crossed the Mississippi. It had dropped through a crack in the lights of Minneapolis, and I hadn't even seen it go. The smile on the face of my London acquaintance would have been so superior that it would have joined up with his eyebrows in a perfect oval. It was a jackanapes' way of ending a pilgrimage and starting an odyssey.

I pushed on deeper into Minneapolis until I found myself driving up a street that felt like the heart of something. Hennepin Avenue. Louis Hennepin had been a seventeenth-century Franciscan friar who had been chaplain to the La Salle expedition which had charted the upper Mississippi in 1680. I'd just been reading about him in Francis Parkman's *La Salle and the Discovery of the Great West,* and was interested to see how his name had been commemorated here. Hennepin Avenue was blocked solid with gay bars, massage parlors, bright little boutiques with vibrators and dildos displayed in their windows, and the offices of pawnbrokers and bail bondsmen, now shuttered and padlocked for the night. Perhaps Father Hennepin had been an altogether merrier priest than Parkman had made him sound. Or perhaps the ruderies of Hennepin Avenue were intended to convey what Protestant Minnesota thought of foreign papists.

I stopped at a bar that looked and sounded rather more straight than its neighbors: MOBY DICK'S—FOR A WHALE-SIZED DRINK. Having just missed out on one American epic by oversight, I had better catch up with whatever classics I could find. A few doors down the street, no doubt, there'd be a sex shop called "The Scarlet Letter."

In the three-quarters dark, the walls of Moby Dick's were bright with sweat. It was the kind of place where all the loose ends of a city tend to shake down together. A glazed-looking Indian in a booth had a pitcher of beer for company. Two black men, wearing enviably sharp hats and suits with lapels as narrow as switchblades, were feeding the jukebox with quarters. At the bar, a drunk was getting nowhere with the bartender as he tried to sweet-talk her into betting on the outcome of the New England–Pittsburgh football game.

"Come on, honey. Just a little bet . . . a *gennelman's* bet . . . Whaddaya say?"

On the TV screen above his head, someone dressed up in medieval armor was running for a touchdown.

"A *dollar*."

The bartender squirted whiskey from a tube into my glass.

"I said a *gennelman's* bet. One dollar. What's a dollar between friends?" He sprawled across the bar toward the girl in a sudden access of inspiration. "Hey . . . you can take Pittsburgh."

"Straight up or soda?" said the girl to me.

"Go on, what's a dollar?"

"Food, clothing and a place to sleep," I said. Bob Hope had said that in a movie once.

The girl faced the drunk for the first time in minutes. "It's too early in the season. I ain't into the teams yet."

Defeated, he settled on me, grabbing at my sleeve as I started to leave the bar. "Where you from, fella? Where you from? I can tell you ain't from around here," he said with the triumphant cunning of a man who has got the better of half a bottle and can still pull off feats of amazing detection.

I headed for the empty booth next to the pickled Indian's.

"Hey, where you going? Where you going, fella?"

Far away, I hoped. South with the Monarch butterflies. Downstream.

2

Casting Off

*O*n *Labor Day*, no one was taking calls. The phone pealed un-answered in the boatyard. I pulled aside the heavy drapes of my hotel-room window and looked down on the emptied streets of Minneapolis, already beginning to fry in the early sun. I wondered where the Mississippi was. Its course must be a well-kept secret, hidden somewhere in the crevices between the city's squat little skyscrapers of smoked glass and steel.

In this high room, with the expensive air conditioner breathing hardly louder than a sleeping child, I felt I was as far from my river as I'd ever been. My morning orange juice stood islanded in a silver tureen of crushed ice. I propped Parkman up against it and went back to my favorite bit, where La Salle, Tonto and Father Hennepin see the Mississippi for the first time.

> The travelers resumed their journey . . . and soon reached the dark and inexorable river, so long the object of their search, rolling, like a destiny, through its realms of solitude and shade.

Here it rolled obscurely through realms of insurance companies, cattle-feed factors, television stations and chain hotels. I put an admiring pencil line under the phrase "through all the perilous monotony of its interminable windings" and tried it out loud. It sounded terrific.

I went to the window to stare at the city, trying to find a gap or a shadow, a sign of a winding, but the man-madeness of it all looked seamless. I had spent a lot of time dreaming of losing myself on the river; it had never once occurred to me that it might be possible simply to lose the river. There must be a reason for the way Minneapolis behaved toward the Mississippi as if the river were the skeleton in the city's family closet. That was something else I would have to find out.

There was no clue on the streets outside as to the whereabouts of my river. Lost by a series of forced right turns, I took a long boulevard where the shadows fell toward me and hoped that that meant east. Mine was the only car about. The traffic-control system of Minneapolis had been switched on specially for my benefit. "Walk" signs flashed WALK and DON'T WALK to whatever ghosts haunt deserted cities. Blinking filter-arrows sped imaginary columns of automobiles down empty avenues. Somewhere, many streets away, a police car went whooping just for the sake of whooping, like a lonely kid whistling to keep himself company. The sweet stink of a brewery lay leaden in the heat. No people. No river.

Then, suddenly, I was part of the crowd. The street had merged into an expressway, and the expressway was jammed solid. We were elbow to elbow in the crush, a grumbling herd of dusty pickup trucks, all windows down, all radios turned full up. I spoke to my nearest neighbor, a colossal jellyfish in a plaid shirt and a cowboy hat with a wide curly brim.

"Where's everybody going?"

"*You* goin' to the Fair, man. Hey, Butch—guy here don't know where nobody's goin'."

"He's goin' right to the Fair," Butch said from the driver's seat.

"I just told him that. Hey, where you from? You ain't a Norwegian, are you?"

"I'm from England."

"England. Shit. Guy's from *England*. Reason I asked if you was a Norwegian fella is because I'm a Norwegian myself. Got a Norwegian name. Olen. That's Norwegian, Olen—ain't that right?"

"Sounds right to me."

"Hey, you talk just like one of them Norwegians. That kills me. Yeah, I come from those parts. From way back. Wanna beer?"

He passed me a can of cold Budweiser clad in a sheath of polystyrene foam.

"That's *Bud-weiser,* that beer." Remembering that he was talking to a foreigner, he carefully separated every syllable for me, and started shouting. "That's a *German* name. Don't come from Germany, though. Comes from the *Yew*-nighted States."

We rolled forward in consort for a few feet, and stopped.

"I'm looking for the river," I said.

Olen's jellyfish face squinched up, then expanded again.

"*Look*in' for the *riv*er."

"The Mississippi."

"The river's back," said Butch. "He just come over it."

"The river's back," Olen said. "Ain't no exits now, not till the Fair-grounds."

"Shit," I said.

"You gonna have a real good time at the Fair, man. They got all kinds of things there. They got freaks. You know what we all call the Fair? It's the great Minnesota get-together."

"That's right," Butch said. "The great Minnesota get-together."

"I wanted to find the Mississippi."

"*Mississippi?* That ain't nothin' much. Any road, you gone past it. It's way back."

With the sole exception of Olen's ten-gallon affair, everyone in our crowd was wearing a plastic cap with a long shovel-brim. The caps gave the cavalcade a vaguely military air, as if we were off to sack a city. The fronts of the hats were decorated with insignia and slogans. OH BOY! OH BEEF! advertised a kind of cake that cows ate. Others ped-dled farm machinery, Holsum Bread, chemical fertilizers, pesticides, corn oil, cement and root beer. Under these corporation colors, the owners of the caps looked queerly like feudal retainers riding around wearing the arms of their barons. A few self-conscious individualists wore personalized caps announcing I'M FROM THE BOONDOCKS and YOU CAN KISS MY . . . followed by a picture of an ass in a straw bonnet. Butch's cap said JOHN DEERE; I took this for his own name, and only gradually noticed that several hundred men at the fair were also called John Deere, which turned out to be a famous brand of agricultural tractor.

The state fair sprawled across a hillside and a valley, and at first glance it did indeed look like a city under occupation by an army of rampaging Goths. I'd never seen so many enormous people assembled in one place. These farming families from Minnesota and Wisconsin were the descendants of hungry immigrants from Germany and Scan-dinavia. Their ancestors must have been lean and anxious men with the famines of Europe bitten into their faces. Generation by genera-tion, their families had eaten themselves into Americans. Now they all had the same figure: same broad bottom, same Buddha belly, same neckless join between turkey-wattle chin and sperm-whale torso. The women had poured themselves into pink stretch-knit pant suits; the men swelled against every seam and button of their plaid shirts and Dacron slacks. Under the brims of their caps, their food projected from their mouths. Foot-long hot dogs. Bratwurst sausages, dripping with hot grease. Hamburgers. Pizzas. Scoops of psychedelic ice cream. Wieners-dun-in-buns.

Stumbling, half-suffocated, through this abundance of food and flesh, I felt like a brittle matchstick man. Every time I tried to turn my head I found someone else's hot dog, bloody with ketchup, sticking into my own mouth.

On either side of us, the voices of the freakshow barkers quacked through tinny loudspeakers.

"Ronny and Donny. The only living Siamese twins on exhibit in the world today. Now grown men, Ronny and Donny are joined at the breastbone and the abdomen, facing each other for every second of their lives."

"We carry the most deadly and dangerous of any in the world. Don't miss it. All alive!"

"Can you imagine being permanently fastened to another person for your entire life?"

"You see the deadly Monocle Cobra from Asia, the Chinese Cobra and the Black-Necked Spitting Cobra. All alive."

"Ronny and Donny, the Siamese twins, are fascinating to see, interesting to visit, and completely unforgettable. The Siamese twins are alive, real and living."

"You'll see the giant, one-hundred-pound pythons. They're alive, and they're inside. Don't miss it. Everything's alive."

"You will remember your visit with the Siamese twins for the rest of your life—"

Crushed between the bust of the woman behind and the immense behind of the man in front, I did not find it hard to imagine what it might be like to be Ronny or Donny. There was no chance of visiting with them, though. As the sluggish current of the crowd passed them by, I was carried with it, deep into the heart of the state fair.

I was going down fast. The air I was breathing wasn't air: it was a compound of smells, of meat, sweat, popcorn, cooking fat and passed gas. Wriggling and butting my way out of the crowd, I found myself in the sudden blessed cool of a vaulted cathedral full of cows. They stood silently in their stalls with the resigned eyes of long-term patients. The straw with which the stadium was carpeted gave the whole place a ceremonious quiet. Grave men, whom I took for bulk buyers from the burger industry, padded from stall to stall. The cattle stared back at them with profound incuriosity. I wondered what they made of the smell of charred beef. Soon they'd be minced, ground up with cereal and soybeans, and turned into Whoppers and Kingburgers. For now, though, the animals had a lugubrious dignity that put the people at the fair to shame. They were the real heroes of the day. Washed sleek as seals, they were the scions of the finest stock of Minnesota, aristocrats in their world. They looked temperamentally unsuited to the garish democracy of the fast-food business.

I was trying to make contact with some kind of pedigreed shorthorn whose face had reminded me of the late Zero Mostel when I noticed the man standing at the next stall along. He was wearing a stripy one-piece pajama suit which hung on him in loose folds. Once, perhaps, he too had had a Minnesotan figure, but he had shrunk inside his peculiar garment until his pajamas flapped like rags on a stick.

He also was attempting to strike up a relationship with a cow. He was dabbing at her ears with a liver-spotted hand as if he'd short-sightedly mistaken her for a dog.

"Lady . . . Lady . . . Lady . . ." he pleaded. The cow regarded him with ageless stupid skepticism. "Hey, Lady—"

He turned toward me. His cap said, HAPPINESS IS BEING A GRAND-PARENT.

"Know about stock?"

"Nothing at all," I said.

"Me neither. That's you and me both. You and me both." His twiggy fingers went dandling away in the fur of the cow's neck. "You ain't from around these parts."

"No—I'm just passing through."

"I could tell. You from the East? From New York? You from New York?"

"No, England."

"England. Oh, yeah. England." His tone was forgiving. He was letting me off the incriminating hook of coming from New York. "I was there once. In the days of wrath. I went all up Italy in the days of wrath."

"In the war—"

"The days of wrath." He looked at the cow and spoke to it in a cracked, erratically remembered parody of a British accent. "Wot yer! Yer bloomin' bloody bloke!" He wheezed with pleasure at this performance. "We had English out there with us. Days of wrath. Yeah. I was there. You ever hear of Monte Cassino?" He made the place sound like a Chicago gang leader.

"Yes. My father was there."

"I was there. Him and me both." He gave his cow another friendly scratch. "Englishman, eh, what? What ho, old bloke!"

26

I couldn't find more than a feeble snicker to answer him with, but my silence seemed to please him more than any words could have done. He left his cow, pulled excitedly at the folds of his pajamas, and launched himself into speech like a parachutist hurtling out of a plane.

"Know somethin', old bloke? You come out here in the summer, huh? Hot enough, ain't it? Hot enough to boil your brains. Boil your brains. That's Labor Day for you. Up in Minnesota here, Labor Day she really means something, you better believe it. Last day of summer. Know what folks are at all over this state right now?"

He allowed himself a thunderous, dramatic pause. His dried crab-apple face was about six inches away from mine. His eyes were wet.

"Eating and drinking and pig roasts and partying! Every kind of partying you can think of! They got barbecues like you never seen . . . and pool parties . . . and euchre . . . Hell, every sonofabitch is having himself the finest goddamn time he can. And you know why, sir? The Minnesota Winter! Now, that is something else. That is really something else. You come here Thanksgiving, old bloke, *that's* when you ought to be up here in Minnesota. Cold? I'm telling you. It'd freeze your nuts off. Freeze your nuts off. Snow? There's whole cities underneath the snow there. Ain't nothing that ain't froze right over. You go out there in that air, that is *cold*, I'm telling you. Twenty below, thirty below—that ain't *nothing* in Minnesota. Hell, we got it worse than the Eskimos here. And that's why when folks in this state go party-ing on Labor Day, we put on the best goddamn show in the whole United States. You hear what I'm saying? I been to state fairs, and there ain't none like the Minnesota State Fair, because there ain't no-body who knows how to party like the Minnesota people do. And it's all because of them goddamn freezing winters—"

This breathless oration was accompanied by a frantic series of clock-work nods and jerks. The brim of the old man's cap wagged an inde-pendent emphasis at the end of each sentence. Happiness, it kept on announcing, was being a grandparent. The whole performance came to a sudden stop when a woman's voice called, *"Hatfield!"* across the cattle stadium.

"Hatfield!" It was a blowtorch of a voice, and the old man was being roasted in it. He shrank even farther back inside his pajamas.

"Hatfield! I been looking all over!"

The man gestured, flutteringly, at me. I clearly was not much of an alibi.

"I had to leave Doug and Mo. They're eating popcorn and wieners. You know Jo-Ann hates to have the kids left *any*place!" Hatfield's spouse was wearing Bermuda shorts. The varicose veins on her thighs were so intricately blue that they looked like the willow pattern on a Chinese plate.

"Beatrice . . . this gentleman is from England—"

I got a brief once-over from behind a pair of clip-on dark glasses. Beatrice could tell a rotten tomato when she saw one.

"Well," she said. "Is. That. So."

"Hello," I said.

"We, uh, kind of got talking . . ." said Hatfield, but I could see that the words sounded improbable in his own ears. Talking was not an area of life for which Hatfield carried a license. He plucked at the knees of his pajamas. Beatrice studied the rows of cows in their stalls. "Cattle," she said, identifying them as if they were a species hitherto unknown to her.

"Been nice talking to you," said Hatfield sadly. I hoped that he was going to muster up one of his cracky tags of wartime-British, but he glanced across at Beatrice, thought better of it, and let the brim of his cap sink down over his face, forestalling further communication. He was led off, silent, rainbow pajamas flapping, to join his grandchildren in the wiener-and-popcorn corral.

I'd never been much good at being one of the crowd. Now, feeding myself back into the flow, I tried to settle in, to feel part of the blood being pumped through the fair. Be a corpuscle. Let go. We oozed down a long sickly tunnel of cotton candy, came up against some invisible obstruction, and were channeled into a mass of separate thread veins and arteries. The going was hot and smelly, the pace jerky, as if the whole coronary system were clogged and subject to frequent breakdown. All nerve ends and elbows, I kept on getting stuck.

I was shown a selection of snow blowers. A lady dog handler demonstrated the latest psychological technique for dissuading Ajax and Hercules from leaving piles of poopie on the rug. I found her frank, instructive, but a bit too academic for me. I nearly bought some vitamin pills. I looked at a display of swimming pools, custom-designed to suit my yard; I did my best to covet a threshing machine; I moved fairly swiftly through the extensive exhibit of chemicals that promised to enhance the nutrient values of my poor soil. I did pause, in mute assent, in front of a placard which asked me: DO YOU SUFFER FROM THE LITTLE PAINS USUALLY ASSOCIATED WITH ARTHRITIS? The handsome orthopedic vibrator, on which I might have massaged all my little pains away, was both expensive and rather too large to carry on a small boat.

The demonstration model was being put to heavy use by a line of sweating agribusinessmen. I came upon a stack of illustrated encyclopedias. Their grained plastic bindings were a deep episcopal purple, the color of seriousness. Their salesman had been got up to look like everyone's idea of a proper scholar. Close-cropped, in chunky tortoiseshell glasses, he was the only man in Minnesota who wore a necktie on Labor Day.

"If I may ask, sir, would you have children of school age?"

"Oh, yes," I said. I like purely hypothetical questions, and have always found it a treat to be singled out by Gallup pollsters.

"Would they have ready access to encyclopedia sources in the home?"

"I very much doubt it."

The salesman brightened up no end. I began to ferret through the volumes. They stank unpleasantly of a mixture of gasoline and lavender.

". . . outstanding aids to education . . . indispensable in the home, school or college situation . . . no article longer than seven hundred words . . ." His voice ran on like a leaky tap. The language of encyclopedia selling is an Esperanto; I imagine that every phrase is duplicated word for word in China, Persia or Peru.

I found LINCOLN–PACIFIC.

". . . world's foremost scholars in their fields . . . expert communicators . . . selected vocabulary . . . uniquely commissioned from leading illustrators and artists . . ."

MISSISSIPPI. I skimmed the entry. Nothing new.

> . . . principal waterway in the U.S., draining all or parts of 31 states in the heartland of the nation. Its name derives from Chippewa, *mici zibi,* or "large river" . . .

I copied out those two sentences and returned the book to its rank.

"Thanks. I was just looking something up."

"May I ask the ages of your children, sir?"

"I haven't got any."

The salesman stopped looking like a scholar. *Jerk. Smartass.* But there were other, real parents about, trailing visible children of genuine school age, and I watched the salesman reminding himself that his own imposture was of more immediate importance than mine. He gave me a cold, waxy, very scholarly smile. The lenses of his spectacles were plain glass.

Ebbing and swirling, we drifted from tent to tent. At every bend there was another pagoda selling brats or franks or dogs or burgers. Church flags flew from their tops. The Lutherans specialized in bratwurst sausages, the Methodists in hot dogs, the Catholics in hamburgers. At each stall, there was a stack of giveaway devotional reading placed handily beside the ketchup squirt. Did all this eating have some sacramental significance? Could munching on an Adventist wiener be the first step on the ladder of conversion?

The crowd was wedged solid from horizon to horizon. There were no signs of an exit from this colossal Roman holiday. In a brief gap in the stream of overamplified country-and-Western I heard a faint familiar voice, and almost thought of it as a friend.

"We offer a reward of a thousand dollars if they're not real and alive, exactly as advertised. We could make it a million dollars, or a billion dollars, it doesn't make any difference, because we won't have to reward anyone a penny. Because the Siamese twins are real, human and alive."

Lucky Siamese twins. As each sticky, claustrophobic minute went by, I felt less real, less human, less alive. I thought how curious it was, this crowd. No nation in the world had ever put quite such a high value on privacy and space as the United States, and nowhere in the country did people live so far apart, in houses islanded in acres of sequestered green, as here in the Midwest. When Minnesotans got together on Labor Day, they did so with the fervor of people for whom being part of a crowd is a rare holiday luxury. The fairgoers were like children playing sardines.

We rolled slowly on past an amphitheater. They might have been feeding born-again Christians to the lions there, but no—it was just a late-model-stock-car race. On the public-address system, the commentator's voice was bawling over the top of the growling animal bass of the auto engines. He was getting the Amzoil Three Hundred under way. Well, we certainly had a beautiful day here today in Minnesota, he said. Plus, we had some real beautiful cars and a lot of real super people.

"They're turning those engines at over seven thousand r.p.m.," he shouted. "So, gentlemen! Let's go racing!"

Please, I thought, please don't let's go racing. The thought was instantly smashed from my head by the noise of what sounded like an intercontinental bronchial hemorrhage, as the stock cars took off from their starting positions and went roaring around the stadium. Christians and lions must at least have been a great deal quieter.

I didn't want to go racing. I didn't want to stuff my face with meat, corn and cotton candy. I didn't feel like rolling dimes for the National

Heart Foundation. I wasn't going to buy a snowblower. I didn't care to ride the Big Wheel or goggle at the Black-Necked Spitting Cobra. I wanted out. I wanted to find my river.

I had crossed and recrossed the Mississippi. There were eighteen bridges over it in as many miles, and it seemed that already I had been on most of them. Yet I was having almost as much trouble as De Soto or La Salle in actually reaching the riverbank. Once, the Mississippi had provided Minneapolis and St. Paul with the reason for their existence. Later, it had turned into an impediment to their joint commercial life, to be spanned at every possible point. Now it wasn't even an impediment. The Twin Cities went about their business as if the river didn't exist. No road that I could see led down to it. From a gloomy little bar on First Street, I could smell the Mississippi, but didn't know how to reach it. Feeling foolish, I called the bartender over.

"How exactly do I get down to the Mississippi?"

"The river? She's on the far side of the tracks." The *wrong* side of the tracks. The river had been consigned to the part of town classically set aside for the American poor. It belonged to the same category as vandalized public housing projects, junked automobiles and dead cats. I was appalled. No one would have dared do such a thing to the river in my head.

I left my beer untouched. Across the street, there was a potter's field of ancient railroads. Most had died. Others were in that geriatric state where death is just a whisker away. It was a sorry strip, half a mile wide, of dingy grass, cracked ties and crumbling rails. The rolling stock looked as if it had rusted solid on its tracks. I couldn't see any locomotives, only the names of the surviving railroad companies, painted in flaky lettering on the sides of the cars. BURLINGTON NORTHERN. CHICAGO AND NORTH WESTERN. MINNESOTA TRANSFER. THE SOO LINE. CHICAGO, MILWAUKEE, ST. PAUL AND PACIFIC. Crickets wheezed and scraped at my feet as I crossed from track to track. The soggy holiday air smelled of diesel oil, rotting wood and river.

I clambered between two standing chains of freight cars, slid down a culvert of cinders, and there was the Mississippi. All that I could see at first was what it was not. It was not a great glassy sweep of water, big enough to make the civilization on its banks look small. It wasn't the amazing blue of the cover of my old copy of *Huckleberry Finn*. Nor was it the terrible chocolate flood of Charles Dickens and Frances Trollope.

It was just a river. From where I stood, the far bank was no more than a couple of hundred yards away. Its color was much the same as that of my domestic Thames: a pale dun, like iced tea with a lot of mosquito larvae wriggling in the glass. I squatted moodily on a bleached rock, looking across at the dead smokestacks of a Victorian mill and listening to the rumble of a weir upstream. I lit a cigarette to frighten off the gnats buzzing in a thick cloud around my head, and flipped the empty pack into the river. The surface of the water was scrolled with slowly moving eddies. My cigarette pack drifted for a moment, slipped into the crease of an eddy, and was taken crabwise off across the stream. How long, I wondered, would it take to reach the Gulf of Mexico? Two thousand miles at . . . what—four, five miles an hour? A month? Six weeks? At any rate, it would arrive long before I did. I watched its red flip-top lid slowly circling in the tepid water until it was carried out of sight.

I realized that I'd seen this bit of river before, in a dozen or so bad nineteenth-century engravings, most of them by untalented but adventurous Germans who had traveled up and down the Mississippi with sketchbooks. The rock on which I sat was exactly where they must have set up their equipment to draw the Falls of St. Anthony. Then the river spilled over a succession of steep limestone steps. It was famously picturesque. The Germans represented the waterfalls by taking a pen and a ruler and making a hatchwork of parallel vertical lines. It must have been a very orderly way of passing an afternoon. They then colored them in with a fierce mat white. The general impression was that at this point the Mississippi was a cascade of toothpaste; one could almost see the army of hired hands squeezing the giant tubes behind the falls. The kindest thing that one could say about the engravings was that they were a vivid illustration of the sheer bewilderment of the European imagination when it tried to confront the raw wilderness of the American West.

For even in 1800, this place had been utterly wild—far wilder than the Alps, or the Upper Rhine, or the English Lake District, or any of the other places to which romantic pilgrims went in search of wilderness. Fort Snelling, just downstream, was the last outpost of white America against the Sioux. In 1805, Colonel Zebulon Montgomery Pike led an expedition to the headwaters of the Mississippi and camped beside the Falls of St. Anthony. A Sioux warrior stole the Colonel's American flag while Pike was out hunting for geese, swans, ducks and deer. In his notebook, he was very hard on the local savages and wrote that he had shot "a remarkably large racoon" on the riverbank.

Then the falls had been harnessed to turn millwheels. The remains of the mills still lined the far shore, their brickwork fallen in, their paddles long gone. They'd ground corn and sawed up forestfuls of timber. The falls had blocked any further navigation of the river to steamboats, and Minneapolis had been the natural place to join the railroad system to the waterway.

In 1861, Anthony Trollope came to Minneapolis by train, but couldn't make up his mind about whether the place, whose name he found delightfully ridiculous, ought properly to be called a village or a town. Mark Twain came here in 1880 and found a city that had swollen to the size of St. Paul, its "Siamese twin." The two cities were the Ronny and Donny of the Northwest, joined at the breastbone and the abdomen, facing each other for every second of their lives, interesting to visit, alive, real and living. By then, sixteen different railroads met up in the desolate sidings at my back, and they were knocking the heart out of the commercial life of the river. In 1904, the Baedeker Guide to the United States, rather at a loss to find nice remarks to make about Minneapolis, was at least able to describe it as "the flour-milling capital of the world."

And the river . . . poor, schooled, shriveled river. All this piling up of one technology on top of another—railroad on steamboat, interstate highway on railroad, hydroelectric dam on watermill—had reduced the Mississippi from a wonder of nature to this sluggish canal on the wrong side of the tracks. Bridged, dammed, locked, piered, she was safe now. Minneapolis had no need to bother with her. It had turned its back on the water, and only odd foreigners like me with dreams in their heads came here to brood over what had happened to her.

Out in the stream, the grubby current humped against the giant steel mooring bitts to which no barges were tethered. I thought I saw a dead fish, but it turned out to be a condom. I remembered the old spelling bee, the voices of little girls chanting in a primary-school classroom:

> *Mrs. M., Mrs. I., Mrs. S.S.I.*
> *Mrs. P., Mrs. P., Mrs. Ippi, Ippi, aye!*

The condom went off in pursuit of my cigarette pack—a "French tickler" with a nasty semblance of swimming life. I suppose that some indigent peasant in Yucatán might find a use for it when it finally washed up on his beach.

It was a forlorn walk upriver, through the chunky, honey-colored arches of the old Burlington Northern railroad bridge. I had not expected to feel quite so elegiac about the Mississippi quite so soon. That was supposed to happen later on in the plot.

Beyond the bridge, I came on the last of the fetters that Minneapolis had built around the river in order to cramp its style, the new lock and dam at the top end of what had once been the Falls of St. Anthony. It had been finished only sixteen years before, in 1963, and it had turned what remained of the rapids into a watery equivalent of a split-level putting green.

It wasn't picturesque at all. No romantic German would have wanted to set up his sketchbook in front of it. Yet one had to admit that the thing was a wonder of sorts in its own right. I was used to the tiny, pretty wooden locks on England's eighteenth-century canals—dripping little chambers seven feet wide and sixty or seventy feet long. This was a monster. Two city blocks could have been comfortably sunk in its basin. Its fifty-foot drop looked more, a dizzying black pit in the river. The lockmen were talking to each other over walkie-talkie radios. With a hundred yards or more of bald concrete between each man, the place felt more like an international airport than a device for ordering a river. Why, too, on this empty afternoon when the only things stirring were the crickets in the overgrown railroad tracks, was all this Oscar-Lima-Charleying going on over the short waves? The lock was a gigantic toy. The lockmen were playing at being lockmen; gates and valves and sluices were being opened and shut for the simple boyish pleasure of watching that staggering quantity of rancid Mississippi water boil up in the basin.

I found the lockmaster, captaining this pointless operation from an upper deck, his handset squawking incomprehensibly. He had the contentedly abstracted look of a man listening to a favorite piece of music. I felt I had a useful hold over him, having caught him out tinkering with several million gallons of river just for the hell of it.

"Just fillin' her up," he said, gazing happily down into his private maelstrom. It didn't sound like much of an explanation to me. If I'd come along fifteen minutes later, I suppose he would have said that he was "just emptying her out" in exactly the same tone of voice.

"She's real quiet today, real quiet . . ." The entire building thrummed under my feet as water from the river raced through the tunnels to fill the chamber. "Feel it?" the lockmaster said. "That's twenty-three thousand gallons a second coming in down there." He stood at the window, alternately shouting into his radio and waving his arms at the men below: Bernstein conjuring the *Dies Irae* through its fortissimo climax. There were the giant bass drums, there the massed choir, there the trumpets, there the trombones. He was a maestro of water. I found the performance splendidly exciting, but from a practical point of view, I didn't like the look of it at all. A sixteen-foot boat would be . . . I tried to measure sixteen feet against the lock wall. Hardly more significant than an empty Budweiser can or a fallen leaf.

"I'm going to take a sixteen-foot boat down the river to New Orleans and the Gulf of Mexico," I said. "At least, that's what I *was* going to do."

"Sixteen feet? That's a pretty good size of boat. You won't have too much trouble at all. I seen guys go down the Mississippi in all kinds of things. Twelve-foot jonboats . . . canoes . . . why, just a month or two back, we had two crazies go through here in a pedal boat like they have in parks. They thought they was going to New Orleans."

The thought of the two men in the pedal boat took the glory out of my own trip at a stroke.

"Did they make it?"

"I never heard nothing of them since."

I had, after all, dreamed of disappearing from the world. WENT DOWN THE MISSISSIPPI, NEVER HEARD OF SINCE, would at least make a tantalizing line on a modest memorial slab somewhere.

"Oh, you'll have problems. You get down in some of the big pools, like the Dubuque pool—that's one of the worst pools, is the Dubuque pool. She's wide open: four, five miles, as far as you can see. There's stump lines. . . . When you're out there . . . boy, when it gets rough it can really get rough in a hurry. Then you'll get wakes. When some of them big tows get down in the flats, they're pushing along at ten, twelve miles an hour, and they'll turn the whole river to a rooster tail."

"What do I do then?"

"You stay right inshore and ride those waves out. If you're in the channel, you'll be running into waves that are seven feet tall. Even up here, we've had boats tipped over, just from wakes. We get drownings every day. You going to ride the Mississippi, you better respect her or she'll do you in."

His lock basin had filled. It had the absolute stillness of the moment after the last note of the finale before the applause begins. He ran his eye along the brimming surface. I felt that the lockmaster was a kindred spirit, a man who simply loved water. He softened every time he looked at his pet element, his long, chipped hatchet face taking on a moony otherworldliness.

"But you've got to watch that sky. You ever see anything queer about it, if the clouds look wrong somehow, you get off the river. Oh, you'll see thunder and lightning. Hell, you could run into a hurricane. There's storms on the Mississippi so bad even the big tows get lost sometimes. There's tows gone down there, just sucked under in a storm on the river. She can be meaner than the ocean. But you'll be okay. Just remember, if there's something in the air that don't feel right, *get off the river.* You'll get to know her. You'll learn the signs. The time you got to start worrying is when she goes dead quiet. That's when she means to get up to something, and that's when you get off that river."

He had put me back in touch with the dream. The lockmaster's river and mine were, thank God, the same beautiful, treacherous place. He had grown up right beside it in the little river town of Lansing, Iowa. When he left school, he had become a commercial fisherman and trapper. Then he'd got a job as a construction worker, building levees to contain the floodwaters of the Mississippi. From there he had gone on to work as a bargeman and had graduated to being a full-fledged river pilot, ferrying barge fleets between Minneapolis and St. Louis.

"In 1960, I got married. Hell, *I* wanted to stay on the river, but my wife was mad. You know the way women change you? My wife . . . she don't care for the Mississippi too much."

So he had settled on his lock. I asked him how much he still missed being a pilot.

"Every time a tow goes through here, I think I'm up there in that wheelhouse."

Upstream of us, a tow was swinging round the bend of Nicollet Island. It looked as if someone had turned several tall apartment buildings on their faces and set them afloat. It was not a "tow" at all, in fact: it was a push. Somewhere far at the back of the fleet of barges, now lost behind the island, now printing blots of smoke on the sky, was a boat that wasn't a boat, but a blunt white four-story house, all balconies and verandas, mounted over the top of an enormous engine. This displaced housing project filled the river. Its wake shook the trees on the banks and sent a curling wave far into the shore.

"Three by three," the lockmaster said. "A little one. A single. You should see a double come through here."

"Uh-huh," I said, as noncommittally as possible. I didn't want to be too soft a touch for Minnesota comedians. "So what's a double, and what do you do with it?"

"A double, she could be fifteen barges, three wide, five long. You push nine of 'em in. Break the couplings. Boat backs out with six barges. Then they lock 'em, raise 'em up, drag a cable on 'em, snake 'em up the wall. Drop back. Pick up the second half. Then they make up the fleet and away they go."

"I think I lost about six barges somewhere."

"You'll see how they lock-through. There's twenty-nine locks between here and St. Louis. After that it's open river. Then you'll see the real big tows. Fifty, sixty barges. That'd be around eight acres. And that's something else."

Looking at the wake of the baby tow ahead of us, I felt an apprehensive surge in my guts, seeing waves as high as houses breaking on my cockleshell.

"That trip you're making . . . now, that's something I'd like to do. You a married man?"

"Not exactly."

"If you was married . . . Boy, if I told my wife I was going to ride the river down through New Orleans . . . reckon she'd be around at her attorney's, filing for divorce."

The huge gates at the head of the lock swung open on hydraulic winches.

"All those river towns . . . they're different than the inland towns—looser, more wild. A few years back, they were really wild, those river towns." He seemed to be thinking of his own past and his present compromises. "Yeah," he said a little sadly, "they were wild."

He locked the tow through. Thirteen thousand tons of grain bound for Baton Rouge, Louisiana. When the pilot's voice came through on the radio, he spoke in the singsong whiffle of the very deep South.

"Well, Cap—wish I was goin' with you," said the lockmaster into his handset. I supposed that he said that to everyone.

On Tuesday, I drove out to see my boat. I had firm ideas about what a boat should be. One of the river books over which I'd pored during the summer had been Henry Thoreau's *A Week on the Concord and Merrimack Rivers*. Thoreau had made his inland voyage in a green-and-blue dory, "a creature of two elements, related by one half of its structure to some swift and shapely fish, and by the other to some strong and graceful bird." I had been tempted to send this lovely specification on an airmail postcard to Crystal Marine.

The boatyard lay far out of town, away from the river, at the end of a dismal suburban boulevard. In the lot at the back, a hundred boats were tipped up on trailers, identifiable only by their numbers. Mine was WS 1368 DD. It was just a mustard-colored shell of aluminum. Blunt-backed, broad in the beam, this bare piece of riveted alloy did not look like a craft in which one might float at all easily into an idyll. It was related to neither fish nor bird, but to some new, efficient brand of nonstick saucepan.

Herb Heichert, the joint owner of the yard, stood by while I walked in a slow circle around this unalluring object, trying to think of something polite to say about it.

"How do you like it?" His voice had the rusty remains of German in it.

"It looks . . . strong," I said. "Would it be easy to sink?"

"No, you got plenty of flotation there. See those seats? That's where you got your flotation."

I was glad that I had flotation. I thought of it more as a moral quality than as a physical property. I'd always wanted to have flotation.

"Now we got to fix you up with the right rig for the river." He leaned on the transom. The boat boomed like a dull gong. Mr. Heichert pointed at the blank metallic space.

"All these hulls, they come in the same, and every one she goes out different. You got to build it around the customer, right? No one's the same. Everybody's different. That's America. That's the American Way. We're in the customization business here. You take a plain old hull and you build a guy's whole identity into it. Look, I'll show you—"

He led me to his showroom. Boats hung on ropes from the ceiling, stood on trailers and were rooted by their keels to the walls. My mind boggled at the identities of the guys for whom they had been customized. One was carpeted from bow to stern in blood-red polystyrene fur; another, in the kind of artificial grass which undertakers spread over fresh graves.

"When a fella gets a boat, he gets real sore if he sees some other fella riding round the lake in a boat just like the one he's got himself. Round here, everyone's an *individualist*."

So it appeared. I tried to focus my eyes on a boat on which every last inch had been covered with swirling rainbows of acrylic paint. The effect was roughly comparable to taking a heavy overdose of lysergic acid. A little dinghy had a ship's wheel that might have been salvaged from the wreck of the *Golden Hind*. I peered into cocktail cabinets and freezers and rang the great brass bell that was mounted over a chubby day boat.

"Know what this is?" Herb was playing with a bit of fun technology that had been screwed to the thwart of a red-and-white-striped skiff. Fifty stars were painted on its stern. "Electronic fish locator. Like radar. See here—switch it on, it finds your fish for you, shows you what size it is, what the depth of water is there . . . all you got to do is put your pole over the side and catch it."

It struck me as immoral.

"We like our gizmos here."

"Will the fish locator tell you what bait to use as well?"

"They must be working on that, I guess."

When we returned to the lot, I saw WS 1368 DD through rather different eyes, as an empty canvas on which Herb Heichert was going to paint a gaudy extravaganza. I had certainly come to the right person: he was the works manager of a dream factory. I was bothered, though, by the fact that the dreams he dealt in bore no resemblance at all to mine.

"So what do you think?"

"I'll need somewhere to put my charts. A chart stand."

Oddly, a chart stand turned out to be the only gizmo that Herb had never been asked to fit to a boat. We set about designing one: a foldaway wooden frame with a button-down front of transparent plastic.

"The guys here stick to the lakes mostly. They don't use charts."

We settled on navigation lights, a steering wheel, an electric pump and a swivel seat. Herb seemed disappointed with my parsimony.

"Fish locator?"

"No, thanks."

"We could run you up a paint job."

"No, it's fine as it is."

With oars, anchor, and the engine that was now running in a tank at the workshop, I would have the vessel I needed to sail into my Cockaigne. Esthetically, it might not be a patch on Thoreau's dory or Huck's raft, but it would be fast enough to run from trouble. And I had plenty of flotation.

I needed to lay in some provisions. Thoreau had taken a supply of melons and potatoes on his trip. Huck and Jim had loaded up with traps, setlines for catfish, a lantern, a gun and a Barlow knife. I went shopping in the city, hoping that if I acquired a few symbols of pioneer self-sufficiency it would bring about a transformation of my character and turn me into a proper outdoor adventurer.

Minneapolis itself, though, had gone indoors. When it had done all it could to tinker with the Mississippi; when the bridges, mills, power plants, locks and dams had been finished; then the city had turned its back on the river and focused inward on itself. Now it was engaged in yet another exercise in utopian gadgetry; building a city within a city, a perfumed maze of artificial streets and plazas set in midair, four stories above the ground.

No wonder the streets had seemed so empty. The city had gone somewhere else and cunningly hidden itself inside its own facade. To go shopping, one had to take the elevator up to this other Minneapolis.

It was a completely synthetic urban space. Glassed-in "skyways" vaulted from block to block, and the shopping plazas had been quarried out of the middles of existing buildings like so many chambers, grottoes and tunnels in a mountain of rock.

Here, fountains trickled in carpeted parks. The conditioned air smelled of cologne and was thickened with a faint, colorless spray of Muzak. The stores were open-fronted, like the stalls of a covered Arab souk. Like all the best utopias, this one was only half-built. It was the nucleus of a dream city designed to stretch out and farther out until Minneapolis-in-the-air would be suspended like an aureole over the deserted ruins of Minneapolis-on-the-ground. If one put one's ear to the walls, one might hear the distant reverberation of workmen with pneumatic drills tunneling out more corridors and plazas in the wider reaches of the city.

The skyway system was as vividly expressive of the peculiar genius of Minneapolis as the roller-coasting freeways are of Los Angeles or the glass-and-cement cliffs of New York. Only a city with really horrible weather could have arrived at such a thing. Here people had left their local nature behind altogether. It was something nasty down below, and the skyways floated serenely over the top of it. "Nature" here was of the chic and expensive kind that comes only from the most superior of florists: ornamental palms and ferns, rooted not in soil but in coppery chips of synthetic petroleum extract.

Voices melted into the musical syrup of André Kostelanetz that trickled from hidden speakers in the palm fronds. Footsteps expired on the carpeted halls. At a mock-Parisian street café, the shoppers sat out at gingham tables, drinking Sanka with nonsaccharin sugar substitutes. Skyway-city turned one into an escapee. It was a place where everyone was on the run—from the brutish climate, from carcinogens, from muggers, rapists, automobile horns. Even one's own body was being discreetly disinfected and homogenized by the deodorant air. Up here, everything was *real nice:* we were nice people who smelled nice, looked nice and did nice things in nice places.

Four floors below, we could see the nasty world we'd left behind. Hennepin Avenue was stretched out in front of us, famous for the Original Sin in which it wallowed. Beneath the skyway, a crummy little store sold rubber wear and shackles. Posters for the blue-movie houses showed nipples and pudenda so imaginatively colored and airbrushed that they'd ceased to look human in origin. A wino pissed in a doorway, watched by his dog. It was a pregnant bitch, and looked vaguely ashamed of its owner.

Looking down on that fallen world from the standpoint of this temporary synthetic Eden, I thought that perhaps Minneapolis and I were really on much the same track, traveling hopefully, never arriving. I loved the audacity of that American principle which says, When life gets tainted or goes stale, junk it! Leave it behind! Go West. Go up. Move on. Minneapolis had lit out from its river. Now it was trying to wave goodbye to its own streets. The skyways were just the latest stage in its long voyage out and away. "Where ya goin'?" said the truckdriver to the hitchhiker at the end of *Manhattan Transfer.* "I dunno. Purdy far." It was the same answer that I'd given to the drunk in Moby Dick's, and on the skyways the whole city seemed to be echoing that classic traveler's statement of intent.

Our voyages, though, led in separate directions, and I seemed to have made yet another knight's move away from the river; so I was cheered to see a rack of corncob pipes in a cigar store. They weren't called corncob pipes—that would have been too straightforward for this realm of artifice and invention. They were advertised as "Missouri Meerschaum," and I bought two of them, along with a tin of Captain Black Smoking Tobacco, which sounded suitably swarthy, and a Zippo windproof lighter. Drifting idly through more chambers of glass and ferns and tea-garden rumbas, I picked up a corkscrew, a thermos flask and a khaki rain hat. I reached my hotel room half a mile away without ever touching ground.

I sat in front of the mirror and tried to construct the man who was going to ride the river. I packed a corncob with Captain Black, lit it with my Zippo, jammed my new hat over my ears and looked in the glass, hoping to see the beginnings of a true voyager. The effect was not good. The face reflected there belonged to a grinning scoutmaster.

Half the luggage in my room was books. For months I'd been collecting them in London. I had found more in New York. They were the stuff out of which I had been making my imagined river, and as the Mississippi grew more real, I would have to start dumping them overboard.

The one I liked best was titled *The Navigator.* Set in cheap, jerky type, it had been published in Pittsburgh in 1814, and it had been written by Zadok Cramer as a pocket guide for immigrants and traders who wanted to travel on the Western rivers. It had detailed maps of the Ohio and the Mississippi, and it was full of notes about where one could find lodgings, where the best places were to tie up one's boat, which were the most dangerous bits of the river, what to do in storms and how to test sandbars for safety. When I had first looked at it, I had thought it a charming curio; now its cracked pages were beginning to take on a riveting up-to-dateness. Cramer's first remarks about the Mississippi were standard pietistic twaddle:

> This noble and celebrated stream, this Nile of North America, commands the wonder of the old world, while it attracts the admiration of the new. . . .

Within a paragraph, though, Cramer was scoring direct hits.

> To a stranger, the first view of the Mississippi conveys not that idea of grandeur which he may have pictured to himself: his first judgement will rest upon the appearance of its breadth, in which respect it is inferior to many rivers of much less note.

Exactly. Cramer knew only the lower river, below its junction with the Ohio at Cairo, Illinois; I wished he'd been able to see it from the railroad tracks at Minneapolis. Flicking through, I went back to his section of general hints for intending voyagers.

> The first thing to be attended to by emigrants or traders wanting to descend the river, is to procure a boat, to be ready so as to take advantage of the times of flood, and to be careful that the boat be a good one.

Well, I had attended to that, all right. Right now, Herb Heichert should be fixing the steering gear to the motor and putting in the circuitry for my navigation lights. Cramer's tone grew sharply monitory. This business of going down the river must not be done impetuously. There were, he said, too many "young and inexperienced" navigators who,

> being flushed with the idea of a fortune before them, hastily buy a boat, load, jump into it themselves, fly to the steering oar, and halloo to the hands to *pull out*. Now swimming in good water, and unapprehensive of the bad, they think themselves safe, until alarmed by the rumbling of the boat on a ripple, or shoving herself into the mud on a sandbar.

In Cramer's day, no one thought of going down the river without a copy of *The Navigator*. It was a much-reprinted best seller—and ironically enough, it became a hazard to navigation in its own right.

At least, that is what it was for Timothy Flint, a Presbyterian minister from Boston who went west with his family, taking the river route, intending to do some evangelizing among the rednecks on the shores. He had a dreadful time of it. His book, *Recollections of the Last Ten Years Passed in Occasional Residences and Journeyings in the Valley of the Mississippi* (1826), was a wonderful inventory of terrors and disasters. The Flint family had innumerable brushes with death on the river, and *The Navigator* was directly responsible for the first of these catastrophes.

> On a sudden the roar of the river admonished us that we were near a ripple. We had with us that famous book "The Navigator" as it is called. The boat began to exchange its gentle and imperceptible advance for a furious progress. Soon after, it gave a violent bounce against a rock on one side, which threatened to capsize it. On recovering her level, she immediately bounced on the opposite side, and that in its turn was keeled up. Instead of running to the oar, we ran to look in "The Navigator." The owner was pale. The children shrieked. The hardware came tumbling upon us from the shelves, and Mrs. Flint was almost literally buried amidst locks, latches, knives and pieces of domestic cotton.

There was a moral for me here somewhere. Like the Reverend Timothy Flint, I was an incorrigibly bookish man. The river in my books was one thing; that sludgy beast beyond the tracks was quite another—and I had better start getting the distinction between the two clear in my head. If I didn't, I was going to run dangerously, perhaps finally, aground.

Herb Heichert was too much of an artist to take much notice of my dull and utilitarian specifications. When I arrived at the boatyard the next day, everything was fixed: the wheel, the lights, the pump that would drain the boat at the flick of a switch, a swivel seat of imitation pigskin and a neatly carpentered chart stand. What I had not bargained for was the canopy that now fluttered over it, a candy-striped sheet rigged up on a folding aluminum frame. Nor was I prepared for the fact that the boat was no longer just called WS 1368 DD. The words RABAN'S NEST had been painted in enormous black letters on both sides.

"Like your canopy?" Herb said. "Now you got a surrey with a fringe on the top."

"The canopy looks fine, but what's this 'Raban's Nest' stuff?"

"Couldn't resist it. Thought it up in the night. Just came to me. Don't you like it?"

We trailed it down to the river at Camden to try it out. The afternoon was rank and sweaty, and the Mississippi here drifted in a listless sweep between two bridges, a mile north of the end of commercial navigation. It looked as tame as a fishpond in a civic park. Root-beer cans bobbed in the scum at its edge, and more condoms dangled from the branches of the trees like a freak show of spring blossoms.

We pushed the boat out from a concrete slip overhung by willows. In the water, it suddenly looked tiny, its canopy riffling in the feeble wind, its broken reflection a scatter of chips of yellow, white and scarlet.

"Floats, anyhow," Herb said.

Swinging there on the current, it abruptly changed sex. It switched from an *it* to a *her*. She looked just right, and I felt a new rush of excitement at the prospect of my voyage.

I sat up in the bow while Herb started the motor and aimed the boat at the bridge downstream. She was alarmingly fast. As Herb pushed the throttle forward, she lifted her sharp nose clean out of the water and settled on her rump, her wake fanning in a wide V to both shores. Herb sent her into a careening series of figure-8s, with the boat heeling over until the river sluiced by the top of her gunwales. As she cut into her own wake, the aluminum hull clanged as if it had hit rock. Clinging on up front, I was high over Herb's head down in the stern.

"You got to see the limits of what she can do!" Herb called over the yakking chatter of the outboard. He spun the wheel and the boat flipped its head, jumped violently on its wake, and headed off on another diagonal.

"Floating log! You got to watch for floating logs! You hit a log, it'll rip the lower unit out!" Not knowing what a lower unit was, I searched the river for floating logs and saw that we were in the middle of an archipelago of the things. Herb was zigzagging at speed between sodden tree trunks whose only indications were a few innocent-looking twigs sticking out above the greasy water.

He turned the boat around on the current, where it slowed, pointing upstream, the motor just ticking over. My turn. I joined Herb in the stern and started off by muddling up the throttle lever and the gear-change stick. Gingerly I set it in forward gear and gave it a cautious dribble of gas.

For me, the boat would hardly steer at all. Its nose wobbled this way and that, and we corkscrewed slowly in the vague direction of the bank from which we'd come.

"Keep to the main channel!" Herb reached for the wheel. "Watch for the buoys! You get out of the channel, you'll run on a wing dam!"

"*Wing* dam?"

"Yeah. The wing dams, they run out twenty, thirty yards into the river. You can't see them when she's high as this, but they're there. Maybe six inches underwater. Maybe a couple of feet. They're real *rascals*. They built them out of riprap . . . rocks and stuff. You run into a wing dam, you'll be real lucky if your motor's the only thing you lose—it can take the bottom clean out of the boat. Hey, don't get too close to them buoys, now! See that log? Watch the piles of the bridge!"

This was probably the safest little stretch on the whole river. Even here, though, there seemed to be more snags and hazards than I would ever be able to comfortably keep in my head at once.

"Those moored barges over there? You keep well clear of them. When the current runs up against them it makes for one hell of a big undertow. Not so much up here, but lower on down the river when the current gets to be stronger, it can suck you right under if your motor stalls ahead of a line of barges. You don't often hear of guys going in at one end of a barge fleet and coming up alive at the other."

"And people do go under?"

"Happens every year." Herb looked pleased with this piece of information. "I don't know nothing much about the river. The only times I go boating is on the lakes. I wouldn't mess with the Mississippi. I guess I'm kind of sweet on the idea of staying alive."

The boat maundered downstream, going hardly quicker than the current. Every time I touched the wheel, its head whipped sideways and threatened to take us straight into a wing dam, a log, a buoy or the piling of a bridge. I found it impossible to keep a steady course.

"You'll get used to it. After three, four days of riding the river it'll be no different than driving a car. You'll be okay. Watch your charts, keep in the channel, look out for them towboats. . . . Remember, you don't have to do *nothing* fast. Think about it. Do it slow. You run into any kind of trouble, think slow and you'll make out okay. Hey! Remember what I said about logs?"

I thought fast, panicked, and we smashed into the log broadside. The hull shuddered and clanged.

"You have to do that a few times. It's the only way you'll learn."

"I'm just frightened that the next mistake I make will be the fatal one."

"We'll rig you out with a life vest."

We were getting into the start of the commercial river. There were more lines of moored barge fleets parked in front of wharves and grain stores. A shovel-fronted tug was crossing the stream ahead of us, throwing up a wake that looked too high for me to handle. I turned the boat around and headed back for the bridge.

"You know how to take a wake? Never get caught sideways to it. Steer into the wave. If they're big and close together, you'll have to ride them out on a diagonal."

He took over the wheel from me and steered for the tug. Close to, its stern waves were running in steep ridges, four feet high and less than twenty feet apart. Herb drove squarely into them, and the boat see-sawed from crest to crest, plunging down, then tilting sharply upward to the oily sky. As each new wave hit the bow, the metal rang out in a melancholy boom.

"Never take it too fast. You don't want to pop a rivet."

My stomach was leading a private yo-yo life of its own.

"See? She hain't taken on a spoonful. You take a wake right, you won't have no problem at all. You let her swing you round broadside, though, she'll roll you right over. Then you'll have to swim down to New Orleans. Guy even tried *that* once. He made, oh, I guess a coupla hundred miles. Then had to climb out. His skin was all boils and sores . . . looked like he had leprosy, they said."

Driving the boat on farther downstream, I went very quiet indeed. Scared by the wake, I'd forgotten my difficulties in steering the boat and was surprised to notice that she was now keeping to a reasonably steady path. I dodged a floating log. I kept to the main channel, watching the twin unfolding lines of red and black buoys. Red to port and black to starboard. This had nothing to do with daydreams and boyhood memories; it was the serious business of learning to ride the river. For the next two hours I crammed myself with everything that Herb could teach me. I rode out the wake of two small tows. I practiced holding the bow into the face of a wave while the wave itself took hold of the boat's nose and tried to swing it around and lay it in its trough. I began to read the surface of the river, hunting for the telltale riffs in the current where the submerged wing dams ran out from the shore. I got accustomed to spinning the boat around, throttling it back and putting it hard into reverse gear. As the traffic on the river thickened, with tugs swinging whole fleets of barges around on the current, I did my best to think slow, feeling childishly dependent on Herb, who stood at my side saying very little except *Easy* and *Okay* and *Watch it,* as if he were gentling a nervous horse. I thought a lot about the warning that I'd been given by the lockmaster. *You better respect her, or she'll do you in.*

Back in the evening inside Minneapolis-in-the-air, I was the one lone diner in a restaurant full of families and couples. I picked at an omelette which had been cooked to the texture of chamois leather and drank, rather more enthusiastically, a bottle of California chablis, feeling my solitude as a conspicuous caste mark.

Most travel involves the reassuring presence of other travelers: one joins that easygoing society of professional solitaries who are themselves just passing through—the salesmen, homesick U.N. peacekeepers, drifters in search of jobs, political scientists pretending to be agricultural advisers, anthropologists who haven't had a bath for weeks, and the rest of that roving crew who prop up bars in foreign places and make for poker schools and conversation. On this trip, though, I was traveling through someone else's domestic interior; a stranger in the American living room. Here, if one didn't have a family one was at least supposed to be a delegate to a visiting convention, with a lapel badge and a light hound's-tooth suit to prove it. Lacking both, I felt that Minneapolis was condemning me to the grim demimonde of Hennepin Avenue.

Trying to look, at least, like an occupied man, I spread out my navigation charts conspicuously on the restaurant table and set to studying them. I had only the volume of charts for the "upper river," the eight-hundred-sixty-mile stretch from Minneapolis down to the junction with the Ohio at Cairo. It was a huge, ring-bound book, broad and thick enough to stun a sheep with, handsomely produced by the U.S. Army Corps of Engineers. By an act of Congress in 1917, the management of the river had been put into the hands of the Secretary of War, and it was still military territory. In a country where really good maps are curiously hard to find, these charts were a cartographer's masterpiece. Brilliantly particular in their details, severe in their exclusion of irrelevant bits of landscape, they gave a practical soldier's-eye view of the Mississippi, breaking it down into a clean summary of all the logistical problems involved in its mile-by-mile navigation. Weeks later, when I got hold of the charts for the "lower river," from Cairo down to the Gulf of Mexico, I was disappointed to find that they were hopelessly inferior—so small in scale, so careless in their inclusion of a distracting mass of surrounding countryside, that the Mississippi wasn't the hero of the book at all, but a minor character following its wriggly career somewhere out on the obscure edge of things.

These, though, were everything that charts should be. At a scale of two inches to the mile, they gave the river a decently heroic size. Turning the sheets, I watched it growing from less than half an inch wide in Minneapolis to sweeps of four and five inches as it suddenly swelled out just a few miles south of the city. Here it became a pale blue tessellation of lakes, islands, "sloughs," chutes, "towheads," "stump fields," bars and creeks. The red vein of the main channel tacked from shore to

47

shore, hedged in by the dotted outlines of "submerged features" that I was going to have to learn to steer clear of—the wing dams, hidden bank supports, pipes, cables, wrecks and stumps.

I was enjoyably lost in the difficulties of getting from Mile 818 to Mile 816 (all distances were numbered from Mile 0 at Cairo). Running close to the Minnesota shore past Boulanger Slough, I'd pass the light and the government daymark on the bank, then begin a long eastward swing out across the river to Wisconsin, keeping on a narrow track between a stump field to my left and a serrated line of wing dams on my right. Buck Island wasn't an island at all, but a miniature Caribbean, backed by another stump field. Past the head of Nininger Slough, I'd graze the Wisconsin shore, following the railroad tracks as they ran along the water's edge, then swing out again, to position-up to enter Lock No. 2 at Hastings.

"Excuse me, sir, but are you the gentleman from England that's going down the river?"

In the electric-candle dusk of the restaurant, all I could see was a stooping business suit. It was pearl gray and filled to capacity.

"That's right. I'm just looking at where I hope I'll be tomorrow on the charts." I pointed to the bloody hairline.

"Lois?" the business suit called to a table somewhere behind him. "Yeah, I was right. It's him. It's the guy I said it was. He's got maps." In an afterthought he said to me, "Read about you in the paper. I was telling Lois—that's my wife—I was saying, 'There's that guy, at that table.' Recognized you from your picture in the paper."

I took this as a prelude to a relationship of some kind, but when I started to reply, his back was already turned to me and he was on his way to finish his dinner across the restaurant. I would have been glad to talk to anybody at that moment, and I found his abrupt departure unsettling. What *was* he doing? I supposed that he must have been settling a bet. I found it saddening that the business suit might have won a dollar by establishing my identity. I would not have risked a bet on it myself.

The charts had lost their vividness. After Lock 2, the river narrowed sharply between Lake Isabelle and Lake Conley. There was a marina on the Minnesota bank, just south of Hastings. After that, I couldn't be bothered to follow it further. The chablis bottle was empty. The waiting check looked rapacious. I saw the face of the business suit turned momentarily toward my table. It was meaty, and it was laughing.

I slept thinly. High wakes from towboats came rolling at me through my dreams. There were floating logs, and the propeller screamed on the rocks of a wing dam, and the boat pitched and clanged, and I tried to remember why on earth I was here, out of character in a Boy Scout hat. Later, with the curtains drawn against the sun, jittery and unshaven, I ordered up breakfast from Room Service and packed my bag.

The waiter who brought my eggs and coffee looked as if he had already done some growing that morning since he had put on his tuxedo. His forearms stuck out of his cuffs, and his collar was popping around his Adam's apple.

"I saw the article about you in the paper. The trip you're making . . . I really envy you."

"Really?"

"That's something *I'd* like to do, go down the river. St. Louis. New Orleans." He named them as I used to name them to myself.

"Why don't you go?"

"I'm buying time. Working through the summer. Most days, when I can, I go down to the lock and dam and look at the river. You're taking a boat, right? I want to build a raft."

"I thought of that too. I think it could be hellishly dangerous."

"People nowadays, nobody does nothing. Everyone plays safe and stays home. I'm going to save myself some bread and get out of this city. I'd like to work on the towboats . . . get a start as a barge hand. . . . But that river . . . shit! I love it, you know?"

I showed him my charts. He pored over them, saying, "Hey! . . . Hey! . . . Hey!" and clicking his tongue noisily against his front teeth. "Just looking at these, man . . . I *am* going to build that raft. There's a place up above the lock, a friend and me, we were talking about putting it together up there."

"On a raft you're going to have a lot of trouble keeping out of the way of the tows, aren't you?"

"Yeah . . . I guess so. . . ."

I had intruded a ponderous detail that had no place in the waiter's vision. He shook out his forelock of Swedish-colored hair.

"I better get back. Hey, have a *fantastic* ride, will you?"

"You too," I said.

"Yeah . . . well . . ." He laughed. "Wouldn't that be something else?"

It had faded into the conditional. Every time the waiter looked at the river he thought of lighting out, and the thought was sufficient in itself —more sustaining, even, than any real journey could be.

I found it harder to leave the city than I'd planned. Herb's partner had been doing some heavy public relations, and by the time I reached the river a crowd was waiting. Two television crews had turned out, and a gang of passersby had thickened around the television crews. No one seemed to know why anyone was here. But whatever it was, it was going to be on TV. There were rumors of a drowning, a rare bird, the arrival of the *Delta Queen* steamboat, and various other wonders. I was introduced to a spruce old man with an Instamatic camera and a basset hound. He was announced as the King of Camden, and very kindly took my picture. As he put away his camera he said, "I got an album of photos of people who've been on TV."

The boat went growling from its trailer into the water. I sprinkled a few drops of five-dollar champagne over her bow and shared the rest of the bottle with Herb, the King and the basset hound. I heaved my case into the front of the boat and was about to take off when the TV crews intervened.

I've always enjoyed slow-motion action replays on television. I now found myself living in one. Acting under instructions, I held the neck of the champagne bottle over the bow of the boat. I shook hands with Herb. I climbed into the boat. I pushed off with an oar. I started the motor with a jerk of the cord. I waved to the King (who was by this time happily engaged in photographing the cameramen). I steered for the railroad bridge downstream. As soon as I had passed under its arches and was out of sight, I returned to the slip, got out of the boat, picked up the empty bottle, held it over the bow, shook hands with Herb, got into the boat, and went through the rest of the mime until I reached the bridge, then turned back to repeat the whole sequence one more time. With each new performance, these movements stiffened until they took on the ritual grotesquerie of a scene from Kabuki theatre. I became a star at taking my leave of Minneapolis: now christening my boat, now waving, now setting my face southward with, I thought, a becoming expression of jowly determination. The twin violet eyes of the cameras followed me with the same indifferent gaze that I'd noticed in the cow at the state fair. My head rattled with a conundrum: if my going away didn't happen on TV, it wouldn't be real; if it did happen on TV, it couldn't be real.

There was one problem with a sound boom; two hairs in the camera gate; one time when my motor wouldn't start; and a hitch involving a small boy and a basset hound. After the sixth rerun, I got back to find the crowd dissolving and the TV crews packing their equipment back into their vans. I turned around. No one remarked my last departure. I slipped into the main channel and let the boat take root in the river.

At last I had the Mississippi to myself, and it seemed that Minneapolis had conspired to make a gift of it to me for the afternoon. Nothing was moving. Barges and towboats were moored at the wharves, but no one was about on them. Cranes and derricks were frozen on the sky, caught at odd angles, as if their operators had been suddenly called away. The air was inert, and the surface of the river was as finely patterned as a fingerprint. Every twist and eddy of the current showed up as a black-pencil curlicue on the water. One day, I'd learn to interpret every squiggle—at least, I'd try to. For now, it was enough to be moving just for moving's sake, like Baudelaire's lost balloon.

A factory went by; an empty dock; a lone man with a paintbrush on the deck of a tug, who looked up for a moment from his work and waved; then summer-dusty trees, massed and entangled on a shore of powdery sand. Rising fish left circles on the water here, and the current squeezed them into narrow ovals, before they faded into the scratched wax polish of the top of the river. It was lovely to be afloat at last, part of the drift of things. All I needed was a pet fox from a Bingham painting to throw his black reflection on the water.

Beyond the riverbank, the city blocks wobbled and tapered in the afternoon haze. They looked so insubstantial that a cooling wind might have wiped them away altogether. Pity the typists, doormen, cleaners, clerks, executive vice-presidents locked in those trembling columns of gas! I had the natural superiority of the truant; out of it all, on my own limb, at a happy angle to the rest of society. The motor chirruped smoothly behind me, the boat kept up an unwavering line between the buoys, and in this still water I could see the floating logs fifty yards ahead and swing casually around them.

The upper lock at the Falls of St. Anthony was already open for me when I rounded Nicollet Island. Up on the platform, Herb, the lockmaster and the King were leaning over the railing. I crashed into the chamber wall, overshot the ropes that had been lowered for me to hang on to, reversed furiously, crashed again, and just managed to grab one of the lines before the steel gates at the back of the lock closed with a hiss and a clunk.

"Okay," said Herb. "You'll learn."

"Wish I was going with you," said the lockmaster.

The lock had seemed huge when I'd stood above it four days ago. Inside the chamber, it felt twice as big. I clung to my pair of ropes. The water began to bubble and boil as the lock emptied. The boat edged down the slimy wall, and the faces above my head grew smaller and vaguer. As I dropped to thirty, then forty, then fifty feet down, it was like entering a new element in which the air was dank and cellarlike; I was far out of earshot of the people I had left back up there in the city daylight, their voices lost in the gurgling and sluicing of Mississippi water. The boat tugged and swung on the ropes, and even in a sweater I was shivering. Looking up at the pale pink blotches of Herb, the King and the lockmaster, I felt that this descent was a kind of symbolic induction, a rite of passage into my new state as a river traveler.

I couldn't hear what they were calling. The front gates of the lock opened on a blinding rectangle of day, and I was out, past the railroad sidings, into another chamber, another drop, more clammy half-darkness, and another wide-open afternoon.

In that sudden alarm which sets in an hour or so after one has started any journey, I ran through the inventory of what I'd packed. My Hostmaster soda siphon with its box of bulbs for putting bubbles into tap water . . . chapstick . . . aerogrammes . . . the ineffective electrical gadget that was supposed to put instant creases in my trousers . . . surely I had left my hotel room quite bare. Then I remembered. On the lower shelf of the bedside table, a fatal place to put anything, I had left my copy of *Huckleberry Finn,* open face down at the bit where Huck plays the mean trick on Jim with the sloughed rattlesnake skin. Damn, damn, damn. Slowing on the current, I thought that perhaps my loss wasn't such a bad augury after all. This was a voyage I was going to have to make alone.

Old Glory

*B*y *the time* I reached Lock 1, six miles farther on downriver, I was feeling cautiously insouciant about locks in general. I rode up to the ladder built into the lock wall, tweaked the bell rope hanging behind it, and was told by a voice coming out of a loudspeaker to stand off while an upstream tow came through.

I beached the boat under the Ford Parkway Bridge and lit a pipe, listening to the grumble of city traffic over my head and to the fanatic whistlings and scrapings of the crickets on the shore. The rising towboat showed over the top of the lock: its smokestack, radar scanner and top deck, then four more decks, one after another in wedding-cake tiers. These modern towboats had inherited a great deal of the glory of the steam-powered stern-wheelers they had superseded fifty years ago. Each deck sported a frieze of white ornamental railing work, slender Corinthian pillars and a fancy portico. Like the old steamboats, they were the floating equivalent of the Southern planter's mansion, brimming with neoclassical swank. Their pilot houses, jutting forward from the rest of the boat in a wide-windowed balcony, had a royal arrogance about them. Even now, a Mississippi River pilot was a definite somebody, and the top-heavy pyramid of the towboat's superstructure reflected all the luster that still attached to his title.

When the lock gates opened, the tow pushed out its fleet of nine barges, sucking the river away from the shore as it came, and sending out a long stern wave which lifted my boat and rammed it deep into the bank. I got my motor started and headed for the open lock chamber. The water there was still threshing from the action of the tow's twin screws, and when I went in I lurched and slid as if I were trying to drive too fast on ice.

I had been warned. Tows had engines of enormous horsepower—anything from three thousand for little ones to eight and nine thousand for the big, lower-river boats. In the open river, they could make wakes and eddies that went on churning for a mile after they had passed. In a lock chamber, they could swill the two-or-three-million-odd gallons of water about like a milkshake.

I wasn't even supposed to be here. In my newly won assurance I hadn't troubled to notice the red light at the entrance, and as my boat slopped and skidded in the lock I got cursed for a blind sonofabitch shit who should've waited for the fuckin' green, *you asshole*. Were they going to drown me in cold blood in order to teach me a lesson? The lockman allowed me my rope only after he'd run through such a lexicon of expletives that the torrent of excrement being tipped on me from the lock wall was roughly equal to the volume of turbulent water on which I was just managing to keep afloat. I was torn between fright, fury and bleating apology. As I sank into the emptying chamber, I heard my own whinnying voice collapse into a stutter of *f*'s. *F-f-f-f-f-f-f-f-f-f-f*, I went, my own attempt at obscenity turning as seemly as a line of asterisks in a Victorian novel.

The lockman called down: "You come in like that, you goin' to have to *luck out!* How far you goin'?"

"Oh . . . New Orleans. . . ."

"*N'Orleans?*" His derision boomed off the wet walls. "I'm telling you, man, you get to N'Orleans, you can send me a fuckin' postcard!"

Mercifully, distance and the noise of the sluices obliterated the rest of what he had to say.

Below the lock, the face of the river changed. Before, it had been a city slicker, hemmed in by streets, yards, piers, warehouses. Now it ran through a rough country of forest, sand and rock. The chart showed Minneapolis and St. Paul keeping pace with the Mississippi, less than a mile away from each bank; but this wasn't parkland so much as a stretch of original wilderness on which the twin cities had never bothered to intrude.

At the sound of my motor, baby turtles the size of saucers plopped from overhanging branches into the water. Big butterflies on floppy wings rode the air like kites, tacking and dipping ahead of me. They were Monarchs, and we were going the same way. The butterflies used the river as a highway down which they made their annual migration. They left the Northern states in late summer and traveled downstream to the Gulf and on to Venezuela and Colombia. Sometimes I took them on as hitchhikers. They would come flickering out of the wind and lie on the thwarts of my boat, where they sunned themselves, their crinkly orange wings veined with fine threads of black. I liked these fellow vagrants. Their style of travel, at once feckless and compulsive, seemed much like my own.

Here the water was a deep olive green, mottled all over with leaf shadows. Its current thickened as the Minnesota River added itself, in a string of miniature whirlpools, to the Mississippi below Pike Island. A tow was heading upstream between the trees, and I pulled in to the bank to keep out of the way of its wash. Setting my anchor in the crook of a boulder on the sand, I felt contentedly Robinson Crusoeish. I wandered along the shore, scuffing up gouts of bleached dust. I never noticed the fisherman, and nearly fell headlong on him as he squatted in the bushes, his cane pole lost among the other branches that ran out over the water.

"Hey, mister—" He was old and black and wore a once-gray suit which had gone to the sheen and color of verdigris. A brown derby hat was tipped back on his head. His half-eaten sandwiches were spread on a scrap of greaseproof paper at his feet. Stale slices of bread had peeled back in wings in the sun from their fillings of cheap corned beef.

"I'm sorry—I didn't see you there."

"I thought maybe you was the warden."

"No."

"So I was layin' kinda low." He flipped his pole upstream and trailed it down with the current.

"What are you fishing for?"

"Just for what I can catch. Crappies . . . catfish . . ."

"How big do the catfish run here?"

"Oh, pretty big." He made the classic fisherman's gesture of showing me with his hands. They began a foot apart, then spread to encompass a giant.

"What bait do you use?"

"Good meat." He pointed at his bait tin. It was true. Corned-beef sandwiches were good enough for him, but for the catfish he'd bought at least a pound of filet steak. Channel catfish must have been picky eaters, for they hadn't been tempted, even by these bloody hunks of prime Midwestern beef.

"Can't seem to get a bite out of them. Sun makes them real sleepy. Been down here for better than four, five hours and I hain't had but one little nibble." He resettled his hat over his eyes. "There's no way you can rely on them catfish. Some days, I've had more of 'em outa here'n you could shake a stick at; other times they're layin' right down at the bottom of that river, and they're so *lazy* they won't raise a whisker."

The tow went by, dragging the river in creases behind it like a trailed skirt.

"Maybe she'll wake them fish up," he said.

My own boat rocked and banged on the beach. I pushed it out onto the current, through a tangle of hanging green, and out into midstream. The western shore was beginning to darken, while the eastern shore was taking on a buttery glow of evening sun which turned the trees to bright cutouts and the sand to turmeric. After the tow's passage, the water tidied itself back between the banks, and the swallows came crowding in over the surface.

It was mosquito hour. All over the river, the bugs were coming to. Crickets, ticks, gnats, chiggers . . . grass bugs, rotten-timber bugs, leaf bugs, water bugs . . . everything with six legs and wings and stings was whirring or whining or chirruping. The din these insects made was enough to override the noise of the motor at my back. It sounded as if a dozen radio stations were all trying to broadcast on a single frequency. It was, I realized, no accident that I had the river more or less to myself. My wrists and ankles were turning lumpy with mosquito bites. When I slapped at the air, it was crunchy with bugs.

The trees went black, then lost out to high warehouses again, while the sandy beaches were shuttered away behind piles and wharves. In the violet light, the riverfront of St. Paul had the pretty decrepitude of a European city; its dusky brickwork floated in long reflection on the water. It looked frowsty, aged, and likable. I found a little shantytown of houseboats moored on the west bank, and tied up to a pontoon there. The whole assembly of floating frame houses was murmuring and groaning in the current as it dragged at their hawsers and scoured their front steps. I lugged my case down a steel catwalk, the inky water hissing under my feet. Behind each lace-curtained window, the same colored picture flickered in each houseboat's darkened room. Bursts of obedient studio laughter broke with the monotony of waves on a beach. *Mork and Mindy.* I crept past as quietly as I could. My own picture was a great deal grander than that livid and jerky image . . . the Gothic silhouette of the highway bridge, the black sweep of the river streaked with city lights, and the tangerine moon lying low over the rail yards.

I was mesmerized by the river. St. Paul was an abstraction on a limestone bluff where I checked into a hotel room for the night and found a bar to kill time in while the Mississippi went on unrolling in my head.

Admiral Benbow's was a convenient enough nowhere in which to let one's thoughts drift. Everything in it was in imitation of something else. The nautical junk that furnished it was faked; so were its walls of plastic leather books; so was the girl singer who was churning out old Barbra Streisand numbers to a Magnavox organ and a drummer who spent the entire evening in a state of near-coma, wiping his skins with a pair of wire brushes.

> . . . *second-hand curls, I'm wearing second-hand pearls,*
> *I never get a single thing that's new* . . .

I licked the frost of sugar from the rim of my whiskey sour, glad at least of the gloom in which the place had hidden its tackier bits of artifice.

> *Even Jake the plumber, he's the man I adore;*
> *He had the nerve to tell me he'd been married before.* . . .

My fellow drinkers looked as if they had been purchased in bulk along with the plastic library walls. They were all aged thirty-four and three-quarters, with identical sets of cropped curly hair, wire-rimmed glasses, and catfish mustaches which gave their faces a single expression of bewildered solemnity. Since the elderly young men were telling each other jokes and showing off an enviable expanse of costly bridgework, these mustaches were ill-chosen accessories. It might have been a good idea if their wearers had come to an agreement to take them off their upper lips and put them in their vest pockets for the evening.

The great-grandfathers of these men could have been in on the beginnings of St. Paul. If one of them had arrived here in 1847, he would have found a dismal collection of traders' cabins set above the river and called, with a frankness uncommon in these parts, Pig's Eye. In 1849, two hustlers named Henry Rice and John Irving decided to turn Pig's Eye into a metropolis. Rechristening it was the first step. Then they laid out a street plan which—like most street plans in the West at that time—was a piece of pure prophetic fiction. Tracts of cut-down timber were labeled as hotels, churches, factories, warehouses, government buildings, tenements, newspaper offices, stores and schools. In five years, amazingly, they had conjured up a population of seven thousand people. St. Paul became the state capital of Minnesota, and by the 1870s, people were writing of it as if it were as old, genteel and venerable a place as Boston. Minneapolis was the "new city," and by comparison with its twin, St. Paul legitimately considered itself a crusty social superior. People who forgetfully referred to it as Pig's Eye were ridden out of town on a rail. In the telescoped version of history that has been a Midwestern necessity, St. Paul has always dated "from way back."

Six months after the evening in Admiral Benbow's, when I was back in London, I found a book titled *Information for Immigrants* published by the United States Immigration Bureau in 1872, right at the peak of German and Scandinavian settlement in Minnesota. It was a manual of homely statistics, covering all the middle and western states and territories, designed to help the prospective settler fix on a destination in which he could afford to build his new life.

In 1872, Minnesota already had more than four hundred thousand people living in the state. It was long past the stage of being anything like a frontier. Most of its railroads were built; cities like Minneapolis and St. Paul were nationally important; the basic pattern of its trade, agriculture and industry was set solid. An immigrant in 1872 would have been a latecomer.

Yet if he pored over *Information for Immigrants,* he might have been astonished to find just how open Minnesota still was. He might, for instance, especially if he was German and used to working on a farm in Europe, think of trying his luck in Pennsylvania among his fellow "Pennsylvania Dutch," who were really Pennsylvania *Deutsch.* Or he might try Ramsey County, Minnesota—the riverside county that contained St. Paul.

As an agricultural laborer, he would earn about $2 a day in Minnesota, but only $1.35 a day in Pennsylvania. A pound of Pennsylvania beef cost 17 cents; in Minnesota it cost 12 cents. A barrel of flour: $4.30 in Minnesota, $7.53 in Pennsylvania. At $5.12, a pair of "strong boots" would cost 32 cents more in Pennsylvania than in Minnesota.

If my imaginary immigrant had a little capital, he might want to buy a "small improved farm"—already fenced and plowed, with a log house and stable. In Pennsylvania, such a place sold for about $200 an acre as against $20 to $30 an acre in Minnesota. If he bought a hog to truffle in his backyard, a Minnesota pig came at $5, while its Pennsylvanian cousin cost $15.

In Pennsylvania there were only scattered openings for labor, and wages were generally a shade lower than in Minnesota. Around St. Paul, though, there was a tremendous demand for all sorts of manual workers: on railroad gangs and public works projects; in the flour and timber mills; in woodcutting; on farms; in machine shops and factories; in carpentry and plastering and every other trade connected with the riot of new-house building.

In 1869, 125,000 Germans and 42,000 Scandinavians had arrived in the United States. No wonder that so many of them had gravitated here.

To me, the idea of "westward expansion" had always had the impressive vagueness of one of those laws of quantum physics, like the causes of black holes and the structure of the double helix. It made a great deal more sense to think of it in terms of the price of hogs and strong boots.

What would my old man, with his log house and his memories of Pig's Eye, have made of his descendants in Admiral Benbow's? Would he have felt a damp-eyed pride to see them here, jiggling the ice cubes in their cocktails?

> *People who need people*
> *Are the luckiest people in the world,*

sang the tired woman on her cabaret rostrum.

> *We are children meeting other children,*
> *Letting our grown-up pride hide all the hurt inside . . .*

Surely Barbra Streisand must have made more rhythmical sense out of the unrhythmical words; yet this rendering had given them an unintentional, rather terrible sincerity. It was smart now to sing of loss and failure and the discovery that life was mostly secondhand. The catch was that the songs were supposed to be sung by successes—international stars of loss and failure. From the mouth of a real loser, they came close to genuine blubbering despair. And in this setting, where the hopefulness of the immigrants who had created it was so close to the historical surface, far from sounding narcissistically wry and self-knowing, they sounded simply and painfully tragic.

The mournful mustaches of the junior executives were in tune with the rest of their faces now. They nodded to the music. They poked at the lemon chips in their vodka martinis with little striped straws. If I had been Great-great-gran'pappy, I would have wanted to whup them good, every one. Hell, those guys, they wouldn't have known one end of a five-dollar hog from the other.

I walked back to my hotel along Front Street. A sodium lamp cast a disk of light on the river below. It looked like a vat of simmering tar: busy water, wrinkling and bulging and coiling in on itself. It didn't just keep rolling along, but kept itself occupied with a myriad of pointless calls and errands along the way. Standing there in the darkness, I felt that the more I experienced of the Mississippi's character the more it looked as if she and I were going to be happily compatible.

The hotel room was a featureless closet somewhere high up in the teens among the elevator buttons. I switched on the TV: the Federal Reserve Board announced that the dollar was being propped up by heavy intervention on the foreign-exchange markets. That didn't seem very interesting, so I sought entertainment elsewhere. A rusty steel box built into the side of my bed promised me a relaxing vibro-massage if I fed it with a quarter. I dropped the coin in the slot and lay on the bed and waited. The mattress on which I was slumped suddenly seemed stuffed with several hundred small, scurrying gerbils. The experience of squashing these animals was mildly interesting but not, I thought, particularly relaxing; and after a minute or two of feeling them wriggling under my buttocks I began to wish that the gerbils would go away.

The TV news went local. An Englishman had left Minneapolis that day in a small motorboat bound for New Orleans and beyond. In interview he said that he'd first read *Huckleberry Finn* when he was seven, and had been haunted by the idea of going down the Mississippi ever since. In the picture on the screen, his face had a cheesy pallor. His countrified hat didn't at all match the urban fatigue of the rest of him. He climbed into his boat, produced a wan grin for the camera, and was soon lost to sight beyond a bridge. He looked to me like a clowning greenhorn, as raw an immigrant as any of those other, weary Europeans who had come to the Midwest with hopes and handbooks. Feeling rueful to see myself so travestied by this foolish character on television, I took comfort from the fact that at least the gerbils had moved out.

Ahead of the highway bridge, the river bunched and narrowed; great wings of blackened timber funneled it through a central arch. I fed my boat into the main channel, where the water ran fast in a glittery swell. The bow clanked as it hit each new wave and kept a permanent corona of spray over my head. When I squinted upward, I could see my own, private, traveling rainbow there.

I had little time for rainbows, though, for now the traffic on the river thickened. Big tows lounged on the current, thrashing the water around their tails, their engines farting loudly as they turned. They maneuvered lugubriously around each other, honking and grumbling, heaving their ridiculous bulk about like hippopotami at a water hole. As I threaded my way through them, one boomed its horn at me, a warning animal note from a very dangerous beast indeed.

Here the river really did mean business. The St. Paul shore was solidly blocked in with cranes, derricks, huge steel drums, gantries, chutes, silos and brick warehouses. I tried counting cargoes . . . scrap iron, salt, molasses, coal, phosphates, sand and gravel, grain. This was harvest time, and there was so much grain that it colored the river itself. Near the elevators, the surface of the water was dusted a pale ocher by the husks of soya, barley, wheat and corn. Closed chutes like elephant trunks fed the moored barges in a continuous stream: twelve or fifteen hundred tons to one barge . . . nine to fifteen barges to a tow . . . and still there were whole fleets of empty barges, tied up off the channel, waiting to be filled.

Until the river straightened out, I didn't realize the strength of the south wind. It was blowing dead against the current, and the water was crumpling into it, ridged with lines of whitecaps running so close together that the boat just rattled across the top of this bumpy, corrugated river. Steering into the waves in the early-morning cool, I felt unreasonably happy merely to be here and now; and the happiness was made real by an underlying tinge of anxiety and fright.

I passed Pig Eye Island, the end of St. Paul and the last reminder of how the city had begun. On the right bank, a long freight train trundled south on the Chicago and North Western railroad, moving hardly faster than I was myself. The tracks and ties were so dilapidated now that trains had to go on tiptoe for fear of falling off the rails. As the train inched past me into the forest, it blew a long, deep chord of organ notes in a valedictory minor key.

It was Saturday, and there were other pleasure boats about, looking tiny and solitary as they nosed out into midstream from behind islands and sandbars. The smartest of them were restored steamboats. Once they had been working tugs and ferries; now, painted up, their stern wheels powered by marine diesels, they were historical toys, hung with holiday bunting, Old Glory flying from the masts on their texas decks. Other bits of history were being reconstructed elsewhere on the river. Wood fires smoked on the sandbars as suburban families played at being pioneers, laying lines for catfish and boiling up their breakfasts in billycans.

The past they were acting out was not, after all, very far away—still within the realm of hearsay and grandfathers' tales. Back for a weekend in the wilderness, in cowboy hats and dungarees, people were taking a day round-trip ticket to a family memory of a time when the essential quality of American life was its freedom from precedent and tradition. Here in Minnesota, between the 1870s and now, America had molded its immigrants into a pattern of manners just as rigid as any that they had left behind in the farming communities of Europe. On the river, though, there was still a smell of uncut forest, and the haunting reminder that things could, perhaps, have been otherwise. Not so long ago, personal identity here was all pliancy and possibility, and camping on a sandbar one might just conceivably remember something—a lost key, a talisman. The plumes of smoke from the fires were flattened by the wind. The houseboats and launches rocked at their moorings. The wilderness was government property.

I pulled in out of the channel to set myself up with a mug of coffee and a filled pipe. There were Man Friday footprints in the sand that blew around my ankles as I hooked my anchor around a fallen tree trunk on the bar. The footprints disappeared over the top of a ridge. Another boat was moored in the inlet there: the most basic of all the sorts of Mississippi boat—a wood-frame garden shed mounted on a floating pontoon, with a flat tin roof and an outboard motor at its back door. It made no concession to the usual fripperies of marine design; it was just a shack built on oil drums. As I stood on the ridge, a German shepherd dog came growling nastily down the plank that joined the boat to the shore.

"Hurricane! Hey, Hurricane! Shut your shit, hey, willya? Willya just shut your goddamn shit, now?" The man might as well have stepped from a sepia photograph as from his boat. Fair-haired, bearded, in denims and lumberjack shirt, he looked as if he could easily be in the market for a log house on a small improved farm at twenty dollars an acre.

"Okay—he won't do nothing."

Hurricane sulked, deprived of his English breakfast.

"I'm sorry, I'm trespassing on your island."

"Ain't mine. Ain't no one's. Ain't posted." He stared at me for a moment, his fingers playing in the thick tawny hair of Hurricane's neck. "You foreign or something?"

"From London, England."

"That so? You want to come on in?"

Inside, his boat was bare and jumping, with water lights playing on the knotted wood. It smelled of creosote and sawn pine. There was a cot, a rocker, a homemade table. Someone was saying, "Downtown we have sunny skies and sixty-eight degrees . . ." on a cracked transistor radio. The remains of a skillet of beans stood on a Sterno camp stove. Playmates of the Month were thumbtacked to the walls. Two six-packs of Schlitz, a can of Alpo, a shotgun . . . the fundamentals of a very rudimentary life.

He was a carpenter. During the week, he worked on a construction site in Minneapolis making slats to spread concrete over. On weekends he left his wife and two young children back in the city and came out here alone to brood and hunt and cuddle his wolf-dog in his floating shack.

"Don't you ever bring your wife and kids?"

"Elvira, she don't care for the river too much. She says it's a dirty place. She weren't raised on the Mississippi like I was. Hell, my family . . . we used to come down here, swim in the river, fish, camp out.

. . . Elvira don't allow for the kids to go swim, even; she read some-place that the river's all full of diseases and such."

We rocked on the wake of a passing tow. Splashes of sun raced each other up and down the walls.

"On the river, you get your head right." He pulled the ring from the top of a beer and sank half the canful at a gulp. "You want a beer? No, what I'd like to do . . . I'd like to build a houseboat the whole family could live on all year round. The whole thing—bathroom, gas central heating, big kitchen, give the kids a cabin each . . . sell out the home I got in Richfield . . . live on the river. Elvira, though, she wouldn't stand for that. She'd go goddamn nutso. *That stinkin' river!* Shit. Hey, give over, Hurricane—give over! But the Mississippi, it ain't dirty, not now. Shit, you can drink the water. I don't know why she hates it so. Lot of women, they do. Guess it kind of scares them."

"It's beginning to scare me."

"Scares me too, sometimes. Specially when she's running high. In the spring, now, with the floodwater and all, this river, she's something else."

The carpenter was on much the same track as Len Mink, the radio gospel singer: he too was going back to the God of his childhood, to the same simple things as the child he once knew. Here he was twelve years old again, a boy in the woods. I tried to guess at the family he had slipped away from, but their outlines were dim. I imagined that Elvira must be big and grown-up, slopping around the house in a floral-print smock and pink fur slippers.

"What do you hunt?"

"Coon. Squirrel. Duck. Coyote. Last fall I got a shot at a polecat, but I missed it. I wanted that polecat real bad, for a trophy. Hurricane, now, he's a great coon dog, ain't you, fella? That dog, he just loves to tree coons. *Coon,* huh? *Coon!* Hey, Hurricane!"

Hurricane looked back at his master with tolerant incomprehension.

"You want to go tree a coon?"

The dog eyed me. A very faint glimmer of hope showed behind the film of rheum. Coons, though, were outside his imaginative range on that particular Saturday morning. Some dim spirit of canine realism asserted itself, and I watched the hope die in his eyes.

"Hurricane?" *Harry Caine?* was how the carpenter actually said the name.

Obliged to respond in some way to this torrent of questions, the dog shifted heavily off his butt and went to eat Alpo out of a bowl with his name custom-printed on it in German Gothic lettering.

"That *is* some coon dog."

"Looks like a fairly keen Alpo dog, too."

"Coon's out of season yet, though. When the coon season starts, that dog . . . shit, there ain't nothing Hurricane likes better than treeing coons."

He laid his shotgun across his lap, posing for his own self-portrait: *The Settler, 187–*. Hurricane broke wind and slept. I said goodbye, leaving the carpenter to his solitary, adolescent make-believe, and went back to my boat to get on with mine.

The rags of blown foam on the water were copycatting the rags of high cloud that came beating north across the sky. I kept the boat headed into the waves. The whole trick, according to Herb, was never to get caught broadside . . . "She'll roll you right over" . . . and I could feel her doing her best, snatching at my bow and tugging it sideways, knocking loudly on my hull and trying to come in.

The river was squeezed into a twisty crevice between high bluffs, and the wind, thickened with sand from the bars, went scouring into every cranny and backwater. The forest came down sheer into the water on both sides, broken by outcrops of ribbed limestone, staring out of the solid cliffs of green like the faces of Easter Island statues. Fall was still a couple of weeks away, and the leaves hadn't yet begun to turn. Shaken by the wind, they caught the sun and winked. The river, barred black and silver, was too bright to take in all at once; I had to watch each wave, looking for the rim of shadow under its breaking crest, and steer the bow into it.

I wound through a string of narrow islands, following the lines of buoys. The path was puzzling. It kept on going straight in to the shore and opening onto another stretch of river whose existence had been a well-kept secret behind a false wall of tamarack and swamp oak. Blunt-nosed tows came foraging out from what I'd thought unbroken forest, and I learned to look for their giveaway inverted commas of diesel smoke tethered above the treetops.

The bluffs widened, and the Mississippi spread itself into a great islanded pool, two miles from shore to shore. It was Boulanger Slough. Two nights before, sitting in the restaurant in Minneapolis, I had crossed it on the charts as casually as if I'd been planning a country stroll. Boulanger Slough in life, though, looked horribly different from Boulanger Slough on paper.

So this was what a stump field was: a barbered forest. For as far as one could see, the rotten tree trunks stood up, some just below, some a few inches above the water. It had been, perhaps, a hundred years since they'd been cut down, and they looked as if they were already halfway to being coal. The river slurped around their blackened roots and boles. The channel here swung out and east through this waste of water, bog and timber. The wind was bowling long gusts from the right-hand shore, where it began as a riffle on the edge of the stump field, then built up a rolling swell as it came north across the mile or so of peaty water.

By the time it reached me, it had accumulated a frightening height and weight: lines of chocolate combers ran straight up and down the channel. They took hold of the boat and rocked it over on its gunwales. I had to find a diagonal course into the rollers, and kept on trying to tack against the grain of the wind. Black to red and red to black . . . but the buoys were mostly hidden by the high waves. Suddenly lifted on a crest, I'd see them, then get pitched down again into the slop. Riding a wave top for a moment, I looked for the two shores. They were both getting farther away. Had I been the Reverend Timothy Flint, I would have rushed for my copy of *The Navigator*; but that was packed deep in my suitcase far up in the bow, with rivulets of Mississippi water dribbling all over its scuffed leather. *Think slow.* One wave at a time.

Turning the boat's head at the end of each tack was my main problem. As I got closer and closer to the lines of rotten stumps, I had to wait for a wider-than-average trough, then spin around and head back up into the wave from which I'd just dropped down. Once, when I seesawed ineptly over a breaker, the propeller was lifted clear of the water and the engine made a vile sound, like the squeal of a stuck pig.

"You don't have to do *nothing* fast."

"Respect her, or she'll do you in . . ."

Wave followed on black wave in a monotonous, lilting rhythm. There were some words that went with it, somewhere . . . and suddenly they came back to me. A British manufacturer of tonic and mineral waters supplies a lot of English pubs with ashtrays to advertise his products. The words go in a continuous circle around the rim:

> In foreign climes there are at times
> Some moments quite appalling;
> But none too fraught to set at nought
> By a stiff drink mixed with Rawlings.

Thank God for Mr. Rawlings. His jingle revolved obsessively in my head like a loop of recording tape. I set it to the waves:

> *In foreign climes* (Drive at an angle up the shoulder of the wave)
> *There are at times* (Perch on the top, look for the next red buoy)
> *Some moments quite appalling* (Race for the trough, like a child riding down a slide) ;

But none too fraught (Steady; square up to the next wave)
To set at nought (Watch those stumps, before going down again)
By a stiff drink mixed with Rawlings (Swivel the boat around
   in the trough and head southeast for the blacks) .

I quite lost count of all the foreign climes and moments quite appalling; I also lost my fright. I didn't notice that I was gaining the lee shore
of a fringe of islands until I was there, and the water was quiet, and
there was suddenly time on my hands under sunny skies at sixty-eight
degrees.

Bluffs closed in on the river again, and it dawdled through deep woody
pools. On the holiday houseboats moored offshore, parties of women
played euchre while their husbands took off in skiffs for the riverside
bars, where they roistered dutifully through the long afternoon.

"Trouble with folks around here," said the man at Diamond Bluff,
"is we don't have no fun at all! No one has any fun here—ain't that
right, you guys? No one's having fun! Look at these guys here—not one
of them's having fun!" He laughed, and dribbled Budweiser, his face
smashed with liquor. "Say, do we look as if we're having fun here?"

"Not very much." It was true. The shaky, aging funsters with their
whoops and hollers looked as if they'd been condemned to having a
good time. They were serving out their sentences as old cons do, with
practiced resignation. The man, though, mistook my answer for companionable irony.

"Not much! Hey, Clyde—give this fellow another goddamn drink.
Can you believe it? You come out to Diamond Bluff any Saturday, and
you'll find it just exactly the same. Eggs-ackly. Do you have fun in
England the same way we have fun here? Betcha don't have no place
there like Diamond Bluff! You just take a look at us guys: nobody . . ."
His voice wobbled into a hiccup. ". . . has fun like we do." He caught
his foot in the brass rail at the bottom of the bar and fell against me,
scattering my half-eaten pizza to the floor.

I went chugging out past the knot of houseboats. The women, waiting for their sodden menfolk, were eking out the hours with ice cream,
brownies, chocolate-chips and cards. Their cracked tenor voices rattled
over the water:

"Pass."
"Pass."
"Left bower."
"Right bower."
"Euchred!"

Below Diamond Bluff, the river slid by an Indian reservation, posted against trespassers. Curious, I ran my boat into a quiet creek off the main channel. Herons lumbered off their fishing stations on creaky wings and the forest glades were speckled with butterflies, but the Indians were away and somewhere else. The burned-out chassis of a car caught high up in the branches of a tree was the only sign that people ever came near this place. I wondered if I was being watched. Turning my motor off, I drifted in the slack water, listening. All I could hear was the crickets, rattling in the brushwood like pocketfuls of chinked nickels, and the plop-plop of baby turtles falling off logs.

The air had gone dead. The boat hung torpidly on the trickle of current that fed Sturgeon Lake. My pipe crackled. I wasn't sure if I was on forbidden territory. The chart said LANDS RESERVED FOR USE BY INDIANS, but made no mention of the water. Still, I felt like an out-of-season hunter. Posted and reserved, the Prairie Island Indians had become just one more endangered species, like the brown bear and the bald eagle. There was another wrecked car stuck in another tree; and where the creek opened into the lake, a row of plastic detergent bottles marked a fishnet or a line of baited hooks. So the Indians must have been about. I tried calling "Hello!" into the woods, but the only response came from a pair of snipe that fireworked out of a brake of fallen timber.

I started the motor again, and flushed a complete Audubon of pigeons and waterfowl. They went cackling and flapping overhead. Angry *American* birds. Bigger, gaudier and more numerous than their British relatives, they made me feel even more of a trespasser as they clattered back onto the water, grumbling like wives at the unmannerly way I had intruded upon their afternoon.

I continued downriver, the shadow of the boat running ahead of me as the Mississippi took a dogleg eastward, then dropped sharply south into Red Wing. The bluff on which the town was built was almost black now; it was hard to tell which was which between the pines and the church spires. I nosed around a floating village of boathouses moored to gin poles; they moaned and rumbled on the wake I made, their tin roofs catching the remains of the sun like heliographs.

An off-channel lagoon had a little colony of houseboats tucked inside it, and I went cruising around other people's patios, looking for a space to tie up. All over the lagoon, the electric storm lanterns were being set out with the barbecue furniture, cocktail cabinets were opening, and the serious business of partying was getting under way. The houseboats were bright with lights and voices; their owners stood in identical leisure wear, caught in the same pose with a cocktail shaker in one hand

and a bottle of bourbon in the other, welcoming their guests to a world which, just for this moment, had the stylized brilliance of a TV commercial.

I was taken in hand and invited to come partying. My boat was made fast for me with fancy nautical knots ("You know the double sheet bend? I swear by it"), and I was shown onto the veranda of the biggest and newest houseboat in the row.

"This is Dick and Alma and Walter and Betty and Don and Bonnie and Ruby and Jay . . ."

"Think of the achievement!" Walter was saying. "Just think of the achievement!"

"Thirty-six hours he's gone," said Bonnie. "Thirty-*six* hours!"

"My God, I wish I had his self-control," said Alma.

"Feels like *weeks*," Walter said. He was a big man with sad-sack eyes. He looked as if running for martyrdom were the nicest thing that had happened to him for ages.

"Two *hours*," Alma said. "That's my top limit."

"Thirty-six hours without one cigarette," moaned Walter. "Hell, gimme a drink, will you, Tom—*gimme* a drink?"

They were all in their fifties, just old enough to be young grandparents. Their children were out of college and had fled Red Wing for faraway jobs out of state, in Colorado, Washington, Florida, Chicago. Everyone had a wallet full of creased photos. The wives carried their sons' and daughters' last letters home in their handbags, as if their children had gone off to some foreign war.

"I got a line from Cathy just this morning."

"Pete called up from Washington last week. They're just fine."

"Gerry says he might come home Thanksgiving."

These absent children were the real stars of the party. Red Wing was not a place where children stayed if they could get out. Once, like Pig's Eye, it had looked forward to a future as a metropolis. When President Hayes visited the town in the 1870s, drumming up votes for one of America's wobblier administrations, he had been able to talk of

> this fine city of Red Wing, whose warehouses, I am informed, receive the largest amount of wheat directly from the wagons of the farmers of any city in the world.

It sounds as if even then he was stretching things a little. The sentence bristles with qualifications, as if Hayes feared that there might be a reporter or two from Minneapolis or St. Paul in his audience. Even so, Red Wing then had been thinking big, and by the standards of the time its hopes for itself were not particularly grandiose or unrealistic. Now the joys of living in Red Wing were being thrust on me as if I might be in a position to whip out an American Express card and buy the joint.

"You seen the St. James Hotel?" Don asked.

"That's just great," said Alma. "Oh, you'll *love* it."

"They've restored it. Hell, they've done a real fine job there. A four-poster in every room . . . all the rooms named after different old-time steamboats . . . it's a piece of living history now, the old St. James."

"Did you know the inventor of puffed wheat was a Red Wing man?"

"No."

"Not many do. That's a fact. The guy who invented puffed wheat . . . Anderson. They named the park after him. Anderson Park. He was born and raised in Red Wing."

I thought of Pete in Washington and Gerry in Florida and Cathy in Chicago. I felt that I could see their point.

I saw a crucifixion look in Walter's eyes as I switched from my corncob to a rather damp and crumpled pack of cigarettes. He followed every movement of my Zippo, and his own lips pursed very slightly as I lit up.

"That's one helluva bag you're carrying in that boat," he said. "If you're going up to the St. James, you'll need a ride. I can run you up there easy."

"That'd be very kind of you," I said, but I was making friends with Dick and Alma, the doctor and his wife. They seemed to have come together on the principle of opposites' making perfect wholes. Dr. Yang and Mrs. Yin. Dick was a slender, gray ascetic. He paused for several seconds before speaking, and then delivered one-clause sentences of ten words at most. Alma babbled. Her voice sounded as if she gargled regularly with Brillo pads. Her shape was basically circular. Dick occasionally moistened his upper lip from a glass of mineral water; Alma drank tumblers of neat bourbon, and lit each new Kool from the glowing tip of her last one.

Alma wanted me to see their boat, which was moored next door across a companionway.

"Come on, Dick!"

Dick came, with a slight, apologetic, silent bow to the rest of the party.

The entrance to *Mississalma* was flanked by two squat plaster baseball batters, gloriously painted—the Red Wing equivalent of Florentine *putti*. Alma rather than Dick, I thought. Inside, it was more house than boat, a rich apartment of leather, teak and glass. Its long picture windows filled it with the violet glow of dusk. On the water beyond, the lights from the storm lanterns were stars on an ebony sky. Alma led me through to her galley. Over the lintel she had fixed up a large metal plaque saying SLAVE QUARTERS.

"The slave quarters," she said. "Dick!"

Dick had been reading a paper under a tassel-fringed lamp. He dropped it fast. "Yes, dear?"

"Take him up to your wheelhouse. Show him the radios."

Dick took his usual time to think. He looked as if he were silently counting his own heartbeats. "Maybe he's not interested in that kind of thing."

"Of course he's interested. He's going down the river."

As we started to climb the steps at the front of the living room, Alma called, "You want to take a shower?"

"No, thanks—"

"Anytime you want a shower, go take one. Make yourself at home. You want me to look you out a towel?"

"Thanks, but—"

"How's your drink? Dick, freshen his drink, will you?"

"His drink's fine," said Dick.

"What do you specialize in . . . medically?" I asked.

"Internal diseases." The slightly exaggerated emphasis he gave to the word "internal" suggested that he held all externals in some disdain. I wondered if he only found people interesting when he opened them up with a knife.

In his wheelhouse, his character suddenly changed. We were high over the top of the parties now; we'd climbed out of the small talk, and Dick was free. He showed me his deck of instruments and named them for me one by one. I once spent some time on a modern cargo ship: its bridge was only slightly more elaborately equipped than the wheelhouse on Dick's houseboat. He had ship-to-shore radio, ship-to-ship radio, a depth-sounder, a wind-velocity gauge, a compass floating in gimbals and enough dials and switches to fuddle the mind of an airline pilot. On his chart table were dividers, rulers, T-squares, pencils. With all this gadgetry, he should not have found it too difficult to make his way to Samoa or the Seychelles.

"You must be able to go a long way in a boat like this."

"Oh, you *could*. Yes, I'd go to Florida . . . the Bahamas, no hesitation. She's got a good deep draft, too. She could take on some weather. Yes, she'd make it on the ocean okay."

"How far have you actually gone so far?"

"Oh, well . . ." Dick's anchoritic face went suddenly sad again. He went into one of his long, thinking pauses. I wished that I hadn't asked the question. "A week or two back, not so long ago, we went up to beyond Hastings." I had passed Hastings earlier that afternoon. "Then other times we go down to around Lake City. . . ." He looked at me with the expression of a miserably compulsive truth-teller. "That's twenty miles, I guess. Could be a mile or two short of that, even."

"I expect the hospital keeps you too busy for anything more than day trips."

"One gets vacations," said Dick, not a man to let himself too easily off any hook.

"It must use up an awful lot of gas."

"Oh, she's about average." Dick turned over the pages of his charts. Another imaginary traveler. "You must have come through Boulanger Slough today." He pronounced it "slew." "Was it rough up there?"

"I thought so, but I'm not used to the river."

"All those wide places, you ought to watch them when it's a day like today. When the wind's from the south, blowing up against the current, that's when it's worst. I was up here around lunchtime, it was gusting up to twenty-five miles an hour. You ought to reckon, with a boat the size you've got, anything from the south at more than fifteen, the best place for you is indoors. With a northerly, it's different. Twenty's fine. But a southerly wind . . . ten's okay, twelve's kind of choppy and fifteen's your limit."

My head was beginning to fill with pokerwork mottoes about riding the river. Dick's had been the most explicit and useful so far. I was cheered, though, to learn that my fear earlier in the day hadn't just been cowardice.

We went back to the party. Encouraged by the idea that I had actually behaved rather heroically under the circumstances, I told the story of how I had crossed Boulanger Slough.

"In foreign climes," I recited, "there are at times some moments quite appalling; but none too fraught to set at nought by a stiff drink mixed with Rawlings."

"Say that again?"

I did.

"That *Rollins,* I guess that's kind of like a club soda, is it?"

"Would you say that was a typical British commercial?" asked Jay. "Sounds kind of old-fashioned to me."

"Look," said Walter, "anytime you want I can give you a ride up to the St. James."

"He can stay on the boat," Alma said. "We've got plenty of room. There's a spare cabin. I can make up the bed . . ."

"Thanks so much—" I said, but Walter cut me short.

"Hey, let the guy make his own decisions. He wants to stay in the St.

James. He wants to see *Red Wing*. You want to see Red Wing, you stay in the St. James. Like I said, it's living history up there."

"He can save himself some money . . ." Alma said.

"Let the guy do what *he* wants to do, for godsake!"

Caught in the crossfire, I tried to signal Alma in dumb show that I'd love to stay on her boat; but Walter now had my suitcase in tow and was walking fast up the plank that led to the shore. The whole idea of the journey was, I thought sadly, to follow the current of things, and no current that I had yet met was stronger than Walter marching me off to his car.

The moment we were inside, he said, "Hey, give me a cigarette, will you?"

"Are you sure you want one?"

"*Sure?*" his voice was a millimeter away from rage.

"But after thirty-six hours . . . thirty-seven now . . . surely . . ."

He raped the packet. Cigarettes spilled over the floor.

"Jesus," said Walter, lighting up.

"So it's defeat," I said.

"Look. I lie a little, okay? Everybody lies a little. I lie a little for my wife. I lie a little for Dick. Hell, I've had one or two. I smoked one this morning. I had one after lunch. You don't know the *pressure* I'm under. Hell, look, I'm even lying to you right now. You know when you went off with Dick and Alma, right? Alma left a pack behind. I sneaked one out of it. I smoked it in the john. I *hate* Kools. I can't stand them. And there I am sitting on the john with a goddamn Kool, for godsake. Oh, Jesus."

"I tried giving up myself once. I lasted for three weeks. I couldn't work. Then I just had to write a piece, and I was back on two packs a day."

"This giving-up-smoking. Oh, my God. Look, I'm an honest man. This business, Jesus, it's turning me into a liar and a thief."

We drove along the bumpy track on the levee.

"Hey, I'm sorry," said Walter. "We could go back. You could've changed your mind . . . but you'll like the St. James, you really will. It's living history." He switched on the air conditioner. "Now, if you were smoking a Marlboro too, I wouldn't have to do that. But you're smoking your pipe. If Bonnie smelled those two kinds of smoke, sure as hell she'd *know*. You see what it's making me do? I'm getting to be a goddamn criminal!"

The St. James Hotel was more like a waxwork museum than a piece of living history. The desk clerk sat behind an antique cash register with wrought-iron eagles on it, his credit-card stamping machines kept discreetly out of sight. The hallway was lined with polished brass spittoons. I wondered what would happen if I actually expectorated into one of these objects, but decided not to try.

There was no shortage of rooms: I could put up in "The *Natchez*," "The *Robert E. Lee*," "The *Buckeye State*," "The *Ben Franklin*," "The *General Pike*," "The *A. L. Shotwell*," "The *Belle of the West*." I can't remember which of these dead steamboats I finally moved into. Everywhere there were steamboats. Brown photographs of their pilots, in wing collars and top hats, decorated the landings. Livid chromos from the 1880s showed steamboats battling through sloughs of whitecaps with black thunderclouds sitting on their masts. More chromos displayed these famous stern-wheelers from a technical draftsman's point of view; with every portico, every balustrade, every detail of rigging and trelliswork scrupulously etched in, while the boats themselves floated in a ghostly white element, neither air nor water.

The place was a monument to the age of steamboat Gothic. It smelled not, as one might have hoped, of sweat, beer, oil and coal, but of little china bowls of potpourri. In my room there was, as Walter had promised, a miniature four-poster, spread with a hand-crocheted quilt. A newspaper had been left for me on the scroll-top escritoire, and I seized it hopefully. The *St. James Journal*. Everything in it turned out to be exactly a hundred years out of date.

> This morning a thunder shower of unusual violence came from the west, accompanied by high wind. The lightning struck a chimney of the St. James Hotel over the front toward Main Street, knocking the brick into the street and carrying some pieces across Main Street. Mrs. Donohue was in Mrs. Dodge's room, and was prostrated from her chair upon the floor where she remained a minute insensible. She afterward complained of headache and a slight injury to one foot. She says she did not see any lightning or hear any thunder.

What I wanted, though, was the weather forecast for tomorrow, and this cute facsimile with its jumpy typography was no use to me at all.

I thought that all American hotel rooms had television; this one apparently refused to acknowledge that the instrument had been invented yet. There was a telephone of sorts, though. I unhooked the trumpet-shaped earpiece from its fluted stand, fearing that all I'd hear would be the cracked recorded voice of Rutherford Hayes or Mark Twain. But a girl's voice came through, singing, "Hi, there!" a century out of sync with the apparatus we were using.

"Is there a TV anywhere in the hotel? I want to see a weather forecast."

"You'll find one in your room, sir." She made it sound as if this were a cozy game of Hide and Seek that the hotel usually organized for its customers.

"Where?"

"You just try that old wardrobe right across from where you're sitting, sir." She must have been the queen tease of Red Wing High; I imagined her in frilly pants and fishnet tights, twirling a drum majorette's baton.

I tried the wardrobe, a handsome reproduction piece of pine Colonial. The drawers, when I pulled at them, turned out to be doors, and opened on an enormous color television. I found my weather report. Nothing does so much justice to the gargantuan scale of American life as its national weather maps. In Europe, one is allowed to see the weather only as scraps and fragments: a cake slice of a depression here; a banded triangle of a ridge of high pressure there. In the United States, every morning and evening, I was enthralled by the epic sweep of whole weather systems as they rolled across the country from the Pacific to the Atlantic, or coasted down from the Arctic Circle, or swirled up from Mexico and Cuba. The weathermen tapped their maps with sticks. Without betraying the slightest flicker of wonder or concern, they announced that people were being frozen to death in Butte, roasted in Flagstaff and blown off their feet in Tallahassee. Each day they rattled off every conceivable variety of climatic extremity in a blasé drawl. I'd never seen so much weather at once, and was deeply impressed. I shivered vicariously for the Montanans, sweated for the Arizonans and ran for shelter with the Floridians.

Tonight, though, Minnesota was the one place in the nation with really boring weather. Our local man from Minneapolis foretold moderate humidity, low precipitation and winds from the south at ten to twelve miles an hour. By American standards, he might reasonably have asserted that for the next day we would have no weather at all.

I closed the false drawers on the TV. I peered down at Main Street through the dinky white plywood shutters on my bedroom window.

There was nothing going on. I tried to distract myself with the *St. James Journal*:

> EVEN UP.—Last Monday evening, after concluding his day's labor on the bench, Judge Crosby repaired to the basement of the St. James hotel for a bath. After concluding his ablutions he enquired of the sable proprietor, Charley Fogg, what the damage was. Said Charley: "Judge, dis is the first time I has had ob getting eben with you, and guess I'll hab to charge you about seventy-five dollars." His honor pondered a moment, and then said: "Do I know you? Have I ever met you before?" "I tink you hab," said Charley. "You sent me up once for three months." Honors were easy.

I went to the bathroom. The toilet cover had been fastened to the seat with a paper seal FOR YOUR PERSONAL SAFETY AND CONVENIENCE. That, I thought, neatly expressed the general spirit of the St. James. The era of the Mississippi steamboat had not, on the whole, been notably hygienic. In this expensive piece of "restoration," American history had been marvelously disinfected. It had been robbed of its vitality and given a smooth patina of fake antiquity. In the St. James version of things, the post–Civil War U.S.A., with its railroad scandals, the Tweed Ring, scallywags and carpetbaggers, had been got up to look as if it was as quaint and remote as the never-never land of Merrie England. With history so thoroughly sanitized, no one need fear for his personal safety or convenience as he sat thoughtfully at stool in its purlieus: here, the past had been rendered incapable of passing on any intimate diseases.

At ten thirty on Sunday morning, everyone in Red Wing was going to church. The town was built around a long rectangle of green which sloped sharply up the bluff, and the churches were dotted around this open park. I went past the Methodists, took a path across the green through an avenue of maple trees, hesitated over the Episcopalians and the Catholics, and finally joined the biggest line, at the door of the First Lutheran.

With its pale stone and crenellated spire, it was a perfect model of a German country church. It might easily have been built in the seventeenth century; in fact its headstone said A.D. 1895. Inside, a hanging scroll was blazoned with the message HE CONQUERED DEATH—THANKS, O LORD. To my ear, that "Thanks" sounded a shade casual.

I sat on a pew and bowed my head; not praying, just thinking and hoping. I wanted to get down the river safely. I was frightened of the weather, the waves and wakes, the simple loneliness of the trip. I thought of the people I'd left behind in London and named them to myself. I wondered what would happen to my mail. I worried about the strength of the lock on my outboard motor, and whether it was likely to be burglarized. I thought about laundry: it would be another five days or so before I ran out of clean shirts. . . . Then I thought of my father, a parson in England; for him it was now 4:30 P.M., an age since his first, dismally attended early Communion. I wondered if "praying" was really like this for everyone else—a random stream of anxieties, communicated to no one in particular, but sanctioned somehow by the mere fact of sitting under these high arches with the organ wandering quietly up and down among the holy chords.

My father, at least, would surely have given his eyeteeth for such a congregation. The Lutherans packed the church to its doors. There was such a press of plaid acrylic jackets, fancy hats, fresh perms, good teeth, scrubbed children, Masonic pins that I thought God himself, if He existed, would have been a little awestruck by the way in which His children had got on so well in the world. Would He, I wondered, feel like me—with a twinge of envious amazement at all the four-wheel-drive R.V.'s, C.B. radios, ranch-style bungalows, video cassette recorders, Japanese cameras, motor cruisers and new Chevy pickups with which the Red Wing Lutherans had surrounded themselves?

This was Rally Sunday, I read in my order of worship. What everyone was actually rallying for, I had no idea; so I listened to the reading of the Lesson, in the hope of finding out.

"Wives," read Pastor Roberts, giving his flock a sweeping glance which combined chumminess and severity, "be subject to your husbands, as to the Lord. For the husband is head of the wife as Christ is the head of the Church: and He is the saviour of the body. Therefore as the church is subject to Christ, so let the wives be to their husbands in everything."

I felt a rustle of assent susurrate through the congregation. In Red Wing, generally, we reckoned that St. Paul was a far surer authority on things than the newfangled prophetesses of the Women's Movement.

We sang Hymn No. 383.

As we sang, I sensed that this despair was something that we had read about in the newspapers rather than actually experienced in Red Wing. The tune was jolly, and our voices sounded more triumphant than sad as we bellowed out that the world was coming apart at the seams. There was a hint of smugness, even, as we sang about the kind of dreadful things that happened in places like, say, Chicago or Southeast Asia. At the end of the hymn, Pastor Roberts told us what was happening in Red Wing during the coming week: a pizza party for teenagers, the Junior High swim, the Sarah Group, the Coffee Hour, the Sewing Group, the Cherub Choir . . . nothing that smacked of despair.

I got lost during the sermon. I had started to think of wakes and wing dams again. I heard Pastor Roberts say that the Bible was "God's greatest free meal." Insurance salesmen, he explained, bought expense-account lunches for prospective clients, and the Bible was a bit like this kind of lunch, only immeasurably bigger and more nourishing. Then, when I listened next, he was saying that the Bible was "a road map." My attention drifted completely. I thought about trying to read my lunch, and what the Rand McNally Road Atlas would taste like if one were ever condemned to eat it. Then I heard the word "oysters" and brightened considerably.

"Are you an oyster or an eagle?" demanded Pastor Roberts. "An oyster-Christian or an eagle-Christian? Now, you've got to make your choice. Will you be an oyster, or will you be an eagle?"

An oyster, I thought; I'd sooner be an oyster every time. But that was not the right answer.

We sang again. Hymn 501.

By waters calm, o'er troubled sea,
Still 'tis God's hand that leadeth me. . . .

I thought of my boat, bucking on the combers of Boulanger Slough.

E'en death's cold wave I will not flee,
Since God through Jordan leadeth me. . . .

I had had just one short glimpse of death's cold wave. The next time I saw it, I would most certainly flee. On Rally Sunday, I was badly out of kilter with the First Lutheran Church. On the way out, I shook Pastor Roberts' hand with an apologetic mumble to hide my foreign accent, and marched off alone down the green to Front Street, where I found an empty bar and drank a Bloody Mary with an overdose of hot Tabasco.

Mississalma had left her moorings. There was nobody to say goodbye to. I crossed the lagoon and got out into the main river. Here the current ran from west to east, and although I could feel a stiff breeze on my cheek, there were no whitecaps on the water and the going was smooth. On both banks, the forest leaned over the river, and the sun, filtered through an opaque bank of low cloud, was just strong enough to throw the shores into shadow and make winking spoons of the little waves in the buoyed channel.

Five miles below Red Wing, the woods abruptly took their leave of the water and the river opened into Lake Pepin, the longest and widest pool in the whole course of the Mississippi. Now the waves were rolling in from a far gray nowhere—a longer, slower swell than I'd met in Boulanger Slough. I climbed them at half speed, slid over their tops and tried to feel out their rhythm as if they were a new dance step: the Mississippi Whoops-a-Daisy or the Pepin Lurch. I tried to soothe my alarm with Mr. Rawlings tonic jingle, but it didn't work. There were twenty-three more miles of this to go, with the river three to four miles from bank to bank, and the channel keeping mainly to a central line down this small, swollen sea.

Just the evening before, I'd heard stories of steamboats' going down with all hands lost in storms on Lake Pepin, of drowned fishermen and capsized cruisers. I waited for a wide enough trough, swung the boat's head around, and ran her back upstream into the shelter of the forest. If I anchored up at the neck of the lake, perhaps the wind would drop an hour or so before sunset, and at least I could make Lake City before it got too black to see the buoys.

I found a shady inlet of stumps and logs, a real raven's nest, and slung out my anchor. The woods here were too thick and tangled to walk in, so I settled down to read John Cheever. I found it difficult not to fall asleep. Lapped in water, with the leaves tinkling overhead, I did my best to follow the talk of Cheever's Connecticut suburbanites. It was oddly tough going. Cheever's world was at once too familiar and too far away. I had lived, briefly, in his landscape when I taught at a college in Massachusetts. Then it had seemed a very foreign place. With the pages of the book blowing over in the wind here in the Wisconsin forest, the East Coast of the United States and the English home counties had blurred into one. London was a city just a little east of Boston.

I heard other voices coming from somewhere on the Minnesota shore.

Children shrilling. A gust of high laughter on the wind. They mixed with the voices in the book and muddled things up: I lost the Wapshots and listened to the leaves instead.

I was woken by the boom of a bullhorn.

"To-whit, to-whoo! To-whit, to-whoo! To-whit, to-whoo!" I thought it said; a giant electronic owl calling across the river.

The *Mississalma* was revolving slowly on the current, a hundred yards out. I cupped my hands to my ears. Next time, the words came in signaled periods.

"I. Said. Dis. Cresh. Un. Is. The. Bedder. Part. Of. Val. Or."

I put both my thumbs up.

The houseboat moved to the near edge of the channel.

"There's a bit of a lick running out there on Pepin!"

"I know!" I shouted. "I tried it and came back!"

"If this wind doesn't die, we'll see you—stay on board here overnight!"

"Thank you!"

"Hope to see you! If we don't, have a good trip, now!"

The *Mississalma* went on upriver. As she disappeared around a loop in the forest, I rather hoped that the wind wouldn't die. When one is traveling, twenty-four hours is long enough to make one think of people as old and valued friends.

I crossed the channel to find where the voices came from. A Stars and Stripes was ripping at its flagpole in a clearing on the far shore. Lawns came down to the river's edge, and I could see figures hunched around trestle tables on the grass. Behind them, a little way up the bluff, there was a wide-windowed timber ranch house. The jokes were coming loudly now, a steady *yak-yak-yak-yahoo* breaking across the water. The small private dock was already filled with boats; I sneaked mine in between two fat white cruisers and set off to gate-crash the affair.

"Hi, there. You a K.C.?"

"What's a K.C.?"

"Knights of Columbus."

"Sorry, no. It just sounded like a good party from where I was sitting across the river. Can anyone join?"

"Hey, Bill, come over here a moment, willya? That's the Chief Navigator, Fourth Grade. He's the head guy round here."

The Chief Navigator said I was welcome to join the Knights of Columbus picnic. I was too late for Mass, he said; that had been at two-thirty. Now there was just beer and beans and barbecued chicken. He gave me a can of Michelob, told me where to find the barbecue and said I should go talk to Father McKinney.

The Knights were burly farmers from across the river at Ellsworth, Wisconsin. From a distance they looked like clones. They wore mail-order suits from J. C. Penney and Sears, all in the same chemical oatmeals and blues. Each face, though, had weathered differently. The hot summers and vicious winters had turned some to jagged outcrops of rock; others were plump and roseate; still more had the grained and knotted surface of old pine. I found Father McKinney, conspicuous in his cassock, at the end of a long table of families.

"This morning I was a Protestant," I said, "up at the First Lutheran in Red Wing. This afternoon I seem to have joined the Catholic Church."

"You know what they say about instant converts?" Father McKinney had a knobbly, bog-Irish face which didn't quite fit his gleaming American dentistry.

"That they're the worst?"

"That's right. The very worst. Real rascals. You don't look *too* bad a fellow to me, though. There might be hope."

I had to confess that I'd never heard of the Knights of Columbus until ten minutes before. Who were they?

"You're talking to the wrong man here. I'm only a first-grader, a novice." But he explained that the Knights had been founded when Catholics were barred from the Masonic orders. Unable for similar reasons to become Elks, Moose or Odd Fellows, the Catholics had dubbed themselves knights. They did charitable works, looked after widows and orphans, had pension funds and sickness benefits, and put on the best picnics and pig roasts for miles around.

"Do they have secret handshakes?"

"If they do, they haven't told me. Maybe you only learn them when you get out of first grade."

A passing farmer pulled a chair up to our table and started talking to Father McKinney about the insides of his cows. The priest displayed what I thought was an unseemly amount of knowledge of the subject. He appeared to have qualified as some kind of cattle gynecologist, and was batting away about uterine growths and lactation.

He told me later that he himself had grown up on a small farm nearby. "My daddy had around two-fifty acres. That was a kind of average little holding. We were hayseeds then. Dumb no-accounts. That was the way people thought. Today it's all changed. Most of these guys here, they've got anything from two hundred to five or six hundred acres. With the way the price of land's gone, a lot of them are rich men now. Some of them . . . gosh, they're millionaires. Nobody thinks they're hayseeds now; they're getting scared. They're worried about the farm vote. . . . The small farmer, nowadays, he's a real important guy. You watch the way the politicians go round these little towns in Wisconsin, Iowa, Minnesota when it gets to be election time. All this inflation; well, it's blown up the small farmer pretty darned big. He's a giant now, compared to what he used to be."

Things were running Father McKinney's way, and he had the reasonable contentment of a prophet who was living to see his forecasts come to pass. "People now, they want to go back to the old ways. I see it all the time in the Church. A little while back, everything had to be *modern*. They wanted the Mass set to jazz. They wanted services in jive talk. If it was new, it had to be good. Now we're going back to the old liturgy, the old ritual. Folks are coming to realize that maybe Gran'pappy knew a thing or two, and if it was good enough for him it must be good enough for them too. Last year, now, we had some of them Moonies come to Ellsworth. They didn't get too much of a welcome. Some folks in town weren't quite as charitable as maybe they should've been."

"How long did it take to run them out?"

"Oh—I'm a bit of a conservative," said Father McKinney. "It might have been a matter of minutes. It sure didn't take no longer than an hour."

Dusk wasn't far off. The shadows of the trestle tables stretched almost down to the river. The last of the chicken bones had been picked clean, and the children were beginning to grizzle. The flag still tossed and shuddered on its pole: I wouldn't be able to make Lake Pepin this evening.

Alma woke me in the middle of the night. "How do you want your eggs?" I couldn't make out where I was. *Eggs?* Framed in the fluorescent brightness of the cabin doorway, Alma looked like Struwwelpeter. Beyond her, Dick passed by: bespectacled, necktied, in a pale gray business suit.

"It's a quarter after five."

It felt like it. If I was to cross Lake Pepin, though, it would have to be within an hour or so of dawn. Last evening, even at her mooring in the lagoon, the *Mississalma* had groaned and stirred on the water in the wind. Now she was silent, except for the breakfast noises from the galley—the sputter of fat in a pan, the dog whistle of a kettle coming to the boil.

We sat out in the glass conservatory on the bow.

"I'm sorry," I said. "It's a dreadful thing to do to anyone, to get a household up at this hour."

"When we stay out here on the boat I'm always up about now. Best time of the day," Dick said. He looked out happily at the dead lagoon. It was like a sheet of gray ice. Trickles of smoke rose from its surface. The sky was bleary. It began as a swath of charcoal overhead, then lightened to the color of pale mud somewhere far away over Wisconsin. It was a primeval morning, the sort of day on which it was easy to imagine one's ancestors crawling out of the slime of things. I wished I had asked Alma to turn my eggs over: their yolks had a horrid brilliance, as if they'd been made and painted in Hong Kong.

I was puzzled by Dick's repose. Perhaps this was how physicians dreamed of a perfect world—unpeopled, gray, requiring no surgery to put it right. Alma was on her second Kool of the morning. Lucky Dick. If he hadn't married her, he might easily have forgotten that he was human.

"When do you have to be at the hospital?"

"Eight," he said, slicing a sausage as if this were a delicate moment in a transplant operation. "You shouldn't have any trouble with Pepin today. She'll be like glass. Watch for the wind around nine, though. Don't get caught in the middle."

Alma was busying herself around the boat, taking my journey in hand. I hadn't felt so mothered in years. She wanted to wrap up everything I had in plastic bags; she wanted to pack me a lunch; she filled my thermos with coffee; she gave me a pocket flashlight and some cookies; she was worried that I didn't have rain gear. I was the still center of a tornado of kindliness, whirling around me in gusts of menthol-flavored smoke. I hugged her when I left, and blew farewell kisses to her across the lagoon. She looked as if that had been more or less the right thing to do.

The air was wet and heavy. The movement of the river showed only in the faint scar lines of the current. At the ranch house where the Knights of Columbus had held their picnic, the trestle tables had all gone. The flag on the pole was limp, its stripes hanging in sculptural folds as if it had been molded in soft plaster.

When Lake Pepin opened out, it was immense. Its islands showed up faintly behind standing anvils of mist. I searched ahead for the first signs of the sun. There it was, low down, a fitful dim bulb guttering across twenty-something miles of unbroken water.

I had entered an absolutely seamless world. Everything in it tended to one color. Its browns and greens and blues had been mixed until they'd gone to the translucent gray of dirty gauze. I couldn't tell what was shore, sky or river. The current, exhausted by the sheer space of Lake Pepin, had stopped altogether. In front of the boat, the water had the gleaming consistency of molasses; behind, it lay smashed and buckled by my wake. I slowed right down until the propeller left only a little string of corkscrew whorls, and even they were the marks of a vandal on an otherwise immaculate landscape.

Lake City went by on the south shore—a foggy smear of holiday cabins and motels. Just beside my boat, a fish jumped. It was a big carp, and as it turned in the air and walloped back, it looked as if someone had chucked a block of gold bullion into the lake. The sky was beginning to brighten now. Five miles or so off, I could see the flat black rectangle of a barge fleet heading upriver, the darker prints of smoke from its funnel just distinguishable from the surrounding mist. There was one other early bird about: on the north side of the channel, a fisherman stood in his flat skiff, casting plugs for walleyes. As the sun came up, his reflection sharpened until he and it joined to make a single cruciform pattern on the water. For me, the moment was unalloyed magic. The picture in my head had been real after all.

4

Garfish and Bullwinkle

ick was right. By eight, the surface was beginning to ruffle. Half an hour later, I was banging and splashing through the last mile to Reads Landing, where the lake turned back into river. A wooden shack on the shore had a cola sign outside. It creaked and rattled in the wind.

"Been out on Pepin?"

"Yes; it's getting rough out there."

A huge old man in a boiler suit turned his head to the window without interest. "Ah, she's just giving her ass a scratch."

I sipped at a mug of coffee. The woman behind the bar said, "You wouldn't get me on the river. No way. I've always been afraid of it. I grew up with it and I never learned to swim. You work that one out."

The old man and the woman ran through a long, sad litany of the names of the people they'd known who had been drowned in the Mississippi. Some were from, oh, a good while back now; others were from last fall, out duck shooting, this spring in the flood, or just last month. The names kept coming: Ron . . . Stan . . . Nancy . . . Neal . . .

"It takes its toll," the woman said.

"The Mississippi water, it does funny things. You go across to Nelson, they got a high school there, the girls is all *giants*. Seven-foot girls. A whole school of 'em. That's Mississippi water. Ain't no other explanation."

"You're putting him on, Ed."

"I ain't. That's the truth of it. You been to Nelson? I'm telling you, across in Nelson, all the girls is seven foot tall."

"What do you do?" I asked him.

"Do?" He stared at me, his eyes vague and placid. "Nothing." Then he reviewed his life in detail. "Fish."

The woman clearly thought the man was giving the industry of Reads Landing a bad name. "Jerry, that's my husband, he's a shingler. He reroofs."

"You've always lived at Reads Landing?"

"All my life. Never wanted to go no place else."

"You've never hankered after the big city?"

"Nope. The way I look at it, places like the Landing and Wabasha, they're the *right* size. Now, I got two daughters in school. If they was in a city, they wouldn't stand a chance. How would they make the team in a graduating class of two hundred? In a class of thirty, forty kids, everybody gets to do what they want to do. What the bottom line says is there's only five on the basketball team. Right?"

It sounded to me like the clearest and least answerable argument in favor of the small town that I'd heard yet.

The old man stirred. "You ever seen the basketball team from Nelson? They're so goddamn tall that when they put the ball in that net they look like they was bending down and tying their *shoelaces*."

"Give over, Ed. He's always been full of bullshit. You grow much older, Ed, you'll get so full of shit you'll bust. It's got to come out sometime. You just make sure it don't come pouring out all over my lunch counter."

"Goddamn. Sonofabitch," Ed said. He was in a good mood.

Wabasha, Minnesota, was just three miles on downstream. Behind me, the lake was white with breakers, but the river, running through a deep grove of tall forest, was quiet. When I pulled into the town jetty at Wabasha, I meant to take a walk around the place and continue on down to the Minnesota-Iowa border before nightfall. It was the sight of the hotel which made me stay. The Anderson House was everything that the St. James should have been but wasn't: a big, creaky, railroad-and-steamboat hotel with a warren of plain little rooms where the double-hung windows stuck and the screens were torn. The whole building had grown a bit bent and shaky in its wooden old age. Its polished floors were hillocky. The walls of the corridors leaned in on one at odd angles. The key to my room was of a kind that might have unlocked the gate to the Castle of Otranto. Given all these attractions, I was prepared to overlook the fact that the waitresses in the dining room had been got up to look like Meissen milkmaids in pink-and-white-checked dresses and rabbit-eared mobcaps. I decided that I was going to like Wabasha.

"War-bashaw," said the lady at the desk, correcting me. "We call it War-bashaw." I'd been insistently referring to it as "W'basher."

War-bashaw was a model river town. In a short walk from the river to Third Street, I saw its classic iconographic pattern unfold. Up and down the Mississippi there were hundreds of places like Wabasha which had grown up at the same date in the same way. Like the key to my hotel room, Wabasha unlocked an unrestored piece of American history.

First there was the river. Then, standing on the levee between the wharves and the railroad track, there was a line of grain elevators. The words BIG JO FLOUR stood out in the sky over Wabasha's head like a flag. I picked my way between the stationary freight cars, smelling the wheat which had given the town its main livelihood, and was on Front Street, a stretch of low white clapboard, with a muddy pickup parked in every drive and a chained dog grumbling at me from every shaven lawn. Until lately, no one of consequence would have lived on Front; it was too close to the river; its old shacks had been swept away by floods, and their smart successors had been built only after the levee had been made high enough to keep the river from turning up as an unexpected guest in their living rooms.

One up from Front was Main; and here the brick began. Brick meant substance, importance, civic pride. There was hardly a building on the street which didn't announce that Wabasha had once, at least, intended to be a really big apple. CITY HALL 1894 said the lintel on a Gothic monster which might have accommodated enough people to keep Chicago going. Across from City Hall (and Main Street, Wabasha, was very nearly as wide as Fifth Avenue, New York) stood a group of fine old pretenders. Kuhn's Block 1874. I.O.O.F. 1882. Smith's Block 1884. H. J. Jewell 1880. Masonic Building 1880. Each one was a chunk of fancy architectural confectionery. The European origins of Wabasha showed in its German-Dutch gables, but their facades had gone Ancient Greek, with dadoes, porticos, friezes and lots of Doric columns. The constant toing-and-froing between South and North on the river had brought about a curious intermixture of taste. Even up here in Minnesota, one could see shadows of cotton planter's Hellenism. Perhaps H. J. Jewell had come upriver, seen the palaces of Louisiana and Mississippi from the Texas deck of a steamboat, and decided that if Natchez had it, then Wabasha must have it—or as much of it as he could remember. His block, at any rate, belonged to a style of architecture exclusive to the river, and evenly distributed down almost its entire length. This Mississippi-Corinthian mode had a marvelous swagger and confident imposture to it. It had class—with a short *a*. It was ritzy. It gave some of the meanest little towns on the riverbank an air of yearning grandeur.

Kuhn, Smith and Jewell, not to mention the Independent Order of

Odd Fellows, would probably have been appalled to see how little had happened to Wabasha since they had put it on its feet. The wind blew down Main Street, rattling the flap of the blue mailbox. One scrawny granny in dark glasses and Bermuda shorts was dragging a toddler in diapers past the drugstore. Otherwise, the only human presence on the street was an acrylic-painted clown in a funny hat who turned out, on closer inspection, to be a fire hydrant, decorated by the local children for Bicentennial Year.

Main Street had been built so that the town, like the rest of the nation, could move indefinitely westward. I went to see how far it had gone. Just two blocks on, Wabasha petered out. There were a row of wooden bungalows, a stretch of dingy grass, Highway 61, a creek, another railroad, and then nothing more than a few hundred miles of corn stubble. In whatever lottery it was that decided which American villages were going to turn into megacities, Wabasha had clearly drawn a dud ticket.

I walked back to Main, and found the granny and her toddler in the hardware store. They were wandering up and down the arsenal of guns. Perhaps that was what had happened to the people of Wabasha. There were enough rifles and pistols to equip both sides of a Middle Eastern war. It was conceivable that the citizens of the town had had some dispute—about street lighting, maybe, or the site of a community swimming pool—and settled their differences in the usual way. I spent a happy half hour buying fishing tackle; flexing rods and sorting through boxes of painted plugs which were supposed to look like fish to fish. Their artists, who had decorated them in Day-Glo stripes and flashes, were deeply under the influence of Mark Rothko and Jackson Pollock. I bought a blinding handful of the things, hoping that Mississippi bass and walleyes understood the conventions of the modern movement. I bought an aerosol spray which promised to repel "mosquitoes, chiggers, gnats, ticks, fleas and biting flies." A block up the street, I found the offices of the *Wabasha County Herald,* and begged a pile of back issues from a girl who had fallen asleep over a typewriter.

"It's pretty busy in town today."

"Yeah," she said, yawning. "You can hardly move for the crowd"— and resettled her typewriter to make it into a more satisfactory pillow. I smiled at her as I went out. "I ain't *sleeping,*" she said. "I'm just taking a good look at the insides of my eyelids."

I carried my booty back to the hotel, and assembled my new rod and line. The room was too confined to allow more than an experimental flick of a bass plug into the old china washbowl on the dressing table. I thought about going down to my boat and seeing if I could raise a fish from there: in the bar by the jetty I had seen glass cases full of huge perch and bass, their enameled carcasses arranged primarily to display their teeth. The general idea was a good one, but the spirit of Wabasha prevailed, as I lay on the bed taking a good look at the insides of my eyelids.

At the American Legion, I sat up at the bar and read over the last few issues of the *Wabasha County Herald*. No wonder the town seemed so exhausted. The summer had been a succession of excitements. WABASHA GRACED BY ROYALTY JUNE 14! said the first copy of the paper. THE "QUEEN" LEAVES THOUSANDS INSPIRED. The front-page photograph showed a meaningless something with a row of portholes. It was captioned: "The 'Mississippi Queen': Shown Is Less than Half of the 385-Foot Stern-Wheeler." The photographer had not been able to get far enough away from the boat to include all of it in his viewfinder: this had been taken as a tribute to the boat's glory rather than as a sign of the incompetence of the man who took the picture. The front page continued with a column of breathless asterisks:

> So much happened in Wabasha last week, that it may take another 10 weeks to try to recall all of it . . .
>
> * We were graced by the visit of the newest, most luxurious and beautiful stern-wheeler, the "Mississippi Queen."
> * We hosted the world's most loved and popular millionaire, one Mr. Percy Ross, who made Wabasha his second home last week.
> * We were treated to perhaps the "finest," biggest parade ever staged in Wabasha.
> * We were given a simply beautiful Pageant at the Pioneer Club, with 11 beautiful, charming young ladies and a great dance following, AND
> * We were blessed by a super managing job done by the Wabasha Chamber of Commerce to see that it all went off as promised.

Beside me at the bar, a row was brewing among four stout men. They had the unlined faces of reddened boys under their caps. They were quarreling about their ages.

"You was two grades ahead of me in school. I remember."

"Bullshit. You was in the same grade, you and him both. *I* was one grade behind."

"Hell, Ivor, you know you're a goddamn liar? You're ten years older than all three of us put together!"

"I wasn't even in school when you guys all grad-yoo-ated."

"Now *that's* the biggest sonofabitch lie I ever heard in all my life."

I went back to the paper. The next issue carried a proud quotation from a daily newspaper published in Rochester, a city of fifty thousand people forty miles out to the west: Wabasha's metropolis.

> The "Mississppi Queen" may have been the big boat in Wabasha's River Boat Days last week, but it certainly had to share with million-aire Percy Ross any claim as top attraction.
>
> Ross captured the hearts of the thousands watching the River Boats parade by first handing out ice cream cones and later by tossing out 10,000 silver dollars.
>
> Like baby birds stretching their beaks for a worm from Mother, the outstretched hands of the festival watchers grabbed for the coins.
>
> Ross is a unique individual who has openly shared his wealth with many Minnesotans.

I hoped that there was a hint of satire in the use of the word "openly."

The argument around the bar peaked. The red man sitting next to me said, "Okay, show your hands. Show your hands!" He spread his out in front of him and turned them over. The three other men followed. I looked at the eight hands on the bar top: they were gnarled, liver-spotted, twisted and lumpy with arthritis. I had taken their owners for men of about my own age.

"Hey, you, you don't know none of us. Now, you judge which one's the youngest!"

It was no beauty competition. I pored over the hands and settled, arbitrarily, on Ivor as the winner. His hands looked as if they might be only about seventy-nine years old; the rest all seemed to be well into their eighties. My verdict was disputed.

"Know why he picked you, Ivor? 'Cause you ain't done a real day's work in your whole goddamn life. Shit, look at that pinky! Only use for that fuckin' thing is maybe you could use it for a corkscrew."

I reached the August 16 issue of the paper. Its giant, astonished headline ran: FIRST FAMILY TO VISIT WABASHA! THE PRESIDENT OF THE UNITED STATES IS COMING TO WABASHA! Jimmy Carter, in a publicity stunt designed to revive his fading popularity in the Midwest, had engaged the *Delta Queen* to take him and his entourage on a trip down the Mississippi from Minneapolis to St. Louis. My eye was caught by the wonderful first sentence of the paper's editorial comment:

> In years to come, in these rural areas, Carter will be remembered as the President who brought an entire town to its knees. For we are gathering at the river in a mass "Pray-In" hoping every man and woman and child will come in from the farms, down from the mountains, out from the valleys to join the Ministers and Priests as they conduct a non-denominational Pray-In at the levee for the success of President Carter's program.

My excitement was almost uncontainable as I hunted for a paper of a later date which would tell how the presidential visit had gone off; but I was interrupted in my search by a Legion official who wanted to know who I was and whether I was a bona fide Legionnaire.

"Don Carr," he said.

"Jonathan Raban," I said. "I'm not a vet, I'm afraid; I'm not even an American."

"The Englishman. I heard there was an English guy in town. Pleased to meet you. Make yourself at home." He had a shy, kindly face. He had hidden his mouth as best he could behind a soft white mustache which wobbled when he talked, giving it an oddly animal look, like a tame mouse. Whenever he spoke, he twisted his Masonic ring on his finger, round and round and round and round.

"I was just looking through the papers to see how Jimmy Carter went down in Wabasha—sorry, *War-bashaw*."

"Oh, gosh . . ." Don Carr said, with a visible fluster of sadness at the memory of it. He twisted and pulled at his ring. "Jimmy Carter shook my hand when he was here, and I just hate to say anything bad about him. Oh, gosh."

"What happened?"

"Well . . . first there was all the Secret Service guys. I reckon there was more of them than there are folks in Wabasha County. They was posted up on every bluff. Sharpshooters. They was all over the Big Jo elevator. Everywhere. It looked like the Civil War was breaking out again. Then the President gets off the boat . . . and we're all lined up to shake his hand . . . and you couldn't hardly see the guy, he was tucked in so close with bodyguards. Gosh, they were big men. Great tall, broad fellows . . . When you got to see the President, he was like some kind of little dwarf beside those guys. He was smiling and smiling, and I was thinking, Gosh, this is History . . . the President of the United States, and he's going to shake me by the hand. Then he comes up real close, and I get to see his eyes. He's got this big grin on . . . and all them teeth and all . . . but it was the *eyes* I was looking at. You know, I was looking into his eyes when he shook my hand, and I could see behind that smile. He was stiff with fright. All he was thinking was someone was going to shoot him. Up on those bluffs above town . . . you get some nut up there . . . he could've picked off the President easier than a squirrel. This was the President of the United States, and . . . gosh, he was just a real scared man. I mean, I felt *sorry* for the guy. I *pitied* him. But I'm never going to be able to look up to Jimmy Carter after that, never again. Last time around, he had my vote. But he won't get it next time. I couldn't vote for a man I felt sorry for like I felt sorry for Jimmy Carter. Oh, gosh . . ."

His ring was giving him little consolation. His mustache wiggled unhappily.

"You know what I mean?"

"Yes, I do. You tell it very well, too. Did many people here feel the same way as you did?"

"Oh, there was a lot of folks was real disappointed after Jimmy Carter came to Wabasha. Everybody was wanting to look up to him and somehow he just seemed so *small*."

We were joined by a man who had the habitual sidewise twist of the head of someone who is deaf in one ear. I could see immediately why Don Carr and Jim Curdue were friends; they had the same dreamy mild-manneredness, the same air of moving in a world which bruised easily and must be disturbed as little as possible. Curdue spoke in a voice as soft as a whisper. Beside him, the stout men at the bar sounded like fairground barkers. When he said that he was going fishing in the morning, I asked if he would mind taking me on as a student/companion. I said that I'd be happy just to watch; I wanted to learn the likely lies in the river, what depth to fish at, whether my postabstractionist plugs would work or not.

"Oh, no," Curdue said; "I'd like that. I'd ap . . . pree . . . ceé . . . ate it." The way he drew each vowel out made me assume that he came from the South.

"I was born and raised right by here, up at Reads Landing."

So his accent, like the architecture of Main Street, was a piece of Mississippi cosmopolitanism. Voices carried on the river, even ones as low as Curdue's whisper. There were sounds in it which must have come from at least a thousand miles away.

He ran me back to the hotel in his gray Oldsmobile. I noticed that it was rigged with a Citizens Band radio.

"What do you call yourself when you're talking on the C.B.?"

"My handle?" He said *hay-andle*. "Oh, mostly, I'm Garfish. Then some days, I don't know why, I'm Gray Goose."

We dragged Garfish's jonboat down the stony shore to the water. It was a shovel-fronted metal punt, the commonest kind of Mississippi fishing boat. There were some errands to be done before we could go fishing. Jim had to visit his father at Reads Landing and deliver the mail and this week's paper. We set off up the main channel into another windless, misty morning, with the forest black and dripping on both sides of us. The surface of the river was smooth enough to show the lines of the wing dams as long, dark humps on the current.

"Every dam here's got its own name," Jim said. "That one there we just passed, that's McCann's dam."

"Why McCann's?"

"Oh, it's been called that from way back. Could've been a guy named McCann used to fish off there. Or maybe that's where he drowned himself. Then there's Noisy Dam—that's over there. And Whistling Dam . . . Oh, all kinds of names. . . ."

We beached at the landing and tied the boat to a stake. Jim picked up a clam shell from the shore and showed it to me: it was less a shell than a brittle filigree of neat circular holes. "Know what that is? That's from the old button factory. There was hundreds and thousands of pearl buttons came out of Reads Landing, once." I saw that what I had taken for a pebbly beach was in fact a dump of perforated clam shells. They crunched underfoot: some still quite intact, others gone to a silvery powder. "Oh, back in Daddy's time this was a real important town; there was hotels, and churches, and bars all over. . . . Now there ain't hardly nobody left at Reads Landing."

His father's house was a shack on the levee. It must have started out as a single room; then every few years someone added a new clapboard box to an end or a side, so that it gave the impression of having gone on a drunken ramble around the riverbank. We kept on passing odd corners of it and eventually reached a front door which was actually situated somewhere in the middle of a maze of peeling white paint and warped driftwood walls.

Daddy was eighty-six; Jim was well into his sixties. Both nearly deaf, they spoke in the same gentle whisper, lip-reading each other's words. When I tried to speak to the old man, I shouted. Jim winced at the loudness of my voice, and his father didn't understand a word.

Mr. Curdue, his side stiffened by a recent stroke, pottered in his drafty warren of knickknacks and notions. He found a coffeepot on a cluttered sideboard filled with framed brown photos, rag dolls and a comical ceramic whiskey bottle called a Wyoming Jackalope.

"Now, this'd interest you," Jim said. "Daddy was on the last raft of timber that was made up at Reads and floated down to New Orleans."

"Yeah," said Mr. Curdue. "That was, oh, that must have been in nineteen and ten."

"Ask him how much he remembers of that trip," I said. Jim asked him, in a whisper.

"Oh, I remember it plain. Real plain. It was in nineteen and ten," Mr. Curdue said, raising his voice to a shout for my benefit, and went off to his kitchen to brew the coffee.

"That was how Reads got big. They used to float the white-pine logs all down the Chippewa and make them up into rafts here, then take them down the river to New Orleans. All the forest now, that's re-growth. When I was a kid, it was just like a stump field for as far as you could see. They'd cut down every last tree."

When the lumber business died, old Mr. Curdue had become a professional fisherman. Jim had joined him, setting fish traps and seines across the river for catfish, walleyes, bass and panfish. He'd been a clam diver too, supplying the pearl-button factory with shells. He'd damaged his inner ear in a deep hole in Lake Pepin where the clams grew as big as dinner plates. Then he had been an oiler on a tow, working the Mississippi between St. Louis and Memphis—which was where, I supposed, he had picked up his long elasticated vowels.

"I'm too young to remember much," Jim said. "Daddy's the one you ought to get to tell you stories. But he has his good days and his bad days. He hain't been feeling too well lately, not since he had his stroke."

"I'm fine," said Mr. Curdue, coming in. He appeared to be able to lip-read around walls and through closed doors. "You just worry too much. Always worrying and worrying." He turned to me. "He's been a good boy to me, Jim has. He just does too much goddamn worrying." As they nannied each other along, the two elderly men looked more like a husband and wife than a father and son.

We floated out across Lake Pepin, following the gulls. Still and brown, gleaming faintly in the thin, diffuse light, the lake had the vacant gaze of an enormous animal's eye. We watched the gulls map the underwater movements of the school bass, zigzagging slowly along the north shore. The lake was dotted with small flotillas of jonboats.

"They're where the fish was *yesterday*," Jim said. "Sometimes I reckon them gulls are a whole sight brighter than the fishermen round here."

We joined up with the birds and cast out, our colored plugs sailing away in twin parabolas on either side of the boat.

"Let it sink deep. Count ten before you reel in."

It was reprehensibly easy. We started to catch fish from the first cast. They hooked themselves with a careless snatch at the plug, and one could feel them thrumming deep down at the end of the line like an electric current. As I reeled them in from under the boat, they changed from one metal color to another, coming up, struggling, through the peaty water: first an indeterminate flash of dull pewter, then a powerful glow of polished brass, finally a brilliant threshing of pure silver as they came wallowing to the net. Killed, their lovely colors went instantly to a cracked gray glaze. Their spiny dorsal fins folded into a ragged heap on their backs. It seemed altogether too close a rehearsal of real life, this violently accelerated transition from excitement to shame.

"They taste real good broiled," Jim said.

"I'm surprised you still enjoy doing it for fun, after being a professional fisherman."

"Oh, I guess it's just something that you never lose. I don't know. Maybe it's more just the being out on the water that I like now, more than the fishing. But I like fishing pretty good. I go out most days, so I must, I guess."

We'd caught a dozen white bass. Their corpses lay in a dulled pile in a plastic bowl in the middle of the boat.

"You want to go try for a walleye?" Jim turned the boat around and headed back for the neck of the lake where it narrowed into river. On the way, we talked about my job.

"You mean, all you got to do is just kind of lallygag around all the way down to New Orleans?"

"It's the writing afterward that's the hard part."

"It don't sound too bad a sort of life to me. Maybe I should've set up to be a writer. That *writing*, though, that's never been much in my line. Lorraine, that's my wife, now, she's an English teacher. Teaches fourth grade. She does most of the writing round our place. She's always picking me up on my grammar and such. I reckon the only way we could work it out is if I was to do all the lallygagging, and Lorraine, if she was to do all the writing." Jim laughed. It was a prospect of Paradise.

The walleyes, with their narrow, sharkish build, canine teeth and large, muscled fins, were the fish I was interested in. They grew as big as salmon. Fast, predatory and hard to catch, they sounded as if they might revive my faltering enthusiasm for going fishing.

"You want to look for the fast water, that's where the walleyes are. Right in those pools behind the wing dams . . . close in to the shore . . . wherever you see a rip in the current, there could be a walleye under there."

We anchored downstream from a wing dam and tried casting under the trees where the Mississippi ran fast and shallow over a sandy bottom.

"They're *rascals*, walleyes. They're rat-sharp, too. If you're going to catch a walleye, you got to think clever and mean."

If a walleye was about, skulking down there in the quick water, he must have thought that we were trying to insult his intelligence. We lobbed our jointed wooden dummies far out and twitched our rod tips to make the plugs dart and dive like real minnows. If I'd been a walleye, I wouldn't have been taken in for an instant. As the plugs came scurrying back to the boat they looked to me almost exactly the same as they had looked in the hardware store—improbable artifacts, too stiff and gaudy to pass for anything in nature. There was one moment of high hope, when I snagged mine on a root; another when Jim claimed that he'd had "a touch"—but I suspected that he was saying that only to keep my spirits up.

"There's walleyes *in* there."

"We're going to need a stick of dynamite to get them out, though."

The wake of a big downstream tow pulled the water away from the wing dam; just for a second it lay exposed, a serrated line of rocks like a jawbone of blackened teeth.

"Look! See why you got to keep to the main channel? Don't ever go messing with wing dams." The river slopped back. Now the dam was a faint, broken shadow on the current; I had to concentrate to see that it was there at all.

We agreed to leave the walleyes to enjoy their private lives of stealth and rapine. Jim ran the boat across the river to the Wisconsin bank, found the entrance to a dark alley in the woods, slowed the motor and coasted up the narrow channel between the trees.

"This ain't something *you* ought to do. These backwaters are kind of tricky. Every month we get some hunter from out of town, thinks he's smart, loses himself up a slough someplace. Oh, there must be better than a hundred miles of cricks and sloughs in here. If you don't know them, they all look the same. And this wise-guy hunter, he's pretty happy, banging birds out of trees, till the sun goes down. Then he gets to be kind of scared. He shoots off up some crick, and it's a dead end. Then he don't know which slough he was in to start with. Then he hollers good and loud. Ain't nobody shouts back. If he's lucky, someone back in town remembers seeing him go out. Then they leave him to roast for a while. Then we have to go out and look for him."

"And all you find is his skull, eaten clean by the ants."

"You got hold of the general idea, there."

The farther we moved up the "crick," the more the air smelled of rot. Big bubbles of gas burst on the water, which opened out into a stagnant lake. The high forest around us grew out of a black swamp of leaf mold and fallen timber. We followed a continual clatter of wings as the ducks and egrets took off at the sound of our motor. On almost every stump and overhanging bough, there were lodged whole families of snapping turtles. Their long, leathery necks were stretched straight up to take the sun. They had the faces of bored elderly clubmen; age had set the skin under their jaws in brittle creases and given their slit mouths a supercilious twist at the corners. Only the babies scrambled into the water as we went by; the big ones merely blinked and went on sunbathing, as if they were too bored with life now to be able to stir themselves to anything as enervating as fear.

If Jim hadn't pointed to them, I would never have seen the snakes. They were perfectly disguised as dead twigs and branches, lying out any-old-how along the trunks of the uprooted trees which had fallen into the edges of the lake. Jim ran the boat alongside one of these trunks to check the snake's I.D. I expected the thing to spring back with a sudden hiss and a show of bared fangs but it went on sleeping. Its only sign of life was a faint repetitive tremor in the flattened, scaly bag of its belly.

"He's only an old water snake. I thought, from over there, he might be a rattler."

"Is it poisonous?"

"No, he won't do you no harm at all. Not up here. The water snakes we've got up North, you could have them in the bathtub with you. Down South, though, they're something else. When you get down to Tennessee and Arkansas, you better look where you're going, especially if you ever have to step out into that water. That's cottonmouth country. You get into a slough off the main river down there, you'll see more cottonmouths than you can count. And they're real deadly. There ain't but a few snakes in the world can beat an old Arkansas cottonmouth for poison."

"Why are they called cottonmouths?"

"When they open their mouths to take a nip at you, it's pure white in there. And if you don't get to a doctor real fast, that'll be just about the last thing you'll ever see. So if I was you, I wouldn't take too much time writing out the description of it in that book of yours."

"Have you ever taken a look inside the mouth of a cottonmouth?"

"Nope. And I don't want to, neither."

We glided past a beaver dam but saw no beaver. Jim navigated the swamp as if it were a city, taking shortcuts down side streets, crossing squares of open water, finding forested avenues and crooked paths through garbage heaps of brushwood and marsh grass. We were in deep forest when Jim cut out the motor on the boat.

"Hear that?"

Nothing at all except the leaves in the trees. Then a faint *tick-tick-tickety-tock;* the sound of dice being shaken in a wooden cup.

"That's a rattler. He's in there somewhere."

Tickety-tickety-tickety.

"He's moving away from us now. He was right close up when I first heard him."

The noise of the snake was lost in the rustle of the leaves.

"A while back, this was a real good place for rattlers. You don't see too many now, though. When I was a kid, we used to come out and hunt them. You got twenty-five cents for every rattle then. They was trying to exterminate them. Then a whole lot got drowned in the summer floods. I was out in my jonboat in the floodwater, and there was rattlers all over, trying to climb aboard. They was just desperate to get on anything that was floating . . . logs . . . boats . . . I guess they weren't discriminating too much. It wasn't me they was after, it was just a ride on my boat. I tell you, I ran the engine just about as fast as it could go, out of that slough. But there must have been thousands of them that died then. This year, you come out, and you're lucky if you see one rattler."

He started up the motor again and turned the boat around. The bass we had caught earlier in the morning were beginning to add their own smell of mortality to the rancid atmosphere of the swamp. The everglades of Pontoon Slough were as close as I'd ever been to real jungle, with their dozy reptiles, bubbling gas, and a forest whose excessively vivid head of spreading green was counterbalanced by the way in which its feet stood in an excessively deathly mire of rotting compost. Jim Curdue was at home here, a man pottering comfortably in his backyard. I wasn't. I was primly shocked by this wanton, spendthrift Nature in which everything was either living too easily or dying too easily.

Yet it explained a great deal about the character of Wabasha. This was exactly how the landscape must have first appeared to the town's founding fathers—the Smiths, the Kuhns, the Jewells . . . the Lowells and Cabots of this particular neck of the woods. As we cut across a putrid lake and headed down Indian Slough toward the open river, I felt that I could see, through half-closed eyes, the inspired arrogance that had gone into the building of the infant city. To lay down that grid of streets in the classic style of American Rectangular . . . to fill it in with dimly remembered bits of Athens, London and Vienna . . . to turn an infested bog and an impenetrable bluff into a humming nineteenth-century metropolis: these things meant flying triumphantly in the face of Nature. Old Kuhn and Jewell were touched with the mania of Phaëthon; the least they could do was set the world on fire with Wabasha. As it had eventually turned out, the first, certain imaginative stroke of Main Street had been the last. Since then there'd been a lot of tinkering, of timid sketchwork on the fringes of the master plan, but nothing to touch Kuhn's Block 1874 under its now crumbling architrave. Just imagining what Wabasha *might* become had somehow exhausted the resources of the town. Now, like the turtles, it was tired and elderly, apparently content to squat by the side of the river doing nothing much except take the sun and let the leathery creases under its chin hang out.

When we got back to town, Main Street was lined with vintage cars. They were on a round-the-state rally and had stopped in Wabasha for tea. The Legionnaires and their wives padded around the automobiles, leaning on sticks or humping themselves along on tubular walking frames. Most of the people were older than the Model T's. Jim and I joined the crowd around an especially handsome Panhard, its polished brassbound radiator snorting steam. The Bermuda-shorted granny whom I'd spotted the day before was saying, "Beautiful. Just *beautiful*. Now, *ain't* that somethin' else?" The nonvintage drivers trooped out of the Anderson House and got their machines going. As the rally trailed, stalling and backfiring, down Main and around the corner of City Hall, we all stood waving them goodbye. After they had gone, we could still hear them rumbling out west on Route 61, and there was a curious, post-something *tristesse* in the crowd that they had left behind. Later, eating catfish and French-fries in Lyla's Idle Hour Restaurant, I tried to puzzle out exactly what it was that we had been saying farewell to. It was certainly a more complex object than a line of old cars.

I had taken a window seat in the restaurant. Outside, a big illuminated yellow sign said IDLE HOUR. Beneath it hung a pulsing heart of scarlet neon. The old, banal symbol of love kept on flashing unrequited in the darkness. I was the only diner in a red desert of oilcloth-covered tables, each with its ketchup dispenser and bowl of Coffee-mate packets. There were no headlights on the highway. A ceiling of low cloud had blotted out the stars. The plastic heart throbbed and throbbed, across the black wheat country, for nobody. My half-finished plate of food was taken away by a speechless waitress. I looked down at my place mat. It said, SMILE—GOD LOVES YOU.

Walking back down the middle of the long, straight, empty highway, I listened to the sounds of anonymous rodents scuffling in the grass at the sides of the road. They sounded large, and I quickened my step to the pace of a jog, then a breathless run. In Kuhn's vision of things, this should, I supposed, have been in the neighborhood of South Twenty-second Street. It should have been bright with wrought-iron gas lamps and tall with fine brick houses. As I raced in panic between the dark harvested fields, I wondered if I was just infecting the town with my fit of private loneliness or whether Wabasha itself was really mourning its own isolation, seeing in those vintage cars some shadow of the past which had left it stranded here as lonesome as a half-built house.

The next day the river was so gentle that it seemed to have forgotten that it was the Mississippi. The sun was up; the wind was barely puckering the water. For the first time since I'd started out on the trip, my nerves didn't tighten with fright as I slipped the boat into the buoyed channel and set off down the long, wide southward swing out of Wabasha. This was picnic weather, and up in the front of the boat I had turkey sandwiches and white wine. Today, I was going to live easy. I would fish and loaf and generally have myself a holiday. By Buffalo Slough, a lounging deckhand on a towboat waved at me as we crossed each other's paths at a safe distance; it was nice to be thought of as a fellow traveler, a paid-up member of the society of the river.

The Mississippi was keeping its true nature hidden in more ways than one. I was afloat on one river while the chart in front of me showed quite another. The river I could see was a neat affair, lined on both banks by forest, so narrow that even I could have swum from shore to shore. It looked no wider or more scary than the Serpentine in Hyde Park. Only the chart revealed that the river was telling me lies. On paper, it was three to four miles from bank to bank. The wooded channel was just a single, arbitrary path through an enormous maze of forest, sand and open water. There it was, mapped in green and blue, a fantastically elaborate scribble of loops, scrolls, dots and spurs: the river writing its signature in its inimitable Gothic script.

Alerted, I looked for breaks in the trees and saw through them to the real river. Slowing on the current, I drifted past a hundred-yard gap in the false shore on the west side; it was no more than a sliver of woodland on a bar. Beyond it a watery stump field stretched away as far as I could see, the low stumps arranged with infinite regularity, like the flat tombstones in a Muslim graveyard. That, said the chart, was Weaver Bottoms. I had to extend my thumb and forefinger full out to measure it . . . four miles by three. It would have been a wicked place in a wind. Now, though, with the sun on the still water, it had the eerie brilliance of a dreamscape, with the jagged reflections of the stumps dancing on the looking-glass blue of the sky.

Weaver Bottoms was blotted out by another false wall of living timber. According to the chart, I must be passing Lost Island to the east. It was certainly lost to me. I wondered how it had come by its name. Perhaps someone had come here once on a day like today and had been tricked, like me, by all the deceptions the river was capable of springing. Mistaking reflections for the things they shadowed, water for sky, the fringe of trees for land, he had settled on the invisible island as a symbol of his condition, so confused by this amazing hall of mirrors that his own identity had temporarily dissolved in Mississippi water.

I had no intention of losing myself here, though; I meant to get my bearings and find things out. In Wabasha I had added a book titled *Trees of North America* to my traveling library. If I could just begin to decode the jumble of the forest, that at least would be a start. I ran the boat into a sandy cove, hitched up the motor, and climbed out, book in hand, to read the trees. In the field guide, arrayed by class, order, family, genus and species, they formed a perfectly articulated society. There were gymnosperms and angiosperms, monocotyledons and dicotyledons. The families sounded like the sort of decent, dullish people one might meet at a faculty party on an East Coast campus. The Dogwoods. The Tupelos. The Lindens. The Buckthorns. The Maples. The Apples. The Hophornbeams. The Birches. Each family member had his or her own full-length color portrait. In such a well-distinguished company, one should never be at a loss as to who was who.

I found that I had landed up in a tree slum, where overcrowding and miscegenation had made it almost impossible to make out individuals in the tangled mass. The leaves of one tree seemed to be reaching out from the branch of another which, in its turn, was growing from the trunk of yet another. They swarmed up the bluff; trees in their incontinent millions. They didn't seem to be aware of the opportunities for trees in North America; far from yearning to be free, these huddled masses looked as if they were getting on very well as they were. I pulled off a few leaves from the branches in front of me. Was this *Salix interior*, the Sandbar Willow?

> Somewhat curved, the leaves are yellow-green but darker above than below, with a yellowish midrib and wide-spaced marginal teeth.

Or could it be *Carpinus caroliniana*, the American Hornbeam?

> elliptical leaves . . . dull green above and yellow green below, with tufts of hair in axils of the veins and doubly toothed margins.

What were "axils"? I didn't know. I saw, or thought I saw, elms, red oaks, cherries, pines, walnuts . . . and lost count. I pulled the cork from my bottle, and started to make some contributions to American botany. Helped by the book, I discovered species hitherto unrecorded in this part of the United States. The farther away they stood, the more exotic they became. I found Jamaica Thatch Palms, Saw Palmettos, Longleaf Blollies, Florida Poison Trees, Swamp Cyrillas, Everglades Velvetseeds. The exhilarating thought occurred to me that I might be a new Darwin as I swept away the pieties of traditional science and prepared to tell the world that a single Mississippi bluff (not very far from Buffalo, Wisconsin) actually contains all the trees of North America.

I drifted on downstream, just letting the river unroll around me. It was no wonder that the charts and the tree book seemed hopelessly thin and theoretical when set against the here-and-now of the Mississippi itself. The river was simply too big, too promiscuous in its nature, too continuously changeable. It would never tamely submit to posing for its portrait. The engineers had done their best to make it presentable, with their locks, levees and wing dams, but these didn't control the river, they merely curbed some of its wilder tendencies to eccentricity, and every so often the river would sweep away these curbs in a flood— a brute demonstration that the Mississippi was not to be messed with lightly, that no human order could safely contain it. My own charts were less than a year old, and already they were out of date. Again and again, the channel would run around the wrong side of a sandbar, turn west not east, or divide around a new, unmarked island which was even now beginning to sprout with a baby forest.

The river defied representation. In the 1840s there had been a craze among painters to produce enormous "panoramas" that would transfer the Mississippi, drawn to scale, onto rolls of canvas. These were exhibited like movies: the audience sat in a darkened hall while the illuminated painting was slowly unspooled in front of them. They were thought of as marvels. It was like enjoying an accelerated steamboat ride all the way from New Orleans up to St. Paul: a three-week journey compressed into the length of a play at the theater. For the American artist, the Mississippi was his inevitable subject. The river was the best embodiment of the sheer space and variety of American life; nothing else in the country could match it for its prodigious geographical reach, as it moved through genteel Southern life, modern industrial cities, frontier farmsteads, budding towns and uncut wilderness. The panorama painters spent months afloat, sketching and taking notes. Then they supervised the design and coloring-in of the roll, using squads of apprentices to put the Pepins and the Pig's Eyes into the picture.

Léon Pomerade, a French immigrant who had settled in New Orleans, did a *Panorama of the Mississippi and Indian Life* which was shown in St. Louis in 1849, and destroyed by fire a year later. The panorama that came nearest to being a serious painting was Henry Lewis' *Mammoth Panorama of the Mississippi River*. This was 12 feet high and 1,325 yards long; and even then it covered only the upper reaches, from the Falls of St. Anthony down to St. Louis. Lewis' painting was a miniature, though, compared with the epic panorama constructed by John Banvard—a three-mile long picture which showed the Mississippi from the Gulf of Mexico to St. Louis. Banvard went on a world tour with this giant spool of canvas. He was invited to exhibit it to Queen Victoria in Buckingham Palace. It is an episode in her life that her biographers seem to have missed. How long did it take? What did she say? Did she start to nod off at Vicksburg, or Natchez, or Greenville? Did she become hypnotized by the groaning noise of the cylinders as they moved the river on in front of the small gilt throne? Was Banvard able to alter the speed of the thing when he saw the suppressed beginning of a royal yawn? Nine hundred miles at a scale of 18 feet to the mile . . . Even if Banvard had bowled the Queen up the river at twenty miles an hour, the trip would have lasted more than eleven hours.

Banvard's panorama was lost in another fire, in Chicago. It was, apparently, the fate of these epic representations of water to be consumed, almost as soon as painted, by water's rival element. Or perhaps these old deities had found a common cause in making people like Banvard repent their temerity. The Mississippi would not be cut down to size.

For me, it was slowly unspooling itself past Kieselhouse Bay and Haddock Slough, around Horseshoe Bend, past Fountain City and into Betsy Slough. A big double tow was coming upriver through Lock 5a, and I stood off among the islands with half an hour to kill before I could lock through. I set up my fishing rod and tied on a homemade bass plug that Jim Curdue had given me. I flipped it out into the shallows where the walleyes were supposed to lie.

It was taken almost instantly, in a splashy lunge under the trees, and the fish came in, swimming fast for deep water, under my boat. I reeled in, first on nothing, then on something strange which was juddering like a road drill thirty feet below. For a minute or two I was lost in the old cruel joy of being back in touch with who-knew-what . . . a monster, perhaps . . . a creature out of legend more than natural history. The fish abruptly stopped fighting against the strain of my rod. When I raised it to the surface, it came up with the limp weight of a bundle of old clothes. I netted it, and it lay on the seat in front of me, gasping feebly in the mesh. It wasn't a walleye—it was too heavy-bellied for that. It was too big to be a white bass. It had spines, and no whiskers, so it couldn't be a catfish. I settled on the notion that it must be a largemouth bass. I unhooked it as gently as I could and gave it back to the Mississippi. Its fins fluttered hesitantly in the water; it swam in a slow circle; then, in a sudden restoration of energy, it dived deep into the black.

All I could see of him was his big, gray porcine face suspended over the lock railing as I was sinking in the chamber.

"Hey—you the *Englishman?*"

"Yes!"

"My wife saw you on TV! Every day she's been asking me if you come through yet!"

Our talking time was running out. I was dropping rapidly down the wall. The hiss of the sluices was getting louder every moment. My interrogation was conducted at a pace of frantic *accelerando*:

"You know Mildenhall, Suffolk?"

"Yes!"

"I was stationed there. In the military." *Millie Teary.*

"Really?"

"You know the Samson and Delilah Ballroom, Norwich?"

"Yes," I shouted, "I used to live in Norwich."

"Ya *did?* Boy, wait till Beverley hears that!"

Another two feet of brown slime went by.

"You stopping off in *Winona?*"

"Yes!"

"Where?"

"Don't know!"

"You wait there! I got an idea!"

I settled finally at the bottom of the pit. The lockmaster's instruction to "wait there" was perfectly gratuitous. I was firmly caged in. The chamber was cold, dark and smelly. Clinging to a rope with one hand, I lit up a pipe with the other and wondered whether the lockmaster's intention was simply to keep me here as an exhibit. Perhaps the railing far over my head would soon crowd with curious faces; perhaps I would have to dodge a hail of bananas, sugar lumps and Cracker Jack. It was several minutes before a message was lowered to me, wrapped around a rock, on the end of a rope.

It read like a list of clues for a treasure hunt. In wobbly capital letters it told me to take my boat to Dick of Dick's Marine, ask Dick to ring Chubby, get Chubby to pick me up and take me home with him, then Beverley would collect me from Chubby's place and the author of the note would see me later. It wasn't signed.

"Okay?" His voice might have come from a far mountaintop.

"Fine! Thank you!" I called back. My first law of the river was always to submit to a *force majeure* when I met one. I carefully pocketed my instructions and rode out of the open lock in search of Dick's Marine.

Lights were coming on all over the city. Winona's riverfront of grain elevators and oil terminals had gone to a deep purple against the streaky evening sky. I found Dick's Marine in a lagoon on Lasch Island; Dick was shutting up shop when I pulled in. Feeling foolish, I showed him the note.

"Oh, yeah. So you're a friend of Bob's."

I supposed that I must be. We walked around the darkening lagoon to Dick's boat store.

"Ever been to Winona before?"

"Never."

"Great place. You know we got twenty-nine millionaires in this city? Now, they don't look like millionaires. You'd never tell they was millionaires. But they're millionaires, all right, you better believe it.

Look—" He pointed to himself. "Thirty-dollar boots. Fifteen-dollar overralls. Ya smoke? Lousy cigarette case. Twenty-dollar watch—in case it drops in the river. Round here *no one* looks like a millionaire. But there's twenty-nine of them, right here in one little town."

I was exhausted by the treasure hunt. It went on for hours. I was shunted through the suburbs of Winona in the night rain, seeing them only as smears and blotches through the streaming windshield of one car after another. I hauled my suitcase from trunk to trunk. In a timber barn of a house, I was besieged by shrilling children who all wore hearing aids. They brought me sloughed rattlesnake skins, swimming certificates and lumps of raw agate, while I dreamed of escaping to a hotel room, a bath, a meal, sleep. Then there were more suburbs, more Pizza Huts and Kentucky Fried Chicken joints, more wet flags billowing over clapboard bungalows, and then, at the end of the trail, Beverley, with her feet up on the sofa, watching the TV and eating popcorn.

She looked like a retired lady wrestler. Slack-jawed, her eyes hidden behind the thick lenses of her glasses, she filled her outside stretch pants to the last stitch. She had insulated herself behind a solid wall of electronic noise. The volume of the TV set was turned full up, and beside her on the floor stood a great black hulk of gadgetry from which distorted voices squawked and burbled continuously.

"What's that?" I called to her, pointing at the thing.

"Radio scanner. So's I can keep a track on Bob."

A comedy show was running on the screen. When the audience laughed, Beverley paused in her popcorn eating, gave a perfunctory cackle and said, "Funny, huh?" to me without moving her eyes from the TV. Once she jerked her head at her radio scanner. "Hear that? That's Bob there, up on the lock. They're bringing the *Delta Queen* up through there tonight. You ever seen the *Delta Queen*?"

"No, I haven't."

"Know what Bob calls it? The Floating Fire Hazard. Funny, huh?"

I agreed that it was.

"You don't like to watch TV?"

"No, it's fine. I'm just not concentrating very hard."

"You like to read books?"

"Yes. I seem to have spent half my life doing nothing else."

"We got the *Encyclopaedia Britannica*. Over there. Anything you want to look up, you look it up."

"Thanks very much. There isn't actually anything I . . ." But Beverley had evidently transferred her entire attention to the popcorn and the people in the comedy show. Beverley and I were not hitting it off, somehow. Whenever I tried out my own notions of conversation on her, something in her circuits made an automatic cutout, and I found myself reduced to stumbling monosyllables on the rare occasions when she tossed me a sentence from the side of her mouth.

"I sure would like to take you down the cellar. Bob'd kill me, though."

What?

"He called up over the radio. He says he's going to take you down the cellar in the morning."

I heard myself give out a high whinnying laugh.

"He wants it to be a surprise, see?"

"What's . . . uh, in the cellar?" I had noticed earlier, without particular alarm, that the main item of furniture in the living room was a locked glass arsenal of rifles, shotguns, pistols and crossbows.

Beverley was looking coy. It was not an expression in which she'd had very much practice, I thought. Something happened behind her glasses. She had winked.

"Radio," she said.

"What?"

"That's where he keeps all his equipment. Bob's a real big ham. Only don't ever say I told you. He'd kill me. He likes to surprise people."

It was nearly midnight when Bob arrived, his shift finished. He was indeed a real big ham. Only a cartoonist like Rowlandson could have managed the bell-shaped curve of his basic construction. An ellipse of bristled stomach showed between his T-shirt and jeans. It was, on the whole, his most expressive single feature. When he laughed, the fat quaked and creased; when he grew solemn, it swelled hugely and took on the shape of a downturned mouth. He and Beverley were one flesh. They must have had six hundred pounds of the stuff between them. Seated on the sofa together, they had a perfect symmetry, looking more profoundly married than any couple I'd ever seen. Bob scoffed a pint or two of his wife's popcorn.

"What ya been doing, then, Vicious?"

"Talking," said Vicious.

"That's what I call her—Vicious. 'Cause she's real vicious—ain't you, Vicious?"—and he tickled her. She heaved, flopped, and swung a right hook at his paunch. "See what I mean?"

We talked about England and the U.S.A.F. base on which Bob had been stationed until I could keep my eyes open no longer. Beverley had given up her own bedroom for me, but I was too tired to sleep. Over my head hung a framed poem set in illuminated Gothic letters:

> Are you passing through a testing?
> Is your pillow wet with tears?

—and so on, for fifty lines or more. There was, surprisingly, a book bound in imitation leather on the bedside table. I opened it. It was full of quotations from the Gospels, neatly copied out in round schoolgirl handwriting.

> There is no respect of persons with God. For as many as have sinned without law shall also perish without law: and as many as have sinned in the law shall be judged by the law.
>
> Abide in me, and I in you. As the branch cannot bear fruit of itself, except it abide in the vine; no more can ye, except ye abide in me.

I read on, torn between a sneaking guilt at having trespassed on Beverley's secret life and the suspicion that she had left her book here deliberately for me to find. I thought that I'd met an enormous slut. That was not the person who was revealed here. Few of her favorite passages were consoling ones. She liked the knotted theology of St. John and the severity of St. Paul. In her book there was more suffering and perplexity than there was hope of redemption. Alone here at night, after the TV had died to a glowing dot and her husband had gone to his own bed, Beverley would feel her way around the gloomier vaults of Christian metaphysics, her pen tracing the letters onto the page with meticulous regularity of space and shape.

I wondered if she ever showed her book to Bob. Maybe he kept one of his own. The real question, though, was why I should be so astonished by this discovery. As I traveled, glancingly, through the lives of other people, I had learned to trust to surfaces and appearances, as travelers must. Reading Beverley's private book, I felt chastened. I knew nothing of her at all, and the notebook, far from filling in some specific depth of character, had made her even more unknowable than she had been with her bag of popcorn and her weak eyes fastened to the colored screen.

After breakfast, Bob exhibited the secrets of the cellar. He had a complete radio studio down there. From his sagging swivel chair, he was in touch with the world. His teletype machine kept up a continuous chatter of small talk. An old-fashioned microphone on a stand was linked to a transmitter powerful enough for him to talk to Korea and Rio de Janeiro. He found a buddy up in Montana for me to talk to after failing to raise a contact in Tunbridge Wells, Kent. I read off the previous day's messages from the yellow roll of teletype paper. Here was Bob, off to work in the afternoon . . .

> WELL DUANE THE WEATHER TODAY IS KIND OF MUGGY I WOULD SAY. DONT HAVE TO DO MUCH AND YOU HAVE WORKED UP A SWEAT. GUESS IT IS SUPPOSED TO RAIN SOMETIME. I BETTER WATER DOWN MY SOD CAUSE IT STILL HASNT GOT IT SELF KNITTED TO THE GROUND YET. ANY WAY KIND OF WARM AND STICKY. WILL HAVE TO MAKE IT TO THE MINE AT 3:30 SO I CAN MAKE A FEW DRACHMAS TO KEEP THE WOLF AWAY FROM THE DOOR.
> W9HWQ DE WBØPRK

Duane had come in later.

> WELL BOB DID NOT DO A HECK OF A LOT TODAY. WENT TO WINONA THIS AFTERNOON TO GET SOME STUFF AT THE FOOD STORE AND THEN CAME RIGHT BACK HOME AGAIN. SO REALLY DID NOT DO ANYTHING EXCITING WHAT SO EVER TODAY. AND IT LOOKS LIKE TONITE WILL NOT WIN ANY EXCITING CONTEST EITHER. OH WELL. SO MUCH FOR THAT.
> WB9KPX.

I said that I couldn't see very much difference between this kind of broadcasting and calling up people on the phone.

"Radio's public," Bob said. "Any ham with a license can listen in. There's a whole community of guys out there. You seen my call cards?" One wall of his studio was papered with them, their foreign stamps looking like pinned butterflies.

> WAS LOOKING THRU THE TV GUIDE FOR TONITE AND SEE THERE ISNT ANYTHING WORTH LOOKING AT UNTIL ABOUT 10:30 WHEN THAT MYSTRY MOVIE IS ON 8 . . .

went the teletype.

"That's Jim, K9ZZ."

A voice on the loudspeaker in front of us was saying something in Japanese. Bob turned it down. "On the radio, you get to meet all different kinds of people. Like I said, it's public, it's a *community*. Hey, you know about radio teletype art? That's a whole new radio art form. Look —you like this? That's 'Miss Black America 1969.' "

Miss Black America was composed in densely patterned x's and z's.

She had been transmitted across the airwaves by a coded system of computerized instructions. To my eye, she had lost a great deal of her allure in the process.

"There's 'Bung' . . . 'Sarge' . . . 'Nancy' . . . 'Cookie' . . . 'Birds.' That's a real nice pic, that 'Birds.' "

I saw from the roll of paper that there were mass-produced radio teletype jokes, too.

GOD AND MOSES WERE HAVING A DISCUSSION ABOUT THE END OF THE WORLD AND GOD SAID MOSES I HAVE SOME GOOD NEWS AND SOME BAD NEWS FOR YOU. MOSES TOLD HIM TO LET HIM HAVE THE GOOD NEWS FIRST SO GOD SAID THERE WILL BE FIRES, FLOODS, PESTULANCE, STARVATION ETC AND MOSES SAID MY GOD IF THAT IS THE GOOD NEWS THEN WHAT IS THE BAD NEWS. AND GOD SAID MOSES YOU WILL HAVE TO FILL OUT THE ENVIRONMENTAL IMPACT STATEMENT!!!!

"Funny, huh?" Bob said.

"Not bad."

"Bob—" The metallic voice came out of an intercom speaker over Bob's head. He picked up a hand mike. "What you want, Vicious?"

"Can you run around to the store in a while?"

"Sure. What you want?"

"Beans," said the voice.

"Okay, Vicious." He put the microphone back on its hook. "You want to come with me to the store? We'll take the Bronco."

The Bronco was Bob's pickup truck. His C.B. set was fancier than any I'd seen before. "You want to know my handles? I'm Moose . . . then I'm Dirty Pierre . . . The Minnesota Grit-Gobbler . . . and Bullwinkle. Bullwinkle, that's the one I use the most." We drove through the outskirts of Winona, taking a very roundabout route since Bob wanted to show me every school and college in the city—not out of any spirit of civic pride but out of simple hatred of all educational institutions.

"You know what that is?" he said, pointing furiously at what was obviously the campus of the College of St. Teresa. "Tax-exempt property! Look over there. There's more of it. Tax-exempt property! Look, I pay my goddamn taxes; why can't those sonofabitch shysters pay theirs?"

"You sound like a man who'll be voting for Ronald Reagan next year."

"I don't vote for no one. If Jesus Christ Himself was running for

President, he wouldn't get my vote. Them politicians, they're a bunch of outlaws. You know the only thing those guys in Washington ever agree about is giving themselves pay hikes? Look! Look at that! *Tax-exempt property!*"

Outside the Piggly-Wiggly, he got on to Vicious over the C.B. and checked his shopping list. As he wandered up and down the avenues of food, Bob went into a long, bemused grumble about how America had let him down. Everything on TV was "junk" made by "Madison Avenue jerks." "Who do they think we are? I'll tell you: to them this is Flyover Land. You live in Winona, you're nobody. They serve you up with junk 'cause you don't amount to a hill of beans to those jerks. They can't even see you, you're so goddamn small." His protesting bulk filled the CRACKERS-'N'-COOKIES alley foursquare, his gut protruding from him like a giant watermelon. "The *beautiful people.* We got some of them beautiful people in Winona. They're a gang of assholes too."

On the way back, Bob said sadly, "You ever get the feeling you was born in the wrong time?"

He had a right time in mind—a notion of an open West where Bob, reconstituted as Daniel Boone, could have walked out of his drafty cabin each morning and shot his breakfast. The only picture in his house was a Remington print of a bull moose at bay. That hung on one wall of the dining room, facing the mounted head of an elk with schizophrenic glass eyes. Each year Bob and two of his friends applied for hunting licenses in North Dakota. Every second or third year their numbers came up, and for two weeks they shared a log cabin, tramped through the snowy forest with their guns and pretended to be frontiersmen. Bob had a wad of Polaroid photos taken on these hunting holidays. He was just recognizable in them: a comically squat Leatherstocking, lost in his fur parka, his belly crisscrossed with ammunition belts. In one, he was sitting on the body of a dead buck. I was surprised that he hadn't crushed it flat.

"That's *me.*" He wasn't simply identifying the character in the picture; he was trying to tell me who he really was.

"You know where I'd be happy? In the woods. I could live in the woods."

"I don't want to live in the woods," Beverley said.

"You don't know nothing about the woods. So don't talk about what you don't know about, Vicious."

"I'll stay right on in Winona."

"And *that's* okay by me."

Snorting, Bob unlocked his arsenal for me. He laid the guns out on the tabletop. "That's my prize baby," he said. "You just take a squint through that." It was an automatic rifle with telescopic sights. It smelled of machine oil and polished mahogany. Its heavy barrel wavered in my hands. Peering into the sights, I tried to adjust the knurled cylinder of the lens. The suburban room swam into and out of focus. Eventually I got the hairline cross on target and saw what I was supposed to see: Washington politicians, Madison Avenue jerks, college presidents and beautiful people. One by one they staggered to their knees like struck deer.

By afternoon I was back on my boat, with an east wind, this time, blowing up hard against the grain of the current and the hull clanking on the sharp edges of the waves. Glad to be alone again, I drove happily downstream into Blacksmith Slough. I was accompanied by a slow-moving train on the Burlington Northern which looked, at first, as if it too were afloat in mid-river. The tracks had been raised on a thin causeway, and for five miles the grain cars walked on water like a line of angular type on an empty sheet of flecked duck-egg blue.

I also had the ghostly company of Bob and Beverley. After lunch, I'd run away from them, but they had taken up a fully furnished apartment in my head and nothing would budge them, not even the heavy wake of an upriver tow. I puzzled over the strange social space they occupied. There must be a connection between Bob's ethereal "community" of radio hams, his dream of living "in the woods," and his furious rejection of all the official ties and responsibilities of organized society. In the disembodied freedom of the airwaves perhaps he had found the illusion, at least, of an open territory where human relations were still improvised, optional, do-it-yourself. As W9HWQ he could be the lone gunslinger prowling the shortwaves, a tough guy to run into over a microphone. Bullwinkle, Moose, Dirty Pierre, The Minnesota Grit Gobbler . . . like his Polaroid pictures of himself as a hunter, his bullish handles asserted that the real Bob wasn't a tax-paying citizen of Winona at all but a displaced person from an imaginary and sentimentalized West. And Beverley . . .

The tow's wake scooped me up and set me down. The water felt as hard and fibrous as muscle tissue, and the whole structure of the boat throbbed as it hit each successive wave. It wasn't frightening now. The river was simply the biggest and most powerful natural force I'd yet encountered, and I was learning with elation that if only I rode it with proper humility it would, in its turn, sustain me and carry me home. Seesawing over the last of the high crests, I watched the sun flash on the bow and catch the toppling edge of a beer can in the wave; and from the corner of my eye I saw the great white mansion of the towboat pass behind me; and I wondered how on earth the young men in the bars produced those yodeling whoops with which they greeted winning kicks in football games. If I'd known how, I would have whooped.

. . . But Beverley. Copying out her texts from the New Testament like a Victorian girl working on a sampler, she was as lost to Winona as Bob in his basement studio. The couple were so grossly corporeal that they looked as if they must be rooted in a very literal world indeed; a world of things as dense and weighty as Bob and Beverley were themselves. Yet exactly the reverse was true. Their fatness was the fatness of balloons; it was as if they were filled with oxygen and floated remotely over the top of the suburb in which they only seemed to be living. Bob was away on his frontier, Beverley out in her metaphysics. No wonder they needed two-way radio in order to talk to each other.

I went through Lock 6 at Trempealeau and the river changed again, into another crazy terra-cotta of islands, lakes and creeks, with the buoyed channel running close under the bluff on the Minnesota shore. Here the water, sheltered from the wind, was as dark as boot polish. I cut the motor, drifted, and tried to measure the depth by dropping a sinker on the end of my fishing line. The reel ran out of line before the sinker touched bottom. The river must be as deep as the bluffs above it were high—a submerged canyon. I wondered what was down there. Wrecked steamboats. Catfish as big as sharks. The rib cages of dead sailors. A million silver rings of stainless aluminum, pulled from the tops of all the Pepsis, Cokes, 7-Ups, Buds, Coorses and Michelobs, littering the black river floor like jewelry on velvet.

Just three weeks before, I had lunched with a New York journalist in a Chinese restaurant off Park Avenue. Our chopsticks had been clicking companionably among the bean sprouts, and he'd said, "I'm afraid you'll find it all kind of samey." If there was one thing the Mississippi wasn't, it was *samey*. Cruising past Shingle Creek and Bullet Chute, I wished I could have taken the journalist and the man in London who had called the river "boring" as passengers—just for twenty minutes or so; they didn't deserve more. The Mississippi could terrify, enchant, delude, but it was beyond the range of its character to bore or disappoint. I was a hundred and fifty miles into my trip; and I had done no more than nibble away at the very top of the upper reaches, but I was in the river's grip. With each new mile, I could feel it tightening, the hold of a creature so complicated and devious that I could sense already that by the end of the journey I would be unlikely to have done more than scratch its surface—unless it chose to turn nasty and drown me somewhere along the way.

Now, with the river beginning to fluff up and an indecipherable change in the color of the trees and sky, I could feel it widening invisibly beyond the screen of islands on my left. I watched for a gap and saw the spread of Lake Onalaska, with the water sucking and spitting around the stump fields. Slowly the islands gave way to single trees standing on sandbars too small to chart, and the wind came straight across the lake, furrowing the river and sending slantwise breakers foaming in to the foot of the bluff. I tacked into them, then rode them back like a surfer, slowing my engine to their pace, until a windbreak of forest abruptly closed in at the head of the next lock and dam.

When I pulled into the harbor of the boat club at La Crosse, Wisconsin, I was jittery with the nervous relief of having *made it*. It was always like this: every time I arrived at a town off the river it was like docking at a foreign port after a real voyage. La Crosse was only thirty miles downstream from Winona; on a car ride one might easily have blurred into the other; but approached from the river they felt like cities in different countries. After all, the stretch of water that separated them was longer than the English Channel is wide; on that afternoon I could have just as well driven my boat from Dover to Calais and come halfway back. When I stepped onto the shore, I would notice that my hands were trembling, and later, when I came to speak, that my voice was trembling too.

I had heard voices from the clubhouse bar as I walked up the steps. Entering it, I knew that I'd broken into the middle of a scene. The faces of the figures on their swivel stools had taken on the sudden rigidity of people playing Statues. Everyone was trying to smile, but their teeth were clenched and the corners of their mouths looked as if they had been fixed into position with nails. One woman was bravely impersonating the attitude of a lady renting out a Hertz car on television, but the effect was marred by the drips of tears and mascara that were running down her cheeks. Only the bartender, rinsing glasses at the center of the horseshoe, gave the impression of being made of flesh rather than wax. Automatically, he laid out a clean glass on the bar as I came in.

"I'm sorry," I said, stupidly staring from fixed face to fixed face, "do you have to be a member to drink here?"

The prospect of my leaving was evidently too dreadful for the group to bear. I was seized, dragged to the bar, installed in the middle of things. A drink was bought for me before I could begin to reach for my wallet. I was besieged by voices, all sounding as if they were set several semitones up from their usual register. *Where've you come from? England? Great. Fantastic. Where're you going? We were there, in '75. We loved it. Hey, that your rig out there? Great. Great. You are? Well, son-ofabitch!*

Thickened by too many martinis, the voices went into a chorus of advertisements for La Crosse. Once more, as in Red Wing, I felt I was being treated as a prospective buyer of small cities:

"This is a wonderful town—"

"You ought to stay here for a month—"

"We have some *marvelous* restaurants . . . nightclubs, too—"

"You want to go on a tour around the brewery. That's a fantastic place, the brewery."

"We have fun here. It's slow by comparison with New York, but we like it that way."

"And I'm not prejudiced—I don't even come from La Crosse."

"This city," said a man, wagging his stubby forefinger under my nose, "has got the best jazz in the country. And that's not excluding New Orleans."

"Right. You like jazz, you've come to the right place."

From my stool I could see the river through the long clubhouse window. Night had fallen with the suddenness of a clicked switch. Under the dock lights the Mississippi had the viscous look of molten tar, its surface ribbed and scalloped with waves. A returning speedboat came bumping into harbor. Set beside the black sweep of the river, the voices around me sounded as tinny and disembodied as if they were playing on a radio somewhere. I nodded politely and watched the water.

"We're going to Smitty's—you want to come with us?"

"Why don't we send out for chicken and pizza?"

Francie—whose blotches of mascara had now dried on her cheeks like powder burns—went to the piano on the far side of the bar. She swayed, bumped into tables and chairs, and collapsed in a heap on the piano stool. She played "Smoke Gets in Your Eyes." I had to concentrate hard to pick out the tune from the welter of missed notes, bad timing and lurches out of key, but she managed to stumble to the end of it. Everyone clapped.

"Great! How about another, now, Francie?"

"It's what she needs to do," said a woman with brutally razored hair. "Everybody does what they need to do. . . ."

Francie attempted a Scott Joplin rag. She murdered one passage and tried to do it over again. Dah-di-dah-dah. *Dah*-di . . . Dah-di-*dah* . . . Dah . . . Dah . . . She slammed the lid on the piano.

"Hey, Francie! You were going great!"

"Great!"

"I'm shit," said Francie. "And you guys all know I'm shit."

"Francie! *Honey—*"

She came over to me and leaned against the bar. I offered her my stool, but she shook her head. "I got to stand up . . ." she said, and laughed tearfully, ". . . for myself." Her face still had the puppyish sweetness of a high school girl's; she was in her mid-forties, and the flesh under her chin had gone to rolls of fat, but her crimped mouth under its Cupid's-bow of rose-petal lipstick and her wide wet eyes gave her the air of someone who has never quite escaped from her teens.

"I'm not a drinker," she said. "Seeing me here tonight you wouldn't know that, would you? You wouldn't. I know you wouldn't." She was having a struggle to pronounce her words. "Basic-ally," she said, "I'm a very . . . happy . . . adjusted . . . outgoing . . . person"; and hiccupped into tears. I put my hand to her cheek, awkwardly conscious of the fact that my action was being closely watched from across the bar.

"Hey . . ." I said. "Come on, love—" She stared at me in total surprise. In Britain, addressing someone as "love" doesn't mean very much; bus conductors do it all the time. In La Crosse, though, it had a different connotation. Francie, interested, immediately stopped crying. She pointed to the piano. "I could have had any career in music that I wanted. I could've been a teacher . . . I could've been a *performer* . . ." And I saw the tears welling up in her eyes again at the thought of the *could-have-beens*.

A beefy fifty-year-old in a leisure shirt designed to display his fine tangle of graying chest hair to its best advantage decided that the intimacy between Francie and me had gone far enough. He thumped his glass on the bar and put on his loudest voice.

"Hey, you guys! You know the difference between the English girl and the American girl?" He waited until he had the giggly silence he needed. "The American girl says, 'Honey, I'm going to come!' But the English girl . . . well . . ." He looked across at me. "The English girl, she says, 'Dahling, Ai do believe that Ai may be just about to arr*ai*ve.'" The boat club thought this was a tremendous joke.

"And did she?" I said.

"What?"

"Arr*ai*ve?"

He sniggered.

"Where was this? One of those hotel rooms you can rent by the hour around the back of King's Cross Station? Or was it over the top of a strip joint in Soho?"

"It was a joke," said Francie.

"I thought he was trying to boast about his sexual prowess," I said. The face of the man was reddening fast with dislike. "Smile, Norbert," said the crop-haired woman next to him. Obediently, he showed his teeth. I decided that for the moment anyway, I wasn't in immediate danger of assault.

Francie said: "As from tonight, I'm not going to be walked over anymore." Soberer now, she told me her story. She'd been married for twenty-two years. She had four children. Her husband went on binges. This afternoon she'd arranged to meet him at four o'clock on their cruiser, to fit it out for their planned weekend trip to Wabasha. He hadn't shown up. He never showed up. He was away in some bar across the city, drinking with the friends he never introduced to Francie; and since four o'clock she had sat here, revenging herself on him with more vodka martinis than she could remember.

"I made up my mind. If he wants to go to Wabasha tomorrow, he can go. I'm not going with him. For once in my life, I've made a decision. Let him go. Hal can go to Wabasha in his stupid boat. I'm going to get a divorce. Look! I said it! You heard me! I'm going to get a divorce. That's the first time I've said it straight to myself in my whole life."

"You're so *tense*, honey . . ." Another big gray man had come up behind her and had started to massage her neck and shoulders.

"This is . . . Joe . . ." she said in her little-girl voice, "and this . . . is . . . Jonathan."

"Hi, Jonathan."

"Hi, Joe."

"He's my . . . therapist."

He was working his hands down and around her ribs now, until they cupped both her breasts. "That's right," he said. "I'm her *therapist*," and winked at me.

"Cut it out, Joe," she said, squirming away from him.

"It's only therapy," Joe said.

"Go away, I want to talk to Jonathan."

"So I know when *I'm* not wanted."

"It's not *like* that, Joe."

"Never is, is it, *Jonathan?*" said Joe, removing himself.

"I mean I've got my whole life in front of me, haven't I?" said Francie. "I don't have to just sit around just watching Hal self-destruct. He's had two heart attacks already. He's been in Intensive Care. Look, I mean *you* wouldn't be that hurtful to somebody else, would you? I couldn't be that hurtful to somebody else. You know the trouble with him? He's spoiled. He's a spoiled child."

Tired, still haunted by the grandeur of the river and oppressed by the squabbles of the clubhouse, I saw them all as spoiled children. The men were beginning to row again, their voices rising to a common pitch of whining complaint. The woman with the jagged hair was trying to catch their attention. "The crap I've had laid on me . . ." she said, over and over again. "The crap I've had laid on me . . ." But the big boys in their fifties took no notice of her at all.

"He's always thinking that the grass in the next field will be greener. He never says no to the next drink."

The woman across the bar said, "You know what life does to you? It . . ." but she was cut off by Norbert, leaning across her to yell his contribution to the argument.

"They're talking about the commodore," Francie said.

"Poor guy."

"I like you. You're your own man. I'd be happy if I was married to a man like you."

"You wouldn't. You'd loathe it."

"I can talk to you."

"That's what strangers are for. It's always easier talking to a stranger."

The bartender had the deep placidity of a man who had learned how to behave as if he were congenitally deaf. He moved among his bottles and glasses, flapping napkins, wiping invisible smears from the cocktail shaker, as if he were in an empty room. I envied him.

The woman opposite said—to me and Francie, now that she had lost all hope of capturing the interest of the men—"Sometimes, honestly, I just want to pass away . . . like *that*." She brushed her hand across the polished leatherette of the bar and let it slide off into air. "Like *that*. I *do*. I really *do*."

"I've learned something about myself tonight," Francie said. "I'm going to get a divorce." She said it rather as if a divorce were a particularly new and desirable brand of food processor. "You've helped me understand myself," she said, putting her head against my shoulder.

"Hi there," said Hal. He was glazed with alcohol. His expensive suit was askew. A tall, cloudless man, he had a vacant dignity about him—a quality that I suspected he must have inherited from somebody else. His father, perhaps, might have been a corporation president, and Hal had caught the habit of presiding. Francie wouldn't look at him or speak.

"Well, Francie—here I am. I thought we were going to get the boat together."

Francie slipped under his arm. She walked, steadily this time, to the window. She passed through a door I hadn't seen and went out on to the levee. I saw her stand looking at the river for a moment, before she disappeared into the dark around the corner of the clubhouse. Hal and I stared after her, two fools together.

"Yes, sir," said Hal, grinning emptily, "that's my baby. What are you drinking?"

As quietly as I could, I asked the bartender to call me a cab. "Hey, where are you going?" Hal said, putting his arm round my shoulder. "A *hotel*? You can stay at our place. Francie loves to have guests."

Tonight, though, I was going to break my rule and be my own man. The cab came. I escaped the clubhouse. As I heaved my luggage into the trunk, I saw a figure in a checked dress standing between the trees. I waved; but Francie must have had her back to me and been gazing into the black Mississippi.

"What you want to come to La Crosse for?" asked the cabdriver. He had Jesus Christ hair and a straggly mustache. "They're not too bright around here. I hate this fuckin' city." He himself had been beached in La Crosse four years before. He and his brothers, from Newark, New Jersey, had been playing in a rock group "out of St. Louis." The group had broken up in a fistfight on stage. The others had left in separate directions. My cabdriver had stayed, to suppurate like Francie over his failed musical career. He was eaten up with resentment. He still wrote songs between rides, and someday, he said angrily, he was going to make his comeback and kick La Crosse in the teeth.

"What I like about music is you can be yourself. Plus the feeling that you've got so much love from so many people. You can feel the vibes coming at you. Waves of love. That's what I like: so much love from so many people."

He dropped me on the edge of the ruins of what had once been La Crosse's grand hotel. Its marbled lobby was grimy and badly lit by a few bare bulbs. It had been built for rich steamboat passengers, grain merchants, visiting politicians: a huge red-brick palazzo. Now it was used by a handful of elderly residents, railroad crews and the poorest sorts of traveling salesman. The desk clerk was idly engaged in hunting down bluebottles with a red rubber flyswatter. He gave me the key to a room on the third floor (cash in advance). It was big and dusty. I guessed that I must be its first tenant in months. I opened the window to air the place, and listened to the wind rattling the chains of the sign that hung outside. It wasn't a cheering sound: if the wind kept up, I might be stuck here for days, moldering like the cabdriver or getting furiously drunk with the boat-club gang. I took my notebook off to one of La Crosse's marvelous restaurants and ate an overdone steak and a limp, shredded salad. I was still writing on my third coffee and second brandy. *My room*, I wrote, *looks custom-built for a very dreary act of suicide. Hitchcock, perhaps, in 1940s black-and-white. The body wouldn't be found for days, perhaps weeks. The corridor smells of burned biscuits.*

On the street, I couldn't face returning to it. Scouting around a corner, I found a line of "club" bars advertising nude cabaret. I chose what sounded like the least noisy one and set up my notebook on the bar. A young black woman was taking her clothes off on a tiny rostrum, jigging mechanically to an acid-rock record. Neither she nor her customers looked at all interested in this activity. She waved her unstrapped bra from side to side and handed it to the disc jockey. She put her thumbs in the front of her pants and rolled them down just far enough to show the tangled fuzz on her pudendum, wriggled a couple of times, and stepped out. She pretended to masturbate, gave that up, shook her buttocks at the audience, splayed her legs, and settled to gyrating sulkily to the music. I went back to my notebook. There was nothing touching or vulnerable in her nudity. Perhaps that was the point: she had the gift of making sex look almost unbearably tedious and ordinary. The men along the bar seemed to prefer staring into space to watching her. The only people who moved were the house hookers, sifting the bar for customers; and even their attempts to drum up trade seemed curiously spiritless.

A fair-haired young woman eventually drifted up to me. She must have been eighteen or nineteen; probably she should have been in school.

"You gotta light?" Her voice was professionally toneless, but her Southern accent came clearly through her studied deadpan. I lit her cigarette for her.

"Okay," she said.

"You're not from La Crosse?"

"West Memphis, Arkansas." She opened her mouth and blew a bubble of smoke in my face. It wasn't a signal of invitation that I was used to, and my eyes stung. She made a long, careful study of the notebook in front of me and the pen in my hand.

"You're *writing*. . . ."

"That's right. Just notes."

She bent over the ball-point squiggles as if she'd never seen such marks before. I wondered if she could read, and hoped she couldn't. She turned from my notebook to me. Her face now was altered by the animation of serious thought.

"You a salesman? Or are you some kind of a student?"

"Oh, I'm some kind of a student."

"Okay," she said, and went on up the bar in search of a better-heeled prospect.

I was halfway through recording this unconsummated dialogue when I was interrupted again. This time it was a man. He was holding his beer glass with both hands to keep it steady.

"You read books, man?"

"Yes."

"You read *Body Count?*"

I hadn't caught the title.

"*Body Count,* man. *Body Count.*"

"No, I haven't."

He had a stubbly black beard, and his eyes were recessed in their sockets like glittering nuggets of iron pyrites.

"You want to read that book. *Body Count.* Look—" He reached for my pen and notebook and wrote the two words out in huge jagged capitals so that they filled half a quarto page. "You read that book, it's like you're there, man. I was there. I know. Eight times I read that book, and every time I'm back there, man. You wasn't in 'Nam—"

"No—"

"Shit." His glass trembled in his hands. "I was there. Seventy to '72. You read *Body Count,* man. Guy that wrote that book, he's got it there. That's the only fuckin' book I ever read. Eight fuckin' times."

He worked as a casual laborer now for the Milwaukee Road, repairing ties. I guessed that his pay did not go very far toward feeding whatever habit he was on. I tried to see whether he might be carrying a knife or a gun.

"Listen, man, you're okay. You like to smoke a little with me, hey? I know a place, we could score. You and me together. The guy's a friend of mine. He's got good stuff. What you say?"

"I'm not into that anymore. Besides that, I'm broke," I said. "I've got about two dollars fifty cents on me."

He studied my face, first with suspicion, then with depressed resignation.

"Two fifty."

"Two seventy-five, maybe," I said, trying to sound as gloomily honest as I could about my penury.

"Shit. You and me, we could've scored, man."

"Yes, it's a pity."

"Well, see you, man." His bony hand gripped my upper arm for a moment and he left the bar. I waited for a long, long time before I dared go out into the street, and as I walked I listened for his following footsteps. The wind moaned in the telegraph wires and blew scraps of garbage down Main Street but, so far as I could hear, I wasn't being shadowed. Perhaps he really had been just lonely, hunting for a friend and not a victim; or perhaps I had given him long enough to find a stray drunk on the way to his car in a deserted lot where no one would observe a pulled knife or a drawn service revolver.

Trying to sleep, I listened to the rattle of the chains outside my window and to the intestinal rumble of the hotel's Victorian plumbing system. Before I switched off the flyspecked bulb, I'd seen an irregular rusty stain on the pillowcase, itself so old that it had gone to the texture of thin muslin. Blood, chains and gurgles in the pipes fed my dreams; by morning, when I woke to a ragged sky and a sudden chill in the air, I was decided that no wind short of a hurricane would keep me from lighting out for some less dismal territory.

Mr. Frick's American Garden

*T**he little towns* were going past as smudges on the far shore: Brownsville, Stoddard, Genoa, Victory, De Soto—every one a temptation to be resisted. I was too immersed in the risky business of keeping moving to care very much about the landscape I was passing through. It was all I could do to keep the boat headed steadily into the waves. Whenever I saw a tow coming upstream, I pulled in to a sandbar and waited for it to go by: having once been caught between the roll of a wake and the chop the wind had raised on the river, I didn't want to get trapped that way again. The boat had heaved and yawed, its motor thrashing ineffectively against the much more powerful counterswell of the water. The clouds of early morning had blown over, leaving the sky a frigid blue. It was shivery weather, and on my sandbars I dosed myself against it with swigs from a bottle of Jack Daniel's. The going was slow—a series of nervous sprints downriver, none of them lasting more than fifteen or twenty minutes before the sight of a barge fleet drove me off the channel to another island shelter; but I meant to put as many miles as I possibly could between myself and the cheerless fun of La Crosse. I watched the wind flattening the smoke from the towboats and blowing it ahead of them in shreds of purple which dissolved in the air long before they reached the leading barges in the fleet.

The whiskey enabled me to keep my nerve in the four-mile crossing of Coon Slough. It was almost bare of islands; only the odd windswept tree stuck up out of the miserable open veld of stumps and whitecaps. Ahead of me, a tow was beating up the channel, foam spuming over the fronts of the barges. I ran as close in as I dared to a stump field; the waves licked at my gunwales as I wallowed there, running the motor just fast enough to keep the bow facing up into the wind. When the wash came, it bared the stumps to their roots, parting the water to expose, with the rapid blink of a camera shutter, the shallow bottom of black sludge and rotted branches.

After that, things were easier. The river stayed wide—four thousand yards from bank to bank—but the islands thickened until they lay as dense as the pieces in a disturbed jigsaw puzzle, with the buoys marking out a narrow wriggling path between them. On the right-hand shore, the Upper Iowa River dribbled into the Mississippi. I'd crossed my first state border, and I burned my tongue with a slug of bourbon in celebration.

At Lansing, Iowa, I stepped out onto a beach of punched clam shells. Another button town. The riverside hotel at the bottom of Main Street had closed down. Someone called Mel had commandeered its lobby for a pizza parlor, but that was shut too. There was a small motel a mile up on the bluff, and I checked into a cabin like an anchorite's cell, with a swept concrete floor and a black-and-white TV whose foggy picture trembled fitfully on the screen. It turned Walter Cronkite into a washed-out fever victim.

The news seemed remote—something about Moon Landrieu—but not as remote as the commercials which intermitted it. The families who populated this bland fiction of American middle-class life looked and sounded like a pack of fancy weirdos. They were skinny fast-talkers, jabbering about laxatives and cake mixes and automobiles. They were as foreign to the America that I was living in as I was myself. Their voices mingled with the crickets on the far side of my screen door.

There was one moment when life and television briefly coincided: when, in an ad beamed by the local station in Decorah, an Iowa farmer spoke stiffly to the camera in testimony to the bags of fertilizer that were heaped in front of him. He squinted into the lights from under his billed cap, his burred *r*'s exaggerated by the microphone. Watching him with the sudden intentness usually reserved for happening on an interview with a friend, I thought how tamely we had all succumbed to the theory that television automatically draws the world together. Surely it had just as strong a tendency to pull the world apart. It was television that had fueled Bob's hatred of the "beautiful people," the Washington outlaws, Angelenos and New Yorkers who bedeviled his imagination. He switched his set on in order to be reminded of their beastliness. Now I was beginning to do much the same thing. From the perspective of this bluff in Iowa, Scotland or Patagonia would have seemed more recognizably familiar than the CBS studios in Manhattan.

. . .

I was awakened before seven by the proprietor of the motel. He'd promised to take me and my luggage to the café where the town ate its breakfast. He'd struck me as morose and growly when I had met him the previous afternoon. Wondering why, I asked him about business.

It was bad. He had bought the motel to cushion his retirement, but as cushions went, it was turning out to be hard and lumpy. The total turnover from his string of cabins was, he said, about four, sometimes five, hundred bucks a week. A few fishermen came to stay, a few hunters, the occasional stranded salesman.

"Look at this place," he said, pointing at the pretty slope of Lansing as it ran down to the river. "It ought to be a *re*-sort. The folks around here, though, they don't care too much for strangers. They see a Dubuque County license plate and they think those people don't have the right to walk on our Main Street. So they freeze every tourist out of town."

Dubuque was seventy miles south. On that basis, the citizens of Lansing should dislike me roughly seven hundred times as much as they loathed the people from Dubuque County.

"Oh, no, *you're* okay. They'll like you because you're a foreigner. They love foreigners; it's just strangers they hate."

I sat up at the counter in the bright clatter of the café, taking my place in the line of identical lumberjackets, boiler suits and muddy farm boots. The man next to me, in his green parka and checked button-down shirt, looked like a holidaying college professor. Hearing me give my order for eggs and hashed-browns, he introduced himself as the owner of the local newspaper, the *Allamakee Journal*. His name was John Dunlevy. His grandfather had come to Lansing as a young man and started the paper in 1880. The population of the town had dwindled over the last hundred years; now the *Journal* was just managing to keep alive on a circulation of little more than a thousand copies a week.

Mr. Dunlevy took me across the street to his office, a long gloomy corridor of a room which smelled of must and printer's ink. His grandfather's original press stood in the middle, surrounded by the wooden founts of Victorian type in which the paper was still set up. The last issue had come out yesterday, and I looked at the headlines: LIONS CLUB HAS SUNDAY PICNIC. RITES HELD FOR LEO J. COLLINS. CLASS OF 1959 MEETS AT CLANCY'S. The news inside was, among other things:

> Mr. and Mrs. Francis Weipert of McGregor and Mr. and Mrs. Pat Cox of Waterloo spent Thursday evening visiting Mrs. Florence Weipert.

Geneva Johnson drove her sister,
Dorothy Foster, from Fennimore,
Wis. to the Gundersen Clinic in La
Crosse for a checkup on Tuesday,
September 11.

There were advertisements for pig auctions, guns, chain saws, silo covers, corn cribs, barbed-wire fences and hog panels, along with the week's menus for meals-on-wheels and school lunches.

Grandfather Dunlevy must have started his paper at much the same date and in much the same spirit as the first proprietor of the *Kansas City Star*. For in 1880 Lansing was clearly bidding to become the state capital; it had been scooped by Des Moines by a mean trick of history. The fine red-brick and stucco buildings along Main were an announcement of grand things yet to come. Streets with names like "Capitol" and "Washington" could not have been designed to hold the little frame houses with their peeling paint that lined them now. Pigeons lodged in the derelict cupola of a closed church. Twentieth-century Lansing was squatting comfortably in the nooks and crannies of the ambitious Victorian city. Main Street was full of unpretentious survivors from the past. In Hogan's Barbershop a farmer was being given a wet shave with a cutthroat razor while he read the front page of the *Journal*. Krieger's Variety Store, under a ragged maroon awning, sold notions pegged on strings in the window: packets of seeds, cheap wristwatches, skin creams, latex sweat absorbers to line one's shoes. The new illuminated sign for a Speed Queen launderette looked like an incongruous trespasser. Perhaps it had come from Dubuque. There was no indication anywhere that Lansing thought of itself as quaint or picturesque; it was just quietly vegetating. Even the button factory was still going—though the buttons now were imported from Japan, and all the "factory" did was employ women to sew them onto printed cards.

John Dunlevy led me up the bluff on the town's north side. I asked him what Lansing people did for a living nowadays. There were a state electricity project, a fish farm, a small auto-parts factory. Farmers came in from the hills to shop and dine out, so there were more stores and restaurants than one might have expected in a town with a population of only 1,500. A handful of professional fishermen supplied the fish market on the levee which drew customers from miles west across the state.

Lansing had set out to be a big city; it was, apparently, much relieved to have failed. In 1880 every two-bit town in the West had wanted to become a metropolis; a hundred years later, the big thing was to be a handsome village. LIONS CLUB HAS SUNDAY PICNIC was a headline to boast of—far better than the tales of murder, theft, riot and rape that covered the front pages of the newspapers of those towns which had succeeded in their original ambitions.

"Look," said Dunlevy, "you know any place else where you can get a view like that?"

We'd arrived at the top of the bluff. The forested cliff on which we stood went down sheer into the river, and the Mississippi Valley was laid out like a relief map in brilliant acrylic color, framed by a tangle of ferns, flowers, oaks and mulberries. Its tesselated pattern of islands and slackwaters had the fantastic elaboration I had seen before only in theory on my charts. The unbroken wooded bluffs on the Wisconsin shore, five miles away, showed as a hard, carved edge of shadowy green. Below us, every strut and hawser of the Lansing suspension bridge was perfectly repeated on the mirror surface of the water, and the interlocking V's of a tow's wake, just downstream of the bridge, were innocent doodles on the glass. The morning sky was empty except for a single pale streak of high cirrus like the track of a faraway airplane.

"Don't you envy me my trip?" I said.

"If I didn't have a paper to get out, I might just ask you to give me a start as a deckhand."

At that moment, no one in his senses would have passed up the chance to go down that river. Looking south, into the lovely unexplored tangle of wood and calm water, I thought of the happy impulse that had brought me here—and found myself faced with a conundrum. When I was a child of seven I thought that I was imagining the Mississippi. Yet seeing it now, in all its old pictorial clarity, I found it hard not to think that somehow I had remembered it. The fit was troublingly exact; and there were details in it that I could never, surely, have got from *Huckleberry Finn*. I had to remind myself that I have no belief whatsoever in ideas of precognition. One can't remember the future, whatever J. W. Dunne may say in *An Experiment with Time*. For a few moments on the bluff over Lansing, though, I felt a nervous tremor of disquiet. The particularity of the dewdrops on the ferns, the rock-crystal blue of the water, the secrecy of the islands . . . it was like wiping the dust from the glass of a picture in an attic and suddenly recognizing the painting that used to hang on the nursery wall. How it had made its way from there to here in the course of thirty years was a problem that I had no means of solving. It was just very odd, and I would have to leave it at that.

Sliding by through the islands, I heard the dry snapping of rifle fire in the forest. I pulled out of the channel, ran under a dripping railroad bridge and rowed the boat up a weedy lagoon where little pickerel scattered in fright as I splashed past. An old man with a broad reptilian face was sitting up at Withey's Bar when I entered; he was wearing a grubby red cravat which was held in place with a pearl pin, and he rested one mottled hand on a silver-topped walking cane. He looked as if he'd been left behind fifty years ago or more by a touring Shakespearean stock company.

I asked him what the shooting was about.

"Shooting?" he said, cupping his free hand to his ear. "I hear no shooting. No bullets, praise the Lord, have yet come . . . ricocheting . . . into the precincts of this quiet tavern. To confess the truth, sir, I move little in this world. I stick to my bar stool, departing only to empty my bladder in the porcelain temple there. But if you assert that there is shooting, I will believe you, my friend; let there be shooting. The question, however, remains: what is to be shot? Women? Children? Dogs? Cats?"

"It's the first day of the Wisconsin squirrel season," said the bartender. The old man's style of speech had evidently ceased to amuse him; he appeared not to notice it, even.

"Ah," said the old man, "we are enlightened. The shaft of dawn breaks upon the mind. What's getting shot? Squirrels are getting shot. Out in the woods, squirrel blood is being drawn, in bucketfuls."

"People *eat* squirrels around here?" I said.

"Eat squirrels?" the old man shouted, banging his stick up and down on the bar floor. "We do not 'eat' squirrels, sir. We may regale ourselves upon them. We might be described, on occasion, as consuming them. We do our humble best to honor the noble squirrel. We make, at the very least, a repast of him."

"What do they taste like?"

"Good," said the bartender.

"The bartender, sir, is a man from whose lips words fall like rocks. He has no poetry in him. The precise savor of the flesh of your squirrel is a subject that only a brave poet would assay." He kissed the inside of his fingers and flourished them in the air. Then he closed his eyes, tilted his head back and affected the smile of a dead saint.

"Don't pay no attention to that old gasbag," the bartender said. "He's been going on that way ever since I can remember. They got a whole ward full of guys like him up at the county hospital. How come they ain't got you there yet, hey? Best place for you, I reckon."

"Sonofabitch," said the old man, with his eyes still closed. "Put another Schlitz in that goddamn glass, will you?"

The bar was filling with the Saturday-morning hunters and their dogs and guns. The first squirrels of the season were skinned, split open and laid out on a grill tray. Cooked, they looked disconcertingly like black bats. I was made to try one.

"Back legs is the best," said the bartender.

The few scraps of meat I was able to disentangle from the bones were tough and tasted vaguely of overhung pheasant. I noticed that the old man dismissed the squirrel that was offered to him with a lordly wave.

Below Lock 9 there was a lunch counter in a wooden shack that ran out over the river on stilts. The woman who sat by the coffee urn was painting a grinning face on a homunculus she had made by glueing pinecones together.

"Now, that is Art, Charlene," said a fisherman in a one-piece suit of green rubber. He looked as if he might be a piece of sculpture himself. "You're a real artist, you know that?"

"It's just something I read up in a magazine," Charlene said, giving her doll a toper's scarlet nose. "Just seemed a kind of cute idea to me."

"Hell," the fisherman said, "that's an original artwork you got there. You take that to Dubuque, or Davenport, or some big city, they'd pay you fifty bucks for it. Maybe a hundred. There's big dough in artworks."

Charlene looked across at me. "Betcha I can tell where *you*'re going," she said. I hadn't realized that my destination was so clearly written on my face. I thought, in fact, that the whole point of the river was that it was too long, too winding and digressive, to yield any certain destination. "We'll be going down there later too."

"Where?"

"The Falling Rocks Walleye Club Annual Pig Roast. Ain't you with them?"

Enchanted by the name, I sought it out. A mile or so downstream, a cluster of jonboats was pulled up on the Wisconsin shore, and I climbed the path up the bluff to the highway and the Falling Rocks Lounge. In a rough clearing behind the bar, the pig roast was circled with campers and pickup trucks, as if the Falling Rocks Walleye Club were taking the usual precautions against Indians. The hog was turning on its spit over a barbecue fire, and trestle tables were laid out in lines under the trees. It was a last-day-of-summer celebration; already the four-o'clock shadows were long and deep, and the bright synthetic colors of everyone's holiday clothes were softened by the low sun. One could feel that fall was just a windy day or two off now; I could smell it in the barbecue smoke and hear it in the tindery rustle of the leaves.

I joined a table of families, feeling a shade regretful that I wasn't myself accompanied by a large fair-haired wife and two slender children in identical jeans and T-shirts, the girl in braids, the boy with braces on his teeth; the basic qualifications for membership of the Walleye Club seemed comfortable and reassuring ones.

"Don't you think it's just beautiful here?" a woman said.

"We come from seventy miles away, over in Iowa," said her husband. "We love it. Where we come from, you know, the land's so flat that all you ever see is water towers and grain elevators. Here, heck, it's beautiful. It must be just about the prettiest place on the whole Mississippi River. We think so, anyhow."

"So the Walleye Club has more to do with the landscape than it has with the fishing?"

"Oh, some of the guys, they get kind of serious about the fishing, but for most of us, no; it's this bar here, and this bluff, and that water. . . ." That water, set out in a wide swath at our feet, had changed its color from morning blue to afternoon green; it was the same deep viridian as the forest that surrounded it.

"So when did you last catch a walleye?"

"Oh, I don't know. Must be a while back, now."

"Years," said his wife.

We lined up to collect our slices of charred meat on paper plates. I wasn't sure whether the echoes I caught of the wagon train at camp for the night—the stockade of drawn-up trucks, the communal meal from the open fire in the center—were deliberate or not. If I'd voiced them, I would have been laughed at; but it must have been nice, I thought, to have one's ancestral past so near at hand that one could unconsciously re-create it at the most ordinary picnic. That was an American privilege, and a European loss.

An old man with a stubbly white beard said that I had to come and meet "the Mississippi Songbird" in the bar.

"When do you sing?" I asked her.

"When I got enough drinks inside me. I ain't hardly started yet."

"This girl here, she's got the most ripplingest voice you ever did hear," said the old man. "She's really something else." So I bought her a Seven and Seven—a Seagram's 7 Crown and 7-Up.

"You just wait till you hear her. Now: I got a kind of hobby. I can tell a man's age, exact. You want me to tell you your age? I'm never wrong. I'll lay you a bourbon on the rocks that I can say what you are to your nearest birthday. Okay?"

"Go ahead," I said, already reaching for my wallet.

"You're . . . This is a specialty of mine. I made a kind of study of the subject. Now, you . . . yep, I got it. You're forty-one years old."

I have rarely been less pleased to win a bet.

"I'm not. I'm thirty-seven. There's my passport."

The man investigated it suspiciously. "I ain't never wrong," he said. "Now, you could've got by for thirty-seven if you'd taken more care with your teeth. That's how I tell. Don't look at nothing else; look at a man's teeth, 'cause teeth don't lie. And I'm telling you, you got the teeth of a man of forty-one." He snapped my passport shut and handed it back to me. It was clear that he expected me to buy the drinks.

"I'm waiting for that bourbon," I said.

"Hell, I don't know. Them teeth you got, they sure look like forty-one years old." He sounded as if he thought that I had deliberately set out to cheat him by cultivating my beastly trick teeth. Grudgingly, he set me up with a whiskey and lectured me on dental care. It was not one of the happier passages of my trip. The time, too, was coming dangerously close to sunset. I said that I had to leave.

"You ain't heard the Mississippi Songbird yet! She'll be singing in a while!"

As I scrambled down the bluff to my boat I was thoroughly disconsolate. The man was obviously right: I had forty-one-year-old teeth. I was four years older than I'd thought, and the burden of this unexpected age sat leadenly on me; with the river getting darker every minute, I felt old-fogeydom closing in.

At Prairie du Chien, Wisconsin, I felt my age. The hotel had closed down years before. The motels were booked solid. The streets were black. Dogs howled at their chains as I walked around the town; they could smell me for a grizzled hobo who had no business being on their block. I hoped that my last resort—the city police department—would take a more charitable attitude toward me than the dogs.

Even in the kindly half-light of Kaber's Supper Club, I was grubbily conspicuous. I sat at a table with my scuffed luggage piled around me, in a denim shirt and old corduroy Levi's, while the other diners—the prosperous small farmers of Wisconsin and their wives—were dressed for a Saturday night out. Never mind. I was going to eat first, and worry about finding a place to bathe and sleep later. Trying to make an announcement to the waitress that I wasn't really the person I appeared to be, I skipped through the cheap wines and ordered a bottle that cost nine dollars. Within seconds, the owner of the restaurant was at my table. I supposed, sadly, that he was going to insist on seeing the color of this mooching bum's money.

"Rex Kaber," he said. "So it's true you're from England. The waitress said so. I told her she must have had a martini too many. Welcome to Prairie du Chien."

I would never get the pronunciation of these places right. *Do Sheen.*
Do Sheen. Remember that.

He joined me and we shared the nine-dollar Burgundy. Since Mr.
Kaber said there was "no way" that he was going to let me pay for either
the wine or the meal, I wished I'd been more modest in my choice.

"Well, this year we're getting Presidents at a dime a dozen, but I
can't remember the last time we saw an Englishman around here.
Where're you putting up?"

I told him about the full motels.

"No problem. Stay in the kid's room. We'll be glad to have you."

His words were easy and openhanded. His face wasn't. It looked as if
it masked a complicated inner life. Twenty years before, it would have
been a simple face, hawkishly handsome, with a tight mouth and eyes
set a little too thoughtfully far back in the skull. Since then it had taken
on a contradictory pattern of fine lines and furrows. Kaber's eyes were
framed by big black-rimmed glasses, and watching them I saw a mixture
of melancholy and good humor, gentleness and curiosity. There were
sleepless nights there too. Rex Kaber looked misplaced as a small-town
restaurateur: a lean, wary man who looked to me as if he had lived more
on his wits and his nerve ends than was good for him.

We steadily talked the bottle down, and Rex called for another. Like
John Dunlevy's newspaper, Kaber's Supper Club was an old family
business; it had been Prairie du Chien's main chophouse since early in
the century. Rex showed me a brown photograph of the place in his
grandfather's time: men in aprons and straw hats in a long open kitchen
which faced onto a street crowded with the overflow from the railroad
and the steamboats.

"Prairie du Chien was really something then. Now . . . you just
have to walk up West Blackhawk Street; half the places are empty and
up for sale. Some of them have been like that for years. The Supper
Club does okay; we get the tourists and the out-of-towners; but the rest
of the city . . . Every year we lose seventy percent of our high school
and college graduates. They just don't want to know. Like my older
son. He's married out in Florida. . . ."

"So will the Supper Club stay on in the family?"

"I'm lucky. My younger son—he's tending bar over there—he just
took a natural interest in the business. He's majoring in hotel management at college. As soon as he gets to be old enough, the place'll be his.
I'll be the one who just tends bar. But Jo-Ann and I, we're real lucky
that way. For most parents, it's heartbreak; they raise their kids here,
and then just have to say goodbye to them at the airport. That's the
way it goes here. You seen McGregor, across the river? They had four,

five thousand people there in 1900. Nowadays . . . well, if you were to count a thousand you'd have to throw in a hundred dogs to make up the weight. They're pretty, these places, but sometimes, 'specially when you see the kids all go, I think we're all dying. Dying on our feet."

When the restaurant closed, we crossed the yard to Kaber's house.

"Would you like to see some of the pictures I've taken? I do photography, just for a hobby."

He brought them out. As soon as I saw them I understood why we had made friends so easily. They were all photographs of water: a frozen creek, its ice splitting away in jagged diagonals; a dead tree standing on its still reflection; a whole colored sky floating in the vacant glass of the Mississippi.

"You like them?"

"I like them so much that I think I took them myself," I said.

The "kid's room" which was my billet for the night had the air of a museum. The kid was a married man with children of his own now, fifteen hundred miles away in Florida, but his room looked as if he'd left it yesterday. His football pennants decorated the walls: I lay under Saints, Colts, Cardinals, Redskins, Oilers, Vikings, Patriots, Raiders, Eagles, Buccaneers and Seahawks. His old singles lay in heaps on the floor, their scratched black vinyl leaking from dog-eared cardboard covers. I remembered them from . . . way back. Patience and Prudence singing "Tonight You Belong to Me"; "Chantilly Lace" by the Big Bopper; Smokey Robinson and "You Better Shop Around." A wooden chest spilled with sports equipment: ski boots, a baseball bat, a tennis racket left out of its press. I felt afloat in time, in this sixteen-year-old's room with my forty-one-year-old teeth, and I cast out what I hoped would be an anchor by trying to read myself to sleep with a novel by Graham Greene. His lizardy tone of weary wisdom toward all times, in which past, present and future were equally corrupted under the eyes of God, seemed appropriate to the moment. I dreamed of bridgework, fillings and extractions.

In the morning I was burrowing in the humming recesses of a strange refrigerator, looking for the orange juice and the coffee beans, when Jo-Ann Kaber, vivid and big-eyed in her bathrobe, found me.

"Hi," she said. "Sleep well?"

"Very," I said, thinking that the actual confusions of my night would strike a stranger as good cause for committing me to an asylum for schizophrenics.

"Rex says that was some evening you had together. I had an early night. I missed out on the fun. You want the Alka-Seltzer?"

"I can't take it," I said. "Reminds me too much of champagne. I hate noisy bubbles in the early morning."

"You want to come to church with us?"

"I'd like that," I said.

Rex had come in. "You want to hear one of Father Finughan's sermons. He's a cracker. He's not one of those milk-and-water priests. He makes you think. That's why we go to St. John's and not to St. Gabe's. That Father Finughan, when he's in form, he can make you shake in your seat. He don't pull none of his punches: he tells you what you *ought* to hear when all those other priests just tell you what you want to hear."

"Oh, he'll just love Father Finughan," Jo-Ann said.

We drove out across town to St. John's. On the way we passed St. Gabe's. Its parking lot was stacked, fender to fender, with new automobiles. Boards outside it advertised Bingo and a Grand Euchre Contest. At St. John's, there was hardly a car in sight and the congregation was thinly sprinkled across yards of empty pews where dusty beams of sunlight showed up the threadbare cushioning and frayed hassocks.

Another beam shone on the bald skull of the priest, who moved quietly through the procedures of the Mass: a small, absorbed figure attended by an acolyte. He had a pointed face like a chipped flint arrowhead. He came suddenly to life when he moved forward from his holy duties to stand at the head of the aisle and deliver his sermon. He gave a dry cough of a laugh. There was more expression in that laugh than in the grand rhetorical flourishes of the American preachers I'd heard before: it held pity, and sarcasm, and disbelief in equal quantities. He looked across the half-empty vault of his church, and laughed again.

"The Church Triumphant," he said. "Sounds good, doesn't it? 'The Church Triumphant'? How many times have you heard those words? They sound mighty fine when you're singing along with the hymns; they make you feel pretty good, hey? You must be quite a guy, to be a paid-up member of this fancy corporation, the Church Triumphant." There was another, wicked little laugh. "Well, don't kid yourself. The Church hasn't triumphed. Take a look at it—if you dare to. Oh, yeah, it's still here, still around, struggling, suffering. The poor old Church. You think it's 'Triumphant,' huh? I tell you, *I* don't. When I see the Church, I see the struggling and the suffering, I see Her being opposed on all sides by the . . . elders . . . and scribes . . . of our time. Oh, yeah. Haven't you heard? They're rejecting us pretty regularly, those elders . . . and scribes."

He had saved a special laugh for me, as he watched me trying to transfer his words to my notebook.

"Yeah, they're turning their backs on us all right, the doctors, the lawyers, the college professors. The big shots. The good guys. The fellows we're all supposed to look up to in our society today." In a crackly whisper, he talked of the legal system in which rich men and their lawyers could buy acquittals for themselves, of hospitals where the poor couldn't afford the treatment they needed, of the bill-collection agencies that terrorized people on welfare. The prospect of twentieth-century America sent him into a spasm of angry chuckles.

"You think the Church is a church of good guys, do you? You think Jesus suffered on the cross for the folks with two cars in their garage, and their fine homes, and their four-figure donations to charities? I tell you, this is the church of bad guys. It's the church of sinners, the church of prostitutes, the church of the poor, the church of Mary Magdalen. You remember how Jesus taught us that we must sacrifice our goods? Think about it. Okay, so you'll give away your house, your car, your farm." He raked his congregation with a skeptical, amused eye. "Yeah? So who are you going to give them to? The good guys? Or are you going to sacrifice everything you've saved for to some bum, some guy who's done nothing—nothing at all—to deserve it?

"That's the teaching of Jesus. Pretty hard, ain't it? That's what He did. He suffered on that cross for prostitutes—not for saints, not for the good guys. Go on—give away your farm to the first bum you see on the street, or the prostitute in some bar . . . pretty crazy, huh? 'That guy's nuts!' Can't you hear the voices? Oh, yeah, all them good guys, they'd talk you out of it real fast, wouldn't they? But that's what Jesus did. . . ."

No wonder St. Gabe's was packed and St. John's was attended by the faithful remnant. Mocking, asperitous, plainspoken, the priest had come near to emptying his church with the rigor of his theology. We left chastened.

"Wasn't that something?" said Rex.

"God, I need a drink," Jo-Ann said.

Passing St. Gabe's we could hear the last hymn swelling out onto the street, the sopranos and baritones competing with each other for the loudest, proudest notes. It sounded like a church of good guys, comfortably triumphant. Back at the empty supper club, with our Bloody Marys lined along the bar, Jo-Ann asked me why I hadn't gone to the altar rail to take Communion.

"Aren't you a Catholic? What church do you belong to, Jonathan?"

I explained that I'd been brought up in the Church of England and that although I still respected the moral force of Christian teaching, I could not accept any of its supernatural claims.

"You're not an *atheist!* I'd hate to think you were an atheist!"

"No. It seems illogical to try to deny what you can't prove or disprove. I'm an agnostic."

"So that'd mean you'd still believe in . . . like, Eternal Life?"

"No. I don't believe in Eternal Life."

"But how can you bear to go on living? There's going to be a really beautiful Eternal Life! I *know* that. If I didn't believe in Eternal Life . . . I guess I'd just want to die. You *have* to believe in Eternal Life!"

"Perhaps I want to die even less because I don't believe in it."

"Knowing that about you, you know it makes me feel so sad. I want to pray for you."

Rex studied the inside of his glass embarrassedly.

"I guess," he said slowly, "when I get to thinking about it, I suppose I feel like Jonathan does, really. There's no proof and no disproof. It's just a kind of a nice idea. . . . I don't know whether I really believe in it or not."

"Rex!" Her voice was shrill with shock. Her eyes began to flood with tears. "You've *got* to believe there's going to be a beautiful, beautiful Eternal Life! How can you sit there saying things like that? Oh, my God, Rex! You can't; you just can't!"

Sitting between husband and wife, the cause of this appalled estrangement, I felt ashamed and mean.

"You never *told* me. I never *knew* that about you. . . ."

I thought: It is always like this. You can share decades of intimacy with someone; then one day you will find yourself sitting across from them in a bar and they will be as strange to you as a casual acquaintance on a journey.

"You—*atheist!*"

Prairie du Chien looked like the priest's vision of the Church: it was still around, still struggling; not triumphant. West Blackhawk Street was dominated by the dead hotel. I couldn't make out what its name had been. Eight wooden letters, cracked and bleached, were still pinned at odd angles to its facade. Once they'd been a bright sky blue; now only a few shreds of paint adhered to the crevices in the grain. They had the tantalizing obscurity of an unfinished crossword puzzle:

O T   C W
  O   H O   L

I looked through the window. The ceiling was falling in, and the wood reception desk was whitened with flakes of rotten plaster. An abandoned tubular chair stood in a waste of carpet that had lost its pile. There were flowerpots on the windowsill, but the plants inside them had died long ago, leaving naked bamboo stakes behind.

All down the street there was the same sad air of dereliction. In each vacated store there was a dusty pile of cardboard boxes; torn screening peeled out from the doorframes. Gokey's Meats and Groceries was a boarded ruin. Rusted metal plaques bore advertising slogans at once chirpy and wan. A Coca-Cola logo from the 1940s had its message eaten almost completely away. Was it PAUSE . . . DRINK or PLEASE . . . DRINK? I couldn't tell. HILLDALE MILK—DRINK THE UDDER KIND was clear; so was REACH FOR SUNBEAM BREAD. Even the realtors' signs that hung outside these places were beginning to rust and fade. Yet the basic fabric of the town, its fine neoclassical brick and white clapboard, retained an unseasonably prosperous look, as if it were just waiting for the arrival of the next train or steamboat to restore it to spanking glory.

In fact, the steamboat had just docked. The *Delta Queen* had pulled in that afternoon and anchored in front of the Villa Louis, a pompous Victorian mansion which had been built by Wisconsin's first fur millionaire on the island that kept the town just out of sight of the river. Teen-age girls, sweating in costume bustles and mobcaps, escorted the tourists around the house. I fell in behind one party and was bored by a succession of bad paintings, old dinner plates, clothes that smelled of mothballs and the oohs and ahs of the *Delta Queen* gang as they took in their compulsory history lesson before getting back on the boat and heading for the next scheduled attraction upriver. No one crossed the bridge to the town. Shooting pool in a bar on Front Street, I mentioned the steamboat to my opponent. "Oh, yeah?" he said, chalking his cue. "I never seed it." The only connection between the *Delta Queen* and Prairie du Chien was that their names rhymed. The old cry of "Steamboat a-comin'!" which used to rouse every town along the river would not today stir a single dozing hound on the levee.

Below Prairie du Chien, the Mississippi ran through a tight wooded ravine. The swell on the river was ribbed and glittery, and I plowed into it as fast as I dared. I could feel the fall chasing me; I must move south before the cold, short days caught me up. I was being overtaken now by my fellow migrants. Each day more Monarch butterflies went by, riding the wind in zigzag swoops and bounds. I had seen the first of the snow geese from Canada, going high overhead in strict formation. They were headed for their winter quarters on the lakes of Kentucky and Tennessee. Lower in the air, skimming the water, there were flights of teal. At first I mistook them for puffs of smoke—gray smudges of a hundred birds or so at a time. Then, suddenly, the puff would atomize into its constituent parts, the ducks scattering wildly at some signal from within the flight. I tried to keep up, but my own progress was hobbled and jerky. All through the morning, the southerly wind had been steadily building; by the time I reached Guttenberg, Iowa, just twenty miles downstream, the wave tops were splashing over my bow, and I had to tie up at a fishing station where the boats were lurching noisily around on their moorings. I watched a Monarch being blown back by the wind like a scrap of burnt paper. It fluttered up, made a foot or two of air, lost it, struggled to regain its hold, and was carried off on some slipstream into the trees, drawn to the south as senselessly as an iron filing in the field of a magnet.

I walked into Guttenberg along the sandy track on the levee, nervously watching where I was putting my feet after I'd spotted two sloughed snakeskins within fifty yards. My entry into town was at least more tactful than Jimmy Carter's. The President had stepped off the *Delta Queen* clutching notes for a speech. Once the crowd was already packed solid around him, he had called to his aides, "Hey, is this Iowa? Is this Iowa?" *Yes*, said the crowd; and Carter sailed into a lengthy tribute to Iowa and the Iowans. Unfortunately, his initial question had been better remembered in Guttenberg than the speech that followed it.

For weeks afterward, wits went putting their heads around the doors of Guttenberg bars and crying, "Hey, is this Iowa?" Someone at the end of the bar was then supposed to growl, "Hey, that ain't Ted Kennedy, is it?"

Now, though, Guttenberg was preparing for some more pressing elections of its own. The town was stuck over with posters advertising candidates for mayor, for the school board, for the city council. We were living through a period when contempt for national politics, for "Washington outlaws," for the mass-marketed big shots in the presidential race was deeper than it had ever been. Yet in the politics of the local community there was a transparent enthusiasm and liveliness, as if people had rejected "America" as an ungovernable abstraction and turned instead to that older, more comprehensible model of the city-state as their political sphere of action. Let Reagan, Connally, Carter, Kennedy, Anderson go hang; in Guttenberg, Iowa, the democratic process was alive and well on names like Farmer, Kregel, Webster, Saeugling, Rodenberg, Willenborg, Tangeman and Merrick. That, at least, was the notion I wanted to explore, and I went off to find the mayor of Guttenberg at the back of his cable-TV rental store.

Mayor Webster pushed a pile of paperwork aside to talk to me. He was retiring from office later in the year, and he called in Karen Merrick, a young doctor's wife who was hoping to become the first woman mayor of Guttenberg.

"Look," Webster said. "I'm a registered Republican. Karen here's a Democrat. If we ever got to talking about national issues we'd split right down the line. I'm a conservative, she's a liberal. But I'll vote for her as mayor. On the city council, we've disagreed on a lot of things; but she's backed me on some issues, I've backed her on others. It's totally bipartisan. And that's where national government has gone all to hell, and where the city council of Guttenberg scores. It's the right person for the job, and not the party line. I think Karen'll make a great mayor—and she's a *Kennedy* supporter!"

We talked about the "issues" of the town. There was the swimming pool I'd passed on the way in—that was something Karen Merrick had campaigned for and won. There was a big sewage project on hand . . . the question of town lighting . . . the electricity and water supplies . . .

"But it's only with things like this that you can have real democracy, with everyone in the community participating," Karen Merrick said. "Democracy's something that works best in a town this size, and the bigger you get, the less democracy you tend to have."

I said that I found that a depressing prospect. Didn't such intense localism simply lead to ugly small-town xenophobia? "Like Lansing, up the road. I gather that Lansing people think of anyone with a Dubuque license plate as an intruder."

"Yeah," said Webster. "But that's special. That's all to do with the hunting party. Didn't they tell you about that? That was, oh, must have been back in the 1950s. Some guys from Dubuque County got up a hunting party and went shooting squirrels over on the bluff there. Farmer comes out on his horse, orders them off his land; they shot his horse from under him. Then they cut all the squirrels they got in two; they took the back legs away with them and scattered the heads and front legs all over the guy's land. . . . That's why Lansing folks don't care for Dubuque County license plates. Now, if they'd been hunting rattlesnakes, that wouldn't have been so bad . . . but squirrels . . ." He laughed. "Don't you ever try shooting a guy's horse *and* his squirrels. That's what's known as testing a man's patience."

I had to admit that I was on shaky ground with the case of Lansing versus Dubuque County.

"No, I think we've got things about right, here in Guttenberg," Webster said. "The family's still the center of things here. And the church.

Kids grow up knowing what's right and what's wrong. They know what it means to be a member of the community."

"And then as soon as they graduate from high school, they take off for the big city."

"That's not true. Sure, some go. But then they take what they've learned in Guttenberg with them. That's how the small town educates the city."

"Where are your own children?"

"Right here in Guttenberg."

Foiled.

"I just see one big problem," Karen Merrick said. "So many kids now are going into trade schools and technical schools, the whole vocational thing, and they're losing out on the liberal arts. Unless we can get them back into liberal-arts programs, they're going to lose their understanding of the whole democratic process. Then you've got an unworkable system. I think that's happening now. We're raising a generation that isn't educated enough to know what it means to be a citizen."

"That's in the cities," Webster said.

"No, I think it's happening here too."

"How do you feel about places like New York and Los Angeles?"

"Those New Yorkers," Webster said, "they think Guttenberg doesn't exist; but if places like Guttenberg didn't exist, then those New Yorkers, they'd *starve*. Well, we know that here, but they don't know it there. So I reckon we just about got the edge on them."

"I spent two years in California, when my husband was an intern. I hated the attitude there. You know, I'd say I came from Iowa. *Iowa?* Half the people there didn't know the difference between Iowa, Idaho and Omaha. They didn't know if it was a city or a state. The other half just said, 'Oh yeah: fields of corn.' It's not *like* that."

"California . . ." said Webster, ". . . where the soap operas come from. Those soap operas, they're really something else. You ever seen *As the World Turns?* I was looking at it this afternoon. There was this girl in bed, naked, with a guy. She gets up; the guy shouts, 'You just been using me.' 'That's right,' she says. 'I've just been using you. For sex.' And slams out the door." The mayor chewed the phrase over again. " 'I've just been using you. For sex.' And that's a *girl* talking. Imagine that in Guttenberg—"

Later that evening, in the bar of the hotel on the bluff, I had reason to remember Mayor Webster's happy disbelief in the possibility of such outrageous lines ever being spoken in his city. Beside me, two women were drinking with steady intent. A husband arrived. There was a quick, quiet row in which a few words were used like razor blades, and the husband left before the whiskey he'd ordered had been set up on the bar.

"What *you* doing tonight?" said the wife, handing me her husband's drink. Then, to her friend, she said, "You were always the lucky one."

"Why? Because mine died before yours did?"

"Yup."

"You know they work together now—Ben and her together? That's why they're so goddamn shit-to-shit."

So perhaps Guttenberg did, after all, turn on the same axis as the world.

The wind blew stubbornly on from the same quarter. From the window of my hotel room on the bluff, the river looked like a pretty sheet of beaten metal; but at water level each hammer dent was big enough to hold my boat, its lip curling with foam above the bow. I wedged my hat hard down over my ears and talked to the waves. In foreign climes there were at times some moments quite appalling . . .

I had another useful incantation, too. Just before I'd left London, the British poet Gavin Ewart had published a clever piece of doggerel in the *New Statesman*. It had won a competition in which entrants had been invited to base an eight-line stanza on any town, mountain or river with four syllables to its name. Ewart had chosen the Mississippi:

> I am old man Mississippi,
> Full of time and mud.
> You all must be pretty nippy
> When I get in flood.
> Swim in me? You would be dippy,
> Foolish flesh and blood!
> Would end woeful, dead and drippy;
> Keep your distance, bud.

I chanted this down Cassville Slough and Hurricane Chute. The sprawl of islands here was thick enough to soften the effect of the wind, and the rhythm of the hull on the rocky water was as regular as the sound of train wheels leaping over the gaps in the tracks. *Mis-sis-sippi. Mis-sis-sippi. Mis-sis-sippi.* On the train, one is supposed to hear the name of one's destination in the noise; on the river, all I could hear was the river itself.

I thought of the Monarch butterfly that I'd seen the day before, fighting its way south, and saw myself in my yellow boat as a bug of another species—committed to the same route more by bug instinct than by any act of conscious intelligence. Sometime—I couldn't remember when—the idea of the river had become fixed in my head like a computer program. I could work out what it meant only by the cluster of vague associations with which it seemed to be surrounded. When the seven-year-old lay on the bank of the piddling little river at the bottom of the road, he saw his childhood only as constriction. It was like a suit of heavy clothes in which he was muffled and gagged. His father was a giant, an almost-complete stranger, who had come back from fighting a war to find that the only man who was still under his command was a spindly, tearful dwarf. Unused to children, the father talked to his son in the language of the officer dressing down an unruly private. In a real army, the enlisted ranks quickly develop a retaliatory strategy; they know exactly how to put officers in their place. The child didn't. He smarted miserably under his father's strict discipline. He found it impossible to predict what was likely to win him praise or send him, blubbering, to his father's study for yet another court-martial. The house was small—so small that the father seemed taller than the chimney pots. It was in a tiny village where the handful of other children were all enemies, since the father had forbidden his son to play with village children because they were not the sons and daughters of officers and gentlemen.

So the boy ran away to the river. It was the only place he knew where his father didn't loom over him like a headachy, angry god. He was often forbidden to go there: rough boys from the village fished at the mill and gave him bits and pieces of tackle. These enviable creatures bred maggots in the carcasses of rabbits they'd snared, and he was once given a whole tin of precious, wriggling larvae—the perfect bait for roach. His father found the maggots in his room; for a time after that, going to the river was roughly equivalent to a British soldier's crossing to the German lines and signing himself into the service of the Axis powers.

At the river, I was free to dream of what it might be like not to be a child; and all I could imagine was that there would be no father, no constraints. In this improbable future, I would somehow move at my own will. I'd breed maggots. I'd make friends with the ragged toughs from the village. I'd waste my days away at the water's edge and be muddy and profane. When I tried to make the River Wensum grow as wide as the Mississippi, I suppose I was attempting to stretch it until it corresponded with the amazing breadth of the freedom I thought I was going to enjoy as a grown-up.

Now, going past Cassville and the black windows of another great derelict hotel, I was living the daydream for real; and I felt that even the seven-year-old, with his hopes of limitless irresponsibility, would have been shaken by the gigantic reach and width of the thing. This long, careless drift through other people's lives, with the boat always moored ready for a fast getaway, and the solitude of the river never more than a stone's throw away from the society of the town, would have impressed him as being grander than anything he'd imagined. He hadn't predicted the fright of it. In those days he hadn't been afraid of drowning. I was. I kept on seeing myself dead in the river, a body strewn untidily on a sandbar, its clothes ridden up over its head. The child wouldn't have anticipated the possibility of feeling twinges of guilt about this life, either: he wouldn't have cared one way or the other about the dangerous morality of an existence of temporary pick-ups and friendships, of people dropped almost as soon as met, of the indifferent, deep egoism of moving for moving's sake. He had, perhaps, been wise in his decision to include maggots in his paradise.

At North Buena Vista, I stopped to fill my gas tanks and make the long steep walk up to the village. Old Glory flew over the wooden post office and the brick schoolhouse, but in other respects the place might have belonged to another continent. A painted statue of the Virgin stood in a grotto cut into the rock face, surrounded by dead flowers, candle stubs and colored stones. A wooded path, noisy with buzzings and rustlings and slitherings, led to a hilltop cemetery, and I sat on the fine granite tomb of Peter and Mary Ludovissy, looking down on the river. The Ludovissys had been born in 1855 and 1860, and they'd died ten years before I was born. Overshadowed by a stand of pines, their mountain grave had a view of first the river, then the green plateau of Wisconsin, then the misty violet of the "East," from where, presumably, they had themselves made the trek out here to Iowa, to make, or find, just such a town as the one they'd left behind in Europe.

Maybe that was what I was doing on my own journey. There was a good deal of conceit in the way that I thought of myself as the stranger from the big city; I wasn't really that at all. I'd been brought up in a succession of villages, always within sniffing distance of a farmyard. The little towns I was passing through—Lansing, Prairie du Chien, Guttenberg, North Buena Vista—were places I could instantly recognize from childhood. They smelled the same. The faces of the people in the bars had a cousinly look to the agricultural workers of Pennington, Hempton Green, Aldwick. It was all, in one sense, a coming back, but a coming back with the liberty to move out and on. Perhaps the Ludovissys had felt much the same. To so many of the European peasantry who had come to the Midwest to build farms of their own, America had given their original life back to them; at the same time, it had released them from the bonds of authority which had chained them like dogs in Europe. It had freed them from patriarchy while leaving them within the sight and smell of home.

I climbed back down the path to the village and stopped in at the bar. The bartender insisted that he was a "Luxembourger," even though he and his father had both been born and raised in North Buena Vista.

"You stay what you are," he said. "Like my wife. She's from Louisiana. She's lived here fifteen years. But folks in town, they still think she's a stranger. Or take these German towns around here. In the war, some of them was on the German side. They was *Nazi* towns, they wasn't American."

He told me the story of how, when he'd been a teen-ager, a German farmer had confiscated his driver's license at gunpoint. His father, who had fought with the U.S. Army in Europe, had driven out to the German's farm armed with a twenty-gauge. "You don't give me that kid's license back," the father said, "I'm gonna shoot you dead. I killed enough goddamn Germans in my time; one more won't make no difference." The driver's license had been returned. The story was told with filial pride.

"You know what's wrong with this country now?" said the bartender. "They should've hung Jane Fonda fifteen years ago. Them sonofabitch 'liberals.' Just look up there—" He pointed at all the forms and licenses that were thumbtacked to the wall behind the bar. "The goddamn state *makes* you into a crook. The income tax makes you into a crook. I'm a crook. Like, talking with you I'm not being crooked, but every other way I gotta be crooked to live. What the hell kind of country is this when it does that to folks?

"You know," he said two beers later, "if only we'd had George Wallace or Barry Goldwater for President, things might've been a whole lot different around here."

It was a line I'd heard a hundred times. It still made me shudder. "Ronald Reagan?" I said.

"That sonofabitch. Look at when he was governor of California! Ronald Reagan, I'm telling you, he's a goddamn *liberal*."

It was possible, I thought, that the bartender spoke truer than he knew. His assertion that Germans were still Germans, Luxembourgers still Luxembourgers, was a denial of America's capacity really to transform its immigrants. It might unlock the bonds of patriarchy, yet three and four generations on, the liberated peasantry was still pining for a *Führer*-figure. These lovely villages like North Buena Vista were full of people demanding a "strong leader" and baying for blood—someone's blood; anyone's blood would do. Put Jane Fonda to death. Elect a good hard-line racist on an antitax ticket. As someone from the fringe of America's colonial sphere, I was frightened a good deal more by this than by the Mississippi River.

Preoccupied, I rode the Dubuque pool without giving it a thought. I slipped, a little bumpily, from black buoy to black buoy. Only when I reached the lock gate above Dubuque did I remember the warning the lockmaster had given me back in Minneapolis. "That's one of the worst pools, the Dubuque pool. She's wide open, for as far as you can see . . ." From the entrance to the chamber, I looked back on a darkening spread of yellow scud and rough water; and I felt grateful to the bartender for having distracted me into this uncharacteristic outbreak of fearlessness.

A sociologist might have created Dubuque as an elementary model of a stratified society. A woman cabdriver took about three minutes to explain to me how the whole structure worked. "I'm nobody around here," she'd said. "I come from the Flats." The 'Flats,' down by the river, was where all the nobodies lived. North Side was German, and Germans were nobodies hoping to be somebodies; South Side was Irish, and the Irish were the nobody-nobodies. The cabdriver came from the Flats, South Side. Between the nobodies and the somebodies lay the four-block-thick cavity insulation of the business district. Then, as the bluffs began to rise steeply above the town, so the people and their houses grew more and more important. Right at the top of Dubuque life was Alpine, a rocky stratosphere of mansions and ranch houses.

"How do you get out of the Flats and up to Alpine?"

"You don't. You take a ride up there by cab, and then you come all the way down again."

Perhaps it was the robust simplicity of this way of arranging life that had endeared Dubuque to Al Capone. He liked plain pyramids, and Dubuque had been a favorite retreat of his. According to the cabdriver, he'd rented the third floor of the Julien Hotel by the year; and when things got uncomfortably warm for him in Chicago, he'd brought his court to Dubuque, a three-hour drive by fast car at night. There were stories that he'd also maintained an underground hideout, accessible only by boat, somewhere in the tangle of islands in Dead Man's Slough. No one I talked to later would exactly confirm, or exactly deny, any of this. I suspected that Dubuque people had spent rather too much time on feeding and watering the legend of Capone's association with their town. The suggestion of romantic thuggery had helped to make up for the famous slight to the reputation of Dubuque that was made in 1925 by Harold Ross. When he defined *The New Yorker,* he said it was *not* a magazine for "the old lady in Dubuque." The town's response had been to hint that that was no old lady; that was a Mafioso in drag.

There was nothing gangsterish about the Julien Hotel now. It was a red-brick giant, clinging to what was left of its gentility by its fingernails. I didn't mind its drafts and cobwebs. I liked its creaking elevator cages. For sixteen dollars I got myself a room on Capone's floor, with a bath, a telephone and a laundry service. When the plump waitress in braids, with a brace on her top teeth, suddenly broke off her routine, one-word inquiry about *Hashrownsmashbakemericanorfrenchfries?* to point at my copy of John Updike's *Pigeon Feathers* and say *Hesagudorthor,* I decided to lay up in the Julien for a day or two. I hadn't had a literary conversation for ages. I asked the waitress what else she'd read by Updike.

"Oh, I dunno . . . *Couplesnrabbitreduxnmarrymenmonthofsundays . . . nsuch.*" The trouble was that too much waiting on tables had turned books into kinds of potato too. She had an Iowa voice, with a high abrasive rattle of silica sand in every syllable.

"How on earth do you learn to talk so fast?"

"I dunno. *Guessitskindajustthewaymymindclicks.*"

She was too quick for me. Feeling pleasantly lonely, I wandered out onto Main Street. It had fallen into the deep, vacant sleep which, each night, possesses only American cities of a certain size. Nothing moves. You mistake leaves guttering on the sidewalks for rats. The noise of a distant bar carries halfway across town. Digital display signs outside the banks go through their monotonous retelling of time and temperature, as if they were being pestered by an idiot child. Electric gas lamps on the new brick shopping mall light up benches on which no one sits and trash cans that were emptied at dusk. One by one, the waxwork theaters of the illuminated storefronts are switched off by automatic clocks, and you are left with only the faint splashing sound of cars going by, miles out west, on the Interstate Highway. It is a moment when you suspect that you are the one person who hasn't been told about the disaster which has hit the place like plague.

I stood in front of a window display of colored plaster busts of Elvis Presley until it went out. I crossed the street to another lighted window: it was full of animals. Stuffed racoons, stuffed fish, stuffed coyotes. FOR YOUR TROPHY ROOM . . . I copied down the name and phone number of the taxidermist. In the last few weeks, I had seen so many lacquered corpses in glass cases that I now accepted them as inevitable bits of furniture, like ashtrays and table lamps. In this part of the country taxidermy seemed as much a part of everyday culture as psychoanalysis in Manhattan. I'd heard people talking about "my taxidermist . . ."; and I decided that I too had reached the point in life when I ought to see a taxidermist.

In the meantime, I found a singles bar. The best that one could say about it was that, unlike its counterparts in Boston and New York which I'd visited briefly and miserably years before, it made no pretense of being anything else. It was a singles bar: loud, gloomy, tense with unshared and unallayable sexual frustration. The singles looked as if they belonged nowhere. They certainly hadn't come from the Flats, or from Alpine. Their dress-to-kill leisure gear hung stiffly on their bodies, as if it were taken out of the closet only on very rare occasions. No one was under thirty. Everyone had run to fat and worse. I could see no face with a glimmer of humor in it. The smiles were glued on, and tired lust showed through every one.

I tried to read Updike and happened on a story in which a Rhodes Scholar at Oxford finds himself in a cinema watching a Doris Day movie set in a Hollywood mock-up of a Midwestern small town. The man comes from the East, not the Midwest. He sees the tacky artifice with which the filmmaker has sentimentally recast down-home America. Yet he discovers that he is weeping over his own real exile. The image fascinated me. I could place that moment exactly in my own life. It had been February 1972, and I'd cried in a poky little movie house in Northampton, Massachusetts, watching, of all things, Twiggy in *The Boy Friend,* for just the same reasons, and with the same qualifications, as Updike's hero. I wasn't sure whether to be pleased or sad that eight years on, even a singles bar in Dubuque couldn't raise a homesick tear.

"Hi, my name's Ellie."

Ellie combined in her person all the reasons why, in my right mind, I should never have sought out a singles bar. She was thirty-five, thirty-six, and looked as if she'd devoted most of her life to ice cream and chocolate-chips. Her frilly pink blouse might have looked party-sweet on a slender ten-year-old. On Ellie it just looked a terrible mistake. She had put on a squeaky baby voice, but it was fogged with bourbon-and-cola.

"You like to dance? My mother . . . she always said . . . I couldn't dance . . . 'cause my butt was too big. . . ." She laughed unhappily, and waited for me to contradict her mother. I couldn't.

"I'm a terrible dancer," I said. "My legs feel too old."

She came from Muncie, Indiana. She worked in a hospital in Dubuque. "My friend—oh, he's going to be in right along—*he* says I'm too brilliant, much too brilliant, to work in a town like this. I tell him,

Look, I lived six months in New York City. Six months. I lived in one of the most socially desirable areas in New York. I couldn't stand it. I couldn't *stand* it."

"Where did you live?"

"Oh, you wouldn't know. It was one of the most socially desirable areas. I mean, I had a wonderful apartment and all. . . . It was, it was . . ." I could see her trying to assemble a drunken inventory of New York place names. "It was . . . in the Village. You know, Greenwich Village? Well, it was right there. Hey . . ." She switched track hastily. "Don't you think Americans are all so *vulgar?* I think American men . . . I been to Yerp. In Yerp . . . Yerpean men . . . They got . . . manners. I mean, in Yerp, they treat you like a *woman.* I *want* to be treated like a woman. I want men to open doors for me and offer me their seat . . . you know?"

I said that if I were a woman I'd be tempted to clout men who opened the door for me, even though I was a man who always opened doors for women.

"You don't believe in *Women's Lib?*" Ellie said.

"I don't think it's a matter of believing in it. It's not a faith."

"They got Women's Lib in Yerp now?" she asked. She made it sound like leprosy.

"There's probably more of it about in England than there is in Dubuque."

"I think Women's Lib is a load of . . ." Then she remembered, and revised her phrase: ". . . cold water."

Her complaining voice filled my head like sticky fudge. At thirty-second intervals I nodded and gruffed and tried to keep one small sane space open in my mind. *Think of the river. Think of wing dams. Think of wakes.* It seemed like hours before deliverance came. "I'll be right back," she promised. "I just gotta powder my nose." As soon as she'd gone, I grabbed my book and escaped. Outside, there was just one storefront still lighted. At first I thought it contained model Mississippi steamboats; then I saw that they were plaster wedding cakes. A holstered cop was staring into the window with the deep concentration of a man engrossed in a movie. He never heard my footfalls on the street, but stood there, hunched, his hands on his knees, studying the silver bells and little brides and bridegrooms, the butt of his pistol sticking out from his hip.

My taxidermist lived at an oblique angle to the rest of Dubuque society, out on a bluff to the southwest of town. Jerry Eiben wore a scarlet T-shirt saying I'M A TAXIDERMIST . . . I'LL MOUNT ANYTHING, with the words framing a picture of an elderly maniac in dubious congress with a long-suffering elk. His pretty suburban house was a dead zoo of squirrels, coyotes, coons, skunks, beaver, fish and pheasants. He and his wife, Cindy, ran their taxidermy business in the basement. Cindy specialized in eyes and paintwork, while Jerry emptied the frozen bodies of their guts, cleaned them, slid them over molds of rubber and polystyrene, and sewed them up. Outside in the yard, their baby daughter bounced up and down on a trampoline, leaving her parents to bloody their hands in the flesh trade. We passed a family of racoons, reduced to absurdity by the strips of cardboard that had been fixed around their ears to keep them in shape and by the bristle of pins and clothes pegs that decorated their mouths and whiskers. Cindy, with mechanical affection, let her hand dawdle through the fur of the mother coon.

"They were road deaths," she said.

Jerry opened one of the two gigantic refrigerators. "Spare parts," he said. I saw wings, fins, legs, heads, paws, tails, laid out on the shelves like the ingredients for a bizarre dinner party.

"Have you ever read the Book of Revelation? You've probably got all the right bits to make the beast with seven heads and ten horns."

"You never know when you'll need like a walleye head or a duck's wing. They'll all come in useful, sometime."

Cindy settled down to an eight-color airbrush job on a dead fish. Jerry showed me how to mount a coon, easing the wet skin over the mold. There was indeed a parallel with psychoanalysis. In life, these animals had possessed the particular identity of their personal quirks and disorders—their sagging bellies, twisted hind legs, scraggy rumps. Taxidermy restored them all to the standard shape of a normal, well-adjusted coon. The molds came in different sizes but made no allowance for any variety of diet or behavior. A coon was a coon was a coon.

"That's why we always say no when folks ask us to mount their pets. You can never get a dog or a cat to look like their owners remember them. It just doesn't work out. Then you get into a heartbreak situation, you know?"

Cindy brought out a tray of glass eyes. Even out of their sockets, they had an unnerving look of watery appeal, these staring irises of flecked hazel, pink, ultramarine, dull gold and umber. I picked one up. Deep behind the glass cornea there were red veins on cream, and the dark pupil gazed back at me from my palm with steady melancholy and boredom.

"Coyote," Cindy said. "Skunk . . ." She fingered a rolling eye on the tray. "Wood duck . . . possum . . . deer . . ."

"That's the thing about taxidermy . . ." Jerry Eiben was wiggling the empty coon's head over its rubber form now, drawing out the damp creases in the pelt around its neck. "It's always something different. You been doing fish all week, say, and you think, What the hell, I'm sick of goddamn fish. Okay, so the next day you go do a bird."

"Right now," Cindy said, "we're into creative groups. Like, see that coyote carrying off a pheasant? Or the otter with the fish. Creative groups. That's where taxidermy turns into an art form."

"Who are your customers?"

"Everybody," said Jerry. "You get the guy off the line at the John Deere plant with a coon; then you get doctors, lawyers, all the professional people—they all got trophy rooms."

"There's a woman lawyer downtown, you ought to see her trophy room. It's bigger than our whole house. She's got everything. Giraffes. Elephants. Oryx. Moose. Bears. Doesn't she have a rhino, Jerry? I think she's got a rhino in there too."

So the Eibens kept the world of Alpine supplied with lachrymose bucks and snarling polecats; in the trophy rooms of the stucco mansions, wild things with glass eyes and rubber flesh served to remind the city's aristocrats that they were frontiersmen at heart. The Eibens themselves, though, were outsiders. They were Protestants from northern Minnesota, "strangers" to Dubuque.

"This is a Catholic city," Jerry Eiben said. "It's kind of clicky. If you don't go to the Catholic church, if you haven't been to the Catholic high school or gone to the Catholic college, or you're not a member of one of the Catholic clubs, then you're out. All our friends here, they're newcomers too. You know, they're from Des Moines . . . Decorah . . . La Crosse . . . Timbuktu. I guess that's one of the things I really like about taxidermy. It's kind of a social thing. You get to know the other taxidermists around, you visit with each other at folks' homes, you talk taxidermy . . . Me and my taxidermist friends, we swap bodies."

I wanted to make my way in Dubuque. If I wasn't a Catholic, at least I could climb hills. Up on Locust Street I found the Redstone, a cocktail lounge where the people looked distinctly more Alpine than the desolate singles of Buddy's Bar. The men wore tweed jackets frogged and elbow-patched with suede trimmings, giving them a curiously apposite resemblance to a group of yodeling Austrian woodcutters. The women smelled of Chanel No. 5. I paid an alpine price for a beer served in a balloon glass that should have held brandy.

"You look like Tom Wolfe—" She was Ms. Alpine to the life, with a puffy spray of French lace at her neck, and a face and hair which revealed less about her than about the dedicated toiling of the beauticians and coiffeuses who kept them regularly serviced. "I know you're *not* Tom Wolfe, because Tom Wolfe wouldn't be in Dubuque. But you look like Tom Wolfe, and if Tom Wolfe was in Dubuque he'd be doing just what you're doing."

"What am I doing?" I'd thought I was in a state of suspended vacancy.

"You're watching people from under your eyelids and spinning that pen around between your fingers. Just like Tom Wolfe. Hey—" Ms. Alpine rescued a doll-like child with ringlets from under her bar stool. "This one's mine. Say hello to the gentleman, honey." The infant looked at me with practiced distaste. Its tongue protruded just a millimeter or so from a pair of tiny lips.

"You live in Alpine?"

"Right on the *top* of Alpine."

She had a degree in journalism from a college in Minnesota. Once, she'd had her own radio show. "It was a phone-in, right? There was me and my goldfish. When no one called in, I used to talk to the goldfish. That was really something else. The goldfish, and all. I was a star. Everyone recognized me. It was the biggest thing in Dubuque."

The top of Alpine . . . the biggest thing in Dubuque . . . I was touching heights I hadn't dreamed of.

"What are you doing for dinner tomorrow?" I asked her.

"I have to watch my step. My ninety days aren't up yet. When I get to the end of my ninety days, I'll be a free woman again. Right now, though, I practically have to have a chaperon before I can say Hi to my own brother on the goddamn street."

"You've got a brother?"

"No. Just figurative. I got an ex-husband. Almost-ex. The worst."

We ran through the list of all the restaurants in Dubuque. Some were too public, others too glaringly clandestine. We fixed on one that was suitably upright and discreet. After Ms. Alpine left the bar, I spent a long time trying to decide whether I was elated or just plain frightened at the prospect of my date.

The Dubuque Packing Company was right down in the Flats. I walked through streets of low houses built of smoky brick, oddly at home. They might have been back-to-back terraces in Hull or Sheffield, with their run-down corner stores and children scuffling on the sidewalks. The wind brought the smell of the stockyards over the houses, and the troubled booming and stamping of the cattle in their pens. Then I saw the great, windowless, rust-colored slab of the Packing Company. It looked like the worst sort of Victorian cathedral.

In an upper office, the hog king of Dubuque was at home. R. C. Wahlert spanned the city from top to bottom: he had a mansion high up on the bluff, he was boss of the Flats, he was Catholic, he was German, and the cigar he was smoking was as big as a submarine sandwich. I was lucky to see him at all; to judge by the clocks which were crammed into his small office, his time was obviously a very precious commodity indeed. There were wall clocks, table clocks, a speaking clock which operated from a button built into his oak desk, and a glass clock in which one could watch steel balls run down chutes, trip levers and register the passing of time like the score on a pinball machine. Young men in Redstone clothes ran around him with little bits of paper. "This needs your signature, R.C." "When you have a moment, R.C. . . ." "Oh—you busy, R.C.?" Meanwhile his clocks ticked and rattled and talked; in the Dubuque Packing Company, a minute was a long time.

"I got a problem," he said. "Next week I got a passage booked on the *Queen*. We're supposed to be going to London. Then Alexandria. Wanna see the Pyramids and Sphinx. There's a hitch, though. Same day, I got an invitation from the President; meet the Pope at the White House. Gonna be a job to fit all that in."

"Tell the *Queen* to sail a day later," I said. Wahlert laughed. He had two bangs of bristly white hair on either side of a bald red skull. His goatee and mustache glistened at their points; they managed to suggest a past crowded with deviltry and shenanigans. "I guess it might be easier to fix the President," he said.

He pressed the button on his desk. "The time is nine forty-seven," said a woman's voice. "Just checking," Wahlert said. He removed a ceramic pig from his blotter and put it beside a plastic statuette of the Virgin, then reached for a toy London taxi. "I just bought one of those— a '66 Austin. Getting it restored here in Dubuque. Thought it'd be kind of fun to run around the city in a London taxi. I love those things. You can turn 'em around on a dime."

His phone rang. Wahlert delivered a five-minute tirade into the mouthpiece. I couldn't follow what it was about. Had the bottom fallen out of the meat-packing business? Whatever it was, it was clearly a disaster.

Wahlert hung up, furious. "That was my accountant. This year they're trying to put up my property taxes by five hundred dollars—"

"Five hundred dollars sounds like a pretty small drop in your financial ocean."

"It's not the goddamn five hundred, it's the principle of it. Hell, this year you let them have five hundred, next year they'll be trying to screw you for a million." The smoke from his stogie hung over him in a thundercloud. "I won't let those guys get away with five unnecessary cents."

I tried to steer him away from his property taxes and onto the subject of Dubuque as a Catholic city. I had learned from the Eibens that the Wahlert family had endowed the Catholic high school.

"My uncle put a lot of dough into that school. Hell, *I* put a lot of dough into that school. Oh, yeah, in the old days, there used to be big fights down here in the Flats between the Catholics and the Protestants. But we're all ecumenical now." He put on his most winning smile. "The good thing about this city is . . ." He quickly touched the wood of his desk. ". . . there are no blacks. 'Cept for a few that John Deere had to bus in for the race laws."

"Why are there no blacks?" It was true, and had puzzled me before. Since leaving Minneapolis, I had seen hardly any black faces; this part of the country was a vast white ghetto.

"I don't know why that is. I guess they just don't like the climate around here. I don't blame 'em. *I* don't like the climate. The winters here, they'd freeze the ass off you. Hell, it's a goddamn awful climate. But it's a *wonderful* climate for hogs. You know we've got ten times as many hogs as people? Two million people in this region; twenty million hogs. And that's about the size of it."

"And no blacks."

"Right. Twenty million hogs, no blacks, and let's hope it stays that way."

He told me about his business. "We kill two and a half, three million animals a year." The hogs were gassed, then stuck in the throat; the cows were killed with a "captive bolt." "We used to have rifles, but the bullets went all over the goddamn place." The bodies were then carried on conveyor belts through the plant, to be dismembered, cured, packaged and sold; at the front end of the Packing Company there was a meat supermarket selling fifty different brands of bacon, lard, sausages and frozen joints and steaks—all those pictures of tranquil dairy farms and cheery farmers' wives which decorated the plastic packets were really disguised versions of the Wahlert production line. He'd "gone into" kosher, too.

"Now, that's some racket. Those rabbis have got it sewn up. They got themselves a *union*. They come down every Monday in a microbus from Chicago. Eight of them. Not proper rabbis. Not teaching rabbis. They're just kind of butcher-rabbis. *Shohetim*. I guess they probably do

152

circumcisions too. They all hole up for the week in some kind of rooming house, and they have to get back to Chicago for sundown on Friday. That's part of their religion. Know how much they make? Fifty thousand bucks apiece. There's no way you can get into kosher without them *shohetim,* and hell, do they know it! Now I want to get into that Muslim thing, *hari . . . halli . . .?"*

"*Halal.*"

"Right. So I guess we're going to get the mullahs' union in here too. The Muslims, they're real particular. They won't take the throw-outs from the kosher. Hell, it's all much the same thing—*halal, kosher;* I guess the Muslims just want to get their own union in on the act."

I was fitted out with a white coat and taken through the factory. At the far end, pigs' bodies were coming in from the slaughterhouse on an overhead belt. Strung up by one hind leg on a hook, they looked disconcertingly human. Blood from the gash in their throats dripped into a long steel conduit, where it swirled and eddied like a river. The pigs went by at a fast walking speed, three feet between each corpse, their front trotters stuck straight out, their pink ears limp as cabbage leaves.

It took them a remarkably short time to stop looking like pigs. We followed them, along steel catwalks, up companionway ladders, down corridors paved with dark red tiles to mask the blood. At every turn there was a man in an apron with a saw, a slicing machine or a knife. In order to be completely disassembled, a pig had to make a journey of perhaps seventy yards, lasting just a minute or two. At the end of his trip, he would be boned, jointed, packed in little paper trays sealed in cellophane; some of him would be smoked, some rendered down for lard; his guts would stand in cardboard boxes lined with plastic bags.

"Is there any part of a pig or a cow that you can't use here?" I had to shout over the noise of the pulleys and belts and machines.

"Nope," said the man who'd been detailed to show me around. "Take the pancreas. That goes to Holland to make insulin for diabetics. Beef tongues—they go to where you come from, London. What there is of the rest—it ain't much, but it goes to make pig food." He didn't seem to notice any possible irony. "You like sausages?" he shouted, reaching into a steel cabinet the size of my London living room. "Try one!" It was all I could do to keep from gagging at the sight of the thing; I held it near my mouth for as long as I could bear, then stuffed it into my trouser pocket. My guide, a step ahead of me, chewed happily on his own sausage.

"Don't you ever get back home after a day here and find you can't face the sight of a beefsteak or a pork chop?"

"Nope."

It was a relief to reach the retail store at the end of this fantastic process of surgical deconstruction. The air was full of soft Muzak. Women wandered among the open refrigerators, toying with shiny packets of ham and bacon and beefsteak. "We kill two and a half, three million animals a year," Wahlert had said. In that time his factory should be capable of depopulating sixty cities the size of Dubuque and turning their inhabitants to grease, tallow, frozen meat and pig food; in three years, you could get through New York . . . in less than twenty years, the whole of the British Isles. . . . I reported the results of this bit of mental arithmetic to my guide. He blanched, backed away and stared frigidly at me; I saw a homicidal lunatic reflected in his eyes. He seemed reluctant to shake hands with me when I thanked him for the tour; and it was only when I was back on the street that I realized—or rather, felt —to just what depths of bad taste I must have appeared to have sunk. For the horrid sausage in my pocket had been leaking hot fat down the side of my leg, and it showed. Appalled, I fled to the Julien Hotel to change my trousers.

At dinner, Ms. Alpine was trembling with zipped-up excitement. Her eyes had an overbright glitter to them, as if she'd just taken a snort of cocaine. She darted and pecked around her food. Spearing a baby carrot, her fork rang loudly on the plate.

"There's an aurora borealis tonight," she said. "We can watch it from my house. It looks right out over the river. You can see half of Illinois and Wisconsin from up there—"

I once knew a rather spotty young man whose chief passion in life lay in his collection of rain gauges and barometers; but Ms. Alpine had not struck me as that type at all.

"I'd never have taken you for a meteorologist."

"No, not *that*. Something else. I got good news today. God, I'm so happy."

"What's happened?"

"I can't tell you. Not in this place. Later. People might hear. You know what small towns are like. . . ."

I tried to distract her with tales of the meat-packing plant, but she was off on a mental trip elsewhere. We rode up the bluff in her car, with the great white houses gleaming in the dark.

"He's got three million," Ms. Alpine said in a stage whisper as the automatic transmission sighed on the incline and dropped to a deeper, rumblier note.

"Who?"

"My ex. My lawyer got the figures out of his lawyer today. Three million bucks." Her tone of voice made the money palpable. It seemed to lie around us in heaps in the car; we were lapped in dollar bills, each one with its severe portrait of Washington and W. M. Blumenthal's fussy, copybook signature. ANNUIT COEPTIS: NOVUS ORDO SECLORUM.

"I knew the bastard had some. But three *million* . . . Ever since we split, he's been saying he was broke."

Her house was, as she'd said, right on the top of Alpine: a floodlit ranch whose stucco had been got up to look like Mexican adobe. She led me through to a long, split-level room at the front. A cocktail bar ran its entire length. So did a picture window. Below us there was a sheer black cliff before the mansions began; then, a mile away, the wide polished ebony of the river.

She twiddled a dimmer switch behind the bar and fixed the room in shadowy candlelight, then pressed a hidden button to bring up a television picture projected on a cinema-sized screen behind us. A football game. The players in their colors packed and charged, larger than life, silent as moths.

"What you want to drink?"

"What have you got?"

"Everything." She gestured at the room, and laughed. "Nothing succeeds like excess."

A brief spatter of rain tinkled on the glass of the window.

"How much of the three million will you get?"

"Half."

"Why? Why not just ask for what you actually need?"

"That sonofabitch. He took four years out of my life. The shit I had to take . . . Did I tell you I used to have my own radio show before I married him? Me and my goldfish?"

"Yes, you said."

"Well, I'm going to get my compensation."

"At the rate of nearly half a million dollars for every year?"

"You can't put a value on human life," she said. "I'm just getting my fair share."

"What are you going to do with it?"

"That's what I been thinking about all day. As soon as that settlement's tied up, I'm going to go to Tahiti."

"Why Tahiti?"

"*No one* in Dubuque's been to Tahiti."

"To live? Or for a vacation?"

"Oh, just a month, maybe two. Then I'm going to get out of this dumb city for good. After New Year's, in the spring, I'm going to move to Chicago. I'm going to do what I want to do for a change. You know the first thing I'm going to do? Buy furs. I want mink. A lot of mink. Then I'm going to sit around and invest in S. and B.'s."

"—In your furs."

"Right. In my goddamn furs."

We searched the sky for the aurora, but there was nothing to see. Banks of low cloud had blotted out the moon and stars. I thought I saw a distant, streaky glimmering, fogged by rain, but that turned out to be only the streetlights down in the Flats. The football players on the screen, flickering gaudily in purple and yellow, were stranger and brighter than any aurora borealis could have been.

I had made a poor confidant for Ms. Alpine's dreams of her new life. She leaned on her bar, cupping her face in her hands, staring at the silent game. In the dimmed light she looked like a pretty college student. The role of strident divorcée didn't suit her: she was an uncertain freshman in this course in vengeance and greed. But it seemed sadly probable that she'd eventually graduate *summa cum laude*.

"I guess I'd better call you a cab," she said, reaching for the phone without taking her eyes off the players. I'd misjudged her. She wasn't a freshman; she was a sophomore, at least.

On Saturday morning, the river below Dubuque had turned into a racetrack for powerboats. They shot past me in swift flashes of psychedelic paintwork, their noses high, their streaming wakes gripping my stern and making me ride them like a surfer. I left the main channel and took to the sloughs on the left-hand side of the river. Wisconsin had ended, and Illinois just begun. Watching the charts for wing dams, watching the water for bars and stumps, I inched down the twisty, still canal of Menominee Slough, so narrow that in places it was completely arched over by trees. It was snake and snapping-turtle country; almost every piece of fallen timber by the water had a sleepy reptile in residence. In a week or two they would start hibernating; now they were just indolent and dusty, enjoying this last remnant of summer weather. I had to duck to pass through a curtain of low twigs and had an unpleasant fantasy about black rattlers dropping into small boats out of trees. Menominee wriggled a few times more, then opened into the broad lake of Deadman's Slough. It was dotted with fishing boats. Each one held a complete black family. The men wore dungarees, the women broad straw hats with brims three feet across. Everyone held a motionless fishing pole out over the stagnant-looking water.

"Any luck?"

"Ain't done nothing yet."

"What bait are you using?"

"Night crawlers!"

I had wanted to visit Galena, Illinois. Once it had been a major steamboat port, but the Galena River had silted up and left the town stranded four miles inland of the Mississippi. I pulled in at Shubert's Landing and found another black family unpacking their tackle from an old red Chevrolet. They'd come from Chicago. They hoped for a haul of catfish. Their trouble was that they had no boat, and the water by the bank was shallow and overfished. I said they could borrow mine for a few hours; I was going to Galena for lunch, and wouldn't be back until four o'clock.

At first the man thought I was trying to pull some ingenious kind of confidence trick.

"How much money you want, mister?"

"Nothing. Just look after it for me. Then I can leave my bags here without worrying about them."

"You saying that you giving us your boat for *nothing?*"

"Until four o'clock, yes."

"Okay, mister." But he looked at me in much the same way that my guide had done at the end of our tour of the Dubuque Packing Company.

Galena was at the end of a long and hillocky country lane. Poor town: it had been the victim of a whole series of booms and crashes. It had got its start as a famous lead mine. In mid-nineteenth-century America, everyone with a gun loaded it with bullets from Galena. By the end of the Civil War the seam was more or less exhausted. The steamboats left the town behind, and when the railroads were built they avoided Galena's little Tuscan hills and kept to the bank of the Mississippi. Galena's latest boom had been caused by an enterprising group of Chicago decorators and architects. They had restored the town and turned it into a museum piece for tourists, a handsomely painted exhibition of Illinois–Queen Anne, Illinois-Romanesque, Illinois–Second Empire, Illinois–Italian Villa, Illinois-Gothic and Illinois-Doric.

For just a year or two, Galena had been rich again. Then the oil crisis hit the place. It was barely possible to get to Galena and back from Chicago on one tank of gas. "No one's traveling anymore," said a disconsolate clerk in a gift shop where I bought a pair of dark glasses to replace the ones which, an hour before, I had watched disappear, winking, into the depths of Deadman's Slough. Now, Galena looked like a movie set recently abandoned by the production crew. Even on this sunny Saturday there were few tourists about. The paint on the restored houses was beginning to crack; the short-order restaurants, done up in "historical" ticky-tacky, were mainly just short of customers. The only place in town that looked as if it were still in business in a big way was the Steinke Funeral Home, a gigantic piece of cake icing with steamboat decks and balustrades and columns. It looked as if, bit by bit, the Steinke Funeral Home were finally taking care of Galena.

I found some local people drinking in a back-street bar. None of them worked in Galena itself; they commuted up to Dubuque or down to the "Quad Cities" of Rock Island, Moline, Davenport and Bettendorf. As we talked, an old man with a flappy rubber swatter wandered up and down the bar, chasing blowflies. So ingrained was the habit of going hunting that if you couldn't pot a squirrel or a coon or a duck, the bluebottle was a respectable object of sporting pursuit. In almost every bar I visited there was the same old man in his duck hunter's camouflage cap, sidling with a flyswatter into the middle of one's conversation.

Thwap!

"Got him." And the old man would point happily to his trophy—a tiny blackish mess of crushed thorax and torn wings. "All afternoon I been after that pertickler rascal."

"You did *what?*" said my neighbor at the bar when I told him about my trip and where I had left the boat. "Holy shit! Hey, you guys, listen to this. Go on, tell 'em what you done."

"What the hell difference does it make?" I said. "I just lent my boat to some people for the afternoon."

"This guy here, you know what he done? He give his boat away to a buncha goddamn niggers down at Shubert's. A loada niggers from *Chicago*. He told them they could go fishing in it."

"Well, there's one born every day, ain't there?" A man down the bar in jeans and snake boots tipped his curly cowboy hat to the back of his head.

"Way I look at it, maybe you done us some kind of a favor. Because all them Chicago niggers, I reckon they'll be saving up the carfare for England. The news'll go all around: there's a whole goddamn country full of guys you don't have to bang over the head to steal from, they just come up to you and *give* their stuff away."

His wife put down her glass. "That ain't right, Harry. Them black people, I think they're more honest than us. You don't know no blacks. You never talked to a black person in your whole goddamn life."

"Shit," said Harry.

"I don't know what it is about them," said the man in the cowboy hat. "but they always catch some fish. No one else does, but the Negroes, they get some. You never see a Negro coming back with no fish."

"Where was you supposed to be going?" said Harry. "*Norlins?* I'm telling you, there's only one way you gonna get to *Norlins* now, and that's by cab."

"You got a helluva big mouth, Harry," said Harry's wife.

"Now, this is something I got to see," Harry said. "You want me to give you a ride down to Shubert's? I'm gonna run you right down there."

"Thanks. I'd be grateful for that. But not till ten to four."

He looked at his watch. "By ten of four, that boat of yours'll most prob'ly be in Davenport or someplace, being sold off for scrap."

Two beers later, we rode to the landing in Harry's pickup. He was chortling all the way. A hundred yards short of the riverbank we had to wait at a railroad crossing for a long freight train to go by. "I could get out here," I said. "No, you don't," Harry said; "*this* I wanta see."

The boat was neatly tied to the pontoon. On the seat there was a jagged scrap of brown wrapping paper, weighted down by a pebble.

GoT 2 GoD cAT HAv A GoD DAy

I showed the paper to Harry. He studied it suspiciously and at length.

"One thing about them niggers," he said. "They don't spell too good."

Ten miles downstream I beached on a shore of riddled clam shells at Bellevue, on the Iowa bank. It was the kind of town whose essential character and history were written clearly on its face. In the decrepit little hotel, the old men in the bar were talking in German. When I turned on the light in my room I saw that the switch itself was set in a plaster molding: an angel in robes and wings was leaning over the tongue of the switch to pat the heads of two American cherubs in school uniform. Above my bed hung an octagonal glass chromo of Christ the Shepherd on which someone had stuck scraps of gold foil and velvet around the frame. So Bellevue was German and Catholic and had once had a button factory. Through the dusty window, I could see the town laid out at my feet: there was Riverside Drive, then Second Street, then a grassy railroad track; and beyond the track lay a tangle of white frame houses. People were sitting out in their small, square yards in foldaway picnic chairs, looking much like the snakes and the turtles as they took in these last rays of summer sun.

It was a good town for sleeping in. Below Christ the Shepherd and the angel, I slept profoundly. I surfaced to church bells at ten thirty, too late to join the faithful. Not since I was a child had I felt such a stir of guilt at missing church, but when the carillon of falling notes suddenly stopped in mid-arpeggio I slept again, to dream of shivery seven-o'clock Communions, of the smell of the censer and the starched linen napkin which covered the Host. The bumpy greystone floor around the altar was a terra-cotta of ancient graves and memorials. Thos. Edge-cumbe, Bart. . . . his wife, Eliza . . . some worn inscriptions in Latin that I couldn't construe. . . . The dead clergymen and baronets would have been contemporaries of the first settlers of Virginia and New England; as I'd knelt in my surplice, serving the officiating priest, I had thought of them more as elderly aunts and uncles than as relics of a distant history. I piped my responses in the same voice that I used to recite multi-plication tables: "Lord have mercy upon us and incline our hearts to keep this law. . . . *Christe eleison*. . . . It is meet and right so to do. . . ." The priest, my grandfather, in his gold-embroidered cope, raised the wafer of rice-papery bread and broke it. Pigeons roistered in the belfry, and my mind drifted from the ceremony; under the Sign of the Fish, I thought of roach and dace and the big pike who skulked at the bottom of the millpool.

It took me till lunchtime to return to Bellevue, Iowa. The river was ridged and whitecappy, and my boat was banging on its mooring. I walked back to a bar on the bluff. The bartender was taking an Anacin tablet.

"I got a headache for some reason; I don't know why. I ain't got any-thing *in* there."

She was framed by cracker-barrel mottoes in pokerwork. IT ISN'T SMART TO ARGUE WITH A FOOL—LISTENERS CAN'T TELL WHICH IS WHICH. DON'T CRITICIZE THE COFFEE—YOU MAY BE OLD AND WEAK YOURSELF SOME DAY. MOST FISHERMEN ARE LIARS EXCEPT YOU AND ME AND SOMETIMES I'M NOT SURE OF YOU. These and other ready-made witticisms formed the staple of so much bar talk: they were swapped like old coins gone smooth with use, and valued the more for their antiquity. IF YOU'VE GOT NOTHING TO SAY, IT'S BETTER TO SAY NOTHING. Mottoes like this provided a basic grammar for everyone's one-line quips. You were supposed to deliver them in an expressionless growl, staring straight out front from under the peak of your plastic cap.

"What you want, Werner?" said the bartender.

"You know goddamn well what I want," said Werner, pushing out his glass for another shot of Coors. He was in his eighties, with a sly face like the top of an old hickory walking stick. He'd been born and raised in Bellevue, and I asked him if he could describe the town as he re-membered it in the tens and teens of the century.

"This town . . . it was goddamn good—once," he said, and didn't speak for another five minutes. The only sound in the bar was that of

Werner's bristly lips chewing at his glass of beer. "There was nine taverns," he said. Then: "There was a harness store." Another mighty pause. "Three hardware stores."

"The button factory?"

"Yeah. There was the button factory. There was another factory, made sonofabitch *pianos*. They had thirty pianos a day coming out of that place. Pinewood, they was; pinewood pianos. There was a big logging business here. Every goddamn woman then, she wanted a piano. They must have turned half them logs into pianos for the womenfolk to play their goddamn hymns on. Sonofabitch. Yeah. In them days, you got a dime of beer and there was goddamn crackers and cheese along the bar." His misty eyes focused wickedly on the bartender. "They give you *free* crackers and cheese. Now they don't give any sonofabitch away. This town . . . this town's gone all goddamn to hell."

"I know why I got a headache," the bartender said; "I been listening to Werner."

"Sonofabitch."

Two men came in. The previous day, they had both been to the funeral of a friend named Earl. With long intervals between sentences, they set about constructing Earl's family tree.

"Earl's father . . . he was George, weren't he?"

"His widow . . . she lived in that tin shack right behind the Catholic church."

"George and her both."

"George . . . now, he wasn't *killed,* was he? He *died* . . . natural."

Werner saw his chance to move in. "That George . . . he *died* . . . of *drinking* . . . too much of that goddamn sonofabitch water from *Sabula.*"

Sabula was at least fifteen miles downstream from Bellevue. Werner cackled happily to himself. Cheered by his own joke, he set on me.

"You can always tell a goddamn Englishman. He's always smoking a goddamn pipe. Sonofabitch."

It was like being challenged to an Eskimo insult ritual.

"You can always tell a goddamn Umurrican," I said. "He's always trying to crack some damnfool joke about the Briddish. Sonofabitch."

"He's got you, Werner. What you got to say to that, Werner?"

"Sonofabitch," said Werner.

Sometime overnight the level of the river had fallen. Gulls appeared to be miraculously walking on the water; then I saw that they were standing on the wing dams whose rocky tops were now just breaking the surface. The going was rough but manageable. The bluffs gave little protection from the wind here. Since Dubuque, they had been steadily falling in height; dwindling from mountainsides down to mere tumps and hummocks. The forest was broken by farms whose broad fields came almost to the river's edge, their earth mat black, their avenues of standing corn as high as single-story houses. I followed the buoys through a puzzle of islands, zigzagging east and west across the river, past Big and Little Soupbone Islands and into Savanna Bay. A man was fishing off the end of a gas dock under the sooty sky.

"Ain't no gas—" he shouted as I came close.

"I was looking for a place to tie up."

"Cost you a dollar—"

"That's okay—"

He was live-baiting for crappies. A shoal of sick minnows swam in a pail by his side. His dock was a tumbledown venture with a one-room shack patched with driftwood and a line of gas pumps that looked as if they dated from sometime in the 1940s. He jerked his head at them.

"Three pumps. No gas in them. I wouldn't pay the price they was asking. The price of gas now, it's goddamn ridiculous. I wouldn't pay that price. I'd rather close up my business than pay what they was asking for it."

"So what do you do now?"

"Fish."

He briefly removed his attention from his red-and-white-striped bobber and directed it at me. I watched him take in my luggage with its airline tags and my grubby but still citified clothes. His face filled with the distaste of the countryman for the urban tourist.

"We can live off the land here. 'Round here . . ." He sniggered, choosing his words carefully. ". . . we fuck dawgs."

"Really. That's something I've not tried."

He inspected my boat. Whatever he saw in it did not please him. "You from Minnesota?"

"No—London, England."

His face didn't flicker. "See? I knew you wasn't from around here."

I lugged my bags across the tracks to the Radke Hotel and a monastic cell of a room at six dollars a night. It was the lobby of the hotel, a vintage American interior, that made me warm immediately to the place. Club rockers, leaking gouts of horsehair, were lined across the wide marble floor. The blades of an old standing fan did an inefficient job of churning up the air, a rich and smelly compound of cheap cigar smoke, dust, machine oil and fly spray. It was so thick that the black-

and-white TV set, parked high on a wall, cast a beam in which Barbara Walters floated in tangible soft focus. A fluted column ran up to a cobwebby ceiling of embossed classical plaster. There were battered spittoon-style ashtrays beside each rocker, and the varnished timber walls looked old enough to be original Tudor, oddly out of phase with the new Dr. Pepper and 7-Up machine and the dispenser housing P-WEE P-NUTS 10¢.

Almost every rocker held a dozing occupant with a cracked leather satchel and an orange lantern. The railroad men. The Burlington Northern met up with the Chicago, Milwaukee, St. Paul and Pacific here, and the lower end of the town petered out into a huge maze of yards and sidings, so that the railway lines far outnumbered the huddle of streets. Engineers and brakemen changed trains in Savanna; they put up at the Radke for their rest periods and colored the town with their raffish, temporary presence. They were up and about at all hours. After dark, they moved by the light of their lanterns, fireflies on Main Street; just in from Chicago, just off for Aurora, Galesburg or Des Moines, the whistles on their engines sounding like a lost patrol of mad tuba players. They were proper travelers. They kept as much of life as they needed in their leather satchels; they were careless about soap and razors; they kept themselves to themselves. In the lobby of the Radke, they growled at each other in some taciturn code of their own. I never made head nor tail of any of the conversations that I overheard, and when I timidly tried to make contact with the railroad men all I got was times and destinations. *Chicago, five after two* was as much as they were prepared to reveal of their identity: I began to try thinking of myself as *The sea, sometime,* and on the whole, it seemed a fairly satisfactory definition.

For conversation, I had to go to Canavan's Pub across the street. Canavan kept extended railroad hours and ran his bar as a social salon. Everyone went to Canavan's and got introduced by Canavan to more or less everyone else. It was much like going to a party given by a skilled hostess. A space was found for me in a characteristically mixed group: a retired jazz musician, a young auctioneer and real estate agent, an attorney and his wife, a factory machinist and an insurance salesman. The talk jumped from the contents of the current issue of *The New York Review of Books* to the prospects for the coming coon season. There are very few places in the United States which even remotely confirm any of the more benign myths of American life, especially that most benign and most untrue myth of American classlessness; and if Canavan's Pub seemed to confirm it, that had more to do with the peculiar character of its owner than with anything else. Canavan just knew how to tend a good bar. With his lumbering figure, broody eyes and squeaky voice, he looked after his customers as if they were plants in a garden; watering here, weeding out there, going at apparently stony ground with a hoe until the soil was broken and things could take root.

I was deep in conversation with Marv, the insurance salesman. Marv was worried. He looked as if he had spent much of his time in worrying. Permanent crinkles of worry had indented themselves around his mouth and eyes. His mustache had, I guessed, once been grown to cheer himself up, but that had evidently become an object of worry too. Every now and again he picked at it, and I could see the pink skin of his upper lip behind the uneven growth of bristle. For the moment, Marv was full of kindly worry on my behalf.

"You *do* wear a life preserver, don't you?"

"Always."

"Never go out without that life preserver on. And always do it up tight. The river's so treacherous . . . it's too easy for a guy to die in it. Your boat don't sound big enough to me. What's the size of your engine?"

"Fifteen horsepower."

"Oh . . . I wish you had a thirty. . . . Thirty would really get you out of trouble fast."

"It seems to be doing fine so far."

"But the farther you go down, the worse it gets. Oh, dear. Look, I want you to listen to a piece of advice. Do you mind me giving you advice?"

"No, of course not."

"Never try to swim against that current. If you go in the river, swim *with* the current. That current, it's a lot stronger than it looks. It'll tire you out, and you'll drown. That's what folks always do. There's an instinct in them that says fight the current, and that's what kills them. Never fight the current. Go with it. Let it take you along where *you* want to go. You've worried me, you know? I hate to think of you in that boat."

"You think I ought to buy a chunk of life insurance from you?" I wished that I had bitten back the remark. Marv's face instantly clouded with hurt. I had to explain, painfully, that it had been a silly joke and that I did value his advice. I did. I suspected, too, that Marv had had some experience of his own of swimming against currents and finding himself helpless in their power. His home-and-auto-insurance franchise business was run from a one-room office on the corner of the block. On weekends he played clarinet, the saddest instrument, in a dance band. His wife taught English at the junior high. Together they were struggling to send their eldest son through law school in Chicago, and it was the clever son's career which was Marv's main claim to success in life.

"I missed out. I went straight from high school into the Army, and for just a high school graduate, there isn't nothing much. If I'd been smart and gone to college like my boy . . . He's a real bright kid. But I could've been something. Like, suppose I'd gotten a Master of Insurance degree . . . With one of those you can work right alongside people like attorneys . . . you could go right to the top."

"But you'd have chosen insurance anyway, not music?"

"There's no security in the music business. I don't know. It's a long way from Saturday gigs in Dubuque to having a career. . . ."

He drove me home to meet his wife. I had said that I'd enjoy talking to her English class, and we went over Jan's school textbooks to see if we could find some passage on which I could pin a lesson. I came across a story by Saki, a story written in a very period British accent, which I thought it might be fun to read aloud.

"I got them to read that last year," Jan said. "They just didn't understand what it was about at all." Saki's "The Story-Teller" was in fact about an ingenious and cynical bachelor who, finding himself closeted in a railway carriage with a pious aunt and two fractious children, keeps the children enthralled and outrages the aunt by telling a tale in which exemplary infant virtue is rewarded with well-deserved death in the jaws of a wolf. I thought that I might be able to carry off the role of the bachelor rather well.

"I guess it was just too British for them," Jan said. She sat framed by pots of prickly cacti. Between us stood a vast balloon glass, two feet high, filled with fine sands of different colors. They had been poured into the glass to make a picture of a setting sun over an ultramarine sea, with sand rocky mountains and a streaky sand sky.

"You like it? That's a real work of art."

"In Chicago," Marv said, "they sell those for a hundred dollars. We got it cheap—fifty dollars. Fifty dollars for a work of art."

As with the Wyoming Jackalope and the pinecone men, its merit lay exclusively in the cute oddity of its manufacture. You couldn't be interested in what it did, but you could be absorbed by the question of how it was done. "I can look at that for hours," Marv said. It was too American for me.

We drove back to Canavan's. Main Street flickered with the lanterns of the railroad men as they sliced through the fog that was beginning to rise from the river. I could hear the towboats calling to each other, their rude horns mingling with the musical chords of the trains. In the bar, I made another appointment to look forward to: if the next night was clear, Bob, the machinist, was going to take his dog and "tree some coons." I was to meet him in Canavan's at 1 A.M., and we'd hunt till dawn. Talking till nearly four, about coons, Saki, the migration of coyotes, Frances FitzGerald's *Fire in the Lake*, land prices, the buoyancy of the soybean and the inedibility of carp, I was impressed that the nightlife of Savanna seemed to have that of London and New York beaten hands down. Already I was beginning to be happily tired out by its rigorous sociability.

"Good morning, sir! We have rain today! A wet morning!" The old man in the corridor lifted his straw hat to me. Groggy, only half awake, I tried to grin back. He wore a thin, neat suit of silver-gray and patent-leather shoes. He certainly wasn't a railroad man. "You're a resident here?" "That's correct, sir. Since my late wife passed over. Fifteen, no, sixteen years . . ." And he went on, chipper as a popcorn, down the corridor, spinning his hat by its brim.

I had to run through the rain to the Lincoln Junior High School. Rain chattered in the leaves of the elms and maples; it hid the river behind a thick curtain of dirty gauze, and turned Quincy Street to a rocky brook of rivulets and little waterfalls. The inside of the school was steamy. It smelled of damp raincoats, and umbrellas.

Facing the eighth grade through a trembly hangover was not unlike squaring up to the Mississippi itself. I had never seen thirty such impeccable children: every nail pared to the quick, every hair of every braid perfectly in place, every smile as polite and expectant as if it had been learned at charm school. I felt like a living example of what happened to naughty children who didn't pay attention to their lessons. *Look at his eyes! Listen to his lungs! Could you but see his liver!*

"I don't know if we have an ashtray in school," Jan said; "maybe I could find you a saucer?"

I looked at the children, blanched under their stares, hid myself behind a fat cloud of Captain Black tobacco, and launched into Saki. It was a wickedly funny story. The silence that met it, though, was at once innocent, well mannered and profoundly intimidating. Had a hair pin fallen, it would have been heard as a crash; except that at Lincoln Junior High, no one would have been sufficiently disheveled to allow a hair pin to drop in the first place.

'She was so good,' continued the bachelor, 'that she won several medals for goodness, which she always wore, pinned on the front of her dress. There was a medal for obedience, another medal for punctuality, and a third for good behaviour. They were large metal medals and they clicked against one another as she walked. No other child in the town where she lived had as many as three medals, so everybody knew that she must be an extra good child.'

'Horribly good,' quoted Cyril . . .

At the word "horribly," one boy in the back row giggled, then put his hand over his mouth. I slowed my reading, exaggerated the accents of the children, exaggerated the blasé voice of the bachelor, and raised another suppressed snigger from the middle of the class. At last they began to laugh: furtively at first, checking with Jan to see whether laughter was an offense against the state, then openly, riding comfortably along with Saki's malicious demolition of "improving" literature. At the end of the story, the park pigs scuttled to freedom and the horribly good Bertha was eaten by the wolf, who left behind only her shoes, a few shreds of her clothing and three medals for goodness.

"Hey, that's a real funny story," said the boy who had started the laughter from his back row.

"Now we've all listened to the story," Jan said, "I want you to tell me: does it have a happy ending, or a sad ending?"

The question certainly had me stumped for an answer, and it clearly bemused the class. Eventually a girl in the front hesitantly suggested that perhaps it had a sad ending.

"Yes, Cathy. A sad ending. That's right. Now, why does it have a sad ending?"

" 'Cause the girl gets eat by the wolf?"

"And that's sad, isn't it, children?"

The eighth grade agreed, reluctantly, that Bertha's end was just about as sad as sad could be. The questions that I wanted to put to the children were rather different. I asked them to guess their lives ten years ahead. Would they stay on in Savanna, or move to another part of the United States? Would they like to live abroad? Would they prefer a big city or a small town? I pressed them to daydream and offered them the freedom to be anything from a New York dentist to a movie star in Cannes. I knew that when I was their age my class would have been almost unanimous in our longing for escape—to the big city, to a success unthought of by our parents, to a cheerful moral wilderness where we could kick the narrow values of the small town firmly in the teeth.

These thirteen-year-olds were just as certain of their destinations. They wouldn't move more than a mile or two from Savanna if they could possibly help it. They hated the idea of the big city. Many had never been to one; perhaps half the class had visited Chicago for a football game or a shopping trip.

"It's so noisy—"

"Everything gets stole—"

"It's a big crowd—"

"It's dirty—"

"People don't talk to each other in Chicago; nobody knows nobody else."

The boys hoped to work with their fathers. One wanted to work on the railroad, one at the John Deere plant, one at his father's gas station. Lots of the girls wanted to be salesclerks; the most ambitious of them said that she'd like to become a beautician. Many women, I said, now had their own careers, and preferred living independently to marrying a man and bringing up a family. This was not an idea that found favor with the girls of Savanna.

"I want to get married . . . when I'm around nineteen," said a girl with an embarrassed, serious smile. Others nodded. 'I want to be a homemaker."

I talked about my own trip down the river and about how, thirty years before, I had become haunted by the idea of the Mississippi after reading *Huckleberry Finn*. I imagined that these children, growing up right on the doorstep of Huck's river, would know the book by heart. They didn't. A small, doubtful scatter of hands went up when I asked how many people in the class had read it. No one, it turned out, had managed to finish it.

"It was too difficult," a girl said. "It was all that Negro talk. I couldn't understand it at all. There was just so many Negroes. . . ."

But the river . . . surely they had been excited by Twain's portrait of their own river? They shrugged. For them, the Mississippi was just a big wet highway. The boys went fishing on it. The girls saw it as a dangerous, dirty place. None of the children needed literature to make it real.

When I left the school, the rain had cleared and the sun had come up. I went down to the dock to check that my boat was safe. The river looked like a cloudscape seen from the window of a high-altitude jet. Crags, pillars and twists of thick mist covered it almost completely, the sun shining on their fluffy tops. Here and there one could see irregular scraps of dark water, but they might easily have lain thousands of feet below. The mist slowly rolled and plumed. A vertical column of it rose over the white shed of Smiley's Fish Market and its waiting line of black women in fur coats and turbans. They'd come from Chicago, in old pickups and sagging, chromium-snouted Buicks and Chevies, to carry off hundredweights at a time of channel catfish, buffalo, crappies, carp, eels and sunfish. The luminous mist flattened them to two dimensions. The fish market, the women, the sprawl of boats drawn up on the shore, the piled hoop nets all came accidentally together in a perfect pictorial composition. I was bailing the rainwater from my boat, and saw that I'd left my camera in the open compartment behind the wheel. I photographed what I believed I was seeing, and was puzzled when the transparency came back from the processor's: it didn't look like a genre painting in refracted Mississippi light; it was a picture of yellowish mist, with the outline of a leaning telegraph pole faintly visible in the background.

At 1 A.M., the party in Canavan's was fully afloat. Bob the machinist had returned from his night shift in the factory at Davenport. "Thunder's in the car out back." Two young men, Ron and Bill, arrived with an absurd hound called Ketchup who whooped and skidded around the bar, legs splayed, tail flying, beside himself in his excitement at being allowed up so late. Tonight we were only going to "tree" coons: the season hadn't opened, and their pelts would be in poor condition still; the hunt was a routine training session for the dogs. We drove out into the black hilly country behind Savanna, past darkened farmsteads and grain elevators looking like pale castles in the starlight. Bob watched the sides of the road for animals' eyes.

"We got a saying around here," he said: " 'When the cats are out, coons are about; when the wind's in the east, coons run least.' Don't know why that is, but it's a true saying." Thunder murmured from the seat in the back. He was an old hand at treeing coons and affected an Etonian air of vague superiority. The cars stopped at the top of a rutted lane. Ketchup came over the tailgate of the second car in a joyful somersault and set himself to rolling energetically on his back. Thunder growled at him; his apprentice was showing bad form.

A big owl came out of a tree over our heads, making a noise like a tumbling cardboard box. Following the roundel of light cast on the uneven ground by Bob's flashlight, we moved off in single file down a gully and into a cornfield. The crickets kept up a constant electrical throbbing. The hounds crashed and scuffled ahead of us. Talking in whispers, we tiptoed through the high-arched corridors of standing

corn. "He's sniffing pretty good now—he's smelled something there."
"No, he hain't. He's just fooling. Ketchup!"

"Be quiet and let 'em hunt, now—" Bob was colonel of the expedition. Bill, Ron and I needed to be kept under almost as strict control as the dogs.

We covered a mile or so of broken country. The corn gave way to a tangle of brush, a grazing pasture, a deep wood. Thunder was quartering the ground methodically, making gurgling noises in his throat. Ketchup was mostly content to chase his own tail, bark at owls and find happy patches of wet mud to roll in. Then Thunder "opened"; raising his voice to a sobbing contralto, he went plunging in a straight line up a long timbered hill. We ran behind him, the points of the flashlight dancing in the trees. "He's onto a coon now. Go get him, Thunder—" But the scent stopped at a creek. Thunder stood on the edge of the water, turning in baffled circles and moaning to himself.

"Where is he, Thunder?"

The dog sniffed along the bank, opened for a moment and lost the trail again.

"A coon," Bob said, ". . . he just loves to go along a crick like this one here, chasing frogs and crawdads and such." He made the coon's own hunting trips sound like innocent and curiously skittish affairs, as if the frogs and crawdads were toys rather than prey. We waded through the creek. Thunder picked up the scent once more on the far side. His strangulated singing sounded like a tone-deaf opera fan trying to do *Aïda* in the shower. We stumbled after him through the tall grass and sodden earth, and caught up with him at the bottom of a great red oak, where he stood on his hind legs, howling and scratching at the bark.

"Yeah. He's treed him. Good dog, Thunder, good dog." Ketchup was standing by, barking at the tree, barking at Thunder, barking at us, stupid with delight at the way life was panning out for him.

"Now we got to find him."

We stood in line on a crumbly ridge, raking the black foliage with our flashlights, turning the leaves to silver while the dogs caroled around the bole. Somewhere in that tasseled darkness, sixty feet up, I saw a twin amber flash. The coon had blinked.

"Look—" I said.

Bob followed my beam. Another, longer glow of bloody orange. The coon was staring back at us.

"Now, if we was hunting for real, you'd have to hold your light in your left hand . . . like that . . . and shoot with your right."

The coon was gazing straight into my own eyes, appalled. I wished that there'd been some way of reassuring it that it was currently out of season and that it had another few weeks at least of chasing frogs and crawdads down creeks.

The dogs were called off. We searched another cornfield, climbed a new hill. Across the narrow valley, a strange dog was baying from a farm.

"Sounds like that's a German shepherd out there."

"I hope they got it chained good."

On a tangled brushwood knoll, Ketchup let out a series of hysterical yelps. When we got to him, he was digging himself furiously into the middle of a sandbank. The men stood over him with their lamps. "Go get him, Ketchup," said Ron, almost as pleased as the dog at this unexpected vindication of Ketchup's talents as a coon hunter. "That's a coon, all right. He's right deep in there. Go on, Ketchup, get him, go on!" All this encouragement was a shade unnecessary; the dog's hindquarters were flailing and shuddering with joy as he tunneled deeper in. With his mouth full of earth, his articulation was a good deal impeded, but he was giving out a delirious *hoi-hoi-hoi-hoi-hoi-hoi* sound, his hind legs cycling crazily in the air.

"Hey!" shouted Bob. "Get him *outa* there! Goddamn *skunk!* Get him *out!*"

Ketchup was hauled, howling, from his ecstatic burrow by all four of us. As he emerged, so did something else: a sickly gust, half charcoal, half rotten eggs, with a zest of ammonia, and very strong. He was put on a leash and taken up to the waiting cars in disgrace. It wasn't Ketchup's night. The skunk's fetor filled the little wood. Days later, I could still catch a faint whiff of it in my clothes. We stood out under the stars, stinking of skunk. Bob got a six-pack from the trunk of his station wagon. The metallic taste of the cold beer seemed to have become queerly mixed up with skunk too. It was four fifteen in the morning. The bright points of the constellation of Orion lay very low indeed in the sky.

I had meant to sleep in, to spend at least one more day in Savanna, but when I woke at nine there wasn't a leaf moving in the maple tree outside my window. It was too good a traveling day to lose. I had seen from the charts that there was a huge pool above the lock and dam at Clinton, just a little way downstream. I was scared of facing it in any measurable wind at all; it was a lake seven miles long and four wide, without a single marked island to give cover and the channel running clean through its middle. I packed my bags in a hurry, keeping one eye on the leaves to make sure that they weren't beginning to stir.

The river was safely dead in the sun. Every flourish and excursion of the current was marked as a neat crease on its top. I was sad to leave Savanna; even the old satirist at the gas dock was unpredictably friendly.

"I hear you was out last night treeing coon. How many you get?"

"Just one, and a skunk. I thought you'd have smelled it on me."

He laughed. "Yeah. Maybe I did."

Perhaps, at last, I'd lost my urban taint. I slid past Sabula on the current, dodged the wakes of a couple of upstream tows, rounded a long string of green islands, and entered the pool above Clinton. The chart called it just "Big Slough." This seemed a strange falling-down on the creative job of naming sloughs. Either they were christened after people or they had memorable names which expressed their shape, or what lay in them, or what grew on their islands: Snag, Hubble, Soupbone, Hickory, Crooked, Dead Man's . . . No one, apparently, had found anything to say about Big Slough except that it was big, and its bigness had rendered every other feature irrelevant.

On this windless morning, the water of Big Slough looked as viscous as thick machine oil. It was blackened by the decomposing forest that lay under it. Miles of it were so shallow that the stump fields on either side of the channel were exposed right down to their spreading roots. Wedded to their own immobile reflections, the stumps, in their hundreds of thousands, made arabesque patterns of flattened hexagons. Away across the slough there was the rigid outline of a man in a punt, fishing for his image, and the image casting back. Not a sound, not a ripple fractured the great, empty symmetry of the place. With the motor killed, I was part of it: doubled in water, I was as lifeless a component of the scheme as a carboniferous stump.

If only one could make the notion of freedom into a tangible object, I thought, it would look like Big Slough—a huge, curved, reflective vacancy. No sea could quite attain this greasy calm, or communicate the essential place of dead things, rottenness, torpidity in the vision. Big Slough could.

In my old, city life there hadn't been a day when I didn't sweat at the sheer fiddle of the thing: the telephone ringing, or failing to ring; the bills in manila envelopes; the rows, the makings-up; the jumpy claustrophobia of just surviving as one small valve in the elaborate and hazardous circuit of ordinary society. *If only . . . if only . . .* and at the end of the sentence there was always somewhere the word *free,* a careless stand-in for a careless notion of benign emptiness. But Big Slough really looked free, and for all its peat-brown beauty, it made me shudder. Floating on it felt like being dead, and I reckoned that there was a lesson to be learned from that sensation.

Freedom, though, would never be so conveniently marked with such a regular, winding trail of buoys. Red and black, red and black, their roulette colors led out past the stumps, away from the enormous weir and into the chamber of Lock 13. For the first time in my trip, I saw a Mississippi lock as a safe, contained place; it felt just the right size, and it was good to be inching down the wall with Big Slough behind me.

It took a long sultry afternoon to reach the outskirts of the Quad Cities, with the sun steadily weakening until water and sky faded to the same uncolor. I tied my boat up at a marina in Moline and made a brief acquaintance with the good-time set in the club bar. It was oppressively male, and I wanted to escape from the company of these aging jocks with their acrimonious divorces, their giant powerboats and their glowering paranoia.

A meaty fifty-year-old in a Hawaiian shirt was saying, "When that black . . . when that black puts a rock through my picture window, I'm ready for him. I got a loaded gun right by the TV, and that black, he's going to get shot."

I asked him if he was talking about some particular black who had been threatening his property. He wasn't. He was just talking about blacks, all blacks, in general. There were sixteen whites to every black in Moline.

"So what happens if a white man puts the rock through your window?"

He paused and stared at me, his eyes foggy with booze. What a goddamn ridiculous question.

"I guess he'd get shot too," he said, but it was clear that his words didn't carry much conviction, even in his own head.

A younger man offered me a room in his apartment. "You could get laid." I tried to imagine myself as an egg in the womb of an Amazonian hen, and politely declined. He put his arm around my shoulder. "You like to smoke? I got some Acapulco Gold. Lay on a coupla broads . . . we could party. . . . What you like to drink? British Scotch? I got a whole case in my cocktail cabinet. Hey, you seen my road racer out there?" It was parked outside the bar window: a swollen phallus painted in acrylic stripes of white and purple. It had a phosphorescent bumper sticker announcing IT'S GREAT TO BE SINGLE.

"There's fourteen thousand bucks in that car."

"I bet there is." I could see him speeding around the city, his money his only companion. A dog, I thought, would have been better for his character.

"Hell, come on, we can have a great time."

His loneliness shone through his boastful face. *Go with the current of things.* I flipped a coin in my head but, to my relief, it came down tails.

I settled into an old, pleasantly frowsty hotel in Davenport. The Quad Cities were a queer agglomeration. Their suburbs had leaked and dribbled into each other, and finally the whole mess had loosely congealed. Rock Island and Moline, on the east bank of the river, were in Illinois; Davenport and Bettendorf were in Iowa. They hadn't come together to make a metropolis, but they had lost their identities as individual towns. For twelve miles, they straggled lumpishly along the wharves, the hard angles of their warehouses, steel tanks and factories hemming in the river. Everything was too low, too spread out, to make much more than a cheeky gesture of encroachment on the Mississippi, like a line of children's sand castles on a seashore.

I ate at the Dock, where they had a fine line in restaurant-English. I could never get used to this strange dialect which so awkwardly combined the ceremonial and the intimate. The captain-waiter met me at the door, a lugubrious figure in black.

"And is there just one in your party this evening, sir?"

I admitted, a little shamefacedly, that there was only me; and I didn't feel at all like a party.

The captain-waiter passed me into the hands of an usher in tights and froufrou.

"Hi, my name is Julie! And I will show you to your table! Your waiter for this evening is Doug, and he'll be just right along. See you later!"

Doug announced himself. "Hi, my name is Doug and I am your waiter for this evening. I hope you enjoy your meal."

It was like dropping into the middle of a puppet show. Where had they learned this extraordinary style of speech? It must have been dreamed up in order to give waiting at table the impersonal professional status of gynecology or the law, yet it succeeded in doing precisely the reverse. It made me feel like a customer at a brothel, all this false solicitude for my physical needs.

"What kind of dressing would you like on your salad, sir, this evening?" I found something faintly menacing in the constant repetition of the phrase "this evening," as if I had been condemned to dine at the Dock every night of my life. I had barely started to poke at the lettuce when Julie sprang on me with a smile that looked as if it had been purchased at a shop selling rubber masks.

"And are you having a good evening this evening, sir?"

"I'm having an . . . ab . . . so . . . lutely . . . a . . . *dor* . . . able evening," I said, my mouth full of soggy tomato. At least I had managed to disconcert her. "Oh," she said, "well that's neat," and fled.

Below my window seat the river lay like a rumpled sheet of shiny black vinyl. Tows were moving, their carbide searchlights raking its surface and turning the railroad bridge to a filigree silhouette. The fort on Arsenal Island was a child's cardboard toy. Beside the river, everything dwindled. It was, I thought, appropriate that the talk in the restaurant should sound so tinny and artificial. There was a pre-emptive reality about that great, intricate drift of dark water, spooling and crumpling as it went, which reduced the captain-waiter and Julie and Doug and me and the Rock Island Railroad and the stone castle of the Corps of Engineers to the status of ham actors and painted theatrical flats. No wonder that the rivermen I'd met talked with a good deal of condescension about "people on the beach." It was an attitude that I was rapidly developing myself. I felt that I had a secret stake in the Mississippi and that it ought to show on my face as a visible mark of aristocracy.

On my way out, Julie said, or rather sang, "Come back and see us soon, sir!" and the funereal captain-waiter said, "Have a good night, now," and I walked around the side of the restaurant and crouched on the wharf, feeling impertinently possessive about my river.

Following the line of the riverbank, I took West Second Street as it trailed south away from the center of the city. There was no one else in sight. I jumped at shadows on the sidewalk, unnerved—not so much by the thought of muggers as by the simple nighttime emptiness of the place. The first leaves of fall cracked under my feet. A single car raced past me from a stoplight, its automatic transmission protesting as it lurched too fast from gear to gear. Two miles on, at the corner of Filmore, there were kerosene lanterns and white faces—company to keep. They were huddled in the shadow of what looked like a huge warehouse. On these deserted city outskirts, their voices carried across Myrtle and Taylor and Marquette.

They were strike pickets at the gates of the Oscar Mayer Packing Company. It was the first strike at the factory that anyone could remember, and it had been going on for three weeks. District Local 431 of the United Food and Commercial Workers was in a holiday mood in the lanternlight; they were just about to settle. "We're in a win–win situation here," said a picket on the main gate, and offered me a can of Bud to toast the restored fortunes of Oscar Mayer.

"What happened?" I asked.

"We used to have fun here," a woman said. "Everybody had fun. It was a great place to work at. Then things got sour. Now it's all cutthroat. Everybody's in competition with everybody else. It's not like it used to be. They introduced this bonus incentive scheme, and suddenly no one had time to talk, even, they was so busy cutting one another's throats. Then there was the health regulations. They had to block in all the windows for health reasons. Look—" She pointed up at the hulk of the building behind us. "Can you imagine what it's like to work in there?"

"I went around the packing company in Dubuque," I said.

"In the winter, you never get to see the sun except on weekends. You don't talk. You don't make friends like you used to. You live under those fluorescent lights . . . sometimes I think it's not *human* to work like that."

The coffee run arrived: two men in a car with thermos flasks and paper cups. I was invited along for the ride, and we went from gate to gate, doling out coffee, hamburgers, crackers and cigarettes. Harvey Schwartz, the driver, was a grandfatherly figure with an outdoor face; he'd worked most of his life at the packing company, but he also kept a small farm out in the country. His few acres of corn and vegetables set him apart from the other workers. He had one foot, at least, in a different American tradition. His companion was much younger, in his mid-twenties; and he too was planning an escape from the packing factory and the stigma of belonging to the industrial working class of a country in which so much stress has been laid on the virtue of individualism that to be seen to be working for someone else is close to being categorized as a failure. Jim was getting himself an education; he was going to become a chiropractor.

At night he worked for Oscar Mayer; then, after breakfast, he took off for morning classes at a college of chiropractice.

"The way I look at it, if you're going to *be* somebody, you got to be a *professional*."

I had been struck before by the number of chiropractic centers and schools I had seen on my journey. Almost every town had one. To be a chiropractor was to be almost—well, not quite, but very nearly—a doctor; and the word "doctor" was a magical one. At a stroke it conferred the glow of special expertise, self-reliance and gentility. Easing the aches and stresses of the nation with clicking bones and cold cream, the chiropractors of America nearly constituted a class in their own right: "professional men" who had worked their way up from dead ends and factory floors via morning and evening classes.

We made a slow, stopping circle around the plant.

"You know," Harvey said, "this used to be a nice city here. Now . . . well, it's just another little Chicago."

He pointed out a side street where a man had been stripped to nudity at gunpoint a week or two before.

"They even took the guy's undershorts," Harvey said. "They cleaned up on *everything*."

"Were they white or black?"

"Oh, they were white," Jim said.

"Poor guy was running halfway through Davenport just like God made him."

The official strike headquarters was in a meeting hall next door to the factory; the unofficial one was in Frick's Bar across the street, where the union men were doubtfully chewing over the terms of the settlement. The air was gritty with talk of side deals and percentages. Frick's was a natural location for such talk: it was a famous political bar, an old Democratic hangout where the party leaders of the city had come to fix and plot and bargain since 1888, when the place was built. The Frick family had always been yellow-dog Democrats, and their bar had become a kind of scaled-down, Davenport version of Tammany Hall. Three generations of Fricks had held important positions in the government of the city, and the walls of the bar were hung with old photographs of boss-Fricks in wing collars, framed citations and keys to the freedom of Davenport. When I'd started my walk up West Second Street, I had been looking for Frick's, not for the packing plant and its pickets.

"Hey," Harvey said, "you got to come to the pig roast I'm giving out on my farm Saturday."

"Now, that's an invitation you can't refuse," said Ross Frick, the elderly grandson of the founder of the bar. "Nobody *ever* says no to Harvey Schwartz when he asks them to one of his pig roasts." Frick was wearing exactly the same stripy one-piece pajama suit I had seen on the old man at the Minnesota State Fair. He was small and limber, a quick and dainty septuagenarian with boxer's footwork as he sailed up and down the length of his bar. Harvey told me how, not long before, Ross Frick had missed being elected mayor of Davenport by a whisker. "He'd've made a damn good mayor, too; he tends a damn good bar." Frick was dealing briskly with a drunk who was a third his age and many times his weight; the drunk disappeared into the street looking as if he couldn't believe what was happening to him.

"He's a good boy," Frick said, returning. "Just a little wife trouble."

Mr. Frick got out the gold and silver keys to the city he had been awarded during his political career. Together with the keys of his father and grandfather, they added up to a burglar's incriminating collection. Mr. Frick, as one of Iowa's senior Democrats, was, I thought, unusually well placed to tell me something new about the presidential election. I asked whether he was going to support Carter or Kennedy as the party's nominee.

"Those sonofabitches! I'll be voting for Ronald Reagan."

"But I thought you were a Democrat," I said, still holding a gilt-alloy key.

"Times change," Mr. Frick said. "I *was* a Democrat. Then I got to see how those sonofabitches, our leaders, managed things. . . . Never again. The only guy I'll vote for for President is Ronald Reagan. He's a local boy, you know? From right across the river: Tampico, Illinois. Then I remember him when he got his first start, talking through the football games for WHO here in Davenport. I don't trust any of those sonofabitches no more, but if I trust anyone, I'll trust Ronald Reagan."

"But what's made you change?"

"I remember when America was a great country. Like, when I was a young man, it was To the Victor, the Spoils, you know? When I was a kid and I got someone down in a fair fight, I said, 'Now you're going to goddamn do what *I* say from now on . . .' and they did it. Now look what happens! If you're the victor now, you got to grovel, then you got to grovel some more. That's all America does, nowadays. It's down on its knees. War reparations! Look, who won goddamn World War Two? Once, I thought we did. But then I look at America now and I look at Germany now, and all I can see is we was taken for god-damn suckers. Same thing with Korea. Same thing with Vietnam. Look at these sonofabitch boat people! We're on our knees to them! We're groveling in front of every welfare sponger and refugee we can find. We're eating dirt for them. That's not the way America was supposed to be. You tell me: what's the sense, what's the right in it? Why are we kissing the asses of these jerks? America didn't get to what it was by kissing no one's ass. So why we got to kiss ass now? That wasn't the way I was raised. No one told me I had to go down on my knees to bums. . . ."

Ross Frick wasn't an ordinary bar bigot. I'd heard this line, or one much like it, many times before; but I'd never heard it spoken with quite such bewilderment and quite such a charge of personal humiliation. If the rhetoric was commonplace, the pain was real; Ross Frick minded about America, and he simply couldn't understand what had happened to the place he thought he loved. "Look . . ." he said, then shook his head sadly; what he was trying to tell me was beyond his capacity to communicate. Finally, he said, "You seen my backyard?"

"No," I said.

"Come out back with me. I want to show it you."

Puzzled at this shift of subject, I followed him behind the bar and into a scruffy little kitchen, where he switched on a raft of lights which flooded the yard beyond.

"Look," said Mr. Frick, showing me out through the door.

Even now, his garden was still an embroidered quilt of summer colors. Plants in pots were arranged in steep pyramids, in banks of deep green ferns, in white wrought-iron pagodas and hanging baskets. He had squashed what looked to me like a complete Chelsea flower show into the space of a living room: slender garden daisies, livid begonias, fuchsias, chrysanthemums, primulas, geraniums . . . Tiny graveled walks trailed in and out among the beds of flowers. The centerpiece was a miniature waterfall. Mr. Frick switched it on, and a little river came bubbling through the ferns over rocks of colored crystal and splashed into a lily-padded pool. In the corner of the yard was a rose bower, the blooms of pink and crimson looking bloody in the floodlight. A signboard with carved rustic lettering was suspended over the top of the bower on silver chains; it said: I NEVER PROMISED YOU A ROSE GARDEN.

"You like it?"

"It's lovely," I said.

"I built it for my wife. But you ought to see it in the spring. It's getting to be late for roses now."

I understood why, lost for words, Mr. Frick had wanted me to see his garden. It was a small, embattled American Eden. I looked up at the high walls: they were spiked with broken glass and barbed wire. Mr. Frick had had trouble with vandals; and beyond the walls lay the faceless ones who were out to destroy this pocket-handkerchief paradise—the muggers, welfare spongers, boat people . . . all the jerks and sonofabitches who would happily tear Mr. Frick's geraniums out by their roots and smash the delicate trelliswork of his rose bower. In his garden he had preserved an idyllic version of America against all odds, and the marauders and despoilers were gathering in the street outside.

The raked gravel crunched under our shoes.

"I'm going to have to start taking the plants inside on the weekend," Mr. Frick said. "There's a frost coming. I can feel it in the air."

6

Where Do the Grapes of Eshcol Grow?

*T*he *Iowa shore* was flat and ragged: an unlovely sprawl of coal chutes, cement factories and black barge fleets, with towboats busying about the river in the sun. The wind, blowing out of the west-northwest, should have been coming from the safest quarter; here, though, the Mississippi ran almost due west for twenty-five miles to Muscatine, and the waves were steep and foamy. I'd caught the river people's habit of thinking of the river as *he* or *she* (the genders were interchangeable—they simply asserted that the Mississippi was never an *it*). Despite myself, I had taken to the practice of a superstitious natural magic: each day now I would question the river. Did he mean to kill me or be kind? Today I could feel his irritation. He wanted me off his back. There was an obscure intimation of bad luck written into the grubby landscape and the too-bright glitter of the breakers.

Warned, I scraped ashore on a button-clam beach at Buffalo, ten miles on from Davenport. The Buffalo Club Bar had a corral of motorcycles parked outside it, and inside it the local chapter of Hell's Angels was at home. In knee boots, jeans, leather jackets and cowboy hats, the chapter was making a noisy job of killing the morning.

"Why'd the Mexican tie his wife to the railroad tracks?"

The question was followed by a smirking, snuffling pause.

"Tequila."

The whoops that met this bit of angelic wit sounded like the blood-curdling gurgles Chinese martial-arts experts make when they come in for the final chop, *Yock-hoi-whee! Ya-hoo!*

Another angel told the story of how he'd found a rattlesnake in a creek. He chawed and twisted his syllables as if they were pieces of gum in his mouth. ". . . ayund thayun Ah bayusted the goddayumn sonofabayitch's hayead off with a rock."

"Shit," said someone, in a tone of entirely innocent admiration.

I went to the men's room. When I came back I saw that my hat, which I'd left on the bar by my beer glass, was gone. I had become fond of that hat. It had lost its Boy Scout air. Bleached, creased, pockmarked by the rain, it was nicely registering my own steady accretion of experience. The angels watched me as I sat down. I studied the space on the bar where my hat ought to be. I should have played this game more circumspectly, but the river had made me jumpy, and I just demanded, angrily, that whoever had stolen my hat give it back.

"Guy's lorst his hayut," said the rattlesnake killer, rolling his eyes back in badly hammed astonishment.

"Well," said my immediate neighbor, "Ah still got mine," and he raised the fingers of both hands to touch his brim. "That's what Buffalo's famous for. Hat-napping." Whoops and whistles.

Rattlesnake said, "Are you trayin' to tell us something, fella? You ain't, by any chayunce, trayin' to say as one of us-guys has committed some kinda mister-die-meaner?"

I didn't like the thought of my own head being busted off with a rock. The bartender was conspicuously attending to matters elsewhere. There was going to be no help from him. I said that I was sorry to have lost my hat. It was my only one, and I'd grown to like it. If anyone saw it anywhere, I'd be grateful for its return. I left the bar and stood outside, hoping that it would be chucked at me through the open window. It wasn't. I felt sour and resentful as I left Buffalo, Iowa (pop. 1,513). The United States is internationally notorious for its thuggishness, but in ten years of visits and temporary residences I had never once had anything stolen from me or been met with even the most indirect threat of violence. It seemed infuriating and absurd that the record should be broken here of all places, and broken over something as trifling as a battered twelve-dollar hat.

I cut straight across the river to Andalusia. Angry with Iowa, I felt that the climate in Illinois was healthier. Besides, shielded from the wind behind a long chain of islands, the still water of Andalusia Slough offered a manageable alternative route for another nine or ten miles downstream. I filled my spare gas tanks at Jack Tillia's Harbor and told Mr. Tillia about my troubles in Buffalo. "You been over there?" he said. "Lucky all you lost was your hat."

A big speedboat was circling in the slough. It came close in to the harbor.

"Hey!" shouted a man on board. "We've been looking out for you. Ain't you coming to my daddy's pig roast? He's *expecting* you."

I had forgotten Harvey Schwartz' invitation in Frick's Bar, two days before. Mr. Frick had said that Harvey was a hard man to refuse, but it had never occurred to me that he'd send out a search party. It was good to be rescued. My bags were bundled onto the speedboat. I joined the two men and a woman in the stern, and we went crashing through the slough and into the main river. I had never seen the Mississippi treated so casually. We skipped from wave to wave at twenty-five knots, with the bow of the boat pointing into the sky. We played in the wake of a tow, treating it like a ski jump. As I felt my stomach being left some yards behind, I hoped the river knew that I wasn't doing the driving. It was going to have plenty of future opportunities to take its revenge.

Harvey's white farmhouse stood on a neat rectangle of green which looked as if it had been gouged out with a chisel from the rolling sweep of high corn that surrounded it. Pickups and station wagons were parked fender to fender in a herringbone pattern up the driveway. On the roof of one truck, a transistor radio was broadcasting a college football game. Iowa State was at home to the University of Iowa, and as the State backfield sprinted for the line and scored, a great yodeling cheer went up from Harvey's party to a sky of empty blue in which a crop-spraying light airplane showed as a distant twinkle in the sun.

All morning and afternoon the pig, harnessed to a generator by an ingenious system of pulleys and bicycle chains, had been turning on its spit above a trench of burning charcoal. Harvey stood over it like Abraham with a knife. Carving a pig was a serious business, and at these pig roasts the host, solemn and absorbed in his office, took on the role of celebrant priest. The flashing knife was ritually sharpened, the first incision made, and then the line of paper plates came out, the jokes, the napkins and the sense of being present at a boisterous social eucharist. The separate smells of corn dust, pork crackling and bruised grass got muddled up together to produce the distinctive, ceremonial odor of pig roast.

Someone should market "Pig Roast" and sell it to homesick Iowans in little crystal perfume vials. Had I been able to put it in a bottle, it would conjure up late summer in the Midwest with far more evocative precision than any photograph. It would bring back the barrels of beer on their cradles, long trestle tables, baseball caps, checked shirts, party dresses, lonely houses set a mile or two apart across the fields, pointed spires of wooden churches, arrow-straight tracks of loose asphalt, and a humpy, treeless landscape looking like the yellow dunes of the Arabian desert. The smell would bring back voices, too—all talking with the loud vigor of farming people who spent most of their weekdays in industrious solitude and for whom these Saturday-afternoon bouts of partying with their neighbors, along with churchgoing on Sundays, made up the essential threads with which they knitted themselves into a cohesive and self-confident community.

I sprawled on the grass drinking beer from a Bavarian tankard with a lid, and talked to Harvey's wife. Mrs. Schwartz worked as a seamstress in the bridal section of a Davenport department store. Her main job there was to take wedding dresses, manufactured in New York and designed to fit the anorexic East Coast figure, and make them big enough for the altogether heftier brides of the Midwest. She was an expert in fillets, gussets and secret panels.

"When you say big, how big do you mean?"

"Oh, some of them are forty-five, forty-six, forty-seven round the hips. And that's when they're young. What are they going to be like when they're old?"

I elaborated my own theory of a fatness map of the United States. Areas where European immigration had been most recent, and ancestral memories of hunger closest, would correspond with the forty-seven hip; while states that had been settled before 1776 would register least in the way of excess fatty tissue. Girth would generally increase from east to west and from south to north. The flab capital of the U.S.A. should be located somewhere near here, in the triangle of Minnesota, Iowa and the Dakotas.

"I don't know about that," said Mrs. Schwartz, "but folks around here sure eat too much. I think it's real sad. You know, I rip those pretty gowns from New York right apart, and I feel sorry for the guys that are marrying those girls."

"Well, the guys themselves aren't exactly willowy."

"Yeah, but it's different for a man. A woman can feel proud of a big husband. It means she's fed him good."

Her own husband joined us. Harvey had a healthy solidity to him, but must have been a disappointment to Mrs. Schwartz. He was chasing up another truant guest. Bill, his nearest neighbor, hadn't shown up, so Harvey was driving out to his farm to fetch him. "Bill's a workaholic. You have to dig the guy out of that farm of his like a coon."

Harvey and I rode off in a pickup to retrieve the malingerer. Bill's house was three long fields away, across a shallow valley and a muddy creek. Bill himself was tinkering with a combine harvester in his barn. "We was just coming," he said. "I heard that one before," said Harvey. "Still, you ain't the worst this time. This guy here, he had to be fetched in off the Mississippi in a boat."

Having extracted a sworn promise that everyone would return to his pig roast within the half hour, Harvey left me with Bill to be shown over the farm. In the fine house with its fenced drive, the new grain silo, the expensive farm machinery, the dryers, cattle pens and pig battery, there were the ingredients of a modern Horatio Alger story. Bill had been born in Germany, and his father had come to Davenport to work as a carpenter. Bill still looked more German than Iowan. Serious-faced, blond-haired, he spoke with a slightly over-emphatic precision which gave away the fact that he'd acquired English as his second language. After high school in Davenport, he had served an apprenticeship as a carpet layer, but had always ached for a job on a farm. He had saved and borrowed and built up his holding acre by acre. To start with, he had gone on laying carpets, working the little ground he'd bought in the evenings and on weekends. Gradually his farm had become big enough to just support him. Now it was an empire, and Bill was one of the new Midwestern millionaires, on paper at least. Ten years ago he was buying his land at $450 an acre; now it was worth around $4,000, and he had nearly 850 acres of it in piece-meal lots scattered over several miles of eastern Iowa.

"See this little gizmo? That measures the exact moisture of the grain as I'm cutting it. Once we had to do it by the feel of the thing. Now you just look at the needle, and you know for sure what you're doing. I'm a believer in technology. Every new gizmo that comes out, I'll try it. You know my motto? If you can do it by electricity or hydraulics, don't do it manual."

He took me to the edge of the field of corn he had started to harvest that morning and broke off a big, glistening cob from its stalk. He turned it gently in his hands. His baby. I'd never guessed that there were so many fine points to admire in an ear of corn: the slight dent in each grain which showed that it had begun to dry out and was ready for harvest; the even number of rows; the dark dot at the top of the cob; the black silk in which it was encased—one strand for every grain, these hairs pollinated the corn and were dangerously vulnerable to all sorts of blight and disease.

"And that's a perfect ear?" I asked.

"Near enough. You won't find one much better in this state."

"You must be a happy man."

"I guess," he said gravely. "Yeah, if I get to thinking of it, I am a happy man."

He was his own builder, carpenter and engineer. He fixed his machines for himself; every shed and stall on his farm was an example of his craftsmanship. He let his age slip out by accident; at thirty-seven he was exactly as old as I was. Wanting, perhaps, to excuse a life so much more casual and ramshackle than his, I had taken him for a man in his fifties. Side by side with Bill, gazing into the smelly recesses of his pig battery, I felt like a green and irresponsible adolescent. When I talked about what I did for a living, I could see the unspoken reproach in his face: why *had* I idled my time away in words when I could have spent it building up something really solid and rewarding like this farm?

His wife and children had gone on to the pig roast. As we got into the car, Bill kept on sneaking wistful glances back to the farm, his head full of undone jobs, his eye on the hour or two of daylight still left to him. Every lost minute seemed to sting him like a flagellant's scourge. Then, as we recrossed the creek, his manner suddenly changed. Partying too was a serious duty, and Bill was a good neighbor. At the pig roast he partied with almost exactly the same degree of single-mindedness he brought to farming. As a Horatio Alger hero should, Bill made me feel that I was one of society's natural inadequates. I had never been equipped to follow the alpine, German path of his example.

The pig roast had divided in two. The under-thirties were out on the lawn playing volleyball, their leaping figures rising high over the top of the corn, in black outline against the low sun. The older parents and their small children had gathered around tables in the shadowy barn, which Harvey was rigging out with storm lanterns. As the sky dimmed, so the space around us seemed to stretch. Our small, companionable huddle of light and talk turned into a fragile ark afloat in the kind of enormous darkness which no European country is sufficiently big, or flat, or empty enough to contain. Some of the stars that I could see through the barn door must have been faraway farmhouses, but in the Iowa night it was impossible to tell what was five miles away and what a billion.

"Do people in England have a social life like we do?" Mrs. Schwartz asked.

"Well, yes; but."

Mrs. Schwartz told me about the ordinary social round of Scott County: the wedding parties, winter dances, card tournaments, anniversary barbecues, June graduation parties, pig roasts and clambakes which cemented the scattered farms into a neighborhood. "What about jokes?" said Bill. "Do the English play jokes on each other like the people here?"

The winter before, a cow had died on a local farmer. It had turned, like Bill's giant snowblower, into a "community asset." For weeks before the thaw, the cow's corpse had made a festive tour from farmhouse to farmhouse. It had appeared outside Bill's window one morning, knee-deep in the snow and covered in show rosettes from head to tail. A few days later it had been seen strung up between two tall barns on another farmer's land. A banner hanging from its feet read: THE COW THAT JUMPED OVER THE MOON. Before it eventually defrosted, the cow paid a call on every house for miles around. It peered through girls' bedroom windows, replaced cars in garages, climbed trees and telegraph poles, and stubbornly blocked driveways at their narrowest points. It was affectionately remembered and its decomposition sadly mourned.

The sense of being members of a real local community absorbed the people at the pig roast. Yet it also somehow absolved them from the responsibilities of American citizenship in the wider sphere. No one, for instance, had bothered to turn out to see President Carter when the *Delta Queen* had stopped at the Quad Cities. The general run of pig-roast opinion was that Carter was an honest man, a tryer, and a bore. His Mississippi trip had been an attempt to win the hearts of the heartland, but he had passed by Scott County without raising much more than a faint flicker of curiosity that an American President was out in the backyard. In two days' time, Pope John Paul was due to arrive in Boston. Next week, he was going to celebrate Mass at Des Moines, a hundred and fifty miles away. *That* was something else. Already the *Des Moines Register* had conducted a statewide poll which had shown that there was a huge majority of people who agreed with the statement that the Pope's visit was "the most important event ever in the history of Iowa."

"When the Pope comes to Des Moines," Bill said, *"everybody* will try to get to see him."

"They'll need telescopic sights," said Bill's wife in a chilling, if unintentional, allusion.

On Sunday morning in Andalusia, I loaded my boat, then went to church. Sitting on a cushioned pew at the back of the Community Baptist Church, I was struck by the hymn numbers that had been put up on the boards at the front. They were all in five and six figures. *Hymn 50620?* I had known that Baptists were strong on hymn singing, but even so, to have more than fifty thousand of the things seemed a little excessive. How could anyone hope to remember the tunes? It took a while for me to realize that all the numbers I could see were not hymns but dollars, and the boards displayed today's takings for various enterprises like the Building Fund and the Faith Mission. In place of an altar there was a backlit scene of what might have been Colorado: a misty lake, pines and snowcapped mountains. A furled American flag leaned against the whitewashed wall.

The pastor was of a piece with his church. His smart beige suit had been manufactured from some kind of petroleum extract. His manners were those of a successful brush salesman. He exuded an air of breezy well-being from every synthetic-fiber pore. Next Sunday, he said, we had a real treat coming to us: Brother Papadopoulos would be along, playing his trumpet, and we'd be looking to have a good time with the Lord.

"Okay, then, Brother Gary—let's have a song!"

Brother Gary pulled out the tremolo stop on his electronic organ, and we were launched into the service. The packed congregation sang:

> *Let ev'ry Giant of Distress and Unbelief and Sin*
> *Get ready now to vacate, for you see,*
> *I've come from out the Wilderness! I know I'm going to win!*
> *I want that mountain, it belongs to me!*
> *I want that mountain! I want that mountain!*
> *Where the milk and honey flow,*
> *Where the grapes of Eshcol grow.*
> *I want that mountain! I want that mountain!*
> *The mountain that my Lord has given me.*

Yelling along with the rest that I wanted that mountain, I did wonder whether I wasn't being a trifle greedy. It was all very well to send curt eviction notices to Distress and Unbelief and Sin, as if one were a slum landlord, but I was not happy with this arrogant demand for the mountain. I knew exactly where it was, too. I had set eyes on it on another journey, and I didn't think that its current tenants would take very kindly to my claims on it. The grapes of Eshcol grow along a brook below the city of Hebron, in the Israeli-occupied sector of the West Bank of the Jordan. Hebron had been a dim smudge, high above the line of Israeli command posts, where I'd watched soldiers with binoculars studying me and my Jordanian companion. Excellent as "I want that mountain" might have been as a marching song for the Palestine Liberation Organization, I didn't feel that its words were quite suitable for the Community Baptist Church of Andalusia, Illinois.

Nor was I much reassured by the pastor's sermon when it came. His theme was "Faith," but his illustrations of what he meant by the word were resoundingly materialist. He asked me to take a payroll check from my boss. If I believed that he was going to deposit eighty dollars in my bank account, that was faith.

"Now, you take me and my family," said the pastor. "We went on summer vacation. To the A-zores. By TAP airlines. In a Boeing 747. Okay?"

It sounded fine to me. He looked as if such a holiday were well within his means.

"Why, just by simple faith, here you are—thousands of feet up in the air! That's exercising Faith! You go to a doctor. You go to a drugstore. You go buy yourself a cold cure. That's Faith!" The words "doctor" and "drugstore" apparently reminded him of a slogan that had proved its worth many times before. "In America now, we got prescription junkies!"

"Amen!"

"Amen!"

"We're not talking to modernists, now! We're not talking to infidels! We're talking to the faithful!"

I was distracted by the interpreter for the deaf who stood by, miming his words like a TAP air hostess demonstrating how life vests should be worn. When my attention returned to the pastor, he was attacking the universities. "How many kids do you know—good, decent kids who've been raised in Faith? And they've gone to the State University of Iowa, and they've come home not believing in anything! Some of those kids, they don't believe in *nothing*. They've been reading the wrong books. They've been listening to the wrong teachers. They've been led out of the way of Faith by modernists. By infidels! Well, Faith is fighting back! Why, only next month, David Gibbs is going to be turned loose against the state of Texas. Right?"

"Hallelujah!"

"*Halleluj*ah!" repeated the pastor. "One bag of French-fries, now, why, it don't even give a *smell* for everybody! But God changes circumstances. What am I trying to say? Am I getting through?"

To judge by the *hallelujahs* and *amens* that were coming in steadily now, punctuating almost every remark that he made, he was getting through very well. I found the drift of his logic unfathomable, but the basic grounds of his appeal were clear. He had raveled up prescription junkies, bags of French-fries, college professors, "modernists," school boards into a single, ugly conglomerate, and he was inviting us to freely vent our prejudices in the name of the Lord. Whatever lay beyond the immediate ken of Andalusia was in the territory of the infidel and the Saracen. *Amen* and *hallelujah* had been transformed from cries of praise to grunts of discontent. Moving steadily from one bugaboo to the next, the pastor roused us to a comfortable fury. When he got to the end of his address, he signaled to Brother Gary at the organ, and we stood up to sing:

> *Every day, as I go my way,*
> *It's* nice *for* me.

I left during the second verse. Walking down First Street to the river, past the wooden chalets on stilts with a sleeping dog on every stoop, I could hear the high voices calling *"nice* for *me"* all the way to the harbor wall, where they were blotted out by the chinking of the crickets.

The ruffled water of Andalusia Slough was quick with ragged slivers of sun and yellow aspen leaves. Sharp gusts of wind cut crinkling tracks across it, making the leaves tip upright. skate. and spin. There was hardly any current here. The slough was cut off from the main river by a straggle of sandbars, thickets, outcrops of forest and stagnant lagoons. For convenience' sake, someone had named this interlocking congeries of land and water "Andalusia Island"; but in fact it was made up of several hundred islands—some a mile or more long, others only just big enough to accommodate a family of turtles piled up against one another's shells like a handful of loose change.

The V of my wake went creaming away from the stern. I was full of the old juvenile pleasure at having escaped from church. Mine was the only boat on the slough; I had Sunday to myself and no certain destination in mind. Tows, waves and wing dams were all safely relegated to the main channel beyond the islands. At the mouth of a wooded creek, in the lee of the wind, I chucked my anchor out and settled down to smoke, drink coffee, meditate and fish. I tied on one of the homemade bass plugs Jim Curdue had given me back in Wabasha and flicked it out into a dark pool where the willows came low over the still water. At the Shetland farm where I had spent teen-age summer holidays with my Scottish great-uncle, there had been just one house rule which it was sacrilege to break: no fishing on Sundays. The best days for the running sea trout had always been Sundays, and I'd gloomed from behind the windowpane in my uncle's gun room, looking down at the black loch at the bottom of the paddock, and watched the fish go free, leaping and splashing as they tried to shake the sea lice from their scales. Now, breaking the Sabbath without a wince of conscience, I drew the line steadily in, waiting for a boil on the water and the throbbing plunge of an Andalusia bass.

I thought of the service from which I'd made my getaway. Its style and tone would have made complete sense a hundred years ago, when places like Andalusia were still young and raw. Then, the conditions of an infant, frontier community had demanded a new kind of religious practice. Its language would be colloquial and democratic: Brother Gary, Brother Zeke and Sister Liza would talk in church in much the same terms that they would use in the town meeting. Its theology would be made directly relevant to the everyday business of carving out a living from the land. Divine truth would be revealed through metaphors involving horses and plows and saws and axes; and frontier life itself, a muddy, difficult, improvised, hand-to-mouth affair, would be sanctified by its more than fleeting resemblance to the struggles of the Children of Israel in the wilderness as they headed for the Promised Land. *The mountain that my Lord has given me* was a bluff on the banks of the Mississippi; and if you worked hard enough you could grow the grapes of Eshcol there. Community Baptism was a religion of straight talking, practical know-how and self-reliance, in which making out as a farmer or carpenter was intimately connected with the doctrine of personal salvation.

Between then and now, though, something had gone terribly stale. The down-to-earth metaphors that once had been exact and fresh had turned to routine exercises in folksy cracker-barrel about paychecks, TAP Airlines and drugstore prescriptions. God had once been seen to smile on the reasonable ambitions of the settler. *I want that mountain! It belongs to me!* might have sounded like an admirable claim if it had come from the mouth of a young sodbuster in an open territory. Now it sounded merely petulant. I want that stereo system. I want that camper. I want that ranch-style bungalow. I want that government off my goddamn back. Saddest of all, the necessary pride in the new community, the sense of mutual solidarity in the face of a rough surrounding nature had been converted into crude small-town xenophobia. Phrases which had been coined to give meaning to a new and radical life were now voiced as expressions of irritable conservatism.

Yet if I was right about this, it did help to explain something important about the nature of the "born-again" Christian movement. It suggested that the powerful nostalgia which animated the born-againers was not simply a yearning for a lost theological innocence, but rather an ache to return to a specific period of American history. Once upon a time, ran the seductive story, there was an age when worldly ambition and spiritual virtue existed in harmony, when there was no gulf between the language of religion and the language of day-to-day life, when the small local community was in the front line rather than in the rear guard, when to be a self-reliant householder with your own plot of ground was to be blessed as a righteous man by God Himself. And in the Western states at least, this golden age, this Eden was still tantalizingly near at hand. It was far enough away for the actual brutishness of the frontier to have been conveniently forgotten, but close enough to be dated with precision and still to exert the pull of a strong hereditary attachment. The era would have begun in the 1840s and it would have survived the Civil War by a good twenty years.

Andalusia, for instance, had even gone on looking like a frontier settlement. Its plain carpentered houses, grouped in a rough square, three blocks by three, had kept their air of being temporary squatters on virgin land. There were cars on the streets, TV antennas on the rooftops, drooping telephone lines on poles; anomalous additions which did very little to disturb the essence of Andalusia, the bare conjunction of shack, forest, river and cultivated ground. If being born again and getting back to Jesus really meant losing a hundred years or so of history in a blink, Andalusia was a perfect setting for such a rebirth. Then, perhaps, the words of "I Want That Mountain" would lose the greed and smugness which I heard in them, and sound inspiring and heroic.

In Andalusia Slough, nothing moved except the leaves and jumping lights. Maybe the fish in these parts were Sabbatarians, under a vow of abstinence for the day. I quartered every inch of the pool with my plug and caught some green slime and a twig. Lallygagging on to the lock above Muscatine with my pipe drawing nicely, I drifted into a reverie of Sundays: the moist, cavelike smell of English stone churches; sleepy afternoons with the *Weekly Symphony* on the fretwork-fronted wireless; the steady *tirra-wirra* of a neighbor's lawnmower; my father's sermons, with their unacknowledged echoes of Lancelot Andrewes and Cardinal Newman; the smell of *his* pipe, crackling and bubbling with St. Bruno Rough Cut; and the rocky Sundays of the foreigner, afloat in countries where Sunday is the sharpest reminder that he's not at home.

At Muscatine, I nosed along the waterfront looking for a berth. The town shelved gently down to the river, an intricate, substantial place of oxblood brickwork and terra-cotta streets. One could tell at first sight that Muscatine had class. Its tall shuttered warehouses (were they shuttered just for Sunday, or for life?) had scalloped pediments and fluted Corinthian drainpipes. Other buildings, lagged in ferns and ivy, had little, closetlike galleries of wood hanging out over the street and trailing ragged flights of wrought-iron steps. The broad market square, open at one end to the river, looked as if it were still in business; and there, just across the wharf over the tracks, was a button factory. It wasn't a gap-toothed ruin; it hadn't been converted into a pizza parlor; its recently repainted sign said J & K PEARL BUTTON COMPANY. All in all, Muscatine appeared to be a nineteenth-century river town that was in remarkably good working order.

It was, I felt, slightly too good to be true. The great, puce railroad hotel was alive and well, with a comfortable, creaky twelve-dollar room and a proprietor who asked me if I'd care to go along to someone's housewarming party at the top end of town. Yes, said Mr. Anson, sure there was a button factory. In fact, there were two—no, three. Buttons were big in Muscatine. Pushing my luck, I asked whether the lumber business was still intact here too. Indeed it was; at least, there was a factory that made office furniture. Then there was the Grain Processing Corporation, which manufactured corn oil, starch and alcohol, and fed whole fleets of river barges with their cargoes. Clearly, Muscatine was in possession of some secret of survival which had escaped almost every other town of its size I had visited. I had assumed that slow dereliction and depopulation were the inevitable fate of such places, doomed now to squat and scrape a bare living in the long shadows of their ambitions of a century ago. There must, I thought, be something peculiarly boneheaded about Muscatine in its failure to grasp the basic principles that should have ensured its decline. To go on making buttons was to fly impertinently in the face of history. What did these dodos think they were doing?

Chuck Anson collected me from my room and drove me to the yard party on the bluff. For dodos, everyone seemed to be unseasonably cheerful. A large bearded dodo was singing comic songs to a guitar on the veranda; other dodos were sloshing quantities of gasoline over the barbecue briquettes. I felt that this was not, perhaps, quite the right moment for me to speak up and tell people that their town was a hopeless anachronism and should by rights be dead.

I was introduced to my host, Brad Funk, a young man so deluded that he'd actually deserted a perfectly good city in Missouri to come to Muscatine, where he worked in the public relations section of the Grain Processing Corporation and was married to the onetime Pork Queen of Iowa. Mr. Funk made me feel old and grubby. He looked like the kind of man who would think nothing of jogging five miles before breakfast; an early-rising, nonsmoking, *Newsweek*-reading deep sleeper. I sensed an implicit criticism of my own tendency to make light of serious things in the way he questioned me, like a solemn graduate student knocking the daylights out of a Freshman English class.

Brad Funk was, frankly, worried. I had met plenty of kindly people who were worried for my safety on the journey; but no one so far had given me such a thorough grilling over my motives for making the trip. I had always seen my own reasons as private and obsessional. Funk, though, saw me as a potential representative of a whole class of people whom he feared and despised—all the metropolitan journalists and television scriptwriters who had conspired to represent the Midwest as a country of ignorant hicks and hayseeds. "Why is it that every time they show a bumpkin on a comedy show he's supposed to come from Iowa?" What were my own "impressions"? Were they "favorable" or "unfavorable"?

"I'm not a newspaper reporter," I said. "I'm just passing through, trying to watch what happens to *me*."

"Just be fair to us."

"But the whole idea of 'fairness' implies some sort of objective overview, as if I were in a position to pass neutral judgments. I'm not in that position."

"But you're going to write a book."

"Yes, but it won't be an 'objective' book. It's not going to be the inside story on America. It might be the inside story on me, but that's rather different."

"I'm worried that you're going to condescend to us."

We stood on his lawn, wrangling awkwardly, while Brad Funk defended the Midwest against a whole raft of accusations I had never made. Indeed, I hadn't realized until then that the area was half so vulnerable and prickly as he made it sound. And when he said "us" and "we," he had taken it on himself to speak for a dozen or so entire states at a time.

"Look," he said. "Back East, you've got the old top-heavy bureaucracy. Then on the West Coast you've got all the excesses of America. We're the calm, thoughtful center. We can moderate between the extremes. We can see both sides of the argument. If you take us out of the United States, you drain all the basic common sense out of the country. I *know* what goes on in New York and Los Angeles. I can make judgments about them because here I'm at a remove."

"But that doesn't make you condescend to them?"

I could see that I'd earned a black mark for flippancy.

"In Muscatine, we're ideally placed. Look: we want to see a New York show, we can catch it in Davenport. We want to listen to an orchestra concert, we go to Chicago. We want to shop at luxury stores, we go down to St. Louis. What I'm saying is, in the Midwest we've got the best of *everything*."

"Well, that's something I'd never think of claiming for London or anywhere else I've ever lived. All places are messier and more complicated than that. I bet Muscatine's no closer to Paradise than North Kensington."

"But people are never *fair* to the Midwest," Funk said, brimming with protective anxiety for his region as if someone with careless hands, like me, could easily break it. My own experience of the Midwest suggested that it was far sturdier than he feared.

Yet this sense of slight and belittlement, this precarious pride was in tune with so much else that I'd heard in the last few weeks. It chimed, at one level, with the general mood of the Baptist church in Andalusia. At another, it linked up with a remark made by a man at a gas dock upriver. He'd been complaining about the way his business had fallen off since the rise in gas prices. This year, he'd said, there were far fewer boats about on the Mississippi than there were last year. "Folks now, they're keeping pretty much to their own territory." In American English, the word "territory" had always been associated with expanse, openness, the freedom to move out and on; now it had come to mean the small, threatened space of one's own plot of ground. So in Brad Funk's talk, even something as huge and rich as the Midwest—the classic "territory" in the old sense—could be seen as a vulnerable enclosure to be defended against the stranger.

In Davenport, I'd seen the television trailers for the latest invasion movie: they showed lidless, alien eyes pressed up against the picture windows of a suburban home. The screaming family huddled together, exposed to the horrid gaze of the creatures from outside. I had dutifully identified with the family when I watched those ads. I wondered now whether I should in fact have counted myself among the staring aliens.

The Funks were planning to turn their own house into a self-sufficient fortress. Mrs. Funk was now a teacher of Home Ec and preferred people to forget that she had once been the Pork Queen of Iowa. She was a born-again conservationist and talked of Waste in almost exactly the same terms as the Baptists spoke of Sin and Disbelief. She was going to dig a solar pond in the backyard. She showed me its outlines on the grass. She explained how there was going to be a layer of fresh water here, and a layer of salt water there, and how the warmed salt water was going to circulate like blood through the house. She was going to install solar panels in the roof. Then she was going to block up the windows of the house.

"Do you know how much energy we waste just through windows?" Her eyes were wide with moral indignation at the thought of this reckless dissipation of vital fluids. She blazed with the force of energy saving as an essentially theological doctrine. It was possible, I suppose, that her scheme might in time cut down the family fuel bills, but that wasn't its main point. It was an act of atonement for past sins. America had been prodigal, had squandered its patrimony like a rake in a Thackeray novel. Now it was going to do penance. It was going to keep to its own territory. It was going to blot out the view from the window. It was going to live in a dark, solar-heated box like a contrite sinner in his cell. That, at any rate, was the general theological drift of the thing. In the meantime, though, there was more beer in the barrel and the sound of big Joe singing "Careless Love" on the veranda and the spitting of the wieners on the barbecue grill.

Rain clogged the screen outside my window. The broken clouds were running north at speed overhead. The wind harped and groaned in the telegraph wires; it tore at the American flags on their poles; it gusted noisily around the gable ends of the hotel, shaking the rickety jungle gym of rusted balconies and fire-escape ladders. In the street below, a truck went by, its tires *shush-shushing* in the wet: WIEDEMANN INDUSTRIES INC. FIBERGLASS BAPTISTRIES, CHURCH SPIRES, STEEPLES, CROSSES.

Marooned in my room, I studied the Yellow Pages of the Muscatine directory, looking for someone to call up on the phone. The surnames there gave away a good deal about the town's history: Kokemuller, Grossklaus, Hahn, Fuhlman, Kranz, Behlen, Smit, Hammann, Elkar, Maeglin, Schwinn, Krogstad, Larsen, Toborg, Blaesing . . . But the names of their businesses were all-American: Chuck's, Bob's, Don's, Ken's, Jerry's, Glen's, Tony's, Kathy's, Jean's, Smiley's, Bart's, Gary's, Dan's, Joe's. Names like this had been as important as clothes when it came to transforming the immigrant into the American. Mail-order fashion, distributed by firms like Sears and J. C. Penney (or their nine-teenth-century forebears), had enabled more or less everyone to dress alike. The shortened first name had allowed Swedes, Germans, Dutch-men, Poles to emerge clean-shaven of all those extra syllables which would have betrayed their original nationality. I found the J & K Button Company. Its box had no names at all. Jorkenheim & Klute? Johnson & King? Joe & Kathy? Javitz & Krogstad? They were clearly hiding something. When I got through to the proprietor, all he said was "Hi, Jayunkay?" Perhaps he was a freshly settled boat person.

The factory was two blocks away down Mississippi Drive; a wet fight against the driving wind. The river was in a dirty mood, churning between its banks, ribbed with scuds of yellow froth. Ocean breakers smashed against the levee, and plumes of spray blew over the railroad tracks. A big tow had moored off Muscatine Island, hugging what little lee shore it could find: in weather like this even the tows were beaten by the river; their barges were liable to break apart and sink or wreck themselves on sandbars.

The button factory was gaunt and stooped: four narrow stories of dripping brick and cross-eyed windows. Inside, it was a vertical maze of machinery linked by steep wooden stairways with gangs of women in head scarves doing peculiar things to bits of plastic. It did not, as I'd hoped, make buttons from Mississippi clam shells anymore; that had stopped in the 1930s. Nevertheless, the building had managed to keep in touch with its past. Most of what was happening inside it now was a simple extension of the old techniques of making pearl buttons from clams, and it had stayed in the same German family since it had started.

The whole process of button making was nicely contained and comprehensible. It started at the bottom of the factory and rose, machine by machine, to the top. On the first floor, the liquid plastic was poured into an oil drum, mixed with dye and hardener, and slopped into a centrifuge like a big spin-dryer, where it was whirled around until it formed an even, translucent sheet of soft rubbery stuff. The sheet was passed into a machine that punched it into a thousand or so round button blanks; the blanks were fed on a conveyor belt into an oven where they were baked hard; then they were cooled and sent on up to the next floor. Here more machines drilled needle holes in them and carved patterns on their fronts and backs. They were polished in a tumbling vat of wooden shoe pegs, and on the top floor they were sorted into cardboard boxes. They looked like pretty trinkets, colored rose, shot pearl, smoke, primrose, cornflower blue, amber and scarlet. I would never have guessed that such a quantity of technology and expertise had gone into the making of every button on my shirtfront.

"And that's what you used to do to clams?" I said, fingering a jade-green button on which an elaborately scrolled pattern had been carved.

"Yep. Only they did it all by hand then." Mr. Jayunkay had said very little. He had pointed out each machine, then stood by while I inspected it, alternately touching his trim mustache and his Elks pin.

"But how have you managed to stay on in business when almost every other button factory on the river has been closed for years?"

"I dunno," he said. "I guess buttons just run in the blood."

. . .

Something—buttons perhaps, or some instinctive, saving sense of history —did run in Muscatine's blood. The button factory was only the most obvious symbol of the town's old knack of keeping up a line of continuity with what had gone before. One could feel its reluctance to let go of anything that had served it well. It stuck by its buttons; it stuck by its old hotel; it went on using its river wharves. It was unfashionably loyal to its small downtown stores. There *was* a shopping mall out on the Interstate, but it had done surprisingly little damage to the family businesses along Second, Third and Fourth Streets. The old city had aged gracefully, letting the ivy grow up its walls. At the same time it had managed to absorb a clutch of big new industrial plants which, along with the buttons, the grain elevators and the truck gardens and fruit farms on the town's rim, gave Muscatine its air of being comfortably, unflashily rich. Most towns on the Mississippi had been outfaced by the river. They'd had their boom, and then they'd dwindled, looking shabby and temporary beside that enormous drift of water at their doorsteps. Muscatine, though, had the pride of a place that had always got along fine with the river, able to match it on equal terms. I hoped the wind would go on blowing hard: it was good to be weatherbound in Muscatine.

For a day or two at least, I could pretend that I wasn't really a vagrant. I had a date to look forward to in the evening. At the Funks' housewarming I'd met a schoolteacher named Judith and invited her to dinner. For Judith I had my whiskers trimmed at the barbershop, my trousers freshly pressed at the cleaner's; I knotted my necktie in three different ways, pared my dirty traveler's fingernails down to their quicks, overdid the Eau Sauvage, then fell into a state not far from panic. She had made her date with a grown-up; would she notice that the person she had actually landed was a nervous teen-ager with senile teeth? It seemed hopelessly probable that she would; and I set to trying to wash off the worst of the cologne. I restored a few years to my age with an X-rated shot of bourbon and soda.

Judith too, I saw, had been to the hairdresser's since yesterday. Her hair contained her pointed face like a wimple. Its ends had been chamfered to a polished edge of dull gold around her cheeks. In her white woolen coat and big tortoiseshell glasses, she looked as if she'd been unable to decide whether she was supposed to be a college girl or a middle-aged schoolmarm. I liked her indecision. The serious glasses (she'd been wearing contacts the day before) gave her a funny owlishness when otherwise she would have been just plainly pretty.

She was sorry she was late. She'd had these . . . things . . . to do.

The kids had been real bad. She felt kinda nutso. She had a sand-papery Iowa voice. In ten or twenty years' time it would sound like a rasp; but now it was nicely, lightly dry.

It felt as if it had been an age since I had been half of a couple. I'd dined too much alone with books broken open on their spines. With Judith, for an hour or two, I could play at being husbandly again, fussing over her white coat, hanging on every detail of her day at the elementary school, quizzing her on the names of the particular beasts in her class. I would willingly have beaten little Gary around the ears for her, and put my boot hard into Glen's fat behind. Our heads came close in consultation over the wine list, her beveled hair swinging forward to hide her face.

We had to learn to talk to each other, negotiating in slow motion like swimmers in a pool. Judith had a story. She told it nervously, searching my face after every other sentence for a giveaway glaze of boredom, but I was completely, tenderly held by it. It contained one kind, at least, of Midwestern life with the literal precision of a mirror.

Judith wasn't from Muscatine. She had grown up in a little Dutch town far out in the northwest of Iowa. Her family was Dutch. Every-one she knew was Dutch. She remembered her grandparents' talking in Dutch, and services in Dutch at the Dutch Reformed Church. It was a very strict small town. No one skipped church, and the minister was a more important figure than the mayor. Judith's father was a truckdriver now, but when she was a child he had been a schoolteacher too. He had been fired by the school board for teaching the theory of evolution.

"And he doesn't even believe in evolution," Judith said. "He was just telling the children that this was something that some people thought. It raised a scandal."

Her father had been as scandalized by his own heresy as anyone else in town. He was a devout churchgoer and, had he sat on the school board, would probably have voted to expel himself from the system. Even to mention the existence of the theory of evolution was, as he now saw, a terrible thing; and he accepted his demotion to the post of truckdriver as a perfectly reasonable consequence of his having strayed into mortal error.

Judith, though, had watched her father's fall with a mixture of in-dignation and skepticism. She was a secret believer in the theory of evolution. She was the oldest of nine children, and had had to be grown-up before her time. She'd been marked out as clever at school. There was just one thing wrong with her: she was a girl. Education was fine, for her brothers; but her parents thought that no girl should learn anything beyond what she'd acquired in the eighth grade.

"They wanted me to be a homemaker, wife and mother. So long as I was engaged to a boy, I could be a nurse, or even a grade-school teacher. But that was the top of it."

There had been a quarrel with her family before she had been allowed to attend the local teachers' college, which was run by the Dutch Reformed Church. She had dreamed of going to a real university—the kind of place where the theory of evolution was taught as a matter of ordinary fact. No chance. Judith had gone to the teachers' college. Then, it seemed, her parents' prayers were miraculously answered. The minister's son began dating her.

"They thought that was real nifty—*me* marrying the minister's son . . . God, that was nifty."

"But he was only dating you; you weren't engaged, were you?"

"It was the same thing. If you were dating a boy, you were going to be married. Everyone knew that. I knew it. He knew it. The whole town knew it."

For months, everybody around Judith had talked of weddings. But the minister's son wasn't the man she wanted to marry. He was nice, good, earnest and dull. Marrying him would have been like marrying the town itself; she might as well have taken the church, the school board and the long flat streets into her arms.

So Judith ran away. In secret she applied for a job she'd seen advertised in Muscatine. To her, Muscatine, with its twenty thousand people, was a metropolis. It was as far away from home as any place she dared to imagine. She was called for interview on a Wednesday. The school was shorthanded: when was the earliest day she could start teaching?

"I dunno," she'd said. "I got to go back and get my things. I guess I could make it back here by Friday."

She had driven home in her old green Ford and packed everything she had into the car. She left a letter for the minister's son; then she made her great trek east. The memory of that journey still amazed her. It had been the most daring thing she'd ever done. Telling me about it, she made herself sound like a third person, someone she had once known who'd frightened Judith with her audacity.

It had been dark when she'd set off. She had a two-hundred-mile drive ahead of her. The interior light in her car had gone, and she'd struck match after match to follow the zigzag track of minor roads in the Rand McNally Atlas. At ten, she'd stopped at a Howard Johnson's and had fallen asleep out of excitement and exhaustion over her plate of eggs and French-fries. A waitress had shaken her awake an hour later.

"I didn't know where I was. I didn't know what I was doing. I didn't have an apartment or anything . . . I guess I reckoned I'd stay in a motel. I'd never stayed in a motel before. I didn't even know if you had to have a reservation."

It had been nearly dawn when she reached Muscatine. She parked her car on the levee and watched the sun color the river. At eight, she was at the hamlet six miles out of town where she had been teaching school ever since.

Judith's story was a classic American autobiography in miniature. She had traveled two hundred miles; people little older than her own grandparents had traveled five thousand. I had met a man whose grandfather had come from Luxembourg, sailing in steerage to New York, from where he had walked across six states, taking odd jobs along the way, to reach the farmlands of Iowa. Yet Judith, a third-generation American, found even Chicago too remote and alien to believe in as quite real. Literal distance was meaningless. She'd flown to Hawaii for a summer vacation with a girlfriend, but that was a trifling little expedition when set against her nighttime drive across the state: a journey that had all the essential features of a myth. It explained to her who she was, in exactly the same way that the epic stories of immigration had defined the identity of her ancestors.

I told her about my own journey and how I saw it as really the same American story. Sitting with Judith in the hotel restaurant, calling up a second bottle of Gamay, I had, as it were, just reached the Howard Johnson's on the empty road, with Muscatine still half the night away. Fellow travelers, Judith and I were suddenly, comfortably close, our narratives interwoven.

Keeping our distance like married people, we walked across the dark railroad tracks to the levee. There was a light over the dock where I'd left my boat. I wanted Judith to see it. It was sitting low in the water, flooded by the storm earlier in the day. Two of my battered gas tanks were afloat, along with a tide wrack of empty Budweiser cans, plastic bags, cardboard boxes and a white football sock.

"Is *that* it? God, it's so little. I thought it was going to be more like some kind of a *cruiser*. . . ."

"Are you disappointed? Did you want staterooms and cocktail cabinets?"

"No. It's just so little and scary."

"Would you like to come on down to the Gulf of Mexico with me?"

Judith shivered, appalled at the thought; but she snuggled kindly against my shoulder.

"You really could. Then it'd turn the trip from an epic into a fairy story."

I was sad that Judith thought I was joking.

In the morning the sky was empty blue, but the high wind was back, to my relief. I walked around the river bluff on the southwest of town where Muscatine's Victorian grandees had built their mansions. Nestling up to their eaves in chestnuts and sycamores, these houses were glorious imaginative flights of unbridled nineteenth-century ambition. I had seen nothing like them. Some, clinker-built like ships in white-painted siding, floated like ships over their lower stories. They had used the airiness of wrought iron and delicate wooden columns to defy the ground on which they were built. Their poop decks and forecastles sailed over the trees, Old Glory flying from their mastheads. Others, in brick and plaster, were English Georgian country houses, four thousand miles adrift from Wiltshire. There was a shingled onion dome from Byzantium; a Roman villa; a German Gothic cathedral; a stone portico from a Florentine palace. Geography and history had been no object for the builders of Muscatine: they had cheerfully looted the world for the best and showiest of everything, from everywhere, and put it up higgledy-piggledy on this wooded hill. Clerical . . . secular . . . Moorish . . . Steamboat Corinthian . . . Queen Anne . . . Cosimo de' Medici. Together, they lorded it over the river in a fantastic and exhilarating display of cosmopolitanism run riot.

In other towns I'd seen the scabby ruins of such houses. In Muscatine they were smartly kept up. Their white paint was fresh, their box hedges trim, their verandas swept for an admiral's inspection. They managed to suggest that—against the odds, in flat contradiction to the standard history of the Mississippi river town—the world was still Muscatine's oyster.

The exuberant, free-floating architecture of the bluff was rooted in the serious town below. Most of the places I'd stopped at had given the impression that the chief part of their day was devoted to lounging, spitting, scuffing their heels and swatting flies in bars. I'd felt that my own profession, of being at a perpetually loose end, fitted in pretty well with the general spirit of things. It wasn't so in Muscatine. The few people who were out on the street walked straight, with appointments and destinations in their heads. The rest were locked up in the factories on the flats, industrious bees in the Muscatine honeycomb.

Brad Funk had offered to show me around the Grain Processing Corporation, and he picked me up in his car looking as trim and shaven as one of the box hedges on the bluff in his blue button-down shirt and tan oxfords. He was spilling a cascade of big figures. Each day, he was saying, *x* hundreds of thousands of bushels of grain were turned into *y* hundreds of thousands of proof gallons of alcohol.

"Then there's cornstarch—that's used as a bonding substance in the paper industry . . . there's dried syrup . . . feed-recovery products . . . corn oil . . ."

"Stop, please; I'm lost—"

It looked, in fact, as if GPC had been deliberately designed for people to lose themselves in. It rambled over the best part of a mile of riverbank in a wild tangle of chutes, smokestacks, pipes, ladders and gleaming steel cylinders like Brobdingnagian soup cans. Even in the strong wind, the air was putrid with the smell of rotten bread. Wearing a shiny scarlet hard hat, I scrambled after Brad as he led me on a vertiginous chase through the maze. We went hand over hand up ladders, marched across high catwalks, climbed a spiral staircase up the inside of a grain elevator, crossed a metal footbridge over a canyon, and reached the roof of the highest cylinder of all.

"You can see the whole operation from here—"

The cylinder topped the bluff. One could see right over Muscatine to the bumpy, browning grain country beyond, with its roads as straight as runways on an airfield, its pale, solitary farms, its fertile desolation. Brad was talking facts and figures again: this happened to that, that happened to this, this was transferred across there to here, where, in simple terms, the basic *a, b* and *c* of it was thus and therefore. The general gist of the thing, as far as I could gather, was that GPC was a massive digestive system. Its tanks and tubes were gizzards and intestines and bowels. It could swallow half the wheat of Iowa at a gulp and whirl it around in its gastric juices. Its rear end jutted out over the river, where the fleets of chemical barges were moored at the terminal. The hoses that fed them were GPC's urinary tract, peeing crystal showers of pure alcohol. The cornstarch and the feed-recovery products went, I think, elsewhere.

"There's a whole lot of stuff here even I don't understand," Brad said.

"Thank God for that. The view's terrific, though."

"Yeah, you can see better than twenty-four, twenty-five miles from up here. Smells clean, too."

We made the long, twisty climb down to the Chemical Division in the basement of the plant, where a man in a white coat gave me a thimble glass of clear liquid.

"This here's the bottom line," he said. "This is what it's all about. Go on, try drinking it."

I tried. I found myself balancing what felt like a live coal on my tonsils, and only just managed to prevent my eyeballs' popping from their sockets.

"Hundred-and-ninety-proof spirit."

"It's a bit much before lunch."

"Now . . ." said the chemist. He cut it with water. He did some fancy work with his "botanicals," adding minute traces of the tinctures of juniper, lemon, coriander and macassar. "There. Best gin you'll ever drink. I think I got some Martini in the closet. Reason they used to put juniper in there was because there was so many impurities in the spirit, juniper was the only flavor that was strong enough to hide them. That's why it's called juniper juice. You say 'juniper juice' where you come from?"

It was like watching the elephant straining to bring forth the mouse, the relationship between this tiny glass of spirits and the gigantic scale of the operation that had gone to produce it. I could sympathize with Brad's irritation when he'd talked of the patronizing way in which outsiders conceived of the Midwest. For Muscatine was a true industrial capital of the unconsidered object—the button on one's shirt, the stiff drink in one's hand. Muscatine's secret was that it knew that it took just as much imagination and intricate labor to manufacture these things as it did to make television programs or newspapers or deals on Wall Street. The TV producer, fingering his buttons, or ordering up his lunchtime martini, never gave a second thought to Muscatine, but Muscatine watched television and saw more than it wanted of Los Angeles and Manhattan. It felt that the imbalance was unjust. The floating mansions on its bluff, or the pipes and cylinders of GPC, were really just as worthy of the loving gaze of the film camera as Rockefeller Center or the roller-coasting freeways of Hollywood and Santa Monica. But, no. When the TV producer bothered to represent a town like a Muscatine, he would show it simply as the birthplace of a comic hick chewing on a straw.

The wind had dropped and school was out, and Judith was sitting up in the bow of my boat. In five years of living in Muscatine she had never been on the river.

"I never even think of it as like a river. It's more a kind of a lake."

We drifted around the bend below the bluff where the Mississippi turned south.

"Hey," said Judith. "It's real nifty."

The water was barely dimpled now. A few strokes of pale cirrus showed up on the clear sky. Gentle, picnic weather.

"*How* far is it to New Orleans?"

"I don't know. Fourteen hundred. Something like that."

"God—"

"Are you coming after all?"

"Uh-uh. I got to teach school. I always wanted to see New Orleans, though. I never thought of going there by river."

The fields came right down to the levee and the strip of white sand on the shore. Judith was studying them.

"You know? Something I notice here—in this part of Iowa, they got dirty beans."

"Dirty *beans?*"

"Yeah. Those fields there, they're real dirty." She could hardly have sounded more morally disapproving if she'd caught her charges playing with themselves in the school lavatories. "Where I come from, they'd never do that. They clean the beans. You know, one year they sow corn, the next they sow beans. Up around Orange City, they get all the corn out, *then* they plant the beans. Here . . . look! See how the old corn's gotten all mixed up with the beans? That's dirty beans."

"Is that what they taught you at the Dutch Reformed Church?"

"No," said Judith, squinting, serious. "It ain't religious or anything. It's just what the farmers do."

"Like apartheid."

"What?"

"Beans and corn. Whites and blacks. You're instinctive segregationists."

Judith laughed and trailed her fingers in the Mississippi. The sun was dropping, and I turned the boat around. Lights were beginning to come on in the mansions on the bluff. Pushing upstream against the current in the dead calm, one could feel the strength of the river, its slow, deep, thrusting resistance to the boat. Judith's long shadow rode out ahead of us.

"You make a perfect figurehead," I called, but the motor was too loud for her to hear. Head cupped in her hands on the bow, she was still mooning over the moral degeneracy of eastern Iowa with its dirty beans, I think.

When we reached the landing, the last of the sun had bled into the river. Because the Mississippi ran due west here, Muscatine was famous for its sunsets, and today's was a small masterpiece of the genre. The waxed surface of the water had a glowing bloom to it. The force of the current made it bulge like a muscle. The color of it started as black under our feet, lightening to blue, then rose madder, then scarlet and yellow as it reached the horizon. In silhouette, the giant drums of GPC had turned to the towers of a Gothic castle afloat on their reflections.

For Judith, though, the sunset was an old Muscatine cliché. Look, I said, look; and babbled about colors and castles. "Yeah," she said, wrinkling her nose uninterestedly westward. "It's real pretty. What am I supposed to do with this rope? You want me to put some kind of a knot in it, or something?"

In the hotel bar, we sat up alongside Ed, the oldest of the permanent residents. He was eighty, and had landed up in Muscatine years before from Idaho. He had a rock of gray limestone for a face, with a single tuft of white hair like a sprig of marram grass. He was interested in my journey, for he had travel plans of his own. The evening before, I had shown him my route on the river charts. Tonight, he had an old railway timetable to show me.

"I worked it all out," he said. "I got all the connections."

The timetable was for 1956. The trains it showed were nearly all dead.

"Round early in November, I'll be going there. Hey, Judith—I tell you where I'm going this fall?"

"Yeah, Ed. You're going down to the Rio Grande."

"That's right. Gonna spend all winter down in the valley of the Rio Grande. Know a girl there. Little town . . . Eagle Pass, Texas, right up from Laredo. Goddamn." He sucked reminiscently at his beer glass. "She wrote me this letter. I had to send word to my mother, back in Idaho, and this girl, she wrote it out for me real nice. She wrote beautiful. Just like a schoolteacher." He looked crookedly across at me, then at Judith. "I had a kind of busted hand, then. That's why I couldn't do the writing on my own. Busted it on the railroad. Then I was someplace else, and, I dunno, we got all out of goddamn touch. Shit. But I'm going to get down to Eagle Pass, later in the fall, and I'm going to see that girl . . . if she ain't dead yet."

"When were you there last?"

"Nineteen and . . . Hell, must've been eighteen . . . nineteen. Can't remember."

Later, over dinner, Judith said, "That Ed, God, he's such a dreamer. Ever since I've been in Muscatine he's been saying that crazy stuff about the Rio Grande. Every fall he talks about going down there. He ain't never going to get south of Hershey Avenue."

I envied Ed the unreality of his trip. It would have been nice to stay on in Muscatine, merely dreaming of the river. But it couldn't be. The weather systems that were arbitrarily circling around America were being unkind. Judith and I had watched the local news and forecast on the bar TV. The weatherman pointed his baton at tomorrow's wind speed: 0–5 mph. I was going to have to join the butterflies and the Canada geese again, and move on south.

The weatherman had been right: there was no wind at all. He hadn't mentioned precipitation, though, and for once the American word for rain seemed an exact description of what was happening. This rain didn't just fall; it precipitated. It descended, gravitated, condensed, deposited and settled. Fine and close, it turned the air to wet smoke. It made the branches of the trees sag under its dull weight. It came in droplets so small that they left no mark on the water. In minutes, I was as thoroughly saturated as if I had been swimming in my clothes. Everything had gone to the color of gray ash: river, trees, sand, fields. There was no sky—or if there was, I was driving soddenly through it. A hundred yards away, the leading barge of a tow showed as a blunt smear, apparently suspended overhead in midair. I ran out of the channel and decided to keep to the wrong side of the red buoys for as long as the rain lasted. When the tow's wake arrived, it came in a series of big, lethargic slurps from the clouds, as if the river had tipped up on its end and were pointing into space. It wouldn't have made much difference if the wake had capsized me: the relative density of the water must have been almost identical to the relative density of the air. The candy-striped canopy over the boat was no help; the wetness precipitated just as wetly underneath it as above it. I tried to light a pipe to cheer myself up, but the tobacco was squidgy, like steaming manure. *Christ that my love were in my arms, and I in my bed again.* The motor growled at my back, stirring the dead river. Then the sky lifted.

It sat now on the treetops instead of on the water, making a wide, low-ceilinged corridor of the river. Shaking myself like a dog, I passed New Boston. The dripping cement works there didn't look inviting. Nor did Keithsburg. The Mississippi fanned out through a dank, wide-open reach of flatland, marsh and forest. I killed the motor, changed gas tanks, and let the boat raft slowly down on the current, turning broadside as it went. In the stillness I could hear scuffles in the brushwood on the bank and the sibilant trickle of water over the sand.

On the Illinois side there was a dead tree which seemed to function as a skid-row hotel for a gang of large, ne'er-do-well birds. As I came close, they lumbered off from their posts, assembled above the treetops in a ragged battle formation, and came out over the river to see whether this floating yellow thing was meat. When I started my motor, I thought the birds would scatter in fright, but they kept on coming, in lower and lower circles, until they were perhaps twenty or thirty feet over my head. Their wings creaked. They made bronchial *kark-kark* noises in their throats. They looked scarred, moth-eaten and hungry, and reminded me unpleasantly of the Buffalo chapter of Hell's Angels. *Karrack. Karrack. Shit. Sonofabitch.* I dug my dark glasses out of my grip, possessed by the thought that the first thing they'd try to peck out would be my eyes.

I hadn't yet found an occasion to use the aerosol froghorn that was stowed away beside the fire extinguisher. I pointed it at the birds and put my thumb down on the lever; it made a hideous noise like a bass saxophone stuck on a flat note. It didn't seem to scare the birds much, but they did climb disdainfully a few feet higher in the air. For a long half mile they kept pace with me, croaking nastily as I blasted at them with the froghorn; then, abruptly, they wheeled back to their dead tree.

In my run-in with the birds I hadn't noticed that something very odd was happening to the sky. It was splitting in two. The cloud had ripped away down a clean diagonal line from horizon to horizon. One side of the line was clear blue; the other was a bank of solid gray. I began to take pictures of this curious meteorological event. Bringing it into focus in the viewfinder, I remembered what the lockmaster had told me in Minneapolis. "Watch that sky. You ever see anything queer about it, if the clouds look wrong somehow, get off the river." The nearest town was Oquawka, Illinois, three miles downstream, and I kept as close as I could to the shore as I ran for shelter there. The wind came up from nowhere. The glazed surface of the river puckered, and by the time I reached harbor, a quarter of an hour later, the boat was wallowing in heavy breakers. I beached it alongside the jonboat of a camouflaged duck hunter. He'd seen the crack in the sky too, and had come in from his hide on the stump field across the channel.

"I was watching you, wondering if you'd make it," he said. "Wind's getting up real fast now."

The waves were bunching more steeply by the minute. They were rolling up out of the blue southwest across a four-mile stretch of open water. We stood on the levee watching them suck and slap at the shore. I told the duck hunter about the birds.

"Oh, them red-headed vultures back there? Yeah, they're weird. They been hanging around that one tree for as long as I can remember. They spook people. You have to shake an oar at them or they'll come right down in the boat with you. You know the weirdest thing? They never cross the state line. They'll fly out to mid-channel, and the moment they touch Iowa, they'll turn back. Even if there was a dead muskrat floating by on the Iowa side, I reckon they'd leave it be."

The wind blew steadily on through the afternoon. Sitting in a bar on Schuyler Street, I watched the swinging Texaco sign of the garage opposite and waited for it to quieten. Four o'clock went by. Judith would be out of school now. I damned the weather forecaster who had stranded me in Oquawka. The Texaco sign was blown out straight; it came back, and another gust shook it like a rag of washing on a line. At five, with just an hour to go before sunset, the sign settled to a gentle rocking, and I went back to the boat. The river was still streaky with whitecaps, but the breakers were flaccid, slopping listlessly about in the hangover of the storm. The going was splashy, but reasonably safe, and I kept the boat tacking at half speed down the channel. By the time I reached Lock 17, six miles on, the pool above the dam had returned to a black, syrupy calm.

The first set of barges from a big double tow was being nudged into the lock at the downstream end. It would be dark before I would be able to go through. I wondered if I should leave the boat where it was till morning, and went to ask the lockmaster's advice.

"You got navigation lights on there? You won't have no problem. There's nothing much coming up that I know of. Just keep to this side of those islands down there, keep right on through Drew Chute, you ought to be in Burlington in the half hour. I don't see what your problem is."

"I've just never driven the boat at night before."

"Oh, you'll see pretty well. Ain't nothing to it, when your eyes get accustomed."

The tow took an age to be disassembled and put back together. Deckhands with flashlights and Arkansas voices skipped from barge to barge, hauling on ropes that were thicker than their forearms. When I was signaled into the chamber, the moon was up, silvering the slime on the lock wall. I was lowered into the black. The sluices rumbled in their underground tunnels. When the gates opened, they framed a puzzling abstract of mat India ink spotted with scraps of tinsel.

My eyes weren't accustomed. I nosed out gingerly, feeling my way through water that I couldn't see. The lights on my boat were supposed to make it visible to other people and were no help in making the river visible to me. I went ahead, giving the motor little, nervous dribbles of gas. A flat-topped black buoy, heeling over in the current, went by so close I could have leaned out and touched it. I could just make out the irregular hump of Otter Island and steered to the left of it. For a few minutes I congratulated myself on beginning, at least, to get the hang of this business of night navigation. Then I saw the pointed top of another buoy five yards ahead of my bow. A red. I hadn't been going downstream at all; I'd just crossed the channel at right angles.

The carbide searchlight of a tow (was it across or down from where I was?) raked the river. I headed for what I hoped was the shore, and the tow disappeared over my head at terrifying speed. It left no wake behind, and it was only when I saw another, racing by at the same altitude, that I realized that the tows were trucks on a highway. I edged on. Another beam swiveling idly on the water suddenly picked out my boat and held me, half blinded. The long, growling blast of the siren was as queerly, then scarily, intimate as the cough of a stranger in one's bedroom. Panicking, I swung the head of the boat and drove it at full tilt. Any direction would do—just not, please not, into the tow. It went past, thirty yards off, a lone towboat without its barges. Its balconied side and back were lit up like a Christmas tree, but from the front it had been as black as the surrounding river. Its high wake caught me broadside; I had miscalculated the direction it would come from; and as I hung in the trough, the boat rolled and the left-hand gunwale began to gouge cleanly into the side of the wave. I was shin deep in water before I could swing the front of the boat around and ride out the swell.

I found myself blubbering with shock. Had the towboat been pushing a barge fleet, I would be dead now, or drowning, unconscious, under its screws. I had lost all sense of the shape of the river. I didn't know where the shore was; I didn't know up from down. The tow's lights had left the river even darker than it had been before. I saw one faint glimmer, and what looked like the distant outline of a tree, but I was frightened that it would turn into another tow, its leading barges a black wedge waiting to suck me under. I drove away from it, then around it, then cautiously approached it. It was an electric light on a pole. Under it, a jonboat, piled with hoop nets, was drawn up on the sand.

There was a house behind, a wooden cabin on stilts, its timbers warped and peeling away in a tangle of frayed ends. The window of its queasy-looking front room was lit up. I shouted "Help!" and "Excuse me!" and "Hello!": if the river was thick with invisible tows, the land might well be full of German shepherd dogs and householders with twenty-gauges. No one came to the window. No dog barked. I climbed a steep companionway that led to the door at the side of the house and knocked on the glass. I could see the people inside: two elderly women and a man. They all appeared to be knitting. They took no notice of me, but went on drawing out hanks and threads. I had to bang and shout before the old man got up stiffly, took a shotgun from a cupboard, and came to the door. We faced each other through the glass panel—the man staring, deaf, pointing his gun at my chest while I yelled that I was traveling down the river, I was English, I had run into trouble, I needed help.

"He says he's from England. He's been on the river. He's asking for help," said one of the women in an ordinary conversational voice, her hands full of yarn.

"What you want me to do with him?" said the man.

"Let him in, I guess. But keep that gun on him."

When they saw the miserable figure I was cutting, they were immediately kind, bringing coffee and cookies to this stammering intruder with his peculiar accent. They were not knitting; they were trying to untangle a knotted fishing line. They had been at it nearly all afternoon. The line had a thousand hooks, spaced at intervals of a foot or two, and it looked as if the hooks had gone into a rabbitlike orgy of interbreeding.

"We ain't got but the one other line, and we live off what we can catch; so you can see how it is. . . ." the woman said. "We got to get it out by morning."

I tried to help, but I wasn't of much use. My hands were too shaky to disentangle anything from anything. I explained what had happened; my words were reported back to the old man at second hand.

"I don't care too much to be out on the river at night," he said; "and I lived on it all my life."

The second woman had said nothing since I'd arrived. "He won't get no cab to come out here." She didn't look up from her lapful of raveled line.

Mrs. Lupus—I learned her name later—said, "I can run him into Burlington. . . ."

I was grateful, and apologetic. I asked if I could pay her the price of the cab fare.

"I wouldn't be beholden to you, mister. You give me what it costs for the gas, and that's that."

In her station wagon, driving up a twisty dirt road through the trees, Mrs. Lupus talked. She seemed glad to be able to make a list of her troubles to a stranger. She spoke flatly, staring ahead through the windshield.

"We lost our only son last year, mister. He'd just gotten his own auto-repair shop. His daddy and me, we'd put our savings together to help him buy it. First week, he was lying under a car on the ramp . . . it fell on him. He was dead before they got him to the hospital. It almost killed my husband, Billy's death. Six weeks after, he had a stroke. Then my hip went. We made the down payment on a trailer home for our retirement. There was a gas leakage. It blew up. There wasn't nothing of it left after the explosion."

We joined the traffic on the highway. Mrs. Lupus said, "That's the way life is for us, just now. Ain't so good."

There was nothing to say. I passed her a cigarette.

"We get by," Mrs. Lupus said.

Every night it was her job to bait the hooks on their two fishing lines. They had one of five hundred hooks and one of a thousand. At six in the morning, Mr. Lupus drove to the foot of Big Rush Island in his jonboat, hauled in the night's catch and laid the other line. They sold the fish to a merchant in Burlington who didn't ask them their names. In return for this anonymity, they got a bad price, but they weren't licensed as professional fishermen, and any declaration of their earnings would have threatened Mrs. Lupus' unemployment pay of $140 a month, their only other income now.

When she dropped me at the railroad hotel, I tried to pretend that her fishy-smelling car had gotten roughly two miles to the gallon. She passed me back five of the seven dollars I gave her. "I wouldn't be beholden," she said. "Besides, it does you good to talk sometimes, you know?"

Too tired to wash or eat, I fell in a heap on the hotel bed in my clothes. It was barely nine o'clock, but I felt that I'd been without sleep for days. Since leaving Muscatine, I had been attacked by vultures, faced a storm, been nearly drowned in the dark, and held at gunpoint. I hadn't bargained for half such an adventurous life. I ached to be able to talk myself down from these jittery heights with a friend. I called Judith's number in Muscatine. Her roommate answered. Judith was out. She didn't know when she'd be back. Late, she guessed. No, I said, it didn't matter; I'd call her up some other day.

Fields of late wheat had been combed back and flattened by the high winds. The Burlington taxi driver had been a farm worker himself once and looked aggrievedly out on the ruined harvest. "See that? Only use for it now is maybe the guy can turn his hogs loose in it. Look at it. Ain't it a goddamn shame?"

We got lost on the dirt tracks that crisscrossed the land close to the river. The driver told me how he had turned to the Bible. "Something was wrong with my life. I didn't have to be a genius to figure that out. My nerves was all shot to pieces. I wasn't sleeping good. It wasn't right. So I went to the Book."

"The New Testament?"

"No. I been reading about Moses. How he led the Israelites out of Egypt."

"I'm surprised. I'd have thought you'd go to the Gospels."

"There's something in them old stories. I don't know what it is. It kind of sorts out your perspective. Now I sleep at night. Ain't had a drop of liquor for, oh, must be a coupla months now. Look—steady hands. . . ."

We went bumping down through the trees.

"Them Israelites . . ." he shook his head and chuckled. "Hell, they still got *their* problems over there. And it's all in the Book. Every word. If you read it right."

I could see the Lupuses' house on its tall stilts in a clearing. In the night, someone had dragged my boat high up on the shore for safety. I pointed it out to the driver.

"You going all the way down the river in that? You *need* a Bible. You could run into more trouble than all them Israelites put together." He helped me load up, clucking over the smallness of the boat. "God bless you, and have a good trip, now!" he shouted as he turned his car around and headed back up the hill.

I found Mrs. Lupus in a tumbledown shed in her yard. She was cleaning catfish with a kitchen knife and laying them out in fruit crates.

"How was it this morning?"

"Just sixty-three fish. None of them's big ones, neither." She smiled, her face taut with tiredness. "Ain't so good. . . ."

"You got your line untangled."

"Yeah. Just about. We was up at it till after three. But it's laying out there now. Maybe tonight we'll come lucky."

"I hope so. You deserve to."

She pulled the innards out of another fish and dropped them in the tin bucket of floating guts. "What you get ain't necessarily what you deserve." She laughed sadly. The catfish heads with their gummy eyes and limp whiskers looked as if they had escaped from a *Purgatorio* by Hieronymus Bosch; their presence was calculated to lower the highest spirit. "Don't you ever go out on the river at night again, mister. There's been too many tragedies. You know what they say about the Mississippi . . . he never lets go of a man with his clothes on. That's a true saying."

I heaved at the bow of the boat and joggled it through the soft sand into the water. The dangerous glitter of the waves, the faces of the dead fish and the warnings of Mrs. Lupus and the cabdriver made my launching more solemn than usual. That morning, I felt as if I were pushing off into the Acheron. All I needed was an obol in my mouth and an old man with a ragged beard to see to the business of navigation.

With the wind in the northwest, the swell was running with the current. The humps of the waves were a comfortable distance apart, and motoring at half speed, I could keep the boat balanced on the same crest for minutes at a time. I let the city of Burlington slide by: a loss that I felt I could afford. I had read somewhere that it was famous as the place where the Westinghouse air brake had been perfected. It seemed a doleful and unalluring reason for celebrity.

Below Burlington the Mississippi divided into two. The channel kept to the Iowa side, protected from the sprawl of the rest of the river by a wooded island eleven miles long. It was like a sunny day on the Thames, with the banks reassuringly close, the water prettily scalloped by the wind, and time to watch the herons and pack a corncob pipe with Captain Black. I should have known by now. These holiday moments were designed by the river to lull one into a sense of false security: they were an inevitable prelude to some new and alarming aspect of the Mississippi's character.

The long island petered out into a trickle of sandbars. The channel swung suddenly westward. Where there had been less than half a mile from shore to shore there was now a mile and a half of roughening water, with the wind blowing hard across the line of the current. I tacked from side to side along the channel. The boat bucked, slopped, and took on plumes of drenching spray over the bow. Seeing a tow ahead, I ran for shelter to a bunch of little islands on the Illinois side.

I hadn't checked the chart. I was afloat over a stump field submerged under just a few inches of water. As a roller sucked the river away, it exposed the bed of black-buttery peat, the sawed-off boles like bad teeth, and the boat grounded with a groan and a bang, the motor stalling as it hit a root. The next wave came in over the stern and carried me fifty yards on, bumping over the stumps. I shipped the motor and tried to row in to shore, but nothing I could do with the oars had much effect against the combined force of wind and waves. I landed, dismally, on a mud patch under a dead tree.

The wake of the tow, as it came in over the stump field, showed that there was a way out. Its troughs bared the rotten forest floor and revealed a narrow gully of deep water running out from a bay to my left. The wake picked up my boat and slammed it down on the mud. When the last roller had washed into the trees, I punted my way to the gully, using the crests of the waves to lift the boat while I made a foot or two of ground at a time. Back in the channel, the breakers seemed steeper than they'd been before. I clung to the lee of Grape Island on the Iowa bank, running at full speed to keep the bow of the boat as clear of the waves as it would go. It was a clanking, scary ride. I was frightened of popping a rivet as the booming hull hit the whitecaps as if they were blocks of concrete. I could see a white grain elevator across the river. . . . Dallas City . . . a harbor . . . a warm bar . . . hot Scotch and water . . . a quiet, well-lighted corner in which to settle over Sterne's *A Sentimental Journey*. Between these comforts and me, though, there was the obstacle of two miles of seething Mississippi water. The waves were running diagonally, across and down the stream; if I turned the boat now, they should take me straight in to Dallas City. I lurched along with them, tuning the motor to their speed. In mid-channel, they were running four to five feet high; beyond, they were as tall as I. So long as I didn't allow the boat to drift broadside to them, they were perfectly safe. All I had to do was keep going in their direction, just a fraction more quickly than they were moving themselves. I was surprised by the excitement of it, this lolloping thrust forward with the rollers crowding at my back and the line of ragged surf stretching out on either side for as far as I could see. The boat was fitting snugly into the weather. As I rode with the wind, the air felt still, and the shoulder of the wave a happy perch from which to watch Dallas City come steadily forward across the river like a steamship.

"City" was a courtesy title. The grain elevator dwarfed everything else in town. A trail of frame houses was bunched around the railroad track, and when a long haul of freight cars came through on the Atchison, Topeka and Santa Fe line, the engineer would be way up north in

Lomax while his brakeman would be back in Pontoosuc; Dallas City was just a dozen carloads of corn and phosphates somewhere in the middle. It had a diner with steamed-up windows, a derelict flophouse and a one-story bar on the waterfront next to the ruined button factory. A historical marker announced that Abraham Lincoln had made a speech in Dallas City on October 23, 1858, and it looked as if nothing much of any interest had happened there since. My own arrival caused an enormous stir among the town's population of chained dogs, and I could hear the news of my visit being whooped and growled from yard to yard; but the enthusiasm of the dogs was balanced out by the profound indifference of the people. In the bar, three wordless fat men in plaid jackets stared at the river. The woman bartender stared at *As the World Turns* on the TV.

"It's getting rough as hell on the river," I said. No one turned his head. One man silently pushed his glass forward for a refill of beer.

"Can you do a whiskey and hot water?" I asked the bartender.

"Ain't no hot water," she said, her eyes on the screen.

"Well, make it a whiskey and ordinary water, then, please."

She dumped three ice cubes into a tumbler with an automatic hand. I gave up my attempt to get on with Dallas City and dug my copy of Laurence Sterne out of my bag. It was a nice eighteenth-century edition, with *f*'s for *s*'s, in a chipped calf binding, which I had once looted from my father's library and left unread for years. In London I had packed *A Sentimental Journey* on the strength of its title. I now treated it like a Gideon Bible, letting it fall open where it would. IN THE STREET. CALAIS.

I pity the man who can travel from *Dan* to *Beerfheba,* and cry, 'Tis all barren—and fo it is; and fo is all the world to him, who will not cultivate the fruits it offers. I declare, faid I, clapping my hands cheerily together, that was I in a defert, I would find out wherewith in it to call forth my affections—If I could not do better, I would faften them upon fome fweet myrtle, or feek fome melancholy cyprefs to connect myfelf to—I would court their fhade, and greet them kindly for their protection—I would cut my name upon them, and fwear they were the lovelieft trees throughout the defert: if their leaves wither'd, I would teach myfelf to mourn, and when they rejoiced, I would rejoice along with them.

The learned SMELFUNGUS travelled from Boulogne to Paris—from Paris to Rome—and fo on—but he fet out with the fpleen and jaundice, and every object he pafs'd by was difcoloured or diftorted—He wrote an account of them, but 'twas nothing but the account of his miferable feelings.

Oh, fweet myrtle. Oh, melancholy cyprefs. I must not turn into a learned Smelfungus. I did feel, though, that all of Mr. Yorick's capacity for boundless curiosity and high humor would have been stretched by the bar in Dallas City. Looking for something to fasten my affections on, I fastened them on the river. Myrtles were native to Florida, and there were no true cypresses this side of the Rockies. There were some willows out on Dallas Island, swirling from side to side and touching their toes like gymnasts, but they couldn't match the dazzling motions of the water. Torn and furrowed, it was like streaky jade. It frothed on the shore in a long rime of cotton candy and shook the few still-standing piles of a smashed jetty. Thick white smoke from a factory on the Iowa bank was flattened by the wind and blown low over the river.

"What's that place over there where the smoke's coming from?"

"Huh?"

"Over there. The factory . . ."

"First Miss."

"Yes, but what does it do?"

The man stared out the window. He'd answered one question. He was damned if he could be bothered to answer two. The next man along the bar growled, "Makes nitrogen."

"Oh. Thanks."

"You're welcome."

I didn't feel it. I went back to Sterne.

> The man who either difdains or fears to walk up a dark entry, may be an excellent good man, and fit for a hundred things; but he will not do to make a good fentimental traveller.

The wind had eased a little during the afternoon. It was only eight miles downstream to Fort Madison, Iowa, where there should be a proper hotel and, with luck, some less surly company. I pushed the boat out into the swell. The waves were much bigger than they had looked from the bar window, and I couldn't keep a steady course through them. For half a mile I flopped about, losing steerage and taking in water over the gunwales. Then I put ashore at a little pier that ran out from the trees.

"Hey! That's my landing there!"

He was Charon to the life. His scraggy gray beard, wrinkled face and soft wheeze all typecast him for the part of the Stygian boatman. He wore a bran-new ten-gallon hat, and the hat was everything that he was not. It curled, swelled and billowed, while he was small, stiff and frail, with matchstick wrists and spindly legs, cruelly outlined by the wind which had pasted the trousers of his dungarees around his crab-apple kneecaps.

I explained how the weather had forced me off the river. As soon as he heard my accent, his wheeze loudened with excitement. Well, hell and goddamn! He'd been to England himself in World War Two. Devonport. Southampton. Bournemouth. He named them carefully. In November 1944—or was it October? he wasn't sure on that point— he had seen a show at the Windmill Theatre, London.

"Now you got me thinking. You got plans for this evening? Can you eat corn bread and beans? Can you sleep in a trailer?"

His name was Wayne Oakman, proprietor and sole hand of Oakman Enterprises. From his stilt house on the shore he dabbled in every Enterprise that took his fancy. He was a commercial fisherman. His shed was festooned with lines, gill nets, seines and traps. He had an old mimeograph machine on which he ran off handbills for the local stores. He dealt in junked pickups, old trailer homes, bits of inscrutable farm machinery covered in weeds, twenty-dollar TV sets and gas cookers which had field mice nesting in their ovens. He pointed at the gas station beyond the railroad tracks. "I'm buying that up, too. I always did want a garage."

He had the glittery, acquisitive eyes of the manic collector. Tonight, he had collected me. He took me to his house to show his latest *objet trouvé* to his wife. "Hey, Ida Belle! Come out of that kitchen and see what I found! Look: an Englishman."

I could see that Mrs. Oakman had had a lot of practice in admiring Mr. Oakman's finds. She was used to plows, arrowheads, dead polecats, electrical generators, bulk lots of barbed wire, rattlesnake skins. She wasn't sure into which category I fell. "Well . . . that's . . . interesting," she said.

I had never yet met anyone whose obsession with the river so far exceeded mine. Wayne Oakman was an enslaved courtier of the Mississippi. The front of his spruce frame house was a long window, so that the water seemed to fill the rooms and color the walls. You could hear it lapping on the beach under our feet. Wayne's old basket chair was placed next to the glass so that he could watch the current uncoiling downstream on another westward dogleg. He was inseparable from the water. When he was out of the room, Ida Belle shook her head over her husband's hazardous extramarital affair with the Mississippi. In the last couple of years, he had had two major operations. One of them had left him temporarily paralyzed in his legs. He suffered from diabetes. He had emphysema. None of this had stopped him. No sooner was he out of the hospital than he had gone ice fishing in January.

Stumbling on his weakened legs, he had fallen through the hole in the river. It was a miracle that he hadn't drowned. Somehow he had managed to hold on to the edge of the ice while the current swept his body back, and he'd been rescued by a neighbor with a long ladder. As soon as spring came, he had decided to make a long voyage south in his leaky fourteen-foot jonboat.

Wayne came back into the room, gulls crying in his chest.

"I was telling him about your river trip. . . ."

It was his odyssey. In the war, he had fought in Europe and in the Pacific, but his journey down the river was much the most exciting piece of traveling he had done in his life. He got out his charts and notebook, and laid them out on the floor. He showed me the narrow chutes where he'd seen the banks whistling past his ears as fast as a pair of railway trains, the slough where he had been swamped by a tow, the sandbars on which he'd been marooned, the bends where his boat had been sent spinning by whirlpools and eddies.

"Once you get down by St. Louis, gosh, this river, she's something else. Wide? I'm telling you . . . it's wide like you never seen. And the tows . . . they got tows down there so big you ain't seen nothing like it. The wakes, they come right up, big screw wakes that'll throw you around all over the river, you better believe it. And the current there . . . *fast?* Hell, it just kind of whips you along with it; you don't know you're moving, it's going so fast. And when it comes up against something, it blows up in a kind of big, whirling boil that'll take a hold of you and you can feel it sucking at you, trying to pull you right around and under."

The river he was describing was a place in a legend, and Wayne was beginning to frighten me with this, his favorite story. It was all very well for him: his trip was over; it lay in a mythological past. Mine, though, was still ahead and wide open.

Wayne had made Cape Girardeau, Missouri, 350 miles downriver. The leak in his boat had worsened steadily, and he'd had to keep on bailing himself out with a bucket. His outboard motor, with half the horsepower of mine, had not been able to cope safely with the strong current of the lower river. Ida Belle, who followed him down by car, persuaded him to give up. He was still sad that he hadn't gone farther. We knelt over the charts showing the junction with the Ohio, the huge loops above Memphis, Sunflower Cut-Off, Scrubgrass Bend, Opossum Chute . . . "Gosh," Wayne said, "you know, one day I'm going to do just what you're doing. I'm going to go all the way. Too bad I had that leak. Gosh, I was sore."

We sat up at the table. The foam on the crests of the black water was speckled with moonlight. The river gurgled on the shore beneath us.

"You have the sort of house I dream of living in," I said.

"I had my eye on this place for years," Wayne said. "I remember it when I was a little kid. Used to belong to a doctor's wife. Hell, she turned it into a *re*-sort. She used to lay on a beach fair every year. Oh, she'd get two, three thousand people down here. There was buggies parked all the way up the road. They had all kinds of things. They had horseshoe pitching . . . baptisms . . ."

"Baptisms?"

"Yeah, baptisms and all *kind* of things."

"You mean they baptized people in the river?"

"Hundreds and thousands of them. It was like the River Jordan. The preacher, he'd wade right out there, and the folks was all waiting in line, and he'd dunk them under, one by one, baptizing them in the name of the Lord. Oh, they had all kind of things at them beach fairs."

I was digging into the strong, sweet-tasting flesh of a catfish.

"Did you catch this?"

"Yeah, that was off of one of my trot lines, a coupla days back."

"What bait do you use?"

"Cats . . . they'll eat just about anything you can think of. Oh, I use congealed blood . . . that's a real good bait for cats . . . meat . . . worms . . . chopped snake. They love a piece of rattlesnake. Then for carp, there's corn and doughballs. You get good money for carp, now. They all go up to Chicago, where the Jew-people eat them. Them Jews, they reckon carp a real delicacy."

"I wouldn't eat no carp," Ida Belle said, wrinkling with disgust at the thought.

"Ah," said Wayne, sniffing the beginning of a philosophical debate, "but if you was a Jew-person, you wouldn't eat no pig. We don't eat no carp, they don't eat no pig; it works out just the same, when you get down to it."

"It ain't the same thing at all. Carp don't taste good. Pig do."

"But for the Jew-people, it's all the other way around."

"But I ain't *Jewish*," Ida Belle said, finishing the argument with an unassailable stroke of logic.

I slept in a prettily furnished trailer home which was parked on its own grass lot across the track. It was another of Wayne's enterprises. In the summer it earned its keep from weekending fishermen. Now its thin walls rattled in the wind. It felt fragile, cold and lonely. All the lights of Dallas City were out. A railway train ambled slowly through town, rousing the dogs for a few minutes. Then there was nothing except for the ragged gusting of the wind.

I doubt if Wayne had ever read Emerson, but Emerson, I thought, would have warmed to Oakman Enterprises. It was a small empire of sturdy self-reliance. Independent, shrunken, chipper, Wayne was an enviably happy man. Captivated by the Mississippi, he had built himself a splendidly various life around the river. He was no one's hired man, unless the river itself could count as his employer. After dinner, he'd taken me to see the barn-sized shed that was his headquarters. It was crammed with treasures. Nets, guns, snares, radio sets, refrigerators, a player piano whose insides had been wrecked in a flood, a wooden boat, a stuffed squirrel with a pointy-toothed grin exactly like Wayne's own . . . He pottered contentedly in this trove of precious junk. "You like it in here?" he had asked. "This is where I get my ideas for my enterprises. See? I can fish right out the door here." And he had opened the door on the river, wheezing with pleasure at the simple, indestructible magic of the thing.

By dawn, the wind had eased off to a murmur. The surface of the river smoked, the water hidden under twists and pillars of mist. Ida Belle was cooking eggs and hash-browns for breakfast, and Wayne was in his basket chair, scanning the long window like a painting.

"You got a good hour or two yet. Then that wind'll be back. They were forecasting eighteen to twenty on the radio."

The commercial fishermen were coming in. One boat slid by under the window, close enough for me to see the live catfish squirming in tubs in its bow. The boatman, huddled in his camouflage parka, saluted us as he went past. Wayne had already weighed the man's catch in his head. "Duane there, he's got better than two hundred pounds. Maybe two fifty."

As the sun rose, the water began to twitch and ripple. Lazy drafts of wind were coming out of the southwest, peeling the mist off the river. The Oakmans came to the landing to see me off.

"There's wing dams down there," Wayne said. "You go right on out till you hit the main channel, then it's just, oh, around twenty blocks, I guess, to the bridge at Fort Madison." I was delighted by this way of measuring distance over open water. What to me was breadth and sweep and emptiness was really as mapped as a grid city. I waved goodbye. I promised to write. I motored four blocks, made a left, and counted down the streets in the river.

At each new block, the wind freshened in my face. By Fort Madison, the boat was bucking hard on the choppy little waves, and the wide pool around Nauvoo Bend was ribbed with shreds of white. It looked like a bad place to be caught in a storm. I put in at a marina so that I could watch the weather and wait for the right time to make the seven-mile run into Nauvoo. A small sailboat had gone ahead of me, and we tied up next to each other. The man and the woman, both in their twenties, looked cold, sleepless and rather dirty. They were looking for a warm place that served coffee. I joined them.

The man did all the talking, while the girl rubbed her hands miserably against each other and stamped up and down in her boots. They were bound for New Orleans. Already they were more than two weeks behind time. Their homemade model of a Boston Dory was not taking well to the Mississippi. They had set off from Madison, Wisconsin, and sailed down the Wisconsin River to below Prairie du Chien, where they had entered the main river. First they'd been becalmed, then stormbound. They had spent days laying up in creeks waiting for the wind to drop. They had a tiny eggbeater of a motor, sufficient only to drive them into and out of locks. In a toneless voice, the man listed their adventures like a talking ship's log. Sunday, they'd run aground. Monday, they'd been swamped by a tow. Tuesday, they'd capsized and lost some gear from the cockpit. Wednesday, their anchor had dragged, and they'd run aground again. Thursday . . . but I didn't listen to Thursday. I was thinking that the man bore an uncanny resemblance to the learned Smelfungus.

"Why are you making the trip?" I asked.

"For the American people."

"Oh . . . yes?"

He wanted to prove something, he said, and went into a grave recitation of slogans about Our Generation, Self-Sufficiency, Initiative and Conservation. *Conservation?* I didn't see where that came into it. Wind power, said the man; it was the utilization of a natural resource. Oh, I said; you mean sailing? Yes, he said; he visualized the sailboat as a symbol of the posttechnological future.

"You're not making the trip sound very much fun."

"So why are *you* going down the river?"

"I'm having a sort of love affair with it, I suppose."

We stared at each other over our coffees. At last we occupied a common ground. Our expressions, of total incomprehension and skepticism of the other's motive, were identical. We must have looked like twins.

The couple went up the hill into town to buy groceries. They might have been mourners following a cortege. I returned to the harbor and went snooping over their boat. It was a lovely piece of pure craftsmanship, as slim as a pickerel, with every joint in its timber perfectly cut and glued. It must have taken years of slow, spare-time labor; of patient fitting, sanding-down, varnishing, rigging. It seemed sad, in a peculiarly American way, that anyone should build a boat as beautiful as this, launch it on a long, absorbing voyage, then swamp it with such a dreary cargo of fashionable abstractions. All the grace of the thing itself had been submerged under these abstractions; yet without them, the boat would never have been built, the trip never embarked on. Poor boat. It was in its way a classic victim of the American language and its fatal preference for theories, principles, concepts over mere material objects and their intractable thinginess.

No one, though, would ever convert this river into an abstraction. Humped and grizzled in the wind, it was too rough to make a safe crossing to Nauvoo. I squatted on the harbor wall, looking across the water to the broad green bluff where the town was. I already knew a little of Nauvoo. It had started as a town named Commerce—a scatter of rough cabins overlooking the river. Then, in 1839, Joseph Smith had led his Mormon followers up here from Missouri. He had knelt down on the bluff and said, "I name this place 'Nauvoo,' which is a word from the ancient Hebrew meaning 'the most beautiful.' " Snide persons, including Smith's best-known biographer, have said that it was lucky that no one had a Hebrew dictionary handy at the time. "Nauvoo," they said, didn't exist in Hebrew or, for that matter, in any other language. In fact, Smith was very close to the mark. In Isaiah, Chapter 52, when the Old Testament prophet writes, 'How beautiful upon the mountains are the feet of him that bringeth good tidings,' he uses the word *na'vu,* the plural form of *na'vah.* Smith was right on the second count, too, as I could see from my perch over the river: the wooded hill of Nauvoo was a beautiful place, far too pretty to be lumbered with the name of Commerce.

It was afternoon before the Mississippi quieted and I made my way around to the landing at Nauvoo, hugging the Illinois shore. The town was not a town at all; it was a *mise-en-scène* in which every log, brick and butter pat of Grecian stucco betrayed the hand and eye of some ghostly theatrical director. The director had caused the sun to fall just so. It used the platinum top of the river as a reflector. It made the trees throw long shadows up a slope of green baize. It picked out the blacksmith's shop and the antique bakery. It lit the fronts of the Victorian houses, each standing on its own four-acre block like a manor with a ha-ha and a park. It fell, with tasteful softness, on the horse-drawn buggies that were ferrying tourists up and down the immaculately graveled streets. I could have sworn that their wheels were going backward, in stroboscopic reverse, like wagon wheels in movies. Lugging my bags uphill, I would not have been surprised to hear a voice shouting at me to get out of shot. I was a trespasser; too real, sweaty and imperfect for this world of cunning historical artifice.

The air felt colder. It had the chill of expensive reverence in it. For Nauvoo hadn't been restored, like Galena, in faddish decorator's chic; it was a holy place, a giant glass reliquary of saints' bones and sandals. Joseph Smith and his brother Hyrum had been martyred here, killed by a lynch mob outside the Hancock County Jail, and the Mormons had fled west to Utah and the New Jerusalem of Salt Lake City. They had returned to Nauvoo to buy it up lot by lot and rebuild it as a pilgrims' shrine. It was a place to bow one's head in and talk in whispers. Here was Heber Kimball's house, there Brigham Young's. In Mormon terms, it was much like being able to stroll around Saint Luke's doctor's examining room or Saint Matthew's tax office.

The hotel at the top of the town was of a piece with all this solemn antiquity. Its bar was hushed and timbered. Nibbling at Nauvoo blue cheese, drinking sweet oily wine from the Nauvoo vineyard, feeling uneasily torn between the roles of postulant and tourist, I tried to read the Book of Mormon. It was tough going. The angel Moroni's gold plates must have weighed a ton, since Smith's "translation" of them ran to more than a quarter of a million words. A good half of these seemed to be either *ye, yea, behold* or *it came to pass*. The whole thing was got up in a repetitive pastiche of William Tyndale's sixteenth-century ceremonial English. Indeed, a lot of familiar chunks of the Old Testament in the Authorized Version had found their way intact into Smith's book.

There was much begetting, travailing and tribulation, and the Israelites had been given the sort of names that are universally dreaded by society hostesses. Trying to remember who was who among Teancum and Morianton and Amalickiah and Riplakish and Zemnarihah and Seezoram and Pagag and Nephihah made my head ache. Yet somewhere in the fog there was a story to be picked out. It was a Western. A mass of hopeful immigrants assembled on the shore of the Eastern world; a great ocean was crossed, and the Lord guided the homesteaders on their trek across the promised land of America where the new Zion was to be built according to prophecy.

I liked the boats in which Jared and his brethren made their transatlantic passage:

> They were built after a manner that they were exceeding tight, even that they would hold water like unto a dish; and the bottom thereof was tight like unto a dish; and the ends thereof were peaked; and the top thereof was tight like unto a dish; and the

length thereof was the length of a tree; and the door thereof, when it was shut, was tight like unto a dish.

These vessels sounded like useful craft for the Mississippi. The migrants were far less troubled by big waves than I was myself:

> It came to pass that they were many times buried in the depths of the sea, because of the mountain waves which broke upon them, and also the great and terrible tempests which were caused by the fierceness of the wind.
>
> And it came to pass that when they were buried in the deep there was no water that could hurt them, their vessels being tight like unto a dish, and also they were tight like unto the ark of Noah; therefore when they were encompassed about by many waters they did cry unto the Lord, and he did bring them forth again unto the top of the waters.
>
> And it came to pass that the wind did never cease to blow towards the promised land. . . .

I was engrossed by the book. It was the archetypal American epic. The equation of America with the new Zion had always been an ingredient in the religion of the country. The very first extended narrative of American history, William Bradford's *History of Plimoth Plantation,* used the metaphor; and it was continually harped on by the Puritan founding fathers. Emma Lazarus, in the famous verse which was put up on the Statue of Liberty, "Give me your tired, your poor . . ." recast the words of Isaiah when he described the promised land: "O thou afflicted, tossed with tempest, and not comforted, behold . . ." The Baptists of Andalusia had sung hymns that drew on the powerful analogy between frontiersmen and the biblical Israelites. But the equation had always been in the form of analogy or metaphor. The Book of Mormon asserted it as literal fact. The frontiersmen, the immigrants and sodbusters, *were* the lost tribes of Israel. America *was* the land of Zion. The angel Moroni's gold plates told the classic American story of travel, settlement and salvation. At the very least, the Book of Mormon deserves a place in nineteenth-century American literature, somewhere between De Tocqueville and the Horatio Alger books.

By morning I was practically a candidate for conversion. As a bona fide traveler in a boat that was exceeding tight like unto a dish, I felt that I had a privileged intimacy with the experience on which the Book of Mormon had been based. I gulped a hasty breakfast, walked across the bluff to the Visitors Center, and put myself in the hands of

Elder Tiptree, who was conducting a party of middle-aged women around the essentials of the story and the faith.

My own eagerness dimmed a little at the sight and sound of Elder Tiptree. He was a young man with the stoop and the weak, synthetic smile of Uriah Heep. He wrung his manicured hands together as he talked. He spoke too loudly, too slowly and too expressively, making a meal of every consonant and vowel, his voice going up and down like a two-tone doorbell. He sounded as if he were addressing a class of deaf infants, while at the same time he managed to suggest that he was very, very 'umble.

We processed around a gallery of paintings of the boyhood and revelation of Joseph Smith. They had been executed by an imitator of Norman Rockwell and showed the young Joseph going about his father's business in Upper New York State; if you looked at the child with one eye, he was Tom Sawyer, but if you looked at him with the other he was Jesus Christ. I found this configuration unsettling, and caught a warning coldness in the eye of Elder Tiptree when it fell on me. He had clearly marked me out as one of the rowdy kids in the back row. My tendency to behave with improper giggliness was exacerbated by an interesting speech habit of Elder Tiptree's which, when noticed once, became an object of obsessive attention. His preferred style of diction was that of the Book of Mormon itself—sonorous, hortatory and pseudo-archaic. However, he hadn't mastered the trick of ending his sentences. They would drift into a trail of dots, then finish on a limp "and such." I waited for these "and suches" to come up and mouthed them silently in sync with Elder Tiptree.

". . . then the young Joseph Smith did go out into the wilderness beyond Manchester, New York, and for three days and three nights he did meditate, he did fast, he did make prayers unto the Lord . . . *and such.*" The temptation laid in my way was terrible. I succumbed.

We got on to the business of the gold plates.

"Excuse me," I said, "but what exactly happened to the plates after Joseph Smith had translated them?"

"The angel Moroni received them unto himself," said Elder Tiptree. "I welcome your questions."

"It makes things more interesting, doesn't it—if you have questions?" said the woman next to me. She had evidently sensed that a certain *froideur* had crept into the relationship between Elder Tiptree and me, and was trying to smooth things over.

"Yes," said Elder Tiptree, smiling below his nose and frosting around his eyes; "it does."

We moved on. The Book of Mormon had been prophesied by Eze-kiel, said Elder Tiptree. Did we remember the passage where the Lord divided the world between the stick of Judah and the stick of Joseph? Now, in those olden days, they didn't have books with covers and pages like we have today; they had scrolls. There was a·picture of a scroll to prove it, and Elder Tiptree showed us how the scroll was wound around a wooden cylinder—or *stick*.

"In the ancient Hebrew, we learn that the word for 'book' wasn't book, it was 'stick,' because all *their* books, unlike ours today, were rolled up on sticks. Okay? So we can now read, not the *stick* of Judah and the *stick* of Joseph, but the *book* of Judah and the *book* of Joseph." Elder Tiptree looked as if he'd just explained the principle of the double helix. "And the book of Judah is what we know as the Bible, while the book of Joseph . . ."

I could see what was coming. "Don't you think that the word 'stick' might just mean 'branch,' as in branches of a family? Wasn't it the family of Judah and the family of Joseph?"

"You ask any distinguished scholar of Hebrew," said Elder Tiptree. "Are you a scholar of Hebrew?"

"No, but I'll try and find one," I said. I did. He identified *na'vu* for me, but could find no trace of books or scrolls ever having been called "sticks" in Hebrew.

We progressed to less contentious things and the story of the persecu-tion of the Mormons in the United States, of how they were hounded from Missouri and led to Nauvoo. It was a tale of brute intolerance lightened at regular intervals by divine intervention.

"To that first harvest here in Nauvoo, there came a great plague of crickets and grasshoppers and such. The people fell into a state of lamentation. They saw their crops destroyed and feared that famine would come upon them and upon their children. They prayed unto God, and a miracle occurred. God sent flock upon flock of sea gulls to Nauvoo, and the sea gulls came down and devoured the crickets and the grasshoppers. And the people gave thanks unto the Lord, for He had delivered them."

We were told how, when the Mormons were forced to leave Nauvoo, God had frozen over the waters of the Mississippi for three days and three nights, so that the people could cross with their wagons into Iowa and move on west. It was, said Elder Tiptree, exactly like the parting of the Red Sea for the children of Israel. I kept to myself my suspicion that the river was fairly often frozen over in February, the month when the Mormons made their flight. But Elder Tiptree was wedded to a world of prophecies and miracles. He stood beside an aerial photograph of Salt Lake City.

"And now we see how Brigham Young prophesied the coming of the automobile. Look at these streets, laid out by Brigham Young many decades before the invention of the first internal-combustion engine. You see how wide they are? When Brigham Young laid out that plan, guided by the Lord, he made provision for a median strip, as you see here. And not only that. Look closely at the picture. Here he arranged a left-turn lane. Imagine that! Forty years before the world's first automobile, a median strip *and* a left-turn lane! So the street plan of Salt Lake City was a prophecy. Okay?" He fixed me. I nodded. Okay.

It was a perfect day for moving on. While the Pope, this time in Washington, was conducting his last open-air Mass in the United States, I slipped my moorings and launched on a long southerly swing of calm water. There wasn't a wing dam marked on the chart; the sky was empty, the river a deep reflective blue. I reckoned that Elder Tiptree was as near to churchgoing as I need come this Sunday. If the weather held, I could catch up on a lot of lost miles.

The day belonged to Pope John Paul. He was in all the papers. His American journey had been more like the ride of Caesar to the Capitol in a Roman triumph, gilded, garlanded and drawn by white horses, than a round of parochial visits by a priest. I had watched him on television, and seen him as a twinkling demagogue. He looked frail, hardly strong enough to take the weight of his gloriously colored robes, but he had the populist genius of a latter-day Huey Long. In the course of a week, a whole industry of memorial junk had grown up around him: there were bumper stickers for the Pope, flags to wave for him, lapel buttons to announce that their wearers loved him. I had listened to hardened drunks in bars going lachrymose as they said that the Pope . . . that guy . . . he told it like it was. And I had learned, without enthusiasm, how to tell it like it is: no contraception; no abortion; no sex outside marriage; no ordination of women; no divorce; no relaxation of the vow of priestly celibacy. *No, no, no, no, no, no.* This recitation of blank prohibitions seemed to me to be narrow and complacent. Yet this, in its present mood, was exactly what America wanted to hear. Wherever the Pope went there had been a few protesting feminists; they had been shouted down by brigades and battalions of "pro-life" campaigners. The Pope had arrived in the United States at a moment when the President of the country was being jeered at as a nervous nincompoop. The week before, President Carter, out fishing, had been "attacked" by a swimming rabbit which he had beaten off with an oar.

Shit, that guy's running so scared, even a goddamn rabbit can tree the bastard. If this massive contempt was one side of the coin, then a deep, unsatisfied capacity for hero worship was the other; and the Pope had walked into an enormous adoring wave of the stuff. Where the President dithered on brink after brink, the Pope came out with his *no, no, no*'s, and America loved him for them. Had he been running for the presidency himself, the Pope would have carried every state. The only consolation that I could see in this holy circus was that by comparison with the Pope, Ronald Reagan was beginning to look tainted with an encouragingly dangerous shade of pink.

I had to stand off the lock and dam above Keokuk, Iowa, to let the *Delta Queen* come through. The great white museum piece was puffing away thoughtfully in the lock chamber, its red stern wheel still splashing in the water. It was no beauty. A new towboat, with a fleet of barges up front, had an altogether dandier line than the *Delta Queen* with its snub front and four tiers of balustraded decks. Its appeal lay in the fact that it was a relic of a storybook American past when life was simpler, more heroic, when moral values were certitudes, when America was really something else. There was a connection between the Pope and the *Delta Queen*. The expensive river voyage up from St. Louis was supposed to take one back into a world of frontier pastoral. The stops along the way were cunningly selected to reveal only the most "historic" and quaintly restored versions of life on the Mississippi. The *Delta Queen* promised the tourist a long, comfortable wallow in a vision of America as a still-uncorrupted Eden. Tour guides would shield him from harmful contact with his own century; sustained by gourmet food and vodka martinis, he would be safely coddled in the illusion that he was refreshing his spirit in the brave simplicities of the 1840s.

The steamboat waddled slowly upriver toward Nauvoo. Elder Tiptree was going to have a busy day. The city of Keokuk drifted past me on the current. Another painted steamboat, drawn up high and dry in the middle of an empty parking lot, made an optical trick come momentarily true. The Mississippi was two rivers. They lay right beside each other, but flowed in opposite directions. The steamboats, the historical markers, the fancy Golden Age hotels, the scenic bluffs and gift shops were all going one way, while the river on the charts, with its tows, grain elevators, slaughterhouses, factories, water towers and gantries, was going in quite another. I had done my share of traveling on the first river, but it was a cute irrelevance compared with the deep, dangerous, epic power of the real Mississippi.

On the second river, the Des Moines River added itself to the stream on the right bank below Keokuk. Iowa was over, and Missouri had begun. My fifth state. I felt that I was within smelling distance, at least, of the South. The little towns, half hidden now behind high levees, looked more elderly and groggy. Only a hundred miles or so back, it had been an object of remark to see a black face on a street. Here there were black longshoremen on the wharves, and less of the disquieting sense that one was moving through a pretty white ghetto.

Keen to first-foot in Missouri, I beached at a town that looked like an unkempt graveyard. The houses on the flats nearest the river had been left behind long ago. A brick cottage, its roof fallen in, its windows out, stood in a garden that had gone to jungle. Someone had painted across its front in large, uneven letters: KEP OFF NO TPESPPINC. The message was ambiguous, to say the least, and I felt guiltless as I snooped around its ruined yard. There were rusted beer cans, a fender from an automobile, the mortal remains of what had once been a chair stuffed with horsehair. A few rotten boards were left of its veranda. Picking my way through the ribs of the thing, I looked through a window frame. A sickly river birch had taken root in the floor of the living room. As I stumbled against a joist, a dozen gobbling pigeons clattered off the branches of the tree and rose through the roof.

It was almost dark when I made Hannibal. Throughout the day, I had grown more and more suspicious of the river's placidity. I had been lapped in its current, moving from sheet to sheet through the charts, barely awake, letting my head drift as the water drifted. *She'll lull you to sleep, and then she'll do you in.* Something had happened to my vision. There were banks and islands; they were marked on the charts. But all I saw was water, scrolled with hairlines around the bow of the boat, darkening with the sky, slick as the top of a vat of molasses. I came to briefly, to go through Lock 21 below Alton, then forgot it as soon as I was out in the main channel again. In some small cavity at the back of my mind, there were alarm bells ringing; this pleasant, hypnotic trance which had been induced in me by the river's unwavering eye was a thing I should be afraid of. I had always wanted to be absorbed by the Mississippi, to feel that I was as much a part of its flow as the logs around which I now steered without consciously noticing them. That afternoon I thought, *I could drown in this river, and it wouldn't matter; I wouldn't mind.* The current would just open to admit one, close seamlessly over one's head, and keep on going. It would all be as easy and idle as a daydream.

I shook myself awake in a cold twilight. The bridges of Hannibal were two miles downstream, and a long string of waiting barge fleets was moored off Zeigler Island, the lights in their towboats making a snug floating town. I could hear lazy voices coming from the open windows of their galleys. Everyone else had settled down to supper and TV. Shivering, alerted to my own solitude, I hurried on down.

The old Mark Twain Hotel on the waterfront at Hannibal was a derelict wreck. Its owner had purportedly gone bankrupt. He worked as a night watchman now. I had tried its locked door, attracted by what I thought was a light inside, and a car had pulled up on the street beside me. "You trying to wake up ghosts, or something? That place has been dead for years. You want a room? I got a new motel, two blocks uptown." It was a disappointment. I had seen the Mark Twain, glooming steeply over the river, and had thought it looked just right as a base to mark the overlapping point between Huckleberry Finn's voyage and my own. Instead I had to settle for a bright, sterile cabin, with *Dallas* on television in hideous acrylic color, and not even the ghost of a ghost to commune with. I was just in time to catch the last serving of dinner in the lounge/restaurant. My place mat said wooo ARE YOU? WELCOME NITE OWLS! It was seven thirty-five. When Twain disguised Hannibal as St. Petersburg, he did describe it as "sleepy," but I felt that if this was what he meant, he might reasonably have been a shade more explicit. By the time the waitress had said "you-all" six times, and I'd seen from the breakfast menu that there were hominy grits with everything, I felt that Hannibal was trying a little too strenuously to live up to its fictional reputation as a sleepy Southern town.

Still, a few adventurous insomniacs were up and talking over beer in the motel lounge. An off-duty waitress in her forties was telling the wife of the owner about another American journey.

"I saw Kansas City last week. God. Made Hannibal look like a real dump. The buildings, you know, they was so *new*. All so *tall*. They was all lit up. It looked like the pictures you see of New York. I kind of hated to come back. I had to go get *Eileen*. She run off."

"To Kansas City?"

"Yeah. God, that's someplace else."

"Why?"

"She missed her mother."

"That sounds like a good old-fashioned reason," I said. I'd gathered that Eileen was her daughter-in-law.

"But she took the baby too. So I had to go get her."

"She want to come back?"

"Oh . . . yeah; she was good and ready."

There was one of those long bar silences in which the patrons all investigated the insides of their glasses as if they hoped to find tadpoles breeding there. The waitress, though, wasn't yet done with her story.

"Eileen's mother's moving to California."

"You won't be able to get *there* and back in one night."

"I sure *hope* that girl runs off to California! I never been to California. Hell, even Kansas City . . . that was something . . . it was that pretty. But California . . ."

She had the grapes of Eshcol in her eyes. A man across the bar said, "Well now, Josie . . . she used to run off once. Same reason. Trouble was, *her* mother only lived up at Palmyra."

The waitress put on her coat and left. The owner's wife asked me if I wanted to watch TV. I said that I didn't.

"Me neither. I don't watch it now, except for the religious programs. I watch *them*. There's a great revival going on now. You ain't religious in England much, are you?"

"Certainly not in the way that you are here. Why do you think this great revival's happened?"

"Oh . . . I guess everybody . . . why, they just kind of tried everything else and somehow they don't seem to have gotten any satisfaction. So they've come at last to the Lord. Take my husband. He never did go to church much. But he was dissatisfied . . . felt there was something missing out of his life. Then one day he was watching Channel Six, and the *700 Club* came up. You know the *700 Club*? They have all these folks on who've had testy-moaney. Like celebs, and such. There was that guy, used to be on the *Today* show . . . what's-his-name? Tom Garraway, ain't it, Harry? He had testy-moaney. Anyhow, my husband was watching the *700 Club* and he heard these testy-moanies, and he got to thinking . . . Weren't that the way it was, Harry?"

"Oh . . . er . . . yeah . . ." said her husband, squinting into his beer, resentful and embarrassed at hearing the story of his own conversion.

"After that, we went around trying just about every church around Hannibal. We went to the Spiritualist church. . . . There's a guy there, he speaks one time in Polish, the next he's speaking Arabic. . . . I believe in Speaking in Tongues. Then there's the Church of the Assembly of God. You ought to go to that; you'd get a real kick out of it—"

"Yeah," said Harry, evidently relieved at this shift of focus.

"Now, Harry's brother, he was a real spiritual guy. Weekends, his home was like a *re*-sort. He'd have a hundred pounds of ribs out there. Every Saturday. And by Saturday night—you'd better believe it—there wasn't one rib left, he was that good a person. Everyone loved Joe."

In 1884, Twain described Huckleberry Finn as "the pariah of the village." Poor Huck. He had made horribly good. A hundred years later, he was Hannibal's darling. The untamable boy who had run away from the smug piety and good manners of Twain's archetypal small town had turned into the pivot of that town's tourist industry. There was the Huck Finn Shopping Plaza out on the Interstate, a huge, windy carpark with branches of Rexall's, Bergner's, Sears and J. C. Penney lording over it like a gang of bland corporate fat cats. There was the Tom 'n Huck Motel, lost in the neon strip of gas stations and fast-food joints that was strung out along the bluff a mile or so west of the river. You could put up in your trailer home on the Injun Joe campsite and make with the pizzas at the Mark Twain Dinette and Drive-In. Meanwhile your poodle could be shampooed at the Mark Twain Pet Center and your buckled fender repaired at the Mark Twain Body & Frame Shop. In the light of all this, the last words of Twain's novel had taken on a further irony which even Twain, the supreme American ironist, would have found hard to swallow.

> I reckon I got to light out for the Territory ahead of the rest, because Aunt Sally she's going to adopt me and sivilize me and I can't stand it. I been there before.

Aunt Sally had won in the end, as Aunt Sally was bound to. Hannibal had adopted Twain's angry masterpiece and civilized it into a nice, profit-making chunk of sentimental kitsch.

Downtown, a cobbled street had been coyly restored around Judge Clemens' law office, the Becky Thatcher Bookshop, a moldy waxwork show, a decent little museum of Twain relics and a stretch of new white wooden fence. This, a guide was telling a party of visitors, wasn't just *like* the fence Tom Sawyer had been set to whitewash on that fictional summer Saturday in the 1840s: it was the fence itself—as material a proof of the veracity of an old book as the thighbone of St. Peter. I looked at the fence for a very long time indeed. I learned the set of each one of its narrow boards, and the slightly bubbled sheen of its starch-white paint. If I'd had a spray gun on me, I would have been content to write one word across that fence: HADLEYBURG. One or two people might have known what it meant before the tourist board whited it out.

Below Main Street, though, the waterfront of Hannibal—its business end—was incorruptible. The catchpenny whimsy of the Mark Twain industry couldn't touch it. Past the closed-up Ice House Theater, the closed-up hotel, the eyeless warehouses, there was a proper river town to escape into. I crossed the dusty tracks of the Wabash and the Burlington Northern to where the air was fogged with grain husks and the chutes and elevators made Gothic-castle shapes in the sky. From all over Missouri, it seemed, the grain trucks were coming in to Hannibal. They stood growling in line, bumper to bumper, queueing to be weighed and emptied. The Hannibal Grain Terminal resembled a city under siege. Everyone was shouting at everyone else. The muddy trucks rolled in like tanks. The dry, gritty air swirled and mushroomed. It stuck in one's throat; it gave people's faces the pale, encrusted look of bomb-blast victims; it turned the whole queer landscape to a sickly yellowish monochrome, like an underexposed daguerreotype.

The battle headquarters of this operation was in a long hot shed. The fans which had been scattered around the place to cool it were keeping several thousand bills and invoices in a state of perpetual flurried motion. Today's prices were chalked up on a blackboard: $6.40 a bushel was the going rate for soybeans, while other grains, like wheat, corn and sorghum, were all floating at around $3.50. I found the field marshal at his desk, teaching his several telephones to talk to each other rather than to him. Since the beginning of the harvest, he had been working a fifteen-hour day, seven days a week, and it showed. Mr. Hooley's narrow, knobbly face was creased and powder-burned. Had I been he, I would have thrown me out, but he said no, sure he'd talk, he'd be happy to, if I didn't mind these goddamn phones going off all over the place. There was a signed photograph of the President lying flat among the paperwork.

"That's an unusual distinction around here," I said. "You actually like Jimmy Carter."

"Oh, *that,*" Mr. Hooley said. "I guess I won't even get around to framing it. You know, when Jimmy Carter came to Hannibal on the *Delta Queen*? It tied up right out there. I had the whole plant full of Secret Service men. I said, 'Sure you can use my elevators . . .' and they went swarming up there, dozens of them. Sharpshooters. So I get a signed photograph from the White House. . . ." He shuffled it under a file of correspondence.

"So what turned you off him?"

"You know what he did? He got right off that boat; he went to the Mark Twain museum and saw the Tom Sawyer Cave; made a speech; then he got back on the *Delta Queen* again. Now, if he'd shown interest in what makes Hannibal tick, this town would've taken the President to its heart. All he had to do was to go up to some fellow and say, 'Hey, what's going on here? What's this elevator all about?' But he didn't do nothing like that. He walked right on past the guts of this town, just like a tourist. Now, if those soybeans had been peanuts, he'd have known what was going on . . . maybe. But he had to act like some dumbhead on a scenic tour. If that Mark Twain museum and such takes a hundred dollars, we take a million: that's the scale of it. You understand what I'm saying? This ain't a tourist town; it's a farming town. There's not one store in Hannibal now that could keep its doors open if it wasn't for the farmers' daughters. But what does the President go see? *Mark Twain.*"

"Did you ever read *Huckleberry Finn*?"

"No, I never did read that book. You read it?"

"Yeah," I said. "I read it once."

Mr. Hooley explained to me how he bought grain from the farmers, dried it and stored it. Its humidity had to be kept to exactly eleven percent, so that it could bounce without shattering. He hired the barges that were waiting off the channel and shipped his grain down to New Orleans, where he sold it to firms of exporters. We went out to the elevator and watched the soybeans coming in. Tip-up trucks fed them into an underground chamber. Thousands of little buckets on chain belts scooped them up to the top of the chute, from where they were hosed into the holds of the barges below. It was just noise and dust to me, and I felt a little guilty at being unable to see the glory of the business. If there was glory in it, it was a glory of figures; of bushels per hour, of percentile moisture, of the delicate correspondence between the silent motion of dollars and the slow, rowdy circulation of these trucks and buckets and barges as they engaged in a kind of elephantine ballet.

"What do you think?" shouted Mr. Hooley.

"I was trying to see it as money. . . ."

"Why, that's ten thousand bushels an hour . . . six, seven dollars a bushel . . . works out at around a thousand dollars a minute, give or take a cent. How much do you reckon that Mark Twain museum takes?"

"At least it makes nonsense of that saying about things' not amounting to a hill of beans."

"You get yourself a hill of beans, I'm telling you, you won't have to do no more book writing. Whoever it was made that saying, he didn't know nothing about beans."

At the Ole Planter's restaurant that night, business was flat. The tourist season was trickling to an end. The owner came to sit at my table.

"This town, it used to be the Gold Coast. On this street here, it was girls upstairs, nickelodeons downstairs, all up the street. Now all we got is soybeans."

"What happens to your high school graduates?"

"They go. If they got brains, they go."

A hundred and fifty dollars a week, he said, was reckoned to be a decent wage in Hannibal. A few wealthy families had the town sewn up "real tight." "You want to get on in this town, you keep your fingers clean and your mouth shut."

Tight seemed the right word for Hannibal. It was too tight for me. I didn't like its prematurely dark and empty streets. If there were adventures to have here, I didn't know where to find them. I went back to my motel room and cheered myself up with bourbon and soda and Laurence Sterne.

> —If this won't turn out fomething—another will—no matter—'tis an affay upon human nature—I get my labour for my pains—'tis enough—the pleafure of the experiment has kept my fenfes and the beft part of my blood awake, and laid the grofs to fleep.

The high school marching bands were parading down Broadway through the morning drizzle. They came in all the uniforms of the armies of Victorian Europe: girls in Prussian shakos and English busbies, their tunics frogged with gold and silver, their fluffy pompons looking like splats of melted ice cream in the rain.

"Well! Ain't that just a lovely thing to happen on!" a black woman laughed at me out of the crowd on the sidewalk. She was weighed down with shopping in brown paper sacks. "That's the best thing I seen in *weeks*. Ain't they so *pretty?*"

Drums, cornets, bugles, pipes. The bands filled the town with bangs and skirls. They were marching through Georgia, burying John Brown's body, Yankee Doodling and hailing the Chief; but the tunes had all leaked into each other like wet colors, leaving the musical and military equivalent of a Jackson Pollock painting in the air.

A boy bandleader went by in war paint and feathers, tossing his baton as high as the roof of the cigar store across the street. I thought I saw the face of a real Indian in the crowd, and studied him; but he had the same expression of empty good humor as the rest of us.

Hurrah! hurrah! we bring the Jubilee!
Hurrah! hurrah! the flag that makes you free!

The band of the Missouri Military Academy brought up the end of the event: boys in spats, white helmets and pale blue battle dress. They were all eyeglasses and Adam's apples, their necks thrown rigidly back, their eyes ceremonially glazed over. Scratch one of those serious children, and he would have bled slogans about Laura Norder, the domino theory and the defense of the West. After the pantomime and the chocolate soldiers comes the real thing. *As He died to make men holy, let us die to make men free . . .* But the jolly iambic rhythm of the tune squeezed out the small print from the line. What the drums and the brass section actually came out with was a message of telegraphic compression and telegraphic foreboding: AS DIED MAKE HO, LET DIE MAKE FREE—and it was this sinister communication which stuck in my head as I carried my bags to the river.

The faint *oom-pah-crump* of the marching bands carried from the town over the water. I was in the river of the novel now, and found in my slipping out of Hannibal odd, weighty echoes of Huck Finn's escape from St. Petersburg. I had hated the stupid literalism of Tom Sawyer's fence, but the Mississippi was different. Twain had been superstitiously careful in his handling of the geographical details of Huck's voyage. I had checked his mileages and directions against the charts, and they tallied exactly. They didn't correspond with the local tourist board's version of things, nor with the academic notes at the back of my edition of *Huckleberry Finn*; but they fitted the river. Pap Finn's hut was in the thick timber on the Illinois shore, tucked behind Armstrong Island; the big slough with its wild duck was The Sny. "Jackson's Island" was *not* Glasscock Island, right across from Hannibal itself; it was the much bigger Gilbert's Island, eight miles farther on downstream and safely out of range of the town. Huck paddles "away below" the ferry landing at Hannibal, and sees the hump of Jackson's Island in the darkness from a distance of two and a half miles. In reclaiming Huck as its prodigal son, the town had managed to turn its stretch of the Mississippi upside down.

I went through Lock 22 and *there* was "Jackson's Island":

> . . . heavy-timbered and standing up out of the middle of the river, big and dark and solid, like a steamboat without any lights. There warn't any signs of the bar at the head—it was all under water now.

In the late morning, in gauzy rain, it was an insubstantial gray. The cottonwoods and willows were losing their leaves. The bar at the head, with its line of spindly saplings, stood eight or nine feet proud of the water. There was no doubt at all that it was Huck's island.

The channel wound around it on the Illinois side. It would still be a good place to go into hiding, with its steep woods and outcrops of limestone like pieces of cheese tunneled by mice. Hanging back on the drift of the current, I let it unroll as slowly as I could. Thirty years ago, I'd smelled the catfish grilling over a wood fire on that shore, and counted the stars and drift logs and rafts. Now, watching the dark places where the boughs leaned far out over the river making dripping caves and grottoes, I was full of the nervous pleasure of being a poacher. Gilbert's Island was posted as a wildlife sanctuary. I was hunting a memory, out of season. The island had brought it so nearly within my range, but the current took me past it and back to being cold, wet and thirty-seven again.

The drizzle had thickened to heavy rain. It was coming down in quills, stabbing at the water. The wind, too, was beginning to freshen, making the waves curl and fleck with foam at their tips. Nine miles farther on, at Louisiana, Missouri, I put in at a landing where other small boats were jostling noisily at their moorings and I had to inch my way along a tippy pontoon which bucked and twisted as the breakers caught it.

Louisiana was laid out as plainly as a diagram. It had the standard components of a river town: one levee; one pair of tracks; a ruined button factory; one grain elevator; one lumberyard; one bluff lined with mansions, mostly in a state of poor repair; one stretch of flats, littered with clapboard and tarpaper shacks, ditto. Its great merit on that particular afternoon was that the Fireside Lounge really did have a fine log fire. Steaming, stamping, feeling the warm whiskey burn my throat, I was very grateful that Louisiana existed. The woman who was tending bar said, "You fell in?"

"No," I said. "Not that it would have made much difference if I had." The woman's face went serious. "I had a son. He drowned in the river."

"I'm sorry."

She used a phrase that I'd heard hundreds of miles upstream, in the mouth of another woman, in another accent: "It takes its toll."

She said she'd known too many drownings. She came from a family of professional fishermen, and drowning to her was as natural a cause of death as heart disease or cancer. Her son had gone duck hunting in winter. His jonboat had lurched on the wake of a tow and he'd gone over the side. "There was another boy with him. He couldn't do nothing. Even if they'd got him out, he'd have been dead for sure, the water was that cold. I don't like the Mississippi. I never liked it. But my father . . . my husband . . . my son . . . they've all loved the river. There was no way I had of stopping them. . . ."

Two women were sitting up at the bar. Both had mops of crinkly black hair which looked as if it had been fried like Chinese seaweed. "That chickenshit!" one was saying. "Chicken . . . *shit.*" Her cigaretty laugh carried down the room.

"You better look out for the river," said the bartender. "Up here is supposed to be the *safe* part; down below St. Louis . . ."

"Yes, I've heard about it," I said. I was in a mood in which I was afraid that it would be all too easy to frighten me off the lower river. I didn't want to hear the horror stories.

"Hey," called one of the chickenshit women. "You come from England?"

"Yes."

"That's what I thought. We got an English lady living here in town. She come over from England when she married Everett Asquith. He's got a paint store up on Main."

I said I'd like to look her up.

"She talks just like you do. She got one of them British accents. Like that *Masterpiece Theatre* on Channel Eleven."

Warm, dry, cabined in a motel on the bluff, I reached Betty Asquith on the telephone. Sure, she said; it would be real nice to see someone from England. She hadn't seen nobody from back home in years. Her voice was a complete puzzle. She did not, admittedly, sound as if she had been born and raised in Missouri, but she had the queerest British accent I had ever laid ears on. Her husband drove around to the trucking café to pick me up.

"Asquith," he said. "That's a good English name, ain't it? Didn't you once have a president, or head minister, or some such, name of Asquith? I guess him and me must've been kin at some stage of the game, but that'd be going back a piece, wouldn't it?"

When he was in the U.S. Army in the early 1950s, he'd been stationed in London. His wife was Welsh, from Cardiff, and she had been working as a nurse in a London hospital when he met her. They had come back together to Missouri in 1955. In their neat house on the hill above town, Mrs. Asquith told me the story of that journey.

They had set out from New Jersey on the thousand-mile drive west. She had never seen such endless space. As the states unrolled—Pennsylvania, Ohio, Indiana, Illinois—she had thought America could never end. Farms and fields to her meant the little stone-walled plots and cottages of Wales; she couldn't take in these unbroken miles of crops and forest. By the time they had crossed the Alleghenies, she felt it was high time for the sea to show up on the horizon. It took them three days to reach Bowling Green, ten miles up the road from Louisiana, where Everett Asquith's parents lived.

"After a couple of days, Everett says let's go downtown. We got to Bowling Green Square. I said, 'Where's the town?' Everett says, 'This is it. You're in it.' *Town?* It wasn't no town at all!"

After twenty-five years, her vocabulary and grammar were totally American. But she talked, singingly, from the front of her mouth, still, and had created a dialect of her own, a sort of Pike County Welsh. Pike County itself, its own memories of immigration long lost now, had been mildly astounded by Betty Asquith. Everett's friends were surprised that she could speak English at all. "Well, they knew I was a foreigner, and they knew foreigners couldn't speak English, and that was that. Then I'd ask the neighbors in for coffee and biscuits. That wasn't no good. *Biscuits?* They thought that was real queer. Then I'd ask for a 'chemist,' and nobody knew what I meant. And I'd walk to the store. They thought I was crazy. Nobody walked anyplace in Bowling Green, and folks was going around saying we was too poor to have a car. But back home, I always walked. Everywhere."

She was determined to turn herself into an American. She got a job as a night nurse at the local hospital, she gave coffee klatches and learned to call biscuits cookies. She collected American words and wrote them down in a notebook. She dressed herself from the Sears catalogue and drove herself to the supermarket in the station wagon.

In Louisiana she was still "the English lady." Yet the one way in which she now kept in touch with her original culture was itself characteristically American. Like the German towns with their Oktoberfests, and the Swedes with their Smorgasbords, Betty Asquith occasionally cooked a ritual British Sunday lunch with roast lamb, mint sauce and Yorkshire pudding. This ceremonial food was the last, necessary reminder that she had once made that long journey, and become someone else.

"You aiming to stay on in the United States?" she asked me.

"No. I'll be going back to London."

"I couldn't go back. Not now. I'd love to go on vacation there, but to live . . . no, there's no way. I *feel* like an American, you know?"

The next morning was bright and rough. I was awakened by the metallic clinking of the leaves outside the window. I inspected the river from the bluff: it was streaked with ribbons of froth. Even so, I meant to go on. I had looked at the charts, and between here and St. Louis the river was either so narrow or so well broken with islands that I doubted if the wind could do me much harm. I was well downstream of all the wide pools now: it was typical of the Mississippi's unfathomable nature that it actually grew thinner as it headed for the ocean. At Louisiana it was only half a mile across—just a domestic trickle, compared with the great dawdling sweep of water on which I'd ridden through Minnesota and Wisconsin and northern Iowa.

Waves watched from the bluff were one thing, though; seen from the boat they were quite another. They rolled me around and jerked the sky about over my head. Then they started coming in over the bow in bucketfuls. I ran ashore a few hundred yards south of where I'd started out.

The bartender at the Fireside Lounge said, "I never thought you were fool enough to tangle with that river on a day like this."

"No," I said. "I was being stupidly overconfident. It only took me five minutes to learn my lesson, though."

"Five minutes is plenty long enough to drown in."

A young man was nursing a beer in quivery hands. He looked like a habitual morning drinker. He was too thin for his clothes; he had wet, spaniel's eyes, sunk in pits in his skull. When he talked he sounded like a sleepwalker.

"You're the Englishman," he said.

"Yes—"

"You seen Jeannie yet?"

"Who?"

"The English lady."

"Yes. *Betty*. Betty Asquith. I saw her and her husband last night."

"She don't live with her husband no more."

"Betty Asquith does."

"Jeannie don't."

Mrs. Asquith had said nothing about there being another G.I. bride in town. It seemed improbable that a place as small as Louisiana should harbor British immigrants who didn't know each other's names.

"Jeannie's good people. She's real good people. I could take you around there. . . ."

It took him two more beers to cure his shakes; then Jerry led me to a pickup truck which, I suspected, he had salvaged from a dump. Its exhaust and brakes had gone. There were knocks in its engine and hollow groans in its transmission. We dithered across town in this wreck, misfiring badly up Third, past the decrepit mansions and a ruinous wooden mock-up of the Parthenon, out into a suburban scrub of yard sales, bungalows, vacant lots and dogs on chains. Jerry wanted me to see the trailer home where he lived with his mother.

It was parked in an overgrown orchard. Inside, it smelled of dust, fried bacon and old clothes. It was stuffed with knickknacks. Jerry had been an adopted child, and he'd furnished himself with a personal history by amassing a collection of junk and trinkets. He showed me his clam shells, his old medicine jars and perfume bottles, the 1938 cabinet radio he'd bought for fifty cents in a sale, a Confederate dollar bill. He had two real treasures. One was the Pike County Atlas for 1875. It represented Louisiana as Louisiana never could have been, as an elegant metropolis of genteel culture. Crudely etched pictures showed the ladies and gentlemen of the town riding past trim estates in horse-drawn buggies, the men in top hats, the women dressed in the newest and most fashionable creations of St. Louis. Whaleboned, bonneted, richly petticoated, they processed through the book like queens. Besotted as the artist was with this vision of fine women, he was even more obsessed with fences. Every stake and wattle in Pike County had been carefully drawn in. They were marvelous fences. They crisscrossed the pictures, out of all perspective, reducing the Missouri landscape to a checkerboard of perfect order. In 1875, civilization had meant good fences; and in the matter of fences, Louisiana would not yield a single picket to any city in the land.

In the maps at the back of the book, each lot was marked with its owner's name. "See? Z. O. Mackintosh . . ." Jerry said. "He's my kin." We worked slowly through every patch of Pike County which had been held by Z. O. Mackintosh. He had evidently collected land much as Jerry himself collected clam shells and old coins and ghostly tintypes of people who might have been his relatives. Mr. Mackintosh's name dotted the atlas: an acre here, a narrow strip of ground a mile off, another acre, another strip . . . "He was a real big guy in these parts," Jerry said. "There wasn't nobody to touch Z. O. Mackintosh. I don't know where it all went. By rights, I reckon, some of that land . . . it should've come down to me. I guess the papers are all lost, though, now. My mother, she doesn't know nothing about it. But then she ain't kin, like I am."

Jerry's Pike County, preserved in his atlas, was his lawful inheritance, out of which he had been tricked by misfortune. In this musty trailer, with his part-time job at a plastics factory and his six-packs of Miller's, he was just the sad, daydreaming shadow of the person he believed he really was. In the atlas, he was Z. O. Mackintosh, land-owner, builder of fences, horseman and escort to beautiful women in crinolines.

"This town . . ." Jerry said, pulling the ring from another can of beer, ". . . it was founded . . . I dunno, it was in the eighteen-hundreds. It's dead now. It's been dead for forty years. Maybe more."

His other great treasure was a brown photograph. I mistook it at first for a genuine relic of Louisiana's heyday, but it had been taken six months before. Jerry had gone to a "Western studio" in Ozark, Missouri, where he had been dressed up like a doll in the clothes of a nineteenth-century dude. An ammunition belt with twin revolvers had been hung on his hips. A long-barreled rifle had been put in his hands. He was standing on the porch of a homesteader's log cabin, and this moment of floodlit make-believe had been printed in historic sepia. It looked convincing enough, until one saw Jerry's hopeless eyes. They stared emptily from the picture in ironic contradiction to all the symbols of frontier manliness with which the photographer had tricked out the body of his subject. If that rifle had actually gone off, the gunslinger would have died of fright.

"She's good people," Jerry said again. He was not a man, I thought, on whom many women would let themselves become dependent, and he was proud of the protective way in which he had been able to look after "Jeannie." He went shopping for her in winter, he found driftwood for her fire, he took her out to the Fireside Lounge in his pickup. "She gets to be real lonesome . . . with her being English. . . . She don't know too many folks in Louisiana."

We stopped outside the most tottering and most splay-boarded of all the crumbling wooden mansions in the town. What should have been its front lawn was weeds and thistles; its upstairs windows were broken; a few shreds of once-white paint clung to its siding like flakes of dandruff. "Jeannie" lived in a single room on the ground floor. She was the house's last surviving occupant, but it looked as if she had just moved in the day before. Her clothes were strung on hangers along the picture rails. There were holes in the ceiling where the plaster had fallen. Two burners on an old gas stove supplied the only heat, and most of the light, since "Jeannie" had pulled down the green blind over her window, and the sun came in through a few ragged chinks where the blind had torn or frayed away. The place was as humid and gloomy as a crypt. "Jeannie" herself was indistinct: an old woman, stiff with arthritis, sitting in a dirty housecoat on an iron bed. There was a doll on the pillow, with the severed head of another doll lying beside it.

"Jeannie," Jerry said, "I've brought a friend. He's from *England!*"

"It's not Arthur . . . is it?"

"No, this is Jonathan—"

"Did Arthur send him? You haven't come from Arthur, have you, dear?"

I had to explain that I'd never heard of Arthur. "Jeannie's" face went slack with disappointment. *Arfur,* she said, *Arfur.* She spoke in the querulous, whiffly accent of suburban East Anglia; there wasn't a trace of American in it.

"Oh, dear," she said, "I do wish you knew Arthur. You could've brought a message from him. He'll be coming over, though, any day now. You'll prob'ly meet Arthur. He's coming, see, to take me away. I'm going home. On the aeroplane. To Colchester. D'you know Colchester, dear? Colchester, in Essex?"

"Yes, I've stayed there. It's a nice town."

"That's where I'm going. When Arthur comes."

It was in a dance hall in Colchester, in 1943, that she had met her American husband. She had come over to the United States on a boat full of English brides, and arrived in Nashville, Tennessee. The marriage had been a disaster. Within a few months, the couple had split and "Jeannie" had landed in this Louisiana rooming house. She'd had no money. England was a world away; only the rich could afford the luxury of a transatlantic fare. So she had stayed on, camping out in the room as if it were an overnight lodging, waiting to be rescued and brought home. She had been waiting for more than thirty years.

"Don't call me 'Jeannie,' dear. Call me Ivy. Ivy's me real name. 'Jeannie's' just the name they give me when I come to America. It was from that song. You know . . . *Jeannie with the light brown hair* . . . I don't know the rest of the words, but that's what they called me. It's my American name. But I'd like it if you called me Ivy."

She hobbled over to the chest of drawers where she kept everything she had which was left of England. There was a big wooden crucifix, wrapped in yellowing tissue paper, which she had brought with her on the bridal ship. There were some blurry snapshots of her English family, all taken in the 1940s, with the marks of rationing and air raids in their clothes and faces. Then a glossy, whole-plate professional photograph, its edges chipped . . . it showed two couples on the edge of a dance floor. "Look—there's Arthur, with me sister. They'd just got married then. There's me. And that's *him.*" *Him* was transparently an American, looking bland, smiling and well fed beside the beaky, strained English people at his side. Ivy put her hand over his image. "I wish *he* wasn't in that picture. I wanted to cut him out wiv a pair of scissors . . . but that'd spoil the photo, wouldn't it dear?" Ivy herself, even in 1943, had been no chicken: big-nosed, bespectacled; her mouth had been lipsticked into a Cupid's-bow large enough to mail a letter through.

"Oh, shoot!" she said, looking at her husband's face. Then: "Is that an English word or an American word?"

"It's American."

"Oh, dear. I don't like to use American words. But I get them mixed up now, sometimes. I say things now, I know they're American, but I can't help it. Living here, you just hear that American talk. That's why I like listening to you; you don't talk American at all; you sound just like people did at home. You've got ever such a nice voice, dear."

She had never met, or even heard of, Betty Asquith. They lived a mile apart, but they were divided by the Atlantic Ocean. It was probably just as well that no one had tried to introduce them; in very different ways, the existence of each could only have distressed the other.

With Jerry, I prowled through the upper stories of the house. It was a sordid warren of deserted rooms. There were broken padlocks on the doors. Stairs, banisters and floorboards had gone for firewood. The roomers themselves had left years before, but their bedsteads and leaky chairs remained behind, along with the pathetic tide wrack of old newspapers, fusty trousers, a rusted Gillette razor, a tin kettle . . . the last traces of people who had learned to travel light and disappear without fuss.

"You can find things up here," Jerry said. "Oncet, there was a whole sack of Confederate money up in the attic. . . . I never did see it, though."

The landlord had been as kind as he could to Ivy. He had let her stay on as "caretaker" after the roomers had gone. He had then tried to arrange for her to move to a decent apartment in a city-owned building for indigent old people. She had refused to go. Arthur was coming. She was about to fly to England. If she could just stay on a few more days . . . So she had squatted in her corner of this miserable house, with her blinds pulled and her possessions ready to be packed at a moment's notice, waiting.

Jerry was staring moonily through the cracked pane of a room on the top floor. The flaking paint on the walls was lime green, the color of a prison or a hospital. "You heard of Jesse James," he said. "He was in my family. That's what folks say, anyhow. I ain't got no direct proof of it."

The wind blew on all afternoon. Bored, idling through the *St. Louis Post-Dispatch,* I read: TREE CLUE BRINGS 5 ARRESTS IN RAPE CASE.

> . . . the real break in the case came when one of the three victims recalled seeing a tree from the window of a third-floor attic where she was attacked . . .

I had heard many bad things about St. Louis. I had been told that "the blacks" had "destroyed" it. A woman in a Fort Madison bar had said, "In St. Louis, hell, you're liable to be killed *walking.*" I'd taken such remarks lightly, thinking that they were part of the conventional stock of received ill-feeling that people who live in small towns have for big cities. This story of the tree was different. It gave St. Louis the horrid particularity of a city in a nightmare. What kind of place could this be, where the glimpse of a tree through a window was as telling a clue as a license-plate number or a fingerprint? The newspaper reporter didn't even sound faintly surprised as he told of how squad cars had quartered the streets of North St. Louis, searching for that telltale tree. I had been to plenty of cities built on desert sand. I'd seen trees from my window in Kuwait and Abu Dhabi and Aleppo and Cairo, and thought nothing of them; but a tree growing in St. Louis had imprinted itself as an oddity on the mind of a woman while she was being raped by a thug in an attic. No wonder that St. Louis was almost universally regarded as an object of fear and dislike. Listening to the surflike sound of the trees outside my own window in Louisiana, I felt a bristle of excitement at the thought of this next stage of the journey. It was like being on the road to an accursed biblical city.

At 8 A.M., the trucks on Route 54 outside the motel were still driving on their headlights. Down by the river, the sun showed as a tarnished dime in the mist. It was so still that the moored boats looked frozen solid in the water. I tucked myself into the edge of the channel and headed for St. Louis, with the Mississippi peeling cleanly away in a fantail from my stern.

I didn't mean to touch the shore today. I had food and coffee on board. My gas tanks were full. If I kept going steadily, I could make the ninety-five miles to St. Louis in ten hours; but I would have to race reach the city and lay up for a while; I felt too hypnotized now by the river to be able to see it properly. Even when I was asleep, I was still traveling on it, dreaming of waves and dark sloughs and the endless scribble of the current on the top of the water. In the last few days I had noticed that every time I stopped at a town it was like going to a movie. One watched and listened, and knew that what one was seeing and hearing wasn't for real. Actual life was the river itself. It was the roll of a wake lifting the boat and slamming it down. It was the monotonous stutter of the motor at my back, the buoys, mile markers, sandbars and the trick the river had of always fading, miles ahead, into the sky, so that one had the illusion of being able to drift right off the surface of the earth into pure emptiness. The river had, quite literally, put me into a trance. In St. Louis, I would sleep it off, wake, and come alert again.

I dropped through Lock 24, skipped Clarksville and came into a long stretch where the channel snaked past a series of low white sandbars. They lay in the river, hundreds of them, like whalebacks, leaving a narrow artery of deep water hissing between them. It was a tight squeeze to cross an upstream tow here; perched on a wave, I could see the inside of its engine room and hear a deckhand hollering something about a can of paint. Farther down, a real steamboat blocked the channel. Unlike the *Delta Queen,* this one was not a fancy piece of restoration work. Rusty, half blackened, it had been converted by the Corps of Engineers into a dredger. It looked splendid. Encountering it in midstream, steering clear of its thrashing stern wheel as it swung broadside, was like spotting some famous old society beauty across a crowded room. Its ravaged magnificence reminded me of Lady Diana Cooper towering over the small fry of the young set in an amazing hat: it was a genuine survivor, and it brought a whiff of 1920s high life to the water.

Islands, islands, islands. Tangles of green willow, mounds of white powder like spilled flour, they repeated one another with the confusing regularity of the box-hedge walls of a maze. Was I really moving? Surely I'd been here before. There always comes a point in traveling when motion itself has become so habitual that it breeds its own deep stillness. There was no wind, no cloud; nothing except the imperceptible velocity of the current. My wake was fixed on the water like a piece of molded plaster; it supplied the illusion of movement to a journey that had stopped dead still.

The channel looped suddenly northeast, as if the Mississippi had changed its mind and were going to head off for the Atlantic instead of for the Gulf. Somewhere behind the forest on the left-hand shore, the

Illinois River was emptying itself into the mainstream. As the twin currents merged and the banks spread out, I could feel the water bulge, straining to be free of the confinement of locks and dams. There was just one dam to go now, at Alton, Illinois, less than twenty miles on. Then the Mississippi would swallow the Missouri and run unchecked for more than a thousand miles to the sea. That was a figure which, for the moment, I couldn't afford to think about. All I needed to watch was the scratched-glass surface ahead of the bow and the sun as it began to settle in the sky behind me.

Below Portage des Sioux, Missouri, an obelisk was sticking queerly out of the water off the channel. It turned out to be a fifty-foot-high fiber-glass Madonna. Our Lady of the Rivers. Driftwood had piled up around its base. There was a prayer, and a plaque which announced that the effigy had been put up in 1951 after the Missouri and Mississippi had joined together in a disastrous flood.

On land, the Madonna must have looked gigantic. She would have made any civic statue look like a mere figurine by comparison. People must have expected her to loom monumentally over the river and radiate her intercessionary grace for miles. They had made a bad miscalculation. Far from dominating the Mississippi, the Madonna looked as if she had narrowly escaped from drowning in it, and was now clinging to a pole and waiting for the air-sea helicopter rescue service to arrive. If an innocent pagan had seen her, he would have been able to draw only one conclusion from her presence here: that this weak, synthetic woman-god had been given up in sacrifice to the big river-god, and that the river-god had spurned her as too trivial an offering.

She was abruptly lost to sight as the river made a southerly swing into Alton and the swiveling sun blackened her halo before it disappeared into the trees. At Alton Lock, there was a warning, violet tinge in the sky, and the deep chamber was cold enough to make my fingertips go white. It seemed an appropriate irony that my own feeble circulation should expose itself at just the moment when the river was gathering its power to course through America as fast as it could go.

It didn't meet the Missouri. It crashed into it. The navigation channel was posted with warnings to cling close to the Illinois bank. Four hundred yards out, there was a line of hound's-tooth breakers as the two rivers struggled with each other; and even in the channel there were whirlpools to show that something really big and dangerous was happening in the middle. Whatever it was, it was forbidden to boats to see it. The line of buoys led one to an exit door behind an island, and a long, dull ship canal. For ten miles, the Missouri and the Mississippi were left to thrash out their differences in private along a reach called, for good reason, the Chain of Rocks.

The lock gate at the end of the canal opened on St. Louis. I should have been able to look across at the face of the city; I couldn't, because the river on which I now found myself was utterly different from the Mississippi that I thought I knew. In this new river, the water boiled up from the bottom in convex mushroom shapes. The boat kept on sliding and skidding as I tried to set a course for the line of bridges downstream. I hardly had time to register the fact that it was there before I was shooting through the arches of the Merchants Railroad Bridge, frighteningly close to the piles. Unnaturally forced into a narrow conduit little more than a quarter of a mile wide, the river was "shoaling," ruckling into ugly little waves three and four feet high. Then the smooth humps of the boils began again, and the lurching, slithery motion of the boat as the motor did its best to keep a grip on the crosscurrents of these greasy swirls of spinning water.

Wharves, cranes and smokestacks were going past in a blur of black type. I caught a momentary glimpse of the Gateway Arch, its scaly steel turning to gold in the sunset, but it was an irrelevance beside the whorling surface of the river. The water here was thicker and darker than I'd seen it before; all muscle, clenching and unclenching, taking logs as big as trees and roiling them around just for the hell of the thing. The Mississippi was on a binge. It had tasted freedom, and was celebrating it with a display of elephantine pirouettes.

There were no small boats in sight. Mine felt fragile and facetious as I ran it jerkily from bridge to bridge, afraid of being swept aside and smashed into the piles, or swamped in the heavy shoals under the arches. I made a bad landing on the cobblestone foreshore where some old steamboats had been converted into restaurants, convention centers and cocktail bars. Stepping over the massive hawsers that moored the *Robert E. Lee,* I noticed my jittery knees. I had difficulty striking a match to light my pipe. My fingers were skidding like my boat.

WELCOME FUNERAL DIRECTORS OF AMERICA. The sign over the steamboat's covered gangway was faintly cheering. I found a big, empty cocktail lounge in the stern. The funeral directors were busy elsewhere, presumably discussing rouges and foundation creams. Nursing five dollars' worth of neat whiskey, I watched the river from the window. No one seeing it from here could have guessed at the inward, pent-up turbulence I had felt from my boat; it looked lazy and innocent. Those fierce boils were gentle eddies; the breakers beneath the bridges were pretty ripples. People came here from the city to calm their shredded nerves by looking out over water which was monotonous and tranquil. The Mississippi had us all fooled. No angle on it was the right one. It was dexterous and deceitful; and I saw it through the steamboat window with an increasingly drunken mixture of regard and revulsion.

7

Marriage à la Mode

H<i>e had just</i> called his wife long-distance. He had listened to the phone pealing in the empty apartment, counted twelve trills, and hung up. For several minutes he had stayed indecisively in the booth, his head full of numbers. He thought about calling her mother. Then he thought of calling Jake and Debbie, but he knew that his voice would betray his unreasonable panic. He collected the little pile of quarters which he'd put beside the phone, bought last week's *New Yorker* at the newsstand, and went through to the scaffolded green coffeeshop–cum–bar, where the air was mushy with taped music and there were a dozen or so men looking exactly like himself: all alone, all in business suits that had been worn a day or two too long, all nipping at cocktails which they purchased by showing the number on their room key and signing a card that was beginning to read like the index to a bartender's handbook. *1 Whiskey Sour. 1 Manhattan. 1 Vodka Martini. 1 Highball* . . . All these men were pretending to read. Some were studying the minutes of meetings whose proceedings they already knew by heart. Others were looking at *Newsweek,* turning its pages backward. Every few moments, someone would glance up, without hope, on the crazy off chance he'd spot a girl in the lobby whom he'd known at college. . . . *Hey, excuse me, but aren't you Cathy Silver?* In these quick, sly twists of the head there were dreams of rescue, of not dining alone, of a miraculous flood of unbuttoned talk in a strange city, and perhaps . . . but then the eyes of the men would drop to their watches. It was already eight-thirty. In ten minutes they would go separately and alone to the restaurant, where each would build a little theater around himself. He would engage the waiter as his audience and do his third-rate vaudeville turn as a regular guy having a darn good time on his ownio.

The man with *The New Yorker* sat at a table a little away from the bar. He had stirred his highball with his purple plastic cocktail stick. He had looked at his watch three times in a quarter of an hour. He had cast the obligatory number of glances at the door. He had turned the pages of his magazine. Considering how things were, he was doing fine.

He thought: If I'd been here a few years back, I would have hunted out a jazz club, a singles bar—anywhere I might have drifted into conversation with a stranger. Now, though, he felt too old for that sort of adventuring. He would be a marked man among the men and women in their twenties, busy with still being young. If they noticed him at all, they would see him as a wrinklie, wearing his pathos on his sleeve. Just that morning he had found himself inspecting his own excrement for traces of blood. No special reason; he had simply come to a point at which it would not have surprised him greatly to learn that he was dying, and his first terminal symptom would be something that he'd notice, more or less idly, one of these days, with a kind of dull recognition, like spotting an unpleasant old acquaintance on the street.

He supposed that if he were someone else, it would be in a mood like this that he would visit a call girl. He had never met a call girl. He believed that the proper thing to do was consult a hotel desk clerk or a cabdriver. After that, he assumed, things sort of took care of themselves. The idea was laughable, though. One, he counted himself as a male fellow traveler with the Women's Movement. Two, he expected that only humiliation could come from such a loveless gymnastic coupling. Three, he was a good deal more terrified of talking to either the desk clerk or the cabdriver than he was of the call girl herself. Four, he had spent the last forty-eight hours in the same pairs of socks and shorts. Q.E.D. Call-girl option closed.

He could try phoning his wife again. On the other hand, he couldn't stand the thought of listening to those long electronic trills, paranoia's own authentic sound; the sound of infidelity and wrecked cars on rainy highways. He looked again at what he had been reading. He had covered the listings of every theater on Broadway. He'd taken in the names of the stars and the belittled, silly plots of all the plays. He never went to New York, and the last time he had been inside a theater was in the 1960s. *Jesus,* he thought; *Jesus!* There must be some part of his mind from which he could take an ironical view of his own self-pity; but he felt that his solitude had paralyzed him as effectively as if he'd had a stroke.

.   .   .

He and I were kinfolks. At least, the copy of *The New Yorker* had been bought by me, and I had been sitting at his table in the coffeeshop/bar. The hotel must have held a good three hundred of us, and we were all loosely in the same bag. We were attending a convention, trying to make a sale or just *in transit*, keeping in pointless motion through the hotel's flesh-colored interior, afloat between floors in the glass-walled elevators, checking with the desk for messages that hadn't come through. On these elevator rides we would make a nervous show of conversation.

"You with A.R.T.M.S.?"

"No, I'm on my own."

"I'm with Harmless Radium Testers. Fred Spacks. From Baton Rouge."

"How do you find St. Louis?"

"St. Louis?" Fred Spacks from Baton Rouge looked surprised by the question. He'd quite forgotten that we were actually supposed to be in St. Louis. "Oh, it's a dump." The words came out in a musical phrase: a long semibreve followed by a careless triolet of descending quavers. The phrasing said everything. St. Louis was a place about which one was expected to have no opinion at all; it was just a conveniently central site for everybody's convention. Sure, it was a dump—but it had an airport, hotels, a conference center. So what else do you want? The Taj Mahal, for godsake? The Latin Quarter? Wake up, man: this is *St. Louis*.

I had spent a miserable Sunday. The only people on the streets had been conventioneers, recognizable by the way in which they wandered, uncuriously, like well-dressed mental patients on the grounds of a hospital. I had stared at the blank wall of the Tums factory, at the deserted football stadium, at the Old Courthouse. Obediently, as if I had swallowed my dose of Lithium and were following the instructions of the head nurse, I had ridden to the top of the Arch.

The giant feet of the Westward Expansion Memorial Arch stood on a stretch of ground so absurdly desolate that it did induce a momentary glow of good humor. It had been "landscaped." A few million tons of Mississippi mud had been molded into the shape of a rolling hill and valley. Some of this area was covered with flapping sheets of polyurethane. Most of the mud, though, had been coated with some kind of bilious green slime. Its texture was thickly fungoid, its purpose quite inscrutable. A gardener might well have recognized it as the best and latest form of soil nutrient. My own guess was that the city of St. Louis had run out of funds, was unable to plant grass on its artificial hill, and had decided that the only affordable solution was to spray the whole thing with the cheapest and nastiest green paint it could find. The coating might at least deceive a few inattentive passengers in high-altitude jets. At ground level, it gave the impression that the very earth on which St. Louis had been built was grotesquely diseased.

We were cranked up to the top of the Arch in a train of tiny van-dalized cars. I was squashed opposite a woman from Sacramento. Since the size of the car forced us to interlock our legs, it seemed natural enough to talk on the bumpy journey up through the dark.

She said: "The Arch is supposed to be to St. Louis what the Eiffel Tower is to Paris." She sounded like a tour guide. We gained another stair in the blackness with a terrific rattle and clank.

"Say that again?"

"The Arch is supposed to be to St. Louis . . ." her voice faltered. "The Arch is . . ." There was a sniff, and she started again. "The Arch is supposed to be to St. Louis what the Eiffel . . ." But she couldn't manage it. She was helpless with giggles. I tried to say it, and nearly reached the word "Paris" before something broke in my solar plexus. There were five people in the car. By the time we were three-quarters of the way up, we were all trying to get the sentence out and falling, helpless with laughter, into one another's laps. We tried to say it in chorus. I suggested that it might be easier if we sang it. When we reached the top, we were gurgling like maniacs. On the viewing plat-form, people shrank from contact with anyone from our car, and we in our turn shrank from each other. When I tried to grin at the woman who had started this riot of happy hysteria, she refused to catch my eye.

There was certainly something deeply sobering about the view from the top of the Arch. One had to peer out through tiny windows the size of building blocks. Had they been bigger, the Arch might have turned into the suicide Mecca of the Midwest; but as it was, one would have had difficulty in squeezing a newborn baby through one of these foggy little apertures. Pushing one's face against the glass, one could see all that any human being could reasonably bear of St. Louis: mile after mile of biscuit-colored housing projects, torn-up streets, blackened Vic-torian factories and the purplish urban scar tissue of vacant lots and pits in the ground. It was The Waste Land. The city succeeded tri-umphantly in doing what Our Lady of Rivers had totally failed at: it made the Mississippi look puny, an open drain which had taken on the St. Louis colors of rust, soot and rotting brick.

Beside me, the conventioneers were identifying another city alto-gether. They were pointing out the fine new home stadium of the

Cardinals, Stouffers Riverside Towers, the tall glass office buildings. To me, though, the isolated sprouts of life in the surrounding blight were just objects of pathos: a few wan geraniums planted on a garbage dump don't make a garden.

The Arch that we were standing in was quite the weirdest of these forlorn gestures of renewal. Eero Saarinen's huge glittering loop might justifiably have been raised as the crowning splendor of some modernist utopia. Set over St. Louis, linking nothing with nothing, rooted in its own bizarre wilderness of green mud, it looked to me like an expensive practical joke.

Down on the ground again, I watched the flag on the courthouse dome flying in reflection on the cold green mirror slab of the Equitable Life building. Life didn't feel equitable at all, and the Old Glory seemed to have a sarcastic emphasis built into the word *old*. The flag, magnified by the glass, snapped and juddered on its pole. Many stories below, the image of a slack-faced man stared back at me. He carried a *New Yorker*.

"Sir? Mister? Please excuse me. . . ."

The man in the glass turned. He had been joined by a portly Indian who looked as displaced as he felt himself. The Indian had a checked woolen scarf wound around his throat and wore an old, heavy camel overcoat. Since the actual temperature was close to sixty degrees, the weather for which the Indian had dressed himself was the special, metaphysical iciness of the city. It had made me shiver too, and I thought how sensible the man had been to wrap himself up against it.

"Please—I am looking for *downtown*."

"So was I. I'm afraid that this is it."

"*This* is downtown?"

"It seems like it."

"Good gracious," he said, with admirable mildness. We held a one-minute silence of appalled wonder at this fact.

"I am looking for Chinese restaurant."

So gaunt was St. Louis that I did remember exactly where I had seen a grubby chop suey joint earlier that afternoon. It was three blocks away, and I said I would take him to it. His loneliness broke like a bubble in a sudden cascade of words. Had I seen Richard Nixon interviewed by David Frost on the TV? Frost came from England, yes? Very good man. Very good. He himself had visited London. Very good city. Did I know the Balls Pond Road? I did? What an amazing coincidence! He had spent one month in the Balls Pond Road. Most convenient for the buses. He had a cousin in Ealing. He was an electrical engineer.

No, not the cousin; he . . . *himself*—and the Indian touched his throat as if he half-expected to find that St. Louis had rendered him an immaterial ghost.

I had assumed that he must have arranged to meet someone at the Chinese restaurant, but it turned out that he was going to eat alone. He had fixed on the notion of a Chinese restaurant—any Chinese restaurant—quite arbitrarily. He simply needed a destination, however contrived, to keep what was left of his identity intact. He pressed me to stay with him. I invented an appointment elsewhere. I thought that we might all too easily drive each other to tears.

Once in every half dozen carefully rationed visits, I would find a message for me at the hotel desk. They all seemed to be in code. They said things like TUESDAY 8:15 FXTN . . . KFUO . . . WPTZ . . . KHRB . . . The unpronounceable clusters of initials sounded like business conventions, but if one applied the right sort of acid to them, or held them in front of a fire, they revealed themselves as local radio stations where I was supposed to go and talk to disc jockeys in two-minute intervals between pop records, Lutheran hymns and ads for laxatives and pre-owned autos. As hungry for talk as the Indian, I treasured these abbreviated opportunities for conversation. I hogged the microphone. In crappy single rooms over the tops of Laundromats, in wooden huts on the outskirts of junior-college campuses, in dark closets at the back of churches, I set off on a gibbering trail of free association. I liked the cab rides down long wet boulevards that took me to these assignations; I liked talking to the receptionists at the studios. When I had no radio station to go to, I had no society; and between trips I sat blankly in the coffee shop, an unperson, turning pages backward and sneaking glances at the door. Then another strange conjunction of consonants would turn up and I'd come temporarily to life again.

In one dawn raid on a gospel station, the black cabdriver said, "So, how do you like this city, man?"

"Not very much, I'm afraid; at least, not yet, anyway."

"Not much, huh? Well, I'm telling you: don't you ever go over the river to *East* St. Louis. St. Louis is bad, but East St. Louis . . . they ain't people over there; they is *animals.*"

When I had hailed him on the street, he was deep in a newspaper. He passed it over to me. The *Evening Whirl.*

"You can scare the shit out of yourself with that *Whirl.* What they print in that paper is the truth. That's the one paper in this city where they don't tell no lies."

It was smudgily printed on the cheapest sort of paper. Its headline

256

read: HOMICIDE DECLARES WAR ON KILLERS AND ARRESTS 9 IN 3 DAYS. Beneath it was a row of mug shots of local murderers, all of them black. The news stories were written up in hot boogie-woogie prose:

> This is strong and wrong, this act of brutality and mortality. Bloodthirsty Catullus Eugene Blackwater, 28, carried out his plan to murder his friend Larry Brown, 23, of 9375 Wells, in his rave and crave to see human blood flow . . .
>
> Sex fiends and fools are on the rampant cornering, grabbing and ravishing women nightly . . .
>
> Hugh Saustell, 25, tried to escape from City Hospital No. 1, but a federal agent saw him, leveled a gun on his head and said, "Ho! Lo! Quit it!" as Hugh was running. He yielded to avoid gunsmoke that would have filled his body with lead.

The inside pages were full of advertisements for clairvoyants and wizards. HAS SOMEONE PUT A HEX, A SPELL, A VOODOO ON YOU? CONSULT: THE MAN WHO KNOWS.

We were deep in the South Side of the city, at the heart of *Whirl* country. Looking out at this battlefield of garbage, ruined streets and housing projects, I was tempted to believe that the awfulness of the place could be accounted for only in terms of hexes and spells.

"You ever hear of Pruitt Igoe?" the cabdriver asked. "That was right there. It got so bad, that place, they had to dynamite it out. Bang!" he clapped his hands happily over the top of the steering wheel. "That was something else."

> WHY did Vitalis Pitts Brown, 27, of 6024 W.N. Market, deem it absolutely essential, entirely necessary and a duty to shoot down Cleophus Threlkeld, 41, of 512 E. Linton? He did it.
>
> . . .
>
> WHY does Lafayette Williams, 28, of 4317 N. Market, deal in so much

257

stolen property and loot? Police
will get you yet, boy. Beware.

. . .

WHY did Cassius Parker, 33, of
4916 Arlington, shoot at Larry
Manning, 26, so many times in an
effort to kill him at 6953 Plymouth?
All of your bullets went astray.
Don't be surprised if Larry kills
you Nov. 4, 1979.

. . .

WHY is Ella Sullivan, 45, making
things so good to Mr. Horace Jones
in her Brown Skinned Beauty
Salon at 7423 N. Grand that police
had to arrest him for getting so
excited and crying like a baby wolf?

Twenty minutes later I had an answer, of a kind, to all these questions. We had left the city behind and arrived at the wooded campus
of a religious college with its own radio station on the grounds. The
receptionist was knitting at her desk, a stout woman in her fifties with
frizzy hair and bifocals. She immediately started to talk about murder.
Two women students had been killed on the campus. One had been
out jogging, one returning from the college Laundromat. Both had
been raped, then knifed.

"I walk in fear of my own shadow," the receptionist said. "One in
every four women is a target for rape. You don't have to be young or
pretty."

She feared downtown St. Louis even more than she feared the campus. She hadn't been into the city in two years. It was now just a place
that she read about in the newspapers, a lurid theater of slayings, stab-
bings, holdups and rapes.

"You know why we got all this now?"

It was the question on which whole conventions of sociologists and
criminologists get wrecked, but the receptionist had the light of salvation dancing behind her glasses.

"It's nutrition. I'm a believer in the nutrition theory. It's fast food.
The junk they raise kids up on now, it's doing things to their brains.
It's changing the molecular structure of the human brain! I've been
reading up on the evidence. They got me convinced, those scientists.
You look at the statistics. Did they have crime like this before dogs and

burgers and French-fries and high cholesterol? They've done analysis on what rapists *eat*. Junk food! They got these concentrations of it in the *body*. I mean to tell you, it's like passing gas into the head. They go crazy on it, and then they go out and do these terrible things. . . ."

My face must have given me away.

"That's a scientific theory. That's not what I say, that's what scientists all over America are saying: it's in the *diet*."

I saw Cassius Parker, 33, with his .357 Magnum, his stomach distended with a mess of chewed burger, frozen pizza, tacos, ketchup, mustard, French-fries, buns and relishes.

REV. MOTHER TAYLOR
Guarantees Help in 6 Hours

> Got bad luck, voodoo? Do you have a hex on you? Do you have a pain in your body and the doctors say there is nothing wrong with you? Do you want your loved one or sweetheart back? Do you suffer from lack of money? Do you want to win in everything that you do? Do you have drinking problems? Did your husband or wife leave you and you did not know why? One letter will convince you that Mother Taylor can help you.

The studio receptionist and the witches who advertised in the *Whirl* were on exactly the same path. They lived in a society so baffling and so bad that only magic could explain it. Mother Taylor sold bottles of "blessed oil" to cure the ills of St. Louis. The receptionist had bought her "nutrition theory," complete with its okay status words like *evidence, statistics, analysis, molecular*. What kind of city was this, where people had been reduced to the practice of helpless witchcraft?

Having no one else to call up on the phone, the man dialed Room Service. Asked to identify himself, at first he couldn't remember who he was, then saw that his number was on his telephone. He read it off into the mouthpiece. It was way up in the 1800s; probably the date of some battle in the Crimean War. At least it gave him what the hotel no doubt regarded as a privileged view. From his window he could see six clogged freeways, a line of giant electricity pylons, and the bald, oily levee at the edge of the river. The blue-brick factories below had names in scabbed lettering which meant nothing to him: CRUNDEN MARTIN, NOOTER BOILERMAKERS, CORNELL SEED COMPANY, PEABODY COAL. On the flight that had brought him here, the words of an old Judy

Garland song had been going around in his head like a repeating loop of tape. They contained more or less all he had ever known of the city.

Meet me in St. Louis, Louie,
Meet me at the Fair.
Don't tell me the lights are shining
Anyplace but there.

Yet in St. Louis itself, even its own song didn't work. Everyone called it *Lewis,* not *Louie,* and the grinding off-rhyme had been annoying the man since his arrival. He'd searched his head for a better-sounding alternative, but all he'd come up with so far was *Meet me in St. Louis, do, Miss,* which made the words read as if they were addressed to the call girl whom he didn't dare call. He sat aggrievedly by the phone, staring at his fingernails and waiting for the daiquiri that he didn't want. What the hell. *Suez? Who is? Where the zoo is?*

He was, perhaps mercifully, ignorant of one important fact. In this city of desperate magical remedies, he had himself been set up as one of the saviors of St. Louis. He and all the other solitary men in their hotel rooms were supposed to be revitalizing downtown. Almost all native St. Louisans who could afford to had left the city long ago, moving west to Forest Park, Clayton, Ladue and the other suburbs out "in the county" where the tax base was rich, schools were good and trees grew thickly on every street. The city, stripped of all but its very poorest residents, was trying to bring itself back to life with passing tourists, conventioneers, the Saturday ball-game trade, visiting electricians from India, and me.

The city had "rehabilitated" La Clede's Landing for us, installing fake gas lamps on the cobbled streets of wine bars, gift shops and novelty restaurants where we could do inspiriting things like "eat in the authentic atmosphere of an old-time political convention"—rooting for Calvin Coolidge over our Delmonico steaks and swinging to Herbert Hoover with our ice cream. It had built the giant ribbed shell of the Busch Stadium and the great Convention Center on the corner of Seventh and Martin Luther King. The hotels in which we were adrift were part of the plan, and so was the Gateway Arch.

The plan, so far as I could perceive it, struck me as crazy. It seemed on much the same level as Nutrition Theory and Mother Taylor's Blessed Oil. Our gang of well-heeled transients was likely to bring only more miseries to the city. Temporarily uprooted, unfamilied, not even knowing each other, we were hopeless material for citizenship. We didn't know which streets were safe and which weren't. With time and money heavy on our hands, we were natural bait for every crook in town. The only industries that really flourished on our presence were crime and prostitution.

I could see no sense in it at all. Baffled, I went to police headquarters and talked to a captain there.

"It's just like chickens and chicken hawks," he said. "How can you tell a guy who comes to a convention with his wife that if he goes north of the Convention Center he's taking his life in his hands?"

"How far north does he have to go?"

"One block. Then you're in the rat run. It belongs to the hoods. You can't police it. The guys can disappear into any door. They just have to say the cops are on their tail, and the door will open for them, and it's 'Here, hide under the bed.' They got it made."

The conventions provided a game reserve which the natives treated as a free larder. We made easy pickings. Better still, we didn't stay in town to give evidence against our attackers on the rare occasions when they were caught. The year before, a dancer in the Bolshoi Ballet had been raped.

"We got the guy. We got a signed confession out of him. And he's walking free out there right now. Where was the girl when his case came up and we needed her to give evidence?"

"Moscow?"

"Well the one place she wasn't was St. Louis. It's the same all over. Guy has his wallet snatched, gets beat over the head, lands in City Hospital, and goes home to Washington State or someplace. We catch the thief. But by the time the case comes up, the guy's saying to himself, 'Hell, what was a hundred dollars and a headache?' He's not going to come back to St. Louis to testify. This is the last goddamn city in the world that he wants to make another visit to."

The captain's reasonable pessimism was lightened by one fact. Around Lafayette Square, on the South Side of the city, there was a cluster of airy brick Victorian houses. Many were in ruins, without windows and roofs; cheap to buy, expensive to knock into any sort of livable shape. Since the gasoline crisis, a lot of young couples had moved in from the county to the Lafayette Square district. While they were rebuilding their wrecked houses, they had had to mount twenty-four-hour guards on them. What was restored one day tended to be stolen or desecrated the next night.

"You need a lot of courage to move into Lafayette Square," the captain said. "It could be a nightmare if you've got kids to worry about, but these folks are mostly too young for that. I admire their guts and I kind of feel relieved that nobody in my family's tried it."

These middle-class pioneers had not, at first, been much helped by the police.

"Again and again I was hearing the same line. My cops had been out on an attack or a burglary around Lafayette Square; all they'd said was 'This wouldn't happen to you if you lived out in the county.' I told them, that's the dumbest thing they can say. We need people to stay in the city. We need them to make the tax base bigger. Then we can have more cops, better schools, everything. I tell my guys, 'It's that tax base that's paying your salary, so *listen* to these people. Keep 'em in the city. If they want protection, give them protection. If they want foot patrols or canine, give 'em foot patrols, give 'em canine.' "

"So if this goes on, how long d'you think it'll take to make the city habitable again?"

"Well . . . if they raised the price of gas to ten dollars a gallon . . . if they gave me another thousand men . . . if . . ." He laughed. "I don't know. Ten years. Maybe. With a big thick lucky streak thrown in."

"Or magic. . . ." I told him about the other potions and theories that were being peddled around his city.

"Yeah. I reckon we ought to send out for a case of that Mother What's'ername's Oil. You know something? Next year, we got a national police convention coming up in St. Louis. I got to do a lot of the organization on that. You know what kind of convention brings more hookers into town than any other? Police conventions. That's the kind of cleft stick I have to live in here in this office."

Or Magic.

MADAM LORAINE
Frank Johnson Speaks

I had bad luck. Everything I did went wrong for me. I felt I had a curse or a spell on me from my enemies because they wanted me to suffer or keep me down. They wanted to put me in an insane asylum or have me go on the operating table. The devil's powers really had me. I went to Madam Loraine. She destroyed the evil curse forever. Now I am successful. I have good luck. She took me out of darkness and brought me to the road of happiness and prosperity in life. Bless God for Madam Loraine. I feel like shouting it to the world.

Do not lose hope. Madam Loraine guarantees to make you well and happy again. Come to Madam Loraine and she will remove the hex or curse from you. She will use her God gifted psychic powers to find your lost articles. What you see with your eyes, your heart will believe. Madam Loraine is St. Louis' greatest. 7208 Chippewa 555-9717

I escaped a consultation with Madam Loraine by a hair's breadth. Somewhere in the deranged alphabet of local radio stations I met a woman who asked me what I was doing for dinner that evening.

Her first word when she arrived was "Plus—" Sally lived in the middle of sentences to which she was making constant additions. She began with afterthoughts.

"Plus I had to stop for gas, which is why I'm late. Plus, I was late anyway."

Her long fur coat looked as if she made a habit of going swimming in it. Her pale hair was making a successful jailbreak from the pins that she had jammed into it. She hadn't yet removed the price tag from the neck of her scarlet cocktail dress.

"Plus . . . I don't know. Oh, hell, just give me what you're drinking, huh? What *are* you drinking?"

"Martini."

"I *hate* Martinis. Yeah. Okay. No, that's what I want. I'd like a Martini."

She brought with her a buzz of static electricity. Tense, slender, she was all sparks and crackling filaments. Thinking, she scrunched up her narrow face as thoughts escaped from her in dozens like her unruly hair. Most of what I got was just the spin-offs and industrial waste of this complicated process. Scrunching, she said, "God! . . . like . . . because . . ." and her hand slapped at the air as if she'd seen a blowfly overhead. ". . . kind of . . . well, *you* know . . . right?" Somewhere in the dots between the words lay a whole succession of rejected ideas. It was hard to tell whether they were of the order of grocery lists or of Einstein's relativity theory.

We ate at Anthony's. The big, half-empty restaurant was unnaturally dark; its napery, by fitful candlelight, was unnaturally white. The waiter, insofar as I could clearly see his face, was Henry Kissinger.

"You're not into *cars*—" Sally said, turning on me in a sudden bristle of angry boredom.

"No, not at all." I felt stung.

"God."

"Why?"

"What? Oh . . . I dunno. Yeah. I remembered. Sorry. No, the last guy I dated here, he was into cars. You know what the conversation was? He was going on about *car washes*. I was pretty well switched off, not listening; then he leans over the table and says in this, like, *intimate* voice, 'Which part do you like best? The washing or the waxing?' That was our conversation, for godsake. I went into hiding in the powder room. God, he was a drag."

"Which part *do* you like best—the washing or the waxing?"

"Have you seen my car? I don't wash it. I hate car washes, period." She gave a dismissive, ponylike shake of her head. Pins tinkled on the plates below.

Sally's voice had kept the dry, sandy tone of the Midwest, but it was a voice that had been places. She'd gone to college first in Philadelphia, then on the West Coast. She spent weekends in New York. Her $220-a-week job in her hometown was a stopover between planes, and she was fizzing with impatience at St. Louis. Technically speaking, she was twenty-seven, but she managed to slip, at almost every sentence end, from being seventeen to thirty-four and back again. She liked to keep things fluid. The rush and scatter of her talk left me limping behind, feeling elderly and slow.

"*God,* no—that wasn't on the kib*butz;* this was in the Chinese restaurant in San Fran*cisco* . . ."

In leaps and swoops, we covered the world. I learned how she'd broken with her last "guy" six months before, how she'd rowed with her Catholic boss that morning, how she'd backpacked through France and Italy, how she hated going into bars alone, how she got "dizzy" on wine, how her mother was having difficulty selling luncheon tickets for the forthcoming visit of Isaac Bashevis Singer to the local Hadassah. Just occasionally, I found a couple of bits of the scrambled jigsaw that did fit together.

When I lit her cigarette for her over the cheese board, she cupped her hand around mine to steady the flame. Two days later, following the tracks of several hundred thousand St. Louisans before me, I moved west; into Sally's apartment in Clayton.

It was a magical transformation. Seen from this new angle, from out "in the county," St. Louis was changed as effectively as if a wand had been waved over it. I, too. Repatriated to domestic life, I took to it with the gratitude of a shipwrecked man rescued from a desert island.

In Clayton, estates of half-timbered Tudor houses, gloomy with conifers, stood behind tall wrought-iron gates. As streets in Clayton went, our own street was mean and ordinary; a long avenue of rippling leaves and gabled villas. Women in our neighborhood went shopping in little British sports cars. The neighborhood laundry sold spray cans of Mace for blinding rapists and muggers—the one reminder that another, nastier world lay just a few miles off beyond the trees, that our own safe green exile might come under attack one day. Our country lanes, broad lawns and leaded windows had the special preciousness of things we'd won against the odds from the ugly city at the wrong end of the highway.

Sally's three-room apartment was a little out of phase with Clayton. It didn't feel precious. It had the temporary air of a motel cabin from which she was about to move out at any moment. Nothing in the place looked as if she had deliberately chosen it. Her possessions seemed to have happened to her by accident. There were a foot-high replica of Rodin's *Thinker*, a Buddha, an African girl in fake ebony, a mildly repulsive wall clock made of petrified wood from Arizona, some tired potted plants with candy-striped bows tied around their necks, a glass cylinder of heart-shaped candies. She had papered the walls of her kitchen with a design, terrifying in the early mornings, of black feet on a blood-colored ground. She said that she'd thought "it looked kind of cute," but the emphasis was on the past tense. I wondered whether she had been given the other objects in her life, or whether, like the wallpaper, they were all the results of some long-ago passing impulse, tolerated now because Sally had ceased to notice them. I wondered, with a premonitory spasm of disquiet, where I fitted in. Was I kin to the Buddha, the wall clock and the potted plants? I half-suspected so, and rather warmed to them.

The bookshelf in her living room didn't give much away, either. *The Amy Vanderbilt Complete Book of Etiquette* stood at one end; Joseph Heller's *Good as Gold* at the other. In the middle, *The World According to Garp* had *The Shikse's Guide to Jewish Men* as its next-door neighbor.

"You want to put a record on?"

I went through the rack. Most of the records there had been put back in the wrong sleeves. Dave Brubeck had landed inside Folk Songs from Israel, Miles Davis inside Dave Brubeck. No detective searching her apartment could have fingered Sally on this sort of evidence. She had contrived to keep herself to herself and all her options open.

Sally had embraced the adventitious as a sort of moral good, and it enabled us to improvise an instant common life. Within twenty-four hours, we fell into a routine that felt as set as if we'd been following it for years.

Each morning, the alarm went off at some dreadful time in the dark. Sally, trailing around the apartment in blouse and panty hose, would lose things—keys, bras, tape cassettes, skirts—and I would retrieve them for her. I burned the coffee and listened to the tinny squawking of the radio. At 6 A.M., the announcer sounded quite mad, his tidbits of news like the delusions of a fever victim.

"Scientists at New Mexico State University have recovered twenty-nine particles of antimatter from the upper atmosphere. Balloons were used for the ascent, and the particles were found at a height of 120,000 feet. This proves . . ."

"What the hell is a particle of antimatter?"

"I dunno. You seen my other shoe anyplace? I guess it's kind of like . . . Oh, God . . . my goddamn shoe."

At six thirty, we joined the slow shunt of suburban traffic down Route 40 in Sally's blue Volkswagen, our headlights slowly paling in the grubby half-light. On the final, looping stretch of elevated section, we'd see the Arch, an ellipse of tarnished silver framed between factory walls.

"You know," Sally said, "I *like* it. It gives me a kick to see it's still there every morning."

I was taken aback to realize that, as a resident of Clayton, looking in on the city from my fastness in the suburbs, I liked the Arch too.

Sally worked in a shiny black skyscraper. Outside it, we kissed decorously, I moved into the driver's seat, Sally was lost behind the uniformed doorman, and I joined all the other wives and homemakers who made up the convoy of cars returning to Clayton, Ladue, University City, Westwood, Richmond Heights and Frontenac.

I liked being a housewife. I didn't want my consciousness raised. I was sluttish over the morning's *Post-Dispatch*. I scribbled letters to friends on Sally's monogrammed notepaper. I dusted the Buddha, watered the potted plants and made a show of pushing the vacuum cleaner around the carpets. At ten, Sally would telephone from her office, and I'd hang on the details of her working day. She had an interview to do, a script to write, a tape to edit, a press conference to attend. I was appalled that anyone should have been able to buy Sally's electric busyness for $220 a week; I could hear her over the phone, being four people at once and trying to be a fifth to me.

I drove to our local supermarket, and came back with groceries in brown paper bags. I pored over Sally's only cookbook, a mint copy of *The Jewish Gourmet*. I worried a lot about how to make soufflés rise. In the cupboard under the sink I found a hoard of strange machinery.

There were electric mixers, whisks, choppers, slicers, graters, mincers, dicers—all still in the plastic cases in which they'd been packed at the factory. I fitted a plug to one of these objects, and succeeded in turning half a dozen egg whites into snow.

"God," said Sally. "What's *that?*"

"White of egg. Where did you get all this stuff? Don't you ever use it?"

"Oh . . . they were gifts."

"They must have cost a fortune."

"I hate to cook. Like, I can boil eggs, you know—"

By afternoon, I would sometimes remember why I was supposed to be in St. Louis. I went to the Museum of Art, where there were three river paintings by George Caleb Bingham: *Jolly Flatboatmen in Port, Raftsmen Playing Cards* and *The Wood Boat.* I stood, rapt and critical, in front of the pictures. Once I had used Bingham as raw material for a dream of the Mississippi. Now I was able to match his river against mine on something close to equal terms. He had exactly caught the way the current twitched and folded over on itself, the leaden sheen of the water and the ruffled lights of the wind on it. I could steer a safe course through his paintings, watching where the river quickened over a submerged sandbar and made a swirling eddy in the crook of a bend. I had seen the faces of the men, too. They were still on the river, in a change of costume. The only picture that struck a really discordant note was *Jolly Flatboatmen in Port.* The surface of its paint was more chipped and cracked than that of the others, as if it had had to make more of a struggle to survive intact. In it, a barge was moored off-channel, by the warehouses of La Clede's Landing; and the St. Louis waterfront was dense with steamboats, skiffs and rafts. I could redraw the whole thing, square inch for square inch. It would show fungoid green mud, broken cobbles and a convention of undertakers discussing (as I had found out) the problems of transportation involved after the mass suicide in Jonestown, Guyana.

When Sally finished work, I collected her from the lobby of her skyscraper looking drained and wan, the exhausted breadwinner. Our route home took us past the front of my old hotel. Who, I wondered, was up in the 1800s now? I guessed he had a copy of *Playboy* instead of *The New Yorker* . . . bourbon on the rocks from Room Service . . . Nooter Boilermakers and Crunden Martin out the window . . . six-o'clock panic with an empty evening ahead . . . my almost-double, the poor guy.

For me, Sally's office was a running soap opera in which I lived vicariously. For the ten miles along the darkening highway, I pestered her for the gossip of the day. I learned the names of her colleagues. Mildred and Bob and Harry and Jean became brilliant two-dimensional characters, with the exaggerated reality of people in *As the World Turns*. Life at the top of the black skyscraper was exciting stuff, with smoldering enmities, clandestine affairs, intrigues, conspiracies and sudden bolts from the blue. I lapped it up.

"So," Sally said, beginning the sad question that all working husbands have to ask all stay-at-home wives, "what did *you* do, hon?"

"I went to the art museum." I told her about the Binghams. As material for anecdote they were, if anything, a little flatter than my morning journey around the supermarket. In any case, Sally's interest in paintings was scant. Had she ever been made to confront the hoary question of grandmother versus Rembrandt in burning house, she wouldn't have hesitated for a second in putting her foot through the Rembrandt on the way to rescuing the grandmother. There was a framed print of Grant Wood's *American Gothic* propped against the wall by her dressing table, and a meaningless geometric abstract over her bed; and between them they made up as much art as Sally cared to handle in her life. She now lay stretched out in the passenger seat, blowing smoke rings at the sun visor.

"God, I ought to take you around to these friends of my family's. They got this art collection . . . Like, I mean to say, they've got sort of ten Picassos in every bathroom, you know?"

"What happens when the steam gets to them?"

"I dunno. What d'you reckon? Wilt. I guess."

At home, I mixed the drinks. I brought her little bowls of peanuts and raisins. Sally's face was scrunched in thought. Finally she said, "Plus: . . . oh, I dunno."

For days the fall wind, hot and wet, blew down our street like a monsoon. It came in gusts of fifty and sixty miles an hour, shredding the last leaves from the cherries, sycamores and maples. It croaked and chirruped in the metal fronds of the air conditioner. It made stoplights toss on their overhead wires; street signs shuddered on their poles; the knee-high swirl of leaves on every road gave Clayton the appearance of a lake city on stilts. One early morning, I made a detour around Wharf Street to inspect the river. It looked like an enormous fleece, with a single towboat struggling upstream in a caul of spray. If things went on like this, my own boat, locked away, off the river, wouldn't be launched again until the spring. Even without the wind, one could feel the press of coming winter. For the last week, the television ads for snowblowers had been falling thicker and faster between programs. On the day that I had collected my new set of charts for the Lower Mississippi from the Corps of Engineers, I had bought myself an Eskimo's quilted parka. I hid both it and the charts in my suitcase and said nothing of them to Sally.

Our weekends were snug and sociable. It occurred to me that my river charts might turn out to be like Ed's old railway timetable in Muscatine; out of date, good for nothing except grist for some fleeting annual fantasy.

Sally took me to the house where Picassos were rumored to be languishing on the bathroom walls. It was near Washington University, a pretty cottage in the St. Louis–Tudor style. From the outside, it looked like the sort of residence a woodcutter in Sussex in the 1540s might have been proud of; inside, it was more suggestive of the private quarters of a Medici prince. The owners were away in Europe, collecting more treasure, but Sally and I were let in by the light-skinned black maid.

A Monet, vast and blue, was hung over the chintz sofa in the sitting room; and the walls were checkerboarded with masterpieces. I couldn't take them in. Instead, I found myself looking at the leftover clutter of family life; the open books on tables, overshoes, half-emptied bottles, ashtrays, papers, coats and hats. Beside these ordinary things, the Picassos, Braques, Matisses, Courbets, Duchamps had the alienated splendor of exiled royalty in a seaside boardinghouse.

Embarrassed at finding my eye so numbed, I asked the maid which picture she liked best. She pointed at a big angular Picasso from the 1920s.

"That's my favorite. I like all the straight lines. I ain't so keen on his figures." Like me, she found the paintings themselves difficult to come to terms with. Her face lit with real enthusiasm only when she explained how the house had been wired against burglars. "You know, you only have to touch a window, just light, like that, and the alarm goes off down in the police station? It's *wonderful!*"

In the study, I tried to concentrate on a lovely Courbet sketch.

Sally said: "What's all this worth? A million? Millions?"

"Tens of millions. Hundreds, probably. I don't know. Billions. Trillions. Squillions."

"God," said Sally, "I'm so innocent about that kind of thing," and suddenly hugged me. With my arms around her, I could feel her pulsing and sparking; it was like embracing a human-sized microchip with all its circuits on Overload. Next to us stood a skeletal Giacometti on a low side table. Its head was on a level with ours. Sally twisted her face around, stared at the sculpture, and looked back at me.

"Hey—do you think I'm too sort of, well, like, *skinny?*"

We went out into the garden. The swimming pool, drained for winter, was soddenly carpeted by dead leaves. Its marble rim was lined with reclining figures: fat ones by Henry Moore, thin ones by Giacometti and Arp. Together they suggested a group of badly out-of-condition old folks at some Californian hydrotherapy clinic. One expected nurses to come from out of the trees and ease them, one by one, into the pool.

That evening we met Sally's father at the St. Louis Club for dinner. Like just about everything else in the city, the club had moved west; it now occupied the fifteenth floor of an office building on a hill in Clayton, where its fumed oak, sporting prints and civic portraits were surreally suspended in their frame of concrete, glass and steel. From the club dining room, the hideous buildings of the central city looked innocuous and pretty. By night, at this height and distance, they looked like a fleet of lighted ships riding at anchor. We were a long, long way away from the St. Louis of gunmen, black magicians and wretched conventioneers.

Sally's father greeted his daughter with a look of deep mock melancholy. He raised his right hand and slowly clenched and unclenched it three times.

"The market's fallen?" Sally said.

"Fifteen points," her father said. "Tomorrow, know what I'm going to do? I'm going to buy some clothes." He encircled her with his arm. "There's a recession on: let's go shopping."

He was a big man with a frost of white hair over a pouchy, humorous face; a wise and wary ironist. I was frightened of his reputation. I'd heard of him before I met Sally, and he'd been described as "the one man in St. Louis who makes Wall Street listen when he talks." He was "sharp as a pistol." In the business aristocracy of the Midwest, Sally's father was a self-made duke. He handled the marriages and divorces of great companies. He was a conjuror with money. He could, so I was told, pull a handful of the stuff through a napkin ring and make it billow out into a fortune.

As he walked through the dining room, his importance was as manifest as the glow of light around a medieval saint. People stopped talking at their tables and nodded gravely to him as he passed. Waiters flew on wings ahead of him. When Sally announced that she was going to the ladies' room, I panicked at the prospect of being left alone with him.

"That one . . ." he said, half-lowering his large eyelids in the direction of Sally's back, "she's bright." It wasn't a father's fond indulgence so much as a neutral, financier's assessment of a stock.

"Yes," I said. "Isn't she. Very bright. Indeed."

I felt that my own rating on this particular question was already beginning to drop through the bottom of the market. I had only one idea I thought might arouse a glimmer of interest in him, and that was borrowed; from Edmund Wilson's *To the Finland Station*. Wilson had described Karl Marx as a man who had made a kind of poetry out of money and its movements. He had been able to apprehend currency as a sensuous object. He might have been a brilliant capitalist had he not felt revulsion for the financial system which, in his writing, he compulsively caressed, half in tenderness, half in hate.

I put the Wilson argument to Sally's father. Yes, he said; that sounded right. Money was something for which it was possible to have an artist's feeling for his medium. There was still for him as much creative excitement in the making of a deal now as he'd had in his twenties. He loved the sense of "swinging from the rafters." He stopped speaking. Something was nagging at him.

"Look," he said. "You take a book, like the one by this Wilson guy. How many copies would they have to print of that, to make a profit? Five thousand? Ten?"

I told him what little I knew of the commercial side of the book trade, fascinated by the way his eyes followed what I was saying. They were Trappist's eyes: serious, peaceful and contemplative.

"This must all seem terribly small beer to you."

"Small? A dollar interests me. Especially if it's a dollar profit."

Sally came back. Her father, swinging from the rafters between dour puritanism and gross excess, made niggardly sips at a glass of Coca-Cola while he lit each new cigarette from the butt of his last.

All through the meal he was courted by young men. They stood deferentially by the table in hound's-tooth jackets, striped ties and tortoiseshell glasses. Sometime . . . if he could spare a moment . . . perhaps . . . they'd appreciate it. One was thinking of buying a television station in Illinois; another had seen that a baseball team in Florida was up for sale.

"*His* family," said Sally of one of these young men, "they've got quite a bit of money, haven't they?" The question struck me as a shade redundant.

Her father sipped, smoked, smiled. "I haven't counted it," he said.

"Do you ever find yourself taking real pratfalls?" I asked.

"Unh-hunh. Something I learned right back at the beginning. You can make any mistake you like; it doesn't matter. Only never make the same mistake twice."

I talked of what seemed to me to be the cruel division between the deep woodiness of the western suburbs and the bald brick of the city ghettoes. I told Sally's father how my first view of St. Louis had been based on the newspaper story about the rapists who had been caught because their victim had seen a tree through a window. He considered the situation from all sides.

"Now, if they'd had the sense to cut that tree down, those guys'd be running free." He laughed. "Next time, I guess they'll pack an axe."

He left on the dot of ten o'clock. He was always in bed by ten thirty: a rule, he said, that he'd never allowed any boom or crash to interfere with.

"You stay on. Sign for all you want."

"Please," I said, "if I may, I'd like to—"

"No," said Sally. "Daddy *loves* to pay."

We went in for Sunday treats: bagels, fresh-squeezed orange juice, the multistoried edifice of the Sunday *New York Times*, its sections scattered around every room. We squabbled over who got to read the Book Review first. We annoyed each other by reading paragraphs of news out loud. Former President Gerald Ford announced that he was definitely not available for the Republican nomination.

"That means he *must* be running," Sally said.

The Shah of Iran arrived in New York from Mexico for a cancer operation.

"Why can't they take his gallbladder out in Mexico, for godsake?"

"You know why the Mexican put his wife on the railroad tracks?"

"Why?"

"Tequila."

"Huh?"

"That's the funniest joke anyone's ever heard in Buffalo, Iowa."

"It doesn't sound funny to me. Is that some kind of hoosier place?"

We visited with Sally's friends, driving downtown to Lafayette Square. It was exactly as the broad Georgian squares of north London must have looked after the Blitz. There were bright little shops on the corners selling hand-sewn quilts and antique bric-a-brac, and London-like wine bars with gardens; but their gaiety was forced and defiant. For every smart "rehab" there was a blind ruin, its oxidized brickwork falling out, and weeds growing through the trash on its floors. In the sacked Victorian streets around the square one could sense the waiting shadows of Catullus Eugene Blackwater, 28, Hugh Saustell, 25, and all the other thugs who hadn't yet been honored by a mention in the *Whirl.*

Yet sprawled, talking, among colored scatter cushions on a floor of varnished pine, slopping wine from a flagon of Gallo into a tumbler, I felt uncannily at home. It wasn't just the bookish run of the conversation; it was St. Louis itself. The city was supposed to belong to the West. The full title of Saarinen's monumental loop was The Westward Expansion Memorial Arch, and the museum below it commemorated the great nineteenth-century drive west beyond the Mississippi; but St. Louis was the least obviously "Western" town I had been in since I'd started my journey. Its architecture had none of the happy eccentricity of places like Muscatine. It didn't go in for fake steamboats and boondocks-Greek. What St. Louis liked was solid Georgian, Queen Anne, Palladian and half-timbered Tudor. It wanted things to be in prim good taste. It would have got on very nicely over the teacups with my Wiltshire aunts.

Old, genteel St. Louis—T. S. Eliot's city—thought of itself as a slice of cultivated Europe. It seemed mystified as to how it had landed here, stranded on the wrong side of the big American river. Sally and I had spent an afternoon in the Forest Park section, drinking draft Bass in the Welsh pub off Kingshighway and rummaging in the bookstores along Euclid Avenue. *Kingshighway. Euclid Avenue.* Between them, the names defined the wistful snobbery of a city that was soft on royalty on the one hand and on the most severe of classical geometers on the other.

"Really . . ." I heard someone say; ". . . *really,*" and the voice had more of the throaty Anglophilia of Beacon Hill, Boston, than of the lolloping drawl of the Midwest. The woman next to me mentioned the word "Missoura." It was a pronunciation that had often puzzled me. Some people said "Missouri," others "Missoura." I had asked why before. I'd been told that the *a* was a south-of-state ending, that it was a west-of-state ending, that it was rural usage as against the urban *i*. No one really seemed to know. I said this to the woman.

"Oh, no," she said. "It's perfectly simple. New Money says 'Missouri'; Old Money says 'Missoura.' "

Somewhere in our garden there was a snake, but neither Sally nor I heard its giveaway rattle. The gales had died down; the temperature had settled. The carpet in the apartment was left unswept one morning while I laid out my river charts on the floor and plotted mileages. I didn't pack the charts away, and that evening Sally turned over their big pages until she reached a nowhere down in Arkansas. Not speaking, she put *Miles Davis in Concert* on the turntable and sat listening to it through stereo headphones.

"Martini?"

"Uh-uh." Her face made a quick, negative squirm.

In the Jewish country club in Westwood, where all the crockery was heraldically imprinted with a tennis racket crossed with a niblick or a mashie, we eked out a moody supper, overlit by crystal chandeliers. Passing friends of Sally's parents would save us from each other for five minutes at a time; we'd brighten for them, then fall back to listening to the noise of each other's knives and forks. Gloomily, I remembered that I'd been here before, and at the back of my mind I could see the oily gleam of the river opening out.

Next day the phone rang at ten. I picked it up. "Hi!" said a warm, kittenly voice.

"Sally!" I said. A new leaf. "I'm sorry—"

"This is a recorded message from several chiropractors in your neighborhood. . . ."

I slammed the phone back into its cradle. Sally didn't call.

For dinner we drove to the most expensive restaurant in Clayton, hoping that its showy glamour would restore a little of our own lost shine. We were met by a whole ship's crew of waiters in dress uniform: captains, lieutenants, quartermasters, stewards. It took half a dozen senior officers to escort us to a table for two, but when a pop singer came in, the entire company marched and piped him to his seat. Sally took in his black hat with a Mexican brim, his permed, shoulder-length hair, his beads, boots and caftan.

"That's what I *hate* to see—" But I knew that the singer, in his arrogant duds, was just a convenient stand-in for the man at Sally's own table.

We made a solemn, engrossed play of snapping the shells open around the rubbery bodies of our langoustes. *Rubber,* I thought . . . *bumper;* and tried to talk in our old, light way about the bumper stickers that had kept me half alarmed, half entertained on my rides around the freeways of St. Louis. GOD, GUNS & GUTS MADE AMERICA GREAT. DON'T GIVE GOD A VACATION: TAKE HIM WITH YOU WHEN YOU GO.

"I think the best one I ever saw was around Boston in 1973, just after Nixon had dumped Cox as Watergate Special Prosecutor. Practically every car in Cambridge had one. It said, 'Sack the Cox-Sacker.' "

"That's . . . obscene," Sally said, pronging a soggy tomato.

"You're being stupid and prudish."

"Plus, it's not even funny."

"I saw the weather forecast. It's okay. I'll get moving again tomorrow."

"You know? Something I didn't kind of see you as? You're a coward."

Dinner was our Reno. Before the check came, we'd had our divorce.

8

Snow Geese

I had slipped quietly out of other towns, but there was no slipping quietly away from St. Louis. The current grabbed hold of the boat, flipped it around, and sent it skidding southward out of the city like a puck on an ice rink. I hardly had time to get the motor going before I was swept past the floating depot where the tows refueled and was into the humping, broken water below the highway bridges.

Today was a new beginning. Everything had changed. On the Illinois shore, the high winds had stripped the forest and left the cottonwoods with the spiky glitter of drummers' wire brushes. Fields of crops in the bottoms on the Missouri side had been flattened into scalloped brown waves. Only a few squat thornbushes grew on the naked sandbars. The wing dams of the upper Mississippi had been replaced by high dikes of rock and shambling wooden piers which funneled the rapid current into the middle of the stream. The water was cold in the morning sun; a fast, forbidding river, its surface littered with dead trees, gasoline drums, garden fences, and lumps of polystyrene packing like sheets of frozen tapioca pudding.

There were sharp rips and creases in the current now, as if the Mississippi were trying to tear itself apart; but the most scary change was the succession of great waxy boils. I could see them coming from a long way off. Most of the river was lightly puckered by the wind, but there were patches of what looked like dead-calm water: circular in shape, a hundred yards or so across. I took them for quiet millponds, good places to light a pipe or unscrew the cap of a thermos flask. Delighted to find that the Mississippi now afforded such convenient picnic spots, I drove straight for one. As I hit its edge, the boat slewed sideways and

I was caught on the rim of a spinning centrifuge. I had mistaken it for calm water because its motion was so violent that no wind could disturb it. I could see the cap of the boil far away in the middle, a clear eighteen inches higher than the rest of the river. From this raised point, the water was spilling around and down the convex face, disappearing deep into the crack in which my boat was caught. Running the engine at full speed, I yanked myself out easily enough; but I had felt the river trying to suck me under, boat and all, and I was tense with fright. I grounded on a sandbar and scrabbled in my grip for tobacco and Valium.

From the top of my small Crusoe island, I sized up the Mississippi as an enemy. It was dappled with large whorls of treacherously smooth water. Wherever the current thrust against the bank on the far side of a bend it created an "eddy"—a local euphemism for a whirlpool as big as a baseball field. *Take bends on the inside shore.*

At least I could see a reason for these eddies and learn to predict them before they swallowed me, but I couldn't explain the boils. They came sprouting up from the river bottom, often in mid-channel, miles from any tongue of sand or rock. Their mushroom tops gleamed nastily, like patent leather. I spotted three of the things and tried to read the river to account for them; it wouldn't yield a clue.

When I was sixteen and my forehead was pitted with acne, I had gone to a chemist's shop, lurking around the pharmacist's counter until the girls were out of earshot. The pharmacist thought I wanted to buy contraceptives; all I wanted was a cure for my beastly spots, and I confided my problem to him in a shrouded confessional voice. "At your age," he said, indecently loudly, "you've got so much energy in your body that it's got to come out somewhere. Don't worry. It's perfectly natural." *Ignorant bloody fink*, I thought, and left. Looking at the boils on the face of the Mississippi, I realized that the pharmacist had had more sense than I had given him credit for. It was just the sheer energy of the river breaking out in these ugly blooms and swellings. There were no prescriptions for the condition; I was going to have to learn to live with it as I'd lived with my spots. The boils did have one good point: because they burst outward, they would tend to throw a boat off them. An eddy could draw one into its vortex like a sea anemone sucking on a child's finger.

I spent half an hour talking myself into setting off again. I was back to being a novice, as callow as I had been when I'd left Minneapolis. There was another parallel, too, with that first start, and it troubled me. The voyage had begun with my running away from London; now I was running away from another city. Sally's word rankled. *Coward.*

It didn't hit any nail quite directly on the head, but it gave a good glancing blow to one nail, at least.

She had been right to tag me as a runner-away. The only marriage I contracted had been walked out of a year later. When I had a steady job, with increments, promotion and a pension plan, I left it fast. Marital life and an office in a university with my name on the door had made the sky seem very low and very gray. I had no gift for permanence, for building slowly year by year until one had constructed a life like a granite-fronted branch of a First National Bank. I wanted to wriggle out from under the stones, and I had developed a dubious talent as an escape artist. Running away was something that had started as simple compulsion; now it was what I was good at. Some men are good at French cookery and putting up shelves; my specialty was the quiet exit through the back door, sneakers across the lawn and the relief of the cool air outside. On my river trip, I thought, I am doing only what I have always been doing: keeping the sky up by keeping on the run.

But *coward?* I kept the boat's nose headed up on the slippery water, made a wide and circling detour to skirt a boil, tucked myself close in to the Illinois shore around the bend at Michael's Towhead, exhilarated and absorbed. If riding the river was like anything else in life at all, it was like writing. One could lose oneself in the delicate business of keeping afloat and on course in just the same way as one could lose oneself in the pleasure and hazard of inching along through the words on a page, feeling for the main drift of the current and trying not to run aground. One needed a degree of disengagement to do either. Maybe Sally was right, and it was a streak of cowardice that impelled me to do both.

At Mile 132 a "towhead," half a mile wide and two miles long, swung out from the Missouri bank and squeezed the river into a tight chute. Three big tows were pulled up in line behind it, waiting to take the fast water. I ran ashore, afraid of getting in their way. The tows on the upper Mississippi had been alarming enough; these were monsters. Because of the locks, tow fleets above St. Louis had been limited to a maximum of seventeen barges. The ones across the river had twenty-five and thirty barges each; six acres of killer steel and rolling wake. The towboats themselves had correspondingly bigger engines. When they passed, they didn't just leave their wakes behind; their enormous screws kicked up a series of swirling humps in the water. For a mile or more after they had gone by, the glistening humps would hang in the river, balls of solid turbulence, capable of doing God-knows-what to a sixteen-foot aluminum boat.

A tow fleet loaded with, I reckoned, forty-five thousand tons of cement approached the head of the chute with the caution of a cat burglar. It was moving so slowly that it seemed to be trying to con the river into thinking that it wasn't there at all. As soon as its leading barges touched the point where the river gathered itself together for the long sprint down, the towboat went thrashing into reverse, its rear end spuming. It was "backing up": driving backward against the current so that it moved down the chute far more slowly than the racing water. Tows which failed to "back up" and decided to just go with the flow were liable to hit the state of Missouri with such a bang that people up in Columbia and Kansas City would report earthquake tremors. Their fleets broke loose, and stray barges of cement and grain landed on sandbars ten miles downstream.

The tricks of the current were so peculiar in this stretch of river that even the most careful tows often came apart. Already I had seen towboats go nannying about the stream in search of their lost charges and found twelve-hundred-ton cargoes nestling deep in mud and willows. A boil or an eddy could wrench at a barge, snap its hawsers and carry it off on a private voyage of its own. If it could do that to a barge . . . but pursuing that thought would definitely be an act of cowardice.

I took the chute between tows. Rocks, sand and winter trees went sizzling past. The river here was just two hundred yards wide, and millions of gallons of water were sluicing through this narrow conduit. The current must have been running at close to ten knots, a terrific speed for a navigable river. Upstream tows, driving at full power against the chute, hung, apparently motionless on the water, the camel humps of their screw wakes trailing out behind them as they muscled their way forward.

Following me down the chute was a white yacht, a millionaire's toy of the kind I'd seen lounging by the dozen, up to no good, around the bay at Monte Carlo. It overtook me, throwing up a wake as big as that of a tow. I caught a glimpse of the jeans, rusty suntans and straggly hair of the man and the girl up in the wheelhouse. The girl waved at me. She could afford to. She didn't have to deal with her sweeping rollers curling above my bow. I didn't wave back.

River people called these yachts "snow geese." They spent their summers up in the Great Lakes, where tycoons from Chicago and Detroit entertained their clients aboard them. In the fall, they were taken down the Mississippi to the Florida Keys and the Bahamas, to be picked up by their owners for Christmas vacations and business weekends. Their professional crews who took care of them during their monthlong voyages in the spring and fall were an odd and scruffy gang. Like me, they were runners-away. Many had dropped out of college. Some had worked as deckhands on the tows. The men wore rings on their fingers and crucifixes on their chests. The women, swathed in layers of jersey, looked like roustabouts and talked pure Ivy League. We kept on bumping into each other in wharfside bars.

"You taught at *Smith?* Well, shit. I was at Bennington. You know Bernard Malamud? I audited his class. Hey, Steve, this guy was at Smith —he was a professor. . . ." And Steve, who had majored in towboating and came from Greenville, Arkansas, turned on me with a long, dark backcountry stare.

"Now, is that so?" He looked as if he were fingering a gun.

"You read his books? Professor Malamud's?"

"Yeah, sure. . . ."

But I was afraid of Steve's eyes. I thought that a cozy discussion of *Idiots First* and *The Magic Barrel* might make him reach for his revolver. This was a pity. Steve, Ms. Bennington and I had a world in common. We didn't have to talk about books: we might have had a useful seminar on the subject of what had made us all run.

I put in at a lime dock and ferry landing just short of Sainte Genevieve on the Missouri shore and pulled the boat up onto a rocky beach under the trees. The town had been a port once, shipping lead and grain downriver. Now it was stranded, a mile inland. Gabouri Creek, up which the steamboats used to run, had silted in long before. My chart showed that the town still had a "Front Street"—just a name: the last relic of Sainte Genevieve's dependence on the Mississippi.

I heaved my cases over the railroad tracks and sat at the bottom of the gravel road that led up to town. Somewhere nearby there was the steady *whup-whup* of gunfire. The shots came closer. They turned into a young man with a sad mustache, glooming along a wooded creek with a Magnum rifle. He was zapping the hell out of beer cans. Soon he was standing right across from me, over the tracks. *Whup-piaow!* Another goner. His face had the heavy, expended look of postcoital *tristesse*. I wondered whom he had been squinting at with such rapt fury: wife? dad? boss? mother-in-law? He took another bead on the can, just to make sure, and missed. "Shit!" he said. "Fuckin' goddamn shit!"

"Hi," I said, thinking it about time I revealed myself before I got mistaken for a beer can or Charlie Cong.

"What you doin' there, man?"

"I don't know. Waiting for a lift up to town. I just got off a boat."

He rattled back the bolt of his gun, and the spent cartridge flipped out onto the gravel siding.

"You see . . ." he said slowly, "what I mean to say is, these goddamn sights ain't right yet. New gun. I got to fix 'em. Oncet I get the blame things adjusted up right . . ."

He didn't need to apologize to me for killing his father. I said, "Sure. I used to shoot myself once. It takes a long time to get sights properly leveled."

"Yeah. I come out here most days . . . shoot along the crick awhile. . . . Them sights, though, they're kind of tricky sonofabitches. So, you want a ride?"

He drove me into Sainte Genevieve in his black Chevy pickup. It was the sort of small American town in which green "historical markers" outnumber all other varieties of vegetation. Sainte Genevieve had been founded in 1735, and there was hardly a patch of ground in the place that didn't warrant a historical marker. The only serious omission was the filling station. Its gas pumps looked to me as if they were vintage 1950s Redcoat-soldier style and had a better right to a historical marker than half the other sites in town. I tried to find a bar that wasn't historic, failed, and ended up in "The First Brick Building West of the Mississippi." I had the nagging sense that it wasn't by any means the first brick building west of the Mississippi that I'd been in. What was beyond doubt was the fact that it was the first brick building west of the Mississippi in which I had met a drunk with an artificial larynx.

He was shriveled and lachrymose. He asked me what I was up to; when I told him that I was riding the river, he chawed and spat and said, "He'll bury your ass, you don't treat him right." The words came out on one note, in a deep mechanical bass like a speak-your-weight machine.

"You got a radio?"

"No."

"You believe in God?"

This particular question always spelled trouble.

"I'm asking you, feller. You believe in God?"

"Well . . . not exactly; no."

"I don't believe in *Jesus*," he said, surprisingly. "Know who I believe in? I believe in the Head Nut. Know who I mean?" He looked significantly toward the ceiling of the bar. "He's somethin' else."

I opened my notebook and made a show of writing *Sainte Genevieve, Tuesday, October 30*. But the larynx was impatient of my literary activities.

"Hey, feller—I'm asking you. How'd you make a baby? How'd you grow a blade o' grass? Shit! There ain't no way. It's really hard for me to figure out. You got an answer to that?"

"No."

"There's gotta be some Superior Being."

"Perhaps."

" 'Course there has to be! That's the proof, I'm telling you. You can't make a baby. You can't grow a blade o' grass. That's the job of the Head Nut. Know what I mean?"

"I expect you're right," I said, and tried to get on with my notebook.

"Know who I admire the most? The one guy I look up to in the world today? The Pope. That bastard, *he* told them how it was. A simple man. He told them politicians and professors . . . Just a simple man . . ." His eyes bloomed with tears. They started to drip down his cheekbones. "A simple man . . . he could tell the whole goddamn world . . . Shit. Pope . . . John . . . Paul. Yeah. He told them how it was."

He pointed shakily at my glass. "What's in there, feller? What you drinking?"

"No, thanks. I'm fine. Really."

"I *asked* you. What you drinking?"

"Scotch and water. No ice."

"*Okay. Baw*-tendah!"

He wobbled, and clung to the brass rail.

"Now. Our forefathers . . . our forefathers . . . they . . . our forefathers, they . . . kinda . . . *made* this country . . ." But he couldn't go on, and cried instead. In the washed-out color of the bar TV, a newscaster announced that the trade deficit amassed by the United States in the last month was 2 billion 830 million dollars. It seemed like a fact to hang on to, more solid than the rail of the bar. Beside me, the old man with the artificial larynx mopped himself up apologetically with a Kleenex.

The northwesterly wind had raised a swell on the water, and I kept as close as I could to the Missouri bank, hugging the dikes and running ashore every time I saw an upstream tow. Below Sainte Genevieve, the river made a sharp leftward swing into a chute. Halfway down it, I looked back and saw I was on a steep hill of traveling water—a three-mile slide, on which the horizon behind me was way above the horizon in front. A tow was coming over the top of the hill, and I could see it tip as it entered the chute. No wonder the river had seemed suddenly calm; it was streaming past the sandbars like a glacier. A mile ahead, another tow was coming up round Kaskaskia Bend. I ran for the shore. The motor stalled as it hit sand a hundred yards out, and I clambered to the front of the boat to get my anchor down before I drifted, broadside, into a dike. Everything seemed to be moving in a different direction. The low sandbars were going away to the west; I was trying to follow them by heading south; the river was flowing east. I couldn't work out what was in motion and what was fixed. If I was moving, then the sandbars weren't; if the sandbars were moving . . . It was like being unpleasantly high on marijuana: a giddy, topsy-turvy world of shifting quantities. *My mind's not right.*

The boat swung and steadied on the anchor line. At least, the stone dike didn't seem to be getting any closer. I studied the chart, and the world went even queerer; there was no doubt about it, this wasn't the Missouri, it was the Illinois shore. Or rather, there were now two Illinois shores. I am not a morning drinker, but I took a long slug of bourbon from the bottle before I made a closer, alarmed study of the charts.

It took a while, but the puzzle did eventually come out. The hill of water was a "cutoff." In the nineteenth century, the Mississippi made a wide meander to the right, enclosing a projecting knob of the state of Illinois. The Kaskaskia River had entered the Mississippi at the apex of the loop, and the town of Kaskaskia, the first French settlement in Illinois and an important steamboat town, sat at the junction of the two rivers. Then the Mississippi broke through down the hill, marooning fifteen square miles of Illinois inside Missouri and leaving Kaskaskia high and dry. My chart showed it as a pathetic little grid, five blocks by three, too small to merit even a mention in the index of the Rand McNally. The river had just chucked it aside, as carelessly as if it were a Dr. Pepper can.

With the channel clear of tows, I eased myself out into midstream and took the rest of the chute, shaving the right-hand shore to clear the enormous eddy that swirled where the river piled into the sandstone bluff on the bend. I didn't dare take my eyes off the water. Somewhere on the periphery of my vision I caught splintered images of red, ribbed rock and bare trees rooted to the crags like resting mountaineers. But there was a boil to swerve aside from, a puff of smoke from a tow beyond Chester Highway Bridge, tongues of dirty sand posted SOUTHERN ILLINOIS STATE PENITENTIARY, an odd black crack in the current; enough material to make a good landscape for a bad dream.

At Chester, Illinois, I ran ashore on solid rock. Dizzied by the river, I needed to come awake. A young man was slouching, hands in pockets, at the edge of the water. Every town on this reach of the Mississippi had its own young man—a doleful riverfront figure with the air of the village idiot. Their faces were twisted into a permanent scowl from staring into the current. They wore cracked snake boots, faded jeans, windbreakers and forage caps. Some carried guns and pretended to be out hunting. Most, though, just gazed emptily at the water as if it were a nonstop television channel.

Chester's version said: "You want me to watch your boat for you, mister? Don't trust them Chester people. They'll steal *anythin'*."

He had come with his mother from South Carolina. For three years he had worked as a professional fisherman, netting cats and buffalo. Fear had got him in the end: he couldn't swim; his mother had begged him to come off the river; he had watched two of his friends drown. Now he worked, miserably and part time, as a taxi dispatcher.

"You could've worn a life vest."

"Don't make no difference, I reckon. I seen people in life vests drown just like other folks."

"But you still miss the river."

"All the time. Every minute." He was looking past my shoulder, reading the squiggles on the water.

There was a rough wooden stairway leading up the bluff. It had been pulled away in places by green creepers: a breakneck affair of missing steps and bulging handrails. At a bar at the top I bought two hamburgers for myself and a six-pack for the young man. We took a can each.

"You got a good rig here," he said sadly. "That's something I always wanted to do: go down the river. Where'd you put in at?"

"Minneapolis."

"That up in Canada?"

"No. Minnesota."

"I thought the Mississippi went all up to Canada."

"Not quite. It starts at Lake Itasca. That's about ninety miles short of the border with Ontario. You can jump over it there. It doesn't really get navigable until Minneapolis. That's nearly two hundred miles south."

"Shit," he said. "And you come all the ways down in this?" He was making a slow, envious inventory of the boat. "There ain't just about anything I wouldn't give, to get away from them people in Chester." *Chay-ester*, he said.

I watched him as I left: another crippled snow goose.

The river was peeling away from under me now. Hurried along by the current, I was making nearly twenty miles in an hour and getting distinctly cocky about boils, eddies and chutes. I allowed myself some furtive enjoyment of the country I was passing through: the water moving like syrup around boulders as big as houses, cliffs streaked red and gray, the wiry forest and the sand which seemed to move like the water itself, in ripples and spools. I found a homemade tune which, with a bit of fiddling around the edges, could be fitted to the words of Gavin Ewart's poem, and I bawled it out over the river.

> *I am Old Man Mississippee,*
> *Full of time and mud, ho!*
> *You all must be pretty nippee*
> *When I get in flood, ho!*

By the time I got to Grand Tower, I was in a state of fizzy nervous elation. Grand Tower itself was a pillar of rock which stuck out of the river like a wrinkled limb; twenty stories high, with a fringe of trees on top. The water divided around it in a greasy collar, swelling up at its base and making the deepest whirlpool I'd yet seen between the rock and the Missouri shore. I wanted the town of Grand Tower, though, and rowed myself over the shallows to a sandy beach as big as a seashore on the Illinois side. The town was a low white village, completely hidden behind a levee. I walked to the café with my thermos flask. I needed a refill of coffee to get on to Cape Girardeau.

Hearing my accent, a man came across to the counter and joined me. He was a construction engineer from Chicago, on a temporary job in the wilderness. He had a boat himself, a big cruiser, and he'd fallen in love with the river. He interrogated me about my own trip. What size was my boat? How big was my engine? What spares did I carry? At every answer I gave, he shook his head.

"You moored up on the beach? I'll run you over there. I want to take a look at this."

We climbed the levee. I pointed down to where my boat was pulled up on the sand.

"*That?* You've got to be *shitting* me."

"It . . . looks bigger when you get closer. A bit."

"You've got to be joking."

We waded through the powdery beach.

"So where's your radio?"

"I haven't got one."

"Jesus Christ. You think you can ride this river in a boat like that without a *radio?*"

"Well, I've made it so far."

"What—fingering your St. Christopher all the way, huh? Listen to me. I'm serious. If you want to stay alive, you've got to get yourself a radio. Marine Band. Three channels. How the hell are you going to know what the tows are doing in the chutes if you can't talk to them?"

"I pull in to the shore when I see them coming."

"You don't travel at night, do you?"

"No."

"Well, thank God for small mercies. Look, I don't like to lose my sleep; and I'm not going to sleep too good if I have to lie around thinking about you going down the river like *this*. You get to Cape Girardeau, you've got to find some guy to sell you a radio. It's going to set you back three, maybe four hundred bucks. You got that kind of money?"

"Yes, I'm loaded."

"You're not shitting me? Because I'm leveling with you, now. Can you afford a radio?"

"Yes. I've got a checking account in a New York bank."

"Well, now, you're going to have to make me a promise. You're not going to leave Cape Girardeau without a radio."

"I promise."

"And I *mean* that."

"I do too. In Cape Girardeau I'll buy a radio."

He helped me push the boat back into the water. "You're not lying to me, now?"

"No. And thanks."

He was right. It had been foolish of me to try to manage the open river without a radio. I couldn't talk to the pilots of the tows; I had no means of calling for help. The gaps between towns were growing wider: soon there would be a hundred miles of empty forest and water between one hamlet and the next.

I was chastened by the fact that a complete stranger had been so alarmed for my safety that he'd offered to lend or give me as much money as he probably earned in a week, particularly since he'd made it quite clear that he had precious little respect for my character or intelligence.

Just below Grand Tower there was another cutoff where a rapid chute had handed a chunk of Missouri back to Illinois. Entering it at an alarming speed, I couldn't see its far end and could only cross my fingers in the hope that there wasn't a big tow pushing upstream out of sight around the bend. Luckily, the chute was empty. If I'd had a radio, I would have known that I was safe or would have been warned to stay clear until the tow came through.

There was an oozing rash of boils and eddies in the water ahead as the Mississippi made a sudden westward hook and Cape Girardeau slid out from behind a bluff. The sun had already disappeared over the top of the hills, leaving the lower sky streaked with orange, mauve and scarlet. High up in the black woods some clever pastrycook had made a whole university of royal icing. It was in the best and crackiest tradition of Mississippi-Attic, with its own Parthenon and lots of odeons and shrines. It must have taken years of work with the palette knife and the pastry tube. Frosted, fluted, scrolled, it caught the last of the sun, and its glacé finish turned to a pale pink. From a mile off, the only details I couldn't see were the satin ribbons, silver bells and little horseshoes.

If the woody top of town was ancient Greek, its bottom was English medieval. Cape Girardeau was a walled and gated city. A gray concrete battlement, twenty feet high, had been raised around it to protect it from the river. A patchwork of shingled roofs and glass towers showed over the floodwall, but as far as I could see the place was impregnable. Its wall announced that it considered the Mississippi a dangerous enemy. The brute ugliness of the thing had fear and dislike written all over it. Here was a town that was having as little to do with its river as it could possibly manage.

I tied up at a floating jetty a few hundred yards short of the wall, where a black fisherman sat with a pail of silver live bait beside him. The jetty lurched and creaked in the current. Yeah, said the fisherman, there was hotels in Cape—real good ones, too—but they was a ways out on the Interstate.

Across the tracks, on Big Bend Road, there was a friendly filling station where the attendants let me use their telephone. If I was going to stay in a hotel on the Interstate and go scurrying after a Marine Band radio, I needed a rented car. A black Pontiac was delivered to me on the levee within fifteen minutes. The car was fine. I was less sure about the salesman who accompanied it. In a wide-wale seersucker suit and round horn-rims, he smelled of hair oil and underarm deodorant. He wasn't just renting me the Pontiac, he was selling Cape Girardeau as a fancy piece of real estate.

He was a talking brochure. Showing rather too much bridgework, he rattled through his spiel of worn and shiny words. *Facilities. Resources. Assets. Services. Active. Strong. Expanding. Recreational Activities.*

"Just so happens, I'm a city official myself," he said.

"Gosh, are you really?"

"Yeah. In Cape Girardeau here, we've got a town we're real proud of. And I ain't just saying that." He nodded at the fisherman on the jetty. "Take *race*," he said, pronouncing the word with the same inflection that other people used for *shit*. "We get along just fine with the color in the town. We've only got twenty percent color, and them and us, we get on fine. No problem. They don't make no problems for us at *all*."

The fisherman was intent on his striped bobber as it swung and circled in the current.

"You been up to St. Louis?" the city commissioner asked. "The color they've got there . . . Trash. Same thing over in Cairo. Boy, have *they* got problems." He looked down on the fisherman with an approving smile which might have been more properly bestowed on a housetrained family pet.

It was Halloween. Grinning pumpkins flickered all the way up Independence Street, and the white shingled houses had witches strung up on their verandas. Trick or Treat had lost its innocence, though. The announcer on the car radio was warning us not to let our children eat Halloween candy before we had carefully examined it. All homemade candies must be thrown away unless given by neighbors personally known to us. We must be on the lookout for hidden razor blades, needles, hypodermic injections of rat poison and L.S.D. A clinic in Texas was offering a free X-ray service tonight so that Hershey bars could be screened for terminal lumps and shadows. AMERICA—LOVE IT OR LEAVE IT said the bumper sticker on the Cadillac in front; I hoped its driver was listening to the same wave band on his radio.

Cape Girardeau had, in its own small way, stepped westward like St. Louis. I had driven through the old riverside town. It was ill-lighted and half deserted—a pretty, crumbling honeycomb of dark Victorian brick and wrought-iron trelliswork. Two miles out, just short of the piled earthwork of Highway 55, I hit the Cape Girardeau of the 1970s —a dazzling neon slum of yawning shopping plazas; chain stores, chain burger shacks, chain motor lodges and that thin chain grass with which property developers try to hide the wounds they have made in the ground. It was an all-American anywhere. It looked as if it had itself been bought by mail order from one of the branches of Sears and J. C. Penney that stood back from the road across oceanic carparks. What it lacked in character it made up in grisly electric color. It was as bright and lonely as the moon.

I took a room in a Ramada Inn and listened to the surf of traffic breaking on the shore of the thousand-mile-long highway from Chicago to New Orleans. Grazing the edge of sleep, I heard the road as a river and slid into a dream in which trucks were tows, their shovel fronts plowing me down. When I woke, the room was spotted with yellow sodium light. My watch said ten, and it took a few moments to work out that this was night, not day. Out, shivering, on a bald plaza, I found an open Pizza Hut. Maybe that woman in St. Louis had been right. It was eating this kind of stuff in this kind of place at this untime of day-in-night and night-in-day that turned one into a rapist, a thief or a man who hid razor blades in chocolate bars on Halloween. It had started to rain. The colors of the neon tubes were running in the window and making a mess which bore a strong resemblance to the surface of my pizza. The eve of the Feast of All Saints.

> Matthew, Mark, Luke and John
> Bless the bed that I lie on . . .

Would any self-respecting saint check into a Ramada Inn?

> One to watch, and one to pray,
> And two to bear my soul away.

I stared out through the streaky glass and tried to see the place with more sympathetic eyes. Someone—an exhausted trucker, perhaps, or a woman with a station wagon full of squalling children—must find it a blessing; but I couldn't. Why had Cape Girardeau tried to bury its river behind a wall of cement? Why had it left its handsome old town behind and come out to this loud wilderness of acrylic junk?

I saw the waitress watching me. Perhaps she had nailed me as a spiker of children's candy. I tried to smile and look like an upright citizen. She came across to my table. Her blond hair was pulled back from her face and knotted in a hygienic braid. Her name, the button on her right breast stated, was Linda. She wasn't really a waitress, she said. She was majoring in Elementary Ed at the University of Southeast Missouri—the sugar-icing college on the hill. Now she was waiting on tables at nights because she was saving up to leave Cape Girardeau; next semester, she was going to Columbia University.

"Why Columbia?"

"Oh, you know. The usual. There was a guy there . . . but him and me, we split months ago. So. One: people are kind of narrow-minded around here, right? Two: I always promised myself I'd get to see New York. Plus, I love to watch football. Columbia's football team . . . they're something else."

"It sounds like an exciting move."

"Yeah. I'm getting to be all psyched up. God, you ought to meet with the kids in my class here. They're into, like, chewing straw, stuff like that. . . . Me, I've been liberated since junior high. I guess it's all the books I read. I'm a real big reader."

"What are you reading at present?"

"Sci-fi. Robert Heinlein?"

"He's only a name to me."

"He's neat."

I pointed out the window. "You must feel quite at home here: it looks exactly like something from a sci-fi novel."

Linda took in the lurid illuminated landscape with a blink as quick as the sprung leaves of a camera shutter. "Looks like Cape Girardeau to me. That's why I'm quitting."

It took me two hours of quarrying in the Yellow Pages, chasing leads and following up red herrings, to find a Marine Band radio. I made an assignation with the manufacturer's representative. At four that afternoon, we'd meet in a parking lot outside a farm twenty miles south down the highway. He promised me a crash course in radio operation and said he'd trust my accent and take a check.

In the meantime, I drove to the river to make sure my boat was safe after the shenanigans of Trick or Treat. The houses of the meaner people in town were easily identifiable: crazy foam had been sprayed over their windows, and their garden shrubs were wreathed in toilet paper. The boat was as I had left it. When I arrived at the landing, it was being studied at a distance by Cape Girardeau's haunted boy. He was leaning against a dented and rusty white pickup, sucking at a can of Miller's. He had a pale, pubic mustache, and his face was pouchy with a deep no-hoping sullenness. When I joined him, he held out a can of beer.

"Thanks very much."

"That yours?"

"Yes."

"Shit. I like to look at boats . . . you know?"

"Yes."

The morning was wide and blue; the sheen on the surface of the river might have been a thick coat of Chinese lacquer. A perfect day for moving on.

"When I was a kid," the boy said, "my uncle, he had a boat. I never did get to riding in it, though. It got took away in a flood."

He lived with his mother in a shack less than a mile from the river.

Once, floods had nearly carried their house away. He had gone swimming in the Mississippi, fished in it, most days he came here to moon over it, but he had never in his life been on it in a boat.

"Would you like to go out now?"

"I wouldn't want to be no trouble, mister."

"I'd like to go myself."

"Well . . . if I was to just, kind of, like, string along . . ." I watched his face. He was trying hard to cover up his excitement.

We walked down the jetty, the boy carrying what was left of his morning six-pack.

"I always wanted to get a start on the towboats. But they're close. I tried, but there wasn't no chance. I don't know. I guess for that you got to have kin on the river."

Like his counterpart in Chester, he had a part-time job. He worked for a firm of movers, but there was no money in it.

"Ain't nothin' to do round Cape, 'cept you have money."

"What would you do if you did have money?"

"I don't know. Shows . . . I guess. Go round the bars . . ."

I started the motor and we headed upstream, lumbering slowly against the current.

"How far did you get in high school?"

"Ninth grade." He must have been barely eighteen. He should have been in school still, but his education was years behind him now; a great misty stretch of failure, boredom, unemployment and ill-afforded cans of Miller's. He sat up in the bow, rigid, not daring to move. I couldn't tell whether he was frightened or simply entranced. I kept close to the sandy Illinois shore, hunting for patches of dead water where the engine wouldn't have to fight so hard against the river.

The boy squinted at the water. "I never did see it from out here. It's . . . *beautiful* . . . ain't it?" He used the word timidly; it came from a foreign language and he found it difficult to pronounce.

Then, suddenly, he tumbled into speech. *There* was the beach he'd gone swimming from as a kid. Least, there wasn't a beach there no more; that too had been took away by a flood. *There* was the rocky point where he'd caught his big catfish. In that eddy there, a friend of his had drowned; and there, where those trees were, a cousin had lived in a frame house before a flood swept it down to the Gulf. The sullenness had dropped out of his face. As he talked, I watched him growing younger; he went back to fourteen, then twelve, then eight, the albino fluff of his mustache looking more ludicrous by the moment.

I turned the boat around. Abruptly, he clouded over. He had remembered. By the time we reached the jetty, his face was set back to morose, unwilling adulthood. He didn't thank me for the trip, but just said, "Be seein' ya" and sloped, hunch-headed, back to his truck and an afternoon life of shouldering other people's bedsteads and three-piece suites.

Downtown, where I lunched, was long-faced with shadows of former glory. The Hotel Marquette, an extravagant copy of the Palazzo Vecchio in Florence, had been closed for more than a decade. The old opera house, restored to quaintness, was enjoying a reincarnation, of a sort, as a restaurant. Half the stores in the city were empty and up for sale or rent. The saddest place was the waterfront. One could reach the river through a steel gate in the wall. What had once been the town's commercial heart, the steamboat landing, was a ruinous site of heaps of stones, broken cobbles and lumps of cement. Two frail old men, a hundred yards apart, squatted in this rubble, smoking pipes and searching the water for whatever images the drifting current could summon. They looked unapproachable. In walking through the gate in the wall they had put society behind them. It was, in any case, a place for old men, and I felt a trespasser there. It didn't hold any of my memories. I noted that the water shoaled in dangerous humps inshore above the highway bridge; plotted a smoother course, off-channel, on the Illinois side; and left.

My new radio was going to admit me to full membership in the community of the river. It stood on the dressing table, a businesslike and reassuring white slab of dials and little lights. I knew the handbook that came with it by heart. I had practiced switching from Channel 6 to Channel 13. I'd called "Mayday" into the dead microphone. I had only just restrained myself from taking it down to the boat and wiring it up in the dark. It had cost $380; in return, a tight knot of funk had been cleanly excised from my stomach. For a piece of major surgery, the radio was very cheap indeed.

Even the vile shopping plazas didn't look so bad tonight. The Pizza Hut was full, and the waitresses were moving between tables at the speed of shuttles on a loom; but Linda came over to talk in breathless respites of thirty seconds at a time. She was full of time warps, holes in space and alternative worlds. I was fascinated by her taste in fiction. Out of place in Cape Girardeau, she had made herself thoroughly at home in the more distant of the undiscovered galaxies. She had gutted libraries of the stuff.

"At Columbia," she said, "I heard you can take courses in it"—and was whited-out into the alternative world of root beer, dough and Parmesan.

Back from her next trip, she pointed at the book on my table. "What's that you're reading?"

I showed her. It was the Reverend Timothy Flint's *Recollections of the Mississippi.*

"Oh," she said with disappointment. "Just history, huh?"

I had only recently entered Flint's stretch of the river. In Minneapolis, he had struck me as a comic figure: easily shockable, disaster-prone, worried half to death at the impieties of the frontier. Reading him now, I thought him an admirable realist. His passage on the boils in the current was superbly vivid and exact:

> The face of the Mississippi is always turbid; the current everywhere sweeping and rapid; and it is full of singular boils, where the water, for a quarter of an acre, rises with a strong circular motion, and a kind of hissing noise, forming a convex mass of waters above the common level, which roll down and are incessantly renewed. The river seems always in wrath . . .

I hadn't heard the hissing noise. Next time, I'd turn my motor off and listen.

Linda had returned. "When you graduate from Columbia," I said, "what do you plan to do then? Teach?" I couldn't quite see her blowing the minds of elementary-school children with tales of interstellar warfare.

"No. I'm fixing to be an airline stewardess. I'd really love to travel."

Travel. It was an intransitive verb. It didn't involve any destinations. It was going for the going's sake, to be anywhere but where you were, with the motion itself its only object.

"Anywhere in particular?"

"Uh-uh. I don't know. The East, maybe? Yeah, I reckon I'd like to see the East."

There was to be no travel for me, though. When I woke, the wind was louder than the traffic on the highway. The newly planted saplings outside my window were bent into shivering loops. The most that I could hope to do was attach the radio to the battery in the boat and practice working it.

Waves sluiced over the floating jetty, and the jetty itself was rocking so tippily that I had to crawl rather than walk along it, carrying only the aerial of the set. I wasn't going to let the river take my radio as a votive offering. I had company. A thirty-something-foot sloop had moored alongside me. It didn't look like the usual run of snow geese; an old wooden boat, its deck festooned with lashed-down bicycles, fuel drums, gas cylinders and chests. *Morning Star,* Chicago.

My own boat was lurching in the swell, and as I tried to fix the aerial to the stern, I kept twisting my screwdriver on empty air.

"Hi. You look as if you could do with some assistance there."

The owner of *Morning Star* was a scrawny man in his fifties with more eyeglasses than face. He looked as if he would be easier working an adding machine in an insurance office than sitting out a Mississippi storm.

"We just looked over your rig and reckoned there must be some guy around who's even crazier than we are."

He had a complete kit of engineer's tools and rooted my aerial to the boat in two or three expert minutes.

"You've come all the way down from Minnesota without a radio?"

"Yes—stupidly."

"No," he said, giving a screw a final pinch, "that wasn't too bright of you."

"I had a deathbed conversion."

I went aboard the *Morning Star* for coffee and brownies. Inside, it was a tiny, dark, untidy family house. Five of us huddled in the galley: Ted, his wife, his son, his daughter-in-law and I.

"We're not going anyplace today. This wind, it's too big even for a boat our size. We've had a night of it. It started up around two A.M.; we were laying up behind an island, but the anchor dragged, so we came on down here. Shipped a deal of water, too. But further down, it gets more dangerous. You've got the Grand Chain through Thebes—that's big rocks both sides of the channel. They've had just about everything wrecked there. Towboats. Cruisers. Yachts. The Coast Guard says you can see the masts sticking up behind every rock."

The galley stove creaked in its gimbals. When a tow went by, Ted's wife landed in my lap and a mug of coffee smashed against a bulkhead.

"It's kind of an art, living on a boat," Ted said. "I don't think we've got it quite sewn up yet." More crockery came down in a heap and slid along the floor.

Ted was a geologist. Until the summer, he had made his living draining watery areas for power plants. Then, along with his son and daughter-in-law, he'd given up his job. They had sold their house in Michigan City, east of Chicago; put their furniture in storage; bought the boat and set out to sail around the world. After three weeks, they had navigated the length of the Illinois River, plus a hundred and eighty miles or so of Mississippi. Originally, they had meant to be in New Orleans by now. The younger couple needed to pay their own way, stopping for two or three weeks at a time to take odd jobs, serving in restaurants or tending gas stations. Already they were running short of money. After New Orleans they'd head on for Florida. With luck they'd reach Puerto Rico before the end of winter. Then . . . they didn't know. They hadn't tested their boat at sea yet. Their attempts at running her under sail had not worked out too well. They were learning as they went along; by Puerto Rico, they would have either drowned or turned into real sailors.

"It was my son's idea," Ted said. "Sometimes I think that instead of listening to him I should have gotten him some psychiatric help."

"That's just when the wind's blowing over forty," his son said.

I said, "I would have thought that living in a space as small as this, the worst things that are likely to blow up are family rows."

"Oh, yeah, we have our share of those." Ted was rubbing his glasses with a dishcloth. Without them, his eyes looked small and naked. "My wife here, she's got a hearing problem. Only on the boat it's no problem. She never gets involved in the arguments."

His wife smiled vaguely at him, trying to look as if she had understood.

The river was slapping at the hull. I could see it through the porthole: shredded into curds, it looked cold, dangerous and ugly.

"Why do you think we're all hooked on traveling like this?" I said. "I have long moments of thinking that I need a dose of psychiatry myself."

"I don't know," said Ted. "Ask a lemming, I guess. But I'll tell you this—you've probably had the same thing too—every guy I've ever told about what we're doing, he's had two responses, one right after the other. The first is *You must be mad!* and he makes out like he's looking at a maniac. But then there's always the second—you know what that is?"

"*I envy you.*"

"Right. Every time. *I envy you.* And the envy's real. They'd kind of like to hear of our family drowning, just to prove that they needn't do it themselves. I don't know. We may get nowhere. We may get as far as Florida and just take the plane back to Chicago. Big defeat. But I'd hate to grow old and die and never have tried it."

Cape Girardeau itself was forgetful, a place littered with things absentmindedly discarded. It had left its river behind. It was vacating its old town. Perhaps, with luck, it would soon forget its shopping plazas and motels. Looking at this amnesiac city, I wanted to meet someone with a long memory. The editor of the local newspaper suggested that I should pay a call on Rush Limbaugh, the oldest practicing attorney in town.

He had moved west too. He said over the phone that I would recognize the building where he worked because it was "white" and "Colonial"; but it was a new suburban mock-up of a planter's mansion, built within earshot of the Interstate. Mr. Limbaugh himself gave to this insipid replica a gravity it didn't quite deserve. His room was darkened with walls of calfskin books and antique oak. His own face was walnutty, his hands liver-spotted. When he talked, he spoke in an accent very different from the liquid twitter of the usual southern Missouri voice. He held words in his mouth as gently as if they were eggs, liable to be broken by a careless movement of the tongue. His style of speech, a whispery plainsong, was one that I associated with the old gentry of Virginia and Kentucky; in Cape Girardeau it sounded stranded out of place and time.

He showed me his copies of Coke and Littleton: lovely eighteenth-century editions, printed in London.

"You know Sir Edward Coke?" He made the Tudor lawyer sound like a contemporary of his. Mr. Limbaugh was eighty-eight and could afford to be on easy, first-name terms with the historical past. He quoted: "Six hours in sleep, in law's grave study six, Four spend in prayer, the rest on Nature fix." He looked like a man who had followed Coke's precepts to the minute.

He wanted to talk about England, I wanted to talk about Cape Girardeau, and we spent half an hour in courtly negotiation over our preferred topics. I told Mr. Limbaugh how Chancery Lane and Lincoln's Inn had been when I'd last seen them and how half the courts in the Old Bailey now looked like split-pine sauna baths. In what I hoped was a smart barrister's move, I wriggled from the architectural nastinesses of modern London to those of Cape Girardeau's new West Side.

Yes, he said, the plazas were the latest phase of a movement that had started way back when he was a boy. He remembered Cape Girardeau as a real river town. He'd seen steamboats double- and triple-parked down at the landing. There had been a big trade in lumber then; and in shoes; and in cement. The "love boats" had come down from St. Louis: stern-wheeled brothels with a girl in every cabin.

"The old people then, they disapproved of the river. It brought lax morals down from the big city, and radical ideas. They feared that if anything was going to destroy their community, it was the river. But without the river, the town was nothing. It was like a good boy with a crook for a father. It was dependent on the river, but it knew the river was bad."

The story that Mr. Limbaugh told had all the elements of a fable. The good child grew up and rejected its disreputable parent. From what it believed to be the best of motives, Cape Girardeau had turned itself into an orphan and inherited the orphan's lot of rootlessness, anxiety and disquiet.

"Oh, it must have started, now, in nineteen and four. That was the year they completed the 'Frisco railroad, and from then on the town began to turn its back on the river. By the twenties, we had automobiles here. Then in the thirties, when the towboats went from steam to diesel, they could go right by the town without stopping off. It was very gradual. The city kind of *tilted* slowly away from the river and over toward the highway."

"And the Wall was the final seal on things?"

"Yes . . . the Wall." Mr. Limbaugh clearly cared as little for it as I did. He half-closed his eyes and leaned back in his black leather chair. "Our wall. It was the city's great enterprise. Everybody was for it. They campaigned for it. They raised money. Oh, *I* was all for it—we all were. We looked on the wall as a savior. Every year, people downtown were getting flooded out, and the wall was going to save downtown for us. Instead, it turned into an eyesore and a barricade. I think, now, the wall was a great tragedy that happened to the town. It turned us into a segregated city."

"But you've still got docks below the highway bridge." I had seen them. Grain, sand, rock, oil and cement were shipped through the port of Cape Girardeau; and there was a big marine repair yard and dry dock where towboats were fitted out.

"Yes," said Mr. Limbaugh, "but that's the problem—they're beyond the wall. The Port Authority is rich, but it doesn't really belong to Cape Girardeau anymore. Look. Just last year, the Rotarians were getting together to fund a big civic project, and they went to one of the top guys in the Port. They wanted him to contribute. He said, 'Why —what's this project got to do with me?' They said, 'Well, it affects us all. It belongs to the whole city.' 'That's the point,' he said; 'it don't belong to me. What has the city ever done for me? Everything that comes to me, it doesn't come from the city, it comes from the river. The river is where I make my living from; why should I care about the town?' I don't know how many divorces I've handled in my time, but I reckon that the divorce between the river and the city is just about the biggest and saddest divorce I've ever seen."

"Even so, surely downtown could have survived?"

"Without the river? No. Business goes where the wealth is. Where's the wealth now? It's out there, on the Interstate Highway. There *is* wealth on the Mississippi, but the city cut itself off from that. So you get the old stores holding out downtown. A lot of folks have sentimental feelings for Bellevue and Fountain and Middle and Main. They'd like to stay. They stay even when they know they're losing business by it. Every year, though, more of them move out to the plazas. They have to. Right now, the First National is moving its offices west. That's a big symbol. The bank has *always* been downtown. When the bank moves . . ." He spread his creased palms upward, and smiled: a lizardy, resigned, old man's smile. He could regret history, but was wise enough to know he couldn't quarrel with it.

"Yes," he said, "the wall was a mistake, but it's too late to pull it down."

I was out, beyond the wall, just after dawn. The *Morning Star* had been awake and away before me, and the river was empty, its far shore hidden behind smoky spirals of mist. In the silence, I listened for the hissing noise of boils, but all I could hear was the steady suck of the current at the reveted bank and the pontoons of the jetty.

I connected the radio and switched on to a crackle of river talk. Invisible captains were nursing one another through chutes and cutoffs many miles away.

"I'm just going to tuck myself right in behind you here, Cap, if that's okay with you now?"

"All righty. Fine and dandy."

" 'Preciate it. . . ."

"We'll take it real nice and easy. I can see you good, now."

"Yeah, I can see you too, Cap—"

It was like overhearing people talk in bed. I had seen the tows as a dangerous herd of very alien brutes indeed. It was disconcerting to listen to them now, snuggling up together and fitting the rhythm of their breathing to their mates'. I had no excuse to try broadcasting anything over the air myself, but was in a state of anxious anticipation as to whether I would be let into this privileged world of whispers between the sheets.

Six miles downstream, I had the bend at Gray's Point marked on my chart as fast and tight. I clicked the button on my microphone and asked it, feeling foolish, whether there were any upstream tows between the Thebes railroad bridge and Mile 46. A voice immediately came back.

"Yeah, *Raven's Nest?* This is the *Sidney Beale.* We're coming up now at Mile 45. What's the problem?"

"I'm in a small boat and don't want to get caught in your wake. I'm just about to come around the bend at Gray's Point."

"You just keep on coming, Cap. We'll look out for you. How big's your boat?"

"Sixteen feet."

"We won't trouble you none with our wake. We'll cut right down. You got some good deep water on your black buoy side off-channel. If I was you, I'd run that bend just about as close as you can shave it. Okay, Cap?"

"Thanks very much—"

"Hey, if you don't mind me asking, where's that goddamn accent from?"

"England."

"England? Shit, up here we had it figured for some kinda crazy coonass voice—"

So I wasn't to be blackballed from the club. There was nothing to be scared of in the fast water on the bend. The boat rode it lightly, its bow high, as I skidded off the edge of a boil, steadied on a rip and found my way into the main current again, where the river was as evenly glossy as brilliantine. I waved to the pilothouse of the tow. It had slowed down to a walking pace for me; its wake came in a series of gentle slurps which barely rocked the boat at all.

Sailing nonchalantly in mid-channel through the Grand Chain, I noticed that I was developing all the characteristics of that particularly despicable figure in Victorian novels which touch on clubland, the New Member. He is easily spotted: the New Member lolls comfortably close to the fire on the padded leather seat of the fender, while the Old Member, whose place this has been for fifty years, growls in a corner. The New Member bags the morning's *Times* and reduces it to a crumpled heap. He borrows five-pound notes from the club servants, exhausts the supply of club notepaper, complains about the inferior quality of the baize on the billiard table, and generally lives under the happy misapprehension that he is the most popular fellow around.

I thought the Grand Chain a pretty piece of scenery. On both sides of the channel, the water creamed around the tips of big redstone boulders. It was a marine graveyard. For four miles, between Thebes and Commerce, the rocks gripped the last remains of every kind of craft that had ever ridden the Mississippi. There were keelboats and flatboats down there; steamboats, tows, rafts, yachts and sixteen-foot-long aluminum fishing boats. With my new radio, though, out in the mainstream, a pipeful of Captain Black drawing smoothly, I was looking at the river with the arrogant familiarity of the New Member. Eddies yawned behind the rocks; boils broke in front of them; all as nicely arranged as the patterned coils of water in a Bingham painting.

The triple blast of a tow's horn violated my inner ear, and the picture frosted over like a shattered windshield. I scraped by between the rocks and the high black wedge of the leading barges, hit the wake, wallowed, slopped, and found myself spinning on the edge of one of the balls of turbulence left by the screws. Someone on the towboat's deck was telling me something, but I caught only his final word, which was *sonofabitch.*

I wanted to call up the *Morning Star,* but didn't dare to for fear of being intercepted by the pilot of the tow, whose advice to me would, I knew, be sound, reasonable and too humiliating to bear listening to. Shamed by my silliness, I inched down the chart, paring to the extreme edge of the channel. That was the third time I had grown careless and cocksure with the river; I doubted very much if the Mississippi was going to allow me any more such chances.

You may draw the line across the middle distance with a ruler. It should slant just slightly up from left to right. Above it, color in a pale wash of pink and turquoise. Below it, paint the Mississippi in a rich dark tan. At the very top, cross-hatch the Kentucky bluffs; use a fine pen and India ink. On the right-hand shore, make sandy marshes, reed pools, flights of waterfowl. There should be no clouds in the sky, and you must stop the wind. Follow the instructions carefully. If you try to circumvent them by taking a camera to the foot of the highway bridge at Cairo, you will—as I did—come home with a banal pictorial lie.

The junction of the Mississippi and the Ohio was a confluence of thick machine oil and rosewater. The two looked so different that it was hard to believe they could fuse into a single element without curdling. The Mississippi held the foreground and the Missouri shore; the Ohio had Kentucky. The clean pencil stroke between the brown and the pink, running due west to east for more than two miles, must have been the one place in the United States where the cleavage of the Mason-Dixon Line had its exact counterpart in nature.

Moored below the bridge with a stale submarine sandwich, I could see the line, and the colors on either side of it, as distinctly as I could see towboats and trees. Trying to follow it in the boat, I lost it. It was true that the water was thicker and browner to my right, thinner and clearer to my left; but it was just water. Mississippi mud was swilling in Ohio eddies, and as the stronger river took hold below Wickliffe and Fort Jefferson, one could feel it instructing the other in the art of being a wicked and dangerous character. It taught the Ohio how to make boils and whirlpools, how to loiter around sandbars and carry off chunks of forest. It had scrapped with the Missouri when they met; it married the Ohio, and it took on the added self-importance of the newlywed groom. There were long, wakelike waves off some of the bars now. They couldn't have been caused by tows, since the river was empty as far as I could see. The Mississippi was just making waves for the hell of it; give it the temptation of a shoal and it would run in dark, serrated combers, three and four feet high, showing off its muscles.

There was something I didn't care for in the look of the landscape. The bluffs on the Kentucky side peeled away, leaving the river surrounded by miles of its old alluvial courses—a bleak flatland of bog, black earth, oak and willow. No docks, no landings, no villages behind the levees; just a lot of sand, a lot of mud, a lot of trees. This was the bit of river that nineteenth-century English writers used to find so scarifying. Most of them had come down the Ohio, and their first sight of the Mississippi tended to shock them. Dickens was appalled by it. Captain Marryat called it a "desolating torrent." Their versions of the Mississippi were—as Mark Twain pointed out long ago in *Life on the Mississippi*—annoyingly monochrome. They were ritually overwhelmed by its awfulness, and left it at that. Riding on it here, where the gloomy color of the earth seemed to have worked its way into the water and the sky, I found their depression easy to understand.

A jonboat came scudding out across the channel from the Kentucky shore. I tacked sharp left to avoid it, but it swerved to intercept me. There were two men aboard; one at the bow and one at the helm. Both had guns laid across their knees. Their boat came up to within twenty feet of mine. I shifted to neutral gear and floated on the current. I had no chance of outrunning them; their 30-horsepower motor could take them at more than twice my speed.

"Yes?" I said. "Hello— What do you want?"

Both wore plaid duck hunter's caps with earmuffs buttoned up around their crowns. They must have been in their twenties, but they had squashed faces with premature deep creases around their eyes and jowls; brothers certainly, perhaps twins.

"Yes?"

No answer. I watched their eyes travel slowly over my boat and its contents. Last of all, they came to rest on my face: dim, indifferent eyes of the kind that a taxidermist might keep in labeled boxes.

The man in the stern gave a slight shrug—half at me, half at his brother. Without explanation he accelerated away toward the shore, leaving me bobbing lightly in his wake. Were they river muggers? game wardens? Why wouldn't they speak? They seemed, at any rate, to belong here; to the black marsh, the trees with their roots deep underwater and their branches strung with lianas.

I kept on glancing back, expecting to see these sinister brothers hanging behind, but they had disappeared into some hidden creek or bayou. Feeling absurd as I did so, I crouched as low as I could in the boat and kept up as fast and zigzaggy a course as I could manage. I was torn between giggling at the idiocy of the encounter and being terrified out of my wits. After another five miles, I settled for a shaky sort of laughter.

The town of Hickman showed a long way off across the floodplain on the Kentucky shore. An ancient volcanic rumble had thrown up the only craggy hill in miles of flat mud, and Hickman was a ruddy stain high in the trees. It had a perfect, hidden harbor. A wide bayou emptied into the Mississippi from behind a wooded bar, and gave Hickman its private lake. It looked as if no one used it much. A few floating wooden shacks were moored among the willows, and the U.S. Coast Guard cutter had its own wharf. I tied up there and talked to the coastguardsmen. There was "nothing" in Hickman. The hotel was dead. Yeah, there was a store or two, but I wouldn't find any place to sleep nearer than Union City, fifteen miles away over in Tennessee.

One of the officers said he had nothing to do. He'd be happy to drive me to Union City in the Coast Guard truck. It was a kind offer, a long way out of his duty; it was also a disappointment. I wanted to stay in Hickman. It had looked so right: a real river town of old brick, old timber, old painted storefronts, stepped and huddled on its hill. Before the Civil War it had been a big tobacco port; since, it had been gently moldering, never turning into a ghost town, never recovering its former importance. There was still the smell of old prosperity around Brooklyn Street, a sense that next year, perhaps, the closed shops would open again and the hotel be busy with traveling salesmen. There was also the sense that people had been thinking exactly this thought about Hickman every year since 1865 or thereabouts.

In Union City there was just another anonymous motor lodge with the same blue spread on the bed, the same stippled peach paper on the wall. The bar, though, was more interesting; it didn't sell liquor.

"You don't have bourbon? You don't even have wine?"

"You're in Obion County now. We're dry here. You want bourbon or wine, you're going to have to find yourself a bootlegger."

"So, how easy is it to find a bootlegger?"

"George!" shouted the woman bartender.

"Yes, ma'am." George came out from behind a pillar. He was tall, shambling and black. He wore dungarees and a floral apron.

"There's your bootlegger for you. Just tell George what you want and he'll go get it for you."

In five minutes George returned with a bottle of Jack Daniel's. At least, he returned with a brown paper bag in which he said there was a bottle of Jack Daniel's.

"Now sir," said the bartender, "you know about brown-bagging?"

"No. I've never heard of it."

"Well, that bottle's got to stay in that brown bag. You want to have a drink with your meal in the ray-ester-rong, you hold the bottle in the bag when you pour it in the glass. Okay? That way it makes it all legal, you understand?"

"Legal? It doesn't sound legal to me."

"Yes sir. Brown-bagging is *legal*. What's *illegal* is carrying around your bottle without your bag."

I suspected that I was being hoaxed. If I was, it was an astonishingly elaborate practical joke. There must have been fifty people in the restaurant and at least thirty brown bags. Brown bags were tipping into glasses with the even rhythm of oil pumps working in line across a desert. Brown bags were stored on the moquette seat beside one. The bootlegger in his floral apron was kept constantly on the hop. He would come in with armfuls of brown bags which he would distribute around the tables. I warmed to brown-bagging. It seemed both far madder, and much more fun, than Prohibition.

Nosing out of the bayou on Sunday morning, I saw an electric ripple twisting away from the boat toward a clump of bullrushes. My first water moccasin. There would be no trailing my fingers over the side of the gunwale from now on; the bite of a water moccasin was supposed to be deadlier than that of a rattlesnake, and the backwaters of the lower river were infested with these vipers. Since passing the border between Iowa and Missouri I had felt the steady accretion of Southern-ness. The voices had slowed and turned more musical in their phrasing; the architecture had aged and sprouted trailing wrought-iron balconies and trellises; the vegetation had grown knottier and more festooned. Now the South was coming in a rush of symbols: squashed-faced pirates, lianas, brown-bagging, water moccasins. That, though, was to see things the wrong way around. The real presence of the South was in its absences. It wasn't new and raw. The towns on the upper river had been founded by the grandparents and great-grandparents of the people who lived there now, and there was still something makeshift and temporary about them. They grazed and gashed the landscape in which they were built, and it wasn't hard to imagine the landscape closing over them again.

The odd thing about Hickman had been that it was somehow unthreatened. Its survival on the hill was dependent on a deep capacity for not being mussed and ruffled. Its old warehouses looked as if they might have been thrown up in the same quake that had made the hill; its walnut trees must have been planted when the far bank of the river was held by Spaniards. It didn't have to prove itself, or make good. It was simply *there,* in the stolid, unselfconscious way that small old European towns are there, because no one has ever thought of questioning their right to be.

The chute below Island No. 8 (no affectionate upper-river names now; just numbered hazards) was busy. A downstream tow was hanging above it, waiting to "back up" down. Its pilot told me over the radio that two more tows were making their way up the chute, out of sight round the bend. They crept painfully forward past a willow bar, their screws thrashing against another glacial hill of water.

"Okay, Cap, you can go in ahead of us now. Ain't nothing coming up, and we'll be taking a while going through—"

"Thank you," I said, not quite having the nerve to say " 'Preciate it" as I knew I should.

"Have a good trip, now—"

It was like riding a long slide on a children's playground. The boat streamed with the current. It was going much too fast to boil or eddy; for a mile and a half the water had the immaculate polish of new silver. There wasn't a scratch on it. The land was moving by at speed, but the river looked absolutely still. Rounding the bend below the chute, I was surprised by the sudden chunkiness of the water; I had forgotten that there was a wind at all.

The springy little breakers and scattered whitecaps slowed me down. It was hard to see boils until I was right on top of them, and I had to guess where the eddies were likely to lie from the shape of the bends. Twice I felt the boat making a crabwise skid from under me, and saw the oily peak of a boil showing above the waves just ahead. I counted off the mile markers on the shore. 908.3. 907.0. 903.6. They seemed to be coming very slowly. At the bottom of the reach, the river started out on a huge meander. It was divided from itself by a neck of wood-land only three-quarters of a mile wide, but I would have to go off around a twenty-mile loop before I reached the water I could see beyond the trees.

At the apex of the loop, all of New Madrid was hidden behind a grassy levee except its water tower, its grain elevator and the white wooden steeple of a church. I lugged the boat clear of the waves and caught the town napping through a long, warm Sunday afternoon. Fall was late here. The trees were thick with leaves, the air loud with starlings, and butterflies blew down Mott Street, scraps of pure color like flakes of marbled paint in the wind. Old men sat out on their verandas smoking pipes; and somewhere in the deep tangle of foliage and frame houses there was the monotonous *cheep-cheep* of a child's swing.

The only place that didn't seem shut up for Sunday was the police station: at least, its door was wide open to the street. No one was there, though. Snooping, I walked past the desk and found New Madrid's solitary cell. That too was open. Sunlight fell through an overhead grille and printed more bars down the concrete wall. There were a narrow metal bed, a thin mattress, a seatless toilet; a miserable little space, just big enough to sleep in, shit, and repent the reasons that had brought one down to this. One prisoner had left his night thoughts penciled in erratic capital letters on the wall.

JOSEPH B PRIDE

WIFE⟶KIM PRIDE
SON⟵⟶JACK DANIEL PRIDE
GIRL⟵⟶JULIE AMBER PRIDE

He was not much of a hand as a writer, but one could see the effort that had gone into the careful shaping of each letter. Over the top of this painstaking map of his identity, another prisoner had written an enormous SUCK.

I asked for Joseph Pride in the bar across the street, in the café at the end of town, at the motel on the highway. No one had heard of him.

"Pride? Pride? That name ain't familiar to me. Sure you got it right? Who is he, this guy—a friend of yours or something?"

"Sort of. I'm just curious about him."

"Whoever he is, he ain't from Noo *Mad*-rid."

Of course he had to be a stranger. Finding himself in a jail cell a long way from home, he was easily panicked into the fear of forgetting who he was. So he had arranged his family around him in a double-entry accounting system. The connecting arrows, the dots over the capital I's done as round *o*'s, had given shape and logic to an accidental life. I thought I knew the fear he'd been through. I hoped that he'd got some sleep after he'd finished making his family tree.

In a motel room that was only a little less sordid than the police cell, I sat writing letters home until sunset. I was sorry, I wrote, that it had been so long since I'd last been in touch, but today I had been prompted by Joseph B. Pride, and if I sounded down in the mouth, this was just a momentary flicker of loneliness in a trip that was not really lonely at all. At six, the lights came on in the Church of Christ across the highway, and I went to the evening service.

It didn't look like a church. It was a brown concrete box like an old-fashioned bomb shelter. It was furnished with bare pine walls, two rubber plants, an electric clock and a green nylon carpet. Everything about it was a tacit reproach to the showiness of other churches. No piano playing was allowed in the Church of Christ. No rhetoric was permitted in its prayers and sermons. It was a strict, homespun, plain-spoken sect. It had broken away from the Baptists in protest against the singing, shouting and idolatry of the parent church.

The congregation was thin. We were all middle-aged. Most of us were women with tight home perms. We listened to Brother Southern talk on the theme of "troublesome times." He spoke flatly and sensibly. He had a "secular job" selling tractor parts, and he chatted to us as if we were farmers who knew our business and wouldn't stand for any hokum from him. He reminded us of the Depression and the Wall Street Crash, of the businessmen in the 1930s who had killed themselves because they couldn't see a way out. He said that no one in 1979 was going through a rougher time than St. Paul had known; and he upbraided those who, in 1979, had been drawn to religion simply because they had fallen on troublesome times.

"Sometimes, I think our religion is like deer hunting. Just seasonal. You get a bad harvest, or inflation goes up, and on Sundays you see the cars lined up and down the streets around the churches. Then things get better and all you see are the cars of the faithful. That's what I mean by a seasonal religion. But such is not to be."

After listening to television gospelers and ranting Baptist preachers, I felt well counseled by Brother Southern. Dry, solemn, moderate, he addressed us as his friends, and sounded as if he really meant it.

"There is a way, friends. We can know the way. To the extent that we can find that way, we can know God. And I believe that the . . . majority . . . of the problems in our lives can be solved by our belief in God." That qualifying *majority* was Brother Southern's hallmark.

We sang:

> *If I walk in Heaven's light,*
> *Shun the wrong and do the right,*
> *I know the Lord will make a way for me.*

Had there been a robed choir and an electric organ up at the front, the words would have sounded grasping and brash. With just the two rubber plants and the wall clock, and with our voices halting as we listened for one another, fractionally out of key and out of time, they sounded modest and groping. In our version, walking in Heaven's light came across as the most difficult accomplishment in the world. Baptists might find it easy to shun the wrong and do the right; but the Church of Christ knew otherwise.

As I beat my way around the second half of the loop, the waves built steadily higher. At eight-thirty, the river had been cold and calm under a salmon-pink sky. By nine, the sky had gone blue, the wave points glittered, and I could feel the wind on my cheeks, coming in long warm gusts like the breath of a panting dog. It was blowing up from the southwest, dead across the channel, and I had to tack up and run, tack up and run, gaining only a few yards of water on each maneuver. At the neck of the loop, where the river turned right and ran straight into the wind, the shores were marked in lines of white froth and the waves were several inches taller than my boat. If I made a wrong move, or met a tow at too-close quarters, I'd be swamped. I beached in a sandy cove on the Missouri side. Even after I had pulled the boat up as far as I could, its stern was being lifted by the breakers and thumped down in the sand.

There was nothing much to do and nowhere much to go. The brush and timber were too densely tangled to walk through. According to the chart, there was a lake a quarter of a mile beyond them, and behind the lake there was an old meander course which would probably be marsh. I was on an island, and apparently, I had company of a kind: in the impacted mud above the sand there were a lot of large animal footprints—probably coyote, possibly bear. It seemed wise to stay close to the boat.

I settled down to read Timothy Flint. He had been stranded in New Madrid over the winter of 1819. "The region is interesting in many points of view," he wrote, and as I looked out from my seashore I thought that it must have changed remarkably little since Flint was here. Around the river, at least, it was still his wilderness of forest, swamp and dead lakes. When he arrived, the town was in a state of reconstruction. The New Madrid Earthquake of 1811 had destroyed almost every log cabin and turned lakes into land and land into lakes. Flint had listened to firsthand accounts of the terrifying events in the night on December 16th, 1811.

> The trees split in the midst, lashed one with another, and are still visible over great tracts of country, inclining in every direction and in every angle to the earth and the horizon. [The people] described the undulation of the earth as resembling waves, increasing in elevation as they advanced, and when they had attained a certain fearful height, the earth would burst, and vast volumes of water, and sand, and pit-coal were discharged, as high as the tops of the trees. I have seen a hundred of these chasms, which remained fearfully deep, although in a very tender alluvial soil, and after a lapse of seven years. Whole districts were covered with white sand, so as to become uninhabitable. The water at first covered the whole country, particularly at the Little Prairie; and it must, indeed, have been a scene of horror, in these deep forests and in the gloom of darkest night, and by wading in the water to the middle, to fly from these concussions, which were occurring every few hours, with a noise equally terrible to the beasts and birds, as to men. The birds themselves lost all power and disposition to fly, and retreated to the bosoms of men, their fellow sufferers in this general convulsion. A few persons sunk in these chasms, and were providentially extricated. One person died of affright. One perished miserably on an island . . .

I looked up from the book and saw a white motor yacht rounding the bend below Toney's Towhead. I raised its skipper on the radio.

"What's it like out there in the channel?"

"Well, it's getting to be pretty rough, now. We're forty foot long, and we got a hell of a lot of spray coming over the front. She's yawing on the boils, too. Ain't too good out here. We got a wind gauge up in the cabin, here, and we're getting readings of up to thirty, thirty-five off it. Whereabouts are you?"

"I'm beached up on the island over to your right."

"How long's your boat?"

"Sixteen feet and open."

"Well, I'm telling you: best place for you is on your island. I wouldn't risk it out here. And if them weathermen are right, I reckon you better start building yourself a house there. Raise yourself some chickens. Stuff like that. Have a good trip, now."

He suddenly came back. "Shit, I just got you in these glasses. I see your boat now. You better wait till this wind dies right down, man. That ain't no boat to ride out the kind of weather we got now."

I counted out my provisions. Having expected to make a new town by lunchtime, I hadn't equipped myself very well for the life of a castaway. I still had half the bottle of bootleg bourbon, a can of Miller's left behind by the boy in Cape Girardeau, most of a can of peanuts, and a package of potato chips. I hadn't touched the fishing rod for weeks, but there were hooks and weights in my grip. All I needed was a worm or two. Using a piece of driftwood as a trowel, I went excavating in the bank of mud and dug out a long, gray, flat-tailed creature. On the hook, it knotted itself into a squirming ball. I used to be tougher-minded about these things when I was seven. I was glad to see it plop into the river twenty yards out where I didn't have to watch it writhing. I propped the rod on a forked stick, tightened the line, and set to waiting.

Three worms later, the rod tip started to joggle, then be drawn down in a series of long sucking pulls. I struck; expected the muscled run of a trout or bass and got what felt like a large plum pudding. I could feel it burrowing dully at the bottom, trying to shake the hook from its mouth. It came in, lumpishly flapping on the end of the line: a catfish of about a pound and a half. It was a sad, spotty, limp-whiskered thing; the best that one could say of it was that it was definitely lunch.

I got a fire of twigs alight in the lee of a boulder, and set up the foldaway Bar-B-Q that Herb Heichert had loaded onto the boat in Minneapolis. My gutted catfish lay splayed on the grill. A mat gray film had covered its eyes, and a leaping flame burned off its whiskers. Its skin wrinkled and split away from its flesh. Catching and eating catfish had once been part of my old dream of the river; in the future, that bit had better be left out. I burned my fingers on it. It tasted oily, charred and sweet. I ate only a little of the stuff: mild hunger seemed far preferable to dead catfish.

The gusting wind kept steady all afternoon, with waves creaming across the sand and long troughs and ridges stretching smoothly in parallel all the way to Tennessee. The tows were having a rough time of it. They pushed up thirty-foot pillars of spray ahead of them. I listened in to their pilots, kidding each other along through the stormy water. Someone's barges had broken loose; someone else was going to mosey on down a ways to help find them.

Shortly before dusk, the river quieted just enough for me to move. I made a long diagonal across the waves to the far shore, hugged the bank and reached a muddy inlet by the Tiptonville ferry landing. The ferry itself was a burned-out hulk rotting on its chains, its cabin sides scratched over with graffiti. There was no sign of traffic on the dirt road on the levee, and the town of Tiptonville was nearly a mile away across fields of late soybeans and cropped cotton. Hoping that the authors of the graffiti were fully occupied elsewhere, I left my luggage in the boat, taking only the radio and the pile of ring-bound notebooks in which I kept my trip.

I trudged through cinders along a raised dike above the fields. Although the cotton had been harvested, shreds of it still clung like tufts of sheep's wool to the dead brown stubble. In the failing light, the cottonfields looked as if they had caught some sort of fungoid disease. The last time I'd seen cotton had been in Egypt, where it had been as thickly white as shaving foam; acres and acres of it under a blinding sky. This Tennessee cotton, or what was left of it, these grubby, solitary bolls on their mangled stalks, gave the black bottomlands an air of tedious desolation. The mile seemed longer than it was. By the time I reached the town it was night, and wolfish dogs were baying for me from their backyards.

No, sir, said an old man on the street, there sure wasn't no taxi service in Tiptonville. There had been, but that was ten years back; hell, maybe it was twenty, even. He took a toothless relish in this information, and grew even happier when I asked him if there was a hotel. He *thought* there was a motel, but it was miles out of town. How many miles, he couldn't rightly say.

"Thanks for your help," I said.

"It's a pleasure," he said, and for once the mechanical expression rang with sincerity.

However, I began to like Tiptonville when, in irritable gloom, I fetched up at the County Sheriff's Department and met Officer Guyland Todd. If I didn't mind waiting a few minutes, he said, he wasn't above turning the police car into a cab for a while. Guyland Todd was kind, courteous and as spruce as a cadet in a graduation parade. He seemed saddened by the fact that my life lacked the orderliness of his own, and he set about taking me in hand: muddying his boots as he helped me unload my luggage from the boat, settling me into a motel cabin on Reelfoot Lake, warning me off the "rough" bars in town, and pointing my path through the trees to Gooch's Dining Room. I wasn't to worry about the boat, he said; he'd see that it was checked regularly by the night patrol. If he hasn't yet been made the sheriff of Lake County, an injustice has been done in Tennessee.

Gooch's Dining Room was alive with the sound of an unfamiliar hyphenated word: *Eye-ran*. Farmers in their working clothes and baseball caps were indignantly hurling the word at each other. Eye-ran this, Eye-ran that. . . . I had to have the whole thing explained to me from scratch. I had been out of the way of news for a good twenty-four hours, and it was possible that I was the last person in the United States to learn that Iranian students had seized the American Embassy in Teheran and taken the entire staff hostage.

As a foreigner, I instantly came under suspicion myself.

"This Eye-ran . . . is that anywhere near where you come from?"

I assured them that it wasn't, though it did occur to me that the distance from London to Teheran was only about twice as far as from Tiptonville to New York; and if one were applying a literal-minded standard of measurement, then I was at least two-thirds of the way to being an Iranian citizen.

The talk was furious and ashamed. I was astonished by how personally the event was being taken in Tiptonville; it was as if the individual honor of all these farmers had been impugned.

"The Yewnighted States ought to go in there and take some of them places over."

"We could do it, too. Hell, them U.S. arms they got, they's rusted all to hell. We could go in there . . . We could bust the asses off them A-rab countries."

"I was in the Marines."

"Hell, *I* was in the Marines."

"We could have whupped them sonofabitches—once."

"Seems, nowadays, like the Yewnighted States is jes' too afraid to stand up for itself."

It was like the final bursting of a long and painful boil. The pus had been building for years. Americans had been smarting under a half-articulated sense of their national dislocation and national impotence. Now a gang of foreign students had presented them with an outrageous symbol. It was like Hester Prynne's scarlet A, and the men in Gooch's were having to wear it in front of the rest of the world. They turned bitterly on the Carter Administration; they turned on "America"; then they turned on themselves.

"You know what started off this whole business?" a farmer said from across the table. "What made us weak like this? It was back in '73, '74. Under Nixon. Beans was standing at, oh, three dollars sixty-four a bushel, right? Then Nixon started selling beans to the Russians, and the price was raised right up to near nine dollars. That's when I date it from, when those beans went up. Now *no* one has respect for America no more."

.   .   .

I was in my cabin when Mr. Nunnery tapped at the door. He wanted my "advice," and I followed him along the patio to the motel office where he had his studio couch, his out-at-the-elbows armchair and his smelly little terrier. The dog, he said, had been bought for protection: last year he had been held up at gunpoint and hit on the head with a pistol butt. I doubted if the dog's falsetto bark and wagging tail would do much to frighten robbers, but he was company for Mr. Nunnery; and Mr. Nunnery needed to excuse his want of company.

The advice he sought from me was on how to trace his ancestry.

"My name's Nunnery, see; that's a kind of a British name, ain't it? I reckon I must have some kin over there, if only I could find them."

"Do you know where your family comes from?"

"Well—I know we was from South Carolina. My gran'pappy came over from some place in South Carolina. But before that . . . we must have been British, I guess. I don't know. Maybe we was Scotch or Irish. Would you have an opinion on that?"

Mr. Nunnery's roots seemed too vague to speculate on with much confidence. He told me how his father had once owned a cotton farm. "But then he was caught in around nineteen and ten. First there was a boom. Then the price of cotton went right down to six cents, then five . . . and that was just about the finish of him."

Now he had seized on my arrival as a chance to shore up the fading fortunes of the Nunnery family with some English history. I said I was sorry, but I couldn't help him. I had once been at school with a boy named Nunnery; that, though, was as far as I could go.

"Now, him and me, could we have been kinfolks, do you reckon?"

I looked at the old man cuddling his dog, and tried to remember Nunnery. No particular image came to the surface, except that of adolescence itself: acne and gangliness, wet towels in changing rooms, frozen playing fields, watery cocoa, loud, ragged hymns at evening prayers. Nunnery must have been there somewhere; on house roll calls, his name came two above mine.

"Oh—distant cousins, possibly."

"Nothing . . . special?"

"No—afraid not."

Mr. Nunnery evidently wanted me to stay on talking with him. His lineage hadn't proved a very successful topic.

"I couldn't help but see you had a camera with you. Do you have an interest in photography? It's a kind of hobby of mine. I take a lot of pictures. . . ."

He brought out a boxful of creased snapshots. Mr. Nunnery was possessed by a real imaginative vision of the world. His photographic technique was crude: he had a genius for making telegraph poles sprout from the heads of his subjects and a rather unsteady sense of what was perpendicular and what was not. Taken together, though, the pictures added up to a grave and pessimistic assessment of the relation between the American and his landscape.

I saw the landscapes first. They showed the local wilderness at its coldest and most inhospitable moments: the Mississippi in flood, ice floes on the river, the forest in winter, Reelfoot Lake frozen solid.

"That lake out there was made by the earthquake of eighteen and eleven. You heard about that?"

"Yes, I was reading about it this morning."

"The river ran the wrong way for forty-eight hours then. Flowed right upstream, from south to north, for forty-eight hours," said Mr. Nunnery, honoring the Mississippi's propensities for the awful.

"I never heard that."

"That's gospel truth. Now, there. See that one. That's a bald-headed guy. Lost all his hair in a night. On'y twenty-five when that happened to him."

We put the bald-headed guy aside. Mr. Nunnery pointed to a picture of a grinning woman wearing wide glasses. "That's a Scotchman." He passed over her quickly. "This guy, now, he had a stroke. Face is kinda stiff all down one side. Can't talk." He picked out a charity Christmas card. "See why I got this card in here? That was made by a girl with her *teeth*. Says all about it on the inside. She's so paralyzed, that girl, the only thing she can move is her mouth." We spent a long time admiring the card. The next picture was scrutinized by Mr. Nunnery for more evidence of human frailty and put aside without comment.

"Who's he?"

"Oh, he's just a guy. Got nine hundred acres up at Kentucky Bend. Now, *him*—" He pointed to a new face in the box. "*He* had a fall a couple of years back. Now can't get about, 'cept with a walker."

Mr. Nunnery's world consisted of cripples and unfortunates set in a landscape of impenetrable forests, earthquakes, icebergs, huge, unpredictable rivers, storms, swamps and prairies. Bald-headed, on crutches and in wheelchairs, they crept through their enormous country like wounded insects. Whenever things seemed to brighten up, yet another catastrophe hit them. The price of cotton went phut, or they caught polio, or had a stroke.

"You like my pictures?"

"Yes, I do, very much." Their technical badness was so much of a piece with their human subjects that it made its own ironic point.

"I reckon I could make a book out of 'em."

Had he done so, it would have been a weird, ugly sort of masterpiece on a classic theme; as close as photography could come to Dreiser's *An American Tragedy.*

"Americans," said P. T. Ferry over breakfast in Gooch's, "they'd spoil a wet dream."

The morning's edition of the *Memphis Commercial Appeal* showed pictures of a triumphant mob outside the embassy in Teheran. President Carter had announced that on no account would he return the Shah to the care of the Ayatollah Khomeini. The Iranian students had promised to kill all the American hostages if the United States tried to mount a rescue operation. Opposite Gooch's Dining Room, two tiny Cessna planes were parked on a grass airstrip. The fifty- and sixty-year-old ex-Marines glanced covetously at them over their eggs and grits. If *they* were running the country, they'd be up in the sky, heading for Eye-ran with hunters' Magnums and World War II carbines.

P. T. Ferry was grimly entertained by today's news. He was on to his fourth refill of coffee, and with each cup he grew cussingly funnier. He was a professional fisherman, he farmed a few acres of beans and he owned a garage in town. We had been talking about America's vulnerable dependence on Middle Eastern oil supplies. I told Mr. Ferry that he would have to abandon his big pickup truck and learn to drive a small car like the one I had in London which did forty-five miles to a gallon of gas.

"You better be careful now; you might get lynched, telling an *American* a thing like that. What you doing? Trying to insult my dignity?"

Perfectly on cue, a midget Italian economy car went east past our window.

"See? Some of you are learning already. Soon you'll all be driving things like that."

"That wasn't an American," said P. T. Ferry. "That was some wetback Hispanic."

"You never saw him."

"I didn't have to see him. I know. No American would be seen *dayud* driving that."

He ran me back to town with my luggage loaded on the back of his truck. We stopped at his garage, where he summoned all his employees to stand in a semicircle around me. They crawled out from under cars and made an obedient, greasy audience.

"Listen, you-all. You ask this guy how much gas costs where he comes from."

P. T. Ferry's usual straight man obliged. I felt like a ventriloquist's dummy.

"Last time I was in London it was selling for about two dollars seventy, two dollars eighty a gallon."

There were a couple of polite whoops of pretended disbelief.

"Hear that? And *that*," said P. T. Ferry, pointing at my luggage like an old ham in vaudeville, "is why he's *walking*." He swung himself up into the driver's seat of the truck and beckoned me around, and we drove on. I did rather hope that I wasn't to be taken on exhibition around the whole of Tiptonville as P. T. Ferry's dancing monkey. He had been forbidden to work after a surgical operation, and he found his leisure irksome; with me in tow, he might fill the day as a traveling showman.

Where Cape Girardeau had tried to ward the Mississippi off, Tiptonville had been casually deserted by it. One day the river had shifted its course two miles west, turning Tiptonville from a port into a land-locked town. The old wharf and levee was still called Betty's Landing. Now it was just a line of run-down shacks looking out over a dry hole of scrub and forest. What was still marked on the charts as Island No. 12 was a willow-covered hill showing over the tops of the surrounding oaks. P. T. Ferry pointed out a gray wooden mansion with a pock-marked veranda which stood a block back from the landing.

"See them shell holes? They were made by the Union forces from across the river in the War Between the States."

He made me a present of a bag of nuts from the pecan tree in his yard and set me on my way again. I paddled out of the shallow scoop of mud where my boat had been parked and was whisked off downstream by the current. As soon as I had the motor going I looked back to wave goodbye, but the ferry landing and Mr. Ferry's truck were already too far behind to wave to.

The surface of the Mississippi was riddled with patches of slick. I zigzagged around them, crossing and recrossing the channel to stay clear of these oozings and swellings the color of thick chocolate. They, presumably, were another product of the earthquake of 1811. It had thrown up reefs of rock under the river bottom, and deep down below me the current was riding at full tilt into sunken crags and chimneys. The boils were simply the points at which the Mississippi was finding it easier to run skyward than to head for the Gulf. The power with which the water came up from the riverbed was tremendous: I had seen a whole tow fleet shuddering in midstream as it hit a boil; thirty thousand tons looking liverish and afflicted by the shakes.

Little Cypress Bend, then Little Prairie Bend were loops as tight as crochet hooks. The word "little" in their titles must have been intended as an old pilot's joke. Big eddies skirled in the shallow water off the sandbars at their points, and there were bigger ones still on their outer edges where the current drove hard and deep into the Missouri bank. By Caruthersville, Missouri, after two hours of nervous tacking and dodging, my eye for the river was beginning to glaze. I spent ten minutes aground on a bar, waiting for a phantom towboat to round a bend. Twice I headed for the wide metallic gleam of open water and found that it was just sunlight on sand.

Caruthersville was a muddy, flyblown town. Its gap-boarded cotton gin had been put out of business by the boom in soybeans; a line of Chryslers with no license plates stood rusting on a dealer's lot; its streets were dotted with small, fluttering heaps of garbage. Muffled in my parka against the bright cold, I walked up Main looking for signs of life. There weren't many. One shrunken old man, in a threadbare boiler suit and a grease-stained green felt cap, was kicking his heels on the sidewalk outside the gun-and-liquor store. He crossed the street to meet me.

"You look to me," he said, "as if you was in the Air Force."

"No. I'm not in the Air Force."

"You ain't *never* been in the Air Force?"

"I've never been in any air force."

"Oh." He chomped on his gums, his face twisted with thought. "Say . . ." he said. Then his voice firmed up. "I *bet* you haven't got forty cents on you."

"You're *betting* me that I haven't got forty cents."

"Yep," he said confidently, "that's what I'm betting you."

I thought he had hit on an interestingly democratic version of being a beggar. I gave him a dollar bill.

"Now," he said, pocketing it without thanks, "I got to get you a drink."

"Don't bother. Buy two for yourself."

"Okay. If that's what *you* want, now, I ain't putting up an argument."

After the old man had disappeared into the store, the only thing that moved in town was the digits on the time-and-temperature clock at the bank. Caruthersville seemed very secretive about what it was up to. Perhaps it was rehearsing for a nuclear alert and everyone had gone underground. I did find a dispensing machine full of copies of the local paper, fed sixty cents into it and hoped that the *Pemiscot Journal* would fill me in on the details of life in Caruthersville.

I read it in the vomit-smelling "Riverside" bar, which wasn't by the river but stood inside the equally misnamed "Sea Wall." The *Pemiscot Journal* seemed almost as bewildered as I was by the absence of excitement in Caruthersville. The most interesting piece of news it had managed to rake up for its banner front-page headline was HIGH SCHOOL GETS NEW WINDOWS. "The Colson Company rewarded its employees with a chili lunch last Friday" also made the front page. Inside, the "Local & Society" section sounded more in my line.

> Margie Malin, Alma Adams and Gladys Tinsley went to Blytheville, recently to shop and enjoy the day.
> Gladys Tinsley, Nita Ownby, and Caroline Newton went to Dyersburg recently to shop.

Gladys Tinsley, at least, was certainly getting around; but why had she not enjoyed the day in Dyersburg? Perhaps there was a germ of something here. I went on to an account of how the City of Caruthersville had spent public money during the month of October.

> Fred Noah, for red rock, $738.10; B & D Service Center, for ice, $3.20; ABC Lock Co., for tear gas, $51.00; R. D. Snow, for toilet repair, $33.75; Little Prairie Cemetery, for deposit, $350; Fred Noah, for more red rock, $201.30 . . .

I wondered if Fred Noah's profitable trade in red rock and the entry for tear gas were obscurely connected. Who had broken the toilet? and who was going to be buried at public expense in the cemetery? I left Caruthersville with a great many unanswered questions and a happy disinclination to pursue them further. Flaubert, I suspected, would have loved the town; it would have made a perfect, oppressive setting for Emma Bovary as she looked forward to shopping and enjoying the day at Blytheville with Margie and Alma.

The river had settled into a smooth, loping stride. Just south of Caruthersville, Missouri dissolved into Arkansas somewhere behind the levee on my right. Around the wide curve of Barfield Bend I saw two tow fleets coming upstream in convoy. There was plenty of room for all of us; the Mississippi was more than a mile across here, and although the channel stuck close in to the Arkansas shore, there was a broad reach of open water on the Tennessee side. I had wanted to stop and look at Tomato, Arkansas; the first town in my eighth state was named so enjoyably that I thought it couldn't help holding other pleasures too. Seeing the tows push up toward Tomato Landing, I decided to skip it and cut away to the far side of the river.

It was easy water. I could fill a pipe and let the boat take care of itself, idling along a few hundred yards out from the edge of the forest. I had gone a mile or so when I saw a line of long, crookbacked breakers with an edge of white peeling from their tops. For a tow's wake they seemed to have traveled an unusual distance across the river, but then, both tow fleets were big, and perhaps their wakes had married. Running the engine as fast as it would go, I turned the boat around and headed upstream toward the shore.

At least, that was what I had meant to do. I couldn't work out what was wrong. I seemed to be going faster than I'd ever been before, with the entire surface of the river pouring by in a glassy race of logs, twigs, cola cans and orange crates. The whole world was going past, a stream of pure motion. Yet I was making no wake at all. The river behind me was as unruffled as the river in front, although I could feel the propellor churning hard against the torrential movement of the water. I had quite lost my sense of place and dimension. I looked across to the trees on the bank. They were moving too: wavering slightly, then slipping back, as if they were being tugged up against the grain of the current. So if I was moving at all, I must be going backward downstream, when it felt as if I were traveling up it at an improbable speed.

There was no question of running in to the shore. The forest grew right out into the river, and the trees were knee-deep in water, with no space to slip a boat between them. I tried to get my bearings by switching my eyes from the boat to the streaming current, to the willows and to the sky. We were all out of sync with each other: all in motion, but in different directions and at different speeds. The line of breakers was now only a hundred yards behind me. I spun the boat around and went with the flow of things. For a few minutes, there was a lot of jolting and splashing, and then the long calm of the main channel again.

It was as near as I had come to meeting the river face to face. The Mississippi had behaved perfectly in character. It had been a neat and nasty confidence trick. That invitingly placid water must have been racing at fourteen or fifteen miles an hour over a shallow ledge of sand. Its speed had made it look deep when in reality there was probably only three or four feet between the surface and the bottom. I was still enough of a greenhorn to have been completely gulled.

Yet there was a queer, scary elation in feeling myself poised so fragilely on that sweep of river, watching the forest and sky tremble and start to run. I had touched the deep stillness of the Mississippi; it was as if the world moved around the river and not the river through the world. For a few moments, I had been the pivot, the dead point in the flux; and if the sky had swiveled above my head and raised a sudden shower of stars over Tennessee, I wouldn't have been especially surprised.

When I pulled up a wooded side channel into the town of Osceola, Arkansas, I felt like a sleepwalker. I was too full of the river to take in anything else. There was a motel room, but all I could see was water; gliding, streaming, spinning in on itself, sweeping up in jets from the river bottom. I sat in a café and saw more water. There were eddies on the streets. In a bar-and-poolroom I tried to steady my hand and thoughts by playing a game of pool. I lost, prematurely, as I sent the eight ball on a twisty, meandering course into the far pocket.

Since my entry into the lower river, I had been following my passage against the notes and maps in Zadok Cramer's *The Navigator*. After 165 years they were still impressively accurate. It was true that many of Cramer's islands had gone off to lodge a few miles upstate, where they were scratching out a landlubberly agricultural existence. When Cramer said that the channel went to the right of an island it now usually went to the left, and vice versa. Nevertheless, the portrait of the river held good in all its essentials. There wasn't a reach on it that was not recognizable from Cramer's descriptions.

Over breakfast the next morning, I was studying Cramer against the charts. My first big landmark of the day would be Chickasaw Bluff No. 2, where the Mississippi ran south into a cliff and made a sharp turn to the west. This was Cramer:

SECOND CHICKASAW BLUFF, THREE MILES BELOW NO. 34,

Here you see on the left hand a bluff bank of from 150 to 200 feet in height, singularly shaped, and variegated with different colours of the earth, of which the yellow is the most conspicuous. The river bearing hard against the bluff subjects it to an almost constant caving down, hence the face of the bluff is kept fresh in its appearance. This bluff extends about two miles down.

The river here turns short to the right, and is very narrow. Close in to the bluff is an eddy, you may keep as near the outer edge of it as you please, and the channel is safe and good though very rapid.

Island 34, along with another substantial chunk of Tennessee, had been pushed over into Arkansas by a five-mile chute which had halved the distance of the reach from what it had been in 1814. From there on, though, Cramer was as good as new.

I could see the ragged overhang of the bluff ahead, its sods of tousled grass falling away from its face and the raw streaks of blue and yellow clay. At the point of the turn, the marker buoys directed me straight into a thicket of rough water. The waves were coming up like tongues of flame, pointed and vertical. They knocked and jostled at the boat as I elbowed my way through them. This was what Cramer meant by "safe and good though very rapid." It was rocky going, but I had to stick with the waves to avoid Cramer's eddy. That was there, just to the left of the breakers: a deep concave circle of smooth black water. I kept as near to the outer edge of it as I pleased—which was rather farther, I imagine, than Cramer would have dared to go himself.

For several days now, the river had been rising. It had come up over the top of the dikes, which showed as long ridges of turbulence and rags of scud. It had drowned many of the trees on the shores and sandbars and turned them into "sawyers," the oddest-looking of all the snags on the river. The current would get into the branches of the tree and slowly drag it down until it was completely underwater. Then the elasticity of the trunk would catapult it up again. The trees at the edge of the channel kept on sinking and arching their backs in a ritual rhythm; waving and drowning, waving and drowning. Eventually the river uprooted them, and one could see them spinning in the eddies— full-grown willows and cypresses, their bare roots and branches rolling over and over.

I hadn't seen a tow all morning. It was a lonely business this, riding the swollen river with the sky bleary and the wind just high enough to raise whitecaps on the chutes and make the boat's hull lurch and clank. The nearest towns were miles inland. I couldn't make a landing on either shore, because there was no shore: just a swamp forest which stopped along an arbitrary line where the trees had got the better of the water. A bare sandbar gave me a brief stopping place, where I ate a handful of P. T. Ferry's pecans and watched the movement of a big boil out in the stream. It was a grotesque, animated flower, spilling enormous petals of water from its center. It was bringing up horrible things from the bottom: rotten stumps, branches gone feathery and white with mold, chunks of black peaty stuff—all the garbage of the riverbed was being scoured out and scattered on the surface. I was certain that if I watched it long enough it would start to spew out bodies, boats, skulls.

Memphis had timed its arrival on the current at a perfect moment. On Brandywine Chute I was depressed and frightened by the Mississippi in a way I hadn't been before. I feared its emptiness and loathed its enormous cargo of dead matter, the jungly shore, the purulent, inflamed water. Then, five miles off, in faint outline through a haze of windy humidity, there was the Hernando De Soto highway bridge. I ached for the comfort of a new big city. For a spell, I wanted to stop being a snow goose.

A Sleep Too Long

I tied up to a pontoon on the Wolf River. The attendant in the office was a frog-faced old man with a mouthful of gold fillings, and he was as snappish as an injured dog. Resentment of the world seemed to have eaten him away from the inside; and since no one else was around, he vented his irritation at the world on me. I was in the goddamn wrong place. I could goddamn well pay in advance. I had the goddamn wrong money. He cussed and grumbled. He made an elaborate show of losing the registration book so that he could blame me for its disappearance. Scowling, breathing heavily on my shoulder, he watched me write my name and the name of my boat, hoping to catch me out in a technical breach of the regulations. His surliness was so intent and elaborate that I was more interested than rebuffed by it. I thanked him apologetically for every new rudeness and trapped him into joining me in a game. His object was to make me lose my temper with him; mine was to make him thaw. We moved our pawns into our opening gambits. I approached the coffee machine with a quarter.

"That's members only," the man growled.

"I'm so sorry. I should have thought to ask you first."

There was a long glaring pause.

"Well . . . so long as you *pay* . . ."

It was almost a disappointment to win so easily. Once the man had been persuaded that I didn't come from Tennessee or Arkansas and that, better still, I didn't even come from the United States, he suddenly ceased to be crabby and started talking of his discontents. They centered on the city of Memphis itself.

"You know we got an election on right now? For mayor? I ain't voting."

"Why not?"

"Because them bastards, they ruined my private life, that's why. What I mean is, they stopped people knowing people. Take twenty years ago. I'd go for a walk in the morning, up round Jefferson and Main, I'd see forty people I knew. I had friends in this city then. Today—know how many I'd see? Two. One, even. Some days I won't see nobody at all. Where they all gone, I don't know."

I couldn't immediately see the connection between the old man's angry loneliness and the mayoral election. My failure to grasp the point made him spit and gulp with irritation.

"It was politicians that *done* it, for godsakes! They pulled down Beale, which they never shoulda done. But when they turned Main into that goddamn *mall*, that's when they ruined people's private life. Nowadays there's only niggers there. You go in the stores—just niggers. Nothing but a lot of niggers. That's what they done to me, and nowadays I don't know nobody."

Leaning heavily on the bar, the man brooded, slack-mouthed, staring out the window at his ruined city. What little light there was caught the gold in his teeth.

"Know what they done? They given Memphis to the niggers. Over on Mud Island there—niggers. You got niggers in all the stores. There's niggers sitting out on all the benches on that mall. There's niggers in offices, now. Whole blocks of 'em—solid niggers. They're giving them five and six hundred bucks a month—to niggers in offices. What they got to do for it? Smoke, sass, and drink Coke all day. When I went to work, they give me eight bucks a week. Eight lousy bucks, and I had to work my ass off for it. Now I have to see them niggers giving sass and riding in new Cadillacs. You reckon that's *fair?*"

"Well . . . there's been a lot of inflation all around since you started work."

The old man snorted and drew a heavy overcoat of silence around himself.

"So who's running in this election, then?"

"Mayor Chandler. *He* did that to uptown."

"And who else?"

" 'Judge' Otis Higgs." He gave a humorless little laugh, a dry rattle in his throat.

"Well, why don't you vote for *him?*"

"*Higgs?* Me vote for Higgs? You got to be joking. He's a nigger."

The stones of the wide, sloping wharf were cracked and soapy with age. I climbed up them into Memphis, and saw immediately what the man had meant by the loneliness of the place. No one could expect to come across a friend here. The freight yards around the tracks of the Illinois Central Railroad had been given over to parking lots, empty now even of cars. On Front Street, the cotton warehouses had bats and pigeons as their current proprietors. The painted names of their previous owners had been bleached out beyond recognition; but because it was repeated on every warehouse, the word COTTON itself could just be pieced together still. The C's and O's and T's and N's had survived in ones and twos. Reading along the line, you could make a long sad noise, like an owl's call or the whistle of a train: NOONTCCTNTCOOON.

A few of the warehouses had been pulled like bad teeth from the row. The quality of the dentistry was rough: it had left an injured gum of muddy holes and broken bricks. The reach and height of this general dereliction were so great that it took a little time to notice the few patches of light and life: the fake gas lamp, the rustic timber shingle on its new chains, the sound of someone coaxing an old tune out of an electronic Moog Synthesizer. The bar/restaurants, dotting the ruined waterfront, were working hard to restore a touch of forced glitter to the old man's abandoned city.

They had taken on a job that was out of all proportion to their powers. They were quarried out of the bottom stories of Victorian monsters, and their picture windows and pine boarding gave the impression that people had been storing little ranch-style bungalows in the warehouses for safekeeping. When their electric gas mantles were switched on, they lit up the ferns and grasses that were growing out of the brick and through the floors all round them. The effect was to make one feel anxious about the moral welfare of the bungalows: what on earth were pretty, inexperienced things like these doing in a place like this? I wanted to escort them to somewhere safer, like the lockers at the Greyhound bus terminal.

One could see exactly how the waterfront should have been. There was the sweep of the open river, then steamboats at the landing, then the wharf, the rail yards, the cotton bales and, finally, as raw and steep as the Chickasaw bluffs, the warehouses; all in scale with each other, on a very grand scale indeed. The trouble with the bar/restaurants was that by these measurements they were toys. Even the biggest and bravest of them, One Beale Street, couldn't reach nearly high or far enough. It couldn't extend its sphere of influence even to the railroad tracks, when what it needed was to be able to square up to the river. Sitting in its bar waiting for a cab, I felt dwarfed. It was Happy Hour, and the place was busy. The saxophonist, his body crouched, his knees bent, joined to his instrument in a looping omega, was doing his best to raise the roof. As well he might. We had all the weight of the nine-teenth century piled up over our heads, and I saw no particular reason why it should not come down through the ceiling and bury us in its rubble.

The election was everywhere. The city looked like a heavy parcel, stuck all over with postage stamps; red ones for Mayor Chandler, blue ones for Otis Higgs. I had rented a car and was trying to count the blues and reds among the bumper stickers down Union Avenue. CHANDLER, CHANDLER, HIGGS, HONK IF YOU LOVE JESUS, HIGGS, CHANDLER, CHANDLER, HIGGS, BE KIND TO MICE—EAT PUSSY TONITE. CHANDLER.

I happened on the Higgs headquarters by accident: a decrepit house on Union whose graying paint had been almost completely papered over in blue. A flapping banner hung from the wooden balcony. It said: YES, WE CAN! I drove on three blocks, wondering vaguely if there was another half to the slogan, then turned back. The Memphis may-oral election was the only eddy on my trip into which I drifted care-lessly and got sucked in.

The house was a dizzying swirl of people running in circles with clipboards, people talking into banks of telephones, people folding handbills and people imitating other people being busy. I joined the imitators. Within a minute, I had been mistaken for someone else and handed a Coke. I drank it with what I hoped was the appearance of a man who hadn't a moment too long for this sort of trifle.

"Hey, where the hell's *Rozelle?*"

"I haven't seen her. Sorry," I said.

"It's a goddamn street, man—"

"Sorry. Of course."

In a momentary island of quiet, I found myself with one of the candidate's personal aides. She was white; and although her voice had the slow, dipping rhythm of Tennessee, it had clearly been to prep school and college on the East Coast. I asked her how far Mr. Higgs was going to be able to count on a white liberal vote in Memphis.

"There are no white liberals in Memphis. They're a foreign breed. Otis needs—some say twelve, some say fourteen percent of the white vote to win, and they'll be voting with passion, with anger, with all kinds of feelings, but they won't be voting for him because they're lib-erals. Liberalism's something that only people in the North can af-ford; it's a luxury. Don't mistake me because of my color—I'm no liberal. Why don't you talk with Otis?"

"Isn't he too busy?"

"He'll make time for you."

He did. I was shown into his office, where the candidate was drinking milk and having difficulty in eating a carry-out hamburger from its toilet-tissue wrapping. It was, too, the package in which he himself was wrapped that one saw first: the serious eyeglasses, the trim crescent of mustache, the funereal three-piece suit, the thick gold bracelet. He was encased from top to toe in a uniform which looked as if it had been chosen by a committee. Intelligence must be represented—give him glasses. Tasteful modesty—the suit. Prosperity, a discreet hint of worldly success—the bracelet. Decisiveness—the mustache. His hair had been barbered to eliminate any suggestion of the ebullient Afro high jinks for which it had obvious aptitude. The committee seemed to have done everything it could with him short of giving him a coat of pale peach distemper.

He talked in a rolling bass of such resonance that he put the length of an imaginary aisle between us. He was up at the altar end; I was away in the back pews. This was disconcerting, since we were sitting about seven feet apart.

"I'm a very humble man. I believe in Humility. I never forget that I'm a man. There's an old story from the Roman times, about the centurion and the slave. Whenever the centurion's standing high in his chariot at the races, he always has the slave riding beside him. Why is the slave there? To whisper in the ear of the centurion: 'You're only a man. You're only a man.' I hear the voice of the whispering slave. 'You're only a man. You're only a man.' "

He stared into the middle distance beyond my left ear.

"I tell that story many times."

"Yes."

There was something in his face that was a good deal more complicated than his uniform or his clockwork oratory. There was a lot of tiredness there, a flash of wistful self-irony, even a glimmer of amusement at my own fate of being made to sit down and listen to this stuff about centurions and slaves.

"Next week, when I'm elected, I'm going to become an instant national figure." He was listening to himself as if someone else had been speaking. "That makes me feel very humble."

"You're looking tired. How long has the campaign been running?"

"Since January."

"Can you live off the adrenaline of it?"

"Yes, I guess that's what keeps me going. You know, I'll be talking to meetings all evening; then I'll come home and just pace around and around. I can feel the energy still fizzing in my veins—I got to let it leak out before I can sleep, so some nights I'll be going to bed at three, maybe four. I get to hear the cocks crow."

"How much sleep do you need?"

"I can get by on five hours now."

The distance between us had shortened by thirty yards. We began to talk about Memphis. Higgs said that the city had broken into as many different pieces as a shattered plate. The tension between blacks and whites was only the biggest and most obvious of these ruptures: there was no common feeling between business and the unions, between the universities and the rest of the city, between the old Southern gentry and the new industrial middle class.

"I believe we can heal these wounds. In a small way we're doing just that in this house. You've been through, you've seen it. Out there are blacks and whites, there are businessmen, lawyers, civil rights workers, guys from the fire service union . . . Go over to Chandler's H.Q. You won't see that there. In this house we've got a complete cross-section of Memphis society. I don't think you'll find another house in the city where you can see that. This campaign has really started to bring Memphis together, and that's what it's all about."

The Reverend Judge Otis Higgs himself contained several disparate characters in his own person. He had taught in the public school system; he was an ordained minister of the Baptist Church; he had gone to law school and worked as an attorney; he had been a judge in the Shelby County courts. When he talked at his best he was part teacher, part lawyer, part preacher. At his worst, just one of these characters would seem to gain a totalitarian grip on his personality, and he would suddenly shrink, reduced to a single dimension.

"I have traveled in this country," he was saying, "and I know what people think when they hear the word 'Memphis.' This is Death City. It's remembered for two things. Martin Luther King was shot here. Elvis Presley died here. That's what Memphis is famous for, for death. But I have a vision. I see the death of Elvis Presley as a catalyst for the rebirth of Memphis—"

He was a church-length away from me again.

"What on earth do you mean?"

He talked of the two million tourists a year who went to visit Presley's grave at Graceland. He was going to attract them to the downtown area with an Elvis museum, an Elvis statue, steamboat rides, restaurants. If only he could turn downtown into an Elvis shrine, he could rebuild it on tourist money.

"I think that's a very frightening idea."

"I am listening to you," Higgs said.

I told him about what I had seen of St. Louis and what I thought were the disastrous consequences of its attempt to renew itself on tourists, conventioneers and visiting football crowds.

"You can't make a city out of temporary people. Front Street looked sick to me, but it didn't look dead the way St. Louis is dead."

"They got the balance wrong there," Higgs said. "You need a base of condominiums downtown. We need to persuade local people to move back to the river. If we could only get folks to think that living in a riverside apartment was the smart thing to do . . . But without the revenue from the tourists, our hands are tied. I know what you mean about St. Louis. I can see the danger. . . ."

He sucked at his milk through a straw.

"The river is this city's greatest natural resource, and we've turned our backs on it. I think the river is a key. We have to return to the river. The big problem is that if you're black in Memphis the river has always meant one thing. Cotton. And cotton means 'Haul that barge, boy! Tote that bale!' So the Mississippi has been hated in the black community. If we can have blacks and whites together, living by the river as a matter of choice, then we'll know that the wounds of this city are healing over."

I left with a Higgs bumper sticker and a YES, WE CAN lapel button. I wanted to lose myself in someone else's journey for a change; I wanted to stay long enough in Memphis to see Otis Higgs reach City Hall.

Higgs's trail led north, into the black suburbs of Hollywood and Chelsea. For me, the journey kept on being broken by short, sidewise trips eastward. In the evenings a number of people kindly opened their doors for me to dinner, and I went out to big Victorian greystone houses with oak-paneled walls and high ceilings of sculpted plaster, to the country club, to white Grecian mansions in the woods with long floodlit colonnades.

We were drinking wine from silver goblets. A line of candles flickered down the dining table. My hostess put her hand on my forearm and said, "It's difficult for you to understand, I know. But integration is as new to us as it is to the South *A*fricans—"

I had been to black ghettos before. In Watts, Roxbury, Harlem, South St. Louis, I'd felt the angriness in their air, as if it were thick with iron filings. I had been ordered out; I was a white tourist, and I had no business on these streets. In Roxbury, my car had been jumped at a stoplight:

"Honky! Hey, Honky! What you think you doing here, Honky?"

It wasn't so in Hollywood and Chelsea. They were poor places. They looked crushed and scabby: streets of paintless frame bungalows, uncollected garbage, Salvation Army free stores and housing projects that might reasonably have been mistaken for prisons. They must have been angry; they had every excuse for anger. Yet it was an anger which hadn't yet crystallized into that automatic hatred of the white stranger which I had met in the ghettos of the North; or at least, the hatred was elaborately masked. I received the odd curious glance, accompanied by a faint smile, as if I'd lost my way and needed street directions to get me home. Several times people went out of their way to make me welcome. *Stay and talk. Stay and see.*

The political campaign went from church to church, and the churches were proud islands of well-being in a landscape where the sun seemed to take a perverse pleasure in lighting up everything that peeled, rotted or collapsed. Their electronic organs were new; the robes of the choirs had been laundered to the improbably dazzling whites and blues of a soap-powder ad; the air-conditioning systems were new; the pale pine floors and pews were slippery with scented wax; the microphones and loudspeakers had the expensive mint look of equipment in a store window. The churches were an extravagant proof that the black community, poor as it was, could come together to create something just as fine as any white country club. They had been built from dimes, quarters, one-dollar bills, collected over years from the dismal tangle of surrounding streets. You might live in a two-room shack with a gaping veranda, but you could have a shareholder's stake in a real brick palace.

I had expected meetings, with long speeches. They turned out to be services, with prayers and gospel singing and sermons. At the Pleasant Hill Missionary Baptist Church, Otis Higgs was getting into his stride. After each sentence he paused, letting the organist syncopate a long riff, low down in the bass with a lot of vibrato, to echo the phrasing of the words.

"Rip Van Winkle," said Higgs into the microphone, "he fell asleep for a hundred years . . ."

"Woweow Boom Wadoopah," went the organ. "Bobalee boba yong-di-woweow!"

From all across the church, answering voices came chiming in:

"Yes, sir!"

"That's right!"

"So he did!"

"Unh-*hunh!*"

"Oh, my Lord!"

Higgs's speech wasn't his alone; it belonged to all of us. Everyone was helping it along. Some were clapping its rhythm on the off-beat; others were providing punctuation marks for it with their *Amens* and *Yes, sirs*; the organist was turning it, line by line, from talk into music. The whole event was more of an improvised symphony than a political address.

Higgs had taken "Sleeping Through the Revolution" as his text. He was wreathing together the stories of Rip Van Winkle and the sleepers of Gethsemane and bringing them home and up to date in Memphis.

". . . our people, fast asleep."

"Yeah!"

"Okay!"

"It's all right!"

"I can hear my Lord saying, 'Memphis! You got to wake up!' "

"A-men!"

"I can hear the God of the universe saying to Memphis today . . ."

"So can I!"

"Oh my sweet Lord!"

"Memphis, yes you can! Wake up! You been asleep too long!"

Now women in hats with tall boa feathers were beginning to go into ecstatic trances. They gurgled and shook. They laughed, then shrieked. They looked as if they had plugged themselves into a high-voltage cable. Writhing and sobbing, they fell in heaps on the floor, where they were decorously surrounded by three or four other women who fanned them with yellow order papers. The order papers waved in strict tempo, in time with each other, in time with the riffs on the organ.

The logic of the speech itself was strange. The breaks between one sentence and the next were so long that each line could afford to start out on a quite different tack. Sometimes the organ, the voices of the congregation and the holy fits would occupy a minute or more after Higgs himself had said only half a dozen words. After a while all he needed to do was contribute single tags and let the church take over and do the rest.

"I don't have an ounce of negativism in my body!"

Organ, voices, shrieks, fits.

"If you can't be a highway, just be a trail!"

O., V., S., & F.

"All you got to do is wake up!"

O., V., S., & F.

"Keep on keeping on!"

O., V., S., & F.

"I feel it. You feel it. Something *Within!*"

Oceanic outbreak of *O., V., S., & F.*

"You be the best of what you are and WAKE UP!"

The whole church now was riding on the pulse. The genius was not in the words but in the occasion itself; two hundred people driving each other on to higher and higher peaks of fervor. I was as excited as anyone. I was too inhibitedly Anglo-Saxon to join in the shouting, but I could feel the *That's rights!* and *Amens!* struggling to get free of my buttoned-down voicebox.

Higgs reached his climax with a cluster of words so familiar that I would have thought it impossible to make them sound fresh again. The church transformed them. By the time we had finished with them, their author would not have recognized them as his own.

"We hold these truths to be self-evident!"

There was a great upward surge from the organ.

"That's right!"

"We do!"

"That all men—"

"Yes, sir!"

"Unh-hunh!"

"Are created equal!"

Another dizzying run of organ notes and sixty voices crying out in tune.

"That they are endowed by their creator!"

"Oh, my Jesus!"

"He's everything to me!"

"With unalienable rights!"

"Yes, he is!"

"A-men!"

"That among these are life . . ."

"Oh, yeah!"

"Give that to me, Lord!"

"Liberty!"

"Sweet Lord!"

"And the pursuit of happiness!"

It was an extraordinary, passionate and ironic moment. Jefferson, the obsessive rationalist, the intellectual heir of the *philosophes* of the Enlightenment, had written a magical incantation, a spell powerful enough to cast out devils and city bosses. We swayed, clapped, shouted, lifted by the organ. Otis Higgs was sweating over his microphone. He looked gray with exhaustion and hope.

. . .

At a family supper in the kitchen of a balustraded house in a green suburb, the man was saying, "It's nothing to do with his being a Negro. His trouble is that he lacks the capacity for leadership."

"He seems absolutely magnetic to me," I said. "I just don't see that."

"I gave him my vote in the primary," said the man's wife. "I don't know. I'm afraid that on Thursday I'll be switching to Chandler. I wish I wasn't. In honesty, I wish I could vote for Otis Higgs."

"Oh, Mom!" said her sixteen-year-old son from across the table. "You only voted for him because he's black and you feel sorry for him."

Was this where Southern guilt came full circle? Guilty for feeling guilty, you switch your vote to the white candidate? I wondered how I could put this proposition in a more polite form, found none, and decided to keep it to myself.

"If Higgs is elected," the man said, "I just know what's going to happen. He'll be a puppet prince. The Fords will be pulling all his strings."

The Fords were the most powerful black family in Memphis. Their wealth, like that of so many black political dynasties in the South, was based on a chain of funeral parlors. Blacks had always wanted to be buried by their own, and the funeral business was one of the very few in which blacks had built up large fortunes over several generations. Running for office was expensive and most black candidates needed the backing of funeral-parlor money. The Fords had been lukewarm over Higgs. He had the lightest of endorsements from them. I had seen United States Representative Harold Ford performing once at a rally for Higgs. He had not said a word about the candidate, but had gone striding around the platform in a white suit, shouting slogans for himself. Anywhere but in the South, he would not even have been black. He was a "high yellow," with a Chinese complexion and the chisel-featured face of a poor white. He had struck me as strident and posturing, but the congregation had roared for him just as loudly as they had roared for Higgs.

"From what I've seen of him," I said, "I doubt if anyone will pull his strings. My impression is that he and the Fords can barely stand the sight of each other."

"The Fords wouldn't *allow* another Negro to govern this city unless the real control stayed with them. The only reason they're letting Higgs run is because they know he's weak enough to be manipulated."

At the campaign headquarters, spooks were phoning in. Their calls were coming with increasing frequency, several times an hour. Some described themselves as "concerned citizens"; others claimed to represent the Klan. A receiver was held out to me so that I could listen.

"If Otis Higgs is elected, I'm jes' warnin' ya . . ." It was a man's voice. It sounded caked with farm mud. "He won't be livin' long enough to take office. Tha's a' Ah gotta say to you, and you better b'lieve it, now." He clicked off.

"That's kind of average," said the woman who had given me the phone. "Some are *real* mean."

Although most of the people who said they were Klansmen were merely using the society as an umbrella to hide under, the K.K.K. was out there, somewhere in the shadows. Burning crosses had been placed on the lawns of white campaign workers, and in the plague of anonymous notes and calls a handful did almost certainly come from the Klan and were taken very seriously indeed.

I had coffee with the aide who had first introduced me to Higgs. I told her that on my evenings in the east of the city I had met a constant complaint that the campaign was being feebly conducted there. Too few canvassers were knocking on too few doors; some people hadn't even received handbills. Yet it was from this part of town that the essential votes would come.

"That's deliberate," she said. "In the white suburbs, particularly the rich ones, we're keeping as low-profile as we possibly can. Look—" She showed me a leaflet which was just a numbered list of the planks of Higgs's platform. It had no photograph. It looked as official and as dull as an income-tax form.

"You see, there are so many people who want to vote for Otis' policies. They want Chandler out. They want a change in the city. But we can't remind them that by voting for Otis they're voting for a black *face*. If they see his picture, all they'll be able to think of is that he's a Negro. I know it's terrible when you put it that way; but that's the way things work in Memphis."

"She was my closest friend. Cora. She was my closest friend."

Later that evening, I had gone around to the aide's house to split a bottle of wine with her. She was telling me about her childhood in Memphis; her closest friend had been her black nurse.

"Cora was from Mississippi. To her, Memphis was the North. Before she came here she'd never seen black people wearing suits and ties and living in real houses. For her, it was a liberation just to be here. And I used to sleep beside her in her bed . . . and I never wanted to eat food from my own plate; it had to be off Cora's plate. She was more than my mother to me—can you understand that?"

Her forefinger was pulsing nervously against the rim of her glass.

"I must have been, oh, six years old . . . My mother had given Cora some money to buy me a new coat. Cora and I, we went downtown by streetcar. I was excited, not because of the coat but because of being alone with Cora. There was a big store on Main, and they had two drinking fountains, one for whites and one for Negroes. Cora was taking a drink of water and I wanted some too. Cora said, 'No, honey—*that's* your fountain, over there.' 'But I want to drink with you!' I said. 'You can't, honey; it ain't allowed,' Cora said. And I started to shout and scream. *Why* did Cora have to drink at one fountain and me at another? We shared *everything*. People started to stare. There was this kid, yelling and stamping, and Cora had to drag me out of the store. I thought the world had gone crazy. It just made no sense at all. I wouldn't go in the store again. I didn't want the coat. I was hysterical. . . ."

She was thrilling herself with the memory of it. What she was telling was the story of a religious conversion.

"When we came home, my mother started laying into Cora. 'Why didn't you buy the child that *coat?*' Then I told my mother about the drinking fountains, and she tried to explain to me about segregation as if it was some kind of law of nature or something. She was talking in this sensible voice about white people and Negroes and how the two races each had to have their own separate *facilities*.

" 'But that's so silly!' I kept on saying. 'That's just *so* silly!' And I was hating my own mother for saying these things. A six-year-old child could see it all perfectly clearly, and my mother was blind. It was so obvious to me. The whole thing was just *silly*.

"Oh, but down in Missis*si*ppi . . . that's another *coun*try! You know even now there are places there where if you're black the whites call you one of two things—you're either a 'field nigger' or you're a 'house nigger'? Just saying those words—they're obscenities to me. They're like poison in my mouth.

"Do you see now? Do you see why I said that nobody in Memphis could be a white *liberal?*"

We had been waiting for Higgs for more than half an hour in the Unitarian church on the river. The three blacks in the audience were conspicuous among the thirty-five or so white businessmen and their wives. There was a lot of looking at wristwatches and irritable harrumphing. People had made a long Sunday-morning drive west from their suburbs for this meeting; if they could make it on time, why couldn't Higgs? We had worked our way through the free coffee and cookies; if he didn't come soon, we'd be condemned to reading the book-review section of the Sunday paper.

He was apologetic when he arrived. When he started speaking, I found him almost unrecognizable. He was clumsy with his notes, shuffling them together on the bare pine table. He was difficult to hear. Keeping his face down, he read out a prepared speech in which he announced himself to be in favor of a series of decencies so low-key and ordinary that they came across as merely deferential. He said that he wanted to appoint a consultative committee of experts to advise him on the industrial development of the city. He hoped that more experts would come up with a plan for a workable mass-transit system. He coughed, lost his place, fiddled with his gold bracelet. My eye wandered beyond him to the window and the chunky filigree of the railroad bridge over the Mississippi. The voice to which I was now paying little attention was that of a stranger. It didn't have Otis Higgs's force or humor. It certainly didn't have his capacity to play with ideas as he spoke. It was the kind of voice for which Mom might just feel sorry enough to give it a vote in a primary and switch her allegiance when it came to the real thing.

His campaign manager said that Judge Higgs would be happy to answer any questions. We turned into an interviewing committee. The men in the room started testing Higgs as if they were the senior professors and he the instructor who wasn't going to get tenure. Where did he stand on crime? on enlarging the tax base? on public schools? For each answer, Higgs dug around among his papers and found another lifeless formulation. His profile was so low that one could see the railroad bridge running clean through the space where his head should have been.

In the largest and woodiest of the floodlit white mansions, a woman was saying, "He has to win. He *has* to. I see this election as Memphis' last chance. If he loses, it'll be as bad a day for this city as the day they shot Martin Luther King."

At the fund-raising breakfast in the Olivet Baptist Church, the other Otis Higgs was back in town.

"I can hear God Himself saying this morning, 'Memphis! I'll show you the way!' "

"Hallelujah!"

"That's right!"

"Yes, we can!"

The walls and ceiling were tricked out with looping colored paper chains. We sat at trestle tables, forking up grits and drinking orange juice while the collection plates moved around at eye level like Frisbees.

"White folks who are right don't mind black folks' being black!"

"Unh-hunh!"

"Yes, sir!"

"If you feel it like I feel it, right down in your soul—"

"Oh, yes, I do!"

"I've got the feeling, now! I've got the spirit!"

"A-men!"

"Oh, yes, I've got it!"

The organ chords were coming in languorous waves behind the words.

"If Birming-ham can do it and Memphis fails, then I'm telling you we ought to crawl back into our holes and never come out!"

"Yes, we can!" someone shouted, and the slogan began to gather voices around it. The organist found and embellished a triumphant do-re-mi to accompany us, and we pumped the line out again and again until the church was solid with the sound and one could feel the rhythm of it in the timbers and the glass.

Yes, we can! Yes, we can! Yes, we can! YES, WE CAN! YES, WE CAN!

There had been many rumors. Canvassers who came back to the Higgs headquarters from the poorest of the black suburbs said that people there had been visited a few days before by white "social workers." The "social workers" had explained the tricky points of electoral procedure to illiterate voters on the register. The chief of these points was that many people apparently thought they were supposed to vote twice. By registering to vote, they had already voted once. The election on Thursday was only for those who hadn't registered. This helpful piece of information was now common knowledge in several of the housing projects and was spreading through northern Memphis.

On Tuesday, a burning cross was pushed through the kitchen window of a frame house where a woman lived alone with her teen-age son. The odd thing about the event was that the mother and son were black and had no known political connections. They seemed an unusual target for the Klan, and some curious reporters went out to interview them. They returned with word that the boy was Otis Higgs's illegitimate child.

I watched Higgs as he stood in front of the TV cameras. He made a brave show of it. He held his dignity. He denied nothing. He said that it had happened a very long time ago when he himself was in his teens; a fair provision had been made for the boy and his mother, and the burning cross was a cruel and disgraceful trick. If it revealed anything at all, it showed only to what moral depths his opponents were prepared to lower themselves.

At dinner that night, I said I was afraid that Higgs's chances of winning had been terribly damaged by this piece of beastliness.

"Oh, no—I don't think it'll affect him at all," said the woman on my right. "You see, for Negroes the idea of virginity, chastity, monogamy, why, it simply doesn't exist for them. I remember when I was a little girl we used to have a nursemaid named Ula Mae. And I saw Ula Mae getting fatter and fatter, and I asked the cook, 'Why's Ula Mae getting to be so fat, Ella?' And the cook said, 'Why, honey-chile, Ula Mae's gonna have a baby.' 'But I didn't know Ula Mae had a husband,' I said. 'Oh, lawdy, no, chile—Ula Mae's not *married*.' "

The woman had the kind of expensive Southern smile in which, if you looked carefully, you could see whole genealogies of cotton planters in frock coats. She looked as if she had explained everything very nicely. Her watermelon-darky accent was evidently a party piece.

"I mean to say, in the Negro community, hardly *anybody* knows for certain who their daddy is. That's just their way—"

"It'll probably bring Higgs a big sympathy vote," her husband said. "It may even turn out to be the thing that wins him this election."

It was at that dinner that the husband had said, "Memphis is still the cotton capital of the world." Yet cotton kept almost as low a profile in the city as Otis Higgs had kept in the Unitarian church. There was the Cotton Exchange on Front Street, and in a week I had seen five or six bales of the stuff standing outside one of the few remaining warehouses still in business. I had wanted to meet a cotton man, and in a grubby, sunny upper room on Madison where the Wolf River Society for the Prevention of Taking Oneself Too Seriously held its daily lunches, I was given an introduction to a cotton factor.

Mr. Deans's office was decorated with photographs of mule carts on the levee and field hands' camps. Until as recently as twenty years ago, cotton had been a shaping social force in the life of the city. Like the steamboat trade, it had been something that everyone could see; it assembled masses of people around it; it caused annual waves of migration between the rural plantations and the river wharves. You could take pictures of it. Now, like the towboat industry, it was a subterra-nean economic force. It was almost invisible. The millions of dollars that cotton brought into Memphis came into the city as secretly as laundered money. Cotton was no longer picked by hand; it didn't create labor camps anymore. It was divorced from the river. Most of it now went by freight train to the Carolinas. The warehouses on Front Street had begun to die when the government changed its regulations and the stamping of an official grade on each bale began to be done out on the farm and not here in the city.

"It may not look big to you," Mr. Deans said. "But it's bigger than ever. In this part of Tennessee we haven't been hit by the Recession like the rest of the country. Cotton has insulated us from it. You see, we can afford to grow it where other countries can't. In places like Egypt and Pakistan, they're giving over more and more cotton land to rice and wheat because they need to feed their people. Here, we've got the space. We've got machines they haven't got, so we can grow it cheaply. Don't let your eyes deceive you: you're looking at a boom right here and now."

He took me upstairs to the warehouse, where the bales were stacked to the roof. He reached into a bale and rolled a staple between his fore-finger and thumb.

"Two thirty-seconds," he said.

"How long does it take you to learn to do that?"

"Oh, it's a knack you pick up. Like playing the piano. In this indus-try you start off as a 'squidge.' That's what squidging is. The first thing you need to get is just the feel of cotton on your finger. As soon as you know by instinct that it's two thirty-seconds, that's the time you gradu-ate."

The sample boxes were all labeled with girls' names. The highest-grade staple was called "Clara" ("She's the best girl"); the lowest, "Trixi" ("She's a kind of mean, low-down kind of girl").

"You know, one funny thing about this business . . . When I started out in it, you worked with Negroes. You always worked with Negroes. Now you see a black face on a farm and you notice it. Nowadays, the Negroes are all too grand to work in cotton." He gave a dry, sarcastic little laugh. "They consider it . . . beneath their dignity."

On election day, the bars were shut. I was drinking behind closed doors with a mild, bleary man who had spent the last few years gently boozing on a private income. He was the heir of an old Memphis family; a sad gay who seemed typecast to represent the end of some-thing.

"You have to remember," he said, his voice thick with bourbon, "you're in the South here."

"It's not something that I'm in much danger of forgetting."

"In the North . . . they . . . love the race and hate the individual. In the South, we love the individual . . . and we *hate* the race."

The Higgs headquarters shone like a full moon on Union Avenue. A cordon of cops, their arms linked, was holding the crowds back. The building was framed in a white blaze of television lights. The figures who appeared on the balcony looked blind and pale. I had been given a card that turned me into an honorary personal aide, and I hustled and butted my way through to the house and its unearthly limelight. The crowds had come for a spectacle, as they might have gone to the scene of a plane crash or a multiple murder: the election of the first black mayor of Memphis, like the election of the first black mayor of Birmingham, Alabama, was going to be a national event. It would be on Walter Cronkite and *Good Morning America*.

Inside the corral, people were jittery with anxious elation. It had been a close-run thing, but yes, touch wood, we should have just scraped through. The ground floor was a maze of pinboards, one for each precinct, dotted with red and blue tags. Everywhere one looked there was another portable television set, and the campaign workers were sending messages to each other in code over the smoky crush of heads and cola cans.

When they came in, the results arrived in a flood, far too fast to follow. The tags were moving on the boards. Someone made a whooping cheer, and was shouted down. Then it was suddenly there, on a TV screen, and no one believed it. Chandler had 52 percent. Higgs had 48 percent.

The woman standing beside me was sobbing. An aide called that there was going to be a recount, that not all the precincts had come in yet, that . . . but the TV screen was showing the outside of Chandler's headquarters, and he had already started in on his victory speech.

"What you want to look at *him* for? Why d'you want to look at *him?* There's only one place I want to see him—in a long pine box!"

Chandler's face looked as if it had been gouged and whittled from a lump of soft Dutch cheese. That morning's *Commercial Appeal* had cartooned him as Goliath about to be toppled by the slingshot of Higgs's David. A fiercely reasoned editorial had argued that any sensible Memphian must vote for Higgs.

Higgs had meant to speak to the cameras from the balcony outside. Now he couldn't face that. Two TV crews came into the building and set up their lights. Higgs stood in the chaotic litter of his failed campaign. Women were crying; men were sullen-faced, biting on cigarettes as if they were bullets.

"Mayor Judge Higgs! That's what he is to me, and I ain't saying any different!"

"Amen!"

A microphone was pushed into Higg's face. He was too shocked to be generous in defeat.

"The loser tonight is Memphis," he said.

"That's right!"

"The people's mayor!"

"Yeah—the people's mayor!"

"There's something here that's missing over in Chandler's headquarters. Black and white. Jew and Gentile. Protestant and Catholic . . ."

"Oh, my Lord!" a woman moaned. "Oh, my Lord. Oh, my Lord."

The television lights were switched off. The crowd leaked quickly away. National news was not going to be made tonight in Memphis after all. In our own headquarters we were left with prickling eyes and brave, bitter little jokes. There was still the rest of the evening to face out: a whole floor of the Rivermont Hotel had been booked for a triumphal party, and we were going to have to toast defeat with canapés and Gallo wine; wormwood and gall.

"I think perhaps I shouldn't go," I said to my friend the aide.

"No, you must. Please—just for Otis' sake. He needs us all right now."

I found a telephone and called the Doric mansion where I had dined with Higgs's most impassioned white supporters. The wife answered.

"I cried when I heard," she said. "I wish it had never been. I wish it had never been."

We were too few and too low-spirited for the ballroom at the Rivermont. Television cables lay like trailing vines across yards and yards of empty floor. There were as many waitresses with drinks on trays as there were guests. The best we were able to do with the piles of food on long tables was make it look as if the mice had been at it, leaving small serrated toothmarks at its edges.

An interviewer with a microphone was posing Higgs with his wife and son and daughter, arranging a family portrait of a loser for the ten-o'clock news. Under the lights, Mrs. Higgs was putting on the bright determined smile of a woman about to tell the watching world about a new brand of laxative or breakfast cereal. The children blinked. A video camera trundled along the room toward them on its dolly. It subjected them to a blank, oxlike inspection and rolled back again.

When the cameras had finished with him, I went up to Higgs and touched his sleeve.

"I'm sorry, Otis. I badly wanted to see you win."

He put his arm around my shoulder and gripped me so hard that it hurt.

"Yes. I know that. Thank you." His face was stiff with the effort of choking back tears of disappointment.

There was one person at the party who didn't seem too depressed by the result of the election. I could hear her laugh across the tables, a rich coloratura laugh, full of runs and trills. The third time I heard it, I turned to see who it was who was having fun at the wake. She caught my glance, waved and beckoned me over.

"Hi! I know who *you* are—you're Jonathan. I'm Deedie. You want to insult me, call me Dolores."

"I'll stick with Deedie."

"I've been keeping my eye on you. It seems like I can't go into a church nowadays without seeing your face there. I'm telling you, it's unhealthy."

"What, going to church?"

"No! The way *you* go to church. You ain't getting religion; you're getting politics, politics and more politics. That's not right. You want to see some real religion, not all this preaching mixed up with politics. You want to feel the spirit. You come with me to my church on Sunday, you'll see religion the way it ought to be—"

"I'd appreciate that."

"You ain't getting out of this, now; you just fixed yourself a date."

Deedie's church was out in Whitehaven, to the south of the city. I had thought of the black suburbs of Memphis as precarious slums. Whitehaven, with its smart two-story houses, its lawns and trees, its new campers in driveways, was such a world away from the stained concrete, tar paper, rotting wood and corrugated iron of Chelsea and Hollywood that I feared I'd got my directions muddled and come to the wrong place. In Memphis my own eyes had grown instinctively racist: Whitehaven didn't look comfortable, or green, or well tended, or decently spaced out; it just looked white. If one's eyes could learn to see like that in ten days, what kind of crippling myopia would a lifetime's experience give them? *The idea of virginity, chastity, monogamy, why, it simply doesn't exist for them. What do they do for it? Smoke, sass and drink Coke all day. Integration is as new for us as it is for the South Africans.*

Deedie met me at the church door.

"You mustn't be embarrassed, now, if the spirit takes me and I get to do some shouting. . . ."

"Okay."

"Maybe you'll shout too."

"Haven't you heard about the Englishman's stiff upper lip?"

"When I come to my church, I want to be *free*."

The Middle Baptist Church had two great organs, mounted on either side of a raised dais where the elders sat in swiveling captain's chairs. The organs kept up a continuous conversation with each other, whispering gently through the prayers, then calling at the tops of their voices for the gospel songs, saving their most intricate dialogue for the preaching, when they debated like a pair of orators over the words of the minister. The choir, in blue-and-cream robes, made a wide semi-circle behind the organs and the club of elders; beyond the choir, a pair of heavy theatrical curtains were parted on an illuminated stage with a painting of Christ as its backcloth.

"I want to see Jesus!" we sang. "I want to see Jesus!"

The choir swayed and clapped. The elders, in enviably sharp suits, lounged in their chairs, legs crossed, letting just one foot keep time with the music. Everyone had a silk handkerchief blooming from his top pocket.

"I want to see Jesus!"

"Sure 'nough!"

"Yes, I do!"

"I want to see Jesus!"

There was a flurry of ecstatic shouts. The swoons and trances were getting under way. A woman went down in the choir, and was ritually fanned back to this world by her neighbors. I looked across at Deedie. She was clapping and stamping her feet. I had my order paper ready, but was hoping against hope that I wouldn't have to use it. Little boys of six and seven, dressed in exact miniature replica of the resplendent elders on the platform, were running between the pews. Deedie quieted them with an automatic, absentminded authority, and I remembered that she was a social worker in the city housing department.

It was the preacher's turn. Passionately, expertly, he nursed us through to a climax. He made a vivid drama of his own beginning, standing limply, microphone in hand, waiting for the spirit to seize him.

"Oh . . . yeah . . . wait a little time. Wait a little. Yeah. Oh, yeah. Wait a little time . . . the Lord will pay . . ."

"Sure he will!"

"Amen!"

Then, in a voice that seemed to come out fogged and bewildered from deep in his solar plexus, he murmured: "I'm going to tell about Jesus. Going to . . . tell about Jesus! I may not be able to preach like Paul. I'm a weak man. I don't have the power. . . . I . . . Oh—Jesus!" And he was away. God's word was a two-handed sword cutting right and left, and he was its embodiment. Bald, brown, with sideburns and mustache, he bulged and shook with the force of his message. His face ran with sweat. He cried out, he fell to his knees. He was revived by the fanning surge of the organs. The congregation chanted, wept, screamed, swept from holy orgasm to holy orgasm.

For the first few minutes, I had been part of it; then something in me recoiled and I went suddenly frigid. I had no place here at all. I was white, I was an agnostic, I was a foreigner. I studied the order of worship and surreptitiously turned my wrist over so that I could see the dial of my watch. I seemed to be looking at the contortions of the preacher through the wrong end of a telescope. His body was thrashing like an amoeba in a droplet of water on a slide.

He came back to human size again right at the end of his address. The knot of his tie was halfway down his chest. He was mopping his face with a handkerchief which had fallen on the floor; and he was staring, smiling, at me.

"Brothers and sisters—I heard yesterday that we got a visitor in church this morning. When I woke up, I got to thinking . . . he's from England . . . he's white. And I hear a voice saying in my ear, 'Brother—today when you preach you got to be so so-phis-ticated. You got to be so cool. You got to be so rea-son-able. Ha, ha, ha!' " He was impersonating a Devil's chuckle. "And now look! I done preach just like I am!"

"Yes, sir!"

"That's right!"

"So he did!"

"Because I can't be nobody but who I am!"

"Hallelujah!"

No, no, preacher. *I* couldn't echo that hallelujah. You offered me the microphone so that I could say a word to the congregation. I shook my head. Here, though, is what I think I should have said:

My whiteness doesn't mean logic, sophistication, self-control. And your blackness surely shouldn't just mean spontaneity, warmth, the "feeling within." Racism is another two-handed sword which cuts right and left, and you really swung it hard at the end of your sermon. You turned me into a half person, and you turned yourself into one too. You were condemning both of us to the dirty old charade of white versus black, head versus heart, male versus female. You said at one point that the election was a defeat which we all had to climb out from under. Yet when you talked of whiteness as meaning reason and sophistication, weren't you becoming one of the architects of that defeat? Otis Higgs told Memphis to *wake up*. I reckon you were still fast asleep when you were talking about me. You were in the grip of the same superstitious mythology that feeds white and black racism alike. You *are* in the grip of it. I know I'm a visitor. I have no right to talk to you like this, but please wake up!

But that, though, belongs to the vainglory of the *esprit d'escalier*—the bold second thoughts on the front steps after the event is over. What actually happened was that I thanked the preacher for letting me visit his church. I said the singing was wonderful, the address moving, and I'd like to come again. Warmly holding each other's hands, grinning like maniacs, we were both talking in our sleep.

10

Beyond Thanksgiving

*T**he river and* the city had merged into a blur in the slanting drizzle. Waterways Marine, a floating plaza of stores and offices, was moored off the slippery stones of the wharf. My boat had been winched up onto the deck of one of its supply vessels, and I was waiting to be taken on board the *Frank Stegbauer,* a southbound tow on which I was going to ride to Vicksburg. All the tows were late this morning. The radio operator kept on coming out of his office and changing their estimated times of arrival on a blackboard which mapped the movements of fleets out of Pittsburgh, Minneapolis, St. Louis, Baton Rouge, Greenville, New Orleans. The *Frank Stegbauer* had been expected at eight. Yesterday afternoon, I had heard that it was off New Madrid. It had been laying up in fog for much of the night, and now wasn't due in Memphis before lunchtime. In the coffee lounge, relief bargemen and deckhands sprawled with their kitbags, watching the *Today* show and reading comics. It was clear that they didn't share my own feeling of eager anticipation at getting onto a tow. They growled, cussed, and shifted irritably from ham to ham. For most of these men it would be fifty days before they would be home again: fifty days without a drink, with the shore severely out of bounds. Some had apparently done their fifty days' worth of drinking last night. Small noises made them shudder. The whites of their eyes were stippled with blood.

I tiptoed out to look at Waterways Marine. A whole collection of industries had been assembled on the string of barge hulls that composed it. It was an employment exchange, supplying crews to the tow fleets; it was an immense gas station, pumping hundreds of thousands of gallons of diesel fuel every day into the tanks of the towboats. It was a wholesale grocery store and supermarket.

"Millions of dollars come into this city off the river," said Mr. Tate, the manager; "and the city just don't seem to notice."

It was almost exactly the same line as I'd heard from the cotton factor and from the attorney in Cape Girardeau. The commercial life of the river was a well-kept secret. Its tonnage and money were huge; but where a single steamboat would have made its presence felt in town a hundred years ago, nowadays the tows passed through the city like undercover agents. A few bankers were in a position to measure the financial wake they left behind, but most of Memphis had simply forgotten that it was still a river town. The river gave it no particular cause to remember, and the city had withdrawn itself from the Mississippi because nearly all the memories it did have of the river were bad ones, of flood, fire, cholera and "Haul that barge, boy! Tote that bale!"

"I'm not complaining," Mr. Tate said. "If too many folks got to know about the scale of our business down here, they might start trying to get their fingers in our pie."

The *Frank Stegbauer* called in. It was off Loosahatchie Bar, and I went aboard the supply boat to meet it in midstream. A mile above the highway bridge, the tow swung around on the current and locked still, its engine thrashing the river behind it. Inching as cautiously as a pair of cat burglars on a pediment, the decks of the two vessels touched and held. My boat was swung onto the deck of the tow along with the frozen meat and vegetables, the mail, razor blades, newspapers and crates of Coke. Hoses were clamped to nipples on the towboat, and it fed for twenty minutes, suckled by the supply vessel on fuel and fresh water.

Up in the pilothouse I was introduced to Al the mate and Captain Mac and Chigger the deckhand. My attention, though, was distracted by the river itself. From this superior height of four balustraded decks, in the glassed-in warmth with its racks of electronic instruments, the Mississippi looked tame and shrunken. Shoaling waves that could have swamped my boat were innocent ripples. The wind and the rain simply added to the snuggery of the pilothouse and its family smell of coffee, waffles and polish. For a day at least, I was going to be able to look at boils, eddies and treacherously fast currents with genial condescension. From here I could put the river in perspective.

The *Frank Stegbauer* was pushing a small fleet for this part of the Mississippi; just nine barges, loaded with twelve million dollars' worth of ammonia. As tows went, it was a tight little rig, as maneuverable as a taxicab. It also had the navigational advantage of being a pariah. When other pilots saw chemical barges heading toward them downriver, they cleared the channel for them; no one wanted to risk collision with several thousand tons of poison gas.

In the afternoon it was Al the mate's watch, and he steered the tow through weather that was thin, brown and greasy like cheap meat broth. Everything was a variant shade of tan: the low sky, the smudges of forested shoreline, the ruckled water. In the rain, other traffic on the river showed only as shadowy streaks in this wash of dirty sepia. A low sandbar changed into a tow, a tow into a line of ragged willows. Al combed his beard with a broken toothbrush and kept his eyes on the radar screen, where the river was as neatly mapped as on a chart. The dikes on our starboard side were laid out on the screen like the prongs of a fork, almost touching the faint glow in the center which was us.

"I suppose it must get a good deal easier after Vicksburg," I said. "The dikes stop then, don't they?"

"Below Vicksburg? Well . . . That's, oh, Mile 437. Now, then. Mile 431, you got the Racetrack Dikes; Togo Island, 417; Yucatan, 410; Coffee Point, 405; Bondurant, 395; Cottage Dikes at 389; Spithead at 386 . . . Waterproof, 380 . . . and that about brings you down to Natchez. You want me to go on?"

I decided to keep my river expertise to myself in the future. We rumbled slowly on downstream, poised so high over the top of the engines that they made only a light churning sound under our feet. A pair of giant windshield wipers scraped backward and forward across the glass. Al reached for a plastic Ziploc storage bag from a pile at his side, undid his fly and took a leak into the bag, which he sealed and put on a shelf. He caught me watching him.

"I'm having me a pregnancy test," he said. "I'm hoping for a girl."

The tow was steered by a pair of parallel steel bars like the handles of a lawnmower. When we ran over a boil the bars shuddered, and one could feel the whole fleet wriggling in the water for a moment or two.

"You run into trouble with eddies yet?"

"I've steered clear of them so far."

"That's how you want to keep it. I've run tows bigger than this into eddies the wrong way, and been turned right around by them. I won't fool with an eddy even in a towboat. Boils ain't no problem, but eddies you got to watch."

He pointed to a substantial stretch of forest on the Arkansas shore.

"See that willow plantation over there? In the springtime, when the river's high, we'll ride right over the top of those trees. Around April, that turns into a good piece of slack water. On an upstream run in high water, you won't hardly use the channel at all. You're hunting all the time for slack water on the sides. If you know where to find it, you can knock days off a trip. Saves fuel, too."

Al came from Caruthersville. He had worked as a carpenter before he started as a deckhand on the tows. As a riverman he could earn at least twice as much as he could on shore. Even Chigger, the youngest deckhand on the *Frank Stegbauer,* was making forty-eight dollars a day. Al was taking home the salary of a corporation executive—although "taking home" was not quite the right expression, since no one on a towboat saw much of home at all. The idea was that you worked thirty days on and fifteen off; in fact the working stretches were usually a lot longer. This was the fifty-second day of Al's current trip. The only times he had left the boat had been to call his family from a pay phone on the levee. The crew was forbidden to go ashore in port. Ashore meant bars, and one drink could lose you your job.

"You must have worked out some system of brown-bagging."

"If they hear there's drink on a boat, the pilot loses his license. When he's got that hanging over his head, he ain't going to allow some dumb-head bargeman to snafu the whole rest of his life for a can of Bud."

So the crew of the tow was as isolated as a capsule of astronauts. The rest of the world lay just half a mile to left or right. You could see it going by through the portholes almost within reach of your hand. Yet even the cities where the tows docked and refueled were unknown for-eign places. Supply vessels came out from them; all the crew ever saw of them was their wharfsides, levees and floodwalls. The tow's only means of contact with the outside were the marine radio and the black-and-white TV set in the pantry.

It was a life more cut off than that of almost any oceangoing seaman. It was far more taxing in other ways, too. Once out of port, a ship at sea can be left to steer itself for days on end. The officers on the bridge keep a casual watch on the autopilot, the radar and the digital readout on the Decca navigation system. The *Frank Stegbauer* had to be coaxed and steered down every inch of river. The stack of Ziploc bags was a measure of the constant nursing which the towboat needed. If you took your eye away from the river for a minute, the tow would happily plunge off and wreck itself on a sandbar or deep in a forest.

"I stopped at Caruthersville," I said, remembering it as a muddy un-place. "I didn't see much of the town."

"Me neither," Al said. He pulled out his wallet from the back pocket of his jeans and thumbed through it for a photograph. His wife and two smiling daughters stood in front of a newly painted frame house. "That's my family. We don't have nothing to do with Caruthersville society. If they don't bother me, I won't bother them none. That's my motto."

His self-containment was almost absolute. He had one family on the tow and another on the beach. Between them, they kept Al supplied with as much of the world as he cared to deal with.

The murky brown went steadily darker into night. Al switched on the carbide searchlights and raked the river with them. Rain caught in their beams showed as a stream of bright Patna rice. The curving line of green glints to our starboard was a string of buoys. We seemed to be hardly moving. Our swiveling lights worked like the antennae of a cautious insect. We felt our way along on them, letting them gently brush the trees, the buoys and the smoky twists of fog that were beginning to riddle the water. Another tow was coming upstream around the bend. Its lights blundered, then tangled with ours, as if we were exploring the idea of mating.

I went down to supper in the galley, where Bill the engineer showed me another photograph. In the dislocated world of the towboat, photographs were precious things. Like Al's, Bill's picture was cracked and fading. I wondered how many times a day he got it out of his wallet and put it back again.

"That's my reason for being here," he said.

There were no people. The Polaroid snap showed a ranch house in a forest clearing.

"I just finished building that. It's up out in the Ozarks. I got forty acres with the house."

"It looks marvelous." It did.

"I'm paying off a ten-year mortgage at four hundred bucks a month. If I was on the beach there's no way I could afford that kind of money. When I got that paid off, I'm going to get off the river, farm that land, buy me some more acres . . ."

Chigger had a photograph too. His was of a young woman.

"You think she's pretty?"

"Very. She's beautiful."

"She's real bright, too. She's at junior college."

Chigger himself looked like an E. W. Kemble illustration for *Tom Sawyer*. He wore a felt hat, bright green suspenders and jeans rolled up to his calves. With his pale fluff of beard he looked too young for the smart young woman in the picture with her serious eyes.

"She's talking about getting married." His voice hiccuped from a squeaky treble to an uncertain baritone. "I ain't so sure. I tell myself:

You've only seen Tennessee, Arkansas and Mississippi, and you're nineteen years old. . . ."

All of Chigger's ambition was focused on the river. On the beach, he had worked in a paper mill for a year and dreamed of becoming a Mississippi pilot. Whenever he was allowed to, he steered the tow. On his off-watches, he studied the charts, learning the river. There was no formal apprenticeship for pilots. Deckhands turned into pilots by a process of slow osmosis. In two years, Chigger would be old enough to apply for a license.

"You know? I could be the youngest pilot on the river. Hell, when I'm, like twenty-five, something like that, I could be a *captain*. Like Mac."

In the pilothouse, Mac had taken over the night watch. He was the grandfather of the boat. His mottled face, dentures and glasses made him look as if he might be more in place sitting by a fire in his slippers instead of pushing nine thousand tons of ammonia through a filthy night on the river.

There were flashes of sheet lightning ahead. The searchlights rested on fog banks as thick and hard-edged as clouds seen from above on a high-altitude flight.

"Shoot," said Mac; then "shit"; then "shoot" again.

The river now was legible only in the bright copper-colored picture on the radar screen. The lights picked out little cattle ponds of water in the gaps between the fog. The hostile weather had made the strangely tender quality of the talk over the radio even tenderer.

"Now you come in here real close with me, Cap."

"I'm tight with you now. Okay?"

"That's fine and dandy."

The captains inquired after each other's wives and children. Everyone was just called "Cap" over the radio. People had made close friends with familiar voices without ever knowing the names of their owners. "Cap" was enough. If your name was "Cap" you were a buddy.

We might have been far out at sea, with nothing but pillars of ocherous fog and narrow, winding tracks of water. Then, suddenly, just a few yards ahead of the leading barges, there would be trees, a caving cliff of riverbank, a rock revetment. Once, the black wedge of a barge came nuzzling out of the fog a hundred feet or so to port.

"Hey, Cap!" called Mac over the radio. "You're running so goddamn close, you want me to spit in your engine room?"

"Sorry, Cap. I got you now. Hey, what you got in them fancy barges, for god sakes?"

"P'ison," Mac said with an air of grand smugness. "Mone-yer."

"Shit, Cap—I coulda cut you half in two."

"That's just what I was thinking. Have a good trip, now."

"You too, Cap. And don't go letting that 'monia out all over the river. This goddamn fog's bad enough for my sonofabitch lungs."

The farther south we went, the more the fog thickened. Our lights made a low tunnel into which Mac fed the tow fleet inch by inch.

"I done enjoying just about as much of this as I can stand," he said. "Times like this, I think if I was at home they'd never get me out again. Shoot." The tow was going on a sidewise slide. "Rat's-ass eddy." We straightened up again. "I wouldn't want to wish this on my worst enemy, not on a night like this."

All down the river, the tow fleets were laying up inshore. Eventually, Mac too gave in. He sent the four bargemen and deckhands forward, where they disappeared into the fog and turned into more voices on the radio. I watched the radar screen. The river made a slow turn around 180 degrees, and the leading barges touched the bank with a grind and a bump. As Mac eased the towboat in on the current, the searchlight beam traveled along the levee and lit up a herd of grazing deer. They looked like silver-paper cutouts. For a moment they were quite still, mesmerized by the light; then they scattered into the forest.

With the engines off, I could listen to the river. As it scoured the hulls of the barges and sluiced past our stern, it sounded as if it were breathing heavily in its sleep, making a continuous line of z's. Mac was brewing coffee in the percolator.

"Well, now you've seen what a bad night on the river's like. They don't come much worse than this."

He had been working on the Mississippi since 1937, when he had started running tugs around Memphis harbor. There were still steamboats then, and Mac could remember them lining the wharf, packed solid with bales of cotton.

"They say now they was the good old days. Seems to me that taken all around, they was bad days, mostly. I never saw too much ro-mance in 'em."

I slept for a few hours in a cabin that had most motel rooms beaten hollow for comfort. When I woke I could hear the stir of the engines in the dark. Al was in the pilothouse.

"We gone by Greenville now," he said. "Ain't nothing to see of Greenville at five in the morning, or I'd have called you."

"Happy Thanksgiving Day," I said.

"I don't reckon we got a lot to celebrate about, this Thanksgiving."

The Iranian students had let thirteen of the embassy hostages go—they were all either female or black—but had announced that they intended to put the remaining Americans on trial as spies. At ten thirty each night, ABC Television was putting out a program titled *America Held Hostage.* The significant thing about this daily reminder of the Iranian crisis was the absence of the *n* and the *s*. The whole affair was seen less as the infliction of an outrage on the people in the embassy than as the ritual, public humiliation of the whole country. The United States itself was being bound, gagged, blindfolded and displayed by its captors to the world. Like millions of others, Al took this slight as an offense to his personal pride. It had soured Thanksgiving for him.

At least, the fog had gone. As dawn came up, the river went to a dim, gauzy gray. We were leaving a trail of ragged creases in the water behind us. Both shores were unbroken cypress swamps. We passed between sandbars as cold and bare as bits of Mongolian desert. I was very glad that I wasn't going alone through this landscape. One's inner resources would have to be in extraordinarily good shape: otherwise the place could only seem like a gigantic reflection of just about everything one had known of emptiness and loss.

"Where is this?"

"Mile 515. Worthington Cut-Off. Island 88."

I stored the names; they sounded like useful symbols of something lowering and bleak. In mid-channel, we plowed slowly down the state line: out of Mississippi, out of Arkansas, in the empty crack between the states. We reached a wide-open tract of water. No other tows were in sight.

"You want to try steering her? See how you get along?"

"Sure."

The nearest I had come before to driving a tow was managing narrowboats on British canals. The experiences are not comparable. This was more like trying to steer six or seven blocks of Madison Avenue down a twisty country lane. If one gave a four-degree shift of the driving bar, the movement of the rudder slowly communicated itself along the length of the fleet, and an hour or so later the leading barges would begin to swing off course against the line of trees on the far bank. I tried to keep my adjustments tiny; a degree here, a degree there, learning to wait for the tardy response of the barges at the front. I reminded myself that this was a small tow; a big one would have been half as wide again and more than twice as long.

"You seen that skiff over there?" Al pointed to a fishing boat a mile ahead of us. It was a flyspeck on the glass. "That's *you.*"

"I'd sooner not think about that."

"If he was in our way now, we couldn't stop for him. You'd go into reverse right now, you'd still run him down. Now, *watch* him. Make sure he don't decide to do some blame-fool thing like come across the channel."

"Do you want to take over?"

"No, you're doing fine. I tell you, I never seen a deckhand steer as good as you, not first time out."

Immodestly basking in this compliment, I let the tow wander, then overcorrected it. Al laughed. "You *was* doing fine. Now I'd say you was about average."

We shook on a boil. Through the bars I could feel the gouts of water trying to wrest the rudder out of kilter. Seeing an eddy ahead, I took the tow wide of it along the same curving course that I would have steered in my own boat.

"Yeah," said Al. "You got a real feel for the river. I guess you must have picked up something, coming down in that crazy little boat you got. I reckon, seeing you now, you could make a pilot."

"That's the best thing anybody's said to me on this trip so far."

"Okay, I'll take her now. There's a chute just on a ways; we got to go down flanking."

"Is flanking the same as backing up?"

"Yeah."

"So, when will you let me back up down a chute?"

"Well, if you're still with us next Thanksgiving . . . *maybe.*"

The weather was coming, uncharacteristically, from the east; an opaque gray wall of rain which sidled across the swampland on the Mississippi side, paused, stretched, included the river at a bound, and went on deep into Louisiana. My tenth and last state.

At noon we sat down to a Thanksgiving spread in the galley. No one said much. The turkey, sweet potatoes and cranberry sauce were too powerfully reminiscent of other, family Thanksgivings, and the men's thoughts were somewhere else, probably lost in the world of the photographs in their billfolds. I tried to remember my long-ago reading of William Bradford. It was Bradford who, in 1621, proclaimed the first Thanksgiving Day, after the sickly remnant of the Pilgrim Fathers had survived the terrible New England winter after landing at Cape Cod in the *Mayflower*.

> And for the season, it was winter, and those that know the winters of that country know them to be sharp and violent and subject to cruel and fierce storms, dangerous to travel to known places, much

> more to search an unknown coast. Besides what could they see but a hideous and desolate wilderness full of wild beasts and wild men? . . . What could now sustain them but the spirit of God and His grace?

Indians had taught the settlers how to grow corn and brought them four wild turkeys.

So, with the rain streaking the galley windows, we dug into our mounds of deep-frozen turkey, brought out to us by the supply boat from Waterways Marine. Away from home, afloat in a real wilderness, we were closer than most, I thought, to the spirit of that original Thanksgiving. I doubted if Bradford and Miles Standish and William Brewster had gone in for a great deal of polite conversation over their turkey either.

Two miles above Vicksburg the tow slowed in midstream and my boat was lowered over the side. It was much like going back to school after the holidays. I said my goodbyes and headed out across a rough patch of shoal water through the stinging rain. The Louisiana shore was a jungly swamp of willows, cypresses, cane and kudzu vines. The bluff of Vicksburg, on the far side of the river, was like a smeared thumbprint. I hung back on the current, waiting for the *Frank Stegbauer* to round Vicksburg bend, then crossed over to the mouth of the Yazoo River, skidded on the slick of an eddy, and reached Vicksburg Harbor feeling cold, sodden and very out of sorts. I had been under the innocent illusion that the sun shone all year on the Deep South. This was a wet English winter day. I tied up to a slippery jetty, my fingers too numbed to make proper knots. The city was as quiet and dripping as the swamp. It rose steeply behind its concrete floodwall in a greasy cliff of banked roofs and rivery streets. The blurred taillights of a car disappeared over the top of the hill. It looked as if it might well be the last car in town.

Even without people, though, Vicksburg spoke more loudly about itself than most places. I had to climb up steps past a Confederate cannon which was aimed at the river across Washington Mall. The first time I saw it, in the rain on Thanksgiving, I mistook it for an empty historical symbol, a curio set up to please the eye of the sentimental tourist. It was more complicated than that.

In 1863, General Grant's campaign came to a dead stop at Vicksburg. Its bluff was too high to storm. It was a natural castle, defending the whole of the lower Mississippi. From Vicksburg to New Orleans, the Confederacy was safe as long as its army held the town. On a night in

May, Union troopships ran south around Vicksburg bend and landed a few miles downstream, and Grant's army marched on Vicksburg from behind. With their ships on the river and their gun emplacements at the back of the bluff, they had the town surrounded. When the Confederates refused to surrender, Grant ordered his army to starve the town out. The siege lasted for forty-seven days. On the Fourth of July, Vicksburg gave in; and until the 1960s, there was no public holiday in Vicksburg on Independence Day. The memory of that Civil War siege was still vital to the character of the town in the late twentieth century. Natchez, the next bluff city down the river, had surrendered to Grant without a fight, and that wasn't forgotten either. In the 1970s, an effort had been made to patch up relations between the two towns by mounting a high school football game. It had ended with riot police, Mace and water cannon.

On the day after Thanksgiving, browsing in the library of the Corps of Engineers in Vicksburg, I found a memoir by a veteran of the siege which had been published by the Mississippi Historical Association in 1903. Colonel J. H. Jones had commanded a section of the 38th Mississippi Regiment. He quoted a song that his men used to sing to taunt the Union forces less than a hundred yards away across the trenches:

> Swear, boys, swear Vicksburg shall ne'er surrender,
> Swear, boys, swear that not one Vandal foe
> Shall e'er tread her soil while one arm can defend her,
> Unless her rations shall get demnition low . . .

He recorded the conversations that took place over the lines at night. Soldiers of the Army of the Confederacy set ingenious riddles for the Union men to solve. They shouted: "Why are greenbacks like the Jews?" According to Colonel Jones, "The Yankees 'gave up.' " The answer, yelled in enormous chorus, was "Because they have Abraham for their father and no redeemer." Jones was good at communicating the surreal personal relations between soldiers from the two armies in the War between the States:

> Our friends of the 17th Illinois fraternized with the 38th and aided us greatly by many acts of kindness. They would go out to their sutler's tent with the greenbacks we had borrowed from their dead comrades and purchase food for us, and doubtless many a starving "Reb" felt that his life was thus saved.

Friends? kindness? borrowed? dead? life?
Colonel Jones's regiment failed to kill sufficient men from the 17th

Illinois to collect enough greenbacks to keep themselves supplied with the Union forces' rations: on July 2 they had to dine off the quartermaster's mule.

Vicksburg did badly on national anniversaries. It surrendered on July 4. Thirteen years later, in the centennial year of 1876, the Mississippi made a cutoff and left it dry. Most towns, like Kaskaskia and Tiptonville, simply shrugged and shrank when the river left them behind. Vicksburg insisted on remaining a port. The Yazoo entered the Mississippi ten miles to the north of town. Vicksburg blocked it off and dug a long canal to divert the river around the Mississippi's old meander course so that steamboats could still use the harbor. It was a city that had made a habit of resisting the inevitable. The pug-nosed cannon on Washington was cast in Vicksburg's most characteristic expression, of scowling independence.

I was waiting for the sun. The river was dark with rain and ribbed with whitecaps. I had taken a room at the Downtowner Motor Lodge and was puzzled by something that happened in the lobby there at noon, when men in expensive suits disappeared into an elevator marked PRIVATE. I changed into my own suit, which had been expensive enough in its day but now gave me the air of an itinerant preacher who had fallen on hard times. I took the elevator. Behind a padded leather door on the top floor, I found the Rivertown Club.

The elevator ride took me into the heart of an abstraction I had heard of but never seen fleshed out: the New South. People had talked of it in Memphis, but they themselves had seemed hopelessly trapped by a very Old kind of South, and when I pressed them to say more about this idea they said, "You ought to go to Atlanta," which would have meant rerouting the course of the Mississippi by four hundred miles. In fact, the New South was in just the right place: high on top of an anonymous motel, right across the street from the lordly greystone hotel which had been out of business for a decade. The New South had the right view, too. It looked down over the slope of the nineteenth-century city to the river and the swamps; and in the middle of miles of boggy green there was the long raised strip, checkerboarded with pale cement and blackberry tarmac, of a new industrial park.

It was the voices of the New South that I noticed first. The men at the bar were making the sort of noises I had heard coming out of national conventions in St. Louis. Some did talk with the elastic, treacly vowels of Mississippi, as if the meandering style of the river had somehow worked its way inside their mouths; but I could hear Harvard Business School over in the corner, Brooklyn Irish on the sofa, the sand-

and-snap of the urban Midwest in the armchair just behind me. The woman who was tending bar was as unsurprised by my own accent as I was surprised by hers.

"You're not from Vicksburg," I said.

"Me? Hell, no, I'm from Manhattan. Lower West Side."

Her husband had taken a job in Vicksburg six months before. She still found it like living in a foreign country. She told me how her mother had flown out to visit her with two suitcases full of New York food.

"The things they *eat* here, I can't get used to it. Know what I miss most? Italian bread. What do you reckon a psychiatrist would say if you told him you had whole dreams about Italian bread?"

"I don't suppose there are very many shrinks in Vicksburg to tell it to."

"Right. You got it there."

The bartender was part of the New South. I had it all explained to me over lunch, with the voices coming from all states north and east of Mississippi.

"I closed down the store in Chicago ten years back. I should've come twenty years sooner."

"No one works anymore in the East. Move your pinky and you're into another goddamn labor dispute."

"Here they want to work. We pay good money. No one joins a union; they don't need to."

"This is mostly black labor, is it?" I asked.

"Sure. There's a pool of labor here that you couldn't find anyplace in the North. They're keen, some of them are skilled; they're real good workers."

"Look at it this way: in an energy crisis, which place is going to win —the place in the sun, or some icebox up in Massachusetts or Minnesota? There are guys here who can save a whole year's worth of Northern profit on their Southern fuel bills."

"But there's something special about Vicksburg. Look at Natchez. That place has just kinda *sunk*. What's Natchez, anyway—just a whole lot of itsy-bitsy old ladies with antebellum homes. Natchez gave up. Vicksburg went on trying."

"You know . . . ?" This was said in a Mississippi accent. "There's a line I keep on hearing from fellows who've come down from the North. They say, 'Look, I don't know whether you're thinking of seceding again, but hell, if you *are,* we're going to join you this time.' "

I looked down at the town from the window. It was a little hard to reconcile what I could see with my eyes with this tale of paradise on earth. The streets were too wide and too tall for the few people who were walking on them. Their grandiose mixture of shabby Greek and shabby Gothic gave the people the air of stretch-panted tourists wandering at a loss around the set of a high Victorian melodrama.

"If you'd seen Vicksburg fifteen years ago . . ." a real estate man said. "Then, *everybody* lived downtown. There was an antebellum mansion on one side of the street, and a black family lived in the house right behind it. Black and white, black and white, black and white. All the way down the street. We *had* integration. Now the whites have moved out. The antebellum mansions, they're museum pieces. Downtown's all black."

"Where did the whites go?"

"Out to the county."

The county. I knew what that meant. It was a code word for something that had much the same effect on the life of American cities as cyanide does on human beings.

"Why, though? In a place like St. Louis, people move to the county because there's a lot to run away from in the city. Surely there's nothing much to run away from in downtown Vicksburg?"

"I don't know. It got to be the fashion. People couldn't afford to run big houses any longer. . . . Now they're trying to get folks back. They're doing up the Vicksburg Hotel there, turning it into condominiums. It *could* work, but most people round here think it's just going to be all walkers and white sticks."

"It's certainly where I'd want to live if I lived in Vicksburg," I said.

"Do you have kids?"

"No."

"If you did, would you want to send them to a Negro school?"

"Hey, you know what they say about Vicksburg? The Syrians own it, the Catholics run it, and the Negroes enjoy it."

In the afternoon I ran my boat up the Yazoo River to the new port and the industrial park. The old harbor on Levee Street had been left to pleasure boats and the U.S. Coast Guard, but two miles up the Yazoo, around a bend in the canebrake, there was the twentieth-century equivalent to the crowded wharves of a Bingham painting. A big fleet of towboats, tugs, barges and small oceangoing ships was hidden deep in the swamp. There was the smell of sawn wood in the wind. Black longshoremen were swinging steel containers out over the river on cranes. A towboat in a hurry threw up a wake that nearly rolled me over, but I wasn't going to be stopped from putting my nose into this unexpected busyness.

For the Port of Vicksburg wasn't just a river town that was still in working order; it was a river *new* town, a river version of life out in the county. Somehow (and the cannon on Washington Mall seemed to suggest as good a reason as any to explain it) Vicksburg had managed not just to hold on to its connection with the Mississippi but to turn its river wharves into the focal point for all its industrial activity. It had set up its own customhouse so that containers could be shipped directly abroad without being unsealed by excise men in New Orleans. It had built factories on reclaimed swampland behind the wharves, and some of them were doing things that had died out fifty years ago in other river cities. *New* sawmills? I had thought that a contradiction in terms. But they were here, their lumberyards packed with oak, gum and hickory. Tows were leaving dock pushing huge cargoes of oil, steel and lime.

None of this looked in the least like *Jolly Flatboatmen in Port*. It wasn't easily fitted into my own picture of the river as a wide, working highway, lapping at the towns it touched and threading them together in an unwinding panorama; there was far too much steel netting, concrete and corrugated iron to make anything pretty of it. But it did work. I had watched town after town divorcing itself from the river, putting the Mississippi out of mind, fencing it off as a dangerous monster; at last I had come across a town that was having a second honeymoon with the beast. What the picture needed was a Muscatine sunset of gold and silhouettes. It was an unkind trick of the weather to have hoisted storm clouds and a light that looked used and grubby even before it touched the parking lots and the prefabricated, cost-efficient warehouses.

I turned my boat around. Sloping up the bluff was a green tongue of the Battlefield Memorial Park, dotted with obelisks, temples, arches and bad heroic statuary of ragged soldiers and generals in frock coats. Vicksburg had arranged itself with commendable legibility, putting the past of its siege behind it on the hill and placing the New South in front of it in the swamp. On the hill, the statues were, mercifully, in silhouette; the swamp stayed stubbornly in three dimensions.

"The Syrians own it . . ." That had puzzled me before I'd heard it. I had seen their names on stores: Monsour, Abraham, Jabour, Nasif, Nassour, Baladi. For me there was an odd personal coincidence in seeing these very un-Southern names here. Just a year before, suffering from a bout of cabin fever in England, I had run away to Aleppo for a month, looking for another foreign space. What on earth had brought these fellow travelers to roost in Vicksburg? I went to The Hub—a

clothing store—to buy a pair of gloves to keep the Mississippi cold out of my fingers and met the owner, Mr. Abraham. He told me that the Syrians—or, as they now preferred to call themselves, the Lebanese—had arrived in Vicksburg at the turn of the century. They had been car-petbaggers, peddling fancy goods from township to township through the Southern states. In Vicksburg they had found a city elastic enough to let them settle in. They had built an Eastern Orthodox Church. Their carpetbags had grown into little grocery stores, the grocery stores into big businesses. Why, said Mr. Abraham, Shouphie Habeeb is the president of the First Federal Savings & Loan Bank; and he only came over in the 1920s.

I went to visit Shouphie Habeeb in his office. The long arc of his career was mapped around the walls. It started with a photograph of a tiny grocery on Pearl Street and came to a peak with Old Glory mounted on a brass stand, inscribed to Mr. Habeeb and presented to him by the Daughters of the American Revolution.

His voice was pure Mississippi, his clothes Fifth Avenue; his round, sallow face and broody eyes were Arab. I remembered a goldsmith in the Aleppo souk whom I had visited every day for a week in a state of panic indecision about a bracelet. He had been gray, patient, gentle, and absolutely immovable on matters of money, which he regarded as squalid intrusions into a conversation that had run from Sufism to Plato to the teaching of St. Paul. Mr. Habeeb could easily have been this man's first cousin.

"I was wondering," I said, "whether I should say '*Ma'a salaama*' to you. Do you ever speak Arabic still?"

"Oh, one or two words. Words of endearment, sometimes, when I speak to my children when they're babies. . . ."

"There must be something in you which reminds you that you're Arab as well as American."

"Oh, yes. We're Byzantines—Phoenicians. That's what I am: a Phoe-nician merchant." He laughed a long, up-and-down-the-scale Missis-sippi laugh.

He told me how his father had opened the grocery on Pearl Street in 1920. It had started with a capital of a hundred and fifty dollars. "Fifty dollars from a Protestant, fifty dollars from a Catholic, fifty dollars from a Jew. They trusted my father. He was a clever man." He gestured at the granite of his multimillion-dollar bank. "You see? Here I am—still in the store."

He talked of his early days in Vicksburg, when the Lebanese were still thought of as carpetbaggers. The Habeeb family had had ambitions: the grocery was just their first foothold on the cliff of American society. Shouphie's brother had wanted to go to medical school.

"You could see he was chosen to be a healer. Look at my hands." He laid them palms downward on his desk. Their backs were dark with hair. "Now, you should see my brother's hands. Not a hair on them. Long fingers. Even when he was a little boy, he had healer's hands. He had to go to college. Every dollar we made, it was to send him to college. Imagine! A Lebanese, from Mississippi, going to college in 1931! It was unheard of. Now my brother is a famous doctor. He was a pioneer of anesthesia. I'm the one who stayed in the grocery." He passed the dusty little American flag on its stand to me. It had been given to him in 1958.

"Acceptance! From the Daughters of the American Revolution to a Lebanese carpetbagger! You see, I bought acceptance with service." He pointed to a row of awards and plaques on the wall. The Lions Club. The Rotary Club. Mr. Habeeb had been honored by almost every institution that I'd ever heard of in white Anglo-Saxon Protestant America.

"I was the first Lebanese they allowed to join the country club. That was really something. In 1961. It was an issue. It was like letting in a Negro. Five years later, they made me the president. There you are: acceptance with service again."

"Aren't you paying another price too? Like losing one identity in exchange for another? Every time you get a new scroll for your wall, aren't you becoming less of a Phoenician?"

"No. I don't feel that."

Yet the congregation at the Orthodox church was getting smaller. It had shrunk to about a hundred people. Twenty years ago, all services had been held in Arabic. Now Arabic was used only for processional chants at Christmas and Easter as a concession to "the old people." Shouphie Habeeb himself had a young wife who was a Presbyterian; his own children went to the Presbyterian church and not to the Eastern Orthodox.

"Surely your kids won't think of themselves as Lebanese?"

"I don't know. I hope they will. We Lebanese have very long memories. Something continues in the blood. Perhaps just a talent, a kind of intelligence. A national character isn't something you can destroy in a generation or two. It keeps on coming back."

He touched his flag again.

"You do know what the D.A.R. *is?*"

"Yes, I do."

Mr. Habeeb smiled. *"Acceptance."*

"The Negroes enjoy it. . . ." That seemed to be the real sting in the tail of the local proverb. I had passed their tumbledown green shacks by the river on Levee Street. I had played pool in the Monte Carlo Lounge, with its signs of the zodiac on the walls, its wrecked lavatory, its loud rock, its thumbtacked posters for local black leaders. The air had seemed heavy with despondent lassitude. The volume of the jukebox had been turned too high for anyone to talk. One drank one's beer slowly, straight from the can. One shot one's pool. One sat on a bench in the half-dark and stared the afternoon out. I made the mistake of mentioning my visits there in the Rivertown Club. *"That* place? What the hell d'you think you're trying to do? Get yourself killed?"

"I should think I'm as likely to get killed in the Rivertown Club."

"Hey—this guy's been going to the Monte Carlo Lounge!"

"He can't have much to live for."

That was nonsense. In the Monte Carlo I simply joined the grim democracy of people who had time to kill and little left over from their welfare checks to kill it with. The New South had passed them by. The first time I went, I was asked where I was from. When I said I came from Europe, it was enough. I wasn't anybody. I was the guy who lost at pool.

Downtown, there were hardly any black businesses. Apart from the Monte Carlo, there were a shop that sold wigs, a record store and a closet-sized men's boutique with a window full of shiny suits and sharp hats. I had to locate a funeral parlor to meet a man who had made real money in black Vicksburg.

Willy Jefferson was in his sixties. The Jefferson Funeral Home had been started by his uncle in 1894, and it was the kind of family empire that was an isolated fortress of black power and influence in a town ruled by whites.

"Blacks," Willy Jefferson said. "I just can't seem to get used to that word. I know I should, but to me we've always been Negroes. I don't feel I'm a 'black.' I'm a Negro." His voice was very low and hoarse.

I told him about how I had followed Otis Higgs to his defeat in Memphis and how deeply segregated I had found the city. Yet I had been told in Memphis that things were far worse in Mississippi.

"Maybe so. Maybe so. But not in Vicksburg. Vicksburg's always been a very open town. The river's kept it open. It's never been conservative like other places in this state. Vicksburg's had the whorehouses. It's had the bars. It's had the gambling joints. It's always been a kind of cosmopolitan sort of place, you know what I mean? There's a saying here: this ain't Vicksburg, Mississippi, this is Vicksburg, U.S.A.

"In Jackson, now, that's different. You'd go in a store in Jackson, they wouldn't let you try on a pair of shoes. You had to buy them first. You couldn't have a Negro putting his feet in a white man's shoes! Not in Jackson. But in Vicksburg, you'd go in a store, and it was always 'Why, hello, Willy! Come on in!' " He raised his gravelly whisper by an octave or two and produced an immaculate parody of a country-club accent. " 'You want shoes, Willy? Well, just try these for size!' "

"So that's why there are no black shoe stores in Vicksburg?"

Jefferson laughed. "I guess . . . *if* you was to look at it that way around. . . ."

His own version of Vicksburg was nostalgically rooted in the past, before the great shift to "the county." When he talked about the town, it was a place where whites and blacks were next-door neighbors, even if the whites did live in mansions and the blacks in clapboard shacks. In 1965 his son had died; and it had been his white neighbor who had been the first to visit Jefferson's house. He was a friend of the president of the First National Bank. He lunched regularly with white businessmen. He had never envied blacks in the North.

"Up in the North, it's hidden. Here it's all on the surface. You know what you're dealing with. And the white people here, they look for you. Of course, you got to show respect. In Vicksburg, we been respectful. All we want is fair play."

I was out of my depth. I wasn't equipped to play this masked, courtly Southern game of black-folks-and-white-folks. Trying to find securer ground, I asked Jefferson about the funeral business.

"We keep bodies longer," he said. "You know, when a white person goes, you read in the paper, *Miss Simms, died yesterday a.m., funeral this afternoon.* It ain't like that with us. There's more mourning to be done. Then there's always some nephew out in California, trying to borrow carfare . . . Oh, it'll be five days or a week before the funeral. And then that's something else too."

"How long can you keep a body?"

"I don't know. My old daddy . . . he kept one for six months. On ice." It was the corpse of a man who had been shot by a white, and the defense lawyer had artfully delayed the trial until he was sure that the D.A. would not be able to produce the vital evidence.

"There was the defense attorney—he was laughing his head off. 'Where's the body?' he was saying. 'How can you have a murder trial without a body?' Then my old daddy comes on. 'That's okay. We got the body.'" Willy Jefferson was croaking with laughter. He remembered he was in his funeral home and put on his undertaker's voice again. "Defense attorney, he goes kinda pale. 'You got the body? *Where?*' 'Right here,' says my daddy. 'Outside the courthouse. In the hearse.' You should've seen them. There was *outrage*. Dragging a six-month-old body through the streets of Vicksburg in a hearse!"

"But the man was convicted."

"Oh, yeah, he was convicted, all right. They didn't have no choice. Then there was an old lady I buried, oh, just three weeks ago, now. Back in '75, her uncle died. I said to her, When do you want the funeral, Miss Ellen? 'Sunday week,' she says. 'Sunday *week?*' This was a Monday or a Tuesday. 'Yes,' says Miss Ellen. 'He's my last uncle on this earth, and I want to keep him around for as long as I can.'"

On Sunday morning I went to the First Baptist Church on Cherry Street, a great pseudo-classical temple in cream and duck-egg blue. I was a minute or two late, and the all-white congregation of nearly five hundred people was riding the crest of a hymn that was making strident demands on God's time and favor. I had listened to it as I ran up the street in the rain; a clamor of wants and needs under the very cursory guise of praise.

Sitting in a pew with my hand over my eyes, I made my own list of wants. I wanted a long letter from home. I wanted calm weather. I wanted something else which I couldn't identify exactly. It was an ending. Not a destination; not the Canal Street wharf in New Orleans. I wanted an ending which was emptier and more open than that. It wouldn't be river and it wouldn't be ocean. It would have no particular color. It would be somewhere from which there would be only one place to go, and that would be home.

The preacher had a squashed face, a hectoring manner and a school globe. I was sitting too far back to spot the loop of the Gulf of Mexico on it. "What in the world shall we do?" asked the preacher. "What in the world shall we do?"

He made his globe spin. The colors of the countries swirled, and England was lost in China or Japan. The preacher was talking about Russian Communism. Then he spoke of the American hostages in Iran, of fanatic Muslims crazed with power, of the infidel Khomeini. He jabbed at the globe with his finger. He was finding heathens and atheists on every continent. *Here* and *here* and *here* went his finger, turning the world to a revolving ball of ungodliness.

Finally he edged the globe around so that we could see the Americas. His finger tapped the metal. He was home to Cherry Street, Vicksburg. His voice suddenly softened. Only he was not speaking of Vicksburg, he was speaking of Antioch.

"And the disciples were called Christians first in Antioch . . ."

He told us about how Barnabas and Saul and the rest of the disciples had set up their church in the small town from which Christianity was to radiate out across the world. We in this building were like the first Christians. Vicksburg *was* Antioch.

"What can we do? I'll tell you what we can do in this troubled world! Share our testimony! Share our people!"

We were going to change the face of the globe. There'd be no threat of nuclear war with the Russians, no hostages in Iran, if only we could send out enough missionaries to convert the infidels to Southern Baptism. I felt profoundly unenthusiastic about this solution. Just the day before, the Ayatollah Khomeini had been speaking of America as "the Great Satan." Now Vicksburg was responding by vilifying the Ayatollah not as an irrational despot but as the Prince of Darkness himself. I feared that the preacher was trying to prepare us for a new age of holy wars, with the God of Cherry Street ranged against the forces of Marx and Allah.

The collection plate was going around. It had been a rousing sermon, and the envelopes and cash were coming out in wads. Rejecting a dime as being too conspicuous an announcement of how I felt, I put a quarter on the edge of the plate. I reckoned that on a quarter even the most cheeseparing Southern Baptist missionary would find it hard to travel any farther east than Battlefield Mall.

"Thank the Lord," whispered Miss Lily. "Thank the Lord."

She was very old. Each day at lunchtime she came down to the motel dining room, limping badly on two sticks, and the black waitresses brought her dishes of mushy baby food which she poked at suspiciously and usually left uneaten. On Sunday, I waited for her to come down and joined her at her table by the wall.

"I can't see too good, now. I can't hear too good. I get things mixed in my mind. But I thank the Lord."

She had scabs on her eyelids, and the skin of her face was like the bark of a dead sycamore. Her immense age was set off by the plastic whiteness of her new teeth: they looked horribly immortal.

"They told me you was from the Old Country."

"England."

"Ah. England. Me, I was from Germany."

She had come to America in 1890. She was ten. There had been a ship, a big ship . . . but she couldn't remember more.

"We had cousins. Not here. Up at Milliken's Bend. That was where we went to live. Milliken's Bend, Louisiana. Ain't nothing left of it now. The river took it away."

To me it was a name on a chart. Twenty miles upstream, the river had moved west, leaving its meander-courses as canebrake and swamp. It had swallowed the town of Milliken's Bend. I had sailed over the top of Miss Lily's family house when I was on the *Frank Stegbauer*.

"It weren't a big place. Not like Vicksburg. It was all swept away in a flood. All of my family was saved, though. Thank the Lord."

She had left Milliken's Bend to go to Vicksburg, where she took a job as a stenographer at the Illinois Railroad station.

"I worked forty-three years there. I had a room in a rooming house right here. That's why they let me stay when they put up the hotel. They give me a real good room here. With a TV. Only I can't see the colors now."

"What programs do you like to watch?"

Miss Lily stirred the slop on her plate with the point of a knife.

"Oh . . . Lawrence Welk. I like Lawrence Welk."

"Can you remember how the town was when you were a girl? How Levee Street and China Street used to look?"

"I never did see much of Levee Street. I wasn't one for going out nights. I worked in the depot all day; then I come home to the rooming house. People then . . . they looked down their noses at a working girl; and I kept myself to myself. Hey, do you have a wife back home where you come from?"

"No, I don't."

"Oh, I do wish you did." Her face was filled with her own long and lonely spinsterhood. "I never married. There was two people in my life . . . we was real close friends. But I didn't love neither of them. Sometimes, I wished I had of done. Too late for that now, though . . . thank the Lord! I shall be one hundred in two months . . . if the Lord spares me. That's *old*, ain't it?"

"It is. Very. Do you think you're lucky to have lived so long?"

"I don't know. I done nothing to deserve it. It must be the Lord's will. You know . . ." She put her hand on my sleeve. ". . . you ought to get yourself a wife, for company—she'd be a lucky girl!"

"I'm afraid I doubt that, but it's sweet of you to say it."

"Oh, yes, she would."

She drifted away from me. I could see her own lost chances multiplying in her eyes. Then she told me again how Milliken's Bend had been swept away by the river.

"You should eat, Miss Lily. I'm taking up your time."

"No. You stay with me. Please. I'd be beholden. I got plenty of time. All I got now is time."

I was looking for a magus. Someone must understand the Mississippi. After riding it for fourteen hundred miles I certainly didn't. Captain Mac could still be deceived by it after forty years of piloting. There were people in the woods south of Vicksburg who were supposed to read the river's character and tell its fortune: the Corps of Engineers had its Waterways Experiment Station there. I went out to meet the Director of Boils, Eddies, Cut-Offs and Fast Currents.

The place was like a University of the River. I was driven through the trees from hangar to hangar, where the Engineers had reconstructed little bits of the Mississippi in concrete, coal and crimped wire. Every time they planned to deepen a channel or build new dikes, revetments, dams or levees, they made a scale model of the reach, fed water through it for weeks at a time, and measured all its changes of height and speed with instruments in the little aluminum drums that dotted each model.

"This," said my guide, "is St. Louis."

The river was a yard across, and I could comfortably straddle the Poplar Street Bridge. Fifteen yards away up the hangar, the entry of the Missouri River was obscured by an electric buggy with a load of wire mesh. The water was six inches deep and ran over a shiny coal bottom. I lay on my face and squinted up it, looking for the scrolls and humps, the scruffy edge of a shoal, the interlocking patches of glaze and mat.

"You haven't got a magnifying glass, have you?"

I couldn't see any difference between the water under my nose and the water in the bath at the Downtowner. It didn't look at all like the Mississippi to me. It might have passed as a convincing model of the upper Thames; the model makers seemed to have built everything into it except its essential personality.

"You want to see another?"

Outside, we stood on a State Penal Farm as big as a fireside rug and looked at where the Red River joined the Mississippi. Here, at least, the wind was combing the water into tiny wavelets.

"Have you ever been on the real river?"

"No," she said, "that's something I never have done. I'd like to, though."

"You'll find it . . . different."

"I guess so."

The Director of Boils and Eddies was in his office. With his broken nose and bristled skull, he might have been a retired heavyweight boxer. He was enormous. He looked powerful enough to deal on equal terms with the real thing.

"When you try something out on a model, how often do your results surprise you?"

"Every time. I've never seen a model yet that didn't show up something real strange."

I said that I had been living too close to the river. Things like eddies simply baffled and frightened me. I wanted him to tell me, in his own professional language, how Mississippi water worked. If, for instance, he was talking to another engineer, how would he describe an eddy?

"Well . . . on the Mississippi . . . you got two kinds of eddies. . . ."

We were really getting somewhere now.

"There's the clockwise eddy. Then there's the counterclockwise eddy."

"Clockwise and counterclockwise? Is that all? Can't you sort of define, like, the structure of an eddy . . . exactly *how* the water swirls in it?"

He crossed and uncrossed his huge hands.

"Well . . . you know, hydrography's still a very young science."

"Yes." I was deeply disappointed. "What about boils, then?"

"Ah, them mushroom-tops. Yeah. I reckon . . . it's those very deep, high-speed currents, and they're racing along the bottom there, and then, *wallop!* they hit some kind of a rock or something; hell, they have to have somewhere to go, so they come b'ilin' and b'ilin' up to the top!" His hands had exploded from his knees and were boiling and boiling above his head. The Director himself had turned into a pluming swell of river water. It was an immensely vivid demonstration, making up in energy what it lacked in science.

"Hey, you know," he said, "I got a small boat on the river myself. You hit the edge of a mushroom-top, it's like driving a car fast right into an ice patch; you don't know which way you're at, do you?"

"Yes, that's exactly how it feels. I've done it tons of times."

"When you come off the river at the end of a day, do you ever feel kind of shaky?"

"Every time. I feel all my nerve ends are showing; I can't keep my hands steady."

"Me neither," the Director said. I was delighted. He had looked as constitutionally unshakable as the pillar of rock at Grand Tower. "I come off my boat, and it's like I'm running a fever. You don't notice it when you're on the river, but as soon as you step on shore the strain hits you. . . ."

"That's just how I've been, almost every day for the last three months."

"The river can really shake a man up. You take the disrespectingest man . . . a man who's never had respect for *anything* all his life. Put him on the river. Just for one day. It'd change him. He'd have to show respect for that."

So I was in the best company. The magi found the Mississippi as alien and mysterious as I did myself. Even their models astonished them; the river itself could reduce them to humble wonder. I felt that they had granted me an official license for my fright.

I edged out of the Yazoo into the mainstream, where the glistering water was tooled with arabesques like an inlay of polished silver on oak. In the channel the bow of the boat kept making sudden twists off course. I was having to fight for the steering with a rival, and the simmering current, rolling over and over on itself, had its own ideas about which directions I should take. I watched the paths down which it was leading other bits of driftwood. The river had been rising steadily for days; it was alive with whole trees torn from islands and plantations upstream. A cypress was making a crabwise crossing ahead of me: it jerked, zigzagged, went smoothly down for fifty yards, spun around, headed for the shore, then slid into the channel again, as if a bored child were playing with it by radio control.

A line of indented woody bluffs ran due south on the Mississippi side of the river, which scoured their overhanging rock, swept sharply west away from them until their green turned to a distant purple, and came back. Louisiana was an enormous level marsh, overgrown with trees, cane and vines. The river had never been happy to run along the same course for more than a few decades at a time: it had tried out miles and miles of Louisiana, leaving half the state behind as a jungly bottom of lakes, sludge and sand. There were black caves running through the tangled green on the shore—curving bayous which were the last remains of experimental meanders the Mississippi had abandoned.

At noon I pulled in at a sandbar on the Louisiana side. The water was running in a fast chute around its western edge. Yesterday, probably, it had been connected with the land. It was an island now. It had a thin fringe of cane and cypress on its spine.

With a bottle of wine and P. T. Ferry's bag of pecans, I could get myself into shape again for the run to Natchez. I set out my picnic and sprawled on one elbow in the sand. Beside my foot was the track of an animal, as firm as if it had been set in plaster of Paris. It was a shade smaller than my hand, with a round heel pad, a knuckled wedge of toes and five claw marks, as fine as carpet tacks. There were more—they went down to the water and returned to the bushes in a diagonal to my left.

I snapped the shell of a nut between my thumb and forefinger. The odd thing was that the wind was scuffing the sand, yet the tracks were dead sharp. They must have been made only minutes, or moments, before.

Black bear.

I half-pushed, half-threw myself over the gunwale of the boat. I banged my shin. The hull ground on sand. I dug into the bottom with an oar, leaned on it, and felt the boat slide clear.

Black bear. Where I came from, bears were whimsical creatures whose sole habitat was the colored drawings in children's books. Bears wore rubber boots and scarves and lived off pots of honey. I found it hard to come around to the idea of real bears skulking in the brush. I didn't know if bears could swim; the one on the island was likely to be half-starved if it had been cut off from land for long.

Mr. Ferry's nuts were spilling from their bag on the shore, thirty yards away now. My unopened wine bottle was lying on its side. I peered into the canebrake. There was a darkness there: log? bear? I couldn't see for sure. It was enough, anyway, to justify my telling people later that it was undoubtedly the bear. In the story, it came waddling slowly from the canebrake and stared after me, looking sad to see me go, not because it needed lunch but because it had run miserably short of company. That wasn't strictly true. The tracks were true; so was the smudge in the cane. Admittedly, the smudge did stay very still, but it had a sort of lonely, watchful, bearish stillness.

The water darkened, and the warmth went suddenly out of the day. A steepening bluff bent forward to meet the river, and as the current drove south into the hill there was Natchez, pitched high in woods of magnolia and pine, its electric lights already stronger than the sun. I sneaked around the back of the big eddy where the Mississippi made a sudden westward swerve and landed on the concrete ramp at the foot of the cliff.

I was eighty years or so too late. The ramp, and a brick house spattered with green historical markers, were all that was left of Natchez-under-the-hill. This cold little step of a beach had once earned itself a marvelous notoriety. In 1814, Zadok Cramer was warning his readers to avoid the liquor houses here. In 1826 Timothy Flint called it:

> a repulsive place, the centre of all that is vile, from the upper and lower country. At the proper season a thousand boats are lying here at the landing, and the town is full of boatmen, mulattoes, houses of ill-fame, and their wretched tenants, in short, the refuse of the world. The fiddle screaks jargon from these *faucibus orci*. You see the unhappy beings dancing; and here they have what are called 'rows', which often end in murder.

Disappointingly, I had it all to myself: no other boats, no boatmen, no music, no dancing, no liquor shops, no houses of ill-fame. The town-beneath-the-town had gone. It had been built on crumbly sand, and the Mississippi had washed it away just as it had taken Milliken's Bend. I made the long solitary climb up Silver Street to Natchez-proper.

The Ancient Greek railroad depot had been converted into a restaurant-and-bar. When I ordered a drink, it was paid for by the plump young man who sat on the next stool. He explained that he wasn't on speaking terms with his girlfriend tonight; he had some serious drinking to do, and the odd whiskey for a stranger wouldn't affect his budget for the evening.

When he told me that he ran a nursing home for old people, I said that I had a mild professional interest in old people myself.

"Yeah, they're a gold mine."

It was just what I'd been thinking. If he could find me a nonagenarian with a long memory from Natchez-under-the-hill . . .

"There's a lot of bucks to be made out of old folks. They *pay*. Seven seventy a month a head, federal money . . . Work it out for yourself."

I did later. If you want an annual turnover of a million dollars, you will need a hundred and eight point two old people. Suppose a modest profit margin of, say, eighteen percent . . . You could run a ranch house, a new Cadillac and holidays in Bermuda on old folks.

"Yes—I suppose you can stack them up like battery hens. They don't eat much, either, do they?"

"No, it's not like that. . . ." He laughed. "But you get racketeers in old folks just like in any other business. Wherever there's a federal dollar, there's a shyster chasing after it somewhere."

I bought him a return drink and told him what I was doing.

"Come out and see us tomorrow. You ought to talk with Miss Mary. She's real sharp. She went to college and all. I remembered when I was a kid she used to live in a house all on her own. She let the weeds and trees grow right over the windows. We all thought she was a witch."

The old people's home was a low, verandaed house standing in its own small forest. Men in pajamas with racy sideburns sat out on the porch in rockers. Inside, colored plastic letters had been arranged on a blackboard to form a shaky announcement:

TO^{D}aY i$_s$ WE^d$_{Nes}$dA^y DE$_c$ 5 19$_7$9
THE Se$_a$SoN IS wI$_n$T^{E}R
THE WEAthER s$_u$NN^Y $^\&$ C^{OL}d
THE NEXT hOLI$_D$aY I$_s$ CH^{ri}$_s$$_t$MAS
THE SEasON ^{T}O B$_E$ JOLLY FA L^A $_{L_A La}$

The inmates, black and white together, were distributed around the lobby, on sofas, in wheelchairs, leaning on sticks. Some were asleep. Others were giving lectures to themselves in loud voices. Miss Mary was called from her room. She came out, painfully trundling herself along on an aluminum walker. Her hair was cut in a jagged fringe across the top of her skull. She looked like Bertolt Brecht.

"So, you've come to see me in my *in*-carcer-*a*-tion?"

"I'm sorry. Is it really like that?"

She sniffed, and winced with hurt as she lowered herself onto a chair.

"What? Sleeping four to a room? Listening to *these* people? You can't keep nothing of your own. It goes. I don't know what you'd call it, but I'd call it incarceration."

She felt around in the pocket of her grubby housecoat and found a cigarette there.

"I wonder if I can get away with this one. . . . They don't allow me to smoke, even. One every two hours. That's my *allowance*. They've taken them out of the machines, now; too 'dangerous.' And I've been smoking Lucky Strikes since 1919. *Tskch!*"

The old people's home had been a terrible new world for Miss Mary.

"See?" she whispered, pointing behind her. *"Integration!"*

On the day she had been brought in, she had been helped up the veranda. The first person she saw was the man who had been her cousin's chauffeur.

"He was sitting right there. With a big smile. In a rocker. 'Why, hello, Miss Mary!' You know what? As soon as I was in here I had to set and learn to call Negroes 'Mr.' and 'Mrs.'? I wasn't raised to *that*. I know what's behind this integration—Yankee greenbacks and a gang of crook lawyers up in the state capitol. That's what's done it. And we ain't only got Negroes in here, neither. There's Catholics, Methodists and a lot of . . ." Her voice dropped again to an angry whisper. ". . . *Baptists!*"

"What are you?"

She looked at me as if I were mad to ask such a question.

"I'm a Presbyterian." She was palming her lighted cigarette, shooting sidewise glances in search of nurses on patrol. "And Baptists and Presbyterians don't *mix*."

All the Southern distinctions of rank and station had been dissolved in the home. Half of Miss Mary's high school class had found themselves in a forced reunion here. They shared rooms and tables with the people who had once been their house servants. They had revived all their classroom enmities and friendships.

"Oh, but I wanted a *weapon* today," Miss Mary said. "You read in the papers about how they've been doing these *terrible* things . . . you know, stabbing of someone twelve times . . . another stabbing, seventeen wounds . . . shot in the face five times with a gun . . . *I know how they feel!*"

An old man in a Hawaiian shirt went tapping past on his stick. He nodded to us.

"Morning, Miss Mary."

Miss Mary didn't reply. She waited until he had gone by, then tapped her skull. "The brain's a funny thing—*when it goes.*"

I had been warned not to excite her. I thought that perhaps the past might be more restful territory. She told me how her father had run coal barges down the Ohio and Mississippi from Pittsburgh to New Orleans. She had been a clever child. She had left high school to go to the University of Wisconsin, where she took a liberal-arts degree. When she came back to Natchez, she refused to go out to work.

"I had me a *royal* time."

"What did you do?"

"Oh, every week they had balls in the mansions. . . ." Her crabapple hand pushed irritably at her walker. "I did so love to dance."

New Orleans had been "Mecca." She had sailed down on the *Tennessee Belle.*

"Yes—I've seen a photograph of her." The steamboat had been owned by the New Orleans–Vicksburg Packet Company: one of the biggest cotton-running ships on the river.

In Natchez there had been the Baker Grand Opera House. She had gone there to see Ben Greet playing Shakespeare, Bud Scott's New Orleans Dance Band, the Algy Fields Minstrels.

"Oh, it was *royal*." Ash from her Lucky Strike spattered the roses on her housecoat. "Then there was the movies . . . They had player pianos with them then. Oh, yes. There was one I saw every day for a whole week. What was it called . . . ? *Nigger Heaven*. That was it."

She snorted with bitter amusement. The title had brought her back to the lobby of the home, its orange sunlit leatherette, its nursery smell of urine, milk and Lysol.

"When they put me in here, I'd never looked at TV. I had to learn all the personalities. You couldn't join in the conversation without you knew the names of all the people on TV. That's all they talk about. Johnny *Carson*. They were all new to me. I'd kept up with college football, but the shows . . . they were all new. I couldn't make head nor tail of them. To me they was just plain dumb. These people, though, they love them. They turn the noise of it up so loud you can't read, you can't think. Huh." She tilted her head back and rolled her eyes so that her pupils almost disappeared into her skull. *"Nigger Heaven."* The father of the man behind her could, I supposed, easily have been a slave.

Natchez was littered with the mansions where Miss Mary had danced in her royal days. Deep in elms and live oaks, they looked out across wide parterres of close-shaven lawn. One kept on seeing bits of them between the leaves: a dome, a colonnade of white pillars, a balustraded gallery, strips of wrought-iron tracery, shuttered windows. Up in Illinois and Iowa, I had been delighted by the late Victorian imitations of these Southern planters' houses. They were pieces of good-humored dandyism, and it looked as if the men who had put them up had had fun in their building.

I found it much harder to like the real thing. This was seigneurial fat-cat architecture, and whatever pretty twiddles and curlicues were incorporated into the fringes of the design, it was brutally straightforward about its main intention, which was to boast and belittle. The Natchez mansion presented a standard face to the world with its triumphal portico. Four vast white columns held up a peaked tent of stucco over a spreading fan of stone steps. To cross the threshold, one had first to be ritually humbled. Just as European cathedrals bully the visitor into bowing his head and drooping his shoulders because their scale is so much grander than his own, so the entry to these mansions was constructed to make one feel shy, impoverished and small. I was happier about the idea of shrinking before the glory of God than I was about abasing myself in front of the amazing amounts of money that cotton farmers had put by. The planters of Natchez had behaved more like Pharaohs than Medicis. Their palaces weren't furnished with masterpieces commissioned from individual artists; they were straightforward monuments to the power of the great fortune when it went hand in hand with a more or less unlimited supply of cheap labor. Even their most intricate work—the wrought iron, the carved wooden trellis—was done to a fixed pattern. Once I had got used to the sight of these places, all I could see was their splendid bulk; and that left me cold.

Since reaching the South I had spent time wriggling, as politely as I could, from invitations to tour the local antebellum homes. When I did succumb, I was made to stand, slack with boredom, in front of collections of objects for which I couldn't raise a glimmer of interest. There were bits and pieces of ordinary Victorian furniture. There were mild novelties, like oval spiral staircases. I was told that a photograph of some Confederate officers, taken in 1863, was one of the "oldest" photographs ever made. There were things to see and hear in the deadest bar in town that made it an infinitely livelier place than the biggest and most authentically restored planter's mansion.

When I stood on the steps of Melrose in Natchez, dwarfed by the usual arrangement of Greek columns, I expected nothing more than an hour of deep tedium. The door was opened by a black butler. His presence, at least, gave the occasion a twist of consoling irony. He led me into the dining room and demonstrated how the punkah over the table had been worked. Ropes went through pulleys across the ceiling, down a wall and out to where a "house nigger" had kept the fan turning over his masters' heads at dinner.

"Kind of neat, huh?" said the butler.

We went on to the next room. I made routine admiring noises about the painted floorcloths. I was shown an antique writing desk which I did like, since it was almost exactly the same, if not quite as old, as the one on which I usually worked at home. Then I looked out the window. The grounds at the rear of the house were full of blacks working on some sort of construction project.

"What's going on out there?"

"Oh, they're just putting up the slave quarters. Now, here, we have a chest made in Philadelphia . . ."

"*Slave* quarters?"

"Oh, yeah; didn't you hear? We got the movie people coming in at Christmas. They're doing *Beulah Land* for the TV."

I skipped the imitation Louis Quinze and the chest from Philadelphia and made for the gardens. The slave quarters were coming along fine. Men were sawing logs, toting wood and swinging roof beams through the trees. A line of long log cabins was half finished already; in a week, Melrose would be genuinely restored.

The making of *Beulah Land* had temporarily solved the problem of black unemployment in Natchez. A casting director from Los Angeles was signing up extras for the film. Some people, with previous experience of playing slaves, would get talking parts and stacks of Hollywood money.

"It's something about the faces around here. The thing about these guys is they really look the part. You bring in black actors from the West Coast, it always looks wrong, somehow."

It was a regular Natchez industry. Whenever anyone was making a picture set in the Old South, the production crews came to Natchez. Many of the blacks had enough experience of screen slavery to qualify for membership in the film actors' union. Being make-believe field niggers and house niggers had become their major occupation.

"They've run into trouble with the N.A.A.C.P. When there's no movie work going, they sit in the ditches playing banjos and singing old darky songs for the tourists. Then the N.A.A.C.P. comes in and tells them they're degrading themselves. So they wait till the N.A.A.C.P. guys get out of town, then they're in the ditches with their banjos again. You know—'Camptown Races,' 'Old Man River,' stuff like that."

Fifty-foot logs were going at speed past my left ear, shouldered by blacks who were stripped to the waist in the December cool.

"George! Hey, where's George?" This was a white supervisor with a clipboard.

"*Yassuh?*"

In his *Republic*, Plato abolished the profession of actor, on the grounds that imitation of life turned dangerously easily into the fabric of life itself. Looking at Melrose's new slave quarters, smelling their fresh pine, I thought that Plato himself could hardly have imagined a more telling illustration for his argument.

I had slept badly in Natchez. In the small hours, catching the glint of the mirror on the wardrobe, I had mistaken it for the river, and I thought that the river was trying to kill me in earnest now. Every day it was getting faster and rougher; I saw my boat sliding out of control into the black eye of an eddy, swamped in shoal water, capsized by a wake. There were no convenient towns along the shore between here and Baton Rouge; and after Baton Rouge the Mississippi turned into an international waterway, full of big ships. If only I could get a ride on a tow to New Orleans . . . then I could take my boat west into the bayous of the Delta and look for an ending there.

I telephoned Vicksburg, where a helpful man named Gene Neill said that he'd try to arrange something for me. He called back. Yes, there was a tow, the *Jimmie L.*; it would be passing Natchez sometime tonight, and I should raise its captain on my radio. "Ask for Boom-Boom Kelley. You'll like Boom-Boom. He's a real character."

Killing time, I walked along Canal and Broadway on the edge of the bluff, feeling saved from the river two hundred feet below. The water was pitted with whirlpools and boils. My own boat, a tiny splash of yellow at the landing, was the only small craft in sight. I passed a row of two-room shacks on stilts, their scraps of garden rowdy with chickens. I played pool in a tumbledown wooden grocery-and-bar. My partner was disconsolate. There was nothing for him in the great work going on up at Melrose; presumably he didn't look like a convincing slave. We spoke at long intervals over the steady *chock-chock-chock* of colliding balls.

"You come all the way down the river?"

"Yes. Pretty much all the way."

"Shit."

He potted the eight ball and reached for the wooden triangle to set up another game.

"Me . . . I hate the river. I done ride on it once. Shit, was I scared!"

"It's scared the shit out of me too, sometimes. I'm frightened of it; but I don't hate it."

"You lucky you ain't drownded."

"Ah, maybe you're playing pool with a dead man's ghost."

"Don't *talk* that way, man; I'm *telling* you . . ."

"Well, one thing the river does, it certainly ages you. I feel about ten years older than when I started out on Labor Day."

"Shit, I done stay in Natchez, and *I* feels ten years older than what I done on Labor Day."

The long carbide beam of the *Jimmie L.* lit a channel for me across the water below the highway bridge. The surface of the river, coiled and thick, was like hot tar. There was just enough of a moon for me to see the low angular plateau of the barge fleet; then, behind it, the stepped pyramid of the towboat. The crew guided me alongside with flashlights. I climbed onto the deck, and my boat was scooped out of the Mississippi on a winch.

Up in the pilothouse, the dim moonlight and the amber glow of the instruments had turned Mr. Kelley to a bearded silhouette at the steering bars. Even in the dark, though, I could see his character written into the furnishing of the pilothouse. He had done his best to turn it into a comfortable men's club, with pine-paneled walls, a black leather chesterfield, brass spittoons filled with gray cat litter for ashtrays.

"It wasn't like this on the last tow I was on," I said.

"No, well, when they built this, they asked me what I wanted. They gave me about half of what I asked for. I kind of like my creature comforts."

He reached into a refrigerator for a pack of cigarettes. I moved his twelve-string guitar along the sofa and sat down. I could see him more clearly now. He had a moody Italian face, with tired eyes deeply recessed in his head. He was staring into the radar screen at his side, his mouth moving silently inside its framing circle of black beard.

I said, "I would have taken you for an Italian, except that Kelley's about the least Italian name I've ever heard."

"Uh-uh. Now, my grandmother, she was a pure Choctaw. My grandfather was Irish. He was a horse trader. My other grandmother, she was Scotch . . . I guess there's a bit of everything in me. Bit of Irish . . . bit of Scotch . . . bit of Indian . . . bit of Mexican . . ." He ran his hand through his spiky bush of black hair. "Must be a bit of nigger in there, too, I reckon. But I ain't never heard of any Italian."

He had always worked on water; first as a seaman in the Merchant Marine, then in the U.S. Coast Guard.

"Could you go back to the sea?"

"No, I never could. Once this river gets a hold on you, you don't leave it."

He nudged the fleet through the tight chute above St. Catherine's Bend, reading the river yard by yard with his swiveling searchlight. I told him about my own trip.

"You notice something different about the people on the river than the people on the beach?"

"Yes, all the time."

"I feel the difference. It's a whole way of thinking . . . something kind of philosophical."

We wound slowly through the swampland in the dark. The edge of the water showed as a line of tarnished silver against the black fuzz of cypress and cane. Bob Kelley led a complicated social life over the marine radio. With every tow we passed he used the microphone half as a confessional, half as a running talk show. He was one of the very few pilots on the river who were not known just as "Cap." His voice was instantly recognized. He was a Mississippi celebrity.

"Shit, that's Boom-Boom, ain't it? Hi, Boom-Boom—where y'at?"

One passing pilot announced that he had left his wife the week before.

"Been catting around?" asked Kelley.

"No, she weren't catting around. She was just going all around the town spending my money."

"That's the name of the game, I always heard. You earn it, then they go around spending it. You're supposed to count yourself lucky for having all that warm pussy waiting for you."

"Ain't the way I look at it. I want some of what you'd call a balance in the bank, for emergencies."

"So you're out hunting again, I guess."

"Reckon so—" said the voice.

"You want a kind of middle-aged one, now? Sort of sixteen . . . seventeen?"

"Yeah. Middle-aged. Or a year or two younger."

"Well . . . Look forward to seeing you with your new one, then."

"Yeah. Reckon she'll be kind of dark-skinned."

"Going after poontang, huh?"

"You know what they say . . . a nigger woman . . . she'll stick right by you."

"You still preaching?"

"Off and on. Occasional."

"Why don't you get one of them Pentecostals?"

"They got hair all over their legs."

There was a pause and lot of crackle on the set.

"I didn't get that," Kelley said.

"I said—I ain't above buying me a razor!"

Just beneath the surface of the talk there was an undercurrent of yearning and loneliness. It had the isolation of life on the river in it, of men on their own cut off from the land that was so tantalizingly close by. It caught their homesickness, their nagging jealousy and the brittle masks of humorous indifference they hid behind.

"Poor bastard," said Kelley. "That guy, he's had shit up to his eyes."

"Is he really a preacher?"

"Sure. He's a born-again."

"He didn't sound much like a preacher to me."

"You should hear him when he's in church. He speaks in tongues."

Like me, Bob Kelley traveled with a library. In his off-watches he slept little and read a great deal. We swapped book titles and put together an anthology of our favorites. " 'This is the forest primeval . . .' " Kelley suddenly said, and recited a five-minute chunk of Longfellow's *Evangeline* at the black water ahead. "You know, when you think about the Cajuns, that *Evangeline* just about says it all."

He liked history: Jean Lafitte and the battle of New Orleans; Huey Long on the stump around Louisiana. In his cabin he kept copies of Steinbeck's *The Grapes of Wrath*, Farrell's *Studs Lonigan*, Caldwell's *Tobacco Road*. They were all books that held some kind of mirror up to Bob Kelley's own life; stories of solitude, long journeys, hard times. His closest kinfolks were these famous loners of history and fiction, and he talked about them as if they were brothers and cousins. He had tried once to settle down "on the beach"; it had been a disaster. He couldn't fit into the regular niceties of the small town. Now, in literature, he had found characters who could cast his own brooding restlessness in a heroic light. Up in the pilothouse in the small hours, Bob Kelley and I seemed very alike.

"You've read *Huckleberry Finn* . . ." I said.

"Only when I was a kid at school."

"Read it again. It fits everything we've been saying."

Our conversation drifted from books to the river, to marriage and on to the inevitable, compulsory topic of *Eye-ran*.

"You know, I reckon we been too good. Whenever anyone's been in trouble in the world, we've gone in there to help them. Hell, we helped *you* out when you was in trouble in World War Two. Now America's in trouble, and everyone's looking the other way. No one wants to help *us*. Even your country, you ain't going to come in with us and lend a hand. Even you."

His jowl was set in a melancholy line of deep personal grievance.

"I reckon in America now, we ain't got but one friend left in the world. Know who that is?"

"I'm sorry it's not England."

"South Korea." He gave an irritable snort of laughter. "Fuckin' South Korea!"

It was impossible to tell where America's friendless solitude left off and Bob Kelley's began.

John the mate came up onto the deck to relieve Bob from his watch. Bob picked up his guitar and sat beside me on the chesterfield. He picked out a couple of tentative chords, tightened a string, and sang 'On Blueberry Hill' very quietly. It was a performance just for himself.

There were scattered anvils of fog standing on the river. In the searchlight beam, the shore looked like a harvested cottonfield. Bob started on another song, whispering the words and dragging out the time between the lines.

Love me tender, love me true . . .

The engines underneath us were making a distant, throbbing bass accompaniment to the tune.

All my dreams fulfill . . .

John, at the steering bars, joined the song with his scratchy tenor.

For you know that I love you . . .

The three of us were singing now; all men, all a shade out of key, all to ourselves.

And I alwayuyus wayull.

By sunrise, the fog had thickened and covered the river with a queer kind of architecture. There were tall arches, long galleries and recessed niches in it. The sun, breaking through, gave it the look of freshly whitewashed catacombs. We wormed our way down a corridor of open water, with the fog forming a high vault overhead. I went out on deck. Overnight we had crossed the line into subtropical America, and even in the early morning the air had a damp, bathroom warmth. Old Glory was flying on a pole behind the twin exhaust stacks. It had been eaten away and blackened by the fumes, reduced to a charred rag. Half the stripes were gone to tatters, and the decay was just beginning to reach the stars. I went back to the pilothouse for my camera and was taking photographs of it from all angles when Bob came out.

"Oh, shit! You ain't taking pictures of my flag! Hey, I got another —let me change it. It's a disgrace!"

"It isn't. It's perfect."

Bob stared up at the ragged stump which was all that was left of his flag.

"Oh, yeah, I got you now. It's supposed to *symbolize* something, huh? What I don't see is why it has to be *my* flag. Hey, be kind to me. Find some other guy's, will you?"

The fog lifted on a herd of cows nibbling at the turf on the levee. The grass was so improbably green that it looked poisonous. The cows stamped and stared as we slid by, alarmed by our acres of rumbling steel and the high slap of our wake as it hit the narrow bank on which they grazed. I had thought we were far out in a wilderness, when we actually were trespassing on someone's farm. Beyond the levee, a chocolate flatland of rice fields went west as far as one could see; a line of telegraph poles; a gas station on an invisible highway; and then the fine seam where the soil was joined to the sky.

We rode in a tight loop around Devil's Swamp and headed for the labyrinthine tangle of pipes and cylinders that was the face of Baton Rouge. Bob pointed to the bridge where the city started.

"Huey done that. If that ain't the cunningest thing . . . See how low it is? There's just sixty-five feet clearance under that bridge. Huey had it all figured out. He was going to keep all the big ships down in Louisiana, see? He was out to stop the gravy going up to Mississippi and Tennessee. So Huey builds himself a real mean little bridge. You try running a big ship under there, she'd cut herself half in two. Up in Vicksburg, they was shouting their heads off when they heard about Huey's bridge, and Huey, he was laughing fit to bust. It was like he'd built a solid wall right across the river. Hell, they don't make 'em like the Kingfish no more. He was the sharpest, double-crossingest sonofabitch on God's earth."

We scraped under Governor Long's ingenious shipping trap, and suddenly the river was jammed with great freighters and tankers. It was no place for a sixteen-foot boat. The rusty slab sides of the ships, rising as high as hotels, made even the tow feel squat and vulnerable. We threaded through pools of shadow cast by vessels out of Yokohama, Piraeus, Marseilles, London and Hong Kong. A pale young sailor at an open porthole was putting his underwear out to dry; he was getting a queer and dismal view of America—a toy Gothic castle, the old state capitol, marooned in what seemed to be a gigantic oil refinery. Baton Rouge offered very little in the way of temptation to jump ship. Nor did it seem to have any ending. It had leaked, in a diluted form, down miles and miles of river, spreading its oil and chemical plants along the levees, turning the landscape into an unlovable abstraction of wire, steel, aluminum and tarmac.

I went below. The internal life of the towboat was far more absorbing than the overintricate gray outlines of industrial Louisiana. I sat in the mess room, listening to the gossip.

"Shit, but ain't she been married to that guy once already?"

"You know he owes the I.R.S. two million fuckin' bucks?"

"Shee-it."

"She's having another baby. In March. They got two kids—two boys."

"He's on vacation, in Brazil or someplace."

"She died. Leukemia. And she was only thirty-one."

"He's an asshole."

"I kind of like the guy."

"I tell you, I couldn't give a rat's ass for him."

"He's okay—"

None of them had ever met these people whose lives provided them with continuous material for talk. They knew each other too well; their own personal affairs had been exhausted as conversational topics. Their isolated existence on the tow didn't bring them into contact with anyone else. So, like the residents of Miss Mary's old people's home, they pretended that they lived in the small town of Hollywood. The mess-room library consisted of stacks of old copies of the *National Enquirer,* and the magazine supplied the crew with enough nail parings from the lives of film and television stars for them to know Barbra Streisand and Roman Polanski and Howard Cosell a great deal more intimately than they knew their neighbors.

Watching TV wasn't a passive activity, it was a participatory sport. A children's quiz program came up. *Jokers Wild.*

"Hey, this kid here, he's a genius kid, this one."

"I was reading in the paper about a genius kid. You know, he could play the piano like Beethoven . . . stuff like that. Lives up in Nebraska. Six years old. Shit. They have genius kids like that in England, Jonathan? Have you ever met a kid like that?"

"Hey—*listen.* This I want to hear."

"Watch him. He's real smart."

The host of the show was saying: "Now, what part of a tree both holds it in the earth and supplies it with most of the water that it needs?"

The camera zoomed in on the child's face. He was squinching up his eyes as he tried to think.

John the mate said "The roots . . . ?" and gave a nervous cough.

Time was up for the genius child. "The . . . leaves?"

"Come again, Gary, I didn't hear you that time—"

"*Leaves.*"

"I'm sorry, Gary, I can't give you that. The correct answer was the *roots.*"

"Hey!" John shouted, "you hear that? I got it! It was the roots!"

By the time we were off New Orleans it was dark, and my boat was ready to go over the side again. Bob had torn a sheet from the exercise book of lined yellow paper in which he kept his navigation notes and was making a careful job of writing some kind of inscription on it. He folded the paper into a small square and handed it to me.

"Don't read that now," he said.

I opened it ten minutes later and read it by the light of a city streetlamp, with the paper dimpling in the warm rain.

> I know very little
> of writers, but people
> I do no. You are a
> good man to ride
> the River with, Jonathan Ravan
>> Bob Kelley
>> Master M/v Jimmie L.
>> Dec. 7, 1979

It was the one certificate I had most wanted to earn. I tried to wave my thanks, but the tow was away across the Mississippi.

11

With the Armadillos

Zadok Cramer described the proper way of landing at New Orleans:

> The navigator having now arrived after an irksome passage at the grand mart of business, the Alexandria of America, he leaps upon shore with ecstasy, securing his boat with a careful tie, mounts the Levee, and with elated heart and joyful countenance, receives the warm and friendly hand of a fellow citizen, in whose integrity he confides . . .

My own arrival was shifty and unconfiding. I had sneaked into the city at night as if I were going to burgle it; by day, I kept it under surveillance and grew more and more suspicious of everything I saw.

I took a room in a tall and creaky house on Esplanade, at the far edge of the French Quarter. The house was full of shadows, beams and ponderous old furniture. Its balconied courtyard was a deep, steamy grotto of mimosa, vines and bougainvillea. I slept alone in a four-poster bed meant for honeymooning in, and woke feeling widowed. I watched the city through the bright slits of the shutters and was nagged by a sense of its wrongness—or was the wrongness just in me?

If only the bride had been there: one breast exposed by the wrinkled sheet, the sleepy tangle of her hair smudging her face . . . Then I would have opened the shutters and called, Look! Look out the window! Isn't it *pretty?* Brideless, though, I studied it coldly, searching for blackheads under the city's makeup.

For New Orleans did look lovely. But I thought I had seen its loveliness somewhere before, and I couldn't remember where. It was so veiled in the black lace of iron trellises, gates, balconies, and shutters that it was hard to see through to its skin; but there were strips and corners of candy pink and bright gamboge lit up by the balmy sunshine. Behind more walls, more ironwork, there were the green tops of secret gardens, with the leaves of palms and camellias signaling that when things happened here they happened in private. I felt I was being teased by the view through the shutters: it was equally full of come-hither looks and keep-out notices. It was also trying for its effects a shade too hard, as if it were using me as a mirror in which to inspect its own fresh paint and powder and ingenious twiddles of mascara. I was supposed to say, Yes, you do look beautiful; no, that's just exactly right. I wanted instead to say what truthful mirrors do: Watch it, or I'll crack, you vain old bitch.

For an hour, I went along with the city's overpracticed charm. There was more obvious promise in New Orleans than in any other town at which I'd stopped. It was impossible not to be won over for a little while by its gentle heat, its intricacy and fuss, its dappled colors. On Chartres Street there were secondhand-book stores. I hadn't seen such things since I'd left London. I found an old edition of *Orley Farm* by Trollope. I listened to the voices on the far side of the shelf.

"She borrowed this book of poems by Rupert Brooke . . . you know, from the library?"

"Right—"

"And they tried to get it back from her. No way. She'd *kissed* the picture away."

"Imagine what she'd've done if it had been, like, *Tru*man or Tennes*see* . . ."

"Right . . ."

It was New Orleans talking to itself in its peculiar bastard accent. It wasn't "Southern" at all. There was Irish in it, and the rolled French *r,* and gay-Esperanto; a soft and lazy blend of sounds, in which words were trailed like the swishing of long skirts across floors.

Still being complaisant with the city, I took *Orley Farm* to the Café Du Monde. I sat in the sun. I ate my three *beignets*. I drank my cup of chicory-flavored coffee. I remembered where I'd seen New Orleans' prettiness before.

Across from the café, on Jackson Square, horse-drawn buggies with fluttering canopies were picking up the tourists for sight-seeing rides around the Quarter. Their black drivers, elderly men who'd learned the role that brought them in the biggest tips, were going *Yassuh!* and

Sho nuff!; their white passengers had the benign glaze of people who meant to spend the day being innocently impressed by every single thing they saw. They were being carted about the streets like plastic dummies in their new vacation wear, their heads turning slowly from side to side. Everyone wore the same smile. The men looked oddly naked without their neckties. Bereft of occupation, they pointed cameras at bits of wrought-iron trellis. They photographed their drivers, then photographed other tourists in other buggies, their smiles as fixed and grave as those of early Christian martyrs.

The square was full of artists. PORTRAITS IN FULL COLOR $20. DOUBLE COLOR $25. A young woman sat with a clutch of shiny pamphlets and guidebooks in her lap. An artist was transforming her into a rigid pink oval with mad eyes and an open wound for a mouth. Over on the far corner of the square, an artist was playing a concertina; nearer by, an artist was scratching a guitar and singing "Old Man River." There were artists with out-of-tune trumpets; an artist with a pet monkey; a tap-dancing artist; a pavement artist doing something unrecognizable, and possibly obscene, to the sidewalk. All the tourists were encouraging all the artists in a mass demonstration of piety to the living culture of New Orleans. The continuous clopping of the horses' hooves was art too; more a sound effect than a sound, as if every artist who had failed to obtain a post on Jackson Square had been given a pair of coconut shells to knock together through the day.

New Orleans had had a long and tiresome history of being ceded, occupied and sold. Now it was selling itself. Or rather, it was selling off its own collection of tourist mementos from its holidays in foreign parts. The buggies and the street artists had been brought back from Florence; Jackson Square was a full-color, $20 portrait of the Piazza Della Signoria.

Up on Bourbon Street, the massage parlors and the blue-movie houses with private booths for masturbation went two by two with "Dixieland" jazz bars. The bands were mostly white, and they too were in the business of execrable imitation, casually fooling with the music of Negro funerals and carnivals. I stopped at one of the few bars with a black band. In an interval between the "Saints" and "South Rampart Street Parade" the drummer came over to order himself a beer. His accent sounded strange to me.

"Where are you from?" I asked.

"Chicago."

"And the rest of the band?"

"We're all out of Chicago."

Toward the end of the morning there was the sudden swell of movement in the streets. Something real was happening. From Bourbon and Royal, Decatur and Canal, a big crowd was homing in on Iberville. I couldn't see what was going on. In my wallet I had an out-of-date telex credit card. I waved it over my head and shouted, "Press." It worked. I pushed my way past a line of fire engines, penetrated a police cordon, and reached the patch of street where everyone had a microphone, a notebook or a film camera.

"Who are you with?"

"The *States-Item*."

"*Times-Picayune*."

"WGSO."

"WVUE . . ."

There was a fire in Harry's Pirates Den. Firemen were smashing windowpanes with long prongs. They climbed ladders, shoved hoses through windows, sprang out onto the balconies of neighboring buildings like characters in a French farce.

There was a good deal of dense, peat-colored smoke, but that, as far as I could see, was all. Next door to the pirates' den, across an empty lot, there was a massage parlor with pictures of gymnastic girls. THIS SHOW YOU MUST SEE! A man came out onto a second-floor balcony to watch the fire. He was wearing only his underpants and carried a can of Schlitz. I could see his graying chest hair and scrawny knees. Behind him, in deep shadow, a woman moved past in a bathrobe.

The crowd was getting restless. We knew what we had come for. We wanted collapsing walls, dramatic rescues, a holocaust with flames disappearing into the sky. We got what we deserved, what New Orleans seemed all about that morning: a lot of smoke without fire. We melted disappointedly away. As I left, a radio reporter was interviewing a fire chief.

"And nobody was *injured?*"

"There wasn't anybody in the building, ma'am."

I picked irritably at a bowl of Creole shrimp gumbo. I had got the message, and hated what it said. New Orleans was being frank: it had some home truths for me, and was wasting no time on polite circumlocutions.

Riding the river, I had seen myself as a sincere traveler, thinking of my voyage not as a holiday but as a scale model of a life. It was different from life in one essential: I would survive it to give an account of its end. The journey would turn into a complete narrative, where life—my own life—could be only an unfinished story with an inconclusive plot.

Now, just a few days away from the end, I didn't yet know where the story would finish, but I knew a conclusion was waiting for me somewhere not far off; it had to be. Here, though, New Orleans was telling me plainly that I was laughably deluded: I wasn't a traveler at all; I was just another rubberneck in a city that made its living out of credulous rubbernecks. Go buy a guidebook! Take a buggy ride! Get your picture painted! Eat *beignets*! Listen to the sounds of Old Dixie! Have yourself a relief massage; then *go home,* shmuck!

Perhaps that was the ending I deserved. It would give the hero his comeuppance and boot him firmly back to where he belonged. He could sit with the other tourists on a flight out of the city, nursing a stripy bag of souvenirs: a T-shirt with THE CITY THAT CARE FORGOT printed on its front in fancy wrought-iron letters, a Preservation Hall L.P., a voodoo doll, a Cajun seafood cookbook illustrated with primitive paintings of bayou weddings and, for his bath, a model steamboat and a plastic alligator. I could leave him there, with the plane's engines drawing in their breath for takeoff, a strapped fool in his seat belt at the end of the road, the beginning of the runway.

Instead, I left the shrimp gumbo. I paid the check. I tore up the message on my way out of the restaurant.

I kept superstitiously away from the French Quarter and took to the moldering streets on the wrong side of Esplanade. Every tourist brochure talked about the "magic" of the city, and there *was* a kind of magic there: a dim and degenerate irrationalism which kept on coming up through the cracks in the talk like a tropical weed.

"Jingle Bell Rock" was playing on the jukebox. At the far end of the bar, two women were sitting with a crippled dwarf. One of the women had a deck of cards and was telling the other's fortune.

"Turn the fifth card—"

Business was bad. The bartender was lost in a newspaper.

"Count fifteen cards . . ." The voice was New Orleans–sleepy. *Car-r-ds.* "See? What holds your destiny . . . what lies beyond?"

"The four of diamonds doesn't mean anything," said the dwarf.

"A lot of space . . . a lot of traveling."

I tried to read.

Lucius Mason on his road to Liverpool had passed through London, and had found a moment to call in Harley Street. Since his return from Germany he had met Miss Furnival both at home at his mother's house—or rather his own—and at The Cleeve . . .

It was hard going. The place names stood too evocatively out of the text and got in the way of the story, whose track I had lost long ago.

"Jack of spades. That's the best. A friend . . . somebody like that . . . What I mean is, he's out to get you, but he'll smile."

It was the time of year at which few people are at home in London, being the middle of October . . .

"Three of hearts. That's the man. That's the main man."

She had gone down to Brighton in August, soon after the House broke up . . .

"Since she chose a bad card, she gets another chance. Life comes back. It always comes back."

The bartender folded his paper and took time off to thrash me at pool. We were setting up the table when the dwarf slid down from his stool and left the bar, hauling himself across the floor on a single crutch.

"You seen that guy? Know what I reckon? He's a reincarn."

"A what?"

"Reincarn. You know about reincarnation? The way I look at it, it accounts for a helluva lot of things you see."

He chalked his cue and shot off first.

"Like I was saying. Look at all the little kids who've got these crazy deformities when they're born. The *re*-tards. Grown men with five-year-old brains. Them *mongrels*. Know what I mean? There's got to be a reason. I ask myself, what've guys like that done to deserve it? They must've done *something*—"

"I don't see why."

"Because there's an order in this universe, that's why. Don't you believe in the Divine Pattern?"

"No."

"Shit, I do. You see something like that guy, there's only one explanation for it. It's retribution. I reckon when he was in a previous life, he did something real bad. I don't know. Maybe he murdered someone, something like that. Could've been anything. Rape. Torture. You know what I mean. And that's why he's been sent back. He's serving his term in Hell right now, that's what I think. Don't that make sense to you?"

I laughed. "Not much, no."

"Hell, you only got to use your eyes. Look at the people in the streets. There's us: we're living out our lives for the first time. Then there's *them*. Reincarns."

I couldn't sleep in the big honeymooners' bed. As soon as it was light on Sunday morning I started to walk with no particular direction in mind, and found myself on Elysian Fields. It didn't look like the place of the blessed dead. It was a long dull boulevard which cut through a black suburb of housing projects in khaki brick and gray frame bungalows, half hidden behind palmetto fans and frizzled banana plants. The wet air was still full of Saturday-night smells: a thin, drifting smog of sausage grease, sour liquor, fried fish and sick.

I started to follow a woman. She had come out from a shack across the street wearing a long blood-crimson robe and a dirty white wimple. She had the build of a Russian lady discus thrower. Mounted on precarious stiletto heels, she wobbled up the sidewalk. No one else seemed to think her appearance was at all odd. Small boys in three-piece Sunday suits zapped past her on roller skates without giving her a second glance. At the corner, she was met by another woman who was wrapped in a sheet of spangled gilt lamé and had covered her hair with a lace cap. Keeping my distance, I trailed the women to the door of an ugly concrete building at the edge of a railroad embankment: the Israelite Spiritual Church.

After a minute or two of shuffling uncertainly in the dirt road outside, I pushed the door open and was met by a man in ordinary clothes.

"You a minister, brother?"

"No, I'm just . . . a seeker."

"Okay, come on in. I thought you was a minister. You come to testify?"

"No. Is that okay?"

"Sure. You go right in."

The church was almost dark. Shabby red curtains had been pulled across the windows, and what light there was came from a small forest of colored candles planted around the altar. The room was stuffy with the smell of incense. The names of the tribes of Israel were painted on the walls, and the candles made a kind of bright theater of the altar, where three plaster figurines had been placed one in front of another. The Virgin Mary, slightly chipped, stood at the back; Jesus Christ just ahead of her; then, much the biggest and best-painted of the three, an Indian chief in a feather headdress. The candlelight picked out the sharp points of his nose and chin and made dark caves of his eyes.

I guessed who he must be. Chief Black Hawk was the leader of a lost tribe of Israel; in New Orleans he had been taken up as a patron figurehead by an eccentric sect of black Israelites.

Even in this small church, the congregation was sparse. The women had their heads covered and wore what I took to be old Mardi Gras costumes. There were only four men, and none of them had a hint about him of the women's wild finery—their Lurex, feathers, bangles and lace.

The ceremony itself was a ragged, improvised assembly of bits and pieces. Nothing happened in any particular order. It was as if these people had come together to try to reconstruct a religion which they had all forgotten. There were fragments of Catholic ritual stirred up with Baptism; a touch of television's *700 Club*; a peppering of black magic and astrology.

The organist kept on drifting out of time with the opening gospel song. Then there was a garbled version of the Nicene Creed. The woman in the red robe and the wimple stood in front of the altar and recommended the 91st Psalm as a surefire specific against disasters.

"Thou shalt not be afraid for the terror by night, nor for the arrow that flieth by day . . ."

"That's right—"

"Sure 'nough!"

"Now, you just say the words of this psalm! They is good for auto accidents . . ."

"Right!"

"You don't want no trouble with *guns* . . . that's all down here. You don't want no *knifings*."

"No, I don't, Lord!"

"No snakes and dragons! That's what I read here. All you got to do, you got to say the words, and you got protection. You got the Lord's protection. You got the protection of His wings!"

"Yes, Lord!"

"A-men!"

Yet there was something faint and lackadaisical even in these answering calls from the congregation in the dark. They, too, were echoes from another, barely remembered kind of Christianity. The service lurched into long silences, as if no one knew what to do now. Haltingly, the testimonies began. A woman stood up at the back of the church.

"I want to give thanks to the Lord and Chief for many *re*-wards both material and spiritual."

"Oh, yes, and so I do!"

"Last Tuesday morning, my daughter and son-in-law, they didn't have no furniture in their home. Didn't have no table. Didn't have no chairs. Didn't have no tee-vee. They didn't have nothing. Friday in the evening, by the grace of the Lord . . ."

"Oh, yeah!"

"Oh, praise my Lord!"

"Friday in the evening, they done have a TV, dining table, four good chairs . . . They didn't want for nothing, praise the Lord!"

"Unh-hunh—"

"A-men!"

Another woman rose.

"I want to give my thanks to Jesus!"

"That's right!"

"For many rewards both material and spiritual—"

"Oh, Jesus, yes!"

"He done lead us in peace all the way from January first—"

"Sure he has!"

"To December nine!"

"That's right!"

Even the operation of the calendar had become a miracle. In the flickery red gloom, the world outside seemed a very sad place indeed. There was nothing in it to rely on, no reasons to account for its workings. One was left with only magic spells and charms, the last rags and tatters of religious tradition. Like the fortune-teller and the bartender, these women were squatters in the ruined house of Christian belief. I slid from my seat. The dreary pathos of the voices and the suffocating smell of incense had caused a sudden nausea in my gut. Later, someone said, "Oh, you must have found a *voodoo* church!"—as if I had hit on one of New Orleans' most exotic tourist attractions. It was not like that at all.

I was awakened by the insistent scratch of the maid's broom on the pine boards outside my door. Diagonal bars of sunlight were falling through the shutters and formed a bright palisade across the posts at the foot of the bed. They were pretty, New Orleans bars, but they still made me feel that I was being held in detention here. I took my charts of the Intracoastal Waterway down to breakfast, packed my bags and took a cab to the wharf.

Tourists were standing in line for joyrides on the restored steamboats, and the river was clogged with tows, tugs and cargo ships. I wriggled my own boat out between the high hulls overhead and forced it up against the powerful grain of the current. Slopping about on the tail ends of steep wakes, I waited for the traffic to quiet down and cut across the channel to the far shore, where I searched for the hidden door in the levee that would let me into the Harvey Canal Lock.

The steel gates hissed shut behind me and blacked out the Mississippi; or rather, they blacked out its official, regimented course. Two hundred years of dredging and levee building had squashed the river into a tight man-made conduit; nowadays it emptied into the Gulf through a mile-wide open drainpipe. The Mississippi itself had held quite different notions of how things should be. At times of high water, it had come bursting apart, breaking its banks and fanning over a thousand square miles of southern Louisiana, scoring the country with seasonal rivers, creeks and ditches. These old floodways had turned into an unmappable jigsaw of alluvium and water: part swamp, part lake, part bayou. For a hundred miles south and west of New Orleans, one could lose oneself in the maze the river had left behind. The charts showed the area as a worms' nest intersected by the broad turnpike of the Intracoastal Waterway, with long thin villages lining the biggest of the bayous. I had a one-dollar Woolworth's compass; I wanted to get just lost enough to know that I'd found an ending.

The Harvey Canal was a city street of shipyards which suddenly petered out into a wooded swamp. One moment there were dry docks, cranes and men driving forklift trucks along the wharf beside me; the next, there was the dense December green of mangroves and cypresses; a jagged pane of water; a pelican hauling in the unwieldy stalk of its neck in preparation for takeoff; a family of turtles lolloping off a log; another country.

I crept into it as slowly and as quietly as I could, trying to let the boat do no more than stroke the water as it went. It was strange water, too. Ahead, lit by misty sunshine, it was a milky, streaky green like polished soapstone. There was no wind and no current. It looked so stable an element that one might have carved ashtrays and telephone stands out of it. Behind the boat, though, where the motor was stirring it, it was thick and peaty like black syrup.

Riding the river had never been like this. I lit a pipe, set a mug of coffee on the seat in front of me and decided to give up being a worried captain and start becoming an idle passenger. At last I could afford to lean over my own rail and let my eyes wander.

The surface of the bayou was littered with clusters of bulbous water hyacinths which kept on tangling with my propeller. Looking back, I saw something else bobbing in the wake . . . a sort of gourd, the color of moldy cheese. I turned the boat around to see what it was.

It was a dead armadillo, floating modestly face down. Its grubby-yellow shell was jointed like a rack of lamb. Its lizardy tail dangled limply behind it and its head was sunk too deep for me to see.

Poor, dim, dogged armadillo. It was one of hundreds of thousands who had set out on a great trek, and nearly all had died like this one. Until not long ago, the armadillos hadn't been able to get out of Mexico. They were nearsighted and no good at swimming. Their ambition to reach the United States was blocked by the Rio Grande. They snuffled up to its south bank at night, missed their footing on the edge, and drowned. They were comically unfitted to be long-distance travelers, but dead set on making the trip. Then an armadillo discovered a highway bridge, and the animals began to sneak past the customs-and-immigration posts in the small hours. A sensible armadillo would have been content to have reached Texas. He might have settled down and lived comfortably for years, like other wetbacks, on a forged Social Security card. By this time, though, the habit of making long journeys had become second nature to the armadillos. They turned east along the Gulf coast. Most of them drowned in the swamps and bayous of Louisiana; a few lucky and intrepid ones made it to the west bank of the Mississippi and drowned there.

Just recently, people had begun to see armadillos in their gardens in New Orleans. They were coming in across the road bridges in ones and twos. In twenty, thirty, forty years, perhaps, the first exhausted armadillo would stagger through the Holland Tunnel and sniff the air of Manhattan. I was with the armadillos. It was impossible not to feel a certain kinship with these purblind foreigners as they hoboed their way along the huge and dangerous length of the United States.

I turned from the Bayou Barataria into the Intracoastal Waterway. It wasn't the dull canal I'd feared; it was just a buoyed clearing of open water through the swamp. The marsh was broken with rafts of forest. The mangroves were poised high on their arched, clawlike roots, while the cypresses were surrounded with black woody stumps that grew out of the water, presumably to take the air. Almost every branch supported a thick parasitic colony of Spanish moss. The romantic associations of this stuff baffled me. It was always said to "drape" or "festoon" the trees on which it grew, as if it were a valuable ornament; yet it looked exactly like the matted dirt which collects inside the bags of vacuum cleaners, a purply-gray mess of carpet sweepings. It didn't festoon trees. It soiled them, as if someone had tipped the contents of a giant Hoover over the forest. The real moss, though, was as brilliant as malachite. Tempted to stop and picnic, I tested it with an oar: the green crust broke; the oar came back coated in black slime.

The surface of the swamp was as fragile as the moss. The wake of an eastbound tow, heading across the neck of Lake Salvador, suddenly smashed its level glaze. All its colors came apart. The water darkened, spread and drowned the marsh grass. Mangroves shivered on their stilts. Flights of small cheeping waders came up like puffs of gunsmoke, and a disturbed eagle flapped from the top of a tall cypress tree. For a minute, the tow drained the land behind it, dragging the water away to reveal shallow valleys of putrescent mud. As the swamp settled back, one could smell the rottenness of the place; it had a dead reptilian stink. Before, the air had been salty and fresh; now it was thick with silage, oil, skunk fetor, alligator guts.

For somewhere that looked so inhospitably wild at close quarters, the swamp was oddly full of signs of human busyness. Long marches of power pylons crossed it, going purposefully off to nowhere. The horizon was marked by a line of irregularly typed A's and I's, where rigs and drills were burrowing in the sludge. In the little bayous that turned left and right from the main channel, I'd seen fishermen in jonboats and wooden pirogues. Their nets hung beneath neat circles of plastic detergent bottles. The bayou towns themselves were hidden behind trees, but their water towers showed as the tallest objects in the landscape: great aluminum mushrooms on slender stalks, with the town names painted on them to be read as mariners' landmarks. LAROSE. CUT OFF. LOCKPORT. VALENTINE.

I reached a crossroads where the Bayou Lafourche went north and south off the Intracoastal Waterway, tossed a quarter to decide which way to go, and turned right, toward the distant water tower of Lockport. The bayou was a crowded street of brackish water. The towns, such as they were, ran one block deep along its bank, their houses built out on poles and jetties and leaning over moored skiffs and fish traps. I stopped at a bar where the bartender was sitting on his front step, baiting a crab basket with chicken necks. He rinsed his hands in the bayou and followed me in.

"Where have all the alligators gone?" I asked.

"Alligators? Oh, t'ey is mostly asleep for t'e winter now. You go furt'er down, into t'e salt marshes, maybe you see t'em t'ere still." His voice was Cajun; a quick, liquid, front-of-the-mouth chirrup. *Biba-biba-biba-bib.*

"But in the summer . . . ?"

"Oh, yeah, we got 'em all along. Down the bayou, there's a big hole you have to watch if you go fishing. They say they's not man-eaters round here. But they'll get in the boat with you. Tat's when tey got teir little ones wit tem."

I joined him out on his step and nursed my beer. Another cheesy-looking armadillo was floating in the scum.

"They can't see too good. They fall in," the bartender said.

"Yes. So I heard."

The afternoon sky was the texture of thick clotted cream. Ripe oranges were growing in the bartender's garden. Behind us, a truck went by on the narrow road that ran in parallel with the bayou and formed the town's outer limit. One could spit right over the top of the long straggle of Larose, yet it had the self-absorbed stir of a city. Oxy-acetylene torches lit the insides of small shipyards on the far bank, and the shrimp fleet was coming in from the Gulf to tie up along the town jetties. The masts and spars of the trawlers formed frames over which their rust-colored nets were spread like tents. The shrimp would be frozen and packaged in factories on the bayou. It was altogether a great deal busier and richer than the Main Streets of most small Southern towns.

A mile or so on from the bar, a two-faced gas station served both the highway and the bayou. I pulled in to refuel and parked behind a shrimp boat. I found the owner of the gas station by the sound of his singing. It came from somewhere under a jacked-up automobile: a cracked and happy warble which eventually turned into a man who looked like a wizened terrapin under his yellow plastic cap. I discovered that he had a whole collection of good reasons for singing. He had harvested his forty acres of sugar cane across the road; his first season with his own shrimp boat was just finishing, at a fine profit; his gas station was humming with business. He was a swamp plutocrat, with one foot on the land and one on the water.

"And I ain't complaining none," he said. His fortune had started with just a few acres of cane plantation. Then an oil company had paid him an annual rental on the land for its potential mineral rights. "So I built me a service station." That had done well. "So I built me a shrimp boat."

"They struck oil just over the other side of the bayou there . . . so I'm keeping my fingers crossed and hoping."

397

"What'll you do if they do find oil on your land?"

"Build me another shrimp boat. Hell, you make more money out of the shrimp than you can out of sugar, or gas, or any other damn thing around here. A man can live easy off a shrimp boat now."

"When they do strike oil, you'll be able to build a whole fleet of the things."

"No," he laughed. "You see how it is with me. I like to keep things small."

He filled my gas tanks, still warbling when he wasn't talking. I had imagined that this swampland would be desolate and impoverished; yet even the most tottering of its shacks on stilts was suspended over a fortune that was just waiting to be scooped out of the water and the mud. The trouble of the shack dwellers was that they had no capital to exploit these marvelous possibilities. They had to scrape hungrily by on a wooden skiff, a gun, a few catfish lines and traps, while the owner of the gas station was singing his way into being a millionaire. It was astonishingly easy to be rich here, and almost as hard to stop being poor.

It was nearly dark when I reached the jetty of Erjie's Bar & Cafe at Lockport. There had been no sunset, but the torches in the shipyards had put on a sunset of their own, making the water of the bayou flare silver and carmine, and lighting the cypresses and willows so that they looked like showering Roman candles. My own pleasure at being afloat, and safely, unworriedly afloat, in this engaging world was slightly cankered by the fear that I wasn't finding an ending so much as starting out on a fresh journey.

In the bar, a group of men were playing three-card skat and talking in French. At least, I supposed it was French. It certainly wasn't English, and the occasional French word was just identifiable.

"*Excusez-moi,*" I said, excusing myself, "*mais pouvez-vous me comprendre quand je parle comme ci?*"

There was a long and thoughtful pause.

"Er . . . yes. But what you talking in now is the French they speak in Paris, France."

"I'm afraid that's not quite true. I wish it were."

"Here. Come see." Or was it *comme ci?* But the man was gesturing to me to sit down.

"You say 'I am' in your French."

"*Je suis.*"

"Shoo."

"Shoo?"

"Yup. That's the way we say it. Now you say to me 'You are.' "

"*Tu es?*"

"*Tay.* 'He is' . . ."

"*Il est.*"

"*Lay.* We kind of shortened it all up, see?"

It was still spoken, but not read or written, and had drifted a long way from its parent root. One man at the table had served in France in World War II.

"Took me, oh, just a week, maybe two . . . then I got what they was saying. But with me, they wasn't so quick. They didn't reckon I was talking French at all."

"What about your children? Do they speak French?"

"Ain't many under forty that still can. The kids now, all they learn is this jive talk. *Like . . . like . . . like . . . like . . . man.* That's all they know."

It seemed a sad way for a language to peter out. The Cajuns had originally been the Acadians. They had come to Louisiana in 1758, when the governor of Canada expelled them from their territory in Nova Scotia. Where other immigrants had lost their national languages within a generation or two of their arrival in the United States, the Cajuns were still speaking in French after more than two hundred years. Very soon, Cajun French would be just another property of American folklore, gruesomely treasured because it was "historical," like the Natchez mansions and the First Brick Houses West of the Mississippi. The Cajuns were not even Cajuns now; they were Coonasses. They had happily adopted the name which Texan oilmen had bestowed on them as a jeer. As the sign that was pinned up over the bar said: COONASSES LOVE BETTER BECAUSE THEY EAT ANYTHING!

"So where are you heading for?"

"I don't know," I said. "Maybe . . . Morgan City . . ."

If I didn't stop at Morgan City, I would probably end up in Texas, heading for the Rio Grande. Perhaps I would meet up with Ed from Muscatine.

"*Morgan City?* Why you want to go there? Ain't nothing in Morgan City."

"Ain't nothing" sounded distinctly promising.

"Nothing?"

"Nothing. At all."

"No tourists?"

"Tourists? In Morgan City? You got to be joking."

"What you want, anyway? A job?"

"No, I don't want a job. Just a place."

"Hey," called a fat man from his bar stool, "You want a place, I can show you a place. Out there in the bayous. . . ." He swiveled around. "Know what's there? A cave. A cave full of froomids. You know what a froomid is?"

"No."

"He's shooting his mouth off. Keep quiet, Louis."

"Froomids is . . . paradise. They is . . . men and women all mixed up together. They got these big titties . . . and the dongs on them . . ." He spread both hands a yard away from his enormous thighs. "That's froomids. They'll eat you alive. But with the froomids, it's like heaven, know what I mean?"

"Hermaphrodites," I said.

"Froomids!" he said. "Listen to what I'm saying to you!"

"Louis Beauregard," said the man next to me, "after you come here, this place done go to the dogs."

Louis Beauregard glittered contentedly. "Well . . . all *you* got to do is: barbecue them dogs."

In the morning the air was so still that I could feel the ripples of turbulence I caused by passing through it. A fine salt mist had put the water towers out of focus. They had lost their supporting pillars and looked like silver dirigibles adrift in the sky.

The earth felt like powdered glass underfoot. It was a mixture of black dirt and the shells of millions of tiny white mollusks. With every step, it crunched and snapped. There were mangled stalks of sugar cane on the road and on the bayou, and isolated stands of uncut cane as high as houses in the fields.

I eased the boat out onto the bayou. A faint tidal drift made the water hyacinths and the cane stalks wander sluggishly away from the direction of the sea. Following their lead, I ran up to the end of Lockport and turned left into Lake Fields: miles and miles of open water with the same veined, soapstony sheen. On the southern bank, someone had raised an improvised levee of crushed automobiles. The salt in the air had rusted them together so that they looked like an earthwork, oddly pasted about with spots and scraps of their old, gaudy Ford and General Motors livery.

A muffled fisherman in a pirogue raised his hand in a salute as I went past. It was the kind of morning and the kind of place where it was important to acknowledge the existence of other people. The sheer, motionless space of sky and water tempted one into the hallucination that one had been given the world entirely to oneself. The intermittent reminders of human tenancy were unfailingly odd. There was a crumbling jetty sticking out of the mud. No road or track led to it. There wasn't a house in sight. Yet on the jetty there was a waterlogged sofa, its stuffing leaking from its sides. It was a queer foreign exile; it looked as if it were badly in need of the company of a coffee table, a television set and a standing lamp. A mile farther on, a line of willows ran out across the water on a neck of land as narrow as a sidewalk. At the foot of the trees, three frame houses had been joined together and mounted on the hull of a barge. I rode up to the front door of one of them. The whole place was a ruin. The glass had gone from the windows; part of the roof had fallen in. I tied the boat to the porch and walked through the gutted rooms. Nothing had been left behind except for a few rags and some bits of old newspaper. The *New Orleans Times-Picayune*. June 1968. It had been preserved under a curling sheet of brown linoleum. I wondered what had driven the people from this ingenious and once beautiful house. The lonely vacancy of the view from its windows? Yet the hull of the barge alone must have been worth a fortune in scrap.

I made a long southwesterly loop and rejoined the Intracoastal Waterway, where towboats were busy stirring up the water and the morning. I was glad to see them. They were difficult companions to live with, but their general boisterousness came as a relief after the weird, evacuated stillness of the reach of swamp at my back.

At Houma, I turned up the arched Venetian canal of the Bayou Terrebonne and went to look for a bar. The one I found had the air of a place that scorned the daytime and had created its own perpetual night; it had a pool table and enough bare, dusty space to run several brawls in at once.

"Have you got anything to eat?" I asked the bartender.

"I can do you a shit on a shingle," she said.

It sounded interesting and disgusting in equal parts. My curiosity narrowly beat my feelings of incipient revulsion.

"Okay, I'll have a shit on a shingle," I said, trying to sound as if I'd been shitting on shingles for years.

Waiting for this object to appear, I played pool with a man who'd arrived in Houma five days before. He had come down to Louisiana from Connecticut and was looking for a job as a roustabout on a Gulf oil rig. Houma had scared him half out of his wits.

"Ain't this country something else, though? You should've been here last night. There was a guy came in the bar waving a three-five-seven

Magnum and yelling that he wanted to shoot some niggers. I'm telling you, man: if there'd have been a black sitting here he would have been a dead man. That guy wasn't joking. I've only been here five days. It's crazy. What I need most in this town is a gun. If you're in Houma, you need a gun."

"That's pretty easy in Louisiana, isn't it? You only have to show your driver's license."

"Yeah. That's my problem. I don't have a driver's license."

My shit on its shingle was put out for me on the bar. It was only corned-beef hash on toast, but its revolting name had somehow worked its way into the flavor of the thing; it tasted foul.

I was trying to rid my mouth of the memory of it by smoking a pipeful of tobacco when I found Houma in person standing behind me. He was short and skinny, in his twenties; but his face had the creased and yellowed look of someone well past fifty. He had the shakes.

"What you think you tryin' to put over on me, man?"

"Me? Nothing."

"Why you come in here?"

I shrugged. "A drink . . . a game of pool . . . something to eat."

"What the fuck is *that?*"

He was pointing to the loose cellophane pouch in which my tobacco was wrapped.

"That's my tobacco."

"Tobacco—shit!"

My pool partner came over. "Hey, what's the trouble?"

"And you keep *your* shit out of this, I'm warning you," Houma said. Connecticut backed off. His alarmed eyes were telegraphing *What did I tell you?* at me.

Houma's face was six inches away from mine. The top of his head came up to my nose. "I'm just asking you, polite, now, to get your fucking shit out of this bar."

"Would you mind telling me why?"

"I don't have to spell nothing out to you—Fed!"

"I'm not a Fed," I said.

"You don't fool nobody. You're a fucking Fed narc. You and your shit *bait.*"

"Look—" I said, and started to reach inside my pocket to find my passport. I could hardly be an accredited Englishman and a Fed narc. My hand had been stopped and gripped almost before it had begun to move. I could feel the fierce trembling in Houma's wrist. He had a knife in his other hand.

"You pull your fuckin' gun on me, man, I'll cut you—"

"Look, please—" I said. The whole episode was so insane and sudden that I hadn't yet had time to be frightened by it. "I haven't got a gun. I was trying to show you my passport. I'm British. I'm not a policeman. I'm not an American. I'm not a Fed. I'm not a narc. Now, please . . . look inside my pocket. You'll find my passport with my wallet." I could see Connecticut at the far end of the bar. He had seen the knife and was watching shamefaced. I thought: If I were in his position, all I'd do would be watch too.

Houma's knife came up and flipped the lapel of my jacket aside. He saw at least that I wasn't armed. His fingers twitched at the contents of my pocket, and they scattered in front of me on the bar floor: checkbook, wallet, passport, pen and, as I saw with real alarm, the business card of Clarence Carter, superintendent of the Shelby County Penal Farm in Memphis. I had visited his jail. At this moment, he was the last person in the world with whom I wanted any visible connection.

"You see my passport there? Now, look at it."

"*You* get it," Houma said. "I'm watching you, man."

I picked it up and showed it to him.

"What is this shit?"

"It proves that I'm an English citizen. I'm a foreigner. I'm a visitor to this country."

"It don't prove fucking nothing—" The madness had gone out of his voice, though. Connecticut, feeling the tension slacken, came over to us again.

"He's just a goddamn tourist, man—"

Houma took my packet of tobacco from the bar and sniffed at it. "Shit. Why you keeping it in this fucking stuff, man? You want to get yourself killed?" His voice had turned to a feeble whine. He was just a little runt with a knife in his belt and an addict's jitters. "Okay . . . so I made a mistake. I was wrong, okay? Will you shake my hand, now?"

Absurdly, ceremonially, we shook hands.

"You're my friend now, okay, man?" He tried to put his arm around my shoulder, but it didn't quite reach. "You want another beer?"

"No, thanks."

"Come on—you and me, we'll shoot some pool, huh?"

"Okay."

His cue trembled in his hands; my cue trembled in mine. The balls on the table went everywhere except into the pockets. When Houma shambled jerkily off to the men's room, I fled the bar, and didn't stop running until I reached my boat.

A single-engined seaplane was coming in to touch down on the Water-way, and I had to pull over to the dock where a fleet of little planes rocked on their pontoons. A pilot came across to talk: he had spotted the Wisconsin registration on my boat and wanted to know what it was doing so far from home.

"God, that's something I'd like to do sometime. That's just the kind of thing I'm into myself."

He was a stranger here too. He had gone broke in the Florida Keys, flying a one-man passenger service. The day before, he had signed on as a pilot here, ferrying crewmen and supplies out to the drilling plat-forms offshore. He and his wife were living in a camper down the street. They had lost their house in Florida: Louisiana was their chance for a new start.

"So where are you going now?" he asked.

"I'm not sure. Morgan City, I think."

"Morgan City? I heard that place is a *real* dump."

"So did I."

I pushed on up the waterway as it cut from bayou to bayou: Bayou Cocodrie . . . Bayou Chene . . . Bayou Boeuf. Ahead of the boat, the water was like jade; behind, it was roiling cocoa. Wherever there was a bump of high ground in the swamp, someone had built himself a shack with a muddy yard full of chickens, a dock, a tethered boat. One could live like Crusoe here. The income-tax man would have to paddle out in a canoe to collect his revenue in crawfish, alligator skins and the pelts of nutria rats; there'd be no mail, no telephone calls—just pelicans and vultures in the garden and the slow tidal swill of the water around one's house. Louis Beauregard's story of the froomids did correspond to something real: somewhere up the Bayou Capasaw or the Bayou Pen-chant there must be secret places where men have been living in hid-ing for years. I had heard rumors of a clandestine colony of Chinese shrimp fishermen who occupied a stilt city in the swamp and shot any-one curious enough to stumble on their hideout; the rumors weren't wholly unbelievable, and the pilots of the seaplanes must often have noticed things that were best left uninvestigated.

The Bayou Boeuf opened into the estuary of the Atchafalaya River, and Morgan City was a ramshackle patchwork of low roofs squatting on the junction. I cruised along its beach looking for a place to land. On the edge of the estuary there was a fisherman's jetty with two jonboats moored to its few remaining piles. I grounded on soft mud, and was met by an old man trailing a line of catfish hooks.

"What you want?"

"I wondered if I could tie up here for the night."

"You could lose your boat. Nothing's safe in this town."

"Why's that?"

"*Lot* of drifters about."

He took in my scuffed cases with a glance of scornful recognition.

"Oh. Why do *they* come here?"

"Looking for work." He looked at me again and gave an amused snort. "They don't get none, though. It'll cost you a dollar—"

"Fine."

"In advance."

Across the street there was a grocery with a pay phone. It took half an hour to raise a cab which was circling the town picking up passengers as it went along. The driver, a huge morose youth, introduced himself as Tiny; the elderly woman in the front seat was Miss Leonie.

"You new in town?" asked Miss Leonie.

"Yes, I've just arrived."

"You come to the armpit of the world," she said, making every vowel of the phrase last as long as it possibly could, like a particularly toothsome sweet.

We came to a scruffy little housing project, with piles of old clothes flapping in yards of unplanted sand. Tiny hooted, and a black teenager came out dressed in a sharp dude suit and wearing pink-framed glasses. He sat beside me. "Know what I'm going to do?" he said. "I'm gonna buy me a machine gun."

"Why's that?" Miss Leonie said. "What you want with a machine gun?"

"Climb to the top of the highest building in Morgan City . . ." He swiveled in his seat, holding an imaginary carbine and spraying us all with bullets. "Rat-a-tat-a-rat-a-tat-a-rat-a-tat-a-rat-a-tat-a . . ." He rolled back and laughed, holding his knees.

I had asked to be set down at the best motel in Morgan City. This had driven Miss Leonie into a cigaretty coughing fit.

"*Best* motel in Morgan City? You ain't asking much, are you, mister?"

"Rat-a-tat-a-tat-a-tat-a . . ."

In the event, I was set down by a cluster of peeling cabins grouped around a courtyard with a dead banana plant in the middle. I was given a key to a room with a bare concrete floor. The sheets on the bed looked slept in; the single blanket was riddled with burns and stains. The floral shower curtain was cracked on every fold. I went back to the motel office to talk to two identically fat girls in tight stretch pants and Hawaiian blouses.

"Haven't you got a better room than that? One with a bath?"

"They don't none of them have *baths*."

"It's about the worst motel room I've ever seen."

"Oh, it ain't *good*. Ain't no worse than none of the others, though."

"Is there another motel in town where I could find a better room?"

"Nope. The rest of them, they're *worse*."

"Jesus." I was deeply impressed by Morgan City's pride in its own scabbiness. "What do people *do* in Morgan City?" I asked.

"Fight. Get drunk. Pick up women."

"You can get rolled around here," said the other girl tentatively, picking at a speck on her scarlet-panted buttock.

I wasn't sure whether "rolled" meant mugged or laid.

"I don't think I much want to get rolled."

"Okay," she said.

I went for a long walk around the town. It had a certain repetitious charm, since it consisted of acre after acre of exactly the same house. Half a dozen rough brick platforms, eighteen inches high, supported a shack with a corrugated-iron roof, a veranda draped in torn screening, a single, gray Grecian column made of wood, a broken rocker and a faded blue statue of the Virgin on the doorstep. There were many more cats than people on the streets, and the cats had the same glandular fattiness as the girls at the motel. They grazed on the little heaps of garbage that stood in front of almost every house, spilling appetizingly from leaky bags.

Three miles later I was back to where I'd started, on Brashear Avenue, which was as near as Morgan City seemed to come to possessing a Main Street. In the middle of the road there was one of the most arresting exercises in civic statuary that I had ever seen. It was called *The Spirit of Morgan City* and had been molded in some kind of lividly colored fiberglass. A life-size shrimp boat was in collision with something that at first I took to be the Eiffel Tower, but later decided was meant to be an offshore oil rig. The hideous glory of this marvel had been a little softened for Christmas: it had been wrapped up in tinsel ropes, stars and bangles, as if Morgan City were thinking of mailing it to someone as a surprise gift.

One building in Morgan City didn't fit at all. On the far side of the street beyond a high wall and a row of trees, a colonnaded mansion with a texas-deck front looked out over the Atchafalaya River. The rest of the town barely came up to the windows of its ground floor. This sugar planter's castle had once been all there was of Morgan City; now it was loftily marooned in a cheerful slum, so grand and tall that its owner might never have noticed the steady encroachment of the shantytown around his feet. From his bedroom, he could probably see clear across to Texas and halfway down to Mexico; with luck, he might not even yet have set his eyes on Morgan City. Perhaps he took its tin roofs for a widening of the river and was wondering whether, granted this addition of a paddy field to his plantation, he might change from sugar cane to rice.

The bars on Front Street looked like places where I was certain to be ringed as a federal narcotics agent. I walked away up Brashear Avenue, searching for somewhere a little more salubrious, and ended up in a lounge crowded with other, bewildered strangers musing on their exile in Morgan City.

"What's *happening* here? I don't get it. I come from Chicago. In Illinois, or Missouri, you never see a dead dog on the highway. Here in Louisiana, Christ, you see more dead dogs than you can shake a stick at. What's happening? People here, they go out of their way to run a dog down. It's a goddamn sport!"

"Yeah, I'm from Tennessee. You don't see none of that there neither."

"Hell, when we was kids, we used to break off a car's antenna, make a zip gun out of it. But now it's *senseless*. Here, they take your antenna, no reason. Shoot! That's thirty-nine bucks!"

"But them dogs on the highway . . . Who are these people? People who'll kill a guy's dog just for fun . . . I never seen anything so crazy, not till I came down to Louisiana."

"Me neither."

Me neither.

The morning was a wide-open door, the sky empty except for a single violet-edged cloud in the far north. I took the boat across Bayou Boeuf and into the seaward neck of Bayou Shaffer, sliding past gleaming mud flats and reedbeds where the tide sucked and whispered in the grasses. Ahead, the color of the water ran from streaky green into an even blue.

It was rich water. Dark with peat, thickened with salt, it was like warm soup. When the first things crawled out of the water, they must have come from a swamp like this one, gingerly testing the mud with their new legs. I trailed my hand over the gunwale and licked my wet forefinger. It tasted of sea.

If the man at Lockport was right, there should be alligators still awake out on these salt flats. If there were, they weren't showing themselves. I made a slow circle around an inlet, watching for something to move on the bank. I took an oar and prodded at a bank of mud. It was as soft and greasy as black butter, and the oar went in as far as my hand. There was no alligator there.

Ain't nothing.

I had crossed, or thought I'd crossed, the line from green to blue.

I turned the motor off and let the boat drift out on the tide for a while, then pointed the bow back, in the same dumb, urban direction that the armadillos set their noses.

Acknowledgments

Mr. *John Tuzee*, of M.G.I., Cleveland, Wisconsin, took a kindly interest in my trip from the moment I proposed it. Had it not been for his help, the journey would have been far harder and more expensive to set up. He arranged for me to borrow a 16-foot Mirrocraft from the manufacturer; also a 15-horsepower Johnson outboard motor. Both boat and motor survived my amateurish maltreatment of them—a powerful tribute to their sturdiness and reliability. The boat was rigged by Herb Heichert, of Crystal Marine, Minneapolis, whose handiwork is admired elsewhere in the book.

Along the river, I met with so much hospitality from strangers that even a page-long list of their names would be invidious in its omissions. Some are recorded in the text; many others are not. I am grateful to them all.

I have been immensely lucky in having two editors, Jonathan Coleman in New York and Christopher MacLehose in London, who have done far more than any word like "encouragement" can reasonably convey. Coleman saw this book through from the start; MacLehose helped me to get it finished. For cheering transatlantic phone calls, for tactful silences, for supper, for jokes, for indecipherable postcards and for a tremendous amount of critical reading and deft editorial work, I am up to my eyes in debt to them both.

J.R.

ALSO BY JONATHAN RABAN

"No one has evoked with greater
power the marriage of land and sky that gives
this country both its beauty and its terror."
—*Washington Post Book World*

BAD LAND

An American Romance

In 1909 maps still identified eastern Montana as the Great
American Desert. But in that year Congress offered 320-
acre tracts of land to anyone bold or foolish enough to stake
a claim to them. Drawn by inventive brochures, countless
homesteaders went west to make their fortunes. Most
failed. In *Bad Land*, Jonathan Raban travels through the
unforgiving country that was the scene of their dreams and
undoing, and makes their story come miraculously alive. In
towns called Terry, Calypso, and Ismay, and in the landscape in between, Raban unearths a vanished episode of
American history, with its own ruins, its heros and heroines,
its own hopeful myths and bitter memories.

*Winner of the National Book Critics
Circle Award for Nonfiction*

New York Times *Editors' Choice
for Book of the Year*

History/Current Affairs/0-679-75906-9

VINTAGE DEPARTURES
Available at your local bookstore, or call toll-free to order:
1-800-793-2665 (credit cards only).